# WALK
# AWAY

BOOKS BY SAM HAWKEN

## THE CAMARO ESPINOZA SERIES

.e    Night Charter
Walk Away

## THE BORDERLANDS TRILOGY

The Dead Women of Juárez
Tequila Sunset
Missing

# WALK AWAY

# SAM HAWKEN

**MULHOLLAND BOOKS**

Little, Brown and Company
New York Boston London

Copyright © 2017 by Sam Hawken

Hachette Book Group supports the right to free expression and the value of copyright. The purpose of copyright is to encourage writers and artists to produce the creative works that enrich our culture.

The scanning, uploading, and distribution of this book without permission is a theft of the author's intellectual property. If you would like permission to use material from the book (other than for review purposes), please contact permissions@hbgusa.com. Thank you for your support of the author's rights.

Mulholland Books / Little, Brown and Company
Hachette Book Group
1290 Avenue of the Americas, New York, NY 10104
mulhollandbooks.com

First Edition: January 2017

Mulholland Books is an imprint of Little, Brown and Company, a division of Hachette Book Group, Inc. The Mulholland Books name and logo are trademarks of Hachette Book Group, Inc.

The publisher is not responsible for websites (or their content) that are not owned by the publisher.

The Hachette Speakers Bureau provides a wide range of authors for speaking events. To find out more, go to hachettespeakersbureau.com or call (866) 376-6591.

ISBN 978-0-316-29926-8
LCCN 2016940866

10 9 8 7 6 5 4 3 2 1

LSC-C

Printed in the United States of America

*For Mariann, because there's nothing she won't do for family.*

# WALK
## AWAY

# CHAPTER ONE

Camaro Espinoza dripped with sweat. There was no time, no place but the moment, and she thought of nothing but fighting. The bag dangled to the floor in a line of others, all undisturbed. She alone forged ahead with the war.

She'd gone thirty minutes on the heavy bag and had ten minutes still ahead. She shifted from a jab-cross-and-takedown combination to a jab, jab, and cross as she circled the bag clockwise. Her hands were swathed in wraps, and the leather bag popped as she laid into it punch by punch.

A punch started at the floor and worked itself up through the rising heel, the turn of the hips, the torsion of the shoulders, and then the final explosion. Camaro's fists ached in time with her muscles, every heartbeat pushing fresh pain through her in a steady, rapid pulse. She breathed in through the nose and out through the mouth, exhaling on the follow-through, emptying her tired lungs completely.

The timer sounded again. Thirty seconds down. She caught the bag between her hands and drove her knee into it, alternating leg to leg. When the timer marked off another half minute, she released her grip and fell back, leaving smears of perspiration behind.

Camaro went down on the mat, back flat against it, and forced herself into a series of spring-ups that felt like torture. She did as many as she could squeeze into the time and then labored onto her feet again to begin a fresh set of jab-cross combinations.

She heard Miguel clapping his hands as the timer wound down. It went off. Camaro stepped back from the bag, panting heavily, her shoulders rising and falling. Her arms were as heavy as lead.

Miguel crossed the empty gym, passing the sparring cage, and stepped onto the mat. "Sixty seconds!" he called. "Get some water in you. Go!"

A liter-and-a-half bottle of room-temperature water sat near the wall in the pool of a ratty white towel. Camaro bent, feeling the strain in her back, and picked it up. She was careful to only sip and not to guzzle.

"Thirty seconds," Miguel reminded her. He was a sturdy man, built low to the ground. His dark hair was shot through with gray. "That's enough water."

Camaro tossed the bottle away. Miguel came close, and they bumped fists. "One more round," she managed.

"You can do it. Focus and power. Focus and power. You don't feel no pain."

The timer sounded, sharp and clear. Camaro turned back to the bag.

She did another five minutes. Jabs, crosses, knees, and takedowns. The last two sets of spring-ups were nightmarish. After the second set she made it to her feet only with effort. Thirty seconds remained, and she bulled through it. When the timer sounded its last alarm, she fell against the heavy bag and hugged it.

Miguel cheered her. *"¡Lo hiciste!"*

He picked up her towel for her and offered it. Camaro mopped her face and then her arms. She had stitches in the brow over her left eye. The gym felt stifling, but it was only her body heat and the remnants of the workout.

"Feeling that, huh?" Miguel asked.

"Yeah."

"You don't pace yourself. It's full throttle all the time."

Camaro fetched up her water bottle. This time she took a mouthful, swirled it around, and then swallowed. "You don't get to call time-out because you're tired."

"True that."

The gym was clean, swept, and quiet. The whir of the fans overhead was the only other sound. Even the interval timer was silenced now. Camaro glanced around. "Where is everybody?"

"Gone. You're the last one."

"What time is it?"

"After nine."

"You could have stopped me."

Miguel shrugged. "I figured you had to get something out. None of my business. As long as I'm home by midnight."

"Let me get cleaned up."

"Take your time."

Like the rest of the gym, the showers were deserted. Camaro rinsed her body until it was free of every trace of the workout she'd done. The hot spray pounded her muscles. She stood a long time with her head bowed under the flow, her honey-brown hair turned dark by the water and falling around her face.

When she was finished, she looked at herself in the mirror for a long moment. The stitches in her brow were marked with a single butterfly bandage. She let it be, shouldered her bag, and went out.

She found Miguel near the front of the gym. His office was a raised cubicle built of wood painted white and red, a desk, and a chair where he sat and looked down on the people coming in. His cash register was a simple metal box. He didn't take credit cards or checks. Those who trained here paid cash on the first of the month. It got them a locker and guaranteed one-on-one time with Miguel or his son, Rey.

"All done?" Miguel asked.

"Yeah. I'm sorry."

"Don't be. It's not like I never went to a New Year's Eve party before. They're getting along fine without me."

"I'll drop something extra in the box when I come back."

Miguel made a face. "I can't be bought."

"All right, then. I'll take a discount."

"I can't be ripped off, either."

"Okay," Camaro said. She turned toward the door.

"Hey, where you headed off to tonight?" Miguel asked.

"Nowhere in particular."

"You want to swing by the house? Have a few beers, watch the ball drop?"

Camaro considered. "Thanks, but I think I'll probably just go home."

"Nobody at home, though, right?"

"Not this time."

"You change your mind, you got my number. We're gonna party till dawn, so..."

"I'll think about it. Happy New Year, Miguel."

"Happy New Year, Camaro."

She went out through the front door and onto the street. Out there the palm trees on Washington Avenue were still ringed with Christmas lights, and the liquor and tattoo shops across the street were open for business. All around South Beach, the holidays lingered in the final hours of the year.

Camaro's bike was at the curb. She strapped her bag to the pillion seat and swung a leg over the saddle. The engine started with thunder, and then she was gone.

# CHAPTER TWO

It was in the low seventies on the ride home. In the north it was cold, very cold, and the news was full of reports about how much snow they were getting, how much school the children were missing, and how the airports were jammed with weather delays. Florida escaped all that. There was a time when Camaro welcomed the kind of isolation only a blizzard could bring, but she was far away from it now.

She paid the toll and took the Causeway to get out of Miami Beach, cut through Overtown, and skirted the northern edge of Little Havana before turning toward home. Off the freeway the Harley glided through well-lit stretches where revelers partied in the streets, and delved into the shadows between the streetlights before coming out the other side unscathed. The sky was stained orange by the sodium vapor of the lights, and she was one woman alone on a bike, moving through the city without being caught up in it. There was the solitude of being free of people altogether, and there was the aloneness of being among more people than could easily be counted. Camaro was overlooked completely, and there was a comfort in her anonymity.

Ahead of her a limousine cruised in the right lane with the sunroof open. Two young women in party dresses and costume-jeweled tiaras drank from bottles of wine and took turns tooting on a plastic horn. The other windows were wide open to the night. Music and laughter spilled out, and as Camaro caught up with them a man leaned out and flicked his tongue at her before cackling drunkenly and blowing her a kiss. "I love you, baby!" he called to her. She accelerated past.

Camaro headed into the heart of her own neighborhood of Allapattah. Here there were no clubs and no limos, and the lights and bustle tourists called Miami were far away. All the whitewashed architecture and pastels were left behind in favor of little houses with one or two bedrooms and bars on the windows, duly kept lawns, and no questions. But she didn't live far from a park, and on New Year's Eve they played live music all night long.

Only the sidelight in the carport was on when Camaro arrived home. Her truck waited silently, abandoned for the evening. Camaro sidled past it and put the bike under the carport roof. She killed the engine, pulled off her helmet, and let her ears adjust to the sudden quiet. She listened. A surge of loud voices from a nearby house carried to her, followed by a few light pops of fireworks set off too early. A dazzle of sparks erupted in the sky, flaring red and dying in green. Her neighbor, old Mrs. Cristiano, was already in bed with hours left to go before midnight, the windows of her house black.

Camaro dismounted and unstrapped her gym bag from the pillion seat. She let herself in through the side door, made sure it was locked behind her, and stepped into the utility room off the kitchen. Her workout clothes were damp with sweat. Camaro fed them to the washing machine and dropped in a detergent pod before switching it on. With the sound of water rushing in the utility room, she went to the kitchen and fetched dinner from the refrigerator. The fluorescent bulbs in the light fixture overhead gently buzzed, an insect noise that only barely registered on the ear.

The rib eye was thick-cut and weighed almost a pound and a half. Camaro set it aside while she steamed carrots and green beans for one. As the vegetables worked, she seasoned the steak with kosher salt and ground pepper, then seared it off in a cast-iron skillet with butter. It went into the oven to finish.

She found a bottle of Jack Daniel's in a bottom cabinet and took it to the kitchen table with a clean tumbler. While she waited on the meat she broke the seal, poured herself a single, and downed it. For a moment the heat in her belly pulsed with the ache of her muscles.

The steak came out extra rare, and she ate it alone at the table with two more fingers of whiskey. When the food was all gone, she put the plate in the sink and carried the bottle to the living room. She turned on the television and switched to *Dick Clark's New Year's Rockin' Eve* to watch Ryan Seacrest and some idiot blonde emcee the musical entertainment all the way up till the midnight hour. Now and again Camaro tilted the glass to her lips before pouring out another measure.

Finally the ball dropped in Times Square, and the new year was begun. Camaro powered the TV off and heard the sizzle and shriek of rockets soaring and exploding all around Allapattah, plus the rattle of firecrackers set off by the string in the streets. Somewhere not so far away, men's voices shouted, punctuated by the higher-pitched noise of excited women. Camaro missed the coffee table with her tumbler, and it fell on the floor. She picked it up and set it right. Threading the cap onto the empty bottle was a challenge for awkward fingers.

She weaved her way to the bedroom and undressed in the dark. She slept in her underwear and woke only once before dawn to pull the covers over her body.

# CHAPTER THREE

Morning came sl owl y, with pain. The blinds were shut, but slivers of light escaped the slats and arrowed across the bedroom to strike where they could cause the most damage. Camaro put a pillow over her face and attempted sleep again. Finally she rose and tried to brush the taste out of her mouth. What toothpaste could not destroy, she attacked with coffee and sausage and eggs. The food helped.

She washed the remains of the previous night's meal away, careful to grease the inside of her skillet before hanging it up by the sink. A liter bottle of water from the refrigerator was cold and bit into her headache while she sat in front of her computer.

Camaro browsed the news, but there was nothing she cared to read. She navigated to Craigslist. She selected the list of U.S. cities and saw them arranged alphabetically from Atlanta to Washington, D.C. Choosing Atlanta first, she found the Missed Connections listings in the personals and scanned the ads there. When nothing caught her eye, she moved on to Austin and from there to Boston.

There was nothing until she reached Detroit. The message was simple:

C THIS IS A. I NEED TO TALK TO YOU. URGENT.

Camaro paused, her finger poised over the mouse button. She read the message again, then clicked Reply.

A THIS IS C. WHAT DO YOU NEED TO ASK ME FIRST?

There was no immediate response. She used a dummy e-mail account for Craigslist and for nothing else. Every fifteen minutes for three hours she checked it, until she couldn't stay in her seat anymore and had to move.

Pacing was good for a while, and then she brought out a yoga mat and placed it in the center of the room. She worked her way through poses, straining muscles and tendons until her limbs felt hot and ached dully. Only when she was done did she allow herself to check again. There was a single e-mail in her box.

WHAT WAS THE NAME OF OUR FIRST DOG?

Camaro typed.

ALPHIE.

The next reply came within minutes of Camaro's message. It was a phone number.

In the drawer of her nightstand there was a simple flip phone capable of little more than calls and texts. Camaro turned it on and checked the charge. It was nearly full. She dialed the number. It rang on the other end three times, then picked up.

"Camaro?"

"Is this your regular phone?" Camaro asked.

"No, I bought it from a 7-Eleven."

"Good."

The woman on the other end of the phone sighed. "I'm glad you called."

"You're my sister. I'll always call."

"It's been a couple of years."

"You're still my sister, Bel."

"And I'm still glad."

"Is there a problem?" Camaro asked.

Annabel fell silent.

"Bel? Tell me."

"Things were going really good here," Annabel said. "I got a job and a place to live. Becca's in pre-K now. I have friends. We have playdates."

"Bel, you wanted me to call you. We can't talk about playdates. If it's not important, I have to go. You won't be able to call this number again."

"No, wait! It's Jacob. Jake. He's my boyfriend. We met about a year and a half ago. He was real nice. Becca likes him. He has a job and everything. He's not like Corey was. We went out a lot. It was good."

"What are you telling me?" Camaro asked.

"It's not so good anymore."

"What can I do about it?"

"You don't understand," Annabel said. "He's in my life. We go out, we stay in…he's always around. Or most of the time, anyway. It's hard to get rid of someone when they're so close to you."

"Why do you want to get rid of him?"

Annabel sounded small. "I'm afraid of him."

Camaro sat forward. "Did he hurt you? Did he hurt Becca?"

"No, he didn't hurt Becca. I don't think he would ever hurt a kid. He likes her. They get along real well."

"Did he hurt you?" Camaro asked Annabel again.

"It was my fault," Annabel said.

"Jesus Christ, Bel."

"We were getting along great, but I can't make him happy. He tells me what he wants and I do it, but it's never good enough. And he drinks. Camaro, I can't deal with this. I need your help. It can't go on."

Camaro reached up to rub her brow and touched her stitches instead. She sighed into the phone. "I don't understand how this happens. Everything you've been through and you can't…I don't understand."

"I know. I *know*."

A sob carried over the line. Camaro frowned at the sound. "Don't cry," she said.

"I'm an idiot."

"You're not an idiot."

"I am. And I need you."

"What exactly do you want me to do?" Camaro asked.

"You have to make him go away. I can't leave this place. It's too good for me and for Becca. We have to stay. He has to go."

Camaro was silent.

"Camaro, I need your help."

"Tell me where you are. I'll come."

# CHAPTER FOUR

The cur tains wer e drawn in the motel room's window, but Lukas Collier knew it was snowing outside. It had been snowing all day, and the day before and the day before that, too. Snow lay six feet deep in places, with drifts twice as high, but somehow the city of Denver went on functioning.

Three days before, Lukas had skidded on some ice in his stolen Buick and crushed the right side of the front bumper. The headlight still worked, but it was pointed in the wrong direction. Rather than draw attention with a wonky headlight, Lukas used one of the credit cards he'd taken from the Buick's owner and bought himself a room to rest and drink and see in the new year.

The room was festooned with beer bottles and a couple of empty fifths. It reeked of cigarette smoke, and the ashtray by the bed overflowed. When one credit card was declined, Lukas switched to another. He had a third for when this one died. They were all lasting a while because the man Lukas took them from was laid up in a hospital somewhere with his head broken open. A man in his condition did not call his bank to cancel cards.

He had the television on. It was a rerun of *Who Wants to Be a Millionaire?*, and he paid no attention to it, nor had he to anything that had come on before it. He lay nude atop the sheets with a beer to hand. He hadn't shaved in a week, and his hair was messy.

The toilet flushed, and the bathroom door opened. A naked girl emerged, her skin looking pinched and tight from the chill in the room. She hurried to the bed and threw the covers over herself. Orange hair spilled on the pillow. Her makeup needed redoing. "You should turn up the heat, baby," she said.

"Cold's good for you."

"I think you just like seeing my nipples get hard."

"That, too."

He pushed himself up against the headboard and fished a cigarette out of the pack by the bed. He sparked his lighter to it and inhaled deeply before exhaling through his nose.

The girl touched his arm and traced one of his tattoos. His right arm was completely sleeved, the left partly done. His chest and stomach were inked, and he had a grizzly bear on his shoulder blade. He wore his hair long.

"You got any money left?" she asked.

Lukas eyed her. He tucked the cigarette into the corner of his mouth and used his free hand to pull the covers from the girl's body. She might have been twenty-one, but she had a teenager's looks. A pink heart inked her right hip. She lay back to let him look at her.

"So . . . you got any money left?"

"Some."

"How much?"

"What does it matter?"

"You don't need to be rude. I'm just asking."

He smoked and watched the television. She started to cover herself again. He stopped her. "Keep 'em off."

"I'm *cold.*"

"You know how to warm up."

Lukas saw her smile out of the corner of his eye. "Yes, sir," she said.

When they were done again, she left the bed to throw away the condom. Lukas sat up and gathered his jeans off the floor. His wallet was fat with cash. He counted out a hundred and put it on the bed beside him. She snatched it up and spirited it away in the little pink-and-yellow-striped purse she brought with her.

Lukas lay down again. He wanted beer, but there was no more.

The girl sat on the edge of the bed with her purse on her lap. She rummaged inside until she came up with a small glass pipe and a baggie the size of a postage stamp. "You want to smoke with me?" she asked.

"That shit? Hell, no. My body is a temple."

"If you let me smoke a little, I'll do you once for free."

"Whatever," Lukas said. He searched for the television remote.

The first blow to the motel room door did not burst the lock, but it bent the cheap metal inward. The second blasted the door open, and a flurry of wind and snowflakes chased into the room. Blazing headlights framed a tall figure made burly by a tactical vest and winter gear.

The girl screamed and dropped her pipe on the carpet.

Lukas saw a heavy pepper-spray canister in the figure's hand as the man surged forward into the room. Lukas's hand went beneath the pillows.

Orange spray erupted, painting the wall where Lukas had been. Lukas rolled off the bed and crabbed sideways, putting the girl between him and the newcomer. The Colt in Lukas's grip was hard and cool. He brought it up and fired, three shots at a range of less than ten feet. The report was thunderous in the small room. The man with the pepper spray buckled and collapsed to the thin carpeting. He didn't move.

"Oh, Jesus!" the girl screamed. She clawed for the bedsheets to cover herself. "Oh, Jesus!"

Lukas shoved her out of the way and jumped into his jeans. He put his boots on without bothering with socks and grabbed a T-shirt and jacket off the back of a chair.

The room was still bathed in light from the vehicle outside, and despite the ringing in his ears Lukas heard the engine rumbling. He paused over the motionless corpse on the floor. "Sorry, Stanley," he said.

Lukas stepped out into the freezing twilight and found a Ford Super Duty idling with the driver's door left open. The dome light was on, and the vehicle pinged a steady warning. He climbed into the truck and slammed the door. He put the transmission in reverse and peeled backward out of the parking space, wrenching the wheel around and skidding the tires on the sloppy, icy asphalt. One glance back, and he saw the girl in the room, still naked and wailing. He put the truck in drive and stomped the accelerator. He was gone before the first siren sounded.

# CHAPTER FIVE

It was raining, a cold rain that alternated between sleet and droplets. Annabel Espinoza sat in the living room on the couch with all the lights off but one. Her daughter, Rebecca, was asleep.

The house was small and welcoming, with big front windows to let in the sunlight when there was any. Annabel had flower beds on both sides of the front walk and in the shadow of the picket fence enclosing the lawn. All were barren now, fallow for the winter months, though the lawn still held a fresh emerald under a mantle of water and ice.

She got up from the couch and went to the kitchen. She set a kettle on the stove to boil and selected a bag of chamomile tea to go with her teacup. After a time the kettle steamed, and the sound of Jake's engine carried from the street. She heard his footfalls on the doorstep before his key in the lock. Automatically she got a second cup and saucer for him and put them on the kitchen table with sugar and milk.

"Michelle?" Jake called.

"I'm in here."

He entered through the dining room, still wearing his wet jacket. When he swept the knit cap off his head, his blond hair stood up crazily. There had been a time when she found his perpetual look of untidiness boyish, even handsome, but that time had passed in bits and pieces until now there was nothing except a pit in the bottom of her stomach. She faked a smile, but it was weak.

"I didn't think you'd be awake," Jake said.

"I wasn't feeling good. Why are you here so late?"

"You don't want me around?"

"No, it's...I didn't expect you now."

Jake drew her close and kissed her on the forehead. Annabel put her arms around him reluctantly. "I'm going to have some tea," she told him. "Do you want some?"

"I don't have tea on my mind." He reached around to grope her behind.

"Jake, I'm really not feeling good."

"Oh, come on. Everybody says sex makes your immune system stronger."

"Jake, I don't—"

He caught her by the hair and gripped it tightly. A muscle in his jaw twitched. "Aren't I asking nicely?"

"Jake, please don't hurt me."

"Don't make me."

Annabel did what he wanted right there in the kitchen. She gripped the edge of the table and closed her eyes to everything until it was over. Afterward he did not seem to notice her brush the moisture from her eye.

"*Now* let's have some tea," he said.

They sat down opposite each other. Annabel poured hot water into their cups. She steeped her tea bag in silence, aware of Jake doing the same on his side of the table. Her lip trembled, but her hands did not shake.

"Quit acting like I kicked your dog," Jake said finally.

"I'm not doing anything."

"Exactly. You're not doing anything. You don't say anything. You just sit there with your tea."

"I told you I feel sick."

Jake put his teacup down too hard. "Then go to bed. I'm not keeping you up."

"I don't want to fight."

"What else is new?"

Annabel held her cup in both hands when she drank. The heat fortified her, and her insides stopped quaking. She thought of Camaro. "Are you staying over tonight?"

"Why? Now you don't want me to? All the time you used to ask me if I'd stay, and then you'd act all hurt when I didn't. Now look at you. It makes me want to pop you one right in the mouth. Help you get that stupid look off your face."

"I only asked."

"You have a lot of questions tonight. Do you have something going on?" Jake asked.

Annabel kept her face still. "No. Why?"

"You put any more thought into what I told you?"

"Yes."

"I really need another loan. Me and Derrick, we're just about to close a deal on a real sweet place out by the water. People can walk right down to the beach and surf. It's gonna be nice. Everything we want."

"I need more time."

Jake checked his watch and tapped the face. "I've already given you three weeks. How much more time do you need?"

"Not much longer."

Jake grunted. "Okay, but you better hurry it up. The landlord's not going to hold the place for us forever, and we have to sign a lease agreement soon. So scrape up whatever cash you got or cut me a check. If you can afford to keep this place, you can spare some for our future."

"Jake, I told you before that all my money's tied up in the house."

"But you always have enough for new clothes. How many pairs of shoes do you have? Huh? How many purses? I've never seen anybody with so many purses in my life. Those all cost money. You've got it all squirreled away, but you have it. I just want what's mine."

Annabel looked into her cup. "I'll try."

He pointed his finger at her, and she flinched. "No, you're not gonna try. You're gonna *do*. It's bad enough I have to practically beg you to do me, but now you're going to hold out when my business is at stake? I don't think so. So get with the program, Chelle."

"Okay," Annabel whispered.

"What?"

"I said okay."

"Good girl."

"So...are you?"

"Am I what?"

"Staying."

"Nah. I just wanted to stop by and let you know what you've been missing."

# CHAPTER SIX

Detectiv e Ter ence Lit tle stood in the steadily falling snow outside the Sunrise Motel and brushed a flake from the notebook on which he scribbled. It was so cold, the ink in his pen was sluggish. From time to time he rolled the pen vigorously between his hands to get things flowing again. The freeze was polar.

The parking lot was full of lights, flickering and solid. A trio of Denver Police Department vehicles stood in the main traffic lane, blocking off one exit and forming a natural barrier to the news trucks gathered in the street beyond. Light bars cast red and blue across the face of the motel while members of the Crime Scene Investigations Section shuttled in and out of the room where the body lay. Bright camera flashes still popped inside the room, but it wouldn't be long before the corpse was cleared.

Terence saw the girl dressed and bundled up and sent away in an ambulance, and his initial notes were complete. Now he marked his thoughts in the margins.

"Excuse me," a man said. "Detective Little?"

Terence looked up, his concentration broken. He saw a man and woman in long, dark coats approaching across the fresh layer of snow. They wore matching black scarves, and they had expensive haircuts, the man with a neat beard. The man was not tall, but he stood rigidly upright.

"It's Detective Little, isn't it?" the man asked when he came close.

"Yes," Terence said carefully. "Who are you? You shouldn't be here. This is a crime scene."

The man produced an identification wallet and displayed his credentials. "I'm Keith Way of the United States Marshals Service. This is Deputy Marshal Piper Hannon. I understand you're the man in charge."

"That's right. What brings you out tonight, Marshal?"

"Deputy Marshal. We just got into town from Wichita," Way said. "We have a fugitive investigation under way, and we think our cases are linked. Can you show us around the scene?"

Terence regarded the marshals. Way had a hard, tan face that was not unhandsome, though his nose had clearly been broken more than once. Hannon was younger than Way by seven or eight years, a small and slender figure in her coat, her expression solemn and her eyes unreadable. When Terence looked at her, she simply looked back.

"Yeah, sure," he said. "Follow me."

They went to the room. Terence stepped aside to let Way and Hannon through the broken door. The two stepped over the corpse with no sign of distaste. Hannon produced a tiny digital camera from the pocket of her coat and proceeded to snap pictures of the room. Way stared at the dead man. "Any witnesses?"

"One. A prostitute who spent the day with our shooter. Problem is, she never got a name, and she's so freaked-out by what happened, her description of the man is almost useless."

"His name is Lukas Collier," Way said.

Terence glanced around the room. "Did you just pull that out of thin air, or did I miss something here?"

Hannon took shots of the dead man.

"Have you identified your victim?" Way asked.

"Yeah, Stanley Yates from Norfolk, Virginia. He's a bounty hunter."

"That's how I know who did the shooting," Way said. "Stanley Yates was pursuing a skip out of Virginia. Felony bail jump on a charge of carrying a concealed weapon. The skip's name is Lukas Collier."

"He's a long way from Virginia now. What's your interest?"

"A little over a year ago, Collier gunned down a marshal in New Jersey. He was already a fugitive on that charge when the court in Norfolk let him make bail on the weapons beef. It's a whole mix-up, and you don't need to know all the details. The thing is, Collier belongs to us."

"How does Yates figure into the picture?"

"The bail was pretty steep. Yates figured he had to make good on the bond. We tried to warn him off, but he didn't listen. Now we see what happens."

"I guess that explains the pepper spray," Terence said.

"He was a professional," Hannon said suddenly. "No license to carry firearms in the state. Pepper spray is something anyone can have."

Terence crouched over the body. It was rigid and bluish from settling blood and the frigid temperature. He used his pen to prod an empty loop on Stanley Yates's tactical vest. "Pepper-spray cowboy," he said. "Makes sense now."

"Where's Yates's truck?" Way asked.

"What?"

"Yates's truck. He drove a Ford Super Duty. Dark blue. It would have Virginia plates."

"There was no truck on the scene."

"Did you check other vehicles in the lot and match them to guests?"

"We did. There was a stolen Buick in the lot we guess our shooter came in with."

"And it's still here."

"Right."

"So, what, did you figure Collier just walked away? What did your witness say?"

"She said he left, but she didn't specify. The woman was in shock and suffering from hypothermia when we got to her. I figured we'd get more once she had a chance to come down in the hospital."

Way fixed Terence with a glare. He had heavy brows that settled down over his eyes. "You listen to me, Detective. You have a cop killer running around in a stolen vehicle *right now*. He might even be close enough to catch on one of the main highways if we're quick enough. I'm going to have my partner write down Yates's license plate number, and you're going to put it through every channel you have. It's a big truck, and it's easy to spot on the road. I don't want Lukas Collier getting out of this state."

Terence straightened up. "I'll get right on it."

"If Collier gets away because you were too busy waiting for your witness to get her head together, I'm going to be very disappointed."

# CHAPTER SEVEN

At midday in Northern California there was a steady, bleak rain. Clouds obscured the sun. Camaro got into a cab at the airport and told the driver where to go. She watched the city of Monterey slip away after they joined the highway and thought ahead to the next thing, a moment long delayed, when she'd see her sister again.

Monterey was a small city, and Carmel-by-the-Sea barely qualified as a city at all, with fewer than four thousand people to its name. Camaro had looked the place up online when Annabel told her about it, and it seemed more like a town that happened to grow a little larger than intended, tucked against Monterey Bay.

As they passed the threshold into Carmel itself, her impression didn't change. It was generously wooded here. The houses fit into the landscape, and in the afternoon streets there was peace. Not a single home had bars on the windows or doors. The asphalt was even and dark, without a pothole anywhere. When they drove down a street lined with businesses, she saw no franchises, no big-box stores.

They drove a little while longer and went down a crooked lane to a cul-de-sac among more trees. The driver stopped broadside to a small house with a picket fence and friendly windows in front. Neat curtains tied up with bows framed the glass. A sign with the street name and house number hung from a flawless white upright, and the path from the gate to the door was lined with tiny, solar-powered lamps.

The driver shut down his meter. "Thirty-eight dollars even."

"This is it?" Camaro asked him.

"Yeah, this is the place."

She paid the driver cash and stepped out into the rain. The taxi slipped away and left her on the sidewalk. The homes on either side of her sister's were likewise quiet. Through the picture window in the front of one, Camaro saw an older woman sitting with a mug of something in front of a large plasma television.

The gate made no noise when she pushed it open. There was only the sound of the falling droplets on grass. A tree without leaves stood in the yard. Its branches were the right height for climbing.

Camaro stepped onto the porch. She paused a long moment before pressing the doorbell. The sound of chimes carried from inside.

Footfalls sounded on the far side of the door. It opened, and Camaro was suffused with warmth and the smell of cinnamon. Annabel was there.

Camaro put down her bag, and they embraced on the doorstep. Annabel was shorter than her by inches, and slight. She clung to Camaro and squeezed her, and when her body trembled, Camaro knew she was crying.

"You came," Annabel said into her shoulder.

"I said I'd come."

Annabel pushed away from Camaro and held her at arm's length. Camaro saw her notice the stitches on her brow. Annabel's eyes glistened with tears. "I know," she said, "but you're here. You're here."

"I wouldn't stay away," Camaro said.

"Thank you." She hugged Camaro again fiercely. "Thank you so much. You're soaked. Get in here."

Camaro stepped across the threshold into the house. The air was scented, and the Christmas tree was still up. The living room had a fireplace, and three stockings were hung. The floors were hardwood.

Annabel pressed the door closed and locked it. "I didn't know when you'd be here. I don't have any lunch for you."

"It's all right," Camaro said.

"Mommy, who is it?"

The little girl Camaro saw was nearly three years older than the one Camaro remembered. She was small, almost five, and had light hair from her father but the soft coloring of her mother. A woolen sweater made her look pudgy. Pigtails sprouted from her head, clipped with pink barrettes. Camaro held her breath.

Annabel rushed to Rebecca's side and put an arm around her. She urged Rebecca forward. "Becca, this is your auntie. Auntie Camaro. You remember her, right?"

Rebecca regarded Camaro with dark eyes. "No."

Camaro knelt. She looked her niece in the face. She extended a hand. "It's okay if you don't. I remember you. Shake hello?"

Rebecca stood motionless for a long moment before reaching out. They touched fingers, and then Rebecca withdrew hers definitively.

"Let's go to the kitchen. We were coloring," Annabel said.

The kitchen was neat, the countertops made of rich wood, the appliances stainless steel. There was room enough for a large table with a view of the backyard. A climber and swings stood lonely and wet in the rain.

Camaro put her bag in the corner and stripped off her wet jacket. She hung it on a peg by the back door beside a child's raincoat. When she sat at the table, she sat opposite her sister. They looked at each other across a scattering of crayon drawings.

For a while they said nothing. Camaro spoke first. "Nice place."

"Thank you."

"Pricey?"

"Kind of. But I fixed it up."

"How much do you have put away?"

"Not a lot. Some."

"Same here," Camaro said.

"What did you buy?"

"A boat."

Annabel smiled. "Like Dad always wanted."

"What do they call you here?" Camaro asked.

"Michelle Amado."

"Michelle. You took Mom's name."

"Yeah," Annabel said. She looked sad. "Who should I tell people you are? What name should I give them?"

"Tell them I'm your sister. And they can call me Camaro."

Annabel nodded. "No lies."

"No lies are the best lies," Camaro said. "I'm your sister, and I came to visit. No one needs to know from where or anything about me at all."

"Right. You're right."

"What do you do?"

"Me? I work in a clothing shop. It's a little place. I know the owner, Wilson, really well. He hired me without any references, and he's been a great boss. He never asks me anything about my past."

"That's good. If he ever does, just tell him it's complicated."

"I think he knows." Annabel took a deep breath. "What do you do with your boat?"

"Charters."

"That's awesome. You're a fishing boat captain. You still ride?"

"Yeah."

"That's good."

Camaro watched Rebecca color. The girl was in the middle of a detailed drawing of a house not unlike her own, except the colors were wild and garish where this home was warm and welcoming. The grass was electric blue.

"You've been fighting," Annabel said.

Unconsciously, Camaro raised fingers to her brow. "Sometimes."

"Are you okay?"

"I'm okay."

"I worry sometimes."

"Don't. Tell me about your problem," Camaro said.

Annabel swallowed. "I don't think we should talk about this in front of Becca."

"Okay."

Annabel gathered up Rebecca's drawings and crayons. "Hey, baby, why don't we take all of this into your room for a little while. Auntie Camaro and I have to talk a little bit about grown-up stuff. That's okay, right?"

"This one is almost finished."

"Well, you get it all done, and then we'll put it on the refrigerator." Annabel hustled her daughter out of the room.

Camaro waited. She heard them talking in muffled voices elsewhere in the house. The walls were thick here, the house old.

Annabel returned. "Do you want something to drink? Coffee? I have tea."

"I don't need anything."

Her sister sat down. "Okay. Okay, I'm ready."

"Tell me," Camaro said.

"His name is Jake. I told you that."

"Who is he? What does he do?"

"He's a surfer. That's how we met. I always wanted to learn, you know? He was teaching part-time for this surfing school. He was always a real gentleman. He treated me right."

"What does he do besides surf?"

"He works at a lumberyard in Pacific Grove."

"Where's that?"

"It's another town. It's not far."

Camaro found a rough spot on the tabletop and picked at it with her thumb. "And he's a bum."

"He's not a bum. He has a job."

"I don't care that he's got a job. He's just another bum," Camaro said. "One more bum on top of every other bum you ever picked up."

Annabel looked as if she might bolt from her chair. "It's not the same. He was good to Becca, and he was good to me, and he never asked me for anything except money once in a while when he was short. It's expensive to live here, Camaro. He did the best he could."

"But he hurt you. He's hurting you."

Annabel's face wrinkled, but she didn't speak.

"If he hurt you, he's not a good guy. He's a dirtbag. I want to hear you say it," Camaro said.

Annabel wrung her hands. "Please fix it, Camaro. Just fix it for me."

# CHAPTER EIGHT

A replay of a college football game played silently on a television in the corner of Jeremy Yates's office as he snoozed. He had his boots on the desk and his ragged office chair tilted to capture his long, rangy form at rest. A cup of coffee sat on the blotter, gone completely cold. Outside the windows, soft snowfall flickered green and red from the brilliant neon signs that announced yates all-nite bail bonds.

The telephone on the desk rang. Yates stirred. It rang twice more before he woke completely. He was seventy-one, and wakefulness came slowly. He coughed and dropped his feet to the floor and stretched his long arms over his head until his back popped. Only then did he answer. "Bail bondsman."

The connection popped, and Yates heard the murmur of voices in the background. He looked at the clock. It was after nine.

"Is this Jeremy Yates?" asked a man.

"Yeah, this is Jeremy Yates. Who is this?" He scrubbed his scalp with his fingertips and stirred up his slightly too-long hair. He was sharper now. He smoothed down his mustache, then ran his hand over his scratchy cheeks and chin. It had been a few days since he shaved last.

"This is Keith Way of the U.S. Marshals Service. You'll remember me?"

"I remember. I don't have any word about Lukas Collier."

"I do."

Yates grabbed a pen from a mug on the desk and found a scrap of paper for writing. "Is he caught? Where's he at?"

"We have people searching for him right now."

"Where?"

"Salt Lake City. A little out of your area."

"Collier's in Utah?" Yates wrote "UTAH?" on his paper, then circled it. To one side he started listing the states adjoining Utah: Nevada, Idaho, Wyoming, Arizona, Colorado. "I'll tell my son. Last I heard, he was headed toward Denver. He could be out where you are by now."

"Yeah, that's the thing. Mr. Yates, your son is dead."

The room shrank. His body buzzed with electricity, and he heard the hum of blood rushing through his ears. "What?" he said at last.

"He's dead. He was killed by Lukas Collier last night in a Denver motel room."

Yates's grip loosened on the phone, but then he clutched it again more tightly. He sat upright in his seat, blinking away a sudden blurriness in his vision. "When exactly?"

"About midnight, local time."

"And you're telling me about this *now?*"

"We've been busy."

"It's been a day! You couldn't spare one goddamned minute to tell me my son was murdered? What the hell happened?"

Way continued. "From what we can tell, Stanley died instantly."

"Stanley? I didn't know you two were on a first-name basis."

"I met with him once after Collier skipped. I *told* him not to pursue the man. It's the same thing I told you on the phone, but neither of you wanted to listen to reason. And this is what happens when people don't listen to reason."

Yates swallowed something bitter. "Where is Collier going?"

"We're working on that."

"How?"

"We have leads."

"What leads?"

Way paused. "Collier fled the scene of the crime with your son's truck. But that's not your concern."

"What is my concern?"

"I'll give you the number of the Denver Police Department so you can make arrangements for the transfer of your son's remains."

There was a vibration at the center of Yates's body that slowly built in intensity as he held the phone to his ear. It was warm and growing

30

warmer, crawling up his spine and through his bones until it put his teeth on edge. He still gripped the pen. The plastic snapped. "It was mighty kind of you to call, Mr. Way. Thank you."

"You're obviously out of the picture, so I won't bother to update you on the Collier situation until it's done."

"You do that. Good-bye."

Yates put the phone in its cradle. He slumped forward in his chair and caught his head in his hands. He cradled his skull for a long time, listening to his heartbeat. The tears he feared might come did not erupt.

A footstep scuffed in the back of the office. Tricia Yates appeared in her coat and boots. His wife had been in and out of the office all day in between shoveling the walks. She never let him do it. "Did I hear the phone ring?"

"Yes."

"Do I need to put some coffee on for you?"

"No. Why don't you go on to bed? I'll lie down on the cot after a while. I'll talk to you in the morning."

"Love you," she said.

"I love you, too."

She went. Yates collected the broken pieces of the pen. He put them in the wastebasket. The desktop computer was sleeping. He woke it and entered his password. On the sheet of scratch paper there were his brief notes. He clicked on the Dropbox icon and entered his son's account information. A folder of text files opened. He clicked the first one.

# CHAPTER NINE

Camaro spent the day at Annabel's house as rain drummed on the roof. For lunch Annabel made toasted cheese sandwiches with four different kinds of cheese and a slice of ripe tomato. Annabel put a couple of logs in the fireplace to warm the room. They sat together on the couch, watching the flames flicker and listening to the pop of the wood as it burned.

Rebecca brought a dollhouse out of her room and set it up in the radius of the fire, playing with cloth dolls and doing the voices of mother and father and baby, too. Camaro listened to the little girl and smiled.

"What is it?" Annabel asked her.

"What?"

"You're smiling."

"She reminds me of you," Camaro said. "When you were her age. She's exactly like you."

"Is she?"

"Yes. Exactly."

Camaro observed Rebecca as she walked her mother and father dolls hand in hand out into the pretend yard, where the baby sat on the ground next to a hairy dog. She spread out a checkered kerchief as a picnic blanket, and the whole family sat around to eat imaginary sandwiches. Everyone laughed, and the mother kissed the father on the cheek.

"She'll ask someday," Camaro said. "About her father. And when she does, tell her the truth. Whatever she does then, it'll be on her and not you."

"Everything is on me. I'm her mother."

"That's the kind of thinking that drove Dad crazy. Kids have to screw up on their own. You can't save them."

"You always tried to save me."

"That's my choice. I do it because I want to, not because I have to."

Annabel put her hand on Camaro's and threaded their fingers together. She said nothing for a while, and Camaro did the same. At the make-believe picnic, the mother was telling her baby the story of the Three Bears.

"I'm glad you came. I'm grateful."

"I haven't done anything yet," Camaro said.

"But you will."

Camaro looked at Annabel. "How bad did he hurt you, Bel?"

Annabel turned away.

Camaro closed her grip on Annabel's hand. "How bad?"

Annabel pulled her hand free.

"Bad enough. Let go."

Camaro watched her sister closely. "Whatever he did to you, it wasn't your fault."

Annabel sniffed and touched the corner of her eye. "I know."

"And he's never going to do it again. Ever. He'll have to come through me first."

"I know."

Annabel patted Camaro on the arm. Camaro felt a surge of heat, and she clenched her teeth until the moment passed. The muscles in her jaw unwound slowly. She looked back to Rebecca. The little girl whispered now, the heads of her dolls pressed together in secret conference. Camaro heard nothing but the breathy susurrus of her tiny voice.

"I could use a drink," Camaro announced.

"I have beer. It's Jake's brand."

They retreated to the kitchen, and Annabel pulled a six-pack of Bud Light bottles from the bottom shelf of the refrigerator.

"You're kidding me," Camaro said.

"He likes light beer."

"I'd rather drink water."

"I'm sorry."

"Don't be. Throw them away. He's never coming back to drink them."

Annabel took them to the sink and twisted off the tops one by one, pouring the beer into the drain. She had a recycling bin next to the trash. They sat down at the kitchen table. Annabel directed her gaze out the window. Her eyes were puffy and rimmed with red. "I'm tired of crying," she said at last.

"He's not worth it."

"You never cry," Annabel said.

"No."

"You know, sometimes I used to wish I were you. When I was little. I remember when you had your thirteenth birthday and I was nine, and you seemed like you were all grown up already. And Dad took you riding around on that ratty old Harley he was always getting you to help him with. I wanted to be grown up, too. I wanted to be on the back of the bike."

"It was never a competition," Camaro said. "He loved us both the same."

"I know that now. But it took me a while. When you were gone and he got sick, I was so mad at you for going, because maybe he wouldn't have fallen apart. You know? Like maybe he would have kept it together if he wasn't worried about you getting shot in some desert somewhere. Because he'd never say so. He'd just watch the news and get drunk and start yelling at me and everybody else. I couldn't wait to get out of there."

Camaro watched the rain. "I never meant to hurt him. Or you. It's just when the towers came down...I had to do something. I couldn't do nothing."

"That's you," Annabel said, then smiled weakly. "Trying to save everybody."

"It's not a good habit to get into. Somebody always needs something."

"Like me."

"Don't start that again."

"I'm sorry."

"And stop being sorry."

"I'm...okay."

Camaro looked around at the kitchen and the neat counters, the cabinets with frosted-glass fronts, and the hanging rack of copper-bottomed pans. She encompassed all of it with a wave of her hand. "You have all of this. And a daughter who loves you. That's the kind of thing people wait a whole lifetime for. Dad never had it. I don't have it. This is what you fight for. So I don't want to hear you say 'I'm sorry' again. You understand me?"

Annabel straightened up. "I do."

"Tomorrow I'll go deal with this," Camaro said. "And then it'll be over. It'll be over."

# CHAPTER TEN

The rain clear ed overnight. Camaro slept in the guest bedroom and woke with the sun through her window and the smell of cooking bacon. She found Annabel in the kitchen, making eggs to match. A stack of pancakes stayed warm beneath a towel.

"I figured you'd be hungry," Annabel said.

"I am."

"Then let's eat. After that I have someone to watch Becca, and I can take you to see Jake."

"What do you mean, you're going to take me?"

"I'm going to be there."

"No, you're not," Camaro said. She sat at the table. "You're going to lend me your car, and I'm going to go see him on my own. You're not going to be a part of this at all."

"But you said I should fight."

"Not this kind of fighting. I need to know you're here safe with Becca. That lets me do whatever I need to do."

Annabel turned out two fried eggs onto a plate, then added two strips of bacon. She laid on pancakes and put it all in front of Camaro. "You're not going to…"

"No, I'm not. We're going to talk. He's going to listen. Then we walk away."

"He's hard to scare, Camaro. He's tough."

"We'll see." She shook pepper over her eggs and cut into them with a fork. The yolks ran. She ate the whites and soaked the bacon in what was left. Afterward she drizzled her pancakes lightly with maple syrup. They smelled of nutmeg, and when cut they smelled even more intensely.

Annabel set places for herself and Rebecca. "Good?"

"Good. Now tell me where I can find Jake."

Annabel gave Camaro Jake's address and explained how to link her phone to the little Subaru Crosstrek parked on the street. She hugged Camaro one last time at the door.

Jake's house was in Salinas. The drive would take half an hour. The Crosstrek had satellite radio, and Camaro played with the channels until she found one playing Black Sabbath's "Paranoid." She left it there as she drove the quiet Sunday streets of Carmel-by-the-Sea before hooking up with the Salinas Highway for the rest of the drive.

Salinas was not Carmel. There were no picturesque houses on its streets, and the stores were in strip malls or planted in the asphalt acreage of parking lots. Camaro found Jake's small, burnt-orange house on a street across from a small apartment building, the concrete of its driveway separated from the concrete of the neighboring house's driveway by a teetering wooden barrier. A centur y 21 sign was posted just inside the chain-link fence in a yard consisting mainly of mud.

Camaro parked by the apartments and got out. The air was crisp from the morning, and her jacket was still damp from the day before. She cracked her knuckles and crossed the street.

She stopped at the gate and listened, but there was no dog. She found the latch unsecured and stepped through. The short walk was uneven and cracked, and the porch was simply a poured slab of cement raised no more than an inch or two off the ground. It was awash in bits of dirt flooded over by the rains.

The curtains were open in the front window. Camaro looked at a room mostly empty except for a couch and a television. Bud Light bottles sat collected at one end of the couch. An Xbox was connected to the TV, the wires strung out on the floor.

Camaro turned to the front door and knocked. A minute passed, and no one answered. She heard nothing on the other side.

Another gate led off the porch onto the driveway. Camaro let herself out and looked down along the house. Three windows were visible along the side, the last a part of some disorganized extension at the rear of the house. She went to the first and put her hands up to peer inside. There was a hallway with a bathroom visible at the end of it. At the second she found herself looking into a bedroom messy with clothes thrown wherever there was a spot.

The window farthest back was blocked by a set of wooden shelves. She rounded the house's back end and found a better angle. A sunroom had been transformed into storage space piled with boxes and disused exercise equipment, a wheelbarrow, and even a pinball machine. Camaro backtracked and headed up the driveway.

"He's not there," someone said.

Camaro spotted the man over the wooden divider between the driveways. He stood under his carport. He smiled at her as she came closer.

"Where is he?" Camaro asked.

"I don't know," the man said. He was dark-skinned and had a broad slab of mustache that looked pasted on. "He hasn't been home for a couple of days. Could be working, could be at one of his girlfriends' places."

"Girlfriends?"

"Oh, yeah. He's got a couple."

"How well do you know him?" Camaro asked.

The man shrugged. "What's to know? He likes to party, and he likes the ladies. I know he gets plenty of tail when he goes out teaching surfing in the summers. Is that where you met him?"

"I've never even seen him," Camaro said.

"You're not one of his girls?"

"Do I look like I am?"

The man considered her. "No. I guess not. You don't look like the rich-bitch type."

"I'm not."

"Actually you look like you want to twist somebody's nuts in a knot."

"Listen, where can I find him? Where does he work?"

"Carlson Lumber. It's over in Pacific Grove."

"You know the address?"

"No, but I have the Internet. You got the Internet?"

"Yeah, I do," Camaro said. "Thanks."

"No problem. You gonna kill him?"

Camaro stepped away. "No. But people keep asking me that."

"I'll look for you on the news."

Camaro went back to the SUV and used her phone to look up the lumberyard. She twisted the key in the ignition, and the engine thrummed to life. The GPS said thirty-five minutes.

# CHAPTER ELEVEN

The yard was an unremarkable place: high walls with great towers of fresh-cut wood stacked against them. A warehouse-sized building dominated the center of the lot, its rolling doors thrown wide open to show the cavernous interior where lumber was measured and sheared to order. A forklift was busy on the sales floor, carrying a heavy load of two-by-fours.

Camaro parked the Subaru among the scattering of trucks in the plain gravel lot. As she approached the warehouse, she saw the manager's office and a sales counter and angled toward them. A man in overalls worked the register.

"Morning, miss," he said when she came close. "What can I do you for?"

"Jacob Collier."

"Jake's around out back. Want me to call him up?"

"No, I'll find him."

Outside she rounded the warehouse and walked in the space between the stacks and the corrugated aluminum wall of the building. Wisps of music carried from ahead, along with men's laughter and voices. Camaro's pace quickened.

The area behind the warehouse was an echo of the front. Large sliding doors allowed the whole rear end of the structure to be opened to the outside, though they were halfway closed now. Another forklift stood idle in a puddle of mud, a portable CD player on the back of its seat playing Kid Rock. Four men in work shirts and jeans loaded planks onto the lift. They stopped when they saw Camaro.

One whistled. Camaro ignored him and came closer.

"Hey, honey," said another. "You lost?"

"Which one of you assholes is Jake?"

Everything stopped. Kid Rock boasted and crowed while the drums bashed and the electric guitars crunched. Camaro looked from one man to the next, and each one stared back at her. The last man on the left stepped forward. "I'm Jake."

He was lean, his flannel shirt worn open over a white cotton T-shirt. His boots were caked in mud, and his pants carried a fuzz of sawdust. Jake removed the work gloves he wore. He tossed them to one of the other men. Camaro stood waiting.

"Who are you?" Jake asked.

"My name's Camaro."

Jake laughed. "The sister! The famous sister. Finally came out from whatever rock you were hiding under, huh? And just to see me?"

He came toward her, and Camaro advanced to meet him. They stopped an arm's length apart. Jake had five inches on Camaro. She figured him for a hundred and sixty pounds or somewhere close. He glared down at her. She stared back.

"What?" Jake asked. "What do you want?"

"My sister's off-limits. You don't come around, you don't call. She never sees you again. That's it. That's all I have to say."

Jake studied her. "You some kind of badass?"

"I'm telling you how it is."

"You came all the way from wherever you were to tell me to get lost? What, Chelle can't do that for herself? Me and her, we're gonna have words."

"No," Camaro said.

"Nobody tells me no. Especially not some bitch."

He pushed her. She hit him in the throat.

The punch was hard and fast. Jake gagged and his face turned a brilliant red. He grabbed for his neck with one hand and reached for her with the other. Camaro gripped his forearm like a baseball bat and cranked it hard at the same moment she pivoted her hips into his.

Jake's elbow went into her armpit, and Camaro applied pressure and leverage to lock the joint. Jake made an incoherent sound, like he was seizing up from the inside. Camaro drove her shoulder down into his arm until the ligaments popped noisily. Jake screamed then.

The other men rushed them. Camaro wheeled around and pulled Jake with her. "Back the hell off or I'll break his arm."

They stopped sharply as Jake keened with pain.

Camaro released him, and Jake fell into the mud. She kicked him in the side of the head, snapping his skull around violently. He collapsed, his eyes rolling, and she kicked him again and again as the other men watched but didn't move.

She stopped. Her heart thumped, and she breathed heavily through the mouth. "She's off-limits. If I catch you within a mile of her, you will die. Do you understand me?"

Jake lolled in the wet, sticking mud. He made burbling sounds.

"Do you understand me?"

"Yeah. Yes. I understand," Jake managed.

One of the other men moved. Camaro fixed him with a glare. "You want some of this?"

The man shook his head. "No, ma'am."

"This is between him and me. He knows why," Camaro said. "Now I'm leaving."

She backed away with her eye on the men. Jake vomited spectacularly, painting the ground and the front of his shirt. The men near him recoiled. Kid Rock played on.

Camaro made it all the way to the Subaru before she heard someone yelling for the police. She got in the SUV and started it up, backing out fast but not spinning her tires in the gravel. At the road she accelerated away. When she had gone a quarter mile she heard the distant wail of a police siren.

# CHAPTER TWELVE

Carl y Russo came through the front doors of the Carmel Police Department's small station at three-thirty in the afternoon and waved to Chris Miller at the desk. She had her civilian clothes on, her uniform tucked away in a bag. Miller buzzed her through to the back. There she entered the locker room and made her way to the last locker on the right. The lock on it was brilliant pink.

She was alone, and everything was silent, including the single shower. Carmel had three women on its tiny police force, though sometimes it seemed like it was only her among the boys.

She stripped off her clothes, and her tattoos were exposed. On the inside of her right arm she had inked in decorative script "And though she be but little, she is fierce." On her side was a branch of cherry blossoms. A pair of wings spread out across her collarbones from a crowned diamond. None were visible when she wore her uniform. At five foot five and 106 pounds, with short hair and light makeup, in uniform she seemed as conservative as any citizen might desire.

Once changed, she went out.

"Anything amazing?" Russo asked Miller when she reached the desk.

"Not unless a visit from Mrs. Salazar is amazing."

"She was in today?"

"Of course. She said some homeless folks were rooting around in her garbage cans all night. I told her it was probably raccoons, but she's not listening to anybody. She wants an officer to stop by later. You can give it to whoever."

"Great," Russo said. "I'm sorry I missed her."

"You'll get your chance. Anyway, I have to split. I promised my wife we'd get on the road early."

43

"Where are you headed again?"

"Spokane, to see her folks."

"Have a good time."

"Always," Miller said.

Russo straightened up the front-desk area and made certain all the flyers and pamphlets were orderly. After that she spritzed down the countertops with cleanser and wiped them until they shone. The phone did not ring, and traffic was whatever passed in front of the station. The scattered desks remained empty. The only sound was the faint buzz of the fluorescent lights.

The phone call came a little over two hours after her shift began. "This is Travis Caldwell over in Pacific Grove," said the man on the other end. "Is this the officer on duty?"

"I can get you the sergeant, but I'm manning the phones. Carly Russo."

"Russo? You're not Shawn Russo's kid, are you?"

Russo smiled into the phone. "That's right."

"I'll be damned. How is Shawn?"

"Good. He's down in La Jolla now with my stepmom."

"Retirement is nice," Caldwell said.

"Yes, sir."

"Well, tell him I said hello the next time you talk to him, will you? It's been too long."

"I will. Was there something I could help you with, sir?"

"Oh, right. I almost forgot. Listen, we had an assault-and-battery case come in this morning we could use a little help on."

Russo grabbed a pad and a pen. "What can we do?"

"Fella name of Jake Collier got himself busted up pretty good at his job today by a woman with a serious chip on her shoulder. He's still at Community Hospital last I heard. Concussion, lost some teeth, cracked a rib. She came damned close to breaking his arm off at the elbow."

Russo tucked the phone between her ear and shoulder and used the terminal at the counter. She typed in "Jake Collier" and was rewarded with an electronic jacket. She saw a string of arrests for disorderly conduct, public drunkenness, and other misdemeanor violations. "Jacob Collier? I'm looking at his record right now."

"That's right. Lives in Salinas."

"Do you need me to e-mail his sheet to you?" Russo asked.

"You can do that if you want. Couldn't hurt to take a look. I imagine it's a lot like the one we have for him. Man likes to party. But that's not why I called. Do you have any record of a woman named Camaro Amado?"

"Camaro? Like the car?"

"That's right."

Russo submitted the request. "I don't have anything here."

"How about Michelle Amado?"

She checked. "Nothing. Who are they?"

"Collier and the witnesses say a woman named Camaro was the one who did all the damage. She has a sister who lives in Carmel, Michelle Amado, which is why I'm calling you. As far as we can see she's clean, but apparently this Camaro put a hurt on Collier at her sister's request. I was thinking about taking a drive over there to look into it myself, but I was wondering if you could have a unit knock on Michelle Amado's door. Where one sister is, the other one can't be too far away. Maybe you could see if either one of them is willing to come in voluntarily?"

Russo scribbled down all the names. "Give me the address, and we'll have someone go right over."

Caldwell recited it for her, and she wrote it down. "Tell your officer to be careful. I don't know anything about this Camaro woman, but I saw firsthand what she did to Jake Collier."

"Yes, sir. I'm on it."

"Good talking to you, Carly. Stop by our shop sometime and say hi."

"I will. Good-bye."

Russo hung up the phone. Immediately it rang again. "Carmel Police Department, Officer Russo speaking."

The line crackled. A man spoke. "Officer Russo, this is Deputy United States Marshal Keith Way."

Russo straightened unconsciously. "Yes, sir. How can I direct your call?"

"I'll make it quick, and you can pass this up the chain. I'm on the road to your area right now. I just got off the line with the Salinas PD. It's about a man named Jacob Collier."

45

Russo blinked. "Jacob Collier?"

"That's right. I understand from talking to Salinas that he gets around the Monterey Bay area. Jobs in different towns. Party type."

"Yes, sir. I know the name. I just—"

"Good," Way said, cutting her off. "I need to get a line on him. We have a fugitive situation, and Jacob Collier may be involved. Give me an e-mail address over there in Carmel so I can send you the fugitive's jacket. His name is Lukas Collier, Jacob Collier's brother. We have reason to believe he's headed for the coast. He's wanted for murder."

"Oh, wow," Russo said.

"Yeah. Wow. E-mail address?"

Russo gave it to him. "Do you want me to—"

"This is how we're going to work it. If Jacob Collier has known hangouts in your town, we need you to do a sweep for our fugitive. If you spot him, *do not attempt to apprehend him.* That's our job."

"You really should talk to my sergeant."

"I'll talk to him soon. Get that e-mail and start distributing copies of the attached sheet. How many officers do you have?"

"Twenty-one, but they're not all on duty."

"Tell your sergeant we need all hands on deck. I'm going to give you my cell phone number, and if there's anything not in that e-mail you people need clarification on, call me."

"Yes, sir. I'll take care of it, sir. But you ought to know—"

"Get working on that, Officer Russo. I'll be in touch."

Way ended the call. Russo stood dumbly for a moment with the receiver in her hand. It clicked and a dial tone sounded. She put it in the cradle.

The e-mail was already in the department's in-box when she checked. She clicked on a PDF, and a wanted flyer for Lukas Collier came onscreen. He was dark-haired with a half-grown beard and eyes like hard glass. He glared out of the screen at her. Russo forwarded the e-mail to all senior officers, including the chief.

She found Sergeant Mullins in his office. "Sergeant," she said, "we have kind of a situation."

"Mrs. Salazar again?"

"No, sir."

Russo told him the story. He checked his e-mail. She stood by while he scanned the other documents attached to the message. He stood up sharply and adjusted his uniform. "This needs to go to the chief," he said.

"I already sent it ahead."

"He's off today. He's not going to check work e-mails. I'll drive out and talk to him directly. In the meantime, do exactly as this marshal says and get Lukas Collier's particulars out to everyone on patrol. Put a copy on everybody's desk. You say his brother's in the hospital?"

"Yes, sir. That's the other thing. Pacific Grove PD wants us to—"

"Never mind what they want. We have a federal fugitive headed our way. Everything else goes on hold. Why are you still standing here? Get moving!"

"But the brother's in the hospital because he got assaulted, sir! Pacific Grove says the assailant's in Carmel right now."

"Didn't I say I don't have time for that? You can type it all up in a memo or something and then put it on my desk for whenever. I promise I'll look at it."

Russo left the office reluctantly.

# CHAPTER THIRTEEN

Lukas Collier  used a plastic comb on his wet hair and dragged it into something presentable. There was a spot of shaving cream behind the point of his jaw, and he used a hand towel to wipe it away. His face was a little pink from the hot water. He ran his fingers over his cheeks and felt nothing but skin. Being shaved closely reminded him of being in the Marines, a memory that was partly welcome and partly disagreeable.

He had new clothes laid out on the bed. He used deodorant under each arm before pulling on an undershirt still scratchy from the package. A loose blue work shirt went over that, and he put on a pair of boot-cut jeans. He'd bought a bundle of thick socks with blue soles. He donned a fresh set of steel-toed boots. His other pair had Stanley Yates's blood staining them.

The curtains on the hotel room's window were open, and the Las Vegas Strip glowed in the dark. Lukas had chosen the place at random, paid cash at the front desk, and put in a call to Konnor Spencer from the courtesy phone. They made plans to meet at nine. It was a quarter of now.

The room came with a phone, but he didn't use it. Lukas went down to the gift shop in the lobby and bought a prepaid phone off the rack, then paused just outside the casino to unwrap it. Once it was activated, he dialed and waited for an answer.

Jacob sounded as though he had the stuffiest of colds. "Hello?" he asked. "Who is it?"

"Jake, it's me."

"Oh, shit, Luke."

"What's the matter with you? You sound sick."

"I'm a little busted up."

Lukas glanced around. No one was watching. "What are you talking about?"

"Chelle."

"What about her?"

"Chelle got me, bro."

Across the lobby, Konnor appeared. He was a big man in a denim-and-leather motorcycle jacket, his head shaved bald. A thick chin beard fell into a braid that nearly touched his chest. Konnor waved. Lukas raised a hand, then turned his back. "What do you mean, she got you?"

"She wants me gone. She didn't say anything to me, and the next thing I know, she called her sister. She came to town and got right up on me. They say I have a fracture in my jaw, man. Some of my teeth are out."

Lukas spoke quietly into the phone. "Are you telling me some chick jacked you up?"

"She's like a ninja or something, Luke. One minute she was telling me off, the next minute I was pickin' my head up off the ground. She's not afraid of anything. She would have taken us all on. She calls herself Camaro. It's crazy."

"Where are you now?"

"I'm at home. Where are you?"

"Never you mind where I am. Do you have cops on you?"

"No. They want Chelle's sister. I told them everything I know. They took me home and left me here."

"So they didn't ask anything about the money?"

"No, I don't think they talked to her, and she won't say anything. She thinks I'm trying to set up that surf shop. She doesn't know where the money's going."

"You better hope not, because I'm not having this thing screwed up because of you. I let you in on it because you're my brother and you said you were ready to take it to the next level. Are you ready to take it to the next level, Jake?"

"Absolutely."

"Good."

Konnor held back at a respectful distance. People flowed in and out of the casino and paid neither man any mind.

Lukas exhaled. "This isn't what I need right now, Jake. Low-profile. Remember when I said low-profile? The people in LA aren't going to understand, you end up on the news."

"I know, I know. I'm sorry. I screwed up. I never knew Chelle was gonna blow up on me like that. And her sister. She tried to break my arm. I have it in a sling, and it still hurts. They wanted to give me a cast so I wouldn't move it."

Lukas motioned for Konnor to wait a little longer. "I don't have time to listen to your problems right now."

"I got to get some payback, Luke."

"You will. We won't go anywhere until you get yours. And then it's all LA. You and me."

"Okay. Just hurry, okay?"

"I'll call again when I'm close." Lukas disconnected before Jacob could say any more. He put the phone in his pocket and turned to Konnor. The two men clasped wrists and bumped shoulders.

"Long time, my brother," Konnor said.

"Yeah, long time. You put on a few pounds since I saw you last."

Konnor patted his belly. "My old lady keeps me fed. Hey, was that Jake on the phone?"

Lukas scowled. "Yeah."

"Trouble?"

Lukas waved it away. "Nothing you need to worry about. Let's drink some booze and play cards."

They wound their way into the casino and sought out the blackjack tables. Their dealer was dressed like Alice Cooper in a white top hat and directed them toward their seats with a flourish. "Welcome to my nightmare, gentlemen," he said.

Lukas threw down some cash. Alice made it disappear, then gifted him with chips. He repeated the same trick with Konnor. A waitress swung by the table, and Lukas ordered beers for the both of them. "I need to make some bank tonight," Lukas told Konnor.

"Runnin' low?"

"Cross-country travel ain't as cheap as it used to be."

"You still going to come through in LA? They're gonna expect you to deliver, and that takes cash."

Cards were dealt. Bets were made. Lukas signaled for a hit. Konnor held. "Jake has a line on some money. He's been stepping it up for a while now, and we have a big score coming. Everything we need."

"All right, 'cause I have to tell them you're going to make good on our order. I can't cover the expense with what I have to spend."

Lukas asked for another card. "It'll be done. Jake's not good for much, but he's good at wheedling cash out of his old ladies. I heard he has some legal assistant he's been getting a bankroll from for a while now. Not enough to take us over the top, but good money."

The cards were turned. Lukas had twenty. The dealer had nineteen. "Winner," Alice said, and pushed the chips to Lukas.

"You've always been lucky, Luke," Konnor said. "That's what I always said."

"It's like the man says: the harder I work, the luckier I get. And I'm working hard on this one."

"You know I'm in it with you all the way. I got people lined up in LA who'll turn your straw into gold."

Lukas smiled thinly. "That's what I like to hear."

The beers came. Lukas tipped Alice a ten-dollar chip, and then they played another hand.

# CHAPTER FOURTEEN

His son was dead.

It was evening of the second day after Stanley died. Trish made them dinner and manned the desk as calls came in after afternoon court set the bond amounts. Yates hadn't told her yet and wasn't sure how he was going to. Every passing hour made the task more difficult. She would want to know why he hadn't said something as soon as he heard. She would be brokenhearted in a way Yates could only partly understand. Stanley was his son, but there was something between a boy and his mother that ran deeper than that.

He didn't cry. He felt, but he did not let it go. There were other things to do. Crying now would only keep him from moving forward. That was not all right with him.

The first thing he'd done was go through the paperwork for Lukas Collier's bond. Trish had made the decision to extend Collier the bond, even though it was a massive $150,000. Collier had ties to the community through friends and a few distant relatives, but more important, his girl put up her house as collateral. It wasn't a palace, but real estate values in Norfolk were good.

Everything was in order. All the documents were signed and filed with the court, and Stanley had made certain to catalog the names and addresses of everyone even remotely connected to Collier who lived in the area. But Collier vanished three days after bonding out of jail, and no one in Norfolk seemed to have a clue where he might have gone.

Yates got this story from Stanley's files. His son kept detailed notes on his phone and tablet and uploaded them regularly to an online backup. Each day of the hunt was given its own folder, and calls and visits were marked with the time they happened and detailed with everything that occurred.

It became clear right away that Collier was headed west. He had old ties to California, from when he was stationed at Camp Pendleton as part of I Marine Expeditionary Force. Yates did not like the idea that he and Collier had anything in common, but they were brother Marines, though a generation apart and worlds different in every other way. Collier served in Iraq for a year and a half, and the First Marine Division saw serious action. If nothing else, Collier had bravery.

But this had only mattered a little bit in the overall picture. Stanley drew on law enforcement and simple legwork to trace Collier along his route. By the time Stanley followed him to Kansas, he had a solid idea of where the man was headed: California. Collier had connections in Los Angeles and San Diego. Camp Pendleton was just a part of it. But he was trending northerly, away from the sunny coasts of the south. That was where the brother came in.

A separate folder held all the information Stanley had on Lukas Collier's brother, Jacob. There was an image lifted directly from the California Department of Motor Vehicles, plus a few mug shots from misdemeanor arrests. From what Yates could tell, Jacob was the more harmless of the brothers. Lukas Collier was a killer at least twice over in civilian life, the number he might have laid to rest in Iraq a closely held secret.

Yates found the number to the Salinas Police Department and dialed. A man answered, identifying himself as Officer Powers. "My name is Jeremy Yates, and I'm a bail bondsman in Norfolk, Virginia," Yates told him. "How are you today?"

"I'm fine, sir. You're calling from a long way away. What can I do for you?"

"I'm doing some background on a potential client. He's given us the name of a brother who supposedly lives out your direction. Jacob Collier. I was wondering if you'd run him through your system to see if he's really there."

"That's a real popular name around here."

"How's that?"

"I can't really go into it. Let's just say you're not the first person to call about him."

"Can you still look him up for me?"

"Of course. I can do that. We should have something for you. Just a second. Wait...yes. Jacob Collier has a Salinas address. The one we have on file is current with the address on his license. Sometimes that doesn't match up."

"Could you confirm the address for me?"

"Sure," Powers said, and he recited the information.

Yates hung up the phone. He tore the sheet of paper off the legal pad and folded it in half with the address above the fold, then sent Jacob Collier's picture to the printer. He already had a wanted flyer for Lukas Collier. Stanley had made that one.

Yates went to his bedroom and spun the dial on his gun safe. Inside he had nearly thirty guns, all secured behind eight locking bolts. It opened with a heavy clank. He ignored the long arms and selected a pistol from among several. It was a stainless steel AMT Hardballer in .45 caliber, kept unloaded. He topped off the magazine with hollow-point ammunition and slid the magazine home but didn't work the slide. In the closet he found a holster for the weapon. The gun would sit on his hip, hidden by the edge of a jacket.

He stepped out of the closet, and Tricia was there. She saw the gun slipped into its leather. "Jeremy, what's going on?"

"I need to get some gear together."

"Why?"

Yates looked at her. When he took a breath, it hitched. He slid the holster into place on his right side. "There's something I have to tell you, Trish."

He watched her expression crumble, and she sagged in the doorway, held up only by the frame. A high-pitched keening sound started in her chest and rose rapidly, chased by torrential sobs that clotted her throat. Yates stood with his hands at his sides for a long moment, and then he went to her. He folded his wife up in his arms and held her close as she cried. Something warm ran down his cheek. He did not have to touch it to know what it was.

"Let it go," he said at last. "Let it all out."

She cried for a long time, and after that she became quiet. She listened to what Yates had to say, and together they packed his things.

# CHAPTER FIFTEEN

Annabel made dinner for them, a Parmesan-basil tomato soup served with crusty bread. There was a different blend of herbal tea, this one with a perky aroma about it, which complemented the soup in a natural, tonal way. Camaro ate quickly, as did Rebecca.

"It's good?" Annabel asked.

"Yes. When did you get so domestic?"

"I don't know. It seemed like something to do. I mean, I have this great kitchen. I have to do something with it, otherwise it's a waste, right? I couldn't keep on heating up chicken tenders and french fries for dinner. Wilson turned me on to the tea shop here in town. They have all kinds of amazing stuff there. When Becca got a cold last year, they fixed me up with a special blend that cleared her sinuses and helped her sore throat. It was terrific."

"Can I play on the computer?" Rebecca asked.

"Sure, baby. Go play some games."

Rebecca got down from her chair and fled the room. Camaro shook her head.

"What?"

"I don't know. Her. You."

"You're making fun of us."

"No, I'm not," Camaro said. "I'm not. I think it's great."

Annabel reached for Camaro's hand, and Camaro allowed her sister to take it. Annabel squeezed lightly. "Everything I've done here is important to me. I'm different. I'm better."

"I know you are."

"But you're still Camaro. Thank God."

"What's that supposed to mean?"

Annabel smiled. "It means I never want you to change. You're perfect the way you are."

"That's not what you used to think."

"I grew up."

Camaro didn't reply.

"Let me clear the table," Annabel said.

Camaro sat while Annabel cleaned up. Her eyes drifted toward a large plastic case and a small folding table in the corner. "What's that?"

"Oh, that? That's my beading stuff. I'm really into beading now."

Camaro finished her tea. The sensation of it faded at the back of her throat and disappeared. Outside it was clear and cold, but bad weather was coming again. It was an invitation to a fire and a blanket and having nowhere to go.

Annabel sat again and waited a while before speaking. It was a good silence between them. "Do you want to tell me what you did to him?" she asked.

"No."

"Did you hurt him bad?"

"Not enough."

"But he's not dead."

"No. I could have killed him," Camaro said.

"I know."

There was more quiet.

"When do you want to leave?" Annabel asked finally.

"Soon."

"I can't convince you to stay?"

"There's no way that would work," Camaro said.

"I understand. But I'd like another chance to be sisters again. These last couple of years and then all the time you were in the service... it's like you were on another planet. Getting pictures of you in Italy and Kuwait and Afghanistan wasn't the same as having you around. You went and disappeared. I think Dad would want us to try."

Camaro looked outside. In the autumn it would be absolutely beautiful under trees whose branches were bare now but would be a riot of color at the change of seasons. It was not the same in Florida. There were no real seasons there, only times when it was hot and times when it was less hot.

She thought of her father, of a twelve-hour flight from Japan and the quiet, oppressive stillness of the funeral home. He had not looked like himself. He was too thin, and his color was all wrong. She and Annabel barely spoke before the funeral, or after, and then Camaro was gone again. Another flight, and then the lights of Tokyo.

"I love you, Camaro," Annabel said.

Camaro found it difficult to look at her. "You know I love you."

"Stay."

"I can't."

"Can we come visit you at least? The door's open now that everyone's seen us together, so it's not like it's a secret anymore. Becca and I can come, and we'll all go to Disney World together."

"Disney World is in Orlando."

"Then we'll take the bus. Whatever. Don't you understand that we're a family, and families belong together? I've seen you three times in fifteen years. I don't want us getting old like this."

Camaro shook her head. "You don't want what I'd bring into your world."

"I've survived so far."

"I know."

Annabel placed her hands flat on the table. "Then that's it. We're going to see each other more, and we're going to change things. And whenever you start to run away from me, I'm gonna run after you. Because it's not just me anymore. It's Becca, too. She deserves to have her aunt in her life."

Camaro let the slightest of smiles crease her face. "You didn't just get domestic. You got crazy, too."

"We're both crazy, Camaro. You and me. That's why we need each other."

"You have to do something for me," Camaro said.

"What? Anything."

"Work out your man issues. You're no good at picking them, and you never have been. I can't keep coming back to fix your troubles. If you want into my life, you keep your complications out of it. I have things the way I want them. I don't need another Jake."

The corners of Annabel's mouth turned down. "Do you think he'll come for me?"

"I won't be here if he does."

"Wait," Annabel said. She got up from the table and left the room. Camaro toyed with her teacup.

Annabel returned with a plastic case and a paper bag. She put both of them on the table. They were heavy and thumped solidly. The side of the case was emblazoned with the name gl ock.

"What are you doing?" Camaro asked.

"It's…my gun."

Camaro looked in the bag. Two boxes of .45-caliber ammunition lay inside. She shoved them away and popped open the case. Inside, laid out in foam rubber, was a Glock automatic pistol and two empty magazines. The trigger was equipped with a lock.

She lifted the gun out of the case. "Where did you get this?"

"I bought it online. It's new."

"You know how to use it?"

Annabel shook her head.

"Where's the key?"

"I keep it with my others."

"Bring it."

Annabel went and brought them back. Camaro unlocked the gun and set the lock aside. "Tomorrow I want you to get a chain or a thong to hang the key on. Keep it around your neck all the time. You don't ever put the gun away without making sure it's secure first. You understand?"

"I understand."

Camaro opened one of the boxes of ammunition. They were fully jacketed, their heads perfect brass circles buttoned with a primer, arranged in neat rows in their plastic case. She gave a magazine to Annabel. "Load it."

"I don't know how."

"That's why you're going to load it now."

Annabel accepted the magazine and took the first bullet from the case. She tried to put it in backward. Camaro corrected her. The next bullet loaded faster and the one after that. By the time she reached the tenth, she had it down. "What about the other one?"

"We're going to use that one for practice."

Camaro's sister picked up the Glock with nervous fingers. She held it awkwardly. Camaro reached over and steadied her grip. She nodded toward the empty magazine. Annabel fed it into the well. It snapped together with a loud, metallic click. "Okay, now we pretend it's loaded?"

"Yes, but you can't make it fire just by putting in the magazine. You need to work the slide. Grab it with your other hand at the top and pull. Good. Now let it go."

"It's stuck."

"That's because the magazine is empty. When the slide locks back, you're out of ammo. There's a lever on the side called a slide stop. Push it with your thumb."

Annabel jumped when the slide ratcheted forward. "Should I put on the safety?"

"There's no safety on a Glock. The gun won't fire unless you pull the trigger all the way through. It's a good gun. Now stand up and I'll show you how to hold it."

They got up together, and Camaro molded Annabel's form to her own. Annabel aimed out the window, hands together around the weapon, body braced. She put her finger on the trigger. Camaro told her to stop. The only time to touch the trigger was when it was time to fire.

"When it's loaded it's going to be heavier than you expect. And it's going to kick when you pull through," Camaro said. "You hold it steady like that and keep a firm grip. Aim for the center of the body. Don't try to hit an arm or a leg. Center of the body."

"I don't want to kill anyone."

"If it's down to this, you don't have any choice. Do you want to die?"

"No."

"What about Becca?"

"No!"

"Then put the shot right in the middle. Don't hesitate."

Annabel lowered the gun. "This is crazy. What am I trying to prove?"

"Is there a range around here?"

"In Carmel? Are you kidding?"

"Then we'll find one. Somewhere you can get practice. Before I go, I want you to be able to draw and fire. You don't own a gun to show off to people or to make noise. It's for killing. You have to know how to kill with it."

Annabel pushed the Glock into Camaro's hands. "I feel sick."

Her sister sank into her chair. Camaro sat down with the gun between them, its muzzle pointed in a neutral direction. "I need to know you're safe when I go."

Annabel covered her eyes with her hand and nodded. "I know."

"I wish it didn't have to be this way."

"I know."

"Just promise me you'll do what it takes. Now and when I'm gone."

"I promise."

Camaro put her hand on the gun. "Okay."

# CHAPTER SIXTEEN

Jeremy Yates drove the rented Hyundai Santa Fe from Monterey to Salinas in less than half an hour. The onboard GPS guided him expertly through the little streets of Jacob Collier's neighborhood until he found the burnt-orange house. Weather that began as a drizzle when he left the airport turned into a full downpour by the time he reached the place. He drove by without slowing, noting the porch light burning but none in the windows.

Yates proceeded to the end of the block and pulled up to the curb. He killed the engine and drew the AMT from its holster to chamber a round. He laid the pistol on his thigh for a moment, breathing deeply and watching Collier's little house in the side mirror.

The rain didn't slow, and no one moved around the property. Most of the neighboring driveways were empty, the owners away at work. Once he was certain no one was headed in or out, Yates turned up the collar of his fleece-lined jacket and stepped out into the rain. Instantly his hair was plastered to his skull. His boots splashed in the little rivers streaming along the asphalt, the curb washed in a swirling current.

Yates walked down to the house and stopped at the driveway to survey the property. It was obvious no one was home, his initial impression confirmed. He let himself in through the front gate and braved the pools of rainwater to stand on the flooded porch and look inside.

He skirted the entire house, peeking through windows. Finally, he returned to the front door. He unbuttoned his jacket and produced a slim leather case from an interior pocket and flipped it open. The collection of picks was matte black.

Kneeling at the door, Yates engaged the lock with his picks. The lock itself was as old as the house and very loose. He tried the knob, and the door fell open in silence.

Yates took one last glance toward the street and went inside.

The front room was carpeted thinly, the furniture ramshackle and cheap. The television was the nicest thing in sight, along with the video game console.

He left soaking prints on the carpet as he closed the door. His jacket was sodden. Water dripped from the tips of his fingers and ran down the back of his neck from his scalp. Anyone who paid attention would know someone had been there.

In the kitchen he found a plate with the remains of a burrito stuck to it. The beans were still moist, though the burrito itself was cold. It had not been there more than a day. On impulse, Yates checked inside the refrigerator and found it empty of almost everything except bottle after bottle of Bud Light. The freezer was packed with microwavable meals. The microwave itself was filthy.

Yates went into the hallway that bisected the house and found a small table with a telephone on it and three different books of Yellow Pages. There was no answering machine. He moved on.

The bedroom was a mess and almost seemed as though it had been ransacked by searchers. Yates checked the drawers in the dresser for a gun or a knife, but there was nothing. His gaze alighted on the bed and a yellow piece of paper mostly covered by the sheet.

He pulled the sheet aside and found three pages of carbon copies. It was a police report, scrawled in an uneven hand that was difficult to read. A drop of water fell from Yates's nose and landed on the topmost page. He brushed it off and kept reading. He made a mental note of two names: Camaro and Michelle Amado. There was an address given. After a moment's hesitation, Yates folded up the carbon copies and stuffed them inside his jacket.

The bathroom smelled of mildew and body spray. On the closed toilet lid there were discharge papers from a local hospital. Yates flipped through them but found nothing as interesting as the two names in the police report. The report said Collier had been beaten. The hospital documents revealed how badly.

Yates abandoned the discharge papers and made his way deeper into the house. He found the cluttered back room and the laundry nook where Collier's combination washer and dryer stood empty and quiet. There was nothing to find.

A car horn sounded outside. Yates froze. He put his hand on the .45 at his hip and waited thirty seconds. The horn did not sound again, and no one appeared at the front door. Noiselessly Yates retraced his steps to the front room. He stepped up to the living room window and stood to one side, peering out around the curtains. A car was parked in the street, its hazard lights blinking. As he watched, a woman came down from the apartment building directly across from Collier's house, a sweater pulled out to shield her head. She dashed to the car and got inside. A moment later it pulled away.

Yates locked the front door behind him and splashed back out to the sidewalk. He ran the rest of the way to the Hyundai and got in. His breath was short, and he coughed forcefully until he produced phlegm. He opened the driver's door and spat into the street.

The police report was still dry as he unfolded it onto the steering wheel. The address for Michelle Amado was in Carmel, which the GPS said was thirty minutes away.

The house sat bereft of life in the side mirror, promising someone's eventual return. The police report indicated Michelle Amado was Collier's girlfriend. Yates looked from the paper to the mirror and back again. He chewed the corner of his mustache.

Yates tossed the police report onto the passenger seat and started the SUV. He twisted the knobs on the dash, and warm air spilled out of the lower vents over his wet legs. He looked at the house again, then put the vehicle into drive and pulled away from the curb.

# CHAPTER SEVENTEEN

Hannon dr ove the U.S. Marshals Service's Suburban while Way balanced a laptop on his knees. His phone was between them, sending out a middling Wi-Fi signal the computer could use while they were still in motion. They passed a sign declaring Salinas ten miles away. They had been on the road for thirteen hours without breaks, save to get gas or use the restroom. Way hadn't slept for forty-eight hours, though Hannon had done better in that time.

"What do you have?" Hannon asked him.

"I have all the information on Jacob Collier, plus the latest off the line from the California Highway Patrol."

"Any luck with the Ford?"

"No. Lukas has to have switched cars by now, otherwise we would have picked him up for sure. So until he pokes his head up on a camera where we can pull facial recognition, we're stuck. He could be driving anything at this point. Car, truck, bike. Anything."

Hannon peered out the windshield at the dark clouds gathering overhead. "This isn't bike weather. We're driving into something nasty."

"I thought California was supposed to be dry."

"Someone tell the weatherman," Hannon said, turning on the headlights.

"Right now the only thing we have is the Jacob Collier lead. He was in the hospital yesterday, he checks out, and then he disappears off the face of the earth. Salinas PD says they're doing drive-bys of Jacob's place, but there's nothing so far. He's not at home, and he's not at work. His car is exactly nowhere."

"You think Lukas is already there?"

"I don't know. He could be. God*damn* it. All I want is ten seconds. In ten seconds it's all taken care of."

"You'll get it."

Way chewed his thumbnail and watched the speedometer. "We have to pick it up."

"We're almost there, Keith."

"We need to be there now!"

"We're ten minutes out. There's no reason to get crazy about it."

"I'm not crazy about it. I'm thinking we don't have time."

"There's time."

Way's knee jiggled as he sat, jostling the laptop like an earthquake. His flesh crawled with the urge to get up and move around.

"Deep breaths," Hannon said.

"Funny," Way returned.

A droplet hit the windshield. A second fell, but the real rain was still ahead of them. Way's leg still jiggled. He put his hand on it to keep it still, but that only worked for a moment.

"Do you want to skip the cop shop completely?" Hannon asked him.

"What do you mean?"

"If you're so hot to track down Lukas's brother, we could go straight to the source. Sit on Jacob's house and see where that leads us. We don't need to check in with the locals first. There's time to bring them up to speed."

Way shook his head. "No. It'd be a waste of time. Lukas will never go to Jacob's place. He may not know for sure we're coming, but he has to know somebody's going to keep an eye on Jacob just in case. No, they're going to be somewhere else together. A friend's house. A girl-friend's place. Somewhere like that."

"Did Salinas PD give a list of KAs?"

"Got it here. As soon as we're on the scene, we need to draft some of the locals to hit the list, and while they're at it they can canvas the whole neighborhood. No stone unturned. Someone has to know his habits, who his people are. We'll dig it up and throw a net over the whole thing."

The SUV's GPS indicated that their exit was coming up. They passed into a sheeting rain, the gloomy skies finally giving up the deluge. Hannon put on the windshield wipers. Way stared out at the rain a moment, then grabbed his phone.

"Who are you calling?"

"I'm going to let them know we're almost there. I want them on their toes."

Way dialed the chief of the Salinas Police Department, his private line. It rang a handful of times and then went to voice mail. Way cursed and cut the call without leaving a message.

"Local bullshit," Way spat.

"What's going on?"

"I tell the chief to be on his line and the asshole doesn't even pick up," Way said, his voice rising in the confines of the Suburban. "Does he not get it? Did I not explain it was important? I swear, this is the kind of shit that gets me every goddamned time. Every time!"

"It could be nothing," Hannon offered, her tone even. "He might be in the bathroom. Call the main switchboard."

"I shouldn't have to call the main switchboard."

"I'm only giving you options. I'm on your side, remember? All the way. That's what I promised."

Way rubbed his eyes with thumb and forefinger. They felt gritty and dry, and the sensation had only gotten worse over the course of the drive from Salt Lake City. "You're right," he said. "You're right. You're right."

"It'll all work out," Hannon soothed. "Lukas just ran out of country to cross. We're at the coast. He's done."

Way looked out the window and felt suddenly mournful. "It'll be done when he's dead," he said.

# CHAPTER EIGHTEEN

Camaro sat on the couch with Rebecca, watching a Disney DVD. It was one of the new movies, and Camaro wasn't sure what it was called. Rebecca referred to it as "the princess movie," and that seemed to be good enough for her. Camaro listened to the songs and smiled at the jokes and didn't care.

"The snowman is funny," Rebecca observed.

"He is," Camaro replied.

She heard Annabel bustling in the kitchen. Dinner had been a cherry-and-onion-stuffed pork tenderloin served with steamed baby carrots. Camaro did not know where these recipes were coming from. Annabel worked without cards or a cookbook, slicing and rolling and tying and roasting as if it were something she did every day.

That afternoon they'd gone to a local shop and picked up six bottles of Corona Extra that Camaro let chill in the refrigerator for two hours before opening the first one. She had her third in hand and drew from it occasionally, tasting the cold more than anything else. Outside the winter rainstorm refused to let up. It came down all day long with only a few respites, and even then the sun never shone. Camaro found it harder and harder to imagine Carmel in the warmer months.

They had just reached the final credits when Annabel slipped into the living room. Rebecca clapped her hands for the end of the movie. "Let's watch it again!"

"In a minute, babe," Annabel said. "First I have something for your auntie."

Camaro saw a cupcake on a small dish in Annabel's hands. It had pink frosting and a white wrapper meant to look like lace. A single candle flickered atop the cupcake. "What's this?" Camaro asked.

Annabel sat on the couch and offered the plate. "It's for you."

"What for?"

"Don't you know what day it is?"

Camaro glanced at her watch. The date showed 5.

"January fifth," Annabel said. "It's your birthday. Happy birthday."

Camaro took the plate and held it with both hands in front of her. The candle wept a single waxy tear. Rebecca clapped her hands again. "Happy birthday!" she said. "Make a wish!"

Camaro closed her eyes. When she opened them again, she blew the candle out. The flame vanished and left a curling tendril of smoke. She was thirty-three years old.

"It's a chocolate cupcake," Annabel said. "I know you like chocolate."

"You didn't have to do this," Camaro told her.

"It's just a cupcake. I didn't buy you a new car."

"Can I have some?" Rebecca asked.

"I'll give you half," Camaro replied.

She carefully removed the wrapper and peeled away the paper. The cake glistened with moisture. Annabel plucked out the candle. Camaro tore the cupcake in half and gave Rebecca the portion with more frosting. Her niece attacked it like a wild animal, getting pink all over her face and on the tip of her nose. Annabel laughed, and Camaro felt lightness inside.

"She likes hers," Annabel said. "You eat yours."

Camaro obeyed. The chocolate cake was rich, the icing creamy. Camaro wanted milk.

"Good?" Annabel asked.

"Great."

"There's a bakery down on Ocean Avenue. They do the most amazing pastries."

"Thank you."

"Let me hug you," Annabel said, and she leaned over to put her arms around Camaro and squeezed tightly. When they broke, Annabel wiped her eyes and sniffed. "I'm just glad we could be together on your birthday. Now give me that plate. I'm loading the dishwasher. Becca, go wash your face."

Annabel left the living room, and Becca trudged off to the bathroom. Camaro was alone when the first blow struck the front door.

A splinter from the frame spun away under the initial impact, and on the second kick the wood began to give way completely. Camaro leaped up from the couch. She took one step, and the door exploded inward, letting in a rush of cold air and the noise of the rain. Jake spilled in behind it, soaked from head to toe. "Chelle!" he bellowed.

Camaro came at him straight on and laid a hard right into his nose. She felt cartilage give, and there was blood. Jake took a wild swing at her, and she let it go by, countering with an overhand left into his temple. He was rocked and fell against the wall.

She heard Annabel scream and the echoing cry of Rebecca as Jake came off the wall with full force. Camaro pivoted and tripped him up with her foot. He spilled face-first onto the floor.

"Camaro!" Annabel cried.

Camaro latched on to him and dropped two hammer fists into the back of his skull. His forehead struck the floor, and he struggled to rise against her weight. She snaked an arm around his throat, grabbed her wrist with her free hand, and cinched the choke in hard.

Jake rolled, and Camaro rolled with him. They crashed against the TV stand, and the Disney movie started playing again. Jake kicked Camaro's shins with his boots and scrabbled at the lock around his neck.

He hit her with his elbow, right on the lowest ribs. Camaro let a short bark of pain pass her lips but held on. Jake hit her again, and she felt her hold slip. He made it to his hands and knees and tucked under, rolling forward and carrying her with him. Camaro hit the coffee table with the small of her back. A shock of hurt passed up her spine, and she lost her grip on her wrist. They fell apart.

Camaro found her feet quickly. Jake was already standing. Annabel and Rebecca were gone. Jake's hand dropped to his waist and came up with the click of a lock blade snapping into place. He brandished the weapon between them, four inches of blackened steel jutting from his fist.

"You want some of this?" Jake asked. "Come on and try it."

"Jake!" Annabel stood at the mouth of the hallway that led to the rest of the house. She held the Glock in both hands awkwardly, extended full length at the elbows, her stance shaky. The muzzle trembled.

"Annabel, wait," Camaro said.

"No. You get away from her, Jake!"

Jake looked from Camaro to Annabel and back again. He smiled, his face battered, scraped, and bruised. He was missing an incisor. "Annabel?"

"Michelle," Camaro said.

"Okay, *Annabel*. You going to shoot me now? Is that it? You gonna kill me?"

Annabel shook visibly. "Don't make me do it, Jake. Go away. Go away and never come back."

He didn't lower the knife. "Your sister already tried that one. I'm not going away. You're mine. You belong to me. No matter what your name is. Nobody is gonna come between us. Nobody."

"Jake, don't!"

"I can take him," Camaro said.

"I'll cut you wide open."

Camaro looked at him steadily. "You'll try."

Jake shook his head. "Crazy bitches."

He moved. The Glock in Annabel's hands spoke, an angry bark. Jake lurched to one side and caught his shin on the coffee table. He flopped and fell, the knife flinging from his grasp to land in the corner, then lay still.

"Oh, my God," Annabel said.

Camaro went to him. The entry wound was wet, directly over the heart. Jake stared at the ceiling. She checked his pulse at his wrist, then his throat.

"Is he dead?" Annabel asked.

"He's dead," Camaro said. Rebecca cried out and stepped into the living room. Annabel knelt to cover her face, but her hand was still filled with the pistol. She dropped the weapon on the floor as if it were hot, then folded Rebecca in her arms.

Camaro left Jake and took up the gun. "Take her to her room. I'll call the cops."

71

Annabel looked up. Her face was streaked with tears, and she trembled violently. "They'll take me away, Camaro. They'll take Becca away."

"No," Camaro said. She lowered herself to Annabel's level. "That's not how it's going to happen."

"Why not?"

"Because you didn't kill him."

"He's dead, Camaro!"

"Yes. But you didn't kill him," Camaro repeated. "*I* killed him."

# CHAPTER NINETEEN

Carl y Russo stirr ed when her phone vibrated on the nightstand. When it buzzed again, she came barely awake and fumbled in the dark to find the switch for the bedside lamp. Blinking back the glare, she took up her phone and checked the number. "Carly Russo," she answered.

"Officer Russo, this is Detective Adkins. Do you remember me?"

"Of course, sir."

"Listen, I need you right now over on Raymond Court. Can you remember an address, or do you need to write it down?"

"I can remember."

"Okay," Adkins said, and he told Russo where to go. "I need you here an hour ago, okay, Russo?"

"I'm already getting dressed, sir."

"See you soon."

Russo threw back the sheets and hustled into the bathroom to wash her face and get the sleep from her eyes. Her uniform had come back from the cleaners that afternoon and was still in its plastic bag, hanging from a hook on the door of her bedroom closet. Russo dressed as quickly as she was able. She hopped on one foot as she put on her socks, and she took her polished shoes from their place by the end of the bed. Her service weapon and belt were on a chair.

With no time for makeup or even coffee, she was out the door of her apartment and down to the parking lot in thirty seconds. Her patrol unit was parked in a reserved space. She got behind the wheel and started up. She was already on the move by the time she clipped her safety belt on.

It was a matter of five minutes' drive to reach Raymond Court, and before she got there she saw the telltale flashing of red and blue lights in the darkness. It was a little past ten, and she saw three other Carmel

73

police units parked in the small cul-de-sac, plus an unmarked vehicle with a light on the dash. A van from the Monterey County Sheriff's Department waited beneath a streetlight.

She parked. The rain had finally slowed, and it was only misting down. Iris Cooper, one of the other women on the force, stood on the front lawn of a perfect house with warm yellow light in its windows. She waved Russo over when she came near. "Russo," she said. "Hold up."

"What's going on?"

"Homicide," Iris said. Where Russo was slight, Iris was stout, and the woman stood taller as well. She had been a uniformed cop in San Francisco.

"Seriously? Who? How?"

"Remember that guy we were supposed to keep an eye out for? Jacob Collier? He's the DB."

"DB," Russo said. "Dead body."

"That's right. Shot right in the chest."

"Detective Adkins said he wanted me here."

"Yeah. He said he thinks you're a people person. Whatever the hell that means."

"I'd better go in."

Russo went to the open front door and saw it was broken. She reached to her duty belt and extracted a pair of latex gloves. She put them on before proceeding into the house. In the middle of the front room, Jacob Collier lay dead, his body awkwardly splayed, one elbow cocked in a position that would have caused pain if he'd been able to feel pain at all. She felt ill.

Adkins stood with his back to her. He turned when Russo cleared her throat. "Oh, great," he said. "Russo. Just who I wanted to see."

Adkins was the Carmel Police Department's only detective. He was an older man, close to retirement age, his face pleasantly like that of a grandfather. Other people were at work in the house, crime-scene investigators from the county. They had tripods set up but were no longer taking pictures. One took note of spatters of blood on a wall. Another was busy putting plastic bags over the dead man's hands.

"What can I do?"

"There are some U.S. marshals coming. As soon as they show up, this is going to turn into a circus. The chief put them off as long as he could. I still haven't had an opportunity to interview the shooter and the witnesses in detail. I want to put you beside one of them and see if you can get her talking. The shooter."

"About the homicide?"

"About whatever. I got nothing from her. We don't have a lot of time. The things people say before they end up at the station can mean a lot. You know that, right?"

"Yes, sir."

"She's in the kitchen. Camaro Espinoza is her name. Sit down, introduce yourself, and see what you can come up with."

"I'll do whatever I can."

"She's through there. Good luck."

Russo found her heart beating rapidly. She passed down a short jog of a hallway into a well-appointed kitchen. Bobby Hill, another Carmel police officer, stood near the stove, watching a woman at a table by the window. The woman's back was to her, hair falling free to her shoulders. She wore a denim-blue Henley, and Russo saw she had no shoes on.

"Carly," Hill said.

"Hey, Bobby. Here to help out."

"She's all yours."

Hill left the kitchen, and Russo was alone with the woman. She waited a moment to see if Camaro would do anything. She didn't. Russo went to the table. She cleared her throat. "Hello. I'm Officer Russo. I'm with the Carmel Police Department."

Camaro looked at her briefly, then returned to staring out the window. Russo found the quick, cold assessment daunting. Up close she saw Camaro was an attractive woman with a strong nose and even features. She wore no makeup, but she was not diminished by that.

"May I sit down?" Russo asked.

"Sure."

Russo took a seat at the end of the table and sat turned toward Camaro. "They want me to talk to you."

"About what?"

"About the man you shot."

Camaro looked away from the window and put her full attention on Russo. "You ever shot anybody?"

"Me? No way. This is Carmel-by-the-Sea. This kind of thing doesn't happen here."

"That explains why your detective doesn't know what he's doing."

"He's not so bad."

"If you say so."

Camaro started to turn away from her again, and Russo spoke quickly. "I pulled my weapon at a traffic stop once. The guy behind the wheel reached between the seats, and I was sure I'd have to shoot him. He was just going for his insurance papers. It could have been bad."

"It is bad."

"Why did you kill him? That man, Jacob Collier?"

"He brought it on himself. He threatened my sister with a knife. I had no choice."

"If that's the case, then there's no reason not to talk about it. Self-defense makes sense. You didn't try to kill him on purpose...did you?"

Camaro regarded her a moment, and the merest smile passed over her lips. "You know it was me who busted him up yesterday."

"Yeah," Russo said. "You really worked him over."

"Like I said, he brought it on himself. If he was able to keep his hands off my sister, he wouldn't have been in that situation. Now he's dead. For what? She was never going to go back to him. That was over. But some men—they can't figure out when no means no."

"He's not a little guy. How did you...how did you beat him down like that?"

"I've had some experience," Camaro said, and then she did look away. Russo felt her closing up.

"You have stitches," Russo said. She touched her own brow.

"It's nothing."

"You get in fights a lot?"

"Not when I don't want to."

"Were you a cop? No, not a cop. Military? Something like that?"

"I've said everything I'm going to say," Camaro told her. "You can find out all about me when you put me in the system. I'm not going anywhere."

"I can help you," Russo said.

"I don't need any help. Go tell the detective what you got out of me."

# CHAPTER TWENTY

Way approached the house with Hannon hurrying in his wake. He proceeded up the walk with his identification out, then burst into the front room, where two men were putting the body in a rubberized canvas bag. A man in plain clothes watched them. A shield hung from the breast pocket of his jacket. He looked up when Way came in. "Whoa. Crime scene here, sir."

"I know," Way said. He thrust his badge and ID at the man. "I've been trying to get here for two hours while your people gave me the runaround. What the hell is this, some kind of game to you? Smallville politicking?"

"I don't know what they said," the detective told him, "but we're just following the procedure. This isn't the sort of thing we're used to dealing with."

"Well, first things first: cut the bullshit. I'm Deputy U.S. Marshal Way, and this is Deputy Hannon. We are your first, last, and everything when it comes to the Collier brothers. Everything you learn, everything you say, everything you do will pass through one of us. I have a double murderer on the loose, and now his brother's dead on someone's carpet. I need answers, and I need them right now."

"I understand, but there are ways to ask, Marshal. Maybe they do things differently where you come from, but around here we still say *please* and *thank you*."

Way said nothing at first. When he spoke, his voice was careful. "I'd like to know everything you do about what's going on here, *please,* sir. *.ank you.*"

"I appreciate that. We'll be as cooperative as we can. I'm Detective Eric Adkins, Carmel Police Department. This is Officer Iris Cooper, and I have Officers Hill and Russo watching the witnesses."

"These are the sisters? The Amado sisters?"

"Well, there's Michelle Amado, but the other one is named Espinoza. Camaro Espinoza."

"Do we have full workups on them yet?"

"No, but—"

"See that it's done. Give everything you have to Deputy Hannon. Tell whoever you have to tell that I want the autopsy of Jacob Collier expedited and the results in my e-mail by tomorrow morning. Wake up everybody. We are on the lookout for Lukas Collier. I know you have his name and face spread around, but now you really need to be on your toes, because as soon as he hears what's happened to his brother, all bets are going to be off."

Hannon stepped forward. "Have you taken statements from the witnesses?"

"Nothing official. We're just trying to get them talking," Adkins said. "One sister is in shock, and the other sister shut down like a robot as soon as I started asking questions. I asked Officer Russo to take a run at her to see what she could figure out."

"Who did the shooting? Amado or Espinoza?" Way asked.

"Espinoza."

Way turned to Hannon and shut Adkins out completely. The men from the Coroner Unit were carrying out Jacob Collier's corpse. "Okay, obviously the situation on the ground is a joke, which we figured. Our first priority is getting everything we can squeeze out of these women, so I want you to talk to Michelle Amado and drive her until she's given us something we can use or she breaks. I'm happy either way."

"What about the other one?"

"I'll handle the other one. If I feel like she's not responding to me we'll see about switching out, but I want to put myself in front of the woman who pulled the trigger. This did not happen by accident. First a severe beating, then a bullet. This was cold stuff. Premeditated."

Hannon nodded. "I've got it."

"Good. Let's move."

Way pointed at Adkins. "Who's where?"

"The Espinoza woman's in the kitchen. The Amado sister and her daughter are back there."

"Show my colleague where to go. I'll be in the kitchen, but don't come to me unless you have something good to tell me."

"Yes, sir."

Way went to the kitchen. He made a note of the hanging pots and the immaculately clean cooking area. The counters gleamed. Everything was in place. Hardwood flooring clicked under his heels. The sound caught the attention of the cop at the table. Russo.

"Deputy U.S. Marshal Way," he told her. "Are you finished questioning the subject?"

"I wasn't . . . Yes. I'm all done."

"Wait out there with your detective. I'll call you if I need you."

Russo nodded and left swiftly.

Camaro Espinoza sat perfectly still. He could barely tell she was breathing.

"I'm Keith Way, with the United States Marshals Service," Way announced.

"I heard."

He approached the table and stood over her. "I am here pursuant to a federal fugitive warrant, and I want some answers."

"Send Russo back in," Espinoza said.

"You're all done dealing with the locals for now. This is between you and federal law enforcement. Now, I'd like to know exactly what went down here tonight, and I want you to tell me in detail. Nothing gets left out."

"Did you see the body?"

"I did."

"Then that's all the detail you get."

Way grabbed the back of the Espinoza woman's chair and kicked it around to face him. He leaned in closely. "Let's cut the shit. You tell me what I want to know right now, or I will be the worst thing that happens to you all week."

Espinoza studied his face. Way saw only composure in hers.

"Gosh. Why didn't you say so?" she asked.

He stepped back but didn't sit down. "The woman who owns this house is your sister?"

"That's right."

"Her name's Amado. Yours is Espinoza. Which one of you is married?"

"Neither. We're half sisters."

"Where do you come from? Carmel? Salinas?"

"No."

"My understanding is yesterday you beat the living shit out of Jacob Collier and put him in the hospital. Today he's dead from a bullet you put in him."

"Jake Collier was an asshole. Someone was going to kill him sooner or later."

"You got to be the lucky one."

"I guess so."

"Where'd you get the gun?"

"It belongs to my sister."

"You know your way around guns?"

Espinoza shrugged.

"I'm going to find out everything about you," Way said. "I'll know your shoe size."

Espinoza looked at him and was quiet. Then she said, "I'm a seven."

Way barked a laugh. "You don't even know how much trouble you're in."

"How much trouble am I in?"

"You just killed my best chance at stopping a cop killer. You do the math."

# CHAPTER TWENTY-ONE

Lukas drove a dark green Honda Accord he'd stolen from a parking lot in Las Vegas. The ignition was wired together, the steering column stripped, but he kept to the speed limit on the whole eight-hour drive to Salinas, passing through sleepy Bakersfield along the way. He considered stealing another car there.

The skies were dark and portentous as he made the last few miles to Jake's Pearl Street address. The signs of rain were everywhere, and when Lukas cracked the window to let cigarette smoke out, he smelled water in the air.

He parked two blocks away from Jake's house, the car partially backed into an alleyway, providing him a quick start in almost every direction. A gusty wind picked at him as he walked the rest of the way. He stopped at the corner by a telephone pole riddled with staples and scraps of wet paper. He looked down the street.

The police cruiser made no attempt to conceal itself. It was parked directly in front of Jake's house. Lukas saw the officer behind the wheel. It was impossible to know if he'd been spotted. He walked forward instead of back, crossing the street as if he belonged there, then stopped as soon as the house on the corner obscured him from view.

Lukas stepped up to the corner again and peered around to get a second look at the car. It had not moved, nor had the cop inside. Lukas pulled back.

There was no sign of Jake's truck. Jake was gone, and Lukas's calls went directly to voice mail.

Instead of crossing the street a second time, Lukas looped around to the next block and crossed there, coming back to his car the long way around. He got behind the wheel and thought. After a long while he called up a memory of the place Jake said he worked during the off-season. He remembered it was a lumberyard, but the specifics escaped him. With the phone he searched for lumberyards in the area and came up with three. One caught his eye. He dialed its number.

"Carlson Lumber, this is Spencer speaking, how can I help you today?"

"Yeah," Lukas said, "I was trying to get ahold of Jake Collier."

"Jake?" the man said. There was something in his voice.

"Yeah, that's right. Doesn't he work there?"

"Sure. Jake's been here for years. Listen, can I put you on hold? I think somebody else can help you better."

"What's going on?"

"Just hang on."

The line went quiet. Lukas thought the man had hung up, but the timer on the call continued to count. He waited until finally someone new picked up. The voice was younger, but his tone was somber. "You're calling about Jake?"

"Yeah, who is this?"

"My name's Derrick. I work with Jake. Who's calling?"

Lukas considered his answer. There was no reason the cops would be listening here. "I'm his brother."

"You're Lukas?"

"That's right. Where's Jake?"

"He's not here."

"So where can I find him?"

"I don't know how else to tell you except to tell you, but...Jake's dead."

Lukas was suddenly breathless. He sucked air. "How?"

"He got shot last night," Derrick said. "It's crazy, man."

Lukas licked his lips. "Who?"

"Do you know Michelle?"

"Michelle? His girlfriend? His girlfriend shot him?"

"No, no, no. I heard about it from some guys I know in Carmel. He broke into his girlfriend's place and started swinging a knife around. The next thing you know, Chelle's sister shoots him right in the chest. Kills him. Just like that."

Lukas felt a twinge of pain in his skull. He rubbed his temple with his thumb. Thoughts of his last conversation with Jake swirled around and emptied into his forebrain. Michelle. Rebecca. "Camaro," he said.

"You know her?"

"Jake told me about her. He said she came out to where he worked and laid a hurt on him. Messed up his arm. Messed up his face."

"I've never seen anything like it," Derrick agreed. "She was all over him in a second. Me and the boys, we were going to get involved, but Jake told us to back off so he could handle it. But she wrecked him, man. She totally wrecked him. Now she killed him. Jake should have let us deal with the situation."

Lukas nodded stiffly. The pain in his head increased. He had to pry his teeth apart to speak. "Where is the chick staying? Does she have a hotel or something? What can you tell me?"

"I don't know anything about that. I'm sorry. But I know where Chelle lives. I can give you her address in Carmel."

"Give it to me."

Derrick obeyed. "You probably don't want to go over there, man. The cops are going to be worked up for a while. Nobody gets shot in Carmel. This is like DEFCON One stuff. Like the president got killed."

"You've been a big help," Lukas said.

"Whatever I can do. Me or any of the guys...you need something, all you have to do is ask. I'd be proud to carry his casket at the funeral."

Lukas almost laughed. "What's a number I can use if I need to get in touch with you again?"

"Yeah, let me give it to you."

Lukas wrote the number on the back of a gas station receipt and crushed it into his pocket. It was easier to breathe now, but only just. He wanted to smash the phone into pieces against the steering wheel to have something to break. He kept his voice even. "I'm going to look into this, and then I'll get back to you. And listen, don't mention you talked to me. Not to anybody. I have some trouble I'm dealing with, and I don't need the cops breathing down my neck, you understand me?"

"Yeah, I understand. No one will hear anything from me."

"Good job. I'll talk to you soon."

"Okay. I want to say sorry about—"

Lukas hung up the phone and dropped it on the passenger seat. He started the car by twisting two wires together and drove away.

# CHAPTER TWENTY-TWO

Annabel woke fr om a dark dream that began to fade the moment she opened her eyes. She felt heavy-limbed and tired, but it was eight-thirty in the morning and it was time to move. On the bed beside her, Rebecca slept with a stuffed hippopotamus clutched to her chest.

She paused a moment to brush Rebecca's hair from her face, then slipped out of bed and into the adjoining bathroom. With the door only half closed, she ran the shower and scrubbed herself thoroughly. She toweled off and blow-dried her hair, and when she looked out again Rebecca was still sleeping.

The house was still. She walked silently down the hallway and emerged into the living room. Before this moment it might have been possible to forget. Now it came to her like a hammer blow. The bloody stain marking the floor was still there. Spatters of red flecked the curtains and the wall.

Annabel stood rooted to the spot. She saw bright spots and realized she was hyperventilating. She slowed her breathing. Careful to skirt the empty space where Jake's body had lain, she went to the kitchen.

"Good morning," Camaro said.

Annabel jumped at the sound of Camaro's voice. Her sister was at the kitchen table, outlined by the light falling through the window. It didn't look like she had changed. It didn't look like she had moved at all.

"You scared the hell out of me," Annabel told her.

"Sorry."

She switched on the lights, and the kitchen became a friendly place again. "Do you want coffee or tea? I was thinking coffee."

"Coffee's fine."

"You want French roast? Hazelnut? Hawaiian blend?"

"Coffee."

She selected a K-Cup marked eight o'clock coffee and put it in the machine. She used a pitcher to fill the reservoir and started the process. "It's just a minute," she said. "The water has to heat up."

"That's fine."

Camaro sat with her hands folded in front of her, as quiet as the house itself. Annabel approached her slowly. When she pulled out the chair, it scuffed slightly, the sound incredibly loud in the hush. Only the buzzing of the machine as it warmed the water cut the silence. She sat down. "Did you sleep?"

"For a while."

"Are you okay?"

"I'm fine."

"They talked to me, and I said everything you told me to say. They never pushed me. You were right."

"Cops like easy answers," Camaro said.

"So what happens now?"

"Now we wait to see if they charge me for killing Jake."

"What will you do if they...if you have to go to court?"

Camaro glanced at her. "I'll go."

"They'll ask you questions under oath. Me, too. It's against the law to lie."

"Do you think Jake would give a shit about something like that?" Camaro asked. "They can ask all the questions they want. Never change your story. If you change your story, then they have you. I can't leave here worrying about whether you can handle it."

"I can handle it."

Camaro looked more closely at her. She put out a hand to cover Annabel's. She squeezed it. "I know you can. *You* have to know you can."

Annabel let Camaro hold her hand. She didn't want to pull away. "I have to get Becca's things together for school. Then I have to drop her off and go to work. You can come with me if you want."

"I think I'll stay here for now."

They had coffee together, and then Annabel went to Rebecca to wake her up. She laid out her daughter's clothes, and while Rebecca dressed,

Annabel cooked a warm breakfast for all of them. Rebecca colored at the table between taking bites of oatmeal, drinking orange juice, and talking to Camaro. The scene was so basic and ordinary that Annabel was almost able to forget the night before.

In the end, Annabel dressed for work and left the house with Rebecca in tow. They went up the walk toward the parked Subaru. She noticed the police cruiser only when the woman officer got out of her car and approached them.

"Good morning," the officer said.

The woman was young and slight and unthreatening, and she smiled easily. Annabel put herself between Rebecca and the policewoman anyway. She glanced back toward the house, hopeful Camaro might emerge, but Camaro was somewhere inside and out of sight. She breathed deeply. "What can I do for you, Officer?"

"I've been assigned to watch over you for a couple of days. I'll take the mornings, and Officer Hill will take the afternoons. It's for your safety."

"Safety? I don't understand. We're not being threatened."

The young officer came close. "Why don't you go ahead and put your daughter in the car, then I'll explain."

Annabel's hands shook as she buckled Rebecca into the booster seat in the back of the SUV. She kissed Rebecca lightly on the forehead and said, "I'll be right back," before closing the door.

The policewoman was waiting. "I'm sorry," she said. "I don't want to scare you. You seem like a real nice lady, and your daughter's nice, too."

"Tell me what's going on, Officer...?"

"Russo."

"Officer Russo. Is there something else to worry about?"

"Did anyone talk to you last night about someone named Lukas Collier?"

"Lukas? That's Jake's brother, right?"

"Yes."

"The lady with the marshals mentioned his name. She wanted to know if Lukas had called Jake lately, or if Jake ever mentioned his name."

Russo took this in. "There's a chance—just a chance—that Lukas

Collier might be in the area. We have the police in Salinas and Pacific Grove and the County Sheriff's Department looking into it. The U.S. Marshals have a warrant for Lukas's arrest. And they're worried, you know, that he might do something when he finds out his brother was killed."

Annabel closed her arms around herself. "Do something? Like come after us?"

"Probably nothing," Russo said. "I mean, this is *Carmel*. And there are way too many cops looking for him if he tries something stupid. But to be on the safe side, we're going to do like I said and make sure everything is okay. All right?"

"All right. So do you follow me, or how does this work?"

"I'll follow you. It's time for your daughter's school? She goes to Carmel River?"

"Yes."

"I'll tail you there."

They parted. Annabel walked toward the driver's side and then stopped with her keys in her hand. "Excuse me, Officer Russo?"

"Yes?"

"What about my sister? Who watches my sister?"

Russo looked at the house. "They didn't tell me, but I think your sister can probably look out for herself, don't you think?"

Annabel was slow to nod. "Okay. But don't forget about her."

"Nobody will. Let's hurry. You don't want to be late for school."

# CHAPTER TWENTY-THREE

Yates watched the home of Michelle Amado for hours without seeing any evidence of Jacob or Lukas Collier. With his energy dwindling, he drove away to a small Italian restaurant, where he fortified himself with a porterhouse steak with sautéed spinach the server assured him was organic, plus potatoes and cannellini beans. It was all very expensive, but everywhere in Carmel seemed expensive, and the restaurant was the closest to a family-style place as he'd been able to find on short notice.

When he returned to Michelle Amado's home, the street was alive with flashing police lights, and over the next couple of hours more and more police arrived. He stayed as far back from the end of the cul-de-sac as he could without moving out of sight and watched the cops do their work. They brought out a body in a bag, and his heart leaped, but somehow he knew it was not Lukas Collier. A locksmith came for a while but left by midnight.

Eventually all but one police vehicle left the scene, and the one that remained showed no inclination to depart. Yates saw a young woman behind the wheel, reading something with the small overhead light on. It rained off and on.

He was still in place when he saw a mother and child go to their vehicle. The cop conferred with the mother for a few moments, and then all of them drove away. Yates waited ten minutes to see if the policewoman would return, but the street stayed empty. He got out of the rented SUV.

The gate to the front walk was slightly ajar. Yates cast a look around to see if there was movement in any of the other three houses near this one, but he'd watched all of those people leave in the early morning hours, off to jobs that didn't include all-night vigils and police. Yates was alone. Almost.

At the front door he depressed the lighted button for the doorbell. He examined the door and saw it had been kicked hard. When the door came open, he saw where the frame had been refreshed with new, un-painted wood. And then he saw the woman.

She looked at him frankly, standing in her sock feet just inside. Her body was relaxed, but Yates saw the coiled spring under the surface. He found himself automatically checking her hands for weapons. She had none.

"Who are you?" she asked.

"Ma'am, my name is Jeremy Yates. Are you Michelle Amado?"

"No," the woman said, and offered nothing else.

"May I ask your name, then?"

"You're not a cop," she said.

"No, ma'am." He produced a badge wallet and showed it to her. "I'm a bail fugitive recovery agent."

"What's that?"

"We pick up people who fail to appear in court."

"A bounty hunter."

Yates winced. "That's one way to put it."

The woman's eyes narrowed. "My name's Camaro."

Yates thought of the police report. "Camaro. Michelle Amado's sister?"

"That's right. What do you want?"

"I wondered if I might have a few minutes of your time."

He saw the decision ticking over behind her eyes until finally she stepped back to let him in. Yates closed the door behind him. His gaze strayed to the middle of the living room floor and the broad patch of crimson that indicated a dead body.

"My sister just left. How did you know there was anyone here?"

"I took a shot in the dark," Yates said. "May I sit?"

Camaro motioned toward the couch. She took a chair near the cold fireplace and watched him while he sat down. He was a tall man, and his legs were too long to fit behind the coffee table. He nudged it slightly out of place, at the same time noticing where something heavy had struck the far edge with enough force to crush a mark in the wood. A picture of what happened in this room began to form.

"Someone got themselves killed here last night," Yates said.

"Yes."

"Would that someone be Jacob Collier?"

Camaro didn't answer right away. He saw the calculation again. "Yes."

"Unfortunate, especially given that you put him in the hospital in pieces not too long before."

"You know a lot. Where are you from?"

"Norfolk, Virginia. It's not really Jacob I'm after but his brother, Lukas. He skipped bail and disappeared on his way out west to see Jacob. Along the way he killed my son."

A deep silence descended between them. He kept his face studiously neutral. "I'm sorry," Camaro said at last. "But if you're looking for him, I don't know where he is."

Yates tweaked the corner of his mustache and nodded slowly. He selected his words carefully. "Ma'am, it's my belief that Lukas Collier isn't far away from here. He might even be in town. And it's also my belief that as soon as he finds out what happened here, he's going to be very interested in talking to the person who killed his brother. The question is, who that might be. Now, it could have been your sister, but I had a look at her not twenty minutes ago, and she doesn't look the type."

"But I do."

"Yes, ma'am. You do. Where'd you serve?"

"Overseas, mostly. Iraq. Afghanistan."

"Army?"

"Yes."

"I was in the Marine Corps myself. Vietnam. A little bit before your time, I'd guess."

Camaro acknowledged this with a nod. "So I killed Jake. Lukas will want me."

"That's right. And I expect the police are thinking along the same lines, because they had a car out there all night and an officer trailing your sister when she left this morning. Though I notice they left you here all by your lonesome."

"If you want Lukas, you're going to have to get in line. There were a couple of U.S. marshals here last night. They were pretty hot to find out all about Lukas."

"I suspect that would be Deputy U.S. Marshal Keith Way."

"You know him?"

"I've had occasion to speak with him on the phone. He was on the scene where my son died. He told the both of us to step back and let the Marshals Service handle bringing in Lukas. I've never been one to sit on my hands. My son, Stanley, wasn't either."

"I don't really know how I can help you," Camaro said.

"The marshals want to bring Lukas in because he killed one of their own. I don't know the whole story, but you have to know that killing a cop anywhere in the world is a real bad idea. Lukas, though, he's meaner than hell, and he doesn't give a good goddamn about what anybody else wants or does so long as he gets the thing he's after. And as of last night, the thing he'll want most in this world is to kill you."

"He can try," Camaro said.

"He can. And he has the background for it. He served some time in the Corps, did some shooting in Iraq. Maybe he's not what I'd call an expert killer, but he would have been trained well enough. He's not the kind you'd want to turn your back on. I'd like to find him."

"You and everybody else in this town."

"I'd also like to float a little offer your way. You give me the high sign before you tell the marshals or the local cops or anyone else, and I will resolve your Lukas problem."

"You want to be the one to kill him."

"Yes, ma'am."

She looked at him directly. "Don't call me ma'am. Call me Camaro."

# CHAPTER TWENTY-FOUR

After Yates left , Camaro went in the bathroom and lifted up her shirt to look at her back. There was a livid bruise where she'd crashed into the coffee table, spreading under the skin like a purple oil slick.

She lingered in the front room for a while, staring out the window, before heading out the front door to walk the streets of Annabel's neighborhood. She felt the day stretching out emptily before her, wanting to be filled.

Her impression of the town on foot was much the same as it had been from the comfort of a car. Carmel was very quiet, with every block seeming isolated from the next thanks to wooded lots and houses like perfect little cameos.

She sensed the police cruiser coming up behind her before she heard the engine. When the car pulled even with her, the passenger-side window went down, and Officer Russo peered out from behind the wheel. "Good morning, Ms. Espinoza."

"Good morning."

"Seeing the sights?"

Camaro stopped and the cruiser idled beside her. "Something like that."

"Why don't you get in and I'll give you a tour?"

Camaro thought and looked both ways down the street. No one appeared. She let herself into the car. They sat with a mounted shotgun and a new-looking computer terminal between them. Russo had the heater going.

After Camaro buckled up, Russo rolled. They kept a slow pace. Russo scanned the street. "Where are you from?"

"Florida."

94

"Oh, yeah? Where?"

"Miami."

"Nice. I'd like to go there."

"I'm guessing you already knew where I come from," Camaro said.

"What makes you say that?"

"Because as soon as your people finished talking with me last night, they put me in the system."

Russo smiled. She had a pretty and delicate appearance belied by the policewoman's gear she wore. "My bosses wanted to know all about you."

"What do they know now?"

"Nothing major. Name, address, outstanding charges."

"I have outstanding charges?"

"Not any they mentioned. But I was sitting in front of your sister's place most of the night. I get stuff through the computer. Lots of interesting reading about you."

They turned a corner. An old woman waved from the sidewalk, and Russo waved back.

Camaro watched Russo drive. The young woman was careful behind the wheel, almost formal. "How long have you been a cop?"

"Three years."

"That's not a long time."

"No, not really. And it's not like anything happens here, anyway. Not like in Afghanistan. You're amazing."

"I'm not."

"I saw your record. You got medals and the whole thing. How many women ever got the Silver Star?"

"Not a lot."

"No kidding. You have to tell me your story."

"I'd rather not."

Russo looked disappointed. "Is it because I'm a cop?"

"It's because I don't talk about it," Camaro said. "With anyone."

"Okay," Russo said, though it clearly wasn't.

"You can tell me something," Camaro said.

"What?"

"How tight were Jake Collier and his brother?"

"So you know about Lukas."

"I heard he killed a cop. And I heard he might be headed this way."

"Who told you all of that?"

"Am I wrong?" Camaro asked.

"No. We're keeping watch over your sister and her daughter until we know more."

"How about me?"

"I guess they figure you can take care of yourself."

"Or they're hoping Lukas pokes his head out and tries to kill me for shooting Jake."

Russo shook her head. "Nobody's expendable."

"Someone's always expendable."

Russo drove on. Camaro looked in the side mirror at the road behind them. She saw a green car make the turn with them. It had made the last turn with them, too. "How much do you know about Lukas Collier?"

"We have a picture and a sheet, and that's it. Some trouble in Los Angeles, but that might as well be on the other side of the world when it comes to Carmel. We don't really do city things here."

"I noticed."

"It's nice, though. We don't get any real trouble here. Not like in Salinas. In Salinas they have gangs."

"Comes with the territory," Camaro said.

"I'm not saying we can't handle things," Russo added quickly.

"Tell me about Jake. What was his story? Was he the kind to do what he did last night?"

"Him? I don't think so. There's nothing in his jacket that would make me think he'd ever break into someone's house with a knife. He was always one of those surfer dudes who's out in the water when he's not getting drunk and disorderly. Seems like every month in the summer we're arresting one of those guys for something."

"My sister knows how to pick 'em," Camaro said.

"She's not the only one. I've seen Jake and his crew with all kinds of girls. In the summertime it's the worst, because they're always taking up with tourists and getting them to give up all their money to buy beer and surf wax. I heard one time this lady up from LA bought Jake a brand-new convertible. For *cash*. Some guys have the gift."

They were away from the residential neighborhoods and in the shopping district of Carmel. One tiny boutique after another slipped past Camaro's window. They passed a simple white church with a red sign that declared it the  chur ch  of  the  wayfar er. The green car was still with them.

"What do you think?" Russo asked her.

"It's a pretty town," Camaro replied.

"But boring."

"Maybe a little."

"Maybe a lot."

"Okay, maybe a lot," Camaro said, letting the slightest smile show.

"My name's Carly," Russo said. "You can call me that if you want."

"Okay."

"But you won't, will you?"

"I don't get personal with people who want to arrest me."

"I'm not here for any of that. We're keeping an eye on things for a while. This is just the two of us talking."

Camaro nodded and looked out the window. She knew when she glanced in the mirror again, the green car would be there.

"Of course," Russo said, "if it's too formal in the car, we can talk somewhere else. You like coffee?"

"Sure."

"Still want the rest of the tour?"

"I've seen enough, but I'll take the coffee. Are you buying?"

"I think this counts as official business," Russo said, and smiled. She touched the accelerator, and the cruiser picked up speed. "Yes, ma'am. A cup of coffee coming right up."

Camaro let her drive and paid no attention to where they were. She watched only the green car as it trailed them turn by turn.

# CHAPTER TWENTY-FIVE

Way and Hannon commandeered a meeting room at the Carmel Police Department for their use. It had an eight-foot-long table, a speakerphone, and chairs for seven. At one end were a whiteboard and a screen in the ceiling that could be lowered at the touch of a button. At the other end, a small coffee station was assembled.

Way spread out his things as he wanted and linked into the department's Wi-Fi connection. He used the locals' printer to spit out color ink-jet pages, many of which were posted and piled around his workstation. He had photographs and printouts from the previous night's crime scene, and he reviewed the Coroner Unit's report.

It had been another twelve hours without sleep. Way drank an entire pot of coffee and directed Hannon to brew more. He knew she was waiting for an opportunity to say something about rest, but he kept her busy enough that there was no time. For now, she was deep into the records of three towns in Monterey County, digging up known associates and piecing together the life Jacob Collier had.

She was out of the room now. The machine burbled, and Way's eyelids fluttered. "No, it's okay," he said out loud. "I just need some more coffee."

He put his head down and the words echoed around his mind. *More coffee... more coffee.* He was vaguely aware of slipping into sleep and tried to raise his head, but it was too late. He slept despite himself, and the memory came with it.

"More coffee," Way said.

"The thermos is empty, man," Jerry told him.

"What?" Way said. "That's a two-liter container."

It was a chilly autumn night in Newark, the city settling down into midnight in fits and starts. It would never truly sleep, but it might doze awhile, half awake and ready to pounce on the unwary. Between twelve and three a.m. there would be a handful of shootings, a goodly number of stabbings, and at least one death. Maybe it would be murder or maybe it would be misadventure, but that person would still be dead. A citizen had a one-in-eighty-five chance of being a victim of a violent crime in Newark. It was a wonder the place did not disintegrate into open anarchy in the streets.

Way was bundled up against the gathering cold. The winter promised to be a savage one, and already the temperatures regularly dropped below freezing at night. They were talking snow, and it was only November.

Beside him, Jerry Washington was dressed in a puffy Jets jacket and a black watch cap. His face was dark, his cheeks scrubbed with the beginnings of a winter beard. When he smiled, he flashed sharp teeth. He shook the empty thermos vigorously, but it was silent. "Drained it dry. You're gonna be pissing all night."

"I've got an iron bladder," Way told him.

"That's you. Iron Man."

"What's it like being Iron Man's sidekick?" Way asked.

"What sidekick? I'm Batman, dude. Everybody's Batman's sidekick."

They laughed in the car, their breath visible.

Way looked out the window. They were in the Central Ward, on a street full of potholes and heavily tagged by the locals. A corner store had a painted sign that said happy liq uor. Its windows were gridded over with metal, the front door equipped with a steel shutter that was already pulled down a little in preparation for the end of the night. Shadows moved around inside, visible through the advertisements that papered the glass. After a while a young couple came out with a grocery sack and crossed behind the car, huddled close against the cold.

The building they wanted was a hundred feet away, made of dark brick with white lintels. A single yellow bulb burned above the street-level door, and those windows that weren't boarded over were half lit and half not. The address was spray-painted on the bricks in bright yellow.

Headlights appeared down the block, and Jerry nudged him. "Hey," he said, "that look like a Caprice to you?"

"How can I tell from just the lights?"

"That's a Caprice," Jerry said.

The car approached slowly through splashes of streetlights until it was near enough to see clearly. It was a Chevy Caprice, burgundy, from the mid-'00s. The pulse quickened in Way's temples. "It's the one."

"You want to call it in?"

"Let's see how it goes."

The Caprice slowed until it came to a gentle stop in front of the old, broken building. A loud rattle broke Way's concentration, and he saw the owner of Happy Liquor closing the shutter on the entrance. The interior had gone black.

It was absolutely dark inside the Chevy, but there were some hints of movement. After a moment the dome light came on, and Way saw a black man behind the wheel, a white man in the passenger seat. The two of them leaned close to say something, then bumped fists. The white man got out. Lukas Collier.

Way waited until the Caprice started to pull away. He drew the Glock from inside his jacket and retracted the slide just enough to see the gleam of brass. He let it go. Beside him, Jerry drew his own weapon.

Lukas stayed on the street for only a few seconds. He pushed open the door into the building. As soon as it swung shut behind him, Way and Jerry were out of the car and moving. They crossed the street at a jog.

"We should call in the car," Jerry said.

"I'll do it," Way told him. "You go on ahead. I'll be right behind you."

Jerry touched him on the arm as he passed, and then he slipped inside.

Way pulled a phone from his pocket and dialed 911. When the operator answered, he was quick. "This is Deputy U.S. Marshal Keith Way. I'm serving a fugitive warrant in the Central Ward and have a vehicle and driver that need to be stopped."

"I'll take that information from you, sir," the operator said.

"It's a burgundy Chevrolet Caprice with New York plates. The driver is Marcus Murray. I'm going to give you the plate number now. Please notify Detective Frank Armisen of the stop."

The operator took the information. "Do you need backup at your location?"

"I think we're okay. I'll call if there's a change."

Gunshots sounded abruptly, popping off inside the building in rapid succession. Way fumbled with his phone and dropped it. The face shattered on the sidewalk. He grabbed for it, but the display was dead. He threw it down and went for the door as he heard the first shouts.

A baby was crying somewhere when he hit the lobby. A staircase climbed upward, the steps worn and wooden. "Jerry, call out!" Way yelled. "Jerry, call out!"

"Third floor!"

Way thundered up the steps with his weapon in his grip. He rounded the first landing and made the second floor before he heard another gunshot. People peeked out of their doors, but he did not have time or breath to warn them back inside. He kept climbing.

The crying baby was louder than ever when he reached the third floor. A light fixture hung loosely from the wall, the bulb and glass shade shattered. He passed a garbage chute with a hatch hanging from a single hinge. A man was shouting and Jerry was shouting and mixed into it was the desperate wail of a woman.

He charged down the hallway and found one door open. Way fell in beside the door and looked in. He saw a messy front room with a playpen and a television and a broken-down couch. Papers and magazines were everywhere, scattered among discarded mail and empty bottles of beer. A few fuzzy toys poked up through the mess.

"Jerry, where are you?" Way called.

"Right here!"

Way looked again, and he saw Jerry backing out of a hallway inside, his weapon up. Jerry didn't look in his direction as Way slipped into the apartment. He had opened his mouth to say something when Lukas Collier bellowed, "I will shoot this bitch right in the head!"

The woman was visible down the hallway in one of the bedrooms, partially obscured by the half-closed door. Lukas had her around the neck, the four-inch barrel of a heavy Smith & Wesson pressed to her temple. The woman was flushed and crying, and so was the baby she held.

"Jesus," Way said.

"I got this," Jerry said. He kept his weapon level.

"My phone is busted," Way told him. "There's no one coming."

"I got this," Jerry said again.

"You back the hell off or she's dead, you understand me?" Lukas said.

Way raised his Glock. "There's no way out, Lukas," he said. "Let the woman and her kid go. This doesn't have to go bad for anybody."

"Fuck you," Lukas spat. "You back out of the apartment. You close the door, and you stay in the hall."

"We're not going anywhere," Way said. He looked to the woman. "Ma'am, we're going to keep you safe."

"Don't talk to her, talk to me!"

"Lukas," Jerry said, "listen to me. There's nothing we can do for you if you hurt that woman or her baby. Or is it your baby?"

"It's not my goddamned baby."

"Okay, man, it's cool. But you have to let them go. You don't have to throw down your gun, but you have to let them out of there."

Lukas pushed the barrel of the gun harder against the woman's temple until she screamed again. The whites showed around both of his eyes. "No deal," he said.

"I got the shot," Way whispered to Jerry.

"Don't do it, dude," Jerry whispered back. "The hammer's cocked on that thing."

"He's gonna kill her no matter what."

"What the hell are you saying? Stop talking to each other!"

Jerry pointed his weapon at the ceiling and put his free hand up. "Lukas, it's cool. It's totally cool. I'm going to make you a deal, all right? It's a good deal."

"I don't want any deals. Get out of here!"

"You know I can't do that. But this is what I can do: I can come in there and you can hold me hostage."

Way blanked for a second, and then the words crashed down on him. "Jerry, what the hell?"

102

Jerry ignored him. "I'm gonna put my gun down now. And then I'm gonna come in the room. You let the lady and her kid go, and you take me instead."

Lukas's face purpled. The veins in his neck stood out. "If you are screwing with me..."

"No way. This is for real."

"Jerry, you are not going in there," Way said.

Jerry put his pistol on the floor. "It's handled, Keith," he said. "Get ready to get that woman out of here."

"Jerry..."

"Are you ready, Lukas?" Jerry asked.

Lukas hesitated. He gripped the woman tightly. The baby squalled, and its mother wept. "No tricks."

"No tricks. I'm coming in."

Way's feet felt leaden as Jerry stepped into the hallway. For a moment Lukas was obscured completely, but then Jerry was into the room and Way could see again. He was conscious of sweat on his face and on his palms. A rapid tremor passed through his body, and his teeth chattered. He stilled them.

"I'm here," Jerry said. "Let the lady go."

Lukas released his grip on the woman and shoved her forward. She stumbled and then rushed past Jerry into the hallway. Way caught a glimpse of Lukas surging toward Jerry before the bedroom door slammed shut.

Way yelled Jerry's name and rushed the door, kicking it open to see the two men. Lukas held his pistol to Jerry's skull. "Outside!" Lukas ordered. "Outside!"

"Keith, it's okay," Jerry said. "I've got this. Close the door and wait outside. We don't want anything to happen here."

"You've got nowhere to go," Way told Lukas. His gaze strayed past the man to an open window. Cold air spilled in through it.

"Keith, step away, man. It's all right."

Way aimed at Lukas's face. "Game's over, Lukas. It's time."

"You son of a bitch," Lukas said. He moved the gun from Jerry's head. Way pulled his trigger without thinking. Both men toppled backward. Jerry slid from Lukas's grasp with a wound in his head. Lukas's gun tumbled away, lost under a couch.

Way was frozen. He held his weapon but could not feel it. He was rooted. Jerry filled his vision.

Lukas clambered to his feet. "Nice shot, asshole."

Way tried to shift his aim. His arms would not obey. His mouth worked soundlessly. Lukas fled through the window. Way watched him go.

A long moment passed. Jerry was motionless on the floor.

Way moved. He ran back into the hall, retracing his steps until he found the broken-down garbage chute. The hatch still opened. He dropped his weapon in, thinking that later he could claim Lukas had taken it with him. He heard the gun descend, thudding and banging. Only then did he return to the apartment. He fell to the ground by Jerry's side. He touched the back of his head and felt nothing but pulp and bone fragments. Jerry's right cheekbone was shattered by the .40-caliber round.

Way took a deep breath. "Somebody help! Somebody help now! Call nine-one-one! Call nine-one-one!"

In the depths of the memory, he felt it. Something seized him by the shoulder and shook him. Way's head snapped up, and he was far from Newark, ensconced in the meeting room of the Carmel Police Department's headquarters.

Hannon shook him again. "Keith?" she asked. "Keith, are you all right?"

Way blinked rapidly. He had not felt asleep, but he did not feel awake either. "What?"

"Where'd you go? I said your name like five times."

"It's ... it's nothing. I'm just tired."

Hannon put a fresh cup of coffee on the table by his laptop. "You need to sleep. Even fifteen minutes is better than nothing."

"When I get him," Way said.

"Keith, we don't even know if he's coming."

"When I get him," Way said firmly.

Hannon didn't answer. Way swallowed a mouthful of hot coffee and turned to his computer again.

# CHAPTER TWENTY-SIX

Lukas foll owed the police unit as it passed through Carmel, but when it made a U-turn at an intersection and slotted into a no-parking zone near a coffeehouse, he elected to drive on. In the last few moments of the tail he'd managed to get another good look at the woman he assumed was Camaro.

The police had closed their net over Carmel. Michelle Amado's house was under surveillance, or at least while she was home, and they had their hooks into the sister, too. But they couldn't cover everything all the time. They would go where they felt the links were weakest and leave the rest of the chain alone.

He brought out his phone and put it to his ear as he drove. It rang a few times before Derrick answered. "When do you get off work?" Lukas asked him.

"At four. What's up?"

"I want to get together with you and anybody else who saw this Camaro chick in action. Is there somewhere we can meet?"

"Where are you now?"

"What difference does it make? Can we meet or not?"

"Yeah, sure, sure. There's a place called Flickers on Lincoln Street in Carmel. We used to go there with Jake all the time."

Lukas kept driving. He checked his mirrors. He saw no police. "I don't need anywhere high-profile."

"This place is as low-profile as it gets, man."

"All right. Five o'clock. Don't let anyone follow you."

"Got it. I'll be there."

Lukas ended the call with a grunt. He made two lefts as soon as he was able and headed toward the sea. He spent the next few hours watching the breakers roll in, sitting on the damp sand as the sun gleamed in the clear, cold sky. A few intrepid surfers were out on the waves, clad in black and blue wet suits, ignoring the chill of the water. It put Lukas in mind of years long past when he whiled away the days and weeks of summer in the company of his brother and his friends. They'd surf all day, then light a fire on the beach to make burgers. Jake always knew the best places to buy weed, and they would smoke it with the surfer girls and afterward get laid.

That was all over when Lukas caught a case and the judge told him jail or service. Lukas chose the Marines, and they took him away from beaches and surfing and put a gun in his hand. Later they put people in front of that gun, and he did what they trained him to do. Maybe it was reflex at that point. Maybe he liked it a little. When it was all over with, he couldn't imagine going back to the life he had before. Those were the years before he was born. He was himself now. But still he had the memories.

When it was close to five, Lukas reluctantly abandoned his place on the beach and made his way back to the car. He navigated his way to the bar and parked on the street.

The bar reeked of old cigarette butts and stale beer. It was barely lit, the better to hide the sticky floor, and it was already mostly full of patrons. This was a bar for locals and serious drinkers. The old man behind the bar mixed drinks with long-practiced mastery, ignoring the patrons violating California's strict indoor-smoking laws and hollering out orders as they came done.

Lukas had no idea who to look for, but when he saw the little brown-haired man in the work shirt approaching him, he knew it was Derrick.

The man offered him his hand. "Lukas?"

"Yeah."

"Glad to meet you. I just wish it wasn't like this. Come on over and meet the guys."

Derrick brought him back into the corner, where two other men sat in a cramped booth with barely enough room for two more, beer bottles in front of them. They looked at Lukas, and he looked at them. He knew at first glance they would be no good at all.

"This is Loren, and this crazy guy is Nic."

Lukas nodded to them.

"Let's sit down and have some beers. You want a beer, Lukas? I'm buying."

"I'll drink."

"Loren, why don't you run up and get four longnecks from Frank?"

"I'm still finishing this one."

"Loren," Derrick said warningly. "Come on."

The man named Loren got up from the booth and left his beer behind. Derrick scooted in, and Lukas took the side that would let him watch the front.

"Were you with Jake when this Camaro chick beat him up?" Lukas asked Nic.

"Yeah. Crazy, man. I've never seen anything like it. She knows kung fu or some shit."

"And he just let her beat his ass?"

"No, it wasn't like that," Derrick said. "He was fighting all the time. She sucker-punched him, and then he was trying real hard to get into her, but she was mean, man, real mean. Like I said, we would have helped him, but Jake said no."

"He said no," Lukas said.

"Yeah."

Loren returned with the beers. Lukas did not volunteer to move, so the other two were forced to scoot to make room for a fourth man. Lukas took a draw from his bottle and felt the refreshment go down. He sighed heavily. "What did he do? Did he try to screw her, or what?"

Derrick shook his head emphatically. "She was there because of her sister, Michelle. Chelle must have found out Jake had another girl on the side, and this was her way of kicking him to the curb. I mean, *really* kicking him. Jake said this sister has been away somewhere and the two of them never talk. But then she shows up like this?"

"Something was always up with Chelle," Loren said.

"How so?"

Derrick cut in. "Jake said she never actually came out and said it, but he was pretty sure Michelle was stashing money away somewhere. He came to her for loans a few times, and she helped him out. He figured there was more where that came from. That's when he started talking about you and LA and how we could get into some serious cash."

"He wasn't wrong about that. What's your interest?"

"Well...we thought maybe we'd be able to buy in. As partners, you know? He said you had the LA connections and it was just a matter of putting the money together. He had a real stash coming together. We were just waiting for you."

"But then his girl calls her sister."

"It's bullshit," Nic said. "Jake always treated Michelle like she was a princess. I mean, he had something going on the side, but that doesn't mean she wasn't his number one."

"Who's this other chick he's got?"

"Vicki," Derrick said. "She lives in Pacific Grove. She's a legal secretary or something. They met when Jake got done up for public urination about a year ago. She was working in the lawyer's office. They were pretty hot and heavy for a while, but it's true Chelle was always Jake's girl. He loved her. That's what makes it so nuts. Him dead."

"Where was Jake keeping his money?"

Derrick looked to the others. There were blank expressions. "I'm not real sure. Got to be at his place. I mean, you can't put that kind of money in a bank where the IRS can find it."

"So I need to get into his house."

"Yeah, it has to be somewhere. You know, under the mattress."

"I can't go near his place," Lukas said. "If I do, the cops are gonna be all over me. I need someone to take care of it for me."

No answers came. Lukas ground his back teeth.

"We were kind of hoping we'd be *silent* partners," Derrick said at last.

Lukas leaned in, and the others shrank back. "You want to make the kind of money we're talking about, there are no silent partners. Everybody puts in their share, everybody takes a risk. And if that means you have to bust into Jake's place to find his stash, then that's what you do. I need that seed money to put things together in LA. After that, the rest of you can pick up your end and start making back your investment."

"But what about the sister? You gonna kill her for what she did to Jake?" Loren asked.

"What if I do?"

"I'd want to help, that's all."

"How are you gonna help me?" Lukas asked. "You couldn't even help Jake when he was gettin' his ass beat by a girl."

"It doesn't make any difference, anyway," Derrick said. "The police are going to be all over this. She'll be untouchable."

Lukas took another drink. They watched him. He took his time speaking again. "Nobody's untouchable."

# CHAPTER TWENTY-SEVEN

It was evening, and the streetlights were on before Annabel's Subaru returned. She smiled when she saw Camaro. "You're still here."

"Where else would I be?"

"I had this idea that I would show up after work and you'd be gone. Maybe a note on the refrigerator, but that's it."

"I'm not going anywhere," Camaro said.

Annabel kissed her on the cheek. "Good. Are you hungry? I'll make dinner."

"Nothing fancy."

"Is chicken breast too fancy?"

"Chicken breast is fine."

Camaro felt a tug on her finger, and she looked down. Rebecca was there. "Will you play dollhouse with me, Camaro?"

Camaro knelt down. "Sure, I'll play dollhouse with you."

"Good. You can be the daddy and I'll be the mommy."

"Typecasting," Annabel said.

"Shut up."

Camaro sat down with Rebecca by the dollhouse, and the little cloth dolls were solemnly distributed. Rebecca then took Camaro on a room-by-room tour of the house itself. Careful attention was paid to decor, and Rebecca was careful to mention that Mommy and Daddy slept in separate rooms.

"Why is that?" Camaro asked.

"Because they fight too much."

Camaro frowned. "My Daddy doesn't want to fight with Mommy."

"Good, because if Daddy tries to hurt Mommy, he'll get shot."

Rebecca began to set a tiny dining room table with plastic plates and put the baby in its high chair. Camaro watched with her doll held loosely in her hands. She felt something she was not quick to identify, and she was slow to speak. "You know," she said quietly, "Jake wasn't your daddy."

The little girl didn't look at her. She loaded a plastic turkey into an oven. "I know. But he still got shot. Have Daddy come home from work."

Camaro obeyed, and they played out dinnertime. There was no fighting.

After forty-five minutes, Annabel called them to the kitchen. Camaro smelled olive oil and the enticing scent of frying. The table was already set, and each plate was presented with a fried chicken breast topped with diced tomatoes, parsley, feta cheese, and some sort of sauce. "I thought I said nothing fancy," Camaro said.

"It's not. It's just chicken fried in a falafel mix with tahini and a salad. You want beer or wine?"

"Beer."

They sat and ate. Each bite of the chicken was a burst of spice. Camaro tasted garlic and jalapeño. The salad was delicate and fresh, the tahini light. She thought of her own meals, taken alone at a plain table in her kitchen.

Rebecca excused herself at the end of the meal, and Camaro was left alone with Annabel. Annabel drank from a glass of Chardonnay. "I guess you know," she said.

"I heard."

Annabel put her hands over her eyes. "I've never even *met* Jake's brother."

"That doesn't matter. When he hears Jake was shot, he's going to go on the warpath. That puts me in danger, but it means trouble for you, too."

"So what do I do?"

Camaro regarded the empty bottle of beer beside her plate. She picked it up and rolled it between her hands before putting it down again. "You should think about getting out."

Annabel looked at her. "Out? Like *out* out?"

"You started over before. You can start over again."

"No. No way. I'm not going through all of that. I won't put Becca through it. This is our home. Everything we have is here. All my friends, my job, my house. I can't walk away."

Camaro took Annabel by the wrist, but gently. She spoke softly. "You may not have a choice."

Annabel shook herself free. "I won't go. I'm not going to go. No-body's going to run me out of my life. I don't care who they are, I don't care what they do."

"This man, Lukas, he's not like Jake. He's bad. He's really bad. Jake came at you with a knife, but Lukas will come at you with a gun. He's trained. A vet. He killed a cop in New Jersey, and he killed a bounty hunter in Colorado. He may have killed more people than that."

"More people than you?"

Camaro fell silent.

"You've always told me to make the right decisions," Annabel said. Her voice quavered. "Ever since we were kids, you told me that. This is the decision I've made: we stand up for ourselves and we fight. Just like you said we should."

"That was before I knew about Lukas Collier."

"It doesn't make any difference. And if he tries anything, I'll kill him, too."

# CHAPTER TWENTY-EIGHT

Lukas waited in the dark.

The apartment was neat and small, very much a woman's space, with soft colors and clean lines visible even among the shadows. It smelled nice, a scent of lavender hanging in the air. No one smoked in this place. The kitchen was tidy and organized, without so much as a single dirty plate in the sink.

He heard her footsteps outside before her keys in the lock. The door came open, and a little boy entered. He was no more than nine, with auburn hair. His mother was right behind him. Lukas waited until they were completely inside and the lights came on before he spoke. "Hello, Vicki."

The woman called Vicki froze with the door almost closed. She snatched at her son. Lukas saw the sudden flash of terror in her eyes, her body poised for flight, but she didn't scream. "Who are you?" she asked in a quiet voice. She had control.

"I'm Lukas. Close the door and lock it."

Vicki was short and redheaded. Her coat was open, and he caught a glimpse of swelling breasts contained by a pale red blouse. She set her purse and keys down on the dining table not far from the door. "What are you doing here?"

"Why don't you take off your coat?" Lukas said, and he smiled.

"If you're looking for money, I have about a thousand dollars hidden in the bedroom. It's all yours."

"That's good to know. Sit down. Take a load off. You must have had a long day."

She came to the couch with her hand on her son's shoulder. The boy had said not a word, nor had he made a single sound. Their coats were wet from the spitting rain. Vicki gathered her son's and then took off her own. She laid them over the arm of the couch despite the damp. Outside the weather had come and gone in waves, and now it was turning drizzly all over again. It made a gentle sound. Vicki looked at him with careful eyes. Lukas wondered if her red hair was real. Judging from the boy's, he guessed so. Without the coat, Lukas was better able to see her curves, and he understood Jake's interest. She had a plain gold chain around her neck with a golden heart dangling from it just even with the top button of her blouse. Her fair skin looked soft and smooth. Lukas thought she was about thirty. The boy was as thin as a stick figure.

"Jake mentioned you were a fine woman," Lukas lied. "I've been looking forward to meeting you for a long time."

"H-how did you get in?"

"Through the front door."

"No, I mean..."

"Relax," Lukas said. "I'm not here to hurt anybody. It just so happens I need a place to stay, and Jake said if I was ever in town."

Vicki looked at the floor before she looked at him. "I guess that's okay. But Jake."

"Yeah, it's bad news about Jake. I know you have to be feeling it, too. Jake wasn't the brightest, but he had a good heart."

"I loved him. Brendan—my son—loved him."

Lukas glanced at the boy, who still hadn't made a sound. "I'm glad. A man needs love in his life. I don't suppose that kid is his."

"No."

"That's all right."

"Can Brendan go to his room?"

"Why couldn't he? I'm not a bad guy, and this is your house. Go have fun, Brendan."

Vicki whispered in her boy's ear, and the child slipped off the couch. He paused only a second, and then he dashed from the room. A moment later a door closed deeper in the apartment.

They stared at each other for a while. Lukas never let his smile fall. Vicki spoke first. "What can I do for you?"

"I'm hungry, for a start."

"Oh. Do you want something to eat? I have some lasagna I can heat up. It's what we were going to have for dinner anyway."

"Lasagna's good."

She went to the kitchen, and he watched her go. He kept his eye on her as she moved around the little prep area, cutting pieces from a tray of lasagna and heating them in the microwave. She got down glasses and took a bottle of Perrier and a bottle of Bud Light from the refrigerator. These she put on the table in the small eating space. She set places for three. She called for her son.

The little boy emerged from his room. He'd changed shirts, but it did nothing to hide his frail form. He sat opposite Lukas and watched with owlish eyes.

"How old's your boy?"

"Eight."

"Good age."

Vicki sat at the table, and Lukas cut into his food. He put a forkful into his mouth and chewed. The taste made him screw up his face. "What is that?"

"It's eggplant lasagna."

"Who makes lasagna with *eggplant?*"

Lukas saw a shot of fear pass through her. "Jake liked it."

"I'm pretty sure he didn't," Lukas said. He twisted the top off the beer and drank directly from the bottle to wash out his mouth. He pushed his plate away. "I'm not eating that."

"Do you want me to make you something else? I can make something else."

"You do that," Lukas said, and he had more beer.

She abandoned her food and retreated to the kitchen. He listened to her awhile. Across from him, Brendan ate delicately from his plate. Lukas scowled at every bite the boy took. He left the table.

He found Vicki putting together a meatball sandwich on a crusty long roll. She glanced at him and smiled weakly. Her hands shook.

Lukas stopped her with a touch on the arm. "You got nothing to worry about. Didn't I say so?"

"I'm sorry. It's just finding you here...it's not what I expected. Brendan—"

"I told you not to worry about him," Lukas said, his voice rising. "Go with it. The sandwich looks good. You look good."

"I just want to put it under the broiler to melt the cheese."

She stiffened for a moment, then kept on with the sandwich. Lukas grinned to himself and went back to the dining area. He waited at the table for her to return. Brendan finished his food. The sandwich was hot and spicy and filled Lukas's mouth with enough good taste to make the disgusting eggplant lasagna go away. Vicki picked at her plate while he devoured it. He hadn't realized how hungry he'd been.

"So you're staying here?" Vicki asked.

"If you don't mind. Everywhere else is too public. I told you, I have people watching out for me. Lots of trouble following me around these days. I was counting on Jake to help me deal with it, but Jake's gone. His friends are no goddamned help."

"Yeah," Vicki said, and she attempted a smile. "Those guys..."

"That's why I need a place where no one knows to look for me," Lukas said. "All of Jake's friends are gonna be watched, but you're a little secret. His girl on the side."

"It's a small place," Vicki said. "Brendan has the only other bedroom. I mean, there's the couch, but..."

Lukas reached across the table and touched her face. "Are you worried about something?"

She closed her eyes, and a visible tremor passed through her.

He got up from his seat and stepped around behind her. He laid his hands on her shoulders and felt the micro-shivers still shaking her. Lukas pulled the hair away from her ear and stooped low to speak quietly to her. "I don't have to sleep on the couch."

"Brendan, go to your room," Vicki said shakily.

"That's a good idea," Lukas said. "Your mother and I have something to talk about."

Brendan hesitated. Lukas glared at him. The boy fled the table.

"Smart kid," Lukas said. He touched the topmost button on Vicki's blouse. "Does he have a smart mama?"

"Please, don't."

Lukas closed the back of his hand at the nape of Vicki's neck. "If I have to get specific about what I need, I might get frustrated. And if I get frustrated, I'll need somebody to take it out on. You get what I'm saying."

"All right," Vicki breathed.

"I thought so," Lukas said. He pulled the Colt from its place and put it down in front of her. He felt her brace herself at the sight of it. "Now, why don't you show me where the bedroom is? And make sure the sheets are clean."

# CHAPTER TWENTY-NINE

Camaro l ay awake in the spare bedroom. She was still dressed from the day. Her phone vibrated on the nightstand, and she answered it. "I don't recognize this number," she said by way of greeting.

"It's Jeremy Yates calling. You gave me your cell."

She sat up on the bed. "Why are you calling, Mr. Yates?"

"Forget the mister. I'm just Yates to my friends."

"Why are you calling me? It's late."

"That it is. I've found it's better to burn the midnight oil when a trail is hot. I spent a few hours talking my way around Carmel and Pacific Grove, trying to scare up some names. And now I have one: Derrick Perkins. Ring any bells?"

"No. Should it?"

"From what I gather, Derrick and your best friend Jacob Collier were good buddies. I missed Derrick pretty much everywhere I tried to find him tonight, but I have an address for him in Salinas. I could use some backup."

"I'm not armed."

"If things go well, you won't need to be. Now, did I make a mistake in calling, or are you interested in helping me track down Lukas Collier before he can cause trouble for your family?"

Camaro slipped off the bed and went for her boots by the door. She keyed on the speaker and set her phone down on the dresser. "I'm interested. You just need to tell me when and where. I have to figure out how to get to you. The police are sitting on the house."

"There's a church not far off from where you're at," Yates said. "If you cut through the woods behind your sister's place, you can probably make it to the road. I can meet you there whenever you're ready."

"Give me fifteen minutes."

"See you soon."

Camaro switched off the bedside lamp before opening the bedroom door. In the hallway she heard the sleeping sounds of Annabel and Rebecca in the master bedroom. Her niece did not want anything to do with her own bed. Camaro crept down the hall and into the living room. Through the front windows she saw the Carmel Police Department vehicle standing in the rain. It was dark in the car, and she couldn't see the driver.

Her jacket was on a hook by the front door. She put it on and stole her way back through the kitchen to the rear door. Light rain pelted against the glass as she slowly turned the knob and exited into the night.

The swing set was silent and unmoving in the dark. Camaro jogged past it to the fence at the back of the yard. She grabbed the top and scrambled up the wet wood until she could throw herself over. On the far side she dropped into a cushion of dead, sodden leaves. The woods stood all around, black bark glistening in the half-light reflected from a neighbor's backyard floodlight.

She set off across the broken ground, counting off the distance in her head. She heard the road before she reached it, a car passing in the night. Emerging from the woods onto the gravel shoulder, she looked both ways. Only a couple of houses occupied this stretch of road, set back behind gates of wood or iron. Camaro spotted the church. It was lit on the outside, though parts were shrouded in darkness. A playground nestled in one of the shadowy pockets, and she cut down the drive until she was out of the light and completely concealed.

An SUV came along. It entered by the same drive and cut its headlights as soon as it was off the road. It slowed and then stopped, the engine idling. Camaro saw Yates behind the wheel, illuminated by the dash lights. She came up on the vehicle and rapped on the window. He popped the locks.

Camaro felt a blast of heat as she got into the SUV. She wiped water from her face. "Right on time," she said.

They exited onto the road, and Yates gave the SUV gas. Camaro noted the manila folder on the armrest between them. It was stuffed with papers. "You mind?"

"Help yourself."

She found Jake's information on top, along with a series of booking photos and what looked like the picture from his driver's license. Underneath were pages of handwritten notes torn from a pad of yellow paper. Underneath those was a flyer with a photo of Lukas Collier. He glowered out at her, long-haired and bearded. "So this is him?"

"The man himself."

Backing up, she looked through Yates's notes. They were detailed, filled with arrows and circles and underlining. She saw the list of names that included Derrick Perkins, along with the addresses of each man, or at least most of them. "Where do you get all of this stuff?"

"Part of my business is knowing how to get information on anyone," Yates replied. "You start by making phone calls, and then you knock on doors. Depending on who you call and who you see, your search won't take too long."

"Derrick slipped you?"

"Not because he's smart. Something's going on with him. People I talked to say he seemed worked up. They thought it might have something to do with Jacob getting killed, seeing as how they were friends and all. But one bartender I talked to said he met up with a man matching Lukas Collier's description."

"Lukas has a lot of balls."

"Like I said before, the man is pissed. You killed his only brother. I expect he'll run just about any risk to make sure you're dead before he moves on."

They were moving fast. "You don't think he's hiding out with Derrick Perkins, do you?" Camaro asked.

"If he is, then I'm the luckiest man alive."

"So, no," Camaro said.

"No. But if they've talked, Lukas might have let something slip. And he might be around again to get Derrick's help. This hasn't been Lukas's place in a while, so he'll need people to keep him safe and secure. It doesn't look like Jacob's crew amounts to much, but they're better than nothing."

Camaro sat back. "I need a gun."

"With the eye of the law on you? Not too smart."

"Neither is being out here with you."

"Fair enough. But you've already done plenty. If there's shooting to be done, best to let me take care of it."

They rode in silence the rest of the way, cruising through sleeping town and country until they were in Salinas. Yates followed the GPS all the way to Derrick's address and parked the SUV out front. He drew his weapon and checked it. Camaro looked at the stainless steel gun and wanted to put her hand around it. Yates stashed it away. They got out of the vehicle together.

It was a quiet street, and the hour was close to midnight. Small homes lined the street, some single-family and some duplexes. Derrick lived in one of the duplexes, and his lights were still on. Camaro approached the house with Yates close behind. "Hold up," he said. "You don't know what you're walking into."

"You said yourself Lukas probably isn't here."

"Even so, I'd feel better if you'd let an old man put in the work."

Camaro allowed him ahead of her, and they passed into the shelter of the carport. A flimsy screen door covered a lime-green inner door. Yates pulled the screen door open and knocked. He had his badge wallet in his hand.

"Who's there?" a woman asked through the door.

There was a small peephole, and Yates brandished his badge in front of it. "Bail enforcement, ma'am. Please open the door."

The locks rattled. A Latina woman opened the door a few inches. A security chain spanned the gap. "Bail what?"

"Bail enforcement. I'm here to see Derrick Perkins."

"Derrick isn't here."

"When will he be back?"

The woman looked past Yates to Camaro. Camaro stared back at her. She saw hesitation in the woman's eyes. "I don't know. He's out drinking. Maybe two or three o'clock."

"Mind if we wait inside?"

"Yes, I mind. I told you he's not here."

"He's here," Camaro said.

The woman looked stricken. "Look, he's drunk. Leave him alone."

"Open the door," Yates said.

She tried to push it shut, but Yates had his boot in the gap.

"Go away! Go away!"

"Fuck this," Camaro said. She pushed her way past Yates and put her shoulder to the door, and the security chain tore free of its moorings. The woman screamed.

Yates drew his gun. The sight of it silenced the woman. Camaro was in a short, darkened hallway leading to a kitchen. Light came from beyond. She passed through quickly and looked left and right at the next corridor. A man poked his head out of one of the bedrooms. He gawked at her for an instant and then vanished, the door slamming shut.

"I got him!"

"Watch yourself, goddamn it," Yates called after her.

Camaro rushed the door. It was flimsy, made of thin wood with just a cheap metal push-button lock in the knob. She kicked it, and the splintery fragments caved in instantly. She lost five seconds pushing the ruins aside, and then she was in the bedroom. Derrick was nearly out the window.

Derrick shouted as Camaro seized him by the belt and the back of his shirt and hauled him back in. He stumbled drunkenly and fell on his ass. The stink of beer came up from him like a cloud. Camaro dropped a knee on his leg, pinning it to the floor, and punched him once. He fell backward, his hands over his face. "Don't kill me! Don't kill me!"

She dragged him to his feet and pushed him down the hall. Yates was at the end of it, his gun held openly to keep the woman silent. The four of them passed into the living room, where the TV played. Yates pointed to the couch. "Sit down."

Camaro kicked Derrick in the backside, and he fell down beside the woman. A trickle of blood ran from a split in his lip. The two of them were pale with fear.

"Remember me?" Camaro asked Derrick.

"This is not how I would have played it," Yates said under his breath.

"We got him," Camaro said. She kicked Derrick sharply in the shin and made him yelp. "Right, Derrick? That's your name, isn't it?"

"Please don't kill us," Derrick said.

The woman began to weep. She threw her arms around Derrick, and the two of them shivered together.

"Nobody's going to get killed," Yates said. "I'm in pursuit of a bail fugitive, and I think you know him. Lukas Collier."

Derrick looked up at the name. "He's not here."

"You mind if I look around?" Yates asked.

"Go ahead."

Yates left the room, and Camaro heard him opening and closing doors. After a few moments he returned. "How long has it been since he was here?"

"Leave Rosalinda out of this."

"Just talk, asshole," Camaro said. She ignored Yates's look.

"He's never been here. He doesn't even know where I live."

"Derrick, Rosalinda, I'm a reasonable man. I know the two of you don't want to be charged with aiding a felony fugitive, so I'm going to ask you once where I can find Lukas."

"I'm telling you, he's not here."

"Where is he?"

"I don't know."

"But you were with him earlier tonight," Yates said.

Rosalinda clung to Derrick tightly. He pried himself loose of her grasp and addressed them. "Yeah. Yeah, I was."

"What did he want? What did you tell him?"

"He wanted to know about Jake's girl. And her sister. Anything at all I could tell him about them. But I don't know anything. I don't know *anything*. I never even saw Chelle's sister before she showed up at the yard the other day." He shot a look toward Camaro, his face dark.

"Where did he go?" Camaro asked.

"He didn't tell me where he was going."

"That's bullshit," Camaro said, and she stepped toward Derrick. He shrank back, and Rosalinda whimpered. "Tell us where he is."

Yates touched her arm. "Camaro? Take a minute. I think he's telling the truth."

"Yeah," Derrick said. "I am telling the truth. Why would he tell me

123

anything? I'm not anybody to him. I was friends with Jake. I don't know Lukas at all. You have to believe me."

"I will beat you until you are dead if you're lying to us," Camaro said.

"I'm not. I swear."

Yates holstered his weapon. "I think it'd be better for all of us if you didn't report this to the police. You lie to us, that's one thing, but there are federal marshals looking for Lukas, and if you lie to them, it's a felony."

"I'm telling you the God's honest truth," Derrick swore.

Camaro moved before Yates could catch hold of her. She grabbed a fistful of Derrick's shirt and pulled him toward her. They were face-to-face, and she smelled him even more strongly now. "If he gets in touch with you, I want you to tell him something. You tell him I will go up against him anywhere, anytime. If he wants me, all he has to do is ask. I'll even leave you my number."

"Camaro," Yates said.

Camaro told Derrick her number. "Repeat it back to me."

Derrick failed, and Camaro reeled it off again. He failed and began to shake afresh. Camaro tightened her grasp on his shirt.

"Camaro," Yates said again.

"Repeat it back to me," Camaro said. Derrick squeezed his eyes shut.

"I know it," Rosalinda said. "I have it."

Camaro waited until Rosalinda repeated it correctly before she let Derrick go. He fell back limply against the couch, and Rosalinda threw her arms around him protectively. Camaro scowled at them both. "You tell him," she said. "You tell him what I said."

"Let's go," Yates said.

Camaro waited a beat longer until Rosalinda could not look her in the eye, and then she followed Yates out into the night.

# CHAPTER THIRTY

In the end, Way could not resist. He went to a small room with two bunks inside and fell asleep for hours. When he woke he was confused about where he was and what he was doing. He felt himself, and everything was there, his clothes rumpled and smelling vaguely stale.

He sat on the edge of the bunk for a while, gathering his thoughts. A soft knock sounded on the door. "Come in," he said.

Hannon entered with a small green folder. She looked fresh, and he wondered if there was somewhere else she might have slept. Her clothes were neater than his. He felt like a pile of discarded laundry.

"Good, you're awake," she said.

"How long were you going to let me sleep? It's almost midnight."

"You needed it."

"I need to find Lukas."

"We will. But you wanted this first." She brandished the folder.

"What's that?"

"It's Camaro Espinoza. A complete package of records, including her military service, tax returns, the whole thing."

"Let me see."

"Why don't you get a cup of coffee first?"

Way nodded and got up. They went into the hallway. The police station was eerily still. "Talk to me, at least. What's her story?"

"She's thirty-three and originally comes from Los Angeles but lives near Miami now. She joined the army in 2001, three days after 9/11, and trained as a 68W Health Care Specialist."

"So she's a nurse?"

"A combat medic. She's served all over the place, in the United States and overseas. Been deployed to Iraq and Afghanistan. She saw frontline action in both places."

"You told me before she had the Silver Star."

"Yes. That's a fun story. In 2009 she was assigned to a combat outpost in Nuristan Province in Afghanistan. The army was going to shut the place down because it couldn't be secured, but before they could get everyone out, the Taliban hit them. They mortared the hell out of the troops there, then overran them and set the whole outpost on fire. Our guys fought for fourteen hours, and Camaro Espinoza was right in the middle of it."

"How'd she get the medal?"

"She repeatedly exposed herself to enemy fire to retrieve injured soldiers or to provide covering fire while they withdrew. She kept on doing it even after she took three wounds, and she dragged one guy a hundred yards under heavy fire to save his life. Two soldiers on the ground that day got the Medal of Honor."

"Sounds like a real shitstorm."

"I wouldn't have wanted to be there."

"So why did she get out?"

"It doesn't say. She did another deployment to Afghanistan after that, and then she was in the U.S. for a while before she resigned in the summer three years back."

"Honorable discharge?"

"What do you think?"

Way found the coffee machine waiting for him. The carafe was full. He poured out a measure, then dosed it heavily with sugar and creamer. "What then? She's out of the army. What does she do?"

Hannon gave him the folder. "You can read all about it."

Way sat down with the file and read. He turned the pages slowly, absorbing details. There were many. "Is all this true?" he asked.

"Yes, as far as I can tell. I'm going to make more calls in the morning. Eventually she turns up in Florida. Owner of Coral Sea Sport Charters, a fishing outfit. And that's where she's been until she came here."

"Does the Marshals Service have a reason to step in?"

"She has an outstanding warrant in New York City for bail jumping. We could leverage that."

"Uh-huh. Is this woman even Michelle Amado's sister?"

"Military records indicate she has a sister, but the sister's name isn't Michelle Amado. It's Annabel Watts. Maiden name Espinoza."

"Wait, the sister is married?"

"Widowed. Her husband was shot to death outside their house in New Orleans under suspicious circumstances. Unsolved homicide. And then the sister vanished, too. You want to know when?"

"When?"

"Three years ago this summer."

"What the hell?" Way asked. "Are we sure this Annabel Espinoza, or Watts, or whatever her name is, are we sure she's Michelle Amado?"

"Keep looking."

Way searched the folder until he found it: a printout of a Louisiana driver's license. "We need to go see the Espinoza sisters. Right now."

"Keith, it's the middle of the night."

"Right now."

# CHAPTER THIRTY-ONE

They cruised nowhere in particular. Yates said nothing. Camaro listened to the rush of warm air from the vents and the comforting bass of the engine. Finally she spoke. "What is it?"

"We don't know each other too well," Yates said, "so I'm not sure exactly how frank I can be with you."

"You can tell me anything."

"All right, then. I don't much care for cowboys and Indians. It's not the way I operate, and it's not the way I like my partners to operate."

"We're partners?"

"For the moment. I agreed to let you in on the search for Lukas Collier, and you agreed that when the time comes I kill him. I find it to be a mutually beneficial relationship, given that Lukas won't rest until he puts a bullet in you."

They slowed for a yellow light and stopped for a red. "So what's the problem?" Camaro asked.

"What exactly did you do in the service, if you don't mind me asking?"

"I was a 68 Whiskey."

"Run that by me again?"

"The old MOS code was 91 Whiskey."

"You said you'd been in Iraq and Afghanistan. I'm gonna guess you didn't spend a whole lot of time in the rear."

"No," Camaro said. "I was out there."

"You have it all over you. Back in the Civil War days they called it seeing the elephant. No man's the same after he's seen the elephant. I can attest to that personally. And I suppose now no woman's the same, either."

"If you have something to say, just say it," Camaro told him.

"All right, I will. You are way too eager to bump up against Lukas Collier."

"And you aren't?"

"It's different for me. I lost someone precious to me."

"My sister and my niece are precious to me," Camaro said. "As long as Lukas is running around out there, they'll never be safe."

"And you think calling him out is the best way to keep them safe?"

"You wouldn't get it," she said.

Yates chuckled to himself. They drove some more. He seemed to make turns at random. They went down residential streets and then out onto thoroughfares bright with lights. From time to time they saw a police cruiser, but they were never pulled over. They were an invisible ship in the night.

"Ms. Espinoza, I went to Vietnam in 1965 and I was there two and a half years, until the goddamned VC shot me in the leg and broke my femur. If you want to talk about seeing the elephant, lady, I've seen it, touched it, and even rode on it. There's not a thing you can tell me about your wars that I couldn't tell you about mine. So don't think I don't understand where you're coming from. I'm old, but I didn't turn stupid."

Camaro looked out the window as a 7-Eleven slid by. She frowned at her reflection. "I'm sorry."

"It's just a reminder that we're in this together. So you want to poke at this particular anthill and see all the ants come running out. I get it. That's how they fought my war; we'd go out into the boonies and walk around, trying to get the VC to shoot at us. Most times they didn't, but sometimes they did. It was a relief sometimes when the bullets started flying, because at least then we weren't waiting for something to happen. It was *happening*. That's why I stayed longer than I should have."

A McDonald's sign drew into view. It advertised twenty-four-hour service. Yates put on his blinker and slid into the parking lot. It was deserted at this hour, and the inside of the restaurant was half dark. A double drive-through waited for them. "I'm going to get myself a Quarter Pounder," Yates said. "And lots of fries. How about yourself?"

"I'll take the same," Camaro said. "No onions. No pickles."

He ordered and drove through and paid, and soon they were back on the road with a bag of hot food between them. Camaro ate the salty fries and drank some of the Coke that came with the meal. She thought of Derrick Perkins and his girl. She saw their faces filled with terror. The memory brought nothing with it.

"That hits the spot," Yates said. "Rule Number One when it comes to doing my kind of work: never go out with an empty stomach. Hunger can do strange things to your head."

"I'm not in your line of work," Camaro said.

"How does Camaro Espinoza make a living?" Yates asked.

"I run a fishing charter."

Yates looked at her sidelong. "All by yourself?"

"What's that supposed to mean? Yes, all by myself."

"No offense meant. Can't be too many lady captains around. Especially not ones with good looks and a hard punch."

"My father liked to fish. He took me out whenever he could afford it. When I was younger, he said he only wanted two things: a cherry 1967 Camaro and a fishing boat."

"Did he ever get them?"

"No."

Yates drained the last of his soda noisily. He shook the cup, and the ice rattled. "I love fishing. I go whenever I can. Get out there looking for cobia, drum, sea trout, maybe some croaker."

"You have a boat?"

"Me? No, ma'am. Maybe someday when I retire."

Camaro looked at him. "You retiring sometime soon?"

"I suppose that's one way of saying you think I'm old."

"That's not what I meant."

"It's all right. I am old. I turned seventy-one last August."

"I would have guessed lower than that."

"Clean living. I don't drink but once in a while, I haven't smoked in thirty years, and I only eat red meat once a week. How about you?"

Camaro shrugged. "I don't smoke."

"Well, you're young yet."

Yates got them on the highway back toward Carmel. They were the only vehicle on the road. The streetlights flashed past one at a time in a silent rhythm, playing shadows across the interior of the SUV. Camaro let him drive for nearly twenty minutes without interruption. "Lukas is going to come at me."

"Absolutely."

"But you wish I hadn't done it anyway."

"It's not my preference, that's true, but I'll take what I can get. Now, let me get you home so you can get a good night's rest. I get the feeling it's going to be the last chance you get for a while."

# CHAPTER THIRTY-TWO

Lukas was asleep when the call came. He stirred at the sound of the phone trilling in the dark and opened his eyes to see Vicki's bedroom take shape around him. Images of somewhere warm and faraway faded instantly.

He felt Vicki lying next to him in bed, her naked buttocks pressed against his hip. She made a disturbed noise at the sound of the phone. Lukas took the call. "Derrick," he said, "it's the middle of the night."

"I have to talk to you," Derrick said.

"What the hell about?"

"Her."

Lukas sat up. The covers dragged from Vicki's shoulders, and she fumbled for them, pulling them back up over herself. He got out of bed. His skin prickled in the cold room, and he snared his boxer shorts from the floor. "Are you screwing with me right now? Because if you're screwing with me I will tear out your lungs."

"No, no, no," Derrick said. "I swear it's the truth. She was here. She was just here. Her and some guy. They came busting in and scared the shit out of Rosalinda. I thought they were going to shoot both of us."

He went into the next room. It was dark there, too. He paced in the middle of the living area. "What did you tell them, Derrick?"

"Nothing! They wanted to know where you were staying or where you'd be, and I told them I had no idea. I didn't say anything about Vicki or any of that. I would never give you up, man. I owe it to Jake."

"You owe it to me," Lukas said. "Jake's dead. I'm alive. What did they want to know? Where to find me? Who I'm hanging with? That kind of thing?"

Derrick made an affirmative sound. "The guy had a gun. Rosalinda said he showed her a badge, but he wasn't a cop. He was bail…bail—"

"Bail enforcement," Lukas said. He chuckled. "Those sons of bitches aren't gonna give up, are they? Was this guy old? White hair? Real lanky?"

"That's right. He didn't tell me his name."

"It's Yates," Lukas told Derrick. "Jeremy Yates, I think. The old fart has to be a hundred and one years old. His son thought he could take me down with a can of pepper spray and some big talk."

"Where is he now?"

"Dead. That's where he is now. I shot his dumb ass back in Colorado. He had a nice truck."

Derrick cleared his throat. "So, uh, this Yates guy wants to take you down? Like back to jail?"

"Something like that. I think he's got other things on his mind now, especially if he's hooked up with that woman. He knows when he's got a good piece of live bait, and he wants to reel me in. He thinks I'm stupid enough to go for it when he's standing around waiting to blow my head off."

"That's the thing," Derrick said.

"What is?"

"Well, he's not the one calling you out. Chelle's sister, Camaro? She told me to tell you something."

"Spit it out, then."

"She says she'll go up against you anywhere you want. Anytime, anywhere, she said. And she gave me her phone number to give to you. I mean, maybe this Yates guy wants to kill you, but I looked in her eyes, man, and she wants you just as dead. She killed Jake. She'll kill you, too."

Lukas shouted down the line. "You think I'm scared of some dumb cunt? I'll tear that whore apart piece by piece if she tries to take me on."

Derrick fell silent. Lukas cast around himself for something to throw, but the apartment was too orderly for that. He made a fist and punched the air.

"What do you want me to do?"

"You need to get that money from Jake's house. All of it. Just because Jake's gone doesn't mean the deal is dead. I got a date in LA that I'm gonna make, no matter what I got to deal with first."

"Do you need help with the woman?"

"Maybe. I'm going to handle this all myself from now on. I might need you, but I might not. You just wait for my call. When things happen, they're gonna happen fast. That woman is gonna know what it means to wave a cape in front of a bull. You understand what I'm saying, Derrick?"

"Yeah, I understand. She's asking for it."

"If she comes back, you let me know. But don't you forget about that money. The money. That's what's important. You get that?"

"I get it."

"Thanks for calling."

"Anytime, man. Anytime."

Lukas ended the call. He stood silently in the middle of the room for a long moment, centering himself. Disordered thoughts fell into line, and an idea began to form.

# CHAPTER THIRTY-THREE

Annabel woke to the sound of furious pounding on the front door, followed by multiple rings of the bell. A jolt of fear and energy shot through her, and she put her hand over Rebecca's sleeping form. The girl was deeply asleep and heard nothing. She breathed steadily even as the pounding resumed.

A robe hung from a hook on the closet door. Annabel slipped out of bed and put it on. She wished for the gun she'd used to kill Jake.

She stopped at the spare bedroom. "Camaro?" she asked. She pushed the door open. The bed was empty, the covers only wrinkled but not pulled back. "Camaro?"

There was no answer. The doorbell jangled repeatedly as she went to the front of the house, turning on lights along the way. She saw the police cruiser parked where it had been when she went to bed. There was another car parked behind her Subaru, unmarked. She recognized the faces through the peephole.

"Marshals," Annabel said when she opened the door, "it's late."

Way pushed into the room past her. Hannon paused before entering, her face slightly pained. She touched Annabel on the arm. "We know it's late."

Annabel closed the door behind them. "You could have woken up my daughter."

"Where's your sister?" Way asked.

"She's not in her room."

"That doesn't answer my question. Where is she?"

"I don't know. Can you please keep your voice down? My daughter—"

135

"Maybe your daughter can shed some light on this situation," Way said.

"How? She's only five."

Way brandished a green folder. "I'll bet she knows more than she ever would have admitted. Like the fact that she was born Rebecca *Watts* and not Amado."

Annabel froze. She felt the muscles in her chest seize together, then slowly unwind to allow oxygen into her lungs. A hand on the wall steadied her. Hannon watched her carefully. Way's eyes were fire.

"And your name is Annabel," Way continued.

Tears welled up. Annabel was blinded. She wiped at them and they stung. "Yes, my name was Annabel Watts."

"Was? If I go looking, will I find a legal name change? What about your Social Security number? Will that match? Who was Michelle Amado?"

Annabel sniffed. "She's me."

Way pointed at the couch. "You'd better sit down."

She took one end of the couch while Hannon took the other. Way blazed with energy, slapping the green folder against his leg. Hannon was quiet, still watching. "This isn't what you think," Annabel said.

"What is it, then?"

"I had to get out of my old life. I couldn't stay in New Orleans."

"Was it your husband? The husband who conveniently turned up dead?"

"It wasn't convenient," Annabel said. "It was horrible."

"What happened to him, Annabel?" Hannon asked.

Annabel wiped her eyes again and took a deep breath that hitched beneath her breastbone. "I loved my husband very much. His name was Corey. He gave me Becca, and I was always grateful for that. I still am. But he...he wasn't a good person. He did things that got him into trouble. A lot. And one day that caught up to him."

"And your sister? How did she figure into it?" Way asked.

"She helped me escape."

"What then?"

"Look, she has nothing to do with this," Annabel protested. "After my husband died I never looked back, not even for her. I kept going until I got to the coast, and I settled somewhere no one would ever find me. We didn't even talk about it."

"But she still found you," Hannon said. "You kept in touch."

"We set up a way to talk without anyone making a connection between us. A code if I ever needed help again. I didn't use it all this time, until...until Jake."

"You brought your sister here to kill Jacob Collier," Way said.

"No! He was no good for me, but I couldn't get rid of him on my own. Camaro, she knows how to make people do what she wants. She's always been stronger than me."

Way laughed shortly. "So she comes all this way to beat the shit out of your boyfriend because you don't know how to change the locks and get a restraining order? Is that what you're telling me?"

"It's the truth."

"Oh, man," Way said. He rubbed his forehead. He giggled crazily for a moment, turning his back to her, as giggles turned into laughter, and laughter into a fit of coughing.

Hannon moved closer to Annabel on the couch and reached to take her hand. She frowned at Way's laughter. "You're not the first woman to start a new life away from a bad situation," Hannon said. "You won't be the last. We're not here to ruin everything for you."

Way turned to face Annabel again. "Unless it turns out that your sister killed your husband, too. If *that's* true, then you are in for a world of pain."

"Did she kill your husband?" Hannon asked quietly.

"No, no, never," Annabel said. "Camaro wouldn't do that."

"But she is a killer," Way said. He showed Annabel the green folder again. "I have the paperwork to prove it. What would I find if I decided to go digging down in Miami?"

"Camaro is a good person," Annabel said.

"Where is she?" Hannon asked.

Annabel pulled her hand free of Hannon's. "I said I don't know."

"Okay," Way said. "Okay. If that's how you want to play it, then that's what we'll do. We didn't have to turn your life upside down, but I guess now we have to. We'll check your financials and everything else all the way down the line until we bump up against something illegal, and you'll go to jail. Your daughter will end up with the state."

Annabel felt more tears coming. "I swear to God I don't know where she is."

"All right. It's done. We'll take you both down."

"I'm here."

Camaro's voice brought Annabel's head around sharply. She saw Camaro in the entryway to the kitchen, her jacket saturated by the rain. Her hair was just as wet and hung around her face in dark tendrils.

Way pointed a finger at her. "Freeze right there. Don't move a muscle."

"I'm not going anywhere," Camaro said.

"Hannon, cuff her."

# CHAPTER THIRTY-FOUR

Way dir ected Camar o to sit in the chair near the fireplace, her hands cuffed behind her back. Annabel gave Camaro one last look before Hannon hustled her out of the room. "Don't say anything, Michelle," Camaro called after Annabel, but Annabel did not reply.

Way stood opposite her for a long time in silence, swatting his leg with the green folder. Camaro stared back at him.

"You called your sister Michelle," Way said at last.

"That's her name."

"It wasn't always."

"So you know."

"I know. What I don't know is why she went through all the trouble to set up a phony identity with a new name and the whole thing, while you went on being Camaro Espinoza."

"I'm not in hiding," Camaro said.

"Aren't you? Maybe you just don't care. I get the feeling that's the real answer. You just don't care."

Camaro waited and breathed and said nothing.

"I've been looking at your life," Way said. "It's all here in this folder."

Camaro didn't answer.

"Who do you think you are?"

"I don't look for trouble."

Way smiled tightly. "But you're always in it, aren't you? Like now. You're in a whole lot of trouble now. You're linked to the deaths of two men involved with your sister."

"What are you talking about?" Camaro said.

"Your sister's in hiding. Her husband is dead. And I'm going to see to it that charges are filed in the death of Jacob Collier."

"Why? What's he to you?" Camaro asked.

"He was my link. He was how I was going to nail Lukas Collier, and you had to go and shoot him. And all because he was doing your sister wrong. What was it? Did he get too rough with her? Because that's the kind of thing little sisters call big sisters to help sort out.

"Good old Jake," Way continued. "He had no idea what he was walking into. Your sister looks like she's the type to get pushed around, and if what I heard about her husband is true, she doesn't have the best taste in the world. But you—coming at you is like diving face-first into a chainsaw."

"Uncuff me," Camaro said.

"Why? You going to make a try for me next?"

"I'm not stupid."

"No, you're not. But you are unlucky, because this mess you got yourself into involves me. I do not like being lied to. I do not like people stepping on my toes. I do not put up with interference in an operation. And most of all, I do not like you. I haven't liked you since we first met, and I like you less now. Where were you tonight?"

"Out. With a friend."

"You have friends in the area? I thought your sister came out here alone. I thought you set up shop in Miami. That's three thousand miles of country. Hard to make friends over that kind of distance. Or did you meet on Facebook?"

Camaro stared at Way. She tested the cuffs. She did not know how to slip out of them the way a magician would. "Are you going to take me in?"

"I could."

"Then if you're gonna do it, just do it," Camaro said. "I'm not answering any more questions. I'll hire a lawyer if I have to, but we're done. Let me out of these cuffs now. I want to see my sister."

Way stood over her. "You don't give the orders around here."

"Even you have to follow the rules. So charge me or uncuff me."

He regarded her. "Stand up."

Camaro stood and turned her back on Way. He used his key on the cuffs, and her wrists were free. She turned back to him. "You still going to have them book me for murder in the morning?"

"Are you going to tell me where you went tonight and who you were with?"

"No."

"Then I am. The Carmel Police Department will be in touch. Or maybe you'll want to just head on over there and turn yourself in. Because if I have to come looking for you, I will. You won't like it if I do."

"Does it make you feel tough to push a woman around?" Camaro asked him.

"Why do you ask?"

"Jake Collier liked that."

"Are you threatening me?" Way asked.

He glowered at her, and she returned his black look. "You take it however you want. Just get out of my sister's house."

# CHAPTER THIRTY-FIVE

Annabel cried in her arms for an hour. Camaro made her drink a cup of tea and take a sleeping pill and then saw her off to bed. In her own room she stripped down to a T-shirt and underwear and got between the covers for the first time that night.

Consciousness dropped away from her like a yawning chasm bereft of floating dreams, and she awoke at the first sign of light through the curtains of her bedroom window. She checked the time and then her phone to see if she had slept through a call, but there were no calls recorded.

She tried again to sleep. Instead she lulled into a half doze that carried her a couple of hours further before she heard Rebecca's high voice ringing in the hall and the murmur of Annabel's replies.

The guest bathroom was well ordered, a small bowl by the sink piled with fragrant soaps that looked like seashells. Good towels were on the racks, but there were no others to use. Camaro washed herself under the hot spray and got the night out of her hair before toweling off and using the blow-dryer and a borrowed brush.

By the time she made it to the kitchen Annabel was cleaning up the remains of breakfast. Her eyes were still puffy from the night before, but she wasn't crying anymore. She rinsed plates and bowls in the sink and set them on a rack to dry. "Do you want something?" Annabel asked. "I can make you anything."

"I'll just have some oatmeal and some juice."

"Coffee?"

"Okay."

Camaro sat at the table while Annabel busied herself preparing a simple meal. Soon there was a piping-hot bowl of oatmeal in front of her, along with a glass of orange juice and a steaming cup of coffee. The oatmeal had been mixed with raisins and had a dusting of cinnamon over the top. "Voilà," Annabel said.

"Thanks."

Annabel sat down with her. Her hands were aflutter, on the table or in her lap. She was alive with skittish energy. They didn't talk.

Camaro finished her oatmeal and drained the glass of juice. Now that her coffee had cooled a little, she drank. Annabel still stared at her.

"Say it," Camaro told her.

"Are you going to turn yourself in?"

"No."

"Why not?"

"Because I didn't do anything wrong. And neither did you. That marshal can talk all he wants, but he's got nothing. If he had, he would have taken me in last night. He's bluffing."

"Where did you go? When the marshals came, you were gone."

Camaro waited before she answered. She drank more coffee. "I went to find out about Lukas Collier."

"He really is here?"

Camaro nodded. She finished her cup. "He's somewhere. I have to find out where."

"I'm not saying this is exactly right, but it could be that this is something the police should handle. If the marshal gets what he's after, he'll leave us alone. He won't turn up the money and then he'll go back wherever he came from and things can get back to normal. It's the best thing for everybody."

"You want to take a chance on that guy?" Camaro asked.

Annabel crossed her hands. They trembled. She squeezed one in the other. "I'm afraid, Camaro."

"You were the one who was ready to shoot Lukas yourself," Camaro said.

"That was when I thought the police would help. But now they know where I come from and they know my real name. Everything I've built here is going to fall apart the minute the secret gets out. No one will ever believe anything I say. I couldn't make it."

"What do you want me to do?" Camaro asked.

Annabel shook her head helplessly, then dragged nervous fingers through her hair. "Stay with us until this blows over. Just...stay close and be my sister. Don't go looking for trouble. Be here."

Camaro listened and watched Annabel struggle with a tangle of emotions. She could feel them coming from Annabel, and they came into her, too. They sat at the bottom of her stomach and lay there, promising turmoil but weighed down by a sense of calm. She reached for Annabel, and they clasped hands tightly across the table. "Okay," Camaro said. "I won't go looking for trouble. I'll be here with you. As long as it takes. I promise."

"That means a lot to me, Camaro. It means a lot to both of us."

Camaro let Annabel hang on for a long minute, then slipped her hand away. "I have to make a phone call. I'll clean this up when I'm done."

"No, no, I'll get it," Annabel said. "You make your call."

"I'll be back."

She heard the clink of dishes in the sink as she left the kitchen. Rebecca was in her school clothes already, playing with the dollhouse near the fireplace, though now the dolls had been joined by a stuffed hippopotamus and a cat with a star over its eye. Compared to the little family they were enormous, but none of the imaginary people seemed to mind.

"We're having a garage sale," Rebecca told Camaro when she came close.

"Oh, yeah? Anything good?"

"Lots of baby clothes that don't fit."

"I'll have to check it out. Be right back."

Camaro retreated to the guest bedroom and closed the door. There she sat on the edge of the bed and brought out her phone. She dialed Yates. He answered on the first ring.

# CHAPTER THIRTY-SIX

Yates put his phone down and adjusted the visor to better block the morning sun from his eyes. His body was sore from sitting behind the wheel for hours.

After leaving Camaro at the church for her trek back home, he circled around and headed out to Salinas again. There he navigated to Derrick Perkins's street and killed the lights and the engine on a stretch of curb that allowed him a good view of the carport and the front and side of the duplex.

He made note of the same two cars that were present when he first visited the location, and he assumed they belonged to Derrick and his girl. Yates scribbled down the makes, models, and colors of the cars, as well as their license plates. Given an opportunity, he might make a call and see what he could learn about them, but for now he was more interested in what he would see at the house.

The watch went on until morning. For a while all the lights in Derrick's place were out, and then in the early hours they came on again. Right around dawn Yates saw Rosalinda flee the house through the drizzle, dashing to her car in a long coat. She started up without looking around and drove past Yates without seeing him.

It was brighter out when Derrick emerged in his work clothes and a denim jacket. He went to his car and started it but let the engine run a while before backing out from beneath the carport. He turned the opposite direction from Yates, and it was easy for Yates to fall in behind him as he headed out.

The call from Camaro had changed things. She had to take a step back and stick close to home. Blood was responsible for blood, and that was something they both understood.

Jacob Collier's house waited silently with its yard of mud. No cop watched the place. They'd given up on that.

He parked and watched Derrick sneak around the side of the house and vanish in the back. Yates's phone rang again. He answered. "This is Yates."

"Yates, it's Anita."

"Good morning, ma'am. How are you today?"

"Busy," Anita Matthews said. "Night court was working overtime, so I had a pile of bonds to post before I could get a look at that information for you. I have it all now. When can you pick it up?"

"Well, I'm in the middle of something at the moment. I'm pretty sure I'm watching Derrick Perkins break and enter at Jake Collier's place."

"Do the cops know?"

"Doesn't seem like it, and I'm not much in the mood to call them."

"You don't expect Collier to show up there, do you?"

"No, but that doesn't mean he won't turn up later. Maybe Derrick and Collier will take a lunch break together. I like my chances. Thanks for putting me onto him."

"Bondspersons have to stick together. So I should hang on to this stuff?"

"Can you give me the highlights?" Yates asked.

"There's not a whole lot here that you didn't know already. Jacob Collier got around, collecting fines and a few days' worth of jail time here and there. Nothing serious, like pulling a knife on someone or home invasion. And sure as hell nothing like what his brother's into. In fact, the worst thing Jacob ever did was get busted for domestic battery against some woman named Vicki Nelson. I tried running her name, but she's clean. The case didn't even go to court."

Yates sighed. "A man who mistreats a woman isn't any kind of man at all."

"Amen to that."

"Is there anything I can work with? Any associates I don't know about? Maybe some more family somewhere?"

"I'm afraid not. Jacob and Lukas are all alone in the world. No mother or father, no aunts or uncles, and no cousins. It's just the two of

146

them. Or I guess now it's just Lukas. If I were in his shoes, I'd be hot for payback."

"That's where my mind is, too." Yates shifted in his seat to relieve the soreness in his back. "I figure Lukas is holed up somewhere in the area, trying to figure out the best way to get at the woman who shot his brother."

"You have me to fall back on if you get any thoughts. I'll make whatever calls I need to make. I meant what I said; we stick together out this way."

"I am much obliged to you. I'll try to come by your office just as soon as I can and get those records from you. And whatever it cost you, I'll reimburse."

"It's on the house. Just be careful, Yates. There's been too much bloodshed already."

"I will do my best. Thank you, Anita."

They said their good-byes, and then Yates was alone again with his thoughts. He stayed that way for ten minutes, until Derrick reappeared with a worn gym bag slung over his shoulder. It seemed loose, not fully packed, but there was something inside.

Yates started the SUV.

# CHAPTER THIRTY-SEVEN

Hannon woke earl y. She had a cup of coffee from the machine in her room, showered and did her hair and put on the day's makeup. Using the room's small ironing board, she pressed her blouse and ran the iron over her jacket for good measure. She dressed and put on her gun, flush against her right hip in a leather holster.

A plastic bag on the handle of her room's door had a wrapped muffin and a banana in it, courtesy of the hotel. She ate the muffin though it was entirely too sweet and put the banana in her bag. Afterward she left her room and went next door to Way's. The continental breakfast was still hanging there, untouched. Hannon considered knocking, then stepped away. She retrieved her bag from her room and left the hotel.

The rental car waited in the lot, spotted with overnight rain. Only a little still fell, hazing down over her until she got behind the wheel, stoked the engine, and headed to Carmel.

She greeted the officer behind the desk and was buzzed into the back area. Way still had the folder of information on Camaro Espinoza, but more had come in overnight about Annabel Watts. Hannon called the New Orleans Police Department.

She drilled down through a layer of push-button menus to find a human being and identified herself as a deputy U.S. marshal. She asked for a detective named Alberta Vaughn. The conversation lasted five minutes. When they were finished, Hannon thanked the detective and hung up. "Shit," she said aloud to the empty room.

She had the paperwork cleared up by the time she heard Way's voice in the bullpen. She slipped the printouts into a marbled folder and faced the door.

Way gave her a black look as he entered. "Surprised to see me?" he asked.

"You needed a break."

"I need coffee."

"It's ready."

She waited until he had caffeinated. They considered each other over his steaming cup. "What are you sitting on?" he asked.

"Nothing. Except the fact Camaro Espinoza didn't kill her sister's husband. Annabel Watts is hiding for exactly the reason she said she was: to steer clear of her husband's past. Whatever happened to him could have happened to her. We've seen it a hundred times."

"I still don't like it," Way said.

"There's nothing there, Keith. This is just a woman looking for a new life."

Way partook deeply of his cup, then topped it off. He thrummed his fingers on the edge of the table as he leaned against it. A thoughtful nod won through. "Okay."

"Do you still want to have Camaro Espinoza charged?"

"I'm thinking about it."

"What else are you thinking?"

Way shrugged. "I'm thinking if Annabel Watts was so serious about protecting her new life, she might have had a good reason to see her boyfriend dead. Especially if he threatened to rat her out to her friends or her boss. Whoever could cause the most trouble for her. She doesn't pull the trigger herself, of course. She gets her sister to do it because she knows her sister has the experience. And now there's a new threat: Lukas. She'll want him out of the picture, too, so she can go on living as Michelle Amado."

"Camaro Espinoza isn't going to hunt down Lukas Collier."

"Do we know that? I mean, what do we really know about her besides what's in the paperwork? Where was she last night in the middle of the night? Talking to her is like talking to a wall. You don't know what's behind it."

"So what do we do?"

Way considered that. "We give her a gun and see what she does."

"You want to arm her again?"

"Yes. And if she knows something about Lukas we don't, we use her to get to him. But she doesn't get to kill him. Nobody kills him but me. Nobody."

Hannon kept her thoughts to herself. She watched Way finish his coffee.

"Let's get this ball rolling," he said.

# CHAPTER THIRTY-EIGHT

Annabel gathered her things for work. She had Rebecca's backpack by the door, already stuffed with school supplies and a set of snacks in an insulated bag. Camaro sat on the couch. "Are you sure you don't want to come along and say hi to Wilson?" Annabel asked. "I'm sure he'd love to meet you."

"I'll do fine here."

"Okay. Becca, come on. We have to leave."

"Coming!"

She paused by the door. "There's stuff in the fridge for sandwiches if you get hungry. I'll be back around five. I thought we could go out somewhere tonight. Carmel has great restaurants."

"Okay," Camaro said.

"Do you have anything dressy?"

"No."

"Maybe I'll see what I can get you at the store."

"You don't know my size."

Annabel smiled. "I'm a professional, Camaro. I can guess anybody's size."

"What's my size?" Camaro asked.

"Wait and see. If I get it right, you pay for dinner."

"Okay."

"Becca, let's *go!*"

Rebecca hurried into the front room with a Barbie doll dressed to ski. "Sorry, Mommy."

Annabel left the house and didn't lock the door behind her. She took Rebecca's hand. They went down the walk together. On the street, a police cruiser sat waiting. Officer Russo was behind the wheel. When

Annabel held the gate for her daughter, Russo got out. She had a black plastic case in her hands.

"Good morning," Russo said.

"Good morning."

"You remember me, right? Carly Russo?"

"Of course. Is that my gun?"

Russo hefted the case. "Yes. It's being returned to you. The city isn't pressing any charges against your sister for what happened since it was self-defense. I don't know if you want to take it with you, or..."

Annabel spared a look back toward the house. She saw Camaro through the front window and waved. Camaro came out onto the porch, then advanced up the walk. Russo turned to her as she came, and Annabel thought she colored slightly at the sight of her.

"Good morning," Russo told Camaro. "I was just telling your sister that there aren't going to be any charges filed in the matter of Jacob Collier."

Camaro glanced at Annabel and then at Russo. "No one's afraid I'm going to shoot someone else?"

Russo smiled awkwardly, and this time Annabel was certain she blushed. "No, no, nothing like that. We'd rather you didn't, but that doesn't mean your sister can't have her gun back."

"Take it, Camaro," Annabel said. "I have to go. Becca's going to be late."

Camaro accepted the Glock case. "I'll make sure it's put away," she said.

"Good thinking," Russo said. "Thank you."

"Have a good one," Camaro told her, and she turned away.

"You, too. It was nice seeing you."

"Is there anything else you needed?" Annabel asked Russo.

"I was asked to talk to you again about Lukas Collier."

"I have to get Becca to school, and then I have to go to work. Maybe we can talk at the school?"

"I'll follow you."

Annabel led Rebecca to the Subaru and made sure she was secure in her car seat. As she pulled out of the cul-de-sac, the police cruiser stayed in her rearview mirror.

She hoped Russo would stay in her car when she reached the school, but Russo got out when she did. Rebecca was already unbuckling herself by the time Annabel got to her. Russo waited quietly while Annabel made sure her daughter put on her backpack for the short walk to the entrance.

"Let's hurry. We only have a couple of minutes."

They walked.

"You work at Garment, right?" Russo asked.

"Yes," Annabel said.

"I love the clothes in there. One time, I—"

They were a dozen feet from the entrance when Russo stopped. Automatically Annabel stopped with her, and she saw Russo's face pale and her eyes widen. Russo's hand went for her gun.

Annabel turned at the instant of the first shot. The man approaching them on the sidewalk had his pistol out, and he squeezed off three rounds, one after the other in rapid succession. The bullets crashed into Russo, and Annabel felt a hot spray fall on her cheek as the young woman went down. Near the front of the school, children screamed shrilly and teachers rushed to gather up as many as they could.

Russo was on the ground. Her legs flexed weakly. The man put his sights on Annabel. "Say good-bye," the man said.

She saw Jake in his face. The hardness around the eyes that Jake sometimes got and the cast of his jaw. Annabel stepped between him and Rebecca. He pulled the trigger, and she felt hot wetness burst inside her. Her world tipped over. She staggered against Rebecca, heard her screaming, then collapsed onto her knees.

The man came closer. The gun was still up. Annabel opened her mouth, and there was blood. She tried to call out to Rebecca to run and keep running, but there was nothing from between her lips. She sagged onto her hands.

He shot her again, the bullet spearing through her shoulder. Annabel couldn't keep herself from the pavement. She crumpled completely, her legs kicking feebly as if she might still make her feet. Her head rushed with her pulse, a coursing river that sounded against her ears. Black spots floated everywhere.

Rebecca wasn't near her. The man stepped back, shooting again. Children were still wailing. Annabel couldn't pick out her daughter's voice.

The sidewalk was covered in slick red, more and more as her heart beat. She fell into the pool. One grasping hand found Russo's pant leg. The policewoman didn't move at all. Annabel gagged on the liquid in her throat.

Her head was so heavy she couldn't turn it. Sounds faded, and then there was darkness.

# CHAPTER THIRTY-NINE

Lukas returned to the car. Vicki was in the backseat with her son, and both were drawn and pale. At a distance they were only figures, but up close it was possible to see where their hands and feet had been bound up with duct tape. He had considered gags but at the last moment decided against them.

He slipped behind the wheel. "Nice and smooth," he said. "Comfortable back there?"

Vicki's voice was unsteady. "Who did you kill?"

"What does it matter to you? So long as it's not you I'm killing, you don't have to worry."

She didn't reply. Lukas ground his back teeth together for a long moment, surveying their faces, before finally turning back toward the front. He started the engine and put the car in gear. They drove. Sirens were audible not far away.

He hummed to himself as he drove. In the theater of his mind, the cop went down over and over, and then Jake's girlfriend. It had been done cleanly, which was more than he could say for some. The message was sent.

"You know what I'd like?" he asked Vicki. He saw her in the rearview mirror. "I'd like to get some ribs. Tender ribs with a good rub, mopped down with sauce. I could eat a whole rack of 'em right now. You any good at making ribs?"

She didn't answer him. Lukas drove a little farther as his thoughts darkened. He was about to shout when she cleared her throat and spoke. Her voice was rougher than before. "I can make you ribs if you want them. But we have to stop at the store."

Lukas considered. He watched her carefully in the mirror. Her eyes

155

were puffy, verging on tears. The sight of them made him angrier. "You want me to pull up in the parking lot so you can make a scene with people around?"

"No! No, it's nothing like that. We'll be quiet. I promise you we'll be quiet."

He grunted. "I'll think about it."

A Carmel PD cruiser came roaring at them in the opposite lane, lights flashing and siren alive with noise. Lukas kept on, his hands on the wheel, and didn't glance over as the car passed. It was gone within seconds. He breathed no harder. His heart didn't speed.

"I'm gonna take you home," Lukas said after they'd driven awhile longer. "And then I'm going out with the kid. I think anything's hinky while I'm out, you're gonna need a closed casket. That's all I'm saying."

He heard her crying. It made him wring the steering wheel in his hands. He didn't look at her, because he knew the sight would make him angry all over again.

Lukas shook his head as the crying went on. He tasted something bitter. "You bitches just don't get it, do you?" he asked. "You and that other one—you don't know a man does what he has to do. Gettin' teary, talking about your *feelings*. You think I don't have feelings? Is that what you think? *You think I don't have feelings!?*"

"No, I don't think that!" Vicki cried out. "I don't think that."

Now the boy cried. Lukas fumed. "You tell that kid to shut his mouth, or I'll shut it for him."

He listened to Vicki shush Brendan. The sound of it was maddening. He pounded the steering wheel with the heel of his hand. They were close to Vicki's apartment now.

"You got until I park this car to shut that kid up."

"No," Vicki managed. "Brendan, it's okay. Just calm down. Mommy's here. You're all right."

"That's how boys come out weak," Lukas said. "You get a boy raised by his mama, he doesn't know what being a man is. Now me and Jake, we had our old man to look up to."

He murmured the last to himself a few times, listening to the boy grow quieter and quieter, until finally they pulled into the parking lot outside Vicki's building. Lukas parked and killed the engine. He sat for a long moment, listening to the hot metal of the engine tick, and mother and son breathing raggedly. Unconsciously he rubbed an old scar on the back of his hand. That day the skin had been laid open enough to expose the bone.

"You two ready to stop wasting my time?" Lukas asked.

"Let him come in with me. I promise we won't go anywhere. We won't call anyone."

"Can't take the chance."

"I've been *good!*" Vicki exclaimed.

Lukas laughed. "Yeah, I guess you have. But I'm still taking the kid. You get things ready, and I'll bring home the meat."

"Please... don't hurt him. He's little."

"Don't give me a reason to," Lukas said, and he turned in his seat again. He fixed them both with his gaze. "Don't ever give me a reason."

Vicki looked as though she might cry again. "I won't," she whispered.

Lukas pulled a knife. "Then you don't have anything to worry about."

# CHAPTER FORTY

Community Hospital of the Monterey Peninsula was in a wooded area west of Carmel. Camaro reached it in the backseat of a Carmel police officer's cruiser. When he released her from the rear, she sprang past him, pushing through the doors into the lobby.

A security guard saw her coming and took an involuntary step backward. He put his hand on his belt, where a canister of pepper spray sat just ahead of a walkie-talkie. "Is there something I can help you with, miss?"

Camaro stopped just short of him. "Where's the emergency room?"

"Right down that way and on the left," he said. She moved, and he called after her. "But you're not allowed in there. Miss, you're not allowed in there!"

She kept going until she saw the signs. Automated doors swung open ahead of her. Soon she registered the sounds of medicine and the scent of antiseptic. Nurses in scrubs walked here and there among curtained bays. Two doctors sat side by side at computer workstations, reviewing files. Camaro went to the central hub, the nurses' station. A black woman in a white coat looked up as she approached. "Ma'am, this is not a public area."

"My name is Camaro Espinoza. My sister is Michelle Amado. She was brought in with a gunshot wound. I need to see her."

"Amado? She's—"

"I'll take it from here, ma'am," a man interrupted. Camaro turned toward his voice. Way was there.

"Where is my sister?" Camaro demanded. "Where is my niece?"

"Your niece is fine. Your sister is in intensive care. She had a round of emergency surgery. They're going to take her back in again in a couple of hours."

"The cops said—"

"They don't have the latest. I have the latest. She's in a room not far from here. I'll take you there."

Camaro made a fist reflexively, then pried her fingers apart with will. "Okay."

"Follow me."

They walked, but not fast enough to suit Camaro. "How badly is she hurt?" she asked.

"Four bullet wounds. From all accounts she was shot with a .45, so it's not pretty. The shooter put one into her at close range, but thankfully it wasn't one to the head; otherwise we wouldn't be talking. She was lucky. Unlike Officer Russo, who wasn't."

"Carly Russo?"

"You know her?"

"I met her. Is she alive?"

"No."

Camaro's arms prickled. "It was Lukas Collier, wasn't it?"

"Yeah, it was. According to witnesses, he came out of nowhere with a gun, shot Officer Russo and your sister, then took off after your niece. But she was quick and slipped him. I know Lukas Collier, and I know if he'd gotten to her she'd be dead right now."

"Where did they take her?"

"She's being looked after by Children and Family Services. When it's time, you can see her. Right now is not the time."

He led her to a new area. It was different here, quieter, and the rooms were kept half lighted. Camaro smelled the nameless odor of the grievously injured, the sick, and the dying. "Don't keep me from her."

"I won't. Believe it or not, I'm not an asshole. I just need certain things."

"What do you want?"

"What do you have to give me?" Way asked.

"Nothing."

"So you had no idea this might happen."

"How could I possibly know something like that? You were the people who had the cops following us around. I've never even seen Lukas

Collier. If I'd known he was going to shoot Bel, I would have been with her every minute of the day."

The elevator ascended. "You may not know much about Lukas, but he clearly knows about you and your family. He knew where to go and when to go, and he knew exactly how to get what he wanted. This is him calling you out. When we hear from him, and I guarantee you we'll hear from him, he's going to want you on the hook somehow. Anything to get you close enough that he can do to you what you did to his brother."

"He's crazy."

"Yes. He is. And the thing is, I've got no leverage. We have no idea where he's laying his head, what he might want you to do. Nothing. And before the end of the day we're going to have the FBI crawling all over this town, your family, and you with a microscope, looking for something they can use. You think I'm difficult to deal with? Try your stonewall routine with a special agent."

They reached an area near a nurses' station. Way stepped through a set of automatic doors and waved Camaro to the left. "I can't give them anything I don't have," she said.

"Then there's not a whole lot left for us to talk about. I'll tell the FBI everything I know about you and your sister, and the secret you're trying to keep will be all over before you know it."

Camaro stopped. "Fuck you."

Way smiled broadly. He pointed at the closed door of a nearby room. "She's in there. Think about what I've said. I'm guessing something's going to pop into your head. I'll be waiting."

She went in. The fluorescents overhead were switched off, but light came through the vertical blinds in the window. It was a private room with only a single bed. Annabel lay on crisp white sheets with a blanket across her body. A saline drip fed into the back of her left hand. A ventilator made her chest rise and fall with regularity. Wires sprouted from beneath the neck of her gown, trailing toward the monitors nearby. Heart rate, blood pressure, blood oxygen, and respiration were tracked. Her eyes were closed. Hannon sat on the chair beside her.

"Hello, Camaro," Hannon said quietly.

"I want to see my sister alone."

"I know you do."

"So leave."

"I have something to talk to you about."

"I already talked to your partner."

Hannon shook her head. "This is something even Keith doesn't know about. And I think you'd like to keep it that way."

Camaro looked at Annabel. She looked at Hannon. "Okay, talk."

# CHAPTER FORTY-ONE

Hannon produced a thin folder from underneath her jacket. She didn't rise but held the folder out to Camaro. Camaro took it. Inside were papers full of numbers and years, a neatly gridded layout under Annabel's name, and Camaro's.

Camaro looked at the columns of numbers. She closed the folder. "So?"

"Part of what we do when we run deep background checks on people is analyze their financial information," Hannon said. "Credit ratings, debt burden, income, taxes paid, taxes owed. It's pretty thorough. We can know everything in a day, from the first car you bought all the way to what's in your retirement account. Nobody can hide from the Internal Revenue Service. The Social Security Administration is a big help, too."

Annabel slept. Her breathing was mechanical. Camaro held the folder in both hands. "Okay," she said.

"Why don't you sit down?"

The room had one more chair. Camaro sat in it and watched Hannon watching her. The marshal seemed barely into her thirties, and the shape of her eyes revealed Asian heritage somewhere, though they were light even in the semidarkness of the room.

"You spent twelve years in the army," Hannon said.

"You know I did."

"Most people when they go in, if they don't leave after the minimum hitch, they stick around for a full twenty. So they can get a pension. You were on a steady promotion track, and you had all the commendations, but you quit. Why?"

"Does it matter?"

Hannon was steady. "How much did your sister steal from her husband before he died?"

"I don't know what you mean."

Hannon smiled thinly. "I mean that your sister lives in a house worth hundreds of thousands of dollars and drives a new car, even though she only works part-time at a clothing store. Before she left New Orleans, she was making nineteen thousand a year working at a McDonald's. And that's more money than she ever made in her life. Her husband was getting disability because of a bad back, but that wasn't much. Then she drops out of sight and comes back again as Michelle Amado with plenty of cash to spare."

"What difference does it make? She's the victim."

"I don't think so. I think she conspired to rip her husband off. And I think whatever she got from him she shared with you."

Camaro glanced toward the door. "Is this where Way comes in?"

"I told you, I haven't shown him any of this. Which is good, because the first question he'd ask after he figured out your sister was living on stolen money was how you managed to swing the purchase of a halfmillion dollars of Custom Carolina for your sportfishing business when the most you ever made in the army was around forty-one thousand a year."

Camaro said nothing.

"You can tell me the truth, or I can give that information to Keith and he'll tear you and your sister to pieces. He won't care if she's hurt or what it'll do to you."

"So what do you want me to do?" Camaro asked.

"I want you to tell me the death of Jake Collier has nothing to do with this money."

"He hurt my sister. That's all."

"Are you sure that's all it was? The two of you go through all the trouble of splitting up, working out a code to get in contact, and she calls you out to California to do something she could have asked the police to do? I've seen your record. I know where you've been and the things you've done. She has to know all the things I do, maybe more, and I think she wanted you to come out here and kill him."

"No," Camaro said. "No."

"I'm not saying she lied about what Jake did to her. I'm saying she let you believe what you wanted to believe."

Camaro fell silent. She thought back to what was said, and then further back to times she'd put behind her. What she'd tried to bury.

"She used you, Camaro. She pointed you at Jake Collier like a loaded weapon to protect the things she has. Did he ever ask her for money?"

"Yes," Camaro said slowly.

"Did he know where it came from?"

"No. No one knows."

"But he still asked for it. She had to protect herself. He was abusing her, and then he wanted to take away the only thing she had going for her and her daughter. That money is keeping her afloat. When it's gone, she's going to have a hard time making it in a place like Carmel. So if Jake Collier tried to take it, he had to go."

"My sister is a lot of things, but she's not like that. She's…she isn't what you think. And I'm not what you think. I wouldn't kill someone for money. Anyone I ever killed had a reason to die."

"You have a lot of faith in her."

"She's my *sister*," Camaro said. "You think you know her? You don't know anything about her. All of these numbers you have, that's not who she is. It's not who I am, either. It's just more bullshit. She had no one who could help her, and she came to me. Because that's how it works. You never turn your back on family."

"I want to believe you," Hannon said.

"Then believe it. Because my sister is not a monster. The man who did this to her, *he's* a monster." Camaro turned the folder over on her lap. She put her hand flat on the marbled paper surface. "You let me find him, I'll finish it."

"I can't be a party to that."

"Then what's the point of all this?" Camaro snapped. "You want me to stand aside while she dies, and do nothing? Because that doesn't work for me."

"Camaro, don't do something you'll regret. Whatever happened in your past, it doesn't have to be like that now. Help your sister. Help yourself."

"I'm done talking about this. Just go."

"Camaro," Hannon said.

Camaro rose and held out the folder. "Take it."

Hannon accepted the folder. "You're making a mistake."

"My sister did not use me."

"Are you sure about that?" Hannon asked.

Camaro didn't answer, and Hannon left.

She was alone with Annabel. She put her hands on the foot of the bed and looked out across Annabel's still form. The cycle of the respirator grated on her. "I'm here," she said. "I'm not going away."

# CHAPTER FORTY-TWO

When Lukas returned to the apartment with Brendan, he let the boy go in first. He secured the door behind him. Brendan ran to his room. Vicki stood with her hands hanging loosely by her sides, as pallid as she had been all morning.

"What are you waiting for?" Lukas asked her.

"I don't...I'm not sure what to do."

"You do like I said. Put those ribs in the cooker and get 'em started. I need to make a call."

"What happens then?"

"Whatever I want. So do it!"

He went to the bedroom and closed the door before he brought out his phone. He listened awhile to be certain Vicki was busy in the kitchen and not fleeing the apartment with Brendan. Only then did he dial the number. Camaro answered. "Did you get my message?" Lukas asked without introducing himself.

"You are dead," Camaro said.

The flat anger in her voice made Lukas laugh. "You're a real hard case, huh? I bet you got Jake real scared before you knocked his teeth out of his head. But I don't scare like that."

"What do you want?"

"What do I want? I want you. I want you sucking blood through a hole in your chest, and I want to see you die. I want you to die like Jake died. And I'm going to piss on your corpse when it's over."

"The cops are all over me. I can't get away from them."

"You better figure out a way, *and* you better figure it out soon. I heard on the radio that your sister ain't quite dead, so I'm gonna give you some time to watch her number come up. Then we'll settle it. You're gonna jump how and where I say you jump. And don't even think about screwing with me. You started this."

Camaro was quiet.

"You still with me?" Lukas asked.

"I'm here."

"You were wrong to prod me like you did. I don't take to that."

Again Camaro didn't answer.

"I spent a goodly amount of time down in Mexico," Lukas told her. "I learned a few things from the boys down there. They take revenge real serious. When there's a problem, arms and legs come off. They like to show off the heads."

There was silence.

"You think about what I've said. You have anything you need to say?"

"I'll tell you when I see you," Camaro said.

"When you see me, you'll be dead."

# CHAPTER FORTY-THREE

An hour l ater a cab dropped Camaro at the Holiday Inn. Yates met her in the lobby. They went upstairs to his room. Camaro beat her fist against her leg as he worked his card key in the lock. He held the door for her, and she went in first. Yates put on the lights.

The room had one king bed, perfectly made, and a desk area where Yates had set up a laptop and a portable printer and a scanner. Post-it notes were tagged to the wall in neat lines above the spot where he worked, each one with marker scribbling on it. There was one other chair, but Camaro didn't take it. She walked to the far end of the room and stopped by the window. It was full dark outside, but it had stopped raining.

"How long ago did he call?" Yates asked.

"A little over an hour."

"You called me right away."

"I did."

"Not the police."

"The police aren't going to be able to help me with this."

Yates sat in the chair by his computer and stretched his long legs out in front of him. He folded his hands over his stomach. His expression was dark. "This son of a bitch doesn't give a goddamn who he hurts."

"We've got to find him."

"This is my fault," Yates said.

"What? How?"

"There was something about his bond that I didn't like. It wasn't just the money, it was the man. You should have seen his girl come in to put her house up for his bail. She was shaking like a leaf. My wife made the call. I could have said no. If I had, he'd still be in jail."

"He would have found some other bail bondsman."

"My son would still be alive."

Camaro stepped toward him. She thought of something to say and then reconsidered it. "Your son's gone," she said when the silence had grown too long between them.

"I know," Yates said.

"My sister is still alive. My niece is still alive. If the two of us work together, we can fix this. You can still get him for what he did."

"Why do I get the feeling I'd have to get in line behind you?"

"He's yours," Camaro said. "I'll help however I can. Whatever it takes. I'm in."

Yates considered this for a long while. Camaro let him think.

"When is he set to get in touch with you again?" Yates asked.

"He didn't say exactly. However long it takes Bel to die."

"How is she?"

"They say she might make it."

"But there's no guarantee."

"No."

Yates turned to his computer and called up a file on the screen. He had a list of names and addresses and phone numbers displayed alongside driver's-license photos of several men. He tapped the screen. "You and I already had a talk with Derrick Perkins, but there are two other bums who've gotten arrested with Jake Collier in the past. Both of them work at Carlson Lumber in Pacific Grove, all of them have Salinas addresses."

Camaro came closer. She looked at the men. They gave dead eyes to the camera. "What are their names?"

"Loren Masters and Nic Thompson. Now I'm wondering if one of the two might throw in with Lukas on something like this. I followed Derrick all day today. He went to Jake's place and came out with something he took to a shipping store and left there. I talked with the nice lady behind the desk, and she was kind enough to tell me the package is headed to LA."

169

"What's in it?"

"I have no idea. Neither did she."

"What address was it sent to?"

"Central Avenue. Right near downtown, or so the map tells me."

"So what do you figure? Do we talk to him again?"

"You'd think that, but if he's running errands for Lukas, he's probably scared as hell of something happening to him or his girl. You know now Lukas will kill anybody he can get his hands on if his first choice isn't available. I'm not sure we can break through that threat without knowing a lot more about what he's up to."

"So we get on these other two and squeeze them," Camaro said.

"Spoken like a true professional. Now, I happen to know Loren Masters came to work in the afternoon, so he's probably there until closing. I'd suggest we pay him a visit and put some pressure on him. Either he comes clean right away, or we crush him and then find out what he knows. I'd rather come at Derrick with the truth in hand already, so he knows lying will do no good."

"If the guys at the lumberyard see me coming again, they'll call the cops," Camaro said. "The Pacific Grove police already have me on their radar because of what I did to Jake."

"I'll run interference. You find Loren and make him pop. Make it quick, though. I'm an old man and I get tired easily."

"Okay," Camaro said.

Yates got up and drew his pistol. He checked it over, then returned it to its holster. "You got yourself a gun?"

"There's my sister's gun. The one I used to shoot Jake. It's back at her house."

"Best to leave it there. You already killed one Collier brother, and I suspect it'll look bad if you kill the other one, too. This isn't self-defense anymore. This is search and destroy."

"Make sure you shoot straight. Lukas isn't going to give you a second chance."

"I'll shoot plenty straight when the time comes."

Yates clicked the mouse attached to his laptop, and the little printer whirred. A single color printout ran out of the machine. Yates handed it over. Camaro looked at it. The faces of Derrick, Loren, and Nic stared up at her. She memorized Loren's face, then folded up the sheet and put it in her back pocket.

"You ready?" Yates asked.

"You don't even have to ask," Camaro said.

"Then let's do this thing."

# CHAPTER FORTY-FOUR

Way skipped lunch and dinner and kept working. Hannon moved in and out, running interference with the local police and the representatives of the County Sheriff's Department. Way had no time for them. When they brought something useful to the table, Hannon relayed it to him. When he had an order to give, she brought it to the right person. It was best this way. He had a headache aspirin couldn't cure.

The door to the meeting room opened and then closed softly. Way felt Hannon at his back. "What is it now?"

"You need to take a break."

"I'll take a break when this is done."

"No, you need to take a break now. You've been at this for eight hours solid. Whatever you're looking for isn't there. At least take a minute to put something in your stomach."

"Leave me alone," Way said.

"Keith—"

"Leave me alone!"

Hannon said nothing. She left the room, and it was quiet. When he heard the door open again, he felt his headache spike, and he growled a sigh. "I'm not taking a break and I'm not hungry."

"I'm not delivering food," a man said.

Way started and swung around in his chair. The man wore a suit jacket, tie, and slacks and held a coat folded over one arm. FBI credentials dangled from his breast pocket. He tapped them and smiled.

"Jesus Christ," Way said.

"Not exactly. Special Agent Lewis Brock. I'm from the resident agency in Watsonville. I've been trading phone calls with your partner all day."

"I hadn't heard."

"Somehow I doubt that," Brock said, though he smiled. "She's really good, your partner. She makes it sound like you're helping out, but what she's really doing is keeping you out of things. It took all day for me to figure out what she was doing. I should have come right away and saved her all that energy."

A tic flickered at the corner of Way's eye. "If you've been talking to Hannon, you know we have the situation under control. We don't need direct FBI support."

Brock put his coat over the back of one of the chairs. "That's not really the sort of thing the U.S. Marshals Service gets to decide. Your bailiwick is fugitives. But this isn't just a fugitive case anymore, is it? Your man is running around killing people. Killing cops. Mind if I sit?"

Way gestured toward a chair. Brock sat in it. "We're hours away from getting our fugitive," Way said. "As soon as we have him, it's over. If you want to help out, that's fine, but—"

"Help out?" Brock interrupted. "You misunderstand me. This is an FBI case, and we're going to take it from here. I have four agents in Carmel right now interviewing witnesses and reviewing the scene. I'm going to personally go over everything you have to see what's useful. The minute your fugitive decided to bump it up to the murder of law enforcement, he became our problem, not yours."

"It's too bad the FBI doesn't give as much of a shit when a deputy U.S. marshal gets killed," Way said.

"How's that?"

Way snatched Lukas's updated wanted sheet from the tabletop and brandished it at Brock. "Lukas Collier killed one of my brother marshals right in front of me. With *my gun*. As far as I know, the FBI didn't send so much as a condolence memo to our offices. But now, just as soon as I have this son of a bitch in my sights, you're all over it and making sure you get yours. That's convenient. Real convenient."

A notch appeared between Brock's brows, and he leaned forward to put his hands on the table. "I think we're getting off on the wrong foot."

"You think so?"

"I'm not the bad guy here. This is a simple jurisdictional matter. You don't have the authority to conduct this kind of operation. I do. But that doesn't mean we're going to freeze you out. No, I *want* you and Deputy Hannon to work this thing with us. You know Lukas Collier better than anyone, and I wouldn't dream for a second of taking away your chance to put away the guy you've been after all this time. So let's not fight. Let's do this together."

Way stood up. "I'm not interested."

"Deputy Way, don't be an idiot."

"You know what? Screw you and screw the FBI. And screw everybody else who sat on their asses and let Lukas Collier run around the country doing whatever the hell he wanted. Because what's happened here is on you people. If he'd been picked up after Newark, this would never have happened. He should have been in a prison cell waiting for a needle by now, but nobody listened to me. So take this whole thing and stick it up your ass because this is my operation and my bust, and that's the end of it. Are you reading me?"

Brock's face was calm. "I'm reading you loud and clear."

"Now, if you'll excuse me, I'm going to go out and do some real police work. By the time you FBI guys are finished stroking yourselves, I'll have my guy. Period. End of story."

Way grabbed his coat and stormed out of the meeting room, slamming the door behind him. A small group of uniformed cops looked up at him, their conversation stopped in midsentence, but none stepped in his way or said a word. He passed them in a hurry, barely aware of Hannon rushing to catch up with him. "Keith, what's going on?" she asked.

"You have that list of Jake Collier's KAs that I asked for?"

"Sure, but the FBI—"

Way turned on her. He was burning. "They can do whatever the hell they want. You and I are going to run down these guys and see if they know anything about Lukas. Maybe they saw him, maybe they talked to him on the phone. Anything at all that might give us a clue about where he's laying his head. So if you're coming, grab your shit and meet me at the car. I'll give you two minutes."

Hannon paused. "Okay. I'll be right there."

# CHAPTER FORTY-FIVE

Yates dr ove the Santa Fe to Pacific Grove with Camaro in the passenger seat beside him. They didn't play the radio or talk and instead let the hum of the tires on wet pavement do the speaking for them. Camaro looked over at Yates from time to time, but his face was blank.

When they finally drew within sight of Carlson Lumber, Yates released a breath that sounded like pressure venting.

"Loren better still be here," Camaro said.

"That's his truck over there in the corner. The white Tundra."

They rolled into the parking lot. Inside the broad open doors at the front of the main building there was bright illumination from lamps in aluminum shades. No one moved among the giant racks of lumber.

When they got out of the SUV, they met at the back bumper. Camaro saw Yates tug the edge of his jacket down to cover his gun. "Once we hit the entrance, I'll peel off to distract anyone working at the front," Yates said. "You keep on walking like you've got business somewhere. I'll keep talking until I see you coming out, and then we'll leave together. Sound like a plan?"

"Let's do it," Camaro said, and they went.

At the counter was a man in a bright yellow safety vest. Camaro didn't recognize him from before, and she didn't keep her eyes on him long. They passed under a blast of heat from an overhead fan. Yates split from her, arrowing toward the man and calling for his attention. No eyes were on Camaro. She went on.

She hadn't spent any time in the interior of the building, but now that she was in it she realized the full scale of the place. There were rows upon rows of lumber, the whole place smelling of the sawdust that lay in drifts and sprays on the concrete floor. The racks went all the way up to the ceiling.

175

The first two men she saw weren't Loren Masters. One smiled and lifted his chin in greeting, but Camaro waved him off. "Just looking," she said, and she kept going.

Loren was at the far end of the building, scribbling on a stack of lumber loaded onto a forklift. The moment he saw her, his face changed, falling slack and turning pale in the instant of recognition. He dropped the black marker in his hand and ran. Camaro went after him.

She caught up to him in the building's rearmost corner and put her foot in the back of his trailing leg. He stumbled hard and crashed to the floor with a cry. Camaro pounced onto his back, trapping his waist with her legs and snaring a free arm in the same moment. She caught the cuff of his pant leg with one hand and rolled, levering off the back of his head with her knee. They tumbled together until Loren was on his back and his arm was caught between her legs, the elbow joint locked open. Camaro dropped a calf over his face and cranked the limb. He yelped in pain.

"Shut up," Camaro snapped at him. "Shut up."

"Oh, shit, my arm, my arm," Loren wailed against the back of her leg.

Camaro put pressure on his elbow until he ground out another sound of pain. "I will break it right now," she promised him. "Just keep yapping."

"Okay," he said. "All right. I'm not saying anything."

"If I let you go, are you gonna run again?"

Loren shook his head violently.

Camaro released the arm bar and back-rolled onto her knees. She rose before Loren did, careful to block him into the corner. She glanced back once, but no one seemed to hear them. They were alone. "I swear, if you run—"

"I won't," Loren said. "I promise. Don't do me like you did Jake."

"I want to know where Lukas is."

"Lukas?"

Camaro punched him low and hard. Loren folded over, gagging. She grabbed him by the back of the collar and threw him against the wall. He put his hands up weakly, still coughing. She cocked her fist to punch him again.

"Don't do it," Loren managed.

"Where's Lukas?"

"I don't know." Camaro moved for him, and he threw his hands up again. "Wait! Wait! I've seen him. I just don't know where he is right this minute."

"This morning he shot a cop and my sister," Camaro said. "The cop is dead. If you don't want to deal with me, you can explain to the cops how you were just helping Lukas out a little bit. I'll only hurt you. They'll take your life apart."

"I saw him a couple of days ago at Flickers. But I haven't seen him since then. I swear to Christ that's the truth."

"What's Flickers?"

"It's a bar in Carmel. We like it there."

"You talk to Lukas on the phone?"

"No."

"Did he say where he's keeping himself?"

"No, nothing like that," Loren said, panting with pain. "He wasn't interested in talking to me. He was all Derrick, Derrick, Derrick. The two of them were all hugs and kisses. You should talk to Derrick."

"I already talked to Derrick. Now I'm talking to you. What's Derrick moving for Lukas?"

"What do you mean?"

Camaro hit him again. He bled from a broken lip. "I'm not going to warn you again."

Loren wiped his mouth. "Jake had some money put away. He picked it up here and there, had it all stashed at his place. He said he was gonna open a surf shop with it, but I never saw him do anything like that. He just kept saying it and saying it, and then one day he told us his brother was coming and he was headed out of town for a while."

"Where?"

"I don't know. Maybe LA? I think he mentioned it once. His brother has some connections down that way. But I don't know what's going on with Derrick, okay? You really need to talk to him. He was besties with Jake. He'd know it all."

"All of *what?*" Camaro asked. "Selling drugs? Is that his thing?"

"You gotta talk to Derrick."

"Goddamn it, if you tell me that again…"

"I'm not on the inside, but Derrick is. I know where you can get all the answers: you can go right to Flickers. I'm supposed to meet Derrick and everybody there tonight."

"Where's Flickers exactly?"

"It's right on Lincoln. Hell, I'll draw you a map."

"I'll find it. And you listen to me, I will come back and kill you if you're lying to me," Camaro said. "I know where you live."

"I promise I'm not lying."

Camaro considered hitting him again. She saw the fear lit behind Loren's expression. She took one step toward him, and he shrank against the wall. He was taller than her by inches, but in that moment she was the larger of the two.

"Don't meet with Derrick tonight," she said. "And do yourself a favor and stay clear of Lukas if you see him. His world is about to get bloody."

"He's out of my life," Loren swore.

Camaro turned away and headed for the way out. Loren did not call after her.

# CHAPTER FORTY-SIX

Lukas l ay in bed beside Vicki with the sheets pooled over his crotch. He smoked and used a water glass as an ashtray. She lay curled up, her back to him. Occasionally she shook, and the tremor passed through the mattress. He touched her idly. "That was good," he said. "You're real good."

"Please don't," she said. He heard her crying.

"Jake was too soft on you. Always a gentleman, right?"

For a while he thought she wouldn't answer, but finally her voice came. "Yes. He was always good to me."

"And now you're good to me. See how that works? It says in the Bible that if a man dies, his brother has to take his woman on. So I'm only doing what God says to do. You hear me? Open up your mouth and talk."

"I hear you," Vicki said, her voice faltering. "I'm really glad you're around."

Lukas smiled. "It's not so hard to be grateful. And I appreciate the help you gave Jake getting this deal together. Working capital is hard to come by for an entrepreneur like me. Can't get a loan from the bank, can't get investors without someone putting their nose in your business."

"If I give you more money, will you...will you go?"

"Why do you want me to go? Didn't I just say I was doing God's work here?"

"You can't stay here forever. They'll find you. People will wonder why Brendan isn't in school. That thousand dollars I have is all yours. And then you can do your business wherever you need to go."

Lukas took a long drag from his cigarette, then exhaled toward the ceiling. The swirling cloud was caught in the failing light from outside, murky and oddly alive in its way. "You ever been to Los Angeles?"

"No."

"Better than this goddamned place, that's for sure. Just sunshine and money and ladies all day long. I've been all over this country, but LA is the center of the world. New York City? It's bullshit. You want to make a name for yourself, you go to LA."

Vicki was completely silent.

An ugly thought crossed Lukas's mind. He frowned. "You don't have to wait too much longer," he said. "It's not like you don't got it going on, but a town like this is too small-time for a guy like me. I was happy to let Jake be the point man here, but he's gone. I got to make new plans."

"What kind of plans?"

"What's it to you?"

"It's nothing, Luke. I was only asking."

"Well, mind your own goddamned business. I tell you what I want to tell you. The rest of the time you keep your mouth shut. You hear me?"

Vicki didn't answer. After a while she slid away from him and got off the bed.

He looked after her. "Where you going now?"

"I want to take a shower."

"All right, you do that. And when you come back, I might want to dirty you up again."

"Okay, Luke."

"'Okay, Luke,'" he said mockingly. He considered throwing his cigarette at her. "You really are a dumb bitch. And your son's retarded. Get on out of my sight."

She fled, and Lukas chuckled to himself. He tipped ash into the glass. He thought of Camaro and the dead cop touring around town in the cop's car. He'd only seen Camaro from a distance, but he'd recognize her instantly when he saw her again. Some things never left his mind. Underneath the sheet he stirred thinking of her.

He heard the shower running. He dropped the cigarette into the glass and got up.

# CHAPTER FORTY-SEVEN

They parked two blocks from Flickers because there was nowhere else to put the Hyundai and walked back, their collars turned up against a cold wind coming off the bay. The streets of Carmel were quiet, and most of the little boutique shops and galleries were closed for the night. It was possible to hear the party sounds from Flickers from a hundred feet away.

A crowd spilled out of the front door and onto the sidewalk. Cigarette smoke whipped away on the air, but a distinct haze was visible inside the entrance, lingering around neon lights and low-wattage bulbs.

Camaro tried to look past the thicket of bodies, but it was impossible to see more than a few feet inside the door. She shook her head. "We're going to have to go in."

"You want me to take point?" Yates asked.

"No. We don't know if he's inside. Watch the front. If he rolls up on the place, somebody has to be out here to catch him."

"Shout if you need me. That's if I can hear you."

She elbowed her way through the first layer of humanity and managed to get inside the door. The throng was like a living organism growing out of the bar on one side of the place, casting out thick feelers in every direction. Camaro was barely able to make out the man and woman tending bar. Voices were raised in a loud jumble, backed by music blaring from speakers placed here and there along the perimeter. Led Zeppelin's "Whole Lotta Love" rocked the house, Robert Plant's vocals cutting through everything like a clean, sharp blade. The walls were festooned with license plates and bumper stickers.

There was no clear place to start. Camaro set out perpendicular to the bar, skirting the edge of the space. Her path would bring her all the way to the far corner, then hook around to the other side and back up again. Tables were scattered all around the center, shadowy figures huddled over them in conversation. Some faces she could see easily and some not. She searched for Derrick's.

Clots of bar-goers fell into her path, and she struggled to get around them. It took a few minutes to make the back of the bar, and there she could better see the booths that were set up along two walls. Little electric tea lights glowed in each one, a touch of class in a place bereft of it. Only a few people looked up as Camaro sidled past. The men gave her a second glance, and the women frowned. None of them were Derrick.

She finally reached the farthest corner and turned back toward the front. Her eyes roved over everyone she passed, scanning left and right, catching glimpses between moving shadows. Up ahead there was a hallway that broke out through the wall opposite the street entrance. A lit sign declared r estr ooms. Camaro used that as her progress marker, getting closer step-by-step.

She was coming to the end of the booths. Camaro reached another, where a man and woman sat opposite each other, yelling to be heard. The man glanced up, and in that instant they locked eyes. "Nic Thompson," Camaro said. She could barely make out her own voice above the din. The woman turned to look at her. It was Rosalinda.

Camaro was shoving her way toward the booth when movement near the restrooms caught her eye. She looked through the sea of bobbing heads and spotted Derrick emerging from the back hallway. He saw her in the same moment and spun away.

"Out of the way!" Camaro yelled as she bulled through the people ahead of her. Men and women tumbled over, yelling in surprise. She stepped over them and kept going, spearing her way between the last dozen of the crowd to reach the restrooms. The hallway was clear, the doors to the restrooms closed.

She hit the men's room first, slamming the door open. A man jumped at the urinal and sprayed himself in the leg. No feet showed under the wall of the single stall. Camaro rushed to the ladies' room next, kicking it open to find two women near the sinks, checking their makeup.

Camaro ran to the back of the hallway. There was a door marked office   and another with the label fir e exit—al  arm will   sound. The latter hung slightly open. The alarm did not sound.

Cold air smacked her in the face as she burst out into the alley behind the bar. Her ears were ringing from the noise inside, but she still heard the slap of running feet. She looked left and saw Derrick at a dead run. Camaro sprinted after him.

He made it to the end of the alley long before she did and hung a right. Camaro's heart pumped as she dashed the final distance and skidded around the corner onto another quiet street. Derrick was twenty yards distant, running hard. She went on.

Derrick crossed a street at speed. Camaro closed the distance. She bounded off the uneven sidewalk onto the asphalt and was suddenly awash in the oncoming headlights of a car. Tires squealed as the car careened to a stop, only inches from Camaro. She was frozen in the glare, momentarily dazzled.

The man behind the wheel lunged out of the car. Camaro saw a gun, and then she saw his face. "Don't move! Hands where I can see them," Way commanded. "Piper, get after that guy!"

Camaro moved to run again, and Way stiffened behind the gun. She stopped. Hannon exploded out of the passenger seat and ran after Derrick, who was a block away and moving fast.

"He's gone," Camaro said. "Shit!"

"Put your goddamned hands where I can see them. Lean over the hood of the car. Interlace your fingers behind your neck."

She obeyed. Way approached her without lowering his weapon. He kicked her feet apart. "Who is that? It wasn't Lukas Collier, so who was it?"

"It's nobody," Camaro said.

"Don't give me that shit," Way said. He hit her on the back of the head, and her forehead bounced off the hood, leaving her momentarily dizzy. "Who was it?"

"Somebody who owes me money," Camaro said.

Way grabbed her by the elbow and wrenched her around until she fell back against the hood. He forced his leg between hers and pressed the muzzle of his automatic into her cheekbone. "Was it Loren Masters? How about Nic Thompson? Derrick Perkins? Which one? You're onto Lukas, so tell me which one knows where he is."

Camaro stared at him. "I don't know what you're talking about."

Way leaned into her, pressing the gun harder for emphasis. "I could put a bullet into you right now. Resisting arrest. I should. You want to kill Lukas Collier as much as I do, except I do not get in line behind you."

"I'm on a public street. I'm not breaking any laws," Camaro said. She looked into Way's eyes. They were fevered.

"You're not breaking any laws? You're chasing a suspect. Do you think you're the law? Because you're not the law."

"I know I'm not the law," Camaro said.

Way scowled. "That's right. I am the law. Me. I'm the man. Who the hell do you think you are?"

"Keith?"

Way tensed. Camaro turned her eyes, but not her head. Hannon was there. Her face was stricken. "Keith, what are you doing?"

"This doesn't concern you," Way said. "Just walk in the other direction."

"I can't do that. Put your weapon away."

"I said *walk!*"

"Keith, I can't. I won't."

"She's interfering with our investigation," Way declared. "That's obstruction."

"Keith, put the gun away."

He was slow to respond. Camaro looked from him to Hannon and back again. Way took the pistol out of her face and holstered it under his coat. He backed away.

Camaro rose from the hood. She felt her cheek and the impression of the automatic's muzzle. She looked to Hannon again.

"Go," Hannon said.

"Piper, she's going to screw this all up."

"Go, now!"

Camaro turned from Way and moved. She expected a bullet in the back. It did not come. She ran to Yates, and neither marshal followed.

# CHAPTER FORTY-EIGHT

"He pulled his weapon on you?" Yates said. "He put it in your face?"

"Yes."

Yates shook his head slowly. They sat in the parked Santa Fe on Lincoln Street, alone except for the occasional car slipping slowly past. Carmel went on as if nothing had happened. "This is a problem."

"You think?" Camaro asked.

"If they were down here looking for Jake's buddies, then they're on the same trail we are. It's only a matter of time before they talk to Loren Masters and find out you rousted him. Unless you think you put enough of the fear of God into him that he keeps his mouth shut."

"He doesn't want me coming back to him," Camaro said.

"Okay, then. So the big question is, who gets to Derrick first. If it's us, we have the advantage. If it's the marshals, then we lose everything. I'm not prepared to let all of this slip through my fingers. Not when we're so close."

Camaro pounded her fist on the armrest. "He's gonna disappear. Now that he knows the sharks are out, he's going to get in his car and drive until the heat is off. We'll never find him."

Yates was quiet awhile. "That's not necessarily so."

"What do you mean?"

"I've been at this a good long time, and the one thing I've learned is that people in general aren't that smart. They like familiar places and faces, and they don't like to stray far from the things that make them comfortable. Now if it were you or me, we'd be gone in a heartbeat. But Derrick, he's not a bright boy."

Camaro digested this. She turned over the conclusion in her mind. "He'll come around again."

185

"I won't say I guarantee it, but I'm leaning that way. We might not see him at that bar again, and he'll probably steer clear of his work, but that doesn't mean he won't pop up at home, even if it's to make sure he gets his toothbrush."

She looked at her watch. "I can't go at this all night. I need to see my sister. We can link up again in the morning. I'll come to where you are."

"I understand," Yates said. "I'll take you to the hospital now."

They drove out of Carmel. A waning moon broke through a temporary breach in the clouds, giving the cold woodlands a silvery mantle. Once Camaro saw a fox at the side of the road, its eyes glowing, before it broke for cover and vanished completely.

"How long have you been doing this?" Camaro asked.

"This? You mean skip tracing?"

"Yeah."

"Got to be forty years at least. Forty...three? Something like that. After the service I kind of bummed around awhile doing this and that. Worked construction, fixed cars, cooked food. Pretty much anything a man could do to earn a paycheck. Lot of lean years. Then I heard from a friend of a friend that a bail bondsman was looking for someone to track down some skips. His usual guy had appendicitis. I didn't know my ass from a hole in the ground, but I figured, how hard could it be?"

"Was it?"

"Sometimes. Like I said, most crooks are lazy as hell. You'd be surprised how many you can round up just by knocking on doors and asking politely. That's why I don't much like the term 'bounty hunter.' People get this idea in their head that it's all about kicking down doors and busting skulls when it's not like that at all. The damned TV shows don't help any.

"Anyway, I've been letting my son handle most things for a few years now. Got my own bail-bonding operation, so it's pretty much paperwork and phone calls every day. Long hours are the worst part, but my wife and I have been putting away a good amount for a while, and when the time comes I'm going to step away completely. Except..."

"Your son," Camaro said.

"My son," Yates replied, and they left it at that.

The Santa Fe wound its way up the drive to the hospital, and Yates let Camaro out with a good-bye and a promise to call. Camaro stayed long enough for him to pull away and then went inside. She knew which way to go, and she went on her own.

A sheriff's deputy was stationed outside Annabel's room, sitting on an uncomfortable-looking chair and reading a copy of *Entertainment Weekly*. He stood when she approached and put up a hand to halt her.

He asked for ID. Camaro did as he wanted. The deputy made a satisfied noise. He opened the door for her, and Camaro stepped into darkness.

The only illumination was the soft light from the window cast by that same moon. Camaro heard the whisper of Annabel's sleeping breath. She could just make out her sister's form beneath the covers, looking small and frail in the dimness. The second round of surgery was complete, and she was still alive.

She sat in the chair next to Annabel's bed and said nothing. For an hour she simply listened.

A soft rapping came at the door. Camaro straightened up. "Who is it?"

The door opened, and a man in a jacket and tie stepped through. He looked as though he was sliding into his sixties, his face lined but not unpleasant. He stopped respectfully just inside the threshold. "Do you mind if I come in?" he asked.

"Who are you?"

"My name is Lewis Brock. I'm a special agent with the Federal Bureau of Investigation."

"I have nothing to say."

"That's all right, I can do most of the talking."

He came in and closed the door behind him. He moved to the side of the bed and looked down at Annabel. "I happened to be here when you came in. I wanted to see how she was doing."

"She's making it," Camaro said.

"Have you talked to the doctor?"

"Not yet."

"You should. She has some good news for you. Internal damage wasn't as bad as they feared, and if your sister makes it through the next twenty-four hours or so, she's going to be all right. Or as all right as you can be after something like this."

Camaro put her hand on Annabel's hand. It was cold.

"I understand you've taken some hits yourself."

"You get that from Way?"

"We have our own resources. We don't have to go through the marshals. But the groundwork they did isn't going to waste."

"I'm glad it's working out for you."

Brock let the silence grow between them. Camaro didn't look at him. Annabel's face was obscured with tape and plastic and blanched almost completely pale. She was bloodless.

"It must be hard to keep the kind of secrets the two of you have kept," Brock said.

"You people don't have any idea. Not about either of us."

"Look, I've talked to Deputy Hannon. I know all about your past. I don't know where the two of you keep your stash, but I know you have it somewhere. That doesn't interest me. You can keep whatever you have. God knows if I got out of New Orleans one step ahead of some of the wrong people, I think I'd deserve some peace and quiet in a nice town like Carmel. Or on a boat in the Atlantic. But now people are dying in my neck of the woods, and I can't ignore that."

"So what do you want?"

"You killed Jacob Collier."

"I did."

"Lukas Collier tried to kill your sister."

Camaro remained silent.

"If it were me, and someone did that to my sister, I'd want payback. Don't you?"

Camaro looked at Annabel instead of Brock. "It wouldn't break my heart if Lukas Collier died tomorrow."

"I don't doubt it. And I'm pretty sure you'd like to pull the trigger on him yourself."

"So what?"

"So I'd rather you not do that."

"What difference does it make?"

"I think your sister's suffered enough. Jake Collier was a bad guy, and I don't need to have much imagination to know what that meant for her. She called on you to help, and you did. He's dead now. Maybe it wasn't the best way to resolve the situation, but he wasn't the kind of man who would let your sister just leave him. I understand how it works, I've seen it more times than I care to remember. Some folks would go after the both of you for what happened, maybe put you in prison. Maybe her, too."

Camaro turned her gaze on Brock. "My sister's innocent. If you want to take somebody, then you take me, but leave her alone."

"I will. Looking at her in this bed . . . she's paid a worse price than doing time."

Camaro regarded Brock carefully. "What do you want from me?"

"Walk away. You did what you came here to do."

"Lukas is still out there."

"And we'll get him. But you need to think about what's best for you, your sister, and your niece. If you go after this guy — if you kill him, or even if you try and miss the mark — I won't have any choice. You'll have to go down. What good is that for anyone?"

Camaro didn't answer. She turned to Annabel again and listened to the hiss of mechanical air feeding her sister's lungs. "You seem really interested in seeing us get through this."

"That's because I'm on the side of the good guys," Brock said. He headed for the door. "Think about it. But don't think too long."

189

# CHAPTER FORTY-NINE

After Camaro Espinoza had gone, they sat in the car together for a long time without talking or going anywhere. The engine idled, and warm air blew from the vents.

Finally Hannon had to speak. "That can't happen again."

Way made a noise that sounded like the start of a protest, but it was quashed. Instead, he said, "I know."

"The deal was Lukas. That was all. Collateral damage is unacceptable."

"I said I know."

Hannon breathed out. "Derrick Perkins is in the wind. We need to change tactics if we're going to scoop him up."

"She rousted him," Way said bitterly. "If we'd gotten here ten minutes sooner…"

"It's done. We don't have to let it ruin everything. This whole area is tiny, and he only has so many places he can hide. We start with the most likely and work our way down the list."

"We need to split up."

Hannon looked at him sidelong. "Why?"

"We can't be welded together at the hip. If we work apart, we can cover more ground. Besides which, there's the FBI situation to deal with. That Brock asshole is going to pull the football out of the way before we have a chance to kick. I can't let that happen."

"So where do you want to go?"

"Salinas. Drop me off at the courthouse. I'm going to start with the Superior Court and work my way up from there. Whoever I have to get out of bed, I will. This is a twenty-four-hour-a-day job. Time people knew it."

Way put the car in gear, and they drove away. Hannon looked out the window, but she thought intensely. "While you're doing that, I'm going to follow up on Perkins," she said. "He's not out of this yet."

"Perkins is going to lead us right to the man," Way agreed. "These guys around here, they're just wannabes. They don't know how we operate. They think this is just like dealing with the local cops. What do you have in mind?"

"His place first. I know it's a long shot, but I have a feeling."

"You better hope Camaro Espinoza doesn't screw it up," Way said. He smacked the wheel with the heel of his hand. "She's a danger to herself and others."

"If I see her, I'll deal with her," Hannon said. "You don't have to worry about it."

"I do worry. We can't have someone running around, getting under our feet. The FBI is bad enough. If she doesn't watch it, she's gonna get herself killed."

"But not by you," Hannon said.

"What? Of course not."

"You had me concerned, Keith. I didn't know what to think."

"You don't have to think about it at all. I have a lid on it now."

"Okay," Hannon said, but she watched Way for any sign in his face. Only when there was none did she turn back to the night view slipping by the window.

They made good time back to Salinas and at last came to a stop in front of the Monterey County Superior Court. It was an Art Deco building with a bas-relief of a sword-wielding and sighted Justice above the main entrance. Carved faces looked out from beneath every second-floor window. Way put the car in park. "You take the car," he said. "I'll work out a ride."

Hannon got out of the car with Way. They exchanged sides. Way looked frazzled, and she wondered how she looked to him. "I'll be in touch," she told Way.

"I know. Be careful, okay? Lukas is out there."

"I won't try to take him alone."

"Good. Because he's mine. He's always going be mine." Way gave her a look filled with a contained darkness and then turned toward the steps.

Hannon got behind the wheel. She stayed until she saw Way go inside, and then she pulled away from the curb.

She drove with the image of Way and Camaro Espinoza at the forefront of her thoughts. She imagined a step further, a moment longer, a decision made, and then she imagined Camaro Espinoza dead on the ground. There had been no question in Hannon's mind that Way could have killed her, would have killed her if the circumstances were only slightly altered. Hannon did not like the road down which that ran.

Hannon felt Jerry Washington's loss. He was funny, he was dedicated, and he was the best friend a person could have when they needed one. He'd been there for Hannon when she needed someone. They never talked about it afterward.

Way and Jerry were bonded in a very real way, like men who'd shared the same foxhole during a terrible artillery barrage and come out unscathed.

The mood had been black when Lukas Collier killed Jerry. The commander handed her the case and instructed her to take on whichever partner would be best suited for the task of finding Lukas and putting him away. Way came to her then and told her what it meant to him to follow the trail. She let him in.

She'd known what she was doing. Way had never hidden his agenda from her. No one would say it out loud, but they all thought the same thing. Cuffs or a bullet. Cuffs led to a stainless steel table and the needle. A bullet was a more efficient way of reaching the same conclusion. She made an agreement with Way, and then they followed the trail. Norfolk had been close, so close, and now they were close again.

No police unit had been stationed in front of Derrick Perkins's home. A request to the locals had opened up an opportunity for Derrick to slip inside. They patrolled frequently, but he was invited into the gaps in the hope that he would expose himself going in or coming out.

Hannon slotted into place in front of an undistinguished-looking white house with blue trim a little way down from Derrick's duplex. She switched off the engine and let the hot metal slowly tick into coolness under the night sky.

She was tired. She made a note of all the cars and trucks on the street.

One light was on at Derrick's house, burning in the carport. The rest of the place was dark.

Two hours passed. Headlights turned in at the far end of the block, then winked out. Hannon yawned and went on watching. When she saw the shadowy figure moving along the sidewalk, she sat up and rubbed her eyes.

The man drew closer, but he was just a shape until he passed beneath the glow of a streetlight. Even at a distance she recognized Derrick Perkins. He moved past the houses, trying his best to stick to the darkness, before slipping across the lawn of his duplex and heading for the front door. Hannon saw the pale oval of his face as he looked around once before disappearing inside.

Hannon reached for her phone. She had it in her hand but then paused. She put it down. In the dark she waited for him to emerge again.

# CHAPTER FIFTY

Yates watched Derrick 's place for hours, parked across the street and down two doors, where he had a full view of the duplex without being too obvious about it. He paid no attention to the cold, not running the engine even for warmth.

His body was hungry, but he did not allow that to distract him. Cars came and went. Yates waited with tension in his spine whenever a new vehicle appeared on the street, and remained coiled until he saw neither driver nor passenger was Derrick or Lukas.

It was false dawn when his phone rang. It was shrill and startling in the absolute quiet of the SUV's cabin, and Yates hastened to silence it. He checked the number and answered. "Hello, darlin'," he said.

"Jeremy," his wife said, "why haven't you called?"

"I didn't want to call until I had something for sure."

"And you don't?"

"I might. I don't want to get either of our hopes up."

"You sound tired."

"I'm fine."

Yates imagined her in their home. She was small and frail, four years older than he was but carrying the years differently. Some days she seemed younger and more vital, but other times he saw the age weighing on her, and it reminded him that fifty-three years was a long time and no marriage lasted forever. In the end there was no choice but to part.

"Are you there?"

"I'm here. Sorry. Maybe I am a little tired. A little."

"Are you eating?"

"Yes."

"You have to eat, Jeremy. Tell me you're eating."

"I'm eating," he lied. "I had a big chicken-fried steak for dinner last night with a baked potato. It was almost as good as one of yours."

"Are you staying safe? Are you letting the police do their job?"

"Yes. I'm only here to help. When it comes time to bring Lukas in, I'll step back and let them do all the heavy lifting. Then it's back on a plane and home again. I promise."

Trish was quiet awhile. "I dreamed about Stanley."

"Don't torture yourself, Trish."

"No, it was a good dream. He told me he made it to the other side and was with Grandma and Grandpa. He looked good, Jeremy. Healthy. And he didn't have that silly chin beard. You know how much I hated that thing."

"I know. I guess Saint Peter doesn't allow any chin beards through the pearly gates."

"Don't make fun of me."

"I'm not," Yates said. "I never would."

"He told me to tell you not to blame yourself. He made a mistake, he said, but it wasn't your fault."

"I think that's all I want to hear about this dream," Yates said.

"He said it, Jeremy. He wants you to know it's not your fault what happened. He knows you're taking it hard, and he wants to take that burden from you."

Yates looked at the dome light above his head and sighed. "I don't blame myself. I blame Lukas Collier and his gun. And Lukas is going to pay for everything he's done. In this life and the next. There's no heaven for him."

"I love you, Jeremy."

"I love you, too. I have to go."

"Call me soon."

"I will. Good-bye, darlin'." He ended the call and put his phone in the cup holder.

"Dreams," he said out loud. He heard the bitter sound in his voice and was angry at himself for it. He turned his mind to the scene on the street, the darkened duplex where Derrick kept his home. It was possible Derrick had beaten him there, but it was unlikely. The woman,

Rosalinda, was sleeping in her bed alone. Maybe she knew where Derrick was, maybe she did not. Sooner or later Yates would have to move, and that move would be toward her.

The hint of motion on the street caught the corner of his eye, and he peered into the shadows. Someone approached, and Yates knew without having to see more that it was Derrick. No honest man moved in this way, starting and stopping in the darkness and skittering past the light like a startled cockroach. Yates drew his gun and put his hand on the door handle.

Derrick came closer, then hightailed it across his lawn to the door before vanishing inside. Yates did not get out. He put his gun away and grabbed his phone. He dialed, and after one ring Camaro answered. "He's here," Yates said.

"I'm coming. Give me the address again. I'll take a cab."

Yates checked the rearview mirror as a car appeared at the end of the block and cruised closer. He waited until it passed and only then realized he'd been holding his breath. "Tell them to drop you at the corner," he said. "Come in quiet. You'll see me across the street. We'll visit him together."

"I'm going now."

"Good, because I don't know how long it'll be before he scoots again."

Camaro hung up without saying good-bye. Yates forced himself still and went on watching.

# CHAPTER FIFTY-ONE

Camaro did as Yates instructed and had the cab let her out a block away from Derrick's place. She approached on the far side of the street, looking out for Yates's SUV and spotting it from fifty yards away.

Yates unlocked the passenger door for her. She got in. It was no warmer inside than out. "You made good time."

"I got lucky. There was a cab making a drop-off in Carmel when I made the call."

"What about the cops? They see you on the way out?"

"They saw me go into my sister's place. They probably think I'm still in there."

"Then we have a little advantage. I've seen a couple of cops cruise the place while I've been waiting, but no one's settling in. They must not think Derrick's worth sitting on, or maybe they're playing a different game. The important thing is that we have a clear window to get this done."

"I have a problem," Camaro said.

"What is it?"

Camaro told him about Brock. She watched his face as she relayed the story. His face was stony, and he showed no reaction until she was done.

Yates sighed. "So I take it because you're here that you're not going to take this Special Agent Brock's advice?"

"That's right."

"I suppose it's your call to make. But I think you ought to consider what might come from this."

"I already thought about it." Camaro checked the house. It was dead. The sky was lightening. "He's still in there?"

"Unless he ducked out the back. He'll move before dawn, though. I can guarantee it."

"Then let's go."

She opened her door. Yates stopped her with a hand on her arm. "Hold on a second."

Camaro shrugged his hand away. "What's the problem?"

"Do we have a plan, or is this cowboy time again?"

"I can go in alone," Camaro said.

"I wouldn't advise it."

"This guy is a leech. He's not gonna hurt me."

"Thinking like that is what gets people hurt."

"Well, what's your suggestion, old man?"

"I'm only giving you the benefit of my experience. You go in there like a steamroller, you might get more than you bargained for."

Camaro eased the door shut again. The dome light went out. She reached for the small of her back beneath her jacket and drew Annabel's Glock. "I'm going in there with you or without you. I'd rather you came along. But if you don't, I have my backup right here."

Yates considered the gun. "You going to kill him, too?"

"If I have to."

"Just like that?"

Camaro looked at him.

He nodded. "Okay, then."

She put the gun away and got out of the Santa Fe. She waited long enough for Yates to join her, then jogged across the street toward Derrick's house. Yates was slower, and she heard him breathing as they came up on the dark side of the duplex, caught only by the light in the carport. "Front door or side?" she asked him.

"Front door. No light."

They went onto Derrick's porch and stood in the shadows. Camaro stepped up to the door and listened, but there was no sound. She drew the gun, stood with her back to the frame, and cocked a leg to kick. Yates waved for her to stop, and she froze. "What?"

Yates produced a small leather wallet. "There are quieter ways," he said, and then he knelt before the door.

Camaro waited the long seconds as Yates picked the lock. She checked her watch twice, but only a minute passed. As the sweep hand finished a full circuit, she heard the tinny click of tumblers falling into place. Yates tried the knob, and the door came open silently.

He drew his stainless steel .45 as Camaro passed through the door. They were in the front room where they'd questioned Derrick and Rosalinda before. No one was in sight, and the space was inky.

Yates pushed the door shut behind them, and they advanced in the dark. Camaro's vision adjusted to the dimness as she searched out ahead of her for sounds of life. A gentle snoring passed down the hall toward her.

They passed a bedroom on the right side. Camaro cleared it with the Glock, checking corners and the space behind the door. It was made up as a guest space, with a narrow bed. At the end of the hall past the room were two more, left and right. She heard sleeping breath on the left.

The door was half closed. Camaro reached ahead to gently press it out of the way. She saw into the darkened bedroom, noted the dresser and the window, the closet, and a chair piled with laundry. On the bed, Rosalinda slept beneath the covers, while Derrick sprawled atop the sheets, fully clothed, a half-packed bag at his feet.

Camaro entered. She motioned for Yates to swing around the far side of the bed, and he did so without a sound. For a moment they hovered over the sleeping bodies. Rosalinda sighed in her sleep. Derrick snored again.

She closed a hand over his mouth and pressed the muzzle of her pistol into his eye in the same motion. Derrick started awake, a shout muffled. Rosalinda was jarred awake, but before she screamed, Yates showed her his .45, and she stifled herself. "Shh," Camaro said.

Derrick's uncovered eye bulged. Camaro kept her hand clamped in place, and breath hissed through his nostrils. She felt an uncontrollable shiver pass through his entire body. Rosalinda made a small noise of abject terror.

"I'm going to take away my hand," Camaro told Derrick. "You don't speak until spoken to. You don't make any other sound."

Derrick agreed with a repeated nod. When Camaro drew her hand back, breath exploded from between his lips, and he sucked at the air as if he had been held underwater for a minute. "I'm not gonna—"

Camaro rapped him with the Glock. "I said *quiet*."

This time he didn't speak. He let one hand fall and sought out Rosalinda's. They clung together, shivering and silent. Rosalinda breathed in gasps.

"You were bullshitting us before," Camaro said. "You know exactly where Lukas is, don't you?"

"I swear I don't."

Camaro put the muzzle of the Glock against his forehead. "And I swear I will put a bullet in your skull right here, right now, if you don't start telling me the truth. And if you go, then your girl has to go, too. That's just how it works."

She felt Yates watching her. She silenced him with a gesture. He said nothing.

"You're running errands for Lukas. You sent something to LA for him. And now you're packing up for a trip. Was that money you sent ahead? What's Lukas doing with it?"

Derrick hesitated. "Can I talk?"

"Talk."

"Luke told me to get Jake's stash and send it to a friend."

"What friend?"

"Uh…Spencer. Konnor Spencer."

"Who is he?"

"I don't know."

"What does he want with Jake's money?"

She saw Derrick's eyelid flicker, and then she prodded him with her gun again. "I don't have all night, Derrick. He hurt my sister. He killed a cop who was only doing her job. This is the *end*. No more games."

"I'm not playing any games. Honest."

"Is he following the money to LA? Is he even in town anymore?"

"I really don't—"

"I'm going to count down from five," Camaro said. "Where is he?"

"I don't know."

"Five."

"You have to believe me, I don't know where he's hiding at."

"Four."

"Jesus Christ, I don't have any idea! I didn't know he was going to kill a cop. I would never go along with that."

"Three."

"Camaro," Yates said.

"Later. Two."

"Camaro!"

"One." Camaro put her finger on the trigger.

Derrick's bladder let go, and the smell of urine rose from the bed. He shook as though he were in the throes of a seizure, and he squeezed his eyes shut. "Oh, God," he said.

"He knows," Rosalinda said.

Camaro looked at her, but kept the gun on Derrick. "Talk."

"They've been on the phone a lot. Jake was putting together some kind of deal with his brother, and they were going to bring Derrick in on it. But they needed cash. That was Jake's job."

"What kind of deal?" Yates asked.

"He'll kill me," Derrick managed. His throat was tight, the cords showing beneath the skin.

"*I'll* kill you," Camaro said. "You are holding at one."

"Okay!" Derrick burst out. "It's all about bringing in grass, all right? Luke would get the stuff wholesale and then we'd retail it out all around Monterey Bay. It was easy green as long as Jake could come up with the seed money. We were all going to be in on it with him."

Camaro glanced at Yates. "Surf shop, my ass."

"Surfers smoke a lot of weed," Yates replied.

Camaro returned her attention to Derrick. "You were going to LA with Lukas?"

"Yeah. No more Jake, so he needed a local guy."

"He's got a lot of balls doing business, with everybody from the marshals to the FBI breathing down his neck," Yates said.

"Luke's crazy. But he said I'd be rich. I just want to make some money. I don't want anyone dying. That's not me. I'm not like that. But I couldn't say no to him once we got started. I'm in too deep."

"If you're still here, then he's still here," Camaro said. "Where?"

"He's staying with Vicki. Vicki Nelson. I can give you the address and everything you need."

"Talk," Camaro said.

Derrick reeled off an address that meant nothing to Camaro. Beside him, Rosalinda sobbed openly. Derrick still shivered and twitched. The room stank of piss now.

"This is where he's holed up?" Camaro asked.

"I only know he used to be there. Maybe he's moved on. He was going to call me when it was time to move."

Camaro spared a look toward Yates. He regarded her in the darkness, his eyes black. He put his .45 away. "We can find him now," Yates said.

Derrick spasmed violently when Camaro took the gun from his head. He reached for Rosalinda, and she gathered him to her. Camaro heard him crying now, too. She looked down on them entwined together. She put the Glock at the small of her back.

"We got what we needed," Yates said.

"Wait," Camaro said.

"He could be moving now. We have to go."

"If we leave here with them loose, Lukas will know before we're a mile away."

"Take their phones."

"Not good enough."

Derrick looked up at her. "You're gonna kill us anyway?"

"You got any rope? How about duct tape?"

"N-nothing."

"Then we tear up the sheets. You get her, and I'll take him," Camaro said.

They shredded the bedcovers and prized the two of them apart in a burst of tears and protest. Camaro bound Derrick hand and foot on the floor and gagged him with a washcloth from the bathroom. Yates mirrored her on the other side of the bed. Sunlight glittered through the bedroom window by the time they were done.

Camaro knelt beside Derrick and spoke directly into his ear. "Never let me see your face again," she said. "Ever. You're still holding at one."

Yates went behind her, and they came outside into the morning. "So that's how we're gonna run this from here on out?"

"You have a problem with that?" Camaro asked.

"Would it matter if I did?"

They crossed the street to the Santa Fe.

"Not really."

# CHAPTER FIFTY-TWO

She watched them go in, and she watched them come out. She knew Camaro Espinoza by sight, but not the old man. In the interim she heard no gunshots, and no one else emerged from the house during the time they were inside. She surprised herself at her own calmness, and her phone remained where it was.

The sun was brilliant behind her when they hurried to the SUV and drove away. Hannon started the car and slipped in some four car lengths distant, invisible to them in the glare. All around them Salinas was waking up.

Her phone rang. She answered. "Hannon."

"It's me," Way said. "What's the story?"

"I haven't seen anything," Hannon said. "I'm thinking this is a no-go. If you think it's worth a shot, maybe the locals can send a couple of unis to knock on the door and see who's home. I'm pretty sure somebody's there."

"I'll make the call."

"How are things on your end?" Hannon asked.

"Slow. The East Coast is up, so I've been on the line with New York and Washington for the last couple of hours. They're sending me up the totem pole to San Fran. I don't know if this means I'm getting somewhere or I'm getting set back. All I know is that no one's told me specifically to answer to Brock. As far as I'm concerned we're still independent."

"Do you need me for anything?"

"No, I'm good. Why don't you swing by the hotel and get some sleep? We can regroup around noon. I should have some answers by then."

"You could use some more sleep yourself."

"I'm doing fine as long as the coffee keeps coming."

"I'll be in touch," Hannon said.

"Yeah. We'll talk soon."

She ended the call. The SUV was still ahead, stopped at a light. Hannon slowed down, trying to time the red light out so they would not come bumper to bumper. She opened up the dialer to input 911.

"This is nine-one-one emergency. Do you require police, fire, or ambulance?"

"My name is Deputy U.S. Marshal Piper Hannon. I need to be put through to the local PD."

"What is your current location?"

"Salinas."

"Please hold while I make the connection."

There was a brief empty space where music would have gone, and then a man picked up the line. "Salinas Police Department, this is Sergeant Philbrick speaking. May I have your name again, please?"

"Piper Hannon. I'm a deputy U.S. marshal. You can confirm my identity with a Detective Wright in your department. I can hold if you have to make the call."

"That's not necessary. We were briefed on you. What can I do for you, Marshal?"

"I need a make on a license number for a black Hyundai Santa Fe. Are you ready for the number?"

"Shoot."

Hannon gave it to him and waited while he consulted his computer. The answer came back in seconds. "That's a rental vehicle registered to Enterprise here in Salinas."

"Can you give me a number for them, please?"

"Of course."

He looked it up for her, and Hannon made a mental note. She thanked him for his help and cleared the line for another call. An electronic switchboard at Enterprise forced her through a few choices before she was connected to a human. She introduced herself to the woman on the other end of the line and made her request. "You have a Hyundai

Santa Fe with that tag number out right now," Hannon said. "I need to know who the renter is."

"Don't you need a warrant for something like that?"

"Do I need to get one?" Hannon asked.

"No, it's just…well, that's supposed to be confidential."

"You can tell me. The information isn't going anywhere, and you'll be helping me out."

"Okay," the woman said. "It's rented to a Jeremy B. Yates."

"Do you have a home address? What city and state?"

"Norfolk, Virginia."

"Thank you for your help. That's all I needed."

"Can I get your number so my boss can call you if I get in trouble?"

Hannon killed the call. They were on the move out of Salinas, headed southwest on CA-1. Jeremy Yates, Stanley Yates's father, was behind the wheel of the SUV.

# CHAPTER FIFTY-THREE

The sun had fully escaped the horizon by the time they reached the apartment building. The city livened as the morning developed, and theirs was just another of a few cars moving through the neighborhood. Camaro watched through the windshield as the street numbers ticked by. Lukas did not appear on the street, nor was there any hint of him.

Yates parked. "Looks like a pretty typical setup. One main entrance, probably another one out the back for garbage collection and whatnot. Got fire escapes on both sides. Those could be a problem. In a situation like this, I'd generally call for an assist from the local PD. They'd cover the exits and make sure things didn't get out of hand."

"No backup," Camaro said.

"I suppose not. We got to make sure we hit fast and don't give Lukas time to think. I think we both know what he's capable of. He'll kill both of us sure as anything."

"I'll drop him," Camaro said.

"You seem pretty confident in yourself."

Camaro didn't spare a glance his way. She watched the building. "I'll drop him," she said again.

"Then I guess there's no sense waiting around."

They got out of the SUV and crossed the street to the apartment building. It was four stories, and Vicki Nelson's was on the third floor. The building's front door was glass but protected by an ornate set of wrought-iron bars. Camaro spotted a speaker and a series of labeled buttons just to the right of the door. "We have to get buzzed in," she said.

"Look a little closer."

Camaro saw the narrow wedge of battered wood jammed in the bottom of the door. Up close she saw that it was barely enough to keep the lock from engaging. She pulled the handle, and the door opened freely.

"What did I tell you about people being lazy?" Yates said. "It's the same all over."

Inside it was warmer, but only just. Camaro passed the rows of metal mailboxes on the way to the stairs. She peered up them, hearing nothing and seeing nothing.

Yates went to the elevator at the back of the lobby and pressed the button. "We'll take the stairs, but we want the elevator on the ground floor when we hit the place. One less way out."

A door opened and closed somewhere overhead, and shortly afterward there were loud footsteps. Camaro caught a glimpse of a woman's hand on the rail two floors up. She did not know what Vicki Nelson looked like. "Coming down," she said.

The elevator whirred to a stop and the doors opened. "Is she alone?" Yates asked.

"I think so."

"Step in here and let her go by. She doesn't see anything, she won't say anything."

Camaro went into the elevator with Yates and let the door slide closed. It had a window in the center, the glass gridded with wires. They looked out through it together until they saw a black woman step up to the mailboxes. The woman rattled her key there for a moment, then headed out to the street alone. Camaro let a breath go.

"Let's hope that was her," Yates said.

The elevator door opened at a press of the button. Yates flipped the stop switch. There was no alarm.

Camaro went to the stairs. She took them two at a time, trailed by Yates, who moved more slowly. He made the second floor and coughed twice, breath coming harder. Camaro paid him no mind, mounting the steps to the landing, then finally to the third floor. A plain hallway with doors on either side presented itself, windows at both ends letting in the sun.

She waited long enough for Yates to catch his breath, then counted off the apartment numbers until she reached Vicki Nelson's. She stopped there, tuned to the sounds of the building. There was a morning energy, and somewhere music came to her quietly. Vicki's door conveyed no sound.

"Let me lead the way in," Yates said in a low voice.

"No way. You're behind me."

"Not this time. Age before beauty."

Camaro let a frown crease her face, then shook it away. "Fine. But don't get in my way."

"Don't shoot me in the back."

Yates drew his pistol, and Camaro did the same. He took a step back to aim his kick. Camaro stopped him with an upraised hand. "What about the quiet way?" she asked.

"This time we want the noise. Be ready."

Camaro placed her free hand just beneath her sternum and laid the Glock across it in Position Sul, oriented toward the ground. She steadied herself on both feet and focused on the door. "Do it," she said.

The door took two kicks to break wide, but it was only a matter of seconds to make the breach. Yates surged forward with his gun up and bellowed, "Bail enforcement! Everybody down on the ground!"

Camaro fell in behind him and saw the living area to the left and the dining nook to the right. A woman in a short robe emerged from the back of the apartment, her face drained of color. For an instant she looked at the two of them coming through the door, and then she screamed.

"Get down," Yates commanded. "Bail enforcement! Hands where I can see them!"

A door slammed farther back in the apartment, and there was a crashing sound. The woman was seized by the neck of her robe and jerked out of sight, still shrieking. Camaro's pulse leaped as she closed on the screaming woman.

"Hold up a second!" Yates commanded. Camaro went on.

The hallway ran side to side along the width of the apartment, punctuated left, right, and center by closed doors. Yates broke right, and Camaro took the middle door. Her door was partly broken, and it came apart into lightweight pieces when she kicked it in. "Bathroom," she announced. "Clear!"

"There's a boy in here!" Yates shouted out, and Camaro heard the terrified bawling of a child.

Camaro cut left and advanced down the hallway. She heard the muffled sound of the woman weeping. A boot to the door split it down the center, and one half tumbled to the floor while the other hung loosely from brass hinges. She was through it before thought, the Glock searching out ahead of her.

Lukas hit Camaro on the side of the head with his pistol in the moment before she saw him. She reeled, her balance unsettled, but she held on to her weapon. In the crazy tilt of her vision she saw Lukas with Vicki Nelson pulled to him. Her face was red and streaked with tears, and she pulled against his arm. Her struggling spoiled Lukas's aim, and he fired a round into the wall.

Camaro came at him hard, passing underneath his extended arm and catching him center mass. The three of them tumbled together, crashing into a dresser and spinning to the floor in a mass of limbs and flesh. Camaro lost the Glock then, the textured grip slipping free of her.

They rolled. Vicki fell loose. Camaro scrambled to mount Lukas, but he was already crabbing backward with the wall behind him, leveraging himself off the floor. His gun came around, and she grabbed his wrist. Lukas wound his free hand into her hair and wrenched her around. She twisted against him. His fingers found the side of her face and then her throat. The gun canted toward her.

Yates was inside the shattered doorway. "Let her go, Collier! You don't have a chance!"

Lukas's fingers closed around Camaro's windpipe. "Shoot him," she managed.

"Let her loose!"

"Fuck you," Lukas shouted. "Shoot me, and the bitch gets it!"

"Shoot him," Camaro hissed. Spots swirled in her vision.

"He won't shoot," Lukas said. "He doesn't want to hit you."

Yates sighted in Lukas. His aim was steady. "I'll drop you where you stand."

"I don't buy it. Throw the gun down or she's dead."

Camaro shook her head violently. She worked a foot backward

between Lukas's. He held the gun to her with his right hand and gripped her with his left. He didn't throttle her more tightly when she reached back behind his grappling arm. "Don't do it," she told Yates.

"I can't let him kill you," Yates said. "I won't have that on my conscience."

"That's right, old man. Drop it, and I let her go. It's that easy."

"Don't," Camaro forced out. She felt the blood trapped in her face. Her heartbeat was deafening in her ears. Vicki lay on the floor, sobbing. No one paid her any mind.

Yates kept his weapon leveled. "I'm not putting away my gun, son. That's not how this works."

"You dumb old bastard! Back out of the room."

"I'm sorry, Camaro," Yates said. He stepped backward through the door.

"And I'm sorry you have to go," Lukas said in Camaro's ear.

At the edge of unconsciousness, she moved. He was taller, and his center of gravity higher. She pulled with her arm and pressed back with her hips in the same movement, driving up through his body and turning herself into a fulcrum. Camaro heard him exclaim once as he went over, crashing hard to the floor on his back, his limbs tangled.

Air rushed back into her lungs, and everything sharpened. Lukas rolled onto his knees and brought his pistol up. Camaro blocked it aside, and another shot went wild. She cocked a fist in the moment he speared her, exploding off the floor and driving his shoulder into her gut.

She hit something, and it gave way in a clamor of breaking glass. Air fell away behind her, and then she landed on metal, something stabbing her leg. Lukas was above her, his face twisted. Camaro got a knee between them and thrust him back. He hit the shattered frame of the broken window.

A gun thundered once and then a second and third time. Lukas launched himself down the skeletal steps of the fire escape they were on, trailing glass fragments as he went. Camaro's lungs bellowed, still pumping oxygen into her system. She struggled to get to her feet. When she sat up, she found herself on the broken windowsill.

She saw Yates entering the room with his gun up, and on the floor

Vicki with Camaro's weapon clasped in both hands. She fired again, though Lukas was gone, and Camaro felt the heat of the bullet. Yates covered her with his body then, forcing the weapon down. Vicki let go, and the Glock tumbled free.

Camaro lunged for the fallen gun, fire in her leg. She made it to her feet. "I'll get him, take care of her!"

"Camaro—"

"I don't have time to argue with you! Take care of her!"

She climbed through the window onto the fire escape. Without looking back, she descended quickly, jumping steps to each landing. Lukas was not in sight. Camaro slid down the ladder to the asphalt alley bordering the apartment building and spun in place, searching for a sign. She chose and moved.

The space at the back of the building was open, with two Dumpsters filled with trash. Alleys split off in three directions. Camaro dashed down the nearest one until she emerged onto the next street. Lukas wasn't there.

She backtracked and headed for the front of the building. Sirens were in the air. The sidewalk came into view, and she bulleted toward it. She reached it at the same moment a car screeched to a halt a dozen feet shy of the curb. The driver looked at her through the windshield. Camaro recognized Hannon.

Hannon opened her door. Camaro spun on her heel and ran back the way she came. No bullet chased after her, and no one cried for her to stop. The sirens were louder than ever, and when she made it to the next block she put her gun away and slowed to a fast walk.

# CHAPTER FIFTY-FOUR

Way got a ride to Pacific Grove with a Salinas police officer. He tapped his thumb insistently on the armrest as they plodded along in morning traffic. They passed through the streets almost lazily. Way simmered. By the time they reached the apartment building the simmer had grown to a rolling boil, and he bailed out of the unit before it had a chance to completely stop in front of Vicki Nelson's building.

A trio of Pacific Grove Police Department vehicles was parked out front with an ambulance, and a police line had been set up, manned by two officers. Way showed his badge and ID to them as he approached. "Deputy U.S. Marshal Way. Who's in charge of the scene?"

"The FBI just got here."

Way ground his teeth. "Okay. I'm coming in."

He ducked under the tape and entered the lobby. From upstairs came the clamor of voices in conversation, and he mounted the steps one by one, feeling a rod of tension in the back of his neck that hooked into the base of his skull and held on like a claw. Blackness hovered over him. The cops were congregated on the third floor, and they stopped talking when they saw his look.

Way showed his ID again. "U.S. Marshals. Is Special Agent Brock here?"

"Inside," one of the policemen said.

Way noted that the front door was broken open and there were black boot prints just below the knob. A man's foot. In the living room was another officer and two men in coats, their backs to Way. When Way cleared his throat, they turned. Brock smiled. "Glad you could make it," he said.

"Where's Lukas Collier?" Way asked. He kept his voice modulated.

"We don't know, but there's a BOLO."

"There was a BOLO before. What are we doing now?"

"We're getting ready to take the witnesses out."

"What witnesses?"

"We have the woman Lukas was shacking up with in custody in the back, plus her son. They're both in shock, so we have a medic with them. We're also holding a man who says he knows you."

"Who?"

"Jeremy Yates."

Mixed anger and surprise stabbed at the back of Way's eyes. He blinked the pain away. "Jeremy Yates the bail bondsman. From Virginia."

"Seems like it."

"Where's Hannon?"

"She's with Yates."

Way turned toward the back of the apartment, but Brock put up a hand.

"What?" Way asked.

"You look a little on edge. Maybe you want to let us handle things for a while. We're taking the whole thing back out of here as soon as the county's crime-scene people have a chance to go over the place."

"I'm fine. I want to see my partner."

Brock looked at him and then shrugged. "Okay."

Past Brock and the rest, Way looked into one of the bedrooms, its door shattered, and saw a woman with blankets wrapped around her, face and eyes puffy from tears, talking quietly to a female paramedic. She clung tightly to a small boy, whose face was likewise distorted from crying. Way made a note of the broken window, the glass scattered inside and out.

He found Hannon and Yates in the second bedroom. It was perfect for a child, with a neat IKEA bed and posters on the walls. A small table was set up for coloring and crafts. Yates sat in an adult-sized chair in the corner, and Hannon had a spot on the bed beside him. They were discussing something when Way entered but stopped as soon as he stepped through the door. Yates regarded him from across the room. Hannon opened her mouth to speak, but Way raised a finger to her. "Not a word," he said. "Out."

Hannon stayed silent and left the room with only one look back toward Yates. Way closed the door behind her and rested his forehead against the thin wood. Seconds turned into a minute until finally he turned toward Yates. He said nothing.

Yates broke the impasse. "Nice to meet you face-to-face," he said. "If you're Way."

"I am."

"Looks like you're a step behind again, Deputy. You missed my son's murder, and now you missed Lukas Collier. You're going to give the Marshals Service a bad reputation."

"How long have you been in California?"

"Long enough to know you folks don't really know what you're doing."

"And you do?"

"I've got boots that are older than you, Deputy Way. Finding people was my business a long time before you got into it."

"So how does it work?" Way asked. "You kick down the door, you come in guns blazing, but you miss the target?"

"I told the whole story to Deputy Hannon. She's an agreeable woman. You're lucky to have her on your team."

"I don't want to talk to Hannon. I want you to tell me how it is that you're here and Lukas is not. And I want you to make it clear to me why I shouldn't have your ass dragged off to jail for interfering with the apprehension of a fugitive."

Yates stuck his booted feet out in front of him and relaxed into his chair, his hands folded over his stomach. "You ever heard about something called *Taylor v. Taintor*? A little case from 1873. They probably covered it at marshal school."

"*Taylor v. Taintor* covers your ass if you're licensed to operate as a bail fugitive recovery agent in the state where you are. You're from Virginia, and this is California. You're a long way from home."

"California allows out-of-state bail enforcement for anyone with a bench warrant establishing cause," Yates said. "All I have to do is deliver my skip to state authorities within forty-eight hours of picking him up. It's all in the law books."

Way's voice shook. "You have one of those warrants, Mr. Yates?"

"As a matter of fact, I do."

Way took a long step toward Yates. "Then where the hell is Lukas Collier? If you're so goddamned smart, why don't you enlighten me on that subject? Since you like dealing with people who are agreeable."

Yates's eyes grew dark. "You better watch how you talk to me."

"I'll talk to you however I want," Way said. He rounded the bed to stand over Yates. "I'll put you in cuffs and bury you under paperwork until you don't even remember what year it is, let alone what your rights are. You think just because the FBI is here that I can't put you down? Because I can and I will. Everyone here seems to think they can skirt the law. It. Stops. Now. You tell me what you know, or I swear to God I'll drag you out of this room in cuffs."

"You telling me you can't run your own circus?" Yates asked.

"Don't you push me, old man."

Yates was still. "Send Deputy Hannon back in. She and I get along."

# CHAPTER FIFTY-FIVE

Camaro kept on until she could barely hear the police sirens. She made it out of Pacific Grove in the back of a taxi she called from the phone at the front desk of a Howard Johnson Inn. She had the driver drop her off at the same church she'd used as her way station beginning with her first rendezvous with Yates and followed the path through the woods to Annabel's house.

She scrambled over the back fence and ran in a crouch to the rear door. Empty flower beds were laid in on both sides of the steps, ringed with black rocks. Camaro found the plastic rock with the house key inside and let herself in.

Several times she tried to call Yates, but he didn't answer his phone. At first it rang, but after a while it went straight to voice mail. The silence gave her pause.

In the quiet of the house she took her boots off in the guest bedroom and set her gun on the nightstand before lying down in her clothes. She closed her eyes and practiced breathing, in through the nose and out through the mouth, until her body felt heavy. She let darkness overtake her, and she fell completely away.

When she woke again it was not from any sound. The house was as still as before. She sat up and tried Yates again. No answer. She dialed the hospital instead and asked to speak to her sister's doctor. They had her on hold for a while. Finally a woman answered. "This is Dr. Fort. Who am I speaking to?"

"My name's Camaro Espinoza."

"Michelle Amado's sister."

"That's right. I wanted to ask about her condition."

"Are you available to come in, Ms. Espinoza?"

Camaro stood up sharply. "What's wrong? What's happened to her?"

"Don't be alarmed. Your sister is out of the intensive care unit. I would consider her condition serious but stable. There's always the chance of complications, but she's improved so much in the past twenty-four hours that I'm feeling confident. I thought you might want to see her."

"Is she awake?"

"From time to time."

"Can she speak?"

"She's off the respirator. The rest is up to her."

"I'll be there," Camaro said.

She ended the call and dropped the phone on the bed while she changed clothes. Something stung at the back of her leg when she took off her jeans, and she noticed the gash on her thigh for the first time. There was blood down her leg and a slash cut in the denim. The bedspread was stained red. Camaro felt for glass in the wound, but there was nothing.

She went to the bathroom and found a bottle of alcohol under the sink and a white washcloth. She twisted to see the back of her leg in the mirror and poured alcohol over the wound. The stinging was sudden and intense, but she made no sound. Afterward she soaked the washcloth in steaming-hot water and dabbed away the blood before exploring the laceration more carefully.

It was wide enough and deep enough for stitches, and it was still bleeding. Camaro rummaged in a cabinet. A square hand mirror with a fake tortoiseshell frame was stuffed underneath a pile of towels. She left the bathroom and passed through the house on bare feet, bringing the mirror, the alcohol, and the washcloth with her. In the kitchen she went to the beading case in the corner and lifted it onto the table.

The case folded open in sections to reveal compartments full of colorful beads, large and small. Camaro searched through the bottom of the case until she found some loops of fine wire, which she set aside. She looked further and found a spool of lightweight fishing line with a four-pound test. Another quick search turned up a needle. She took these.

She turned on one of the stove burners and let the flames rise, blue tipped with orange. Afterward she ran the sink until the water steamed. She measured out a length of fishing line and clipped it with a pair of kitchen shears. The line she scrubbed under the water, and then she doused it in alcohol in a cereal bowl.

The needle was not fine, but it fit the line. Camaro held it over the burner, just letting the flames touch it, until the metal was almost too hot to hold. She lifted the dripping fishing line out of the alcohol and fed it through the eye of the needle.

She set the mirror on a chair and held the needle behind her back. When the hot tip touched her flesh, she groaned through gritted teeth. As the metal penetrated, she made herself breathe normally. She drew the edges of the wound together with a continuous locking stitch, then tied off the end and cut it close with the kitchen shears. She tossed the bloody needle into the bowl of alcohol and sighed.

Back in the guest room she changed into a different set of jeans and put on her boots. She raised her phone to call Yates again, then stopped. She opened her call log and saw the recently dialed numbers there. A press brought up received calls. She looked at the numbers listed.

Camaro found her bag, put it on the bed, and packed quickly. Afterward she ensured that a round was in the Glock's chamber and slipped the gun in the back of her waistband. She took the bag with her when she left.

# CHAPTER FIFTY-SIX

Way cl osed the door on her, and Hannon found herself in the apartment's hallway alone. She heard Brock and the other special agent talking to each other in low voices. She went to the other room and peeked in. The woman, Vicki Nelson, was whispering something to the paramedic, whose name Hannon didn't know. Her son was rigid and silent, looking as though he might erupt into a scream at any moment. Hannon knocked quietly on the door frame, and their conversation stopped. "May I come in?" Hannon asked.

"Sure," the paramedic said.

Hannon entered. Pieces of door were all around her on the floor. A stiff, cold breeze blew through the broken window, lowering the temperature into the forties. Vicki had been barely dressed when Hannon arrived on the scene. Now she was in sweatpants and a sweatshirt, thick socks on her feet, a quilted blanket draped over her like a cloak.

The paramedic had latex gloves on, and her jump kit was open on the floor. She stood up as Hannon stepped over the threshold and came close. She spoke to Hannon quietly. "You can't keep her here. She's going to need a full examination at the hospital, including a rape kit. She's riding right on the edge. I gave her some Klonopin, and that's enough to keep her from getting hysterical again, but this is not a good situation for her. The kid's in bad shape, too. He needs a counselor from Social Services."

"I'll take care of it," Hannon said. "I'll talk to her for a few minutes, and then we'll see about getting them both out of here, all right?"

"I'll clean up my gear."

Hannon stilled her with a hand on her arm. "Leave it for now. Wait out front with the officers and tell them what you told me. When I'm done, I'll let you know."

The paramedic seemed reluctant to go, but Hannon patted her and gave her a smile. Hannon went to the corner and grabbed the chair there. She dragged it around so she could sit almost face-to-face with Vicki. The woman stared into the middle distance and shivered as if she were nearly frozen.

"Do you remember me?" Hannon asked Vicki. "I'm the deputy U.S. marshal who found you and Mr. Yates."

Vicki was silent, staring, and Hannon thought perhaps she was lost to any further conversation. Then slowly Vicki's eyes turned toward her, and she nodded slightly. "Yes," she said.

"Great. Then you know I'm one of the good guys."

"He made me," Vicki said.

"Who did? Lukas Collier?"

"Yes. He made me do it all."

"What's your son's name?"

"Brendan."

Hannon addressed the boy. "Did he do anything to you, Brendan?"

The child shook his head slowly, his eyes brilliant and wide. Vicki stifled a sob and pulled him closer to her. "He said he'd kill my boy if I didn't..."

"I understand. He's a real bad man."

Vicki said nothing. She shivered again.

"How badly did he hurt you?" Hannon asked. "If you don't want to talk in front of your son, you don't have to."

Fresh tears welled up, and Vicki shook violently. "No. I'll tell you. He came in and he told me to take care of him like I took care of Jake. I knew he'd kill Brendan and he'd kill me if I didn't do what he told me to do. Even when he...when he took me to bed and I had to—"

"Shh," Hannon said. She reached out to touch Vicki, but the woman flinched away. Hannon dropped her hand. "I don't think Brendan needs to hear that. They'll do a rape kit on you at the hospital. Whatever he did to you, they'll make sure it's all recorded. But he's not going to hurt you anymore. That's done. He's never coming back here again."

"He hurt me," Vicki said.

"Yes, I know. Do you understand you're under protection now? There's going to be a police officer with both of you every step of the way until Collier is in custody. You are safe."

"Okay," Vicki whispered. It was barely audible.

"Do you have any idea where he might have run to? Any people he talked about? Any places? Did he mention what he planned to do with the police looking for him?"

She didn't answer.

"Vicki, listen," Hannon said, "I can't help you if you don't help me. Anything he told you, anything at all, you need to tell me now."

"He talked about that woman," Vicki said.

"What woman?"

"The woman he wanted to kill."

"Did he mention the name Camaro Espinoza?" Hannon asked.

"Yes. Camaro. It's a funny name. He said he was going to get her to come to him and then he was going to hurt her bad. And then he was gonna kill her. But she came for him. She came with that old man, but I don't know where she went. Out the window after Lukas. Gone. Both of them gone."

"To where? Try to remember. To where? Did Lukas ever say?"

Vicki continued, her voice gaining strength. "He was talking a lot about Los Angeles. How he had friends there and he was going to make a whole lot of money. I didn't want him to tell me anything. I thought he was going to kill us so we couldn't say anything about him. I thought he was going to kill us!"

"It's okay, calm down," Hannon said.

"You have to believe me, there was nothing I could do. If I tried to tell the cops anything, he would have gone crazy. He would have killed us both. I couldn't let that happen."

"I understand. No one's judging you. But, listen, I need you to do something for me, okay? Can you do something for me?"

"Anything you want."

"When someone asks you who came into the apartment, you tell them—"

222

A man's voice cut in. "Deputy Hannon?"

Hannon looked behind her. Special Agent Brock stood in the doorway. "Yes, Agent Brock?" she asked.

"When you're done questioning Ms. Nelson, I understand she needs to be seen at a hospital. We'll take over from there. Tell Deputy Way when he's finished talking to Mr. Yates that I'd like to see him outside."

"I'll do that," Hannon said.

Brock smiled thinly. "Much appreciated."

# CHAPTER FIFTY-SEVEN

Way clamped his jaw shut and listened to everything Brock had to say. He endured the passive-aggressive scolding and the smarmy declarations of interagency cooperation, and then he walked away. He found Hannon waiting by the car, and a new wave of ire passed over him. "You and I need to have a serious conversation."

"Let's have it," Hannon replied.

"Not in front of them. Let's go."

They got into the car. Hannon turned the engine over and let the car idle. Way stared straight out through the windshield, watching Brock confer with the county crime-scene examiners. His thumbs hands ached from clenching them.

"I guess what I want to know is how you ended up here without me," Way said after he saw Brock and the other FBI agent walk toward their dark blue Lincoln Navigator. "Because that seems kind of odd to me. Seeing as how we're supposed to be on the same page."

"There wasn't time to wait for you. I had to follow."

"I could have been on the scene with a police unit. I could have been right there! But you follow Yates all the way here without so much as a phone call letting me know what's up. So when I finally hear, it's all over with. The lady and her kid are saved, and the old bastard's in custody."

"I didn't even know who he was," Hannon said. "I've never seen the man."

"But you followed him anyway. Why? Because you had some kind of divine inspiration? A random old man wanders down Derrick Perkins's street, and you make the connection between him and Lukas? Is that how it works? Tell me how it works, because I'm not sure I'm completely up to speed."

He glared at her. "I made a spur-of-the-moment decision to follow up. I didn't know he was going to lead me directly to Lukas. I had no idea if he was involved at all. It was a guess, and it paid off. Until the shooting started, I could have been following anyone."

Way thought of Yates and scowled. "I told them to charge him with reckless endangerment. And he's not allowed to kick down a door in the state of California. I checked that. He thinks he has his ass covered, but it is hanging out there. Man, it is *hanging*."

"Did they let him go?"

"Yes," Way spat. "Free as a bird. They told him not to leave the area, but you know that's going to do no good. The first chance he gets, he's going to fly out of here and never come back. And if you think these idiots are going to go through the bother of trying to reel him in again, you're crazy. No, he's totally clear of all this. Walked in and screwed up the whole goddamned thing for the rest of us, and now he's out with no consequences. They're even letting him keep his gun."

"I'm sorry."

"Yeah, to hell with that. Everybody's sorry for something. What I want to know is where he got his intel and if he has a line into Lukas we don't know about. Because if he's set to make another run at Lukas somewhere else, I want to be there."

Brock's Lincoln drove away. Way resisted giving him the finger as he went.

"Unless you want to tail him everywhere he goes, we can't know where Yates will be," Hannon said. "And that's assuming he doesn't give up and leave like you said he will."

"He's not gonna give up. Lukas killed his son. He flew three thousand miles just for the chance to put a hole in the man. He'll do what he has to do, and then he'll run like hell. But first he has to find Lukas, and there's no way Lukas stays around here after this. No way."

Hannon offered nothing. She turned on the heater, and a warm flow of air passed over Way's feet. He was sweating in his coat already, but he didn't object. Other thoughts turned over and over in his mind. They slowly coalesced around Yates, settling into detail. His gaze drifted across the GPS screen in the center console.

"What's Yates driving?" Way asked.

"A Hyundai Santa Fe."

"Rental, right?"

"Sure."

"You think a vehicle like that has a built-in GPS?"

Hannon turned to him. "It might."

"Get the rental company on the horn and find out where their offices are. We'll go straight from here to there."

"Keith—"

"Just do it," Way said.

He listened while she made the necessary calls. It took five minutes to get what they needed. Hannon put the car in gear and rolled.

"They're going to talk to the woman some more at the hospital," Way said. "She's gonna be useless. What's her deal? She his girlfriend or something?"

"Or something. She was his hostage. He used her like a piece of meat. If Yates hadn't come in there when he did, he might have killed her and her kid."

"What else did she tell you?"

Hannon was slow to answer. "Keith, maybe this isn't worth it. We're too exposed. There's no way Lukas is going to let himself be taken alive, so no matter who finally nails him, it's going to be done."

Way felt darkness pool in his stomach. "What are you saying?"

"I'm saying maybe it's time to let it go."

Way ground his teeth until they ached and made no reply at all.

# CHAPTER FIFTY-EIGHT

Camaro asked for Dr. Fort at the front desk and was directed to an office near the emergency room. She waited ten minutes until the woman arrived. She was black and slim, with a serious face. She seemed very young. "Ms. Espinoza?" she said when she offered her hand. "I'm glad to meet you."

"Is my sister awake?"

"I think she might be."

They went to Annabel's room together while the doctor reeled off the damage done by Lukas Collier's bullets. Cracked scapula. Punctured lung. Bullet fragments in the liver. A kidney too damaged to function. Camaro heard with half an ear, her attention focused ahead of them, step-by-step, all the way. At the door, Dr. Fort held it open, and Camaro went through.

A soft light over Annabel's bed glowed white, painting a pale shroud over her. At first Camaro thought she was asleep, but at the sound of her footsteps, Annabel stirred. Her eyes opened. They were wet and dark.

"So she is awake," Dr. Fort said. "Michelle, I'm going to have a look in your eyes for just a moment. Be ready for a bright light."

Camaro watched Annabel submit to the doctor's examination. She flinched when the penlight shone in each eye.

"We were worried about a concussion when she was first brought in," Dr. Fort told Camaro, "but she's looking good. Everything's great. Your sister is tough."

"Yeah," Camaro said.

"I'll leave the two of you alone."

Dr. Fort stepped out and closed the door behind her. Camaro stayed where she was. She looked at Annabel, and Annabel looked at her. Neither said anything as a minute turned into two. Finally Annabel sighed, and her hand twitched like a fallen bird. She lifted it from the covers and held it up shakily.

Camaro came close and took her hand. There was more heat in it than there had been before, but it was still cool.

"I'm still here," Camaro said.

Annabel nodded. Her lips were badly chapped. She breathed raggedly, but it was real breath. "Becca?" she asked. Her voice creaked.

"They tell me she's okay. I'm not sure where she is."

"He tried to kill her."

"I know."

"That policewoman is dead."

"Yes."

A tear formed in the corner of Annabel's eye and rolled heavily down her cheek. Her lower lip trembled. "I'm so scared."

"The doctor says you're going to make it. Everything looks good. But it'll take time. It all takes time. You can't rush it."

"Where is that man?"

Camaro frowned. "He's out there. Somewhere."

"Are you going to find him?"

"I'm going to try."

Annabel inclined her head very slightly in the merest of nods. "Good."

"Annabel," Camaro said.

She saw Annabel's eyes quicken at the sound of her full name. Her rough breathing hitched in her chest. Camaro heard the thick wetness deep in her lungs. Annabel said nothing.

"You're going to have to do the rest of this without me. With Jake's brother gone, I have to follow. So whatever happens next, you're going to be alone."

Annabel's hand twitched. She felt around her until Camaro closed her hand over hers. "You can't let him kill you," Annabel said.

"I won't. But listen to me, I need you to understand something. Even if I get him, I have to stay away for a while. Maybe for a long time.

There's too much heat here, and there are too many questions. It's better if we don't see each other until all of that goes away."

"You're leaving me?"

"Not forever. And I promise you one day it'll be different. You said you wanted to be a family. I can do that. I think I can, anyway. But for now it's too complicated."

"I don't want to go on being apart," Annabel said, and she clung to Camaro's hand with sudden strength. "It's what killed Dad. As soon as we stopped being together, it went bad. First Mom, and then you. We can't lose everything."

Camaro touched Annabel's hair and tried a smile that died on her lips. "It was always more complicated than that."

"Promise me you're telling the truth. Promise me you'll come back to me someday."

"Someday," Camaro said.

"Promise."

Camaro felt the corners of her mouth turn down. She felt a weight on her that she hadn't been conscious of before. Annabel still squeezed her hand. "I promise."

"Then go kill him. Kill him and get it over with."

"I will," Camaro said, and she bent over Annabel to kiss her sister lightly on the forehead. Annabel's skin was cool.

"I love you, Camaro. Always."

"Always."

She left before the doctor could return. No one called her back.

# CHAPTER FIFTY-NINE

Camaro sat in the coffeehouse where she had spent a quiet half hour with Carly Russo a lifetime before. She had a turkey sandwich with Swiss cheese and a hearty mustard and drank a large cup of hot tea that was redolent of cinnamon and other, unidentifiable spices. Her bag was stuffed under the table, and she kept her back to the rear wall so she could watch the street.

The coffeehouse burbled with sound, the other tables busy with customers taking lunch or tapping away on laptops with earbuds plugged into their skulls. A pair of servers worked their way around the room, delivering food and fresh drinks, while still more customers lined up for take-out service and that important noontime burst of caffeine.

She had the ringer turned down on her phone, but it vibrated on the table. She checked the number and answered. "Where have you been?"

"Police custody," Yates said. "I missed you there."

"I got out. I'm in Carmel now. It's a place called the Roastery, on Ocean Avenue. Do you think you can find it?"

"Yeah, I think I can find it. The question is, what do we plan to do once we meet there? Lukas is long gone. He's in the wind."

"What if I told you there was a way to find him?" Camaro asked.

"I'd say I'm interested to hear it."

"Come meet me. I'm not going anywhere."

She waited twenty minutes and then saw Yates's Santa Fe cruise past the front of the coffeehouse. Another five minutes passed, and then he was there, stepping out of the cold into the warm, scented air. He spotted her and wove his way through the tables to hers. He sat down opposite her.

"You're looking run-down," Camaro told him.

"I always look this way."

"Order something to eat. We have time."

Yates flagged down a server, and she brought him a menu. Camaro waited until he made a selection, and they stared at each other.

"How's your sister?" Yates asked.

"She's going to make it."

"How does she feel about you haring off after the man who shot her?"

"She's okay with it."

"Runs in the family, I guess."

"She knows I can't let it go."

"I suppose that's something you and Lukas Collier have in common."

"I don't have anything in common with him."

Yates made a gesture of surrender. "Forgive me."

"Forget it."

"You said you had a way to find Lukas," Yates said. "I'm all ears."

"He's gonna run. You said yourself he'll run."

"That's true. Lukas may be a nasty son of a bitch, but he's not completely stupid. He had a pretty good shot at getting you for a little while there, but as soon as we rolled up on him in that apartment, he had to know the game was up. Whatever he planned on doing, that's totally shot. His best bet now is to run and keep running until he leaves the heat behind. They'll never stop looking for him, though. Not after he killed a cop. There's not a corner in this country where they won't search."

"Could he lose himself in a big enough city?"

"Sure, for a while. People have been known to stay lost for years. But here's the thing: sooner or later they slip up. And you have to remember it's the Feds and the Marshals Service after him. Doesn't matter if it's one year or ten years, they won't forget about him. They even got Whitey Bulger."

"Who?"

"Never mind."

"My point is that everything says Lukas will run to LA," Camaro said. "He sent money ahead, and he's got some kind of plan. So maybe he's only going to run a little way before he turns and fights."

"It would be foolish of him."

"We have an address where he sent the money. We have a name: Konnor Spencer. Those have to be good for something. And there's something else, too."

Yates's order came, and Camaro sat back while he ate his soup with a piece of crusty bread to sop up the last drops. He slurped his coffee when he drank it, and the corners of his mustache got wet. Camaro said nothing.

After a while Yates colored slightly and wiped his mouth. "Quit staring, will you? I'm a little bashful when I eat."

"I wouldn't waste your time if all I had were a couple of clues and nothing else to go on. What I have can put us right on top of him, and he won't even know it's happening."

"Well, don't keep me in suspense. What do you got?"

"We need to get to LA. Like right now. If we get there fast enough, we have a real chance."

# CHAPTER SIXTY

They got on the road. Camaro gave Yates an address in Los Angeles. They would be on the road for hours, and for a while they simply listened to the satellite radio and drove on US-101, skirting Los Padres National Forest and skipping through farmland carved out of the space between high-riding hills and low mountains. They were two hours out when Camaro's phone rang. She checked the number and answered.

"I understand you left today," Special Agent Brock said.

"That's right."

"It's good you took my advice. There's nothing left for you here."

"I won't be back," Camaro said. "Not for a long time."

"I didn't think you would be. Thank you for that. It makes my life a lot less complicated."

"I had to kill Jake, you know. I didn't have a choice."

"I know. I never questioned it. And it turns out he was putting the screws to his other woman as well. She gave him six thousand dollars over the last twelve months, all in cash. Don't know where it went or what it was for, but he wasn't exactly living the high life. Who knows? Maybe he was going to get into his brother's business."

"What is his brother's business?"

"Whatever he can buy, sell, or trade. If it's illegal, Lukas Collier wants a piece of it. Before he set out for California he was neck deep in a trafficking scheme, bringing guns up from places like Virginia and selling them in New York and New Jersey. That got him on ATF's radar and eventually the Marshals Service's. We have a hand in that, too."

"So who goes after him? All of you people want him."

"We're working on that. I'm finding Deputy Marshal Hannon very easy to work with."

"The other one's a prick," Camaro said.

"He is. But you don't have to worry about it. Good-bye, Camaro. Enjoy Miami."

Camaro ended the call without saying anything else. Her heartbeat was up, and it made her stitches throb. The fishing line was holding. She toyed with the phone for a few moments before stuffing it back into her pocket. Yates glanced over at her, but she directed her attention away from him, out into the winter fields that dragged by beyond her window.

"So which one was it?" Yates asked.

"Who?"

"On the phone."

"The FBI."

"He doesn't seem like a bad kind."

"I wouldn't know."

"Why don't I believe you?"

Camaro shot Yates a look. "Believe what you want. I'm here for my sister."

Yates made an affirmative sound. "You're the one she always came to? Big sister? Always there?"

"Something like that."

"That's a good thing. I had a younger sister who died when she was about your age. Stomach cancer. Ate her up from the inside. I was there every step of the way, and before that I was the one who ran off the bad boys who'd come sniffing around her skirt. I made sure she got together with a good man. I always wished she'd had sons and daughters of her own so we could see how things turned out for them."

Camaro didn't speak for a while. She watched the lane line slip by on the highway ahead. "When my sister was fourteen she was seeing this guy in secret. He was nineteen. One day she tells me she thinks she's pregnant and she doesn't know what to do. The guy won't talk to her anymore. She can't tell our dad or he'll go crazy."

Yates listened.

"So I went to the guy's apartment and I knocked on the door. When he opened up, I kicked his ass. I kicked it hard. He had a girl with him, and she was so scared she locked herself in a closet and called the police."

"What happened then?"

"I left. The cops came, and he wouldn't identify me. A few days later he drops an envelope full of cash in our mailbox with Bel's name on it. So she could take care of things. Then he moved, and neither one of us ever saw him again.

"My sister doesn't make good choices," Camaro said. "Whatever helps a person steer clear of trouble, she doesn't have it. And that's definitely true when it comes to men."

Yates spared a look in her direction. "How about you? What are your men like?"

Camaro's mouth turned down. "I don't have that problem."

"Don't like men, or don't pick the wrong ones?"

"I don't keep them around at all," she said. "That's the easiest way to do it."

"Loneliest, too."

"I'm not lonely."

The miles passed with no more conversation between them. Yates fiddled with the dial and found a station playing classic country from Willie Nelson, Waylon Jennings, and others who fit the mold. Camaro listened with her face pressed into a frown. When the radio played "Okie from Muskogee," she reached over and turned it off completely.

"Not a Merle Haggard fan?" Yates asked.

"I'd rather listen to nothing."

"That's classic music from my youth. Ol' Merle wrote that to support the troops over in Vietnam. I was back by then, but I appreciated the sentiment. Only got a few folks these days who'd write a song like that."

"I still don't want to hear it."

"Fair enough. What's your song?"

"My song?" Camaro asked.

"Sure. Everybody's got a song. My wife and I, we like 'Unforgettable.' They sang that at our wedding reception for the first dance. I have an old record I bought back in 1961 with all of Nat King Cole's hits on it. We play it on our anniversaries and dance right there in the living room. I won't say it makes me feel young again, but it does make me feel a little less old."

"I don't have anything like that," Camaro said.

"That's too bad. It's hard going through life without a song."

"I'll take your word for it."

Yates eased back in his seat and was quiet for a while. Finally he said, "I know it's none of my business, but the old man in me makes me want to impart some wisdom."

"Like what?"

"I looked at you, and first thing I knew you were tough. You went ahead and proved it, too. But the thing is, it's not enough to be hard. You have to let the softer side show through now and again, or you lose it, sometimes for good."

"I don't have time for that right now."

"Do you ever?"

"Hey, you don't even *know* me," Camaro said.

"Not in particular, but I know your type in general. Got a fight in you the whole world is welcome to. Some deserve it, most don't. All I'm saying is, don't let somebody like Lukas Collier turn off the lights in there."

Camaro turned away from Yates and looked at the hint of her reflection in the window. "Lukas isn't taking anything from me. Not anymore."

"That's good to hear, because you seem like someone worth knowing, Camaro Espinoza. I'd hate for you to turn away from that."

She looked back toward Yates. "You going to tell me to save my soul?"

"Souls are God's lookout, not mine."

"I just want to see him die."

"I hope your wish comes true. I surely do."

They said nothing else. After a while Camaro heard him humming the Merle Haggard song to himself. She did not stop him.

# CHAPTER SIXTY-ONE

It was in the upper sixties under clear, bright skies when Lukas passed Santa Clarita and drove into the sprawl of LA. He put the windows down and let his left hand play in the air streaming past the car. He angled down into the Hollywood Hills on the way downtown. Almost at random he took the Alvarado Street exit and ended up on Sunset Boulevard.

He saw no stars, but there were out-of-season tourists on the sidewalks and filthy vagrants who hadn't yet been driven off by LA's finest. He spotted a Super 8 motel, painted canary yellow and wedged into a corner lot. For a moment he considered passing by, but instead he slowed and turned into the parking lot, taking the spot farthest from the street.

The manager behind the counter was a short, round Filipino man in a crisp white shirt. Lukas filled out the registration form with a lot of nonsense and passed it over.

"May I see your ID, please?" the man asked.

"I'm paying cash."

"We still need to see an ID."

Lukas scowled. He put a hundred dollars on the counter, then laid another hundred next to it. "One's for the room, and the other one's for you. I just want a place to lay my head until tomorrow, and I like my privacy. You got your form."

The manager examined the form doubtfully, then swept the bills off the counter. He made a card key for Lukas and handed it over. "It's on the second floor. I'll mark a map for you."

"Thanks, friend," Lukas said.

He had nothing to take with him except the clothes on his back, and he ascended the outdoor staircase to the second floor. The ice machine and a couple of vending machines were at the far end of the building, well away from his door, which meant peace and quiet for the time he'd be a resident.

Inside, the room was small and plain, without even a piece of generic art to adorn the off-white walls. Lukas locked the door and set the bar guard before heading to the sink. He washed his face with cold water, then scratched his scalp vigorously. He made a decision and took a towel from the wall rack, letting himself into the small room with the tub and toilet. He locked this door, too, before stripping out of his clothes.

The Colt went on top of the toilet tank. Lukas washed himself all over, twice, aware of tiny stinging cuts on his arms and neck that he hadn't noticed before. After he dried off, he examined his clothes for glass fragments and found a few in his shirt and clinging to his jeans. He dressed and went out into the room.

For a while he allowed himself to vegetate in front of the television, surfing channels, but eventually he realized he was only delaying the inevitable. He drew his phone out of his pocket and dialed.

It didn't take long for Konnor to answer. "My brother! I was starting to worry about you. No calls, and I got your package."

"Everything in there like it should be?"

"Close to ten thousand. Your brother came through."

"Is that going to be enough to make the buy?" Lukas asked.

"Plenty. We won't be able to tip, but who cares? I have people coming to make delivery at the toy store tomorrow, so all we need now is for you to make the connection."

"It'll be done. I got to make a call."

"Maybe you, me, and Jake can go out and grab some drinks tonight. See about picking up some ladies. Make a party out of it. What do you think?"

Lukas didn't speak for a long moment. "Jake's dead."

"What? When the hell did this happen?"

"A couple days ago. He got himself shot dead in his old lady's place."

"The same old lady you were talking about before?"

"It doesn't matter. We still have a connection in Salinas. One of

Jake's asshole friends. Guy doesn't know much about anything, but that doesn't mean he can't learn. But I can't head up there while he figures it out. I've got more heat coming down on me. I might have to keep my head down for a little while."

"Whatever you need, man. Semper fi."

"Semper fi," Lukas said without enthusiasm. "We make this first deal, I can afford to take a vacation for a while. Catch some waves. Maybe I'll shack up with one of those beach bunnies down by the boardwalk. Work out my grief."

"Well, you know I'm here for you. Anytime, anywhere."

"I'm gonna hold you to that. Talk to you later."

Lukas ended the call. He muted the TV and sat up in bed, then dialed a second number. This one took longer to go through. In the background he heard the thump and rhythm of hip-hop playing. "Yo, who's this?" asked the man on the other end.

"Otilio, it's Lukas."

"Lukas? Hey, Lukas! I was starting to wonder if I was gonna hear from you again, cuz. You keep me waiting too long, I make deals with someone else, you feel me?"

"Yeah, I feel you. I had some things to take care of, but it's all better now. My people tell me we can have the goods ready for you in forty-eight hours. We meet, we settle up, and everybody goes away happy until the next time."

"Are we still talking about the same amount of merchandise?"

"No change. You get everything you ask for, so long as I get everything I'm asking for."

"Have I ever cheated you before?"

"Never. That's why I like you."

Otilio laughed. "White-boy love! Okay, listen, I can get you exactly what we agreed on and deliver it anywhere at any time."

"You'll deliver when we deliver. Even exchange."

"You don't trust me?"

"Just doing business. I'll give you an address twelve hours in advance," Lukas said. "I don't want to see a huge crew."

"No *problema*. Talk to you soon, Lukas."

When the phone beeped and the call was over, Lukas took a deep breath and held it for a count of three before letting it ease out of his lungs. He wanted a cigarette, and he wanted something to drink with it. There had to be a liquor store nearby. But first he had to talk to Derrick. The deal was incomplete without someone to haul the load.

He called and called again. He left two messages. Derrick didn't answer. Lukas's mood grew dark. He left the room and lit a cigarette down in the parking lot, and then he went in search of beer.

# CHAPTER SIXTY-TWO

They were in Los Angeles with some time to spare before sundown. Traffic was dense and unforgiving. Camaro projected herself past all the slow-moving cars, trying to ignore the spring that coiled up steadily inside her, waiting for release.

"Take the exit onto the 10," Camaro said after a while.

"What next?" Yates asked.

"Watch for the 710 exit. Go south toward Long Beach."

"Will do. You think this is going to pay off?"

"As long as he still has the same phone."

"He might have ditched it. He might be over the border already."

Camaro glared at him. "You got any better ideas?"

Yates shook his head. "No, ma'am. I'm just being the voice of reason."

"You said crooks are stupid. They do dumb things and slip up."

"I did say that."

"So this is my play."

"I'm pulling for you. I really am."

"Watch for that exit. It comes up fast."

They were east of downtown, and if they kept on they would end up in Monterey Park, but the exit would carry them farther south. When the signs for I-710 south appeared, Yates followed them, and from there Camaro directed him off the freeway and onto the surface streets. They hadn't gone far when she called for a stop.

The street was narrow and ran along the length of the Long Beach Freeway, closed off on that side by a concrete wall. Houses had barred windows and sturdy fences built into low ramparts. Camaro pointed out a stretch of empty curb, and Yates parked. He killed the engine. "Where are we?" he asked.

"This is the house where I grew up," Camaro said.

She saw his eyes drift past her to the little white house with flowering vines overgrowing the fence in spots and a single tree on the lawn. When Camaro looked at it she saw through time, and in the driveway was parked a '74 Plymouth Barracuda with the cover pulled off and the hood up. A shiny V-Max motorcycle stood just inside the mouth of the open garage door, sharing space with a well-loved FXST Softail bought off the line in 1984.

"This is where it happens?" Yates asked.

"No, but it gets us there. Wait here."

She climbed out of the SUV without waiting for an answer and stepped off onto the dead grass adjoining the sidewalk. Two more steps brought her to the fence. A gust of wind caught her as she put her hands on the white-painted metal. She stood for a long while looking at the house. She had not seen it for a lifetime.

A glance back showed her Yates was still in the SUV. She nodded to him and set off along the street, heading two doors down to a house sided in red brick. The gate was unlocked, and there was an old Ram 1500 with scratched and dull black paint in the driveway. Camaro let herself into the yard and went to the front door. She rang the bell.

The curtains in the front window rustled, but she did not see the person looking out. A few moments later the door opened with the safety chain still in place. A gray-haired woman peered out. "Who are you? What do you want?"

"Mrs. Trujillo? It's me. Camaro Espinoza? I lived up the street from you. My father's name was Hector."

The woman looked at her, thoughts ticking. "Espinoza?"

"Yes. You remember us? My father died in 2007."

The moment was a long time in coming, but Camaro saw the light dawn. Mrs. Trujillo's face brightened. "Oh, yes! *You* are Camaro? You're so much older now!"

Camaro smiled. "Yes."

"One moment."

The door closed. Camaro heard Mrs. Trujillo unfastening the chain. The door opened again, wide this time, and Camaro saw the roundness of the old woman in her housedress. She stepped out and took Camaro by both shoulders before moving to kiss her cheek. Camaro had to stoop to allow it. Mrs. Trujillo was small.

"Come inside. Come in and see me. I haven't seen you in a long, long time. How is your sister?"

"She's good. She has a daughter now."

"Incredible! You must have a husband and a family, too."

"Not yet," Camaro said.

Mrs. Trujillo tsked. "You are a beautiful woman. Don't let it go to waste. Find a husband and then come back to the neighborhood. We miss Hector so much. He was a gentleman and a good friend to Roberto."

"I was hoping to see your husband."

"He's here. He's having a nap before dinner. Come sit down in the kitchen, and I'll wake him up."

The kitchen was not large, because none of the houses in this neighborhood were large. Camaro had a vague recollection of the Trujillos' house being like theirs, with three undersized bedrooms. It was difficult to raise any family of size in a home like this one, but it was done and had been for time out of mind.

Mrs. Trujillo stationed Camaro at the kitchen table and went to fetch her husband. She was back in a few minutes and bustled around the space, making fresh coffee and putting out cookies. After a short while Roberto Trujillo appeared.

Mr. Trujillo was the same age as Camaro's father would have been, and he was fleshy and well fed, like his wife. He wore a red plaid work shirt open over a white T, and his hair was mussed from sleep. When he saw Camaro he smiled, and she rose to let him hug her and touch her cheek. "Camaro, Camaro," he said. "Where have you been all this time?"

"She was in the army, remember?" Mrs. Trujillo said.

"Of course I remember. How is your sister, Camaro?"

"She's great."

"That's good to hear. We hoped she'd keep the house when your father died, but I guess she didn't see the point in staying. It would have been nice if she had, though. The new family is not the same. It's been ten years, but it's not the same."

"You'll stay to eat?" Mrs. Trujillo asked.

"I can't, actually," Camaro said. "I have someone waiting."

"Outside? Tell them to come in."

"We don't want to be any trouble."

"It's no trouble."

"Don't worry about it. He's fine out there. Really."

Mrs. Trujillo sighed. "If you say."

Roberto Trujillo reached across the table to take Camaro's hand, and she let him. "You have to tell us everything," he said. "It's been forever since we saw you last."

"Okay," Camaro said. "But I have a question for you."

# CHAPTER SIXTY-THREE

Yates sat in the SUV for an hour waiting for Camaro. He almost didn't see her when she left the house down the street. She approached quickly and got in. "West Third Street," she said. "A place called iFix."

Yates set off. Camaro stared out the windshield at the road, saying nothing and doing nothing. She could be utterly still.

"How did it go back there?"

"Fine."

"How long has it been since you saw this place?"

Camaro shot a look in his direction. "I was here when my father died."

"How long before that?"

Camaro was quiet, until Yates thought she wouldn't answer.

"Six years," she said.

"Long time."

"It's complicated."

"I imagine."

"I don't want to talk about it."

"Then we don't talk about it," Yates said. "Everybody has secrets."

They drove awhile. Yates considered turning on the radio again for the first time in two hundred miles.

Camaro said, "It's not a secret."

"No?"

"When I joined the service after 9/11, my father wasn't happy. I guess he thought I was better off doing something else."

"Like what?"

Camaro shrugged. "Meeting a guy. Getting married. Like any guy would want to marry a girl who breaks down bikes for fun and can kick his ass."

"Father teach you all that?"

"Yeah. I put my hands on an engine when I was seven. He had me in Jeet Kune Do after that, showed me boxing at home. I got on the wrestling team in high school. After that...I didn't have anywhere to go. He didn't have any good ideas."

"What did your mother say?"

"She was gone a long time by then."

"I'm sorry to hear that."

"It happens."

"At least you were honest with him. Honesty's always the best way. In fifty-three years I've always told the truth to my wife but once, and I regret that every day of my life. I taught my son to be the same way. Have it out on the table. Get down to the truth of things."

"Sometimes people don't want to hear the truth."

"Doesn't mean lying is better. Your father probably appreciated you talking straight."

"I don't know. He just thought it would all work out. So I came home after Basic and we had it out, and then we didn't talk at all. He had a stroke that messed him up pretty bad, and then he had another one that killed him. I got home in time for the funeral."

Yates nodded slowly. "It's tough not getting a chance to say good-bye."

"Yeah."

"My son and I got along better than it sounds like you and your old man did, but we had our disagreements. It would have been nice to hash those out in our own time. But now that's not gonna happen."

Camaro kept her silence.

They were close to their destination. Yates took the La Brea exit. "You want to tell me what we're walking into?"

"There's a guy who used to live in our neighborhood who worked on electronics. He could do all kinds of crazy stuff, like wire the lights in your house to turn on and off by radio. Things like that. I know he does computers and phones, too."

"How long has it been since you've seen him?"

"The same."

The directions on Yates's phone led them in a tight combination of lefts and rights until Yates saw the sign among a string of others on both sides of the street. There was a nail place on one side, and a psychic reader had a storefront two doors down. There was just enough room to squeeze in across the street and not overlap into the red zone. He turned off the engine. "So you really think he can do this?" he asked.

"If anybody can find that phone, Mr. Cabrera can."

"It's illegal. He up for that? You haven't seen the man in an age."

"You got some extra cash?"

"I'm doing all right so far."

"Then let's find out."

# CHAPTER SIXTY-FOUR

They switched seats halfway through the drive to Los Angeles, and now Way was behind the wheel. He had a direct connection with a woman named Marjorie Banner at Hyundai's Blue Link service, and he'd left strict instructions with her to contact him whenever new addresses were entered into the Santa Fe's navigation system, but there had been only one additional call between the time they left the Monterey area and when they finally reached LA.

It was easy for Way to spot the rented SUV once they were on the right street. He breathed deeply, but his pulse was up and he was getting a headache. He'd already swallowed six ibuprofen. The pain was tenacious. He was aware of Hannon next to him, seeing what he saw, thinking whatever it was she thought.

They couldn't park close, but Way found a spot fifty yards past the address and slotted the car into place. He left the engine running.

"I think we should talk," Hannon said. It was the first time they'd spoken in nearly three hours.

Way adjusted the side mirror to better see the entrance of iFix. He rubbed his temple with his thumb. "We already had a talk."

"I need to know what we're going to do here."

"We're going to look and listen." Hannon said nothing. He felt her watching him. He glared at her. "What?"

"I don't like the way we left things before," Hannon said.

"We're on the road six hours and you finally have something to say about it?"

"Keith—" Hannon began.

"Let me cut you off right there. I'm not having a replay of our last conversation. You have objections, and I understand that. But you knew going in how I felt about this, and you said you were clear on what we were going to do."

"I knew," Hannon said.

"Okay. You know Jerry and I came up together. We joined the marshals together, we worked together. He was like a brother to me. He *was* my brother. Anybody, and I mean anybody, who stands between me and taking out Lukas Collier is going to pay the price. So I'm sorry if you're having second thoughts, but I'm not. I'm doing this."

"I need to know if you're going to do something to Yates and Espinoza."

"I'll do whatever I need to do. If they're smart, they'll stay out of my way. If they're not, I'm not going to take responsibility for them."

"That concerns me, Keith. These people aren't the bad guys."

"They are interfering with my duties," Way said sharply. "I don't give a flying fuck about Yates's rights as a bail bondsman. That means shit to me. And what the hell is Camaro Espinoza even doing with him? Her sister's in Carmel; her niece is there, too. They need someone looking out for them. She should be back there playing house and keeping her business to herself. But, no, she's decided to make Lukas Collier her problem."

"He came after her family," Hannon said. "She has cause to worry if he'll come around again."

"He's never coming around again. He's not going to come around anywhere again."

Hannon didn't reply. She turned around in her seat to see iFix. "What do you think they're doing in there?"

"I have no idea, but I don't think they're trying to get their computer repaired."

"We know where they are now. We should get on Lukas."

"We are on Lukas. These two are going to take us right to him."

"How do you know that, Keith? How do you know?"

"It's the vibe I get off Yates, and it's definitely because of the sneaky shit going on with Camaro Espinoza. Yates is harder to fit into the picture, but Espinoza—she has dirt all over her. We didn't have to dig down an inch before we found everything she's been mixed up with."

Hannon turned away. She brought out her phone and fiddled with it. Way kept one eye on her and the other on the shop. She did not stop looking at her phone. Way shifted in his seat. "Man, I wish I had some sound in there. Some video, too."

"We have what we have."

"And that's dick."

"Can you at least tell me you'll try to keep them clear of whatever happens?"

Way wanted to grit his teeth, but he knew that would only make his headache worse. "Do you want out?" he asked.

"You're making it hard for me. I'm only—"

"It's a real simple question. I'll handle it on my own. You sign off as the lead on the case, but I'll do what has to get done."

Hannon fell silent. Way watched her, and she turned her face away from him so he could not see her expression. "I don't think I'm asking a lot," she said.

"You're asking me to take the chance that I won't get Lukas. That is unacceptable. I will not allow that to happen."

She looked at him. "What if it's me between you and Lukas? Would you kill me, Keith? Because that's what I'm thinking might happen."

Way stared back at her. "Don't get between us, and you'll never have to find out," he said flatly.

Hannon shook her head and looked away. Way went back to watching the shop. No one went in or came out. His headache boiled.

# CHAPTER SIXTY-FIVE

Juan Cabrera wrote an address on the top sheet of a pad of yellow paper and tore it off. "Who wants it?" he asked.

"I'll take it," Camaro said. She looked at Cabrera's scratches. "Sunset Boulevard."

"Where exactly?" Yates asked.

"I don't know the place, but I know the area. It's about twenty minutes east of here if traffic's all right."

Yates laid five hundred-dollar bills in Cabrera's outstretched hand. "Thanks for your help, *amigo*. And if we need an update?"

Cabrera folded up the money and put it in his pocket. He was a very thin man with a few strands of hair pulled across a bald pate. His shoulders were spindly in his yellow iFix golf shirt. "You only have to call. Anything I can do to help old friends."

"Let's go," Camaro said.

Camaro jaywalked in a hurry and waited for Yates to get the SUV open. She got into her seat and buckled up. As soon as the engine turned over, she called up the GPS and entered the new address. It lit up on the map of Los Angeles, tracing a route north to the location of Lukas's phone. The blue line pulsed in time with her heartbeat. As they drove, Camaro checked her weapon.

"We get there, let's make sure we get the lay of the land first," Yates said. "I don't want to rush into anything."

"Okay," Camaro said.

"I want him, too."

They drove until they reached Sunset Boulevard, and then Camaro's eyes searched ahead. She saw the Super 8 and pointed. "There," she said. "That has to be it."

251

"You have reached your destination," the GPS said.

"I'm going to put us on the street," Yates said. "If he gets past us, I want to be able to pull out fast."

He found a place along the curb and parked. Camaro steadied her breath.

"Let's go."

The breeze plucked at them on the street. It was cooling rapidly toward dark. Camaro forced herself to walk alongside Yates and not ahead of him. They reached the entrance to the motel's parking lot together. She peered around the corner and scanned the lot. Any car could have been Lukas's.

"I'll take the manager's office. You watch the rooms," Yates said. He had his bail-enforcement badge out.

"Don't take too long," Camaro said.

He vanished inside the office, and Camaro stood half hidden by a pillar on the ground floor. The visible rooms all faced the parking lot, the stairwells exposed so no one could ascend or descend without being seen. There were security cameras at the front and rear of the lot.

Yates returned. "Second floor. Room Two-one-three."

"Where is that?"

"Right above us. The manager marked up a map."

Camaro consulted it. A red ink arrow followed halfway down one side of the lot and ascended. Another arrow directed them to Lukas's door. She nodded and pushed the map away. "I got it."

She went, and he followed. She slipped the Glock into her hand as she reached the stairs. She held the gun in both hands against her body in the compressed ready position. With Yates at her back, she approached the corner and peeked around it. Lukas was not there.

They advanced past still rooms with drawn curtains until they reached 213, then fell in on opposite sides of the frame. Camaro touched the door. It was metal, and the frame was also metal. She shook her head at Yates. He put his gun away and reached for his picks.

The sound of an ice machine dumping a load of cubes carried to them from the far end of the walkway. Camaro looked up as Lukas came around the corner.

A pause lengthened between them in which time seemed to suspend. Lukas stood with a bucket of fresh ice in his hand, his shirt unbuttoned to expose the pistol tucked in the front of his waistband. He froze, his mouth dropped open.

Camaro pressed the Glock out and up, aiming past Yates, squeezing the trigger, and feeling the gun recoil in her grip. Her bullet struck the wall ten feet behind Lukas. The sound spurred him into motion. The ice bucket tumbled from his hand, spilling chunks of frozen water across the concrete in a silvery fan. He twisted and drew his .45 from his jeans.

Yates stepped in front of Camaro as Lukas's gun went off. Blood spattered the wall, and the old man groaned. He sagged against Camaro, and she lowered him to the ground. "Go," he said through gritted teeth. "Get him."

Camaro moved. Lukas had vanished around a corner. Camaro dashed quickly past the remaining rooms, rounding the same corner to find a through hallway that punched out onto the far side of the building, where more rooms lay. She charged down it and turned the next corner. She had only an instant to see the butt of Lukas's gun coming at her face. Then she saw lights.

Her knees folded, and she crumpled. She saw Lukas swinging his weapon around again, the gaping blackness of the muzzle coming into line with her face. She'd lost her gun somewhere. Her hands went up instinctively, closing over Lukas's pistol. She felt his hand flex, and the hammer fell on her finger, a sharp metal bite.

She wrenched the gun one way and then another. Lukas cursed, his finger caught in the guard. Camaro twisted until she felt something give and Lukas cried out. The gun came loose between them and clattered to the concrete.

He kicked her in the side, and pain shot through her ribs. He kicked her a second time as she rolled, clipping her as she made it to her feet. She raised her guard too slowly, and Lukas punched her squarely in the jaw. Her head snapped around, and she saw lights again.

Camaro staggered and drove out a leg. Her heel glanced off his thigh, and then he was on her, swinging her around by arm and neck to crash headfirst into the wall. Blood was in her mouth. She pivoted and ducked, but a rising left snapped her teeth together and sent her reeling.

They exchanged a rapid flurry of blows. Camaro managed to get inside and bloody Lukas's nose. He hit her with an elbow in the temple that nearly took her off her feet.

She drove into him with her shoulder, but he outweighed her by thirty pounds and flung her back. She barely deflected a swinging right that would have closed her eye, but caught a sudden left in the stomach.

They clashed together. She hooked his ankle and sent him down to one knee. He charged back to his feet and rocked her. Camaro had something hot and sticky in her hair, and the only thing she could smell was more blood. A sharp strike directly to the point of her chin sparked stars. The ground came up, and she fell completely.

"Federal marshals! Don't move!"

Way's voice boomed out behind her. Camaro saw Lukas take up his gun and run. She scrambled for her own, a persistent spinning in her skull tilting her balance askew.

"I said stop!"

Her hand closed on the Glock. Camaro raised the gun to fire. Lukas was nearly at the far end of the building.

"Stop where you are, Collier!"

Lukas turned at the moment Way stumbled over Camaro. Camaro was flattened again, the Glock skittering out of her grasp as she and Way became entangled. A burst of exhalation exploded in her ear, almost as loud as the ringing pair of shots from Lukas's gun. Camaro heard a woman cry out.

Way flailed on top of her, cursing as they unraveled the knot of their limbs. He fired his weapon twice, the report profoundly deafening at such close range. Then he was up on his feet, running after Lukas.

Camaro tried to make it upright. She saw Hannon on the ground, clutching her chest. Her gun was loose beside her. Camaro ignored it and went to Hannon instead. There were two distinct entry marks in the front of her dark jacket, but no blood.

"I..." Hannon said breathlessly. She grabbed Camaro by the arm.

"Don't move," Camaro told her. Her brain struggled to put together the next steps, the right words. She kept seeing spots. "Just lie still. Breathe."

Camaro opened Hannon's jacket and saw where the bullets had passed through the material of the marshal's blouse as well. There was still no blood. Her searching fingers felt the stiffness of a layer of Kevlar underneath.

"Way," Hannon said.

Camaro sagged to the ground beside Hannon. She could only place a hand on Hannon's vest. She sucked air, and little by little it cleared her head. "I said lie still," she managed to say. "You could have...cracked ribs."

Multiple gunshots sounded nearby, the reports of at least two different weapons. Camaro distantly heard Way shouting, and Yates, too. She forced herself back onto her knees and leaned over Hannon. She tore open her blouse to expose the body armor the marshal wore underneath her clothes. Two slugs were embedded in the white material.

Hannon shuddered. Camaro felt her hands, and they were cold. "You're going into shock."

"You're hurt," Hannon said. "You're bleeding."

Camaro shook her head. "I'm fine. Breathe like I told you. You're going to be all right."

Camaro didn't hear the footsteps falling behind her, but the sudden blow behind her ear sent fresh sparks into her vision. She wobbled, one hand still on Hannon, the other on the unyielding concrete walk.

She turned enough to see Way standing over her, his gun in his hand. Blood stained his left arm. He hit her with the butt of his weapon again, and something hot dripped into Camaro's vision. She fell on her back and put a hand up. Way hit her again. He panted, knelt over her, and stuck the barrel of his pistol in her face. "Don't you move. Not one muscle."

# CHAPTER SIXTY-SIX

Lukas was gone. Yates surrendered himself into custody, and Way kept them both under the gun until the local police and EMTs arrived. Hannon was taken away on a gurney, and Camaro didn't see her anymore. Yates went, too. Way said nothing to any of them and spoke only to the LAPD officers who bundled Camaro into a unit. The car drove northwest to Van Nuys, where the LA County lockup was.

The processing was the easy part. A female officer was assigned to Camaro and took her photograph and her fingerprints. She was asked a series of questions about her drug and alcohol history. They wanted to know if she was suicidal. She told them she wasn't.

"You're banged up. We'll have a medic check you over."

"I saw one already."

"We'll have them check you again."

She was escorted to a large area filled with rows of chairs locked together. It looked like a DMV, and there were televisions bolted to the ceiling in two corners so the men and women waiting in the chairs could occupy themselves. The deputy informed her that she had free access to the phones on the far wall so long as no one else was waiting to make a call. For the rest of the time she was obliged to sit in a seat and wait.

Camaro took a spot in an empty row. The television was tuned to a basic cable channel, and the show was *Cops*. She sat and willed stillness into herself. Her body ached profoundly, but it did not hurt in the place where she went. There was a constant murmur of noise from the bank of phones as detainees made calls for lawyers, for bail bondsmen, for loved ones. She didn't hear them.

She looked at the holding area. A pair of deputies sat behind an island of counters to one side of the room, working at computers and only occasionally glancing up to scan the assembled men and women. Now and again another two or three officers would pass through the area, either to talk or to escort a new body to one of the holding cells that dotted one long wall. Some of the cells were small enough for a single occupant, but most were large, with broad windows impregnated with wire, through which Camaro saw idle men and women deemed too uncontrollable for the plastic chairs and the reruns of *Cops*.

On the far side of the counter island was the processing area. Through there a direct exit to the outside opened into the loading zone where Camaro had been brought in. There were other hallways leading out, but those were certain to be secured by locks Camaro had no means to bypass.

No one carried guns inside the jail, but the officers were armed with Tasers and collapsible batons. On the way in Camaro had watched her escort check her weapon into a locker outside the detention area, so even the police who passed from the outside into processing were unarmed. Traffic was slow. There were never more than two or three cops present at any given time.

She shook her head. There would be no jailbreak.

A nurse came as they promised, and Camaro was taken to a side room and asked to strip. She had her wounds cleaned for the second time, and the nurse clucked her tongue at the bruises on Camaro's face. When she saw the gash on the back of her leg, she made a disgusted noise. "Who sewed this up? Is that *fishing line?*"

"It's all I had."

"Well, it's torn now. I'm going to put a real suture in, but you need to get looked at by a doctor."

"I'll be all right."

It was done, and she was returned to the chairs. After three hours a deputy came for her. "Up," she said.

Camaro stood. "What's going on?"

"Walk ahead of me along that row of doors."

Camaro did as she was told, and the two of them walked past the cells to another hallway, also lined with cells. They went four doors down, and the deputy instructed her to stand with her nose against the wall and her hands behind her back. The deputy opened a cell then and took her arm to guide her in.

The door was closed. Camaro looked around the space. The cell was empty. There were no chairs, only benches molded from concrete. A short wall at the back sheltered a toilet. There was no sink.

She sat down, but it was only a minute before she heard the deputy's key in the door again. The door swung wide, and Way entered. Camaro didn't move.

They were shut in together. Way stood over her, watching her, and said nothing. Camaro glanced away from him and stared at the opposite wall instead. She heard him breathing. A tense vibration emanated from him, tangible in the still air of the cell.

A minute passed before Way broke the silence. "You look bad," he said.

"Thanks."

"I thought you should know that you're going to go in front of a judge in a few hours. You're being charged with unlawful possession of a firearm, assault with a deadly weapon, and a few other things you probably don't give a shit about. But the fun part comes when the U.S. Attorney's office gets involved, because we're going to step in on the federal level and run your ass all the way to prison."

Camaro remained silent.

Way waved his hand in front of her face. "This registering with you? Because now is the time to help yourself. Felony interference with a federal agent isn't a joke. Your friend Yates, he might make out okay with the right lawyer, but you have no leg to stand on. You're a straight-up criminal, and you got my partner shot."

She looked at him for the first time. "How is she?"

"She'll be fine."

"And Yates?"

"He's a lucky old man. The bullet hit him at an angle and glanced off his shoulder blade. He's going to be stiff, but he's gonna live."

"That's good."

"You're damned right it's good," Way said. "If either one of them had died, I'd look to put you away forever. And I mean forever."

Camaro looked away again. "It doesn't matter."

"Why not?"

"Because Lukas is gone. You screwed up the whole thing. You'll never catch him."

"I screwed up? I am the only one with the authority to pursue Lukas Collier. I don't give two shits about whatever bond he skipped out on. I'm pursuing the wanted felon who killed a federal marshal and a cop. And that's before we even bring kidnapping and every other person he's killed into it. I am the big dog. I told you that back in Carmel, but you wouldn't listen. And now what do you have? Nothing."

"I'm tired of talking to you," Camaro said.

Way stalked the small cell. "I don't think you realize the barrel I have you over. We are talking about prison time. Hard time in a federal penitentiary where you get one hour outside your cell every day. I have the power to put you there and keep you there until your tits fall and your hair turns gray. You get me?"

She saw him grinding his teeth and smiled inside.

"You know, I've been thinking about it," he said. "Identity fraud is a federal crime. You want your sister to be in the same pen with you? Of course, your niece would have to go into the system, seeing as how her father is dead and you have no immediate relatives. Rebecca's coming up on five years old, right? The maximum sentence for identity fraud is fifteen years. So she'll be almost old enough to take her mommy out for a drink when she gets out. What do you think about that?"

Camaro didn't speak.

"So I guess that's what we're going to do. Innocent people are going to be hurt because you won't come clean. I'm glad I'm not in your family."

"What do you want from me?"

"I want you to tell me everything you know about where Lukas is going and what he's going to do when he gets there."

"How the hell would I know that?"

"You knew he was headed south. How?"

Camaro pressed her lips together and didn't answer. Out of the corner of her eye she saw Way smile.

"You had Lukas's personal cell phone number and used it to track him to that motel. Yeah, yeah, we talked to that stupid bastard who traced the signal for you. We know all about it. I want to know when you talked to Lukas, what you talked about, and everything you learned. And if you do that, I'll see about getting you a spot in minimum security instead. That's not so bad."

"I can't help you," Camaro said.

"Don't screw around with me," Way said.

"I want a lawyer, and I don't want to see your face again."

Way said nothing. He stood staring at her, and she felt his eyes boring into her flesh. She didn't look his way and didn't move. She sat and waited and took each breath as it came until finally he moved to the door. He rapped on the thick glass. "Open up."

The deputy unlocked the door.

"Hey, Deputy Way," Camaro said.

Way paused in the doorway. "What?"

"There's one more thing I want to say."

"Spit it out."

"Better luck next time."

Way stepped out. The door was closed again, and the lock engaged automatically.

Camaro rested the back of her head against the wall and let the corners of her mouth turn up just a little as she heard him walk away.

# CHAPTER SIXTY-SEVEN

For the second time in a day, Lukas fled the sound of sirens. He saw a bus stopping for passengers up ahead in the failing light of sunset, its interior brightly lit. The doors were already closed when he got there, but he thumped his fist on the glass and the driver let him on. "Hey, man," Lukas said, "is there a Greyhound station on this line?"

"Not on this line, but you can transfer at Long Beach and Hill."

"Great." Lukas fed some bills into the fare taker and went to sit down. The marshal had clipped him with a shot. His leg was bleeding, and he had no way to stop it. Droplets fell on the floor of the bus. No one seemed to notice or care.

He watched the stops light up on an LED sign just above the driver, and fifteen minutes later he was off waiting for his transfer, a slip of paper in his hand. He threw his phone away in a trash can mounted on the side of a lamppost.

The Number 60 bus picked him up and drove east until it reached his stop. The driver instructed him to keep walking another half a mile to reach the Greyhound bus station. He did as he was told and made it to the station without spotting a single police cruiser along the way. He stopped once to pull up the leg of his jeans and examine his wound. It was only oozing now, though it hurt to put his full weight on that leg.

There was a bank of disused public phones tucked away in a neglected corner of the station. Lukas scrounged in his pocket for change and fed one of the phones. He called Konnor and waited through an interminable series of rings until Konnor picked up. "I've got trouble," Lukas told him.

"What's happening?"

"I got jumped at the motel. Couple of bounty hunters and some U.S. marshals. I got away okay, but I'm hit in the leg and I'm bleeding. I need you to pick me up and get me somewhere I can get patched up."

"How bad's the leg?"

"It doesn't have to come off, but it needs stitching."

"I can handle that, so long as there's no bullet in there. Where are you?"

"Greyhound station off Seventh."

"I know it. Give me half an hour."

"Don't be late."

"Just sit tight."

Lukas left the phones and found a spot on a scratched wooden bench. It wasn't busy in the station, but there were eyes enough that he felt uncomfortable being out in the open. Without thinking he tried to cross his legs, and pain shot through his bullet wound. Lukas gasped and saw an old woman glance his way. He forced a smile and nodded, and she looked in the other direction.

The time on his watch ticked away until thirty minutes had passed. Lukas didn't see Konnor, and another ten minutes went by without the man appearing. He started to count out change again when he heard his name spoken across the room. "Hey," Konnor said. "I'm here."

Lukas got up. His leg throbbed. "About time."

"Traffic. What are you gonna do?"

"Let's get out of here."

They went out to the parking lot, and Konnor directed Lukas to a white Chevy pickup with a Harley-Davidson decal spread across the entire rear window. Lukas managed to climb in and stuck his wounded leg out from his body as far as he could.

He saw Konnor look at his bloodied pant leg. "Hurting?"

"What do you think?"

"We'll get it taken care of. I've got a stash of Vicodin that'll take the edge off."

"Still living with the beaners?"

"Yeah, the neighborhood's got plenty. But you know how it is."

"Sure."

Konnor drove. For a while they didn't talk. It was Konnor who broke the silence. "How close are these people to you? The bounty hunters and the marshals?"

"Too close. I have a pretty good idea how they found me before. I dumped my phone, so I need a new one. I thought that shit was illegal, but I guess not. They homed right in on me."

"Is it gonna be a problem? You know, for the deal?"

"We can still make the swap. I talked to Otilio, and he's ready to make delivery so long as we hold up our end."

"It's all arranged. We're on for tomorrow. Pay the cash, get the goods. Then we make the exchange on Sunday. The candy store is closed that day, so we'll have it all to ourselves. How's your pickup man doing?"

Lukas cursed. "I can't get ahold of him. If he's running scared, we might be stuck holding the load for a while until we can arrange for someone else to take it. If Jake hadn't gone and gotten himself killed, this wouldn't be a problem, but Jake's still causing me trouble. Him and his goddamned friends."

"Amateurs."

"That's the size of it."

Konnor let the silence grow between them. "You want to talk about it?"

"Talk about what?"

"Jake."

"What's there to talk about? He was stupid. He was always stupid. As soon as he told me he could sell weed all around the bay, I should have known it was gonna be trouble. He couldn't be counted on to wipe his own ass."

"But he was still your brother."

Lukas shot Konnor a look. "What are you, my mother? Yeah, he was my brother, and I don't take it lying down when someone messes with my blood. But business is business, and I have to go on. One day I'll nail that bitch when she doesn't expect it."

"Who is she?"

"I don't know. She's got skills, that much I can tell you. She's no

Marine, but she could really get into somebody's ass if they aren't careful."

"You look a little banged up. Her?"

"Yeah, it was her. What of it? I put her down when it came to it. She was mine."

Konnor shook his head slowly. "It's a shame. Even if Jake was a screwup, he was all right sometimes."

"He never would have made it in the Sandbox. You and me, we came out the other side. He would have bought it there. He wasn't strong enough. He was never strong enough. But that's what happens. I did my best with him."

"We'll pour one out for him."

"Yeah, we'll do that. Then we get down to making money. I might have a long vacation after this."

# CHAPTER SIXTY-EIGHT

Hannon enter ed the jail through a secure passageway bookended by heavy doors set with glass inches thick. Whenever she breathed, she felt a painful pressure in the center of her chest. At the hospital they had stripped off her body armor, jacket, and blouse to reveal the blackened cluster of a bruise directly over her sternum. The bruise had twin centers, one for each of the slugs that crashed into her vest.

She stopped by an island staffed by Sheriff's Department deputies and showed her identification for the sixth time. "Deputy U.S. Marshal Hannon," she said. "I'm looking for my partner, Deputy Way."

"I think he's in that office over there," the deputy told her.

Hannon thanked him and followed his pointing finger to a small office set at the end of a line of cells. One wall was half reinforced glass. The door was shut. She saw Way sitting at the desk, his cell phone pressed to his ear, speaking intently. He glanced up, saw her, and beckoned her in.

The office was unlocked. Hannon stepped through the door and let it close behind her. Way continued his call. "So we can have the indictments put together by morning," he said. "Yes, I understand. I'll check into it. Sure. You can reach me at this number. I'll be up all night. Thanks."

He hung up and put his phone away. They looked at each other across the desk.

"Was that the U.S. Attorney's office?" Hannon asked.

"Yes. What are you doing here? You should be resting."

"I'm bruised up, I'm not dead. I want to stay on top of things."

"I have it under control."

"What's happening?"

Way paused, as if considering not answering her. Then he said, "Espinoza's been processed into holding. The old man's out of the hospital, and he's going through the system right now. We're set to see the local judge tonight. We're still going to let them file charges, but we have the priority. They'll be transported to federal court in the morning, and at that point our people take over completely. The locals can get them when we're finished with them."

"Have you talked to either of them yet?"

"I talked to Espinoza."

"What did she say?"

"What do you expect? Nothing. She thinks she's bulletproof. But I have her dead to rights. We're going to run right over her."

Hannon sat down in the chair opposite the desk. "What about Yates? Have you questioned him?"

"Not yet, but I will."

"I'd like to be there."

"You're recovering."

"The vest took the slugs, Keith. I'm fine to work."

"You just got shot. Give it some goddamned time. You could have died."

Hannon heard his voice falter at the last. "I didn't die. I'm not dying."

"Well, I'm not losing anybody else."

"I want to talk to Espinoza," Hannon said.

"Why?"

"She stopped for me, Keith. She could have gone after Lukas, but she stopped for me. I don't know about you, but that means something to me."

"Camaro Espinoza is a stone killer," Way said. "You think she stopped for you? She was probably just trying to get hold of your weapon."

"That's not what happened, and you know it."

"Yeah, well, the FBI will want another crack at her once I get a chance to talk with someone in charge over there. I'm convinced she was on the scene when Yates took down Vicki Nelson's apartment. She's a liability with a gun, and she's not telling everything she knows."

"What do you think she knows, Keith? What do you really think she's going to tell us?"

Way's eyes shone. "She was in contact with Lukas. She had his number. They talked. I've subpoenaed her phone records, and I'm willing to lay odds that when I get them, it's going to show at least one phone conversation between the two of them. She's hip deep in this somehow, and I'm going to use her to find Lukas."

"Lukas is gone," Hannon said. "It's over."

"No! He's in the city somewhere. He has ties here going way back. We punch up his KAs from when he was last in California and we start running them down, one by one. Somebody's gonna give, and then we'll have his ass."

Hannon shook her head. "This has to stop."

Way's mouth flattened. "I'm not having that conversation again. This is happening. We're about two steps ahead of the Bureau right now, and I want to keep it that way. By the time they figure out what we're doing, he'll be taken care of and we walk away clean."

She waited, and she thought. Way stared. "I want to work together with you on this, Keith. I want to be a part of it. I won't let you go on alone."

"Then you'd better get on board with what's happening, because we are going full ahead on Espinoza and Yates."

"When will you talk to Yates?"

"Soon. Everybody who's anybody is off tonight, so I have to roust some people out of bed to get things moving. He can sit and stew for a while. Maybe if he gets enough time to think about what's at stake, he'll be more cooperative than Espinoza was. And I'm not letting any of that *Taylor v. Taintor* bullshit knock me off his ass this time. He's stepped over the line, and he knows it. The minute he pulled Espinoza in on his fugitive recovery, he broke the law. The only thing that's going to get him out of this mess is if we step in and put pressure on the right people, and that's not gonna happen."

Way stood and Hannon did, too. Hannon felt the air between

them, thick and uneasy. "Do you mind if I talk to them before you do?"

"Yes, I mind."

He went for the door, and Hannon stepped aside. She let him leave. He walked away, visible through the window until he passed down an adjoining hallway. The weight of his absence remained.

## CHAPTER SIXTY-NINE

After Way left , Camaro sat in the stillness of the cell, listening to the burble of voices passing through the vents in the door. She stayed quiet and stared at the blank face of the wall for a long time until she heard keys in the lock.

"Stand up," said a deputy with a crew cut. "Face the rear of the cell."

She did as she was told. She was cuffed again and taken out through a side door. The deputy escorted her with a hand loosely on her elbow, guiding her through nondescript hallways and out through a secure exit into another building. She expected to find a courtroom at the other end, but she was brought to a darkened office. The deputy turned on the light to reveal a reception area with a small couch and chairs. Camaro was directed onto the couch. She sat facing a tiny coffee table strewn with magazines she could not pick up and read. The officer went outside.

The office had a clock on the wall. It was just past midnight. Camaro heard the click of hard soles on the tile floor outside, and the door opened. Yates entered first, handcuffed as she was. They put him in a chair. Hannon followed. "Thank you," she told the deputies with him, and then they were left alone with the door closed.

Camaro looked at Yates. He nodded to her silently. She turned her attention to Hannon. "I thought I was due in court."

"You both are. You're supposed to be there now."

"Then what's happening?"

"What did you intend to do when you found Lukas Collier in that motel room?"

"Don't you know?"

"Say it."

"We were going to kill him."

"Even though your sister's going to make it and your niece is all right?"

Camaro indicated Yates with her head. "His son is still dead. And I can't have him come back at Annabel again."

Hannon took one of the chairs and dragged it around to face them. Camaro saw her wince at the effort and touch her chest. When she sat, she was slightly pale. "If I take the two of you to that courtroom, it's going to be over. You'll both be remanded into custody pending a date in front of a federal judge."

Camaro watched her carefully, Yates doing the same.

"Keith—my partner—is playing phone tag with all the people we need to have you charged by the U.S. Attorney's office. I figure we have an hour, maybe a little bit more. Two if we're lucky."

"So what does that have to do with us?" Camaro asked. "You have us. We're not going anywhere."

"The District Attorney's office is ready to file the paperwork that lets you walk on local charges. It doesn't get a federal prosecutor off your backs, but it buys you some more time on the street."

"Why would you do that?" Yates asked.

"I have my reasons. The question is, can you find Lukas again?"

Camaro glanced at Yates. He inclined his head just slightly. "Maybe not where he's hiding, but where he's going to be."

"How do you mean?"

Yates spoke up. "Lukas's brother put together a pot of money for a drug deal. Lukas had that money sent on to LA before he left Carmel. We have the address."

"Let me have it."

"Not until we get some assurances," Camaro said.

Hannon shook her head. "I don't think the two of you get it. You will go to *prison* if I don't help you out of this jam. If you know something, you need to share it, because I already have one person in my life who's shutting me out."

"Right now that address is the only thing we have to go on," Yates said. "You can keep us out of jail, but what can you do to help finish this?"

Hannon pursed her lips in thought, then spoke. "I have some room to maneuver. But whatever you do, do it fast. Because this won't last. Once Keith knows you're back on the street, he's going to lose his shit, and I mean that."

"What the hell is his problem, anyway?" Camaro asked.

"He lost a good friend. He hasn't been the same since. Anyone he thinks will get between him and Lukas Collier, he'll take apart. He doesn't care anymore."

"You care?" Camaro asked.

"I do. I understand the world's a better place without Lukas in it, but there's a line between good guys and bad guys. You don't hurt good guys to stop the bad guys."

"How do you know we're good?"

"I don't. Not for sure. But when you picked me over Lukas, I got a pretty solid idea."

"If your partner's going to go as crazy as you say, we're going to have a whole new set of problems besides Lukas Collier," Yates said. "Can you put a muzzle on your boy?"

"I wish. He got me turned around pretty badly. He got me thinking we were doing the right thing by putting Lukas in front of a gun. But that's not going to bring Keith back from the edge. He needs somebody to save him from himself, otherwise he's going to go somewhere he can't get back from."

"So it's okay if we do it," Camaro said, "just so long as he doesn't."

"I don't expect you to get it."

"Oh, I get it."

"I'm not going to argue about whose honor is worth more," Hannon said. "All I know is Keith can't think straight, and he's never going to think straight as long as Lukas is out there. I'm barely hanging on to him now. If he gets a whiff of Lukas again, I can't control what happens next."

"We'll do it," Yates said. "You don't have to be a party to it."

Hannon stood and went to the door. She cracked the door slightly and peered out, then pushed it shut again. She sat down with a sigh of pain and looked at them for a long time in silence. "All right," she said finally. "Let's do it."

# CHAPTER SEVENTY

They called a cab and quickly walked a few blocks away from the Los Angeles County Superior Court to wait for it. Yates made a series of phone calls while they waited. Camaro didn't listen to his side of the conversation. Instead, she watched the empty street for any sign of Deputy Marshal Way. He did not appear.

The cab arrived, and they slipped into the back. "Santa Monica and Fairfax," Yates told the driver.

"West Hollywood?" Camaro asked.

Yates looked at Camaro. "There's an all-night coffee place there. My man will link up with us. He's bringing us some wheels. No rental cars, no paperwork, nothing the marshals can use to track us. Which reminds me, it was nice of the deputy to give them back, but we need to get rid of our phones as soon as we can."

"We can pick up a couple anywhere," Camaro said. "They're cheap. Hardware is going to be a bigger problem."

"That's been on my mind," Yates said. "I'm still working on that part. I'm gonna miss that Hardballer. My wife gave it to me as a present."

They rode. The driver seemed uninterested in making conversation. He glanced into his mirror occasionally and Camaro saw him looking at her, but he said nothing. There would be a record of their trip from the courthouse. It would not be difficult for Way to find it.

"What do you think?" Yates said when there had been enough quiet.

"About what?"

"This lady marshal. Do you think she meant a thing she said?"

"I do."

"That partner of hers is going to eat her alive."

"He'll try."

"The way I figure it, if we don't get Lukas within the next twenty-four hours, we're gonna be out of options. Way? He'll have everybody but the National Guard out looking for us. Looking for you in particular. From what you tell me, he has the hots for you in a big way."

The streets were washed in clean, white light. Los Angeles had done away with the old sodium-vapor streetlights years ago in favor of LEDs. The look of the city by night was wholly different from the city Camaro remembered from her youth.

"He's not the first one to come gunning for me. He won't be the last."

"You run right up to a dangerous edge," Yates said.

"I don't have a choice."

"Don't you?"

Camaro shot him a look. "I don't go looking for it."

"That's good, because if you did, then that would mean you have a problem. The kind of problem only dying seems to fix."

"Lukas is the one who's gonna die."

"So you figure we still have a shot at him?"

"You don't think so?"

"Let's just say I want to believe," Yates said. "In my time I've gone out on some shaky limbs, but I can't recall a situation where the limb was quite so shaky as this one. We got two tries, and he slipped us both times. Are we third-time lucky? I can't say for sure."

"I'll follow him alone. You don't have to come," Camaro said.

"You think I'm saying all of this because I want to cut you loose?"

"Aren't you?"

"We've got too much invested to walk away now. I only want to make sure we keep our feet on the ground, that's all. Too easy to get blown away otherwise."

Camaro caught the driver looking at her again. She glared into his mirror until his eyes flicked away. "I'm sorry about your son," she said. "I don't think I ever told you that."

"You didn't have to. You never knew him."

"I'm still sorry. My sister, she's still alive. Your son...he's never coming back. No matter what we do, he's never coming back."

Yates turned his gaze toward the window. "No, he isn't."

They let silence grow between them until they were off the freeway and into the streets of West Hollywood, weaving past the Dolby Theatre and finally at their destination, a coffeehouse planted directly on the corner of Fairfax and Santa Monica Boulevard. Yates moved to pay, but Camaro brushed his hand away and gave some bills to the driver. "Stay safe," the driver told them.

The coffeehouse was surprisingly busy for the hour, mostly with young folks taking their caffeine in the middle of the night so they could talk until the break of dawn. Camaro scanned the tables and booths until she spotted the man they were looking for. She didn't know him by sight, but he was the only person in the place over forty, and he was seated alone. Yates waved to him, and the man waved back to confirm it.

"Camaro Espinoza, this is Ronnie Curtis," Yates said when they reached the man's table. "Ronnie, this is Camaro."

"Great name," Ronnie said. "You two sit down for a minute. I have a slice of pie coming."

Camaro sat angled toward the door. Yates settled in beside her. The table was small and round, designed to bring groups of people together in an intimate circle. Ronnie had a newspaper he set on an empty chair.

"You got a ride for us?" Yates asked.

"Right up the street. Red Mustang. You like ragtops?"

"In the winter?" Camaro asked.

"Hey, what do you want? It's short notice, and it's what I could spare. Picked it up at a police auction a couple of years ago. It runs okay, and it'll get you where you need to go in a hurry if that's what you're after."

"How much do I owe you?" Yates asked. He reached for his wallet.

Ronnie waved it away. "Nothing. As soon as Anita called and told me what was up...It's a goddamned tragedy. When one of us gets shot, it's like we lost a brother. Take that car and do whatever you need to do with it. And if it you can't return it, no sweat. Small price to pay."

"I'm much obliged to you," Yates said.

"It's the least I can do."

"There's just one more thing."

Ronnie nodded. "Sure, I know. Check the trunk. Two pieces, like you asked. They're clean, so don't worry about anything blowing back on me."

"You're a real godsend, Ronnie."

"Just make sure you get the son of a bitch, Yates. That's all I'm asking."

# CHAPTER SEVENTY-ONE

Way was very quiet for a very long time. When he finally spoke, his voice barely rose. He did not look at Hannon. "So what you're telling me is that without my knowledge or consent, you filed the paperwork necessary for two known felons to walk out of custody and disappear without a trace into one of the biggest cities in the country?"

They had stepped into a conference area designed for attorneys and their clients outside the courtroom. The door was shut, and no sound entered from the hallway, where a steady stream fed into and out of night court in a ceaseless dance. Way sat. Hannon stood.

"Is that what you're telling me?" Way asked.

"That's one way to interpret the situation."

His eyes flickered toward her. They were dark and sharp, but there was too much white around them. "Okay. Tell me another way to interpret it."

"They're trying to resolve the situation, Keith."

Way brought his fist down on the scratched surface of the conference table. "They're trying to resolve the situation? What in the hell does that mean?"

"We don't have any idea where Lukas is," Hannon said. "He could be in LA, he could be in Mexico, or he could be in Las Vegas by now. Who knows? Those two have a line on him, and with them on the street we have a chance to finish this the way you said you wanted to."

"I wanted to do this myself. I'm not farming it out to some ancient skip tracer and a war hero who's probably so screwed up from PTSD she doesn't even know what country she's in. You know what I found out when I was making some calls? She cage-fights. She fights in a god-damned cage like an animal. And this is who you decide you're going to trust? Her? Not me, but her?"

Hannon took a deep breath. She put her hands on the back of a wooden chair and held on. "Yes."

Way's face reddened. His expression screwed up, and he spat out his next words. "Of all the stupid goddamned—"

"Stop right there!"

Way went silent and fell back in his chair, a startled look passing over his features.

"I have been with you every step of the way through all of this," Hannon said. "I was there for every crazy thing you did or said from coast to coast. I have taken your shit and listened to your ranting, and now I am *done*. You clear it with me when we decide what we do next."

"You don't have the authority," Way said.

"Yeah, I *do* have the authority. You are only in on this because I convinced them you could handle it. But you can't handle it, Keith. You've tried to walk over me from the start. It's over. I can get on the phone right now with the commander and tell him that you are out of your goddamned mind. You are unstable, you are reckless, and you are unprofessional in a way I have never seen in my life. You loved Jerry? We *all* loved Jerry. And when he died, we *all* took it hard. Why do you think I didn't bat an eye when you told me you didn't want to bring Lukas in alive? Why do you think I stuck with you through everything that went down until we ended up at that motel and I got shot? I am on your side, but you are so out of your mind you can't even see that. I'm just another problem to you. Well, I'm not the problem here, Keith. You are the problem."

A dense silence fell between them. Hannon still clung to the chair, her nails dug into the wood. The back of one leg trembled. She felt the chemical surge of adrenaline rising up through her spine, exploding into her brain, and making the lights overhead brighter, the colors of the room sharper.

"Is that all?"

"You need to hear this. You are way too close to this, and you are coming apart. I've tried to hold you together, but I can't do it alone. You have to do your part."

Way put his hands on the table and blew a breath. He looked down at his knuckles and stayed that way for a time, unmoving. Hannon waited.

"Maybe I've been unfair," Way said after a long while had passed.

"There's no maybe about it."

"I have my reasons."

"I know all about it."

"You don't know! You weren't there. It wasn't your gun that killed Jerry. Now we have one shot to make this right."

"Keith, what are you going to do?"

"I'm going to coordinate with LAPD and throw a net over this city so tight a mosquito couldn't get through. Then I'm going to hunt down Lukas, and I'm going to do what I said I was going to do from the beginning. On my own."

"I'll be there, too," Hannon said.

"Maybe it's better if you're not. You have your doubts, and I can't guarantee it won't get ugly. You don't want to go down with me? That's fine. I can do this on my own."

"There's no need for that, Keith. I just need you to take it down a notch. It's the best thing."

"Sure," Way said. "Whatever you say. Let's go."

"I'll be just a minute. I have to make a quick call."

"It's the middle of the night."

"You're not the only one with things going on. I'll be right there."

Way cast a doubtful look toward her, then shook his head. He left the room and closed the door behind him. Hannon brought out her phone and opened text messaging. She keyed in a number from memory. *He's on the move*, she typed. *I'll tell you more when I get the chance. Watch your back and be careful. Steer clear of local PD.*

She sent the text, and no reply came. Hannon tucked her phone away, stood, and straightened her clothes. She let herself out and hastened to follow Way down the hall.

# CHAPTER SEVENTY-TWO

The headquarters of the Los Angeles Police Department was on the 100 block of West First Street. It was aggressively modern, composed of sharp concrete shapes and a patchwork of illuminated glass hallways. There was no street parking, and it took nearly ten minutes for Way and Hannon to get their vehicle squared away and make it to the entrance to the lobby. The doors were unlocked, and two uniformed policemen guarded the space.

One moved to intercept them. "Sir, ma'am, is there something you need?"

Way brandished his ID. "Deputy U.S. Marshal Way. This is my partner. We're here to see a Captain Cobb."

"It's four in the morning."

"Captain Cobb has made herself available. So if you could just show us where to go, we'll be on our way."

The policeman looked at them both, then shook his head. "Okay. Elevators are over there. Room Ten-thirty-nine. Office of Operations."

"Thank you," Way said, and he turned away from the man without another word. Hannon hurried behind him. She slipped her phone from inside her jacket and opened up a text window. *Downtown with LAPD,* she wrote. *Where are you?*

The phone was silenced, so the reply only vibrated in Hannon's hands. *Close.*

*Will keep you informed,* Hannon texted as they reached the elevators. *Stand by.*

"What are you doing?" Way asked her.

"Nothing." Hannon put her phone away. "A friend of mine's going through a breakup."

279

"It's seven o'clock on the East Coast," Way said. "Tell her to go have a coffee."

They took the elevator to the tenth floor and emerged in a corridor that was only half lit. Way ticked off the offices as he went. Hannon sensed the vibrations emanating from him. He snapped his fingers when he saw Room 1039. He went in. Hannon followed, her hand on the phone in her pocket.

There were multiple offices inside the space, and all but one was dark. A woman emerged from it. "Are you Deputy Marshal Way?" she asked.

"Yes. And this is Deputy Marshal Hannon."

The woman came close with her hand extended. "Priscilla Cobb. I'm glad to see you got in all right."

"Do you have some coffee?" Way asked.

"There's a machine. I'll put on a fresh pot. In the meantime you can wait in my office."

Priscilla Cobb's office was large and comfortable, with a table for meetings and a broad desk. American and California flags stood in miniature on both sides of her nameplate, and she had a plastic Slinky and a container of Play-Doh next to her blotter. Photographs of children were on display.

"Did you get those files I e-mailed?" Way asked when Cobb returned.

"Jeremy Yates and Camaro Espinoza? These are your fugitives?" Cobb asked.

"Sort of," Hannon said. "They—"

"They're two of them," Way interjected. "Our primary target is Lukas Collier. You're working from his biometric data."

Cobb nodded. "That's all been processed and sent through."

"I'm sorry," Hannon said. "Biometric data?"

"That's right. We have CCTV cameras all around the city and county, and all that information comes back to one of our operations centers for analysis. We can take any booking photo, any snapshot, even images from another camera, and create a three-D model of the subject's face that can be matched across the board almost instantaneously. I just sent the photos for Yates and Espinoza on. They should be in the system in an hour or two. We can sweep for faces individually or cross-index them with others in the search group, so if they gather in one area, they're more likely to be identified. So far we haven't had any hits. Are you sure Collier's in the city?"

"It's—" Hannon said.

"That's the theory we're working from. These other two are involved with him somehow. We expect them to turn up where we find him, or close to it. They have pending federal charges against them."

"I should tell you that we received an inquiry from the FBI last night regarding your fugitive."

"Local field office?"

"Yes, and a Special Agent Brock from up north. He said some things I don't really understand. This *is* a fully authorized fugitive pursuit, isn't it?"

"Yes. Special Agent Brock's interest is parallel to ours, but we don't fall under his authority."

"All right, then. Our capabilities are at your disposal. Everything our people see, you'll be able to see. When we're done here, I'll make you comfortable in our briefing room, and you'll get real-time updates."

"Thank you. And we'll need you to move when the time is right. Do you have the manpower to handle that?"

Cobb smiled. "Deputy Way, we have enough manpower in Los Angeles to fill a football stadium. We're ready to mobilize twenty-four hours a day, every day. We wouldn't be doing our jobs if we weren't ready for anything."

"Okay," Way said. "I think we're on the same page."

# CHAPTER SEVENTY-THREE

Konnor took Lukas to his place in Alhambra and spent the better part of an hour tending to his leg wound. Lukas knew Konnor had been an EMT for a while after Iraq, but things went a different way for him when he got hooked on painkillers and couldn't get off. Konnor was still taking, but it was the kind of thing he could keep under control now, and he had suppliers better able to maintain his needs than he could ever get from his jump bag.

"Where's your old lady?" Lukas asked.

"Out of town for the weekend, visiting her folks in San Diego."

"Good."

He gave Lukas three pills from his stash and told Lukas to chew them. Lukas washed the bitter taste away with beer. In an hour he was floating away, dimly aware of the recliner underneath him and the vague discomfort of his wounded leg. He might have slept, or maybe he was in a halfway dream.

It was early morning, before dawn, when he returned to his senses. He limped around Konnor's small house, digging some bacon and a couple of eggs out of the refrigerator before frying all of them in a skillet. He was sitting at the kitchen table, finishing them off, when Konnor came in. The man scratched the back of his neck and then stood in front of the open fridge for a long while as if mesmerized.

They sat together as Konnor chewed cold cereal. The two of them looked out through the window blinds at the quiet, dawning street. Lukas was the first one to say anything. "This is not how I figured it to go."

"Shit happens."

Lukas shook his head. "I've been sloppy. Lately I've been wondering if I'm losing my edge. Gone soft."

"I don't think you have. You're still one tough son of a bitch. They don't make soft Marines."

"Oorah," Lukas said without enthusiasm.

"You thinking about that woman? She gave you a pretty good shiner."

He resisted touching his face. He could feel the bruise. "That's what I'm talking about. No way would I ever let some chick get the best of me."

"She didn't get the best of you. You said you put her down."

"She's still alive, ain't she?" Lukas returned. "She should be *dead*. I should be toasting over her body."

"One day."

"One day. Listen, I'm gonna call up Jake's boy and see if he's on his way. When do we pick up our toys?"

"Eleven o'clock."

"Whereabouts?"

"Skate park about half an hour from here."

"Real public."

Konnor shrugged and then drank the milk from his bowl. He wiped the corners of his mouth with his thumb and forefinger. "It's a real smooth transaction. They bring a rental truck with the goods in the back. We check it out, if it's all good we give them the cash and they leave us the keys. We just drive on out. Nobody knows anything about what went down. Trust me, I've done it before."

"I'll take your word for it."

Lukas went in the other room and used the new phone he'd bought from a convenience store a mile away. He listened to Derrick's line ring and then got voice mail again. He killed the call without saying anything. His leg was hurting again.

Konnor appeared with a pair of jeans. "Hey, I got some pants you can try on. Get out of those bloody ones. I got some shirts, too, but they'll probably be big on you. If you don't mind that, at least you'll be clean."

"Thanks. Got to look my best."

He was left alone with the jeans. Slowly he stripped out of the ones he wore, and he took another look at the bullet wound. It was sewn together tightly now, but it had lain open like a mouth before. He'd been running full tilt when the marshal shot him. He'd seen enough to know the man's face. They'd been five feet apart in Newark and one trigger pull away from ending it for good. "Asshole," Lukas said aloud to no one.

The pants fit well enough when cinched tightly with Lukas's belt. Konnor brought more clothes, clean socks and an undershirt and a checkered blue button-down that hung on his body. Konnor was broader than him, and thicker than him, and wearing Konnor's clothes made Lukas feel like he was dressing up in a big brother's hand-me-downs.

For the next few hours he tried Derrick off and on, but it was always the same. Every time he heard the beep of Derrick's voice mail, his tension notched a little higher. Even taking another one of Konnor's Vicodin was not enough to quell it. Konnor stayed clear. He knew when to talk and when to be silent.

They were forty minutes out from the deal when Konnor entered the living room, tapping his watch. Lukas called Derrick one last time and got nothing. He wanted a cigarette, but he hadn't carried enough cash to buy a pack at the store. He chewed the inside of his cheek instead.

Konnor waited until they were on the road to talk again. The bag of money was between them. Lukas kept his hand on it. "You good to drive?" Konnor asked.

"Yeah. Why?"

"Somebody's got to bring the truck back to the candy store. I figure we split up. You bring my truck home, and I take the goods. It's probably a good idea to keep you off the streets as much as possible."

"Don't try to shut me out of the deal."

"What? No way! We're together on this. But there's no reason for you to show your face at the candy store until it's time."

Lukas didn't reply. He watched the city slip by. Weekend traffic wasn't as dense as it got during the workweek. LA freeways were parking lots from Monday through Friday. The only way to take a breath was on a day like today.

Eventually they found their way into a residential neighborhood, and Konnor kept to the speed limit. The skate park was tucked in among the houses, hemmed with a gray cinder-block wall painted blue along the crest. It had a modest parking lot with only a few cars sitting under the bright late-morning sun. The yellow Penske rental truck was parked in the corner. Konnor pulled up alongside.

Two men got out of the rental truck. Unconsciously, Lukas touched the .45 in the back of his borrowed pants, and then he dragged the bag of money out. The men were middle-aged and white, their military-style haircuts heavily gray. One of them had an American flag pin on his breast.

Konnor shook hands with both men. Lukas stood out of arm's reach. The men studied him, and he did the same. "This the guy you were talking about?" asked one of them.

"Yeah, he's my boy. We were both in Anbar Province."

"He see any action?"

"You can talk to me directly," Lukas said.

The man turned another appraising look on him. "You kill some of them hajjis?"

"I killed enough."

"Then you're all right with me. Bunch of savages. Let's have a look at what we got for you."

The rental truck had its rear door pointed toward the wall, and the four of them stepped into the narrow space that was left so the men could undo a heavy steel lock. They rolled the door up. Inside it was dark, but Lukas's eyes adjusted. On the floor were dark green crates, each locked. From nearby came the *click-clack* of skateboard wheels on concrete and the shouts of teenagers.

Konnor glanced down at Lukas's leg. "I'll climb up."

The men got in the truck with Konnor. The man who'd quizzed Lukas took a second set of keys and began undoing the locked crates one by one. His partner laid them open. Even from where Lukas stood, he could see the guns.

"We got a half-dozen carbines, like you asked," said the man with the keys. "All brand-new with magazines. Tactical rails so you can customize to order. Thirty automatic handguns, mixed calibers, guaranteed never fired."

"Or my money back?" Konnor asked.

The men laughed. Lukas did not.

"Let's see your green."

Lukas tossed the bag of money into the truck. He wanted to get his weight off his bad leg, but there was nowhere to rest. "It's all there."

The man with the flag pin knelt down and unzipped the bag. He looked over the banded stacks of cash, riffling each one before putting it back. When he was done, he nodded to his partner.

"Gentlemen, a pleasure as always," Konnor said.

"Likewise. Keys are in the ignition."

"Keys to the locks," Lukas said.

"You can have those, too."

Lukas stepped back to let the men climb down. He jerked his head toward Konnor. "We'll wait until you drive away. Everybody's friends."

"Good hunting."

The two walked to a waiting Chevy across the lot and got in. Lukas watched them drive off. He returned to Konnor as he finished relocking the crates. They conferred at the rear bumper. "That's it," Konnor said. "I'll take these to the candy store, and you can call your people again. What do you think?"

Lukas clapped Konnor on the shoulder and smiled for the first time in a long time. "I'm feeling better already."

# CHAPTER SEVENTY-FOUR

They parked on the street because there was nowhere else to park. On one hand was the back side of the Seventh Street Produce Market, a long structure without rear-facing doors and with high windows it was impossible to reach from the ground. Farther down the block was a spice and garlic company with a warehouse open to the public. It advertised nuts, grains, and fruits and had a bright red jalapeño painted on the white wall.

The sun rose slowly, fat and lazy, spreading over the city and casting long shadows onto the Mustang. Yates sat behind the wheel, utterly quiet, watching the same thing as Camaro: a blue-and-white building festooned with candy signs and the block letters wholesale  candy  &  toys over the shuttered front doors. The side door was also sealed behind steel.

No one came or went. Camaro began to get sore in her seat. She shifted uncomfortably. There had been no word from Hannon.

"Want to get out and walk around?" Yates asked Camaro after the silence had gone on for hours.

"I don't want to move in case he comes."

"You think he's gonna have a taste for some Tootsie Rolls at dawn?"

Camaro sighed. She felt fatigue on her like a smothering blanket, but she knew she couldn't sleep. "He's not coming here," she said.

"You sure of that?"

"It's a goddamned candy store. What's he going to do here?"

"He sent that money on for a reason."

"Do you think it's in there?"

"Couldn't say. Can't rule it out."

She brought out her phone and texted Hannon. *Still waiting. Status?*

The answer came instantly. *No sign of L. Cameras have your faces. Keep your heads down.*

*Your partner?*

*I'll run interference here. Good luck.*

*Thx.*

"What does she say?" Yates asked.

"She says it's handled."

"You think that's true?"

"I don't know."

"That fellow Way is like you; he's not going to sit still for very long."

"She says they have our faces. Cameras."

"I figured as much. Wave of the future. You know they have satellites that can read a license plate from orbit? Pretty soon they'll be able to find anyone, anywhere, just by punching a few buttons."

"Then you'll be out of a job."

"Somebody's still got to knock on the door."

Camaro turned in her seat and looked down the long block. "I don't see any cameras around here."

"There's gonna be dead zones wherever you go. We stray out of this pocket, Way will come down on us hard."

Camaro rolled her head and listened to her neck crackle. "Hannon just has to keep him off us for a little while. Long enough for us to finish what we started. After that he can have whatever's left. I don't care."

Time passed, emptiness looking for something to fill it. Hunger gnawed at Camaro. Her belly made a noise, but Yates didn't comment on it. The sun rose higher, and the shadows began to shrink.

A car turned the corner well ahead of them and crept down the street. The breath caught in Camaro's throat. She felt Yates tense beside her.

"It's not him," Yates said.

The car passed them, then right-handed into the parking lot. It went to the far corner and stopped. The taillights flashed once, and then the driver got out. It was a woman in a pink collared pullover. She slung a backpack over her shoulder and went to the side entrance. Camaro watched her unlock the shutter and slide it open. She let herself in.

"Opening time," Camaro said.

"You want to go in and check it out?"

"In a minute."

After a short while the shutter over the front doors was unlocked from the inside and rolled up. The same woman in pink checked the doors, then vanished inside.

Two more cars arrived in short order. The people who climbed out of them were all employees, marked by the same pink shirts the color of bubble gum. Once they vanished into the warehouse-sized store, the street grew still once again.

"I'm going in," Camaro said.

"Get me a ring pop."

She got out of the Mustang and crossed the street. She used the side entrance facing the parking lot. When the door opened, the smell of sugar came rushing at her. An electronic chime sounded a tone.

Inside it was cavernous, broad aisles marked out by heavy metal shelving fully loaded with brightly colored merchandise. Jolly children's music played on the PA. Camaro passed pallets loaded with plastic party favors, boxes and boxes of candy bars, and then a gumball dispenser taller than she was. She heard voices ringing out here and there, the employees talking over the music. Dozens of brilliant piñatas dangled overhead.

The front of the store was given over to massive displays stacked high with more sugary delights. The center was jammed with shelving, which reached all the way to the high ceiling. Rolling yellow stepladders stood in each row, allowing access to the highest stacks.

Camaro went deeper until she reached the working heart of the store. Here the candy had yet to be unboxed and was held in titanic blocks of brown cardboard stamped with brand names and bound together with bands of heavy-duty plastic. Some blocks were wholly shrink-wrapped. A couple of forklifts stood idle near a loading dock.

"Help you?"

She turned at the man's voice. She saw him, heavyset in his pink shirt, his face young, broad, and friendly. If he noticed the marks from her fight with Lukas, he didn't react to them. "I was just looking," Camaro said.

"Anything in particular? We have a *lot* of stuff in here, and it can get really overwhelming."

"You just sell candy and stuff?"

"Like it says on the sign. Candy, toys, party favors, decorations, kids' games—anything you want. Having a party soon?"

"No," Camaro replied, and she felt suddenly sluggish, as if the candied air were fuzzing her brain. "I'm only... Hey, do you know a guy named Lukas Collier?"

The man thought. "I don't think so. Did he use to work here?"

"I don't know. I thought maybe you might know his name."

"Doesn't ring any bells, sorry. I'm Randy, by the way."

"Randy, do you remember anybody getting a special package here in the last couple of days?"

"You mean not candy-related?"

"Right. Something unusual."

"Well, we got a guy who does loading and unloading for us who gets packages here sometimes. I think one came in. He doesn't like having stuff go to his place, because he's here so much. People steal things off his doorstep, I think."

Camaro took a step toward Randy. "What's this guy's name? Konnor Spencer?"

"Yeah, that's right. Do you know him?"

"I've heard his name around. How about you? How well do you know him?"

Randy's brows knitted. "I, uh, don't really know much about him at all. He's older than me, kind of looks like a biker. I think he is a biker, actually. He has a Harley."

"When does he work next?"

"Later today, I think. Only a couple of hours. Hey, is there something I should know about? Is he in some kind of trouble? Because I try to mind my own business."

"No trouble," Camaro said. "Don't worry about it."

"Okay, but—"

Camaro walked past him without another word. She stalked out from among the stacks of candy and out into the light. Yates sat behind the wheel of the Mustang, still as ever. Camaro ran to the car and got in.

"You get my ring pop?"

"Konnor Spencer definitely works here." Camaro brought out her phone.

"Who is he to Lukas?"

"I don't know, but it's something."

"Hannon?"

"Working on it."

He fell quiet again, and Camaro's thumbs worked as a new car pulled into the candy-store lot.

# CHAPTER SEVENTY-FIVE

*WE NEED TO know more about Konnor Spencer.*

Hannon looked at her phone. *What do you have?* she texted back.

*He's real. He has the money. Works at the candy store. What can you find out?*

*I'll check.*

*Let me know.*

She watched Way through the glass door into the briefing room. The room was dominated by a long conference table, but at one end of the room was a massive bank of monitors feeding out real-time information from across the city. It was a nerve center where the LAPD brass could see and hear everything as it happened. Data was processed and spat out in columns of text or captured images, still or moving, the influx unceasing. Priscilla Cobb had put Way in the path of this deluge, and he hadn't moved from that spot.

Around eight o'clock in the morning, members of the Office of Operations had begun to filter in, just a few on a Saturday, meandering to their offices without much interest in Hannon or Way. A man in shirtsleeves and a tie who looked like he might have been an accountant joined Way in the briefing room. They talked quietly. She could not hear them through the door.

Cobb stopped by the door and looked in at Way. "He's a dog with a bone," she remarked to Hannon.

"That's one way to put it."

"When will he take a rest?"

"Never."

"What about you?"

"I could use some information if you're willing. I could go through our people, but it might be faster if I lean on the LAPD."

"What can I do?"

"A man named Konnor Spencer. Konnor with a *K*. Any record he might have, home and work addresses, registered vehicles. The works."

"I can do that. I'll put the request in right now. Meanwhile, do you want to lie down in one of the empty offices? There's one with a couch."

"I don't think I can."

"Take an hour. If something comes up, you'll be the first to know. I'll have a full jacket on this Spencer."

Hannon took a deep breath, which turned into a yawn. She acceded reluctantly. "An hour," she said.

"I'll show you where it is."

The office was easily twice as large as Cobb's and had its own meeting area, complete with a small conference table, comfortable chairs, and the promised couch. The walls were hung with plaques citing decoration after decoration. "Whose is this?" Hannon asked.

"The assistant chief's. But don't worry, he's not in today."

Hannon took off her jacket and lay down on the couch. "Don't let me sleep too long. And if Keith moves, I have to know. Don't let him leave here alone."

"You don't trust him, do you?"

"It's not that."

Cobb tilted her head slightly. "It's not?"

"Okay, maybe a little. He has some issues with perspective."

"And you keep him on track."

"I try to."

"I won't let him slip away."

"Thank you."

Cobb closed the door. Hannon pulled her jacket over her and shut her eyes. She was asleep in seconds.

There were unformed dreams, cold and dark and full of icy rain. Way's face floated to the surface more than once. And Jerry Washington's. She caught a glimpse of Camaro Espinoza. The old man was more indistinct, but he was there, too.

Someone shook her. She woke. It seemed like she'd lain down only a few minutes before. Cobb stood over her with a sheaf of papers in her hand. "Deputy Hannon?"

Hannon sat up slowly, her thoughts sluggish. Her eyes felt gritty. She rubbed them and yawned. "How long was that?"

"About two hours."

She felt a stab of adrenaline. "Is Way still here?"

"He is, just like I promised. He's coordinating with Herman, one of our data guys. They're sifting a lot of faces. It could be a while. As it was, it took me a little longer than it should have to get Konnor Spencer's information."

"Let me see."

It was dim in the empty office, but Hannon saw enough. They had Spencer's driver's-license photo and a list of minor infractions mostly related to traffic. He had never been in jail, and he had no convictions for anything serious. They had a work address for him Hannon recognized and a home address on Danzig Place, right in Los Angeles.

"Everything you were hoping for?"

"How far away is this? His house."

"Not far. You could get there pretty easily. Mind if I ask how he ties in to your fugitive?"

Hannon got up from the couch. "I'm still working on that. Could you e-mail this information to me?"

"Sure, just give me a couple of minutes."

Cobb left the office. Hannon shrugged on her jacket. She sorted through the pages again. Very little. A truck and motorcycle registered to his name, something they could feed to the maw of LAPD's software. But that meant Way would know. She folded the papers and slipped them into an inside pocket.

She texted. *Have a line on Spencer.*

*What is it?*

*Home address. Vehicles. I'm going to forward an e-mail to you. Not much longer.*

She walked over to the briefing room. She pushed her way through the glass door. Way did not look in her direction. He stood watching the monitors with the man Cobb had called Herman. "What do you want?" he asked.

"Anything?"

"Not so far."

"Then maybe it's time to shut it down."

"No. They're here. It's just a matter of time."

"You've been at this for hours. You haven't slept, you haven't eaten. If you blinked, you could have missed them."

"I didn't blink. These cameras don't blink. Right, Herman?"

"That's right. Just because they haven't passed in full view of a camera yet doesn't mean they won't. Coverage isn't total, but it's good."

"It's over, Keith."

Way turned on her. "It's not over. I made some calls. Those KAs we talked about? LAPD started knocking on doors an hour ago. We can cover the whole list by the afternoon."

"You can't call for that kind of thing yourself. You don't have the authority. The commander—"

"The commander can hear about it when it's done! I'm not going back to him with my hat in my hand, begging for a chance to follow up. They'll hand it off to the marshals in the Southern District and we'll be out. That's not happening."

Hannon exhaled. "You aren't listening to me again. You're not listening!"

"Maybe I should step outside," Herman said.

"Yeah, do that," Way replied. "But don't go far. This won't take long."

They waited until Herman left the room. Hannon spoke first. "I agreed to keep working with you if you got a handle on yourself, but you are cutting too many corners. There are procedures to follow, and if that means someone else takes over from here, then that's the way it's going to go. You have to be prepared to fail."

Hannon's e-mail tone chimed. She didn't look down at her phone.

Way raised a shaking finger. His face was dark. "I am not going through this again with you."

"Fine. Then I'm calling it. My detail, my prerogative."

Hannon turned on her heel and left the room. She grabbed her phone and texted *Trouble on this end.*

Cobb was in her office. Hannon saw the recognition on the woman's face when she entered. "Something's wrong?" Cobb asked.

"We have a difference of opinion."

"Is there anything I can do?"

"Brace yourself."

Hannon's phone vibrated. *How bad?*

*LAPD mobilized in force. Keith on the warpath.*

*How much time do we have?*

*Not long. Spencer's jacket is coming your way. Do what you have to do and get out.*

"What are you doing?"

Hannon looked up sharply. Way was in the door. He grabbed at her phone. She clung to it, but he twisted her wrist and the phone came free. He looked at the screen. His face darkened. "Who is this you're texting? And don't say it's your friend."

"It doesn't matter."

"If you are undermining this operation..."

"What, Keith? What are you going to do? What *can* you do?"

Way held up the phone. "Is this Espinoza? Is that who it is?"

"What difference does it make anymore?"

"You're communicating with her?"

"I've been in contact with Camaro. She's keeping me advised."

"'Do what you have to do and get out,'" Way read aloud. "What does that mean? What have you done? Who's Spencer?"

Hannon was acutely aware of Cobb watching them. She considered her words. "They can help us. They can get to Lukas. We can use them."

"They're using *you*," Way said. He threw the phone at Hannon. She caught it. "Goddamn it, who is Spencer?"

"Konnor Spencer," Cobb interjected. "Deputy Hannon asked me to look into him."

She saw the interplay of emotions on his face, none of them good. "She did? And nobody told me? That changes right now. I want his information, I want to know what his connection is to Lukas Collier, and I want to know *right now*."

"I don't like your tone, Deputy Way."

"I don't give a shit whether you like my tone! Are all of you people stupid? I am in pursuit of a federal fugitive! That supersedes any kind of territorial claims you have on this city and gives authority to me. Me! You're going to tell me everything. Where they are, where they're going. Everything."

"We're not doing it," Hannon said. "You're finished."

Way stepped toward her. "Don't play games with me!"

"You're done, Keith. I'm making the call. We're out."

"You get out. I'm staying in. You have screwed me for the last time," Way said. He wheeled on Cobb. "The information on Konnor Spencer. On my phone in fifteen minutes, or I'm going to make sure your life turns upside down."

He left the office. Hannon glanced at Cobb. The woman sat frozen in her chair, her mouth slightly open. "I don't know what to make of that," Cobb said finally.

"If you don't send it to him, he'll find out another way," Hannon said. "Do it. Let him hang himself."

She went after Way and found him back in the briefing room, gathering his coat. He was shouting at Herman, and the man wilted under the onslaught. "If they're walking, I want to know what sidewalk. If they're on a bus or a train, I want you to tell me every stop they make. If they're driving, I want make, model, and license plate number. Don't wait, don't think, just do it. Do you understand?"

"Yes, sir, I understand."

Way stopped when he saw Hannon. "Out of my way," he said.

"Keith, don't do this. I did what I did to protect you from yourself. You gave it your best shot. It's not too late to step back."

"You know I can't do that. I have to play this all the way to the end."

"If you kill one of them, I'll tell them everything. The whole story. You won't get out from under it. They'll take your badge. You'll go to prison. Is that what you want?"

"We'd burn together. You think I wouldn't tell them how you let it happen?"

"Just try, Keith. They'll never believe you."

"I guess we'll find out. In the meantime, I want to see Lukas Collier dead. And if those two stop that from happening in any way, I'll see them dead, too. Get out of my way."

Hannon stepped aside. Way pushed through the door. She watched him go.

# CHAPTER SEVENTY-SIX

Konnor Spencer 's informa tion came. Camaro shared his photograph with Yates. She paged through the document. "His home address is here. We should check it out."

"One of us should."

"Where are you going to be?"

Yates surveyed the candy store from where they sat in the Mustang. "A long time ago I learned to trust my feelings when it comes to this kind of thing. You said Spencer's supposed to come here today?"

"For a couple of hours."

"What time do they close up?"

"Four. What are you thinking?"

"I'm thinking this is a pretty good place to do a deal. If Spencer has access to the inside, he can make his buy off the street and in private. Nobody looks twice at a candy store. It's got loading and unloading in the back, so depending on the size of his load he's good to go."

Camaro thought. She looked at the parking lot. It was half filled with cars. People had been going in and out steadily as the morning wore on, coming out laden with bags and packages. Some pulled around back with pickup trucks or vans and came away with heavy stacks of shrink-wrapped blocks of candy. "We could be waiting awhile."

"Lukas has to be feeling the heat right about now. He knows they're on him up north, and the marshals already put two and two together. The only thing he has is this deal. That'll buy him some time somewhere the cops aren't watching every corner."

"We still have to check the house."

"You should. I'll stay here."

"Where?"

"Missy, I've been watching places incognito since before you were born. I think I can manage for a couple of hours on my own."

"And if Lukas shows up while I'm gone?"

"I'll be sure to give him your regards."

Yates reached to the small of his back and drew the weapon he had hidden there. It was a Springfield Armory 1911, the finish Parkerized, the walnut grips lustrous. He dropped the magazine, then pressed it back into place before working the slide. He eased the hammer down. They exchanged gazes for a moment, and then Yates stepped out of the car. The gun had already vanished.

Camaro got behind the wheel. "Don't get yourself killed," she said.

"Not today."

She drove away. Yates shrank in the rearview mirror. When she reached the corner, she saw him walking into the parking lot of the candy store. She turned. He was gone.

The 101 wasn't a nightmare on most weekends. Camaro put the radio on but listened for only a few minutes before snapping it off again. She got off on the 10 to cut across the city eastward. She felt tense in the pit of her stomach, the muscles drawn tight.

Off the highway it was harder to find her way around. She used the GPS on her phone to make it through the neighborhood streets. The houses here were not palatial by any standard, but the roadways were clean, and there were even a few white picket fences. Kids felt safe enough to play outside, though the windows everywhere were solidly barred. Los Angeles was a city of bars, of sheer concrete walls and restricted access. The rich kept the best for themselves, while everyone else had to grab some small part of the endless sprawl.

She passed dead lawn after dead lawn, deprived of moisture for so long, the only thing that remained to mow were patches of hardy desert grass that couldn't cover the bald earth. Finally she found it: a blue house with white trim and the same, inevitable bars, perched on the corner of his street.

Camaro passed the mouth of the street and parked well out of sight. She checked the gun that had been given to her, an anodized black P220 with eight rounds in the magazine and one in the chamber.

It had no hammer, no safety. Every trigger pull was double-action. She put it away.

The sun glared almost directly overhead as she made her way back to the house. It had a separate garage on the side and a low chain-link fence cordoning off a barren backyard. Three houses down there was a group of kids shooting baskets on a hoop at the curb. They didn't look her way.

Konnor Spencer owned a truck. It was nowhere in sight. The motorcycle might have been inside the garage, but Camaro saw no windows to peer in. She felt exposed on the street and went quickly to the fence. She hopped it like she was meant to be there and passed into the rear yard.

All the rear-facing windows had blinds, and they were completely shut. Camaro made her way to the back door. Its blinds were half open, and she could see through the gaps into a darkened kitchen. A hallway opened up on one side, also dark. She could not see past the corner on the opposite end.

She examined the door. It was barred like the rest, the window broken up into nine identical panes, but it was possible to reach between the bars and touch the glass. Camaro thought a moment, then stopped to remove her boot. She stripped off her sock and wound it around the knuckles of her fist.

She chose the lower left pane. She put her knuckles against the glass and punched once, hard, in the space she had. The pane cracked. She punched again and a third time, until the pane was riddled with spidery, broken veins. Then she stopped and looked and listened and heard nothing.

It took three more short punches to break the glass. Camaro picked at the broken edges. She pushed back the sleeve of her Henley, then snaked her arm through the opening. Tiny teeth bit her skin. The fit was tight. She pressed in elbow deep, aware of blood running from fresh cuts. She felt around for the doorknob, then above it to where the dead bolt locked. The angle was bad, and the tendons in her wrist ached as she turned it with her fingertips. The lock clicked.

Camaro pulled her arm back out. The cuts would heal. The door opened easily now.

The utter stillness of the house told her no one was there. In the kitchen she found evidence of breakfast for two, a greasy skillet in the sink, an inch of water inside, suspending globs of congealing fat.

There were two bedrooms, the smaller of which was used for storage, boxes piled high. In the other the bed was unmade, but Camaro didn't know whether one person had slept there or two.

In the bathroom she found a pair of dirty socks in the wastebasket, one bloody. When she checked the trash in the kitchen, she discovered a pair of jeans with a blood-soaked lower leg, along with the remains of treatment: red-stained gauze and cotton balls, discarded packets of alcohol-infused wipes. She followed through to the living room and saw the medical kit. There were traces of blood on the leg rest of a nearby recliner.

"Camaro Espinoza?"

The voice carried from the kitchen, and Camaro froze.

"Camaro Espinoza, it's Deputy Marshal Way. I know you're in there. Come out where I can see you and keep your hands up."

# CHAPTER SEVENTY-SEVEN

Camaro heard the back door open. She looked left and right. The front door was ten feet away, but anyone coming through from the kitchen on that side could see straight through to the front of the house.

Way's footsteps were on the linoleum in the kitchen. Camaro moved away from the front door, deeper into the house. There was a closet to her right, the bathroom on her left. She eased open the closet's bifold door and checked inside. It was full, but with room for her to just squeeze in. Camaro slipped inside and tugged the door silently shut behind her.

Light filtered in through slots in the closet door. She heard Way moving around. His footfalls were muffled. He was on carpet now. "I don't know where you are in here, but I know you can't get out. I put in a call to the local PD when I saw you'd broken out the glass back there. They should be on the scene in ten or fifteen minutes. You won't get away."

It was dusty inside the closet. Camaro breathed shallowly. Her nose itched.

"Was he here? Did you just miss him?"

She kept her silence. She knew he was in the living room.

"I don't have to tell you what I'm gonna do to you when I find you. All those promises I made? They're going to come true. I will put you away forever. I'll put that old son of a bitch Yates away forever. I read you're from LA originally. Maybe it's good that everything ends here. Poetic justice. What do you think?"

He advanced down the hall. Camaro heard him breathing now, a raspy sound roughened by adrenaline and fatigue. A shadow fell across the opposite wall as he came closer. She held her breath as his weapon came into sight, followed by the rest of him.

Way stopped directly in front of the closet. "I don't want to play any games with you. If you make me, I'll have to shoot you, and you don't want that. So how about you just come out and give yourself up and we talk like a couple of adults? You tell me where Lukas is, or where he's going to be, and I'll make sure they send you somewhere that's not half bad. What do you say?"

Specks danced in Camaro's vision. She held on until Way moved forward. He looked into the bathroom, and she heard him rattle the shower curtain. He made a noise. She knew he'd found the socks. She let her breath go slowly.

"So Lukas was here," Way called out. "I knew I hit him. Not bad enough, but I hit him. You know, his friend Konnor has medical training. Got it in the Marines. Put Konnor and Lukas together in one person and they're you, you know that? There's not any difference between you and Lukas at all. He thinks the law doesn't apply to him and does whatever the hell he wants. Kill anybody, hurt anybody. Lie, cheat, steal.

"It's my job to put people like you behind bars. You don't belong with good folks, with *decent* folks. You think that Silver Star of yours buys you any sympathy from me? I don't care what you did in the ass end of the world. You and Lukas both. He got a medal fighting in Iraq. Doesn't mean a thing."

He was out of the bathroom now and moving deeper into the house. Camaro couldn't see anything except the space directly in front of the closet door. She pressed the hinge delicately, and the door folded open on quiet tracks. One glance showed the hallway was clear.

She stole out of the closet and shut it behind her. Way had said nothing else. She wasn't sure exactly where he was. She turned toward the living room.

Way's shoes thumped on the carpet. Camaro darted into the bathroom. She left the door open and slipped the patterned shower curtain aside. Plastic rings clicked against one another on the rod. Her tread was light inside the tub. She closed the curtain and pressed herself into the corner.

She heard him jerk the hall closet open. "Goddamn it," he said. "Just come out! Come out!"

Camaro willed stillness into every part of herself.

"I'm talking to myself," Way said. "I'm standing here talking to myself."

He was in the hallway. He was in the living room. The locks on the front door shot, and it opened. Camaro heard his fading voice as he made a call on his phone.

It was time to move. She stepped out of the tub and rushed down the hallway. On her left she saw the living room and the front door hanging open, daylight spilling into the dim interior. Way's voice was more distinct now. On her right was the kitchen. She went right.

In the backyard she jogged to the fence and vaulted it again. She forced herself not to run on the street, only walking fast back to the Mustang. As she started the engine, the first black-and-white LAPD unit passed her, turning onto Spencer's street. She eased off the curb and drove without looking toward the house and Way, who was sure to be on the front lawn.

She dialed her phone and left it sitting on the passenger seat as she drove. She counted the rings until Yates answered. "He's not here," she told him.

"Lukas?"

"Neither one."

"I can explain part of that. Spencer's here."

"At the candy store?"

"He rolled in a few minutes ago, driving a rental truck. Parked it out back and unloaded something into the store. I told you I had old man's intuition."

"Then tell me where Lukas is."

"I couldn't venture a guess, but now we know he won't be far."

Camaro didn't tell Yates about Way. "I'm headed back."

"I'll keep it warm for you."

She drove on.

# CHAPTER SEVENTY-EIGHT

Lukas saw the police cruisers as soon as he turned onto the last street before Konnor's house. He didn't slam on the brakes or touch the accelerator but kept on going as if the sight made no difference to him. He glanced toward the house as he passed it and saw two uniformed officers in conversation with a man he recognized from the motel. His leg twinged at the sight of him.

He drove out of the neighborhood in no direction in particular. He called Konnor. "Don't go home," he said when Konnor answered.

"Why? What happened?"

"Cops are at the house. If I'd been there fifteen minutes earlier, they would have had me. We got to figure they've been inside and they know everything."

"Shit, do I need to get out of here? They have to know where I work."

"They'll jerk each other off for hours before they get down to you. First they'll want to take your place apart for fibers or some shit, and then they'll start using their heads. But this means we have to step up the timetable. How long till the candy store closes?"

"A few hours."

"I'm going to call Otilio and tell them we're moving up the exchange. We get it done today, then you and me will head up the coast."

"Salinas?"

"Nah, Salinas is screwed. Carmel, Pacific Grove—that whole place. We're gonna need to take it farther north. I don't have the same connections up that way, but when you've got ten keys of weed to unload, you can make friends in a hurry."

"I don't like it."

"So what? Since when has this been a democracy? This is my deal, and I run it my way! You want to take your chances with the Feds, be my guest, or you can pull up stakes and start making some serious bank up north. I just wish those assholes in Oregon hadn't legalized it. Screws up the whole deal for the rest of us."

"Okay, we'll play it your way."

"That's what I thought. Talk to you soon."

"You're coming here now? People are here."

"No, I'm gonna find someplace to stay cool until it's time to move. We're better off if we're not seen together. Not yet."

"Tell me it'll be all right, Luke."

"It'll be all right. Don't get your panties in a bunch."

He stabbed the phone with his thumb, ending the call. He was headed farther east. He knew a mall in City of Industry that would be busy on a Saturday afternoon. Konnor's truck would be lost in the parking lot, and Lukas would be another face in the crowd.

The decision made, he made a second call. Otilio answered. "Hey, my man," he said. "What's happening?"

"The deal is happening. Today. Four o'clock."

"Hey, what happened to giving me twelve hours' notice?"

"My timetable's changed. I need to unload my shipment and get the green in the next few hours or it's off. This is a limited-time offer, so if you can't deliver, I'll take my business elsewhere."

Otilio spoke in Spanish to someone away from the phone, his voice muffled; then he came back on the line. "I might be able to get you what you want. But it's gonna cost you."

"Same deal as before. I deliver the guns, you give me the weed. No bullshit and no renegotiation."

"You're stressing me out, cuz. This was supposed to be smooth and quiet. I don't like all this rushing around. You got heat on you?"

"It doesn't matter. What matters is I got what you want, and you got what I want. So let's do it."

"Fine. But if this goes the wrong way on me, some people are going to be very upset about it."

"I'm shaking," Lukas said, and he cut Otilio off.

He glanced into the rearview mirror and saw a cop a few cars back and one lane over. Immediately he checked his speed. He was going no faster or slower than anyone else on the road. The touch of a knob tilted the side mirror so he could have a better look at the cop without lifting his eyes. The cop behind the wheel didn't look his way.

Lukas kept steady. When an exit presented itself, he put his signal on and gently changed lanes, careful to monitor the cop's progress relative to him as he made the maneuver. He started to lose speed for the ramp. The cop didn't slow down. A moment later they were abreast, two lanes apart. The cop didn't even turn his head, his eyes fixed on the road ahead.

Lukas let out a breath as he descended on the ramp. A gas station was just ahead. He slotted in next to one of the pumps and got out. His hands trembled slightly. He made fists until it stopped.

Traffic passed. People filled their tanks. Lukas opened the gas cap and put the pump nozzle in, but he didn't pay for any gas. He stayed where he was for ten minutes, and when the time had elapsed, he took the nozzle out as though he had finished up like everyone else and then got back in the truck.

His hands were rock-steady now. As he pulled out on the road, he had an image locked in his mind of flat packages bound with tape and shrink-wrap. Break the seal with the point of a knife, and the air was filled with the rich, unmistakable odor of resin. It was the smell of money.

# CHAPTER SEVENTY-NINE

*Where is he?*

*At Spencer's house. Where are you?*

*Candy store.*

*He'll come there.*

*I know.*

Camaro stood near Yates behind a wholesale produce business that seemed closed for the day. There was an alley that traversed the length of the entire block, branches letting out between buildings. There were Dumpsters filled to the brim with rotting vegetables and fruit, others snarled with plastic packaging and cardboard. Where they found shelter, the shadow of a Dumpster fell over them, and they had a clear view of the candy store's loading dock.

"How's our friend?" Yates asked.

"Worried. She's right. It's just a matter of time until Way comes here. He was ten minutes behind me at Spencer's house."

"Let's hope we have more lead time than that here. If Lukas comes now, there are innocent people inside that store. And we've already seen what happens when innocent people get in the line of fire when Lukas is around. I won't have that on my conscience."

Camaro watched a couple emerge from the side entrance of the candy store with a gigantic piñata between them, their wrists laden with plastic bags. She made a note of the yellow rental truck. "The place will close soon," she said. "After that, they have the whole store to themselves. Lukas has to show then. We see him, we move on him."

"That's the general idea."

"Is your shoulder all right?"

"I can move it, if that's what you mean."

"If we have to do this the hard way, do I have to worry about you?"

Yates turned from the candy store to look at Camaro. He squinted in the late afternoon sun, and his mouth was almost hidden by the brush of his mustache. "You worried about me, Ms. Espinoza?"

"Yeah. I am."

"Maybe you're not as cold as you like to think you are."

"I'm not Lukas," Camaro said.

"No, you're not. I can see that now. I trust you to watch my back. Lukas? I wouldn't trust him to watch my clothes at the laundromat."

"I'll still kill him."

"That I don't doubt for a second."

Together they waited. Not far away, a police siren called out among the concrete walls of the city and was ultimately smothered. Time passed. People came and went, but never Konnor Spencer, and never Lukas Collier.

Camaro sweated, a thin band of perspiration on her spine. Every time a car passed on the quiet street, she tensed anew. The parking lot thinned out. She checked her watch. "Almost time," she said.

"Keep your eye out. He's coming. I can feel it."

The last of the customers departed. The employees at the candy store stayed inside another ten minutes, and then they filed out in their pink shirts. Randy was among them. They closed the shutter behind them.

"Spencer's still inside," Camaro said.

"Waitin' for Lukas."

The employees drove away. Randy's little Toyota was the last out of sight.

"Truck," Camaro said.

A black pickup appeared on the street. The windows were tinted, but Camaro knew the profile. She took a step forward. Yates put out his hand to stop her. "Hold up. There's more coming."

"Where—?"

As she spoke, three other vehicles cruised into the parking lot from the opposite direction. One was a van painted white, dirty and badly abused. The others were immaculate, a red '67 Impala that sat low on its wheels and a Ford Shelby GT500 painted blue with a twin stripe splashed from nose to tail.

The van circled around to the rear while the cars parked in the center of the small lot. Camaro saw movement on the loading dock. Konnor Spencer was there.

"Update our lady friend," Yates said.

Lukas was out of the truck and shaking hands with a lean, muscular Latino, the sides of his head shaved and his arms heavily inked. There were four others with the leader. They scattered around, casting looks here and there but not seeing Camaro and Yates where they hid.

*It's happening,* Camaro texted.

*I've lost W.*

*When?*

*An hour ago. Not on Spencer scene.*

*We need time.*

*Calling him. No good. Not answering.*

"Damn it," Camaro said out loud.

*You are exposed.*

*L could leave. Got to move.*

*I'm coming.*

*Careful.*

"I suspect the news is not good," Yates said quietly.

"Way's loose. Hannon's coming."

"How far out is she?"

"Minutes. If we want this, it happens now."

Lukas and the Latinos climbed the steps to the loading dock and vanished inside. Camaro's heart raced. Her mouth was dry.

"I'm going to let you call it," Yates said. "Last chance to step back and let the good guys take him."

"Do you think he'll let that happen?"

"Can't say. But it's a crowd in there. It's not going to be one-on-one anymore. The question is whether you still want him, and how bad."

Camaro watched the store. She tried deep breathing to slow her pulse. "I have to look him the eyes," she said.

"Even if you can't take him out?"

She flexed her hands. The muscles in her back were locked. She was frozen in place with competing visions in her head. Lukas dead. Lukas

311

taken away. She licked her lips. "If it comes to it, Hannon can have him."

"But you want him to know it was you."

"Yes. And you."

"Then I guess the decision's made. Let's go."

Camaro emerged from cover with Yates a step behind. They skirted the low wall that offset the parking lot from the alley, steel bars preventing ingress, then made their way in from the street. She fell in along the wall of the candy store and moved forward.

She heard voices ahead, slipping easily from English to Spanish. Camaro understood enough to know they were only shooting the breeze. The business hadn't started yet.

They reached the corner of the building. Yates touched her on the arm. She bent close to let him speak into her ear. "Step in like you got a hundred men behind you. Don't let 'em see you sweat."

Camaro acknowledged him with a pat on the shoulder. She drew the pistol from her waistband. Yates's was already out. They advanced on the concrete steps leading to the loading dock. She held the P220 low ready, against her belly. She took the steps one at a time.

More than half the lights were off in the candy store. Camaro had the sun at her back when she stepped into the open. She brought the gun up smoothly as all seven men came into view. Lukas was framed in the center, three men on each side of him, standing over an open case with a trio of black carbines inside. The hollows of the store were murky behind him, filled with deep shadows. The place had no windows.

"Hey," Camaro said quietly.

The men reacted at once. They reached for guns under the loose tails of shirts or at their bellies. Lukas simply stood, and when Camaro's eyes met his, he smiled.

Yates ghosted in behind her. "Guns down!" he commanded. "First man who moves gets shot."

Lukas still smiled. "Relax, *amigos*," he said. "It's old friends."

"What the hell?" asked one of the Latinos. The bottom of his Lakers jersey was pulled up and hooked on the butt of a Glock at his hip. His hand hovered over the weapon. "Is this a rip-off? Goddamn it, Luke, you son of a bitch!"

"No rip-off," Camaro said. Her gaze held Lukas's. "I'm here for Lukas."

"Gonna shoot me now? Is that how it goes down?"

Camaro's finger rested lightly on the trigger. "Is that how you want it?"

"Cops," said the man in the Lakers jersey.

"No, they ain't cops," Lukas said. "They're concerned citizens."

"Why don't you gentlemen put down your weapons?" Yates asked. "Nice and slow. Nobody gives us trouble, nobody has to get hurt. Like the lady says, it's Lukas we want. The rest of you can go on about your business."

"You can't shoot all of us," said Konnor. He stood two from Lukas, his hand behind his back. Camaro knew his fingers were on his weapon. She heard it in his voice.

"Who wants to volunteer to be first?" Yates asked.

Camaro's vision narrowed. She closed out Konnor, she closed out the man in the Lakers jersey and all the men he'd brought with him. She saw Lukas's face, Lukas's eyes. He didn't blink. Her finger tightened just a little. "You lose, Lukas," she said.

"Boys," Lukas said, "I think it's time to finish our deal."

He blinked. Immediately the collection of men snapped into Camaro's focus. Konnor whipped a pistol from its hiding place and squeezed the trigger in the same motion. She felt a slashing pain in her arm just as Yates's .45 boomed.

The men scattered and left Konnor kneeling on the floor, blood soaking his pink shirt. Camaro moved right and Yates left. She put a bullet into the leg of a fleeing man and saw him go down on his face.

Return fire began to explode from inside the store, sounding like cannon. The gunmen melted into the shadows, and only the sharp flashes of their muzzles revealed them, like burning fireflies.

"You hit?" Yates asked her.

Camaro glanced at her arm. It throbbed, the fabric ripped and fresh blood underneath. Flexing the muscle was painful. "It grazed me," she said. "I'll be all right."

"I'll go high, you go low."

"Let's do it."

They entered the store as one. Camaro picked out a shape in the half-darkness and squeezed the trigger. A short yelp was followed by silence. All the shooting had stopped. Her stunned ears could barely make out the voices sounding farther inside the cavern of the store.

Together they skirted the cases on the floor and moved through the loading area. Camaro used a pallet of candy boxes nearly as high as herself for cover. Yates knelt behind a forklift. She pointed to herself, then gestured with her head. Yates gave her an okay.

She stepped out from behind the candy and dashed for the nearest aisle. Yates triggered his pistol twice into the dark, and the vaulted metal ceiling slammed the report down onto them like an open hand.

A peek around the edge of the shelving revealed a dark, open aisle shadowed at the far end. Camaro saw no one. She emerged from cover, crouching low and moving quickly, weapon up. Her arm was wet with blood and burned more and more by the minute.

A shape loomed out of the dark, and Camaro zeroed in on it. The contours of the giant gumball machine solidified. She took shelter in its shadow just as its plastic globe exploded.

Gumballs showered Camaro and sprayed out across the concrete floor. She sighted on another vague shape in the dark and fired. She saw the shape sink to the ground and lie still.

She slipped on the gumballs as she crossed open space to reach the man she'd killed. Up close she could see it was the man in the Lakers jersey. An automatic lay inches from his hand. Camaro left it and advanced.

More shooting erupted behind her. She dropped to the floor and scrambled toward a display of plastic party favors, their colors dulled by the poor lighting. A man screamed. Another gunshot silenced him. Camaro listened. "Yates?" she called out. "Yates!"

His voice carried over the stacks from somewhere: "Still alive. You see him?"

"Working on it."

The deeper into the store she went, the spottier the light became. It shone in pools ahead of her where the registers and the office were and in spots and splashes. Camaro spotted the end of an aisle and made for it, her boots scuffing as she moved forward.

She reached cover and stopped. She breathed hard, and her vision limned with silver. She exposed herself to peer around the corner.

Lukas seized her by the gun arm and whirled her around, jerking her halfway off her feet. She squeezed the trigger, and her pistol went off between them, a sudden flashbulb of muzzle flare that lit Lukas's face. He hammered her wrist, and her grip on her weapon loosened. His hand closed over hers, and her fingers strained as he twisted the gun from her grip. The gun clattered on the floor.

He backhanded her across the face, and she felt the healing stitches on her brow open up. She came at him low, driving her elbow deep into his ribs. The wind rushed out of him as he fell back. She kicked him hard, and he went off his feet entirely.

Gunfire detonated close by, and a bullet skimmed off the floor between them. Camaro scrambled for her gun. Her hand closed over it, and she fired instinctively.

Lukas threw himself on her. Two hundred pounds, and his breath was in her face. He had a hand on her gun arm, and he slammed her weapon against the concrete. Camaro brought her knee up hard. Lukas cried out.

They rolled. Camaro tried to bring her gun to bear, but Lukas's grip was unbreakable. He closed his other hand around her throat. She gouged him in the eyes.

He torqued her wrist, and she felt something give. Her hold on her weapon slackened. She fired into the floor by Lukas's head, and they both screamed at the close-range report. Dark blood oozed from his ear.

Lukas got a leg between them and pushed her up and off. Camaro went over, striking her head on the floor as she tumbled onto her back. She still had the gun in her hand, but her grip was weak.

Shooting sounded all inside the confines of the store, echoing and reechoing. Someone called for his mother in Spanish. Yates was yelling for Camaro, but she was breathless and hurting.

She saw Lukas make it to his feet. A string of gunshots sounded as rapidly as crackling fireworks. Camaro was misted with blood, and Lukas reeled. She couldn't raise her right hand to fire as he retreated into the dark. She grabbed for her gun with her left, opened fire at his retreating back as it merged with the shadows.

Yates was there. "Are you down? Are you hit?"

"I can't move my arm. I think I tore something. Help me up."

Men shouted to one another in the dark. Yates looked around. "I don't know how many more we got to deal with."

"Get me on my feet."

He helped her rise. She opened her mouth to speak in the same moment a shrill alarm sounded. A red light flashed two rows down, and then there was the sudden burst of white light from outside. "Fire exit," Camaro said.

"I'll go," Yates said.

Camaro shook her head. "No. Hold them off for me."

"You're hurt."

"He's hurt."

"It should be me."

Camaro looked at Yates in the dark. "It has to be me."

"What about Hannon?"

"She's too late."

# CHAPTER EIGHTY

Camaro burst out of the store into the space between it and the chili wholesaler next door. She heard renewed gunfire inside, but there was no time to think more of it. Alley access was fifty feet away. Lukas was already out of sight, but there were scattered red droplets on the dirty ground.

High up in the air, the sound of skirling police sirens carried. Camaro ran to the alley, skirting a Dumpster filled with discarded packaging. Her lungs bellowed.

Her arm was hurting more and more. Blood ran down her hand in a steady stream. She knew she'd feel foggy soon, and after that she'd feel nothing. Her fingers were numb. She dashed ahead, heedless of her own booming pulse. She made the main alleyway just in time to see Lukas vanish thirty yards distant, limping hard.

Camaro ran on, the gun in her left hand, her right arm hanging. She tripped on a loose chunk of concrete and stumbled to one knee, splitting open her jeans. Bracing herself with her weapon, she found her feet again.

She reached the alleyway Lukas had ducked through and saw it reached the street. Heedless of the flecks in her vision, she sprinted after him until she was on the open thoroughfare. Lukas was across the street and pulling away. Camaro fired after him, but her aim was faulty. She saw him pitch forward and then struggle onward, dodging between another pair of buildings.

The racing of a car engine made it to her good ear, but she did not look back. She made it to the break between buildings and skidded around the corner into a barrage of bullets. They crashed into the brick wall on one side and cut the air so closely she felt the heat of them. She

317

spun away behind cover, chased by rounds that chipped at the building she sheltered behind.

Camaro dared a look. Lukas was framed by the space, a chain-link fence behind him blocking the way completely. The slide on his .45 was locked back. He dropped it and ran to the fence, catching it with both hands and digging in with his toes. He began to climb.

Camaro followed. Lukas was halfway to the top when she shot him twice in the back.

He plummeted six feet and crashed to the asphalt. He squirmed there, bleeding. Camaro approached him. Her left hand shook. Her body felt cold. Her limp right hand was covered in blood. "Don't move," she said.

She did not expect him to smile. He did. "You don't look too good," he said.

Camaro stood over him. His arm looked broken. He had blood on his teeth. One of Yates's bullets had gotten deep into his side. "Neither do you."

"Seems like every time I see you, I can't seal the deal," Lukas said. He coughed. "Why is that?"

"I'm lucky, I guess."

The police sirens were much closer.

"You gonna let them take me?" Lukas asked.

"Should I?"

Lukas didn't answer but coughed violently until a gobbet of bloody sputum spattered his face. He shivered from blood loss. Camaro knew it would only get worse. "It doesn't matter anymore."

"Then I guess this is it."

"My brother said you were a soldier."

Camaro only nodded.

"Let me go out like a Marine. One to the head."

"I don't think so," Camaro said. She raised her boot and stomped down on his throat. She put her weight on him as he began to struggle. Lukas scrabbled at her leg with weakening fingers, his eyes turning bloodshot and his face gone purple.

She kept on until finally he was still.

Camaro put her pistol away and turned from the body. She walked back the way she came, aware she was swaying slightly. Out on the street, she looked back the way she'd come. The first bullet struck her low, just above the belt line. Another crashed into her shoulder, and she lost her equilibrium, collapsing backward.

Camaro saw only sky. Consciousness wavered. She tried to focus on the things around her.

Way approached her with his weapon up. Camaro struggled to lift her hips to reach the pistol at her back, but the blazing pain immobilized her. She scraped her heels against the dirty sidewalk and managed to push herself a few inches. Way closed the space.

Camaro was breathing too fast, too shallowly. She could not bring her pulse rate down. Blood on the ground soaked her back. She gasped out loud.

The marshal stood over her with his gun at his side. His eyes were hollow from lack of sleep, and dark. "Where's Lukas?"

Camaro could not draw a breath deep enough to make words.

He looked toward the space between the buildings. Camaro saw the moment he recognized Lukas's body.

"You killed him," Way said. His face turned into a rictus. "That was for *me! I* was the one who was supposed to kill him!"

She tried for her pistol again, but he stepped on her wrist.

"Do you have any idea how long I was after him? Do you know what I sacrificed? Everything. Everything. I called in every favor anyone ever owed me, and I burned bridges. But people knew how much I wanted it. They knew."

When he talked he gestured with his gun, the mouth of the barrel passing over her dangerously. His finger was on the trigger. Camaro felt the bones of her wrist straining under his foot. She would have two ruined hands, and then it would be over.

"And then you. You and that goddamned old man. My own partner turned on me because of you. I've got nobody. All I had was this."

He knelt and laid his full weight on her wrist. He pushed the muzzle of the pistol against the raw wound in her shoulder until Camaro cried out. She thought she tasted blood. The smell of it was thick in her nostrils, even stronger than the odor of spent gunpowder. The fingernails

319

of her trapped hand scraped the dusty ground, but she was not strong enough to pull clear. Her vision narrowed.

Way stood and leveled the gun on her head. "I'm going to kill you now," he said. "We're all done."

Camaro heard the shot, but there was no blackness. She felt no fresh pain. Way stood above her, and his expression melted away into confusion and then slack nothingness. He collapsed sideways, and his gun clattered on the ground.

Hannon appeared. She holstered her weapon and knelt over Camaro. She touched Camaro's wounds lightly, but even that was enough to bring pain. Camaro grunted. "Can you walk?" Hannon asked.

Camaro managed a nod. Her throat rebelled against words. She forced them out. "I think so," she said.

No part of Camaro was free of pain. Hannon muscled her into a sitting position, and Camaro put her good arm around Hannon's neck. Her right was immobile. Every movement jarred her and brought new agony.

Camaro got to her feet and half walked. Then Yates was there. He rushed forward to take her from Hannon. Hannon ran from them, and for a long moment Camaro thought she wouldn't return. An engine rumbled, and a black Charger with LAPD markings surged up the street toward them. Hannon got out to open the rear door. Together she and Yates slid Camaro in the backseat.

Doors slammed, and the police sirens were everywhere. Hannon gave the Charger gas, and the V8 engine pushed Camaro into the cushions. They made two sharp turns, wheels screeching, and then picked up speed. Camaro's head whirled.

Yates twisted around in his seat. He offered a bloody hand, and she took it. He squeezed her fingers. "You're gonna be okay," he said.

Camaro let her eyes slip closed. In her mind she heard the thunder of approaching rotors and the sting of grit kicked up by the wash. All she felt was the heat of coursing blood and the pain that went with it. And the grip of Yates's hand in hers.

"Don't go, Camaro," Camaro's father said.

She faded into darkness.

# CHAPTER EIGHTY-ONE

The pocket beach was barren of people, ten minutes north of Malibu and hidden among the rocks and along a rugged trail that usually dissuaded the casual visitor. Seagulls rose and dipped in the offshore breeze. The sun was low on the horizon, coloring everything orange and bloody red, the sun itself a stained disc.

She sat with her shoes off, letting her bare feet sink into the sand. The pain in her side when she held herself seated was tolerable, held back by a pair of pills taken every four hours. Her right arm was in a cast to the elbow. The bullet wound in her shoulder barely hurt at all.

Camaro heard Yates coming. She looked back and saw him aglow in the colors of the western sun. He held a large paper grocery bag with loops for a handle. "Is anyone sitting here?" he asked.

"Not right now," Camaro said.

Yates lowered himself onto the blanket and put the bag between them. He brought out food wrapped in wax paper and a pack of six beer bottles. "I got cookies, too," he said.

"Open one of those for me?" Camaro asked.

Yates did as she asked and passed it over. Camaro drank deeply. He watched her. "How do you feel?"

"Alive."

"Better than the alternative."

Camaro nudged the wax-paper packages. "What are these?"

"Fish tacos. You like fish tacos?"

"I'm a local girl. What do you think?"

"Then I'm glad I guessed right."

She dug a hole for the beer bottle and set it beside her before going after the tacos. They were good and clean-tasting, like the sea. She said nothing to Yates while they ate.

"No deputy," Yates observed. He wadded up his wax paper and stowed it in the bag.

"She's late."

"She has work to do. Can't be easy explaining how two people you deputized ended up in a gunfight in a candy store with a stack of dead bodies to show for it. Especially when you didn't file the paperwork. It's always the paperwork that gets you."

"She'll come."

Yates nodded. "I never did thank you."

"For what?"

"For Lukas."

Camaro didn't answer. She ate her last taco.

"You know, my wife wants to meet you."

"Why?"

"I expect she'd like to see the woman I've been spending so much time with. She's the jealous type, the missus is. I think it probably won't help much when she gets a look at you."

"Maybe one day I'll get to Norfolk," Camaro said.

"Maybe."

They watched the Pacific for a while. The ocean lapped at the wet expanse of sand. "I need to see my sister," Camaro said.

"Get your niece to sign your cast. Kids like that."

"You want to sign my cast?"

"I'm not a kid anymore. But thanks for offering."

Camaro picked up her beer. She drank until it was empty and reached for another. Yates opened it without being asked. It hissed quietly, the sound almost lost in the murmur of the sea.

"Camaro?"

"Yeah?"

"I've been meaning to ask you something."

"So ask."

"Do you get too much charter business in the winter months?"

"Sometimes. Depends. It's the slow season."

"I was wondering," Yates said. "Just wondering."

Camaro waited for him to finish. The sun grew lower still, fattening as it touched the water and turning the long shadows of the rocks into pools of darkness. There were no lights on the beach. The beer was good. The quiet was good. The city teemed with life, but here it was only the two of them.

"I find myself in a situation," Yates continued. "And I could use some help."

"With what?"

"Have you ever considered a career in bail enforcement?"

# ACKNOWLEDGMENTS

I'd like to thank first and foremost my wife, Mariann, for once again keeping me on course when it comes to my work. I could not function at the keyboard without her. I'd also like to thank Elizabeth A. White for her guiding hand during the pre-editing phase, as she was a breeze to work with and made critical recommendations that made the book better. In addition, I would be remiss if I didn't thank my editors at Mulholland Books and Mulholland UK, Wes Miller and Ruth Tross, for making bang-up suggestions that transformed *Walk Away* into a lean, mean thrilling machine.

Finally, it would be inexcusable if I didn't thank my agent, Oliver Munson, for all his help getting me to this point and for the services he continues to provide in terms of insight into my writing and making it possible for people to read me at all. I am greatly indebted to him.

# ABOUT THE AUTHOR

Sam Hawken is author of the Camaro Espinoza series, which begins with *The Night Charter*, as well as the Crime Writers' Association Dagger–nominated Borderlands trilogy. He was born in Texas and currently lives outside Baltimore with his wife and son.

THE APPEAL TO THE GREAT SPIRIT

# ABORIGINAL
# AMERICAN ORATORY

## The Tradition of Eloquence
## Among the Indians of the United States

*by* LOUIS THOMAS JONES, Ph.D.

*Introduction by*
CARL SCHAEFER DENTZEL

SOUTHWEST MUSEUM
LOS ANGELES, CALIFORNIA
1965

*Printed by*
SOUTHLAND PRESS, INC.

To

MARK RAYMOND HARRINGTON

*for his abiding confidence*

# Introduction

CHRISTOPHER COLUMBUS gave the people of the Old World their first look at native Americans when he returned to Spain, after his great discovery in 1492, and presented the picturesque aboriginal Americans to Ferdinand and Isabella. The Spanish court was first to learn of the wonders of the New World and first to hear the strange speech of the visitors from far across the western seas.

Columbus, Admiral of the Ocean Sea, was the first of many who were destined to plant the flag and cross of Spain in what was to become, as exploration continued, North, Central and South America. History chose him to mark the great delineation of time sequence in the Western Hemisphere by dividing the development of man in that continental system into two parts: the first, Precolumbian America; the second, European Colonial America and subsequent cultural, economic and political evolutions.

The European Colonial Powers found the indigenous

Americans living in various stages of an advanced stone age. Aboriginal America was a complex of many individualistic cultures, some high, some low. The conquests of the Spanish thrust their Colonial power headlong into numerous highly developed Indian societies in the New World. The Aztec, the Maya and the so-called Inca cultures were the outstanding examples of the higher civilizations of Precolumbian America.

The Mayas, the Toltecs and the Aztecs of Central America and Mexico had developed a skillful system of picture writing. Although there was no written language of cursive style in the Americas several means for the retention of knowledge and for teaching through the use of oral literature were highly developed.

In the codices of the Mayas, the Mixtecs and Aztecs were found the history and traditions of those Indian people in what had become the vice-royalty of New Spain. In the **quipus** of the ancient Peruvians the legends of the Inca dynasties were recalled by the Indian scholars and priests in what became the vice-royalty of Peru and New Granada.

Frequently seen in the codices—the picture writing of the Mayas and Aztecs—are representations of persons in the act of speaking. From the hieroglyphs, usually shown issuing from the lips of the speaker like the "balloons" of a modern cartoonist, it is quite obvious that the spoken word in aboriginal society was an important thing. The knotted cords of the Peruvian **quipus** retold the tales of the great orators of the Inca culture: the Chan-chan, the Chimu, the Mochica and Nazca.

Early in their conquest of the Americas the Spanish commented on the eloquence of the Indians. In Malinche, the remarkable Tarascan woman, Cortés found a highly intelligent ally—a talented diplomat. According to contemporary accounts Malinche spoke beautifully in various native languages in serving her master Cortés and the cause of the Conquistadores. Hers is one of the first recorded examples of Indian eloquence. Moctezuma, the Aztec ruler, and many of the officials of his incredible empire were great orators capable of moving large numbers of their people when addressing them and who greatly impressed the Spanish with their eloquence.

Cuauhtémoc, who first treated with the Spanish and later fought bitterly against them, was renowned as an orator, diplomat, warrior and statesman. Unfortunately, neither the eloquence of Moctezuma nor that of Cuauhtémoc could stem the tide of history or avert the fate of the Aztec empire. Tenochtitlan, the Aztec name for what was to become the capital of New Spain and later Mexico City, was the center of Aztec learning. Náhuatl, one of the basic languages of Precolumbian America, had developed a great literature of which poetic recitation was a principal part. Consequently, it was only natural that many learned people—nobles, priests, chiefs or any leader of society—were skilled in their native language arts, particularly speech.

Atahualpa, the last Inca ruler of Peru, and his nobles pleaded eloquently for his life before Pizarro and his Conquistadores. History records much treachery in the conquest of Peru, however, and all the diplomacy and pleas of the Indians for the preservation of their empire availed them nothing.

One of the great Indian revolts in New Spain occurred in what is now the heart of the American Southwest. The Pueblo rebellion (1680-1692) was begun by Popé, a San Juan Indian of outstanding ability. He told the natives that their Great Father and Chief of all the Pueblos had commissioned him to order his countrymen to rebel against the invader and drive him from the land so that they could live as their forefathers had done, free and independent. The uprising came as the culmination of a long period of friction between the Pueblos and Spaniards. Through his inspiring speeches Popé was able to arouse the Indians and drive every colonist from the land. Popé continued as leader of this last great Pueblo revolt until his death in 1688.

To the north, in French America, explorers adding to the realm of the King of France, and the priests who followed them to propagate the gospel, often expressed amazement at the interesting state of culture they found among the aborigines. While there was no written literature, they remarked upon the abilities of the Indians to recall events, recite history and speak eloquently to one another—especially in council. The Jesuit letters which were sent back to France from the New World often described the Indian speech arts as an interesting phenomenon among the people of the St. Lawrence River Valley, the Great Lakes country and the Mississippi Valley. The French found Indian society so interesting that they actually encouraged miscegenation between Europeans and American Indians. Consequently, throughout much of the 17th and 18th centuries in French America, Indians who could speak well in both their native language and French were employed in various aspects of government service. Records reveal that many well-known trappers, settlers, agents, guides, scouts, soldiers, tradesmen and minor frontier officials utilized the spoken word in a most useful way in French America. With the culmination of the French and Indian wars (1755-1763), however, this tradition of fraternization was not maintained by the victorious English.

The annals of English America are filled with references by the early colonists and officials of the Crown to the Indians of New England and Virginia and their speaking ability. Particularly noted was the eloquence of Pocahontas, who saved the life of Capt. John Smith. In Plymouth Colony the pilgrims commented on the long speeches made by their Indian neighbors. It is not unlikely that the first after-dinner speeches in what was to become the United States followed that renowned banquet known as the first Thanksgiving. But it is doubtful if the Indian orators, long-winded as they were, could have outdone some of the pious Pilgrim fathers. That great warrior, King Philip, roused the Indian nations of New England with his fiery oratory delivered in the true spirit and ancient tradition of the Northeast tribes.

During the American Revolution and in the formative period of the young Republic of the United States representatives of the Continental Congress, and later the Congress of the United States of America, made many treaties with the Indians in the old Northwest Territory in expanding the boundaries of the growing United States. Representatives of the state and war departments, who carried on these negotiations, became accustomed to the long speeches and haranguing of the Indian chiefs and statesmen. It seemed that because they lacked a written language they took extra pride in their ability to recall their ancient traditions, so that hours were dedicated to their traditional eloquence.

Many chiefs were very wise—often getting right down to the point without delay. Their logic, concern and prognostication are truly remarkable. Representatives of the American government often recorded with great respect the wisdom gleaned from such speeches. Actually, quite a body of literature exists which represents a great tribute to the intelligence and eloquence of the American Indian.

The intrepid captains, Lewis and Clark, who on President Jefferson's orders set out to explore the Louisiana Purchase, found in the Indian maid Sacajawea the most remarkable ally of all. Her knowledge of the terrain, of tribal customs and of various Indian languages contributed greatly to the success of the expedition. Sacajawea was a diplomat of the first order. Her superb woman's intuition, coupled with her ability to size up a situation, made her a perfect negotiator. As an interpreter, translator and wise speaker Sacajawea has become one of the great legends of all time—a tribute to the American Indian as well as to all womanhood.

Throughout the hundreds of years that the five leading European Colonial powers—Spain, France, Holland, England and Russia—held their American possessions, one of the consequential experiences of each was the common problem of treating and trading with the Red Man. The tradition of oratory in the culture of the Indian was something encountered and commented upon by all.

If the Indians had had a written language, one naturally would wonder if the treaties made by the white man would have had greater meaning. Since reading and writing words meant little to the Red Man, and the Indian's oratory seemed of no real lasting significance to the white man, it is little wonder that most of the treaties between the aboriginal Americans and European Colonials were broken.

It is even more unfortunate that the efforts made by the young United States at the end of the 18th century and beginning of the 19th century to treat the Indians fairly on the North, Central and Southwestern frontiers were not continued. Thomas Jefferson, who was greatly interested in the American Indian and his culture, first as Secretary of State and later as President, endeavored to treat the aborigines fairly. As the 19th century progressed, however, Jefferson's good example slowly waned.

By mid-century the American Republic reached from the Atlantic Ocean to the Pacific Ocean and the power of the Red Man was broken in all but a few isolated regions. His power was broken principally because the treaties made with him were broken. Indian oratory of this sad period of the history of the United States concerned itself with protests against the destruction of Indian culture, of Indian removal, and of the curtailment of rights and the theft of lands.

Pity indeed that Indian oratory could not stop the white man's inhumanity to man in the guise of a policy of national manifest destiny!

Throughout the 19th century many American artists were in the vanguard of that body of intrepid adventurers, explorers, trappers, soldiers, Indian agents, traders, surveyors, wagon and railroad builders and pioneer settlers who moved westward. The history of American Art has been enriched by the artist's participation in extending the pioneer frontiers of the United States. To him the American aborigine was a romantic as well as a fascinating subject. Early journals of travel, government reports and a vast body of literature, both prose and poetry, written by people from all over the world attracted by the dramatic pageant of 19th-century American life were often illustrated by distinguished artists who were well acquainted with the Indian and the pioneer frontier.

It was also the custom, when important Indian delegations would visit the Great White Father in Washington in the course of transacting business between the aboriginal Indian nations and the United States of America, for official artists employed by the government to paint portraits of the chiefs or interesting events. Karl Bodmer, George Catlin, Charles Bird King, Rudolph Frederick Kurtz, James Otto Lewis, Alfred Jacob Miller, Frederick Remington and a host of others lent their esthetic talents and artistic skills to capturing the noble Red Man and dramatic events of his life.

The universal interest shown in aboriginal American life is reflected by many fine 19th-century publications. Particularly in the United States superb productions representing a combination of excellent scholarship as well as good art were created for a public eager to see the likenesses of important Indian characters. Indian life and conflict with the new order in dime novel form or in sensationally illustrated editions found a ready market. Color lithography reached a new height with the production of many Indian works. Historically and artistically these remarkable records are of great importance to American ethnologists.

Foremost among such publications are "History of the Tribes of North America," by Thomas L. McKenney and James Hall, 1836-1844; "Scenes in Indian Life," by Felix O. C. Darley, 1843; "The Aboriginal Port-Folio" and "The Romance of Indian Life," art by Captain Seth Eastman, text by Mrs.

Eastman; "Historical & Statistical Information Respecting the History, Conditions & Prospects of the Indian Tribes of the United States," collected and prepared under the direction of the Bureau of Indian Affairs, per Act of Congress of March 3, 1847, by Henry R. Schoolcraft, illustrated by S. Eastman (6 vol.), 1851-1860. Currier and Ives and other print makers created a new vogue in American decoration with their colorful, popular arts.

With the advent of photography some artists turned photographers, carrying this fantastic new equipment into remote corners of the United States and its territories. So, from the very beginning of photography in America, the Indian and his interesting ways fortunately became a matter of record before the complete demise of the Red Man and the destruction of his culture. L. A. Hoffman, William H. Jackson and Adam Clark Vroman are among those earlier skilled photographers who established a great tradition in the photographic art of using the camera to record American Indian life.

One of the high points of this important and informative esthetic development was the production, between the years 1907-1930, of "The North American Indian; Being a Series of Volumes Picturing and Describing the Indians of the United States and Alaska," written, illustrated and published by Edward S. Curtis. It was edited by Frederick Webb Hodge, with a foreword by Theodore Roosevelt, and consisted of 20 volumes and 20 portfolios of magnificent photographs.

In the preparation of Dr. Louis T. Jones' book on Aboriginal American Oratory the Southwest Museum was most fortunate in receiving the cooperation of many internationally known institutions such as the Boston Museum of Fine Arts, the Huntington Library of San Marino, California, and the Smithsonian Institution, Washington, D.C. It is a pleasure to also acknowledge the generous assistance of many well-known dealers in books and prints. We are particularly grateful to Dawson's Book Shop and the firm of Bennett & Marshall of Los Angeles, and The Old Print Shop of New York. Through their willingness to assist we were able to reproduce a number of rare prints and photographs.

It is a privilege to acknowledge the many years of interest that Dr. Jones has maintained in the Southwest Museum. For more than a quarter of a century he has been an enthusiastic supporter of the Museum's program. He has been among the foremost scholars of American Indian history and culture. As a follower in the tradition of William Penn, one of the few European Colonial developers who treated the American Indian fairly, Dr. Jones' long life bespeaks devotion to the principles of the founder of Philadelphia—the City of Brotherly Love. Dr. Jones' book is not intended to be a definitive study of the American Indian, but rather an appreciation of his eloquence. In his own words the Indian has always revealed himself to be an honorable human being, willing to cooperate, willing to yield at times—but always ready to fight for his own race and rights.

Dr. Jones is a Quaker of New England extraction. Many of his ancestors underwent the experiences cited in his book. He has lived and worked in many parts of the United States from Florida to Maine, the Central West and the Pacific Coast. He is well known as an educator. His undergraduate degree of D.Sc. was earned at Wilmington College, Ohio. In addition he holds the degrees of M.A., M.Sc.Ed., and that of Ph.D. earned at the State University of Iowa, Iowa City, Iowa.

While on the faculty of Earlham College, Richmond, Indiana, Dr. Jones was a frequent visitor at the Indiana State Library in Indianapolis. There he studied the rich resources covering the American Indian. For two years he served as research assistant at the State Historical Society of Iowa, with access to its fine collections. Upon coming to the Pacific Coast he engaged in constant research at the Southwest Museum, the Huntington Library and the San Diego Museum of Man. Three times Dr. Jones has gone abroad for additional study in Europe. These lengthy trips brought him into contact with the British Museum and other English institutions. On one such occasion he was guest of the British Minister of Education in London, which formulated his itinerary to numerous British schools and universities.

Over the years Dr. Jones has pursued much field work as a basis for his ethnohistoric studies. This has been done among Indian schools and kindred agencies. He has paid many visits to Haskell Institute, Lawrence, Kansas; Sherman Institute, Riverside, California; and numerous similar establishments. He has also maintained personal acquaintances with the Zuñi, Hopi and Navajo peoples, as well as other tribal groups, for interpretive purposes.

The list of scientists and scholars with whom Dr. Jones has

prospect of practical extinction with the bravery and dignity of the American Indian. The Indian was a *doer* more than a *talker*, but when there were words to be spoken he could utter them with a direct simplicity that went straight to the heart of the matter, shaming and confounding the white man's circumlocution. Yet anger and scorn, pathos and irony, were not unknown to him. And whoever claims that the Indian has no sense of humor is ignorant of the truth.

The Indian had no written language, but there are words that are deathless in any tongue, whether written down or not. Most tribes had spokesmen, many of whom became skilled in the art of choosing words that could move or stir their listeners. Their words were usually simple and to the point, but the Indian lived and thought in metaphor—consequently even the most mundane of his speeches are like brightly colored pictures reflected in the minds of his listeners.

It is the purpose of this book to give the reader a sampling of these words against a background of the events that inspired them, and to demonstrate that for inherent eloquence the red man had no peer.

As Matthew William Stirling has remarked: "The depth and beauty of his [the Indian's] philosophy and religion has been but little understood by the white man. As an artist, poet, orator and dramatist, he has never been excelled."* Impartial examination of the native Indian's ability in the use of the speech arts must convince of the truth of this assertion.

A mysterious charm has always hovered over the American Indian, this uncomplicated child of Nature who asked no more than life gave him and who thanked the Great Spirit for the privilege of freedom to which he was born. His numberless myths and legends, the rich and varied nature of his folk songs and folklore, at first bewildered the white newcomers from across the Atlantic, but they were nonetheless fascinated. We are still fascinated today.

Years ago, while rummaging through the loft of an old log cabin on the Iowa prairies, the writer came upon a collection of printed Indian speeches, set down just as they had been delivered around the council fires of an earlier day. Despite their mutilated form these bits of manifest eloquence, some of which are included in this volume,

* *Scientific Monthly*, February 1931, p. 175.

# Author's Preface

THE STORY OF THE WHITE MAN'S conquest of America constitutes one of the most dramatic chapters in human history. It takes its beginning with the exploits of the daring Leif Ericsson, and continues through the adventures of many discoverers, explorers and later empire builders. This expansion of Western civilization presents a thrilling epoch in the annals of men as the swiftly moving centuries brought into physical conflict two of the most virile peoples of the earth—the red men of America, primitive but energetic, and the white men, masters of mechanized power. When these two cultures clashed it was like striking steel on flint.

Needless to say, though the Indian was forced to yield to this overwhelming white advance, the heroism of his self-defence has claimed the admiration of the world. And many of the words he has uttered, in peace and war, will echo forever down the corridors of Time.

Few peoples have accepted inevitable defeat and the

corresponded on Indian oratory has been large. These include such persons as Chief Nippo Strongheart (Yakima), Dr. Arthur C. Parker (Seneca), and Dr. A. L. Kroeber, dean of California anthropologists. One could go on with a long list of distinguished men of American Anthropology interested in Dr. Jones and his significant work. Suffice it to say that this appreciation of aboriginal oratory has been of interest to many well-known anthropologists both living and deceased.

The Southwest Museum is delighted to sponsor this long overdue work. In associating itself with the production of so useful and inspiring a book, the Museum salutes the work of Dr. Jones and offers tribute to his devotion to an ideal—that of giving the native American his true and rightful place among the world's great orators in all times and places.

CARL S. DENTZEL
Director

Southwest Museum
Los Angeles, California

exuded an irresistible appeal. That discovery was the beginning of a quest which since has had no end, a research that has led the author through libraries and museums throughout the United States and has even necessitated a number of arduous journeys among the scattered Indian tribes.

Certain difficulties were encountered, of course. One was the incredulous attitude of a great portion of the general public. Did the Indian have a language sufficiently advanced in form and content to justify the term "speech arts"? With his simple form of social organization how, when and where could he acquire the use of language sufficient to be called *eloquent?*

And should attention be confined to a given tribe, or a given era, such as the Colonial period, or should the study embrace the entire extent of the white man's contacts with the Indian? Moreover, if attention were confined to tribal groups within the territorial United States alone, would not conclusions drawn thereby be faulty? What about the more advanced Indian cultures to the south of us—the Aztec and the Mayan civilizations, for example? It was concluded that, while others may find more polished examples of Indian eloquence there, this work should confine itself to the oratorical talents of the North American aborigines exclusive of Mexico.

Naturally, the unwritten character of the early Indian languages offered stubborn resistance to progress in this study. But scores of white men, as well as Indian authorities of unimpeachable integrity, have recorded how they have been swayed by Indian orators, on both official and unofficial occasions. It is to these sources that the writer logically turned.

Carried like driftwood in the stream of passing years, many speeches of great historical worth have found lodgement in the most unexpected places. Some of these are the private journals and writings of early white traders and trappers. Some are to be found in the letters and reports of Christian missionaries who sought to spread their faith in the American wilds. Still others appear in government documents—colonial, state and national—testimonials to the Indian spokesmen's ability to plead the cause of their people when pressed to do so. It is largely from such sources that this work has been compiled.

Most of the speeches of record, translated by interpreters, were transcribed in a continuous, running form, with no paragraphing and little attention accorded to sentence structure. Hence, to discover and preserve the meaning intended by their authors a certain amount of editing has been required.

As with most such undertakings, this work could not have been completed by the writer alone. Many agencies and individuals, too numerous to be listed in this restricted space, have contributed to the enterprise. To all of these the author extends his sincerest thanks.

LOUIS THOMAS JONES

# Contents

# Illustrations

# Aboriginal
# American
# Oratory

# The Struggle
# for a Continent

W**HEN**
history's curtain first rose on the American scene a primitive
people inhabited this continent from ocean to ocean. Called
Indians, they represented many levels of social and cultural
development—some simple, others more advanced, most
savagely warlike. Today, however, due to their decreasing
numbers and broken strength, they are regarded as the
one "vanishing race" of mankind. Consequently, these
illusive but colorful "ghost men" of the past have seized
upon the imagination of the rising generation in many
ways.

Yet they are but little known to most people today.
Dressed in everyday white man's clothing, as most of them
are, the descendants of these first Americans move among
our population almost unknown and unnoticed. Still, as
time recedes from those events which marked the bitter
struggle for the mastery of this continent, the enchantment

of their racial personality seems to become ever stronger. More and more people want to know more about them— their past, their accomplishments, their native arts and talents.

One of the best avenues through which to reach an understanding and appreciation of the true nature of Indian life in general is that of the social position and work of the native Indian spokesman, or tribal orator. The part which he, as an individual, played in the destiny of his people reflects perfectly the cross-currents and points of difference between two great races. It was only through such individuals that the two peoples could meet on anything like a common ground.

Such spokesmen are to be found at the crossroads of all that affected the Indian's destiny. Through them the soul of the red race found its best expression. Indeed, many of them, as this study will demonstrate, are men of eloquence who could have held their own with Demosthenes, Cicero or any of our more modern orators.

Naturally, the Indian orators reflected the minds and feelings of their people—a people who found emotional inspiration in their forests, their lakes, their streams, their sky, and in Nature's ways in general. Unlike the white man, who changes everything to fit his needs and desires, the Indian had long ago learned to adapt himself to his natural environment.

The vaulted heavens above his head comprised the Indian's spacious cathedral and to that which almost universally he called the "Great Spirit," insofar as he understood deity, he directed much of his prayer life. In awed silence the red man can feast his soul upon a gorgeous sunset and be satisfied, while the white man must attempt to transpose all such objects of reverence and worship to canvas or film, never content with the mental image alone. This has led one observer to remark that "the European thought objectively, while the intelligent Indian felt subjectively."

Like his sign language, the Indian's speech is picturesque and garnished with metaphor. He constantly refers to Nature and Nature's ways. Moreover, the buoyancy and freshness of his thought life, so lacking in European models of oratory, are characteristic of the red man's manner of delivery. Hence, to comprehend that which an Indian spokesman attempts to say, the listener must adapt his thought to this natural imagery. Otherwise its implications may appear at times to be very far fetched.

Closely associated with the red man's general speech arts was the council fire. An almost universal institution among the aboriginal peoples of North America, it was conducted along strictly ritualistic lines, varying only in minor details among different tribes.

The force and effectiveness of the Indian speech arts can scarcely be measured by European standards. To attempt to do so usually ruins their innate beauty and stultifies their inherent charm. The Indian communed with Nature, he was an expression of Nature, and consequently his eloquence was Nature's very own.

All that has transpired in connection with the clash of cultures in North America since the coming of the Europeans is in full keeping with the white man's own racial past. From time immemorial the white man's civilization has been built by the use of force in the mastery of lesser or weaker peoples. In contrast, except for his intertribal feuds and conflicts, the Indian's way of life rested in general on the simple principle of mutual aid, often expressed in his orator's speeches.

Under his form of social organization the individual owned only the materials necessary to the maintenance of his personal life. His food, clothing, weapons; his wigwam or transient home; the seed for his impending harvest— these alone were his. Otherwise, all belonged to the tribal group of which he was a member.

The land, the streams, the lakes from which he drew his livelihood belonged to the tribe, not to the individual. Their use was granted to the people by the Great Spirit. Therefore they belonged to the Great Spirit alone. However, the manner in which many tribal groups have been induced to part with their age-old homelands by placing their finger-prints in the white man's heated wax, affixed to treaties carrying the terms of agreement, is shown in the illustration on Page 63.[1] Such treaties are to be found by the hundreds in the government archives in Washington, as well as in those of other nations across the seas.

This ceaseless conflict of interests has left a seemingly

indelible imprint on the minds of the two peoples. From the long struggle evolved an antagonism and racial bitterness which inevitably developed into mutual dread and hate. Indian wars were bloody and merciless, brutal hand-to-hand conflicts that did not necessarily end with death. All too frequently mutilation followed. For many generations the white settlers and their descendants would remember the sound of the Indian's savage war cry, together with the horror which attended the work of the tomahawk and the scalping knife.

As for the Indian—can he ever forget the merciless displacement of his people from their beloved hunting grounds, the terrible carnage wrought by the white man's powder and ball, and above all the broken pledges? How could the Indians of the West, hearing of the treatment of their cousins in the East, trust the white pioneers?

Few Indians have met with the best of the whites. It was from the unscrupulous land trader, the lawless frontiersman, and the corrupt rum seller that these first Americans acquired their initial impressions of the character of the white man's civilization. Of the white man's home life and his better nature the American Indian has known but little. The social and political implications of European refinement, his heritage of literature and art, his religious precepts, his mastery of science and mechanics—preserved for generations through his written language—these assets were strangers to the Indian's total thought life.

Compared to his own simple mode of social organization the white man's complex ways of doing things were baffling to the Indian—and sometimes suggested the supernatural. What the Indian could not comprehend he naturally feared. What he feared he tended to resist, even at the risk of unequal conflict.

In turn, to the devout religionists from across the seas anything which smacked of heathenism or idolatry was abhorrent. In their eyes the primitive religious practices of the American aborigines stood condemned. Why, in their ceremonials, did these red men bedeck themselves with gaudy feathers, with wild bear's teeth, and go about half naked? Why did they smear their bodies with horrid paint and utter savage yells amidst their pagan devotions? Did they not worship animals, as totems, as had the ancient

Hittites and Jebusites—peoples whom Jehovah had ordered his chosen people to go forth and destroy?

So these open chasms widened between the two racial groups. Many of the pioneers believed they were doing God a service when they murdered outright these red barbarians of the forest. Some thought no more of killing an Indian than they did of slaying a deer. With them such action involved no moral issue. Indeed, most of them were convinced that "the only good Indian is a dead Indian!"

Welcomed at first by the friendly Indians, the white man brought to the New World his own long-established social customs and institutions, his libraries, his universities, his museums and art galleries, and the recorded history of his long past. But with America's aborigines it was quite different. For their past they depended on tradition, on the memory of their old men, and the meaning of their prayer sticks, their wampum belts and similar transient materials.

Today conditions are much changed. Of the half million or more native Indians who now make their home within the continental United States, the vast majority are poor, even very poor. Many of their middle-aged and older members do not speak English, hence find it difficult to adjust to the changed environment, social as well as economic, in which they are forced to live.

To some Indians modern civilization has brought an appreciable degree of joint social and economic advancement. Today they have at their fingertips the cumulative benefits of our common cultural heritage. Many of them are skilled agriculturists, successful financiers, educators of note, outstanding scientists, musicians, artists, statesmen, warriors—and even prominent orators.

Taken as a whole the American Indian still chooses segregation, yearning to live apart after the manner of his own free ways. Nevertheless, according to one competent observer, this segment of our population today constitutes the "finest body of raw material for citizenship purposes" which our nation holds within its borders.

This part of our population is moved to action by the same emotions which impel other members of our body politic to self-expression. Indians laugh, cry or get angry as do other people, and for the same reasons. The most pitiful wail of sorrow which ever struck the writer's ear came from the lips of an unlearned Indian woman as she sang her tribal "death song" over the prostrate form of her lifeless husband, found dead at another's hand.

As with most Americans, the passionate love of home and native land lies deeply implanted within the red man's breast. The fact that he has had little or nothing to say about the way in which either he or his country is governed has not dampened his patriotism. In World War I, despite the fact that he and his people were still regarded as "wards of the government" (a status actually equivalent to prisoners of war), 18,000 Indians sprang to the nation's defense.

No less ready was the Indian's response in World War II when 22,000 Indians enlisted in the United States Army and about 3,000 more joined the Navy, Marine Corps and Coast Guard.

# The Native Indian Languages

LANGUAGE in its many forms, spoken or written, is the chief way by which we humans exchange ideas. Men have used this medium to pass on to future generations the lessons they have learned as well as the discoveries they have made, growing out of past experience. This is the framework of all history.

Strange as it may seem humans are the only creatures given to the use of speech, whatever its form or kind—though certain animals, birds and even fish make sounds which seem to be more or less intelligible to their kind. So far as is known, however, none of these rise to the plane of formal language as used by the most primitive of mankind.

As people use these little thought tools, called words, their ability to think tends to grow and expand. This is true with racial groups in all parts of the world. Some of these languages are found in tiny, remote areas of the earth, seemingly isolated from all others, except for the most shadowy connections. To understand their meaning calls for intensive specialized study. Modern languages such as French, German, English, Italian, Hebrew and the languages common to the Orient represent the racial experiences and amalgamations of great cultural groups over a span of thousands of years.

It is a recognized fact that the degree of culture inherited by any group of people is more accurately determined by its language than by any other media known. No society can be more advanced or complex than its members have language to express. Hence, in our efforts to evaluate the worth of the native American speech arts, it is essential that this simple truism be borne in mind.

Those familiar with the many Indian tongues native to North America believe that these languages have shown themselves capable of elevated *oratorical* expression—using that word in its limited sense. As one distinguished authority has pointed out, no single sentence used in any of these native Indian tongues has yet been found which does not readily yield to ethnic analysis, once the racial culture of those concerned is understood.

Hubert Howe Bancroft, a lifelong student of American Indian culture, remarked: "Indeed, throughout the length and breadth of the two Americas aboriginal tongues display greater richness, more delicate gradations, and a wider scope, than from the uncultured conditions in which the people were found, one would be led to suppose." Continuing, he declared: "Nor is there that difference in the construction of words and the scope of vocabularies between nations which we call civilized and those called savage, which, from the difference in their customs, industries, and polities we should expect to find . . ."[2]

Contrary to public opinion, however, the American Indians did not speak a common language. Much less did they enjoy a common culture. Their physical and lingual differences were as varied, in a sense, as were the numerous racial and linguistic stocks from which the white invaders from Europe were derived. At the time of contact no less than fifty primitive Indian root languages were spoken in North America, with at least two hundred or more varying dialects, independent of those to be found in South America.

As for native physical traits, there was no "typical" Indian then any more than there is now. Some were tall, others were short; some were of light complexion, others were dark—according to the area occupied. Some tribal groups, such as the Iroquois and the Sioux peoples, were bold and warlike; others, such as the Pima, the Papago and the so-called Mission Indians of the Southwest, were less aggressive and inclined to docility.

Structurally, the Indian languages as a whole are very different from those found in western Europe, and each must be judged on its own merits in regard to extent of vocabulary and expressiveness. Gender, for example, as used with most tribal groups, was based on the quality of the object described rather than upon sex distinctions. Moreover, whether a thing were animate or inanimate, large or small, noble or ignoble might be determined by the way in which it was treated.

The factor of tense, or time, might be imperfectly conveyed, though in this respect some tribal languages were more accurate and advanced than others.

An added feature of importance, common to many Indian tongues, was the Indian's tendency to use suffixes attached to base words rather than prefixes. In this way qualifying chains of cumulative thought are built up by what has been termed the "incorporation process," often highly confusing to the uninformed. This merely means the obtaining of concrete mental impressions by the naming of things, rather than by a corresponding use of action words or verbs.

James Adair, an English trader who made his home among the southern Indians of the early days, was much interested in the speech of the aborigines. For forty years or more he lived among them, selling and trading his wares, much as did their own merchantmen. He met them in their homes, ate with them, spoke their language, and lived as they lived during the middle of the expanding 18th Century.

In his book, *The History of the American Indians,* published in London in 1775, Adair wrote: "Their words and sentences are expressive, concise, emphatical, sonorous

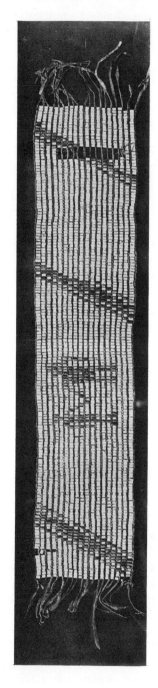

WILLIAM PENN TREATY BELT: This belt of wampum, now in the Smithsonian Institution, was used to commemorate the famous Quaker's purchase of land from the Indians.

and bold . . ." "The Indians express themselves with a
great deal of vehemence, and with short pauses, in all their
set speeches . . ." But in everyday discourse, he states,
"they always act the part of a stoic philosopher in outward
appearance, and never speak above their natural key."[3]
This was the first-hand reaction of an informed European
of that day as to the red man's mode of speech in both
public and private life.

Adair's impressions are clearly sustained by his contemporary Du Ponceau, a noted Jesuit father who
labored among the Indians far to the northward.
"Whether savages have or have not many ideas," he said,
"I do not determine; but if their ideas are few, their words
to express them are many. I am lost in astonishment at
the copiousness and admirable structure of the American
languages."[4]


Another early and close observer of the Indian's ability
in the use of language was William Penn, owner and
founder of the province of Pennsylvania. An Oxford
scholar in his younger days, it is to be assumed that he was
familiar with other European languages in addition to his
native English.

Once on American soil, Penn stated, "I have made it
my business to understand the Indian language, that I
might not need an interpreter on any business." In this
same connection he also declared, "I know not a language
spoken in Europe, that hath more words of sweetness and
greatness, in accent, or emphasis than theirs." And, in a
more analytical vein, he continued, "Their language is lofty,
yet narrow; but like the Hebrew, in significance, full . . .;
imperfect in their tenses, wanting in their moods, participles,
adverbs, conjunctions,"[5] and so on. Such discrepancies were
natural, however, for such terms were altogether unknown
to Indian ears.


So much for the estimates of earlier observers. Let
us now turn to more recent studies—but in doing so we

must always bear in mind the vast area to be covered, both as to time and space, in dealing with relative virility of the American Indian speech arts.

Much attention of late has been centered by American ethnologists on the structure of the numerous native languages. Naturally the Iroquois culture has served as a constant challenge in this regard. Writing of the language of which the silver-tongued Red Jacket was so versatile a user, Horatio E. Hale remarked that, "a complete grammar of any Iroquois language would be at least as extensive as the best Greek or Sanscrit grammar." In this same connection he declared that, "the Iroquois and Algonkin languages possessed all the excellences [of] . . . the Indo-European languages, and surpassed in almost every respect the Semitic and Chinese tongues"[6] in their power of thought transference.

Moreover, after a thorough study of the Mohawk tongue, a branch of the Iroquois, the distinguished linguist Max Muller had this to say: "The structure of such a language as the Mohawk is quite sufficient evidence that those who worked out such a work of art were powerful reasoners and accurate classifiers." These evaluations are to be found in the authoritative work, *The Iroquois Book of Rites*.

But what of the present fertility, or fecundity, of the numerous Indian tongues?

We are told that our unabridged English dictionaries of today carry a word list of approximately 450,000 of these little thought tools, each with its own distinct meaning. Yet how many of this vast storehouse of words are to be found in the vocabulary of the average adult English-speaking American? What studies have been made along this line seem to indicate that perhaps a usable vocabulary of 5,000 or more words might be enough to enable a grown individual to make successful adjustment to his surroundings —barring, of course, the demands of specialized fields of employment such as engineering, medicine, law and kindred professions. By way of comparison, how many such sound tools used as words in the varying Indian tribal tongues comprise the average Indian's vocabulary? Indeed, this raises an interesting issue.

In his study of the Klamath Indian group, a tribal

people located in southern Oregon, the late Dr. A. L. Kroeber, eminent anthropologist, found that this rather primitive people used about 7,000 word sounds in conveying their normal needs to one another. Further, it has been found that the Navajo tongue contains no less than 11,000 words, along with their infinite variations; while the Dakota language, used mainly by the Sioux peoples, commands no less than 19,000.[7] These facts tell their own story.

Perhaps the most convincing statement regarding the adequacy of most Indian languages comes from Dr. Mark Raymond Harrington of the Southwest Museum, a lifelong student of the American aborigines. "Any competent linguist will back me up," he declares, "on the statement that the Indian languages as a whole have vocabularies complete enough to deal with everything of which the natives have knowledge." He adds that, while differing greatly from tribe to tribe, "some languages are capable of expressing every shade of meaning that we can express in English, and in some cases even more delicate shades."

# The Indian Orator

T HE
ability to speak well in public, whether before a highly
cultured group or before a primitive people, is one of the
natural talents most cherished by mankind. Irrespective of
differences in racial background or cultural attainment, the
gift of eloquence has been vouchsafed to certain individuals
through all ages of the past, men as well as women. Nor
is it lacking today.

Fortunate, indeed, is he who attains the mastery of the
fine art of oratory. Some seem to inherit it, as claimed by
Red Jacket, the well-known Seneca Indian chief. Others,
like Demosthenes, the famous Greek spokesman, gain it
only through long training and self discipline. But through
whatever channel its acquisition may be achieved, its possession must be regarded as a trust whose value outweighs
the price of rubies; for its attendant responsibilities often
change the lives and destiny of men and nations.

There are few powers exercised by men like that of influencing human beings by the sheer persuasion of vocal sounds. Julius Caesar, the warrior, controlled men by exciting their fears. Cicero, the statesman, captured their affections and swayed their passions to ends which he himself determined. Much of the influence of Caesar perished with Rome. That of Cicero lives on in the hearts of all who glory in the power of words.

Oratory has been defined as the fluid expression of ideas in the choicest of elevated language; hence, the orator is the person who speaks convincingly on problems related to the needs of his times and his people. Oratory has never been restricted to any one race, creed or era in history. Nature has produced eloquent black men, eloquent yellow men, even eloquent red men, as well as white men. But we know more about the great words of the white races because these people recorded them from very ancient times. However, language which comes from the heart goes to the heart, in whatever tongue it may be spoken. And in any language undue wordiness repels rather than attracts. The Chinese people, who also have their great orators, have a way of reproving those who talk too much. To them they attach the little word *Ko-ti*, which means he has "no mouth richness."

Oratory is first cousin to poetry and is closely akin to music, philosophy, religion and all the other arts which are associated with human emotions. The skill required of him who wields the painter's brush or the sculptor's chisel is no different, basically, from that required of the orator as he shapes life's pictures with the elements of shifting words.

The three major essentials of all oratory and eloquence are these: First, there must be both breadth and depth of thought which commands the respect of those who hear. Second, sentiments expressed must be clothed in language of sufficient elegance to give their content force and charm. Finally, the manner of delivery must be polished and refined to a degree which leaves satisfaction with those who listen.

But individual and group satisfaction is not the end and goal of eloquent utterance. Ordinarily it attains its objective only in meaningful action which grows out of personal and collective need. As Daniel Webster once put it, with true oratory there must be "the man, the subject, and the occasion," all receptively attuned and expectant. Bearing such minimum requirements in mind, how does so-called Indian oratory measure up to these standards?

As to the length of an acceptable oration, naturally there exists no predetermined standard. Each case must stand on its own feet, so to speak, wherever found. This is just as true of orations which found expression in the Greek Areopagus, the Roman Forum, or the British Parliament as it is of those delivered before an Indian council-ring.

Often it is the occasion itself which serves to inspire both the speaker and the listeners. Such was the case when Abraham Lincoln delivered his immortal Gettysburg Address. History tells us that the preceding program had been long and tiresome, interspersed with speech after speech of little interest to most of those present.

Fortunately, Lincoln had the good judgment to be brief. That, together with lofty sentiments expressed in simple but beautiful words, imparted to this address a stately grandeur that has never been surpassed in all the utterances of Man.

Brevity is also an outstanding characteristic of Indian speech making. Some of their most effective appeals of record are both short and simple of content, as we shall see. But there were occasions when their pleadings at the bar of the white man's justice covered hours at a time.

Having no written language, the Indian orators naturally had to speak without notes or manuscript. Hence much that they had to say was spontaneous. For thoughts and materials presented they drew largely on the experience of their own tribe, in consultation with their sachems and wise men. For them there were no books of reference, no libraries, no research centers of any kind—only the tribal "rememberers."

A case at hand well illustrates this type of experience. A contest between a representative of the United States Government, in council with the Indians concerned, was in progress over the content of a land treaty entered into years before. The government agent claimed that the contract read one way; while, from memory, the tribal orator declared that it read just the reverse.

With agitation, the agent said, "You have forgotten.

( one )

Eloquence of the North American Indians.
By Caleb Atwater.

The poverty of their languages tends strongly to excite exertions to express ideas by figures of speech. Hence, their violent gestures and repetitions, in all their public speeches. Their ideas are drawn from sensible objects and these being few in number give a character to their eloquence, which differs materially from ours. Like the rays of light brought to a focus by a lens, their ideas being few, with only a few words to express them, Byron would call them "ideas of fire." Unaccompanied by enthusiasm, genius produces only uninteresting works of art. Enthusiasm is the secret spirit which hovers over the eloquence of the Indian. All the senses of the Indian, from his mode of living in the open air, and indeed from necessity, exist in the greatest possible perfection. Their persons are the finest forms in the world. Standing erect, his eyes flaming with enthusiastic ardor & his mind laboring under an agony of thought, the Indian is a most impressive orator. He speaks in the presence of his assembled nation on some important subject and shows that he feels an awful responsibility. At Prairie du Chien, in the summer of 1829, while listening to many Indian speeches, I was forcibly struck with the evident marks of the awful responsibility which the orators felt during the time they were addressing the United States' commissioners. I have seen an Indian orator when in the course of his speech he began to touch on

**CALEB ATWATER'S JOURNAL:** A page from this interesting account, written in 1846, in which Indian eloquence is praised.

We have it written down on paper."

"The paper then tells a lie," was the quick retort of the tribal spokesman. Touching his brow with complete self assurance, he continued, "I have it written down here."[8]

In due time the document which recorded the contract was brought into the council-ring. There, to the astonishment of all except the Indians, the paper confirmed the tribal orator's words.

Some critics see in the red man's public utterances only the choppy babblings of the untrained savage mind. Others, more tolerant, admit that there may have been occasions when his verbal efforts attained a semblance of what the sophisticated world calls oratory. But those who are intimately familiar with the Indian's ways of expression and who have compared them with those of other races in all ages are agreed that no human being can surpass him in pure and unadulterated eloquence. Metaphor and allegory come naturally to his lips, but he has no use or need for clichés or superlatives.

Henry Rowe Schoolcraft, early authority on American Indian life and customs, spoke from experience when he said, "During long intercourse with numerous tribes, I have often been surprised by the noble nature of their thoughts and their capacity to rise above selfishness" . . . "If these flights are not always sustained, it must be said they are sometimes so."[9]

In 1846 Caleb Atwater, a migrant Indian trader, wrote to his friend, John Bartley of Circleville, Ohio. "Enthusiasm," he declared, "is the secret spirit which hovers over the eloquence of the Indian. All the senses of the Indian, from his mode of living in the open air, and indeed from necessity, exist in the greatest possible perfection. Their persons are the finest forms in the world. Standing erect, his eyes flaming with an enthusiastic ardor and his mind laboring under an agony of thought, the Indian is a most impressive orator."

Continuing, "I have seen an Indian orator, when in the course of his speech he began to touch on the sales of lands of his country, turn pale, tremble in every limb, and sit down perfectly exhausted in body from the operations of his mind."[10]

While we all know that impetuous delivery is not vital
to eloquence, a message delivered with enthusiasm often
sways an audience to conviction.

Suspicious of those whom they did not know, Indian
leaders of the middle period of American history were prone
to anticipate harm. Fearful that a misunderstood word, look
or even gesture might endanger the safety of themselves,
their families or their nation, their opening addresses before
mixed conclaves of Indians and whites were characterized
by a typical laconic reserve. Once assured of his audience's
interest, however, the speaker's emotional appeal might grow
in intensity from stage to stage until all self control was
lost, as illustrated in the letter just quoted.

As with many related matters, the literature of that
early day is replete with case reports of Indian speech-
making. John Heckewelder, a noted Moravian missionary
who spent many years among various tribal groups then
resident in western Pennsylvania and Ohio, has this to say
of native spokesmen:

"The eloquence of the Indians is natural and simple;
they speak what their feelings dictate without art and without rule; their speeches are forcible and impressive, their
arguments few and pointed, and when they mean to persuade as well as convince, they take the shortest way to
reach the heart"[11]—which naturally was by arousing the
emotions of those present.

While members of this vanishing race have had persistent prejudices to meet in their adjustment to the white
man's ways, neither those of the present generation nor their
forefathers should be regarded as dullards. The ability of
their leaders to think in logical and convincing channels is
attested by many who have risen to positions of prominence
in every walk of life over the past 300 years of our inter-
racial relationships on this continent.

No American Indian needs to be apologetic for the
racial blood which flows in his veins. Said the late Dr.
Arthur C. Parker, a distinguished archaeologist and himself
a Seneca Indian: "The red man, once understood, did reason with astounding clarity."

**4**

# About
# the Council Fire

Could the ashes of the forgotten Indian council fires which once stretched across this continent from coast to coast be given the power to speak, what deeds of bravery and barbaric chivalry might they relate! What scenes of tribal despondency and horror might they reveal; what wails of sorrow unbosom! But above all, what bursts of thrilling native oratory might be re-echoed in the crackling flames!

High on the banks of the Hudson, on the palisades of Quebec, at old Fort Stanwix, at Fortress Niagara, at Cahokia, at Council Bluffs, at Fort Defiance—to name but a few— these vanished campsites call back from the past reminders of the embittered eloquence of the red men, poured forth in defense of their homes, their hunting grounds, even their very lives.

Few institutions have had greater influence in shaping the destiny of a people than the council fire of the North

American Indians. So, in our present age, when histrionics
and drama are so strongly emphasized over the air, on the
stage, and in motion pictures, it is not surprising that this
fascinating ceremonial should take on new life with the
American public.

Human beings, of whatever racial background, are
prone to resurrect those institutions of the past which
played a significant part in their mental evolution and
social development. Witness, for example, today's form of
the old outdoor theater and the Roman Colosseum—the
vast athletic "bowls" in various parts of the United States.
These are but reminders of the white man's past.

Fire, too, has always been a vital element in human
happiness and progress. With it men have learned to cook
their food, warm their homes, protect themselves from wild
animals, clear their paths, light their cities, and even battle
their enemies. Around its many symbols men also have
evolved their numerous social practices and conceived their
religious ideas and rituals. It has also aided in disposing of
their dead in a clean and honorable manner.

It is little wonder, therefore, that the American Indians
came to reverence fire as a divine gift if not an actual
manifestation of the Great Spirit.

Still less is it to be wondered at that a central fire was
an integral part of their meetings, whether for council,
prayer or to do some person honor. Indeed, their council
assemblies served much the same purpose as do our pulpit
and press, our lyceums and legislative halls of today. There
friend met friend and foe met foe, under the protection of
that institution's sanctity. There the tribal sages pooled
their wisdom for the shaping of public policy. There, too,
binding agreements and treaties were formulated which
otfen determined the destiny of the tribes concerned.

For the most part such Indian assemblies were democratic in their procedures, but were conducted with a ceremonial formality. In general they were held in the daytime,
but if the safety of the tribe demanded secrecy they might
be held at night. Under normal conditions an elevated
piece of ground might be chosen for the assembly, flanked
by trees for shade, or a rocky precipice for added acoustic
advantage. Such, for example, was the site of Council Bluffs,
Iowa, a noted rendevous for many of the Plains Indians.

Some tribes, such as the Iroquois and the Creeks, built substantial palaver houses for their council centers, made of timbers or stone. These, of course, offered shelter against the elements and better speaking facilities. But even these had ceremonial fires.

Whether in the open or under cover, however, a native protocol was rigidly observed. All sat in a semicircle, to face the speakers, with the more important personages up front. The younger braves and those of lesser renown sat or stood in back.

On matters of purely local concern any mature male member of the tribe might speak his mind freely and in a democratic fashion. Moreover, each such spokesman delivered himself where he stood, and with a voice which was supposed to be heard by all. However, when intertribal matters were to be discussed a spokesman was selected to speak for the tribe.

As has been intimated, most of the talking in these Indian councils was done by the older and more experienced men. Their orations were delivered while standing, unless the age or weakness of the spokesman necessitated his remaining seated.

The spokesman for a tribe usually confined himself to one address at any given council gathering. This, of course, was expected to reflect the thoughts and will of the tribe. But there are known occasions when the tribal orator has seen fit to exercise his prerogative to speak time and again at such councils, and even to "ad lib" when the situation seemed to call for extemporaneous remarks.

To him who called the council likewise belonged the right and duty of kindling the council fire. This was often an integral part of the Indian formal ceremonial. So, too, with the closure of such an occasion: to him who opened likewise belonged the sacred right of concluding the conclave. Until he threw dead ashes over the live coals the conference theoretically was still in session.

Whether called for purposes of peace or war, the first official act of the average Indian council was the smoking of the ceremonial pipe or calumet. Commonly called "peace-pipes," they were of various sizes and designs and frequently were ornately carved or otherwise decorated. There were tribal calumets emblematic of certain Indian communities which served the purpose of passports, carried by messengers and ambassadors. Also there were individual chieftain's calumets, which went with their owners to the grave.

To smoke the peace-pipe with another person or group had a significance ranging all the way from proclaiming a merely temporary truce to the actual endorsement of a treaty of peace between erstwhile belligerents. A later innovation, that greatly appealed to the Indian sense of humor, was the combination pipe-tomahawk—no doubt invented by a white man but extremely popular with the red man.

Indian councils were usually opened by the ranking chief by applying a live coal to the tobacco in the bowl of the tribal calumet. A few puffs would be taken, the smoke gravely expelled, and the pipe passed on to the next in rank. When the pipe had gone the rounds the council was regarded as opened. Only he who has participated in such a council can appreciate the formality and dignity of this simple but impressive ceremony.

Among the Indians themselves no oaths were taken in confirmation of agreements reached. Nor were any permanent records kept of proceedings, except the memoranda entered upon their wampum belts. For the Indians no oaths or records, receipts or other guaranties were needed for the enforcement of agreements entered into. A standard of integrity prevailed which made such warranties unnecessary, except among the most barbarous tribes.

The relation of the Indian orator to his tribe was one of singular importance. To be a war chief did not in itself entitle an individual to this high honor, though the war chief's counsel was usually solicited at Indian "powwows." Nor was the position a matter of heredity. The tribal spokesman was selected because, in addition to his knowledge of the history and traditions of his people, he had a talent for persuasive speech. Likewise, he was expected to have some acquaintance with the language and social customs of those with whom his tribe maintained relations. These facts, in themselves, would imply a reasonable standard of intelligence on the part of the orator.

An excellent word-picture of an actual Indian council of a century ago is to be found in Lawrie Tatum's book, *Our Red Brothers*. The text was written while its author was serving as a government agent in Indian Territory, with some 60,000 tribesmen under his jurisdiction.

The council was held at Okmulgee in the spring of 1871, while the West was still very new. The tribes represented included Cherokee, Muskogee (Creek), Seminole, Chickasaw, Shawnee, Delaware, Caddo, Wichita, Comanche, Kiowa, Apache, Cheyenne and Arapaho—quite a picturesque gathering.

The day set for the council proved to be rainy; hence few of its leaders appeared on time. Almost a week's waiting took place before enough Indians had assembled to justify the conclave's opening.

A spot of rising ground, overshadowed by trees, had been selected as the council site. An improvised amphitheater had been built, with log seats arranged in a semicircular position after the custom of the Indians. Blankets of many colors were spread on the ground for the leading chiefs to sit upon. And, since each tribal group could be expected to speak only its own language, competent interpreters were on hand.

Following the lighting of the fire James Van, a Cherokee sub-chief, opened the council with the approval of Mr. Tatum. He began by saying, "I am glad to see my red brethren and smoke the pipe of peace with them. We will smoke the Cherokee pipe and tobacco."

Having touched a live coal to the bowl of his two-foot pipe, he took a few puffs and passed the calumet to the next chief in rank. After the pipe had made the round of all those seated in the semicircle, including Agent Tatum, the council was regarded as officially in session.

First to speak, with the tobacco smoke making the air fragrant, was the Cherokee chief. Said he with calm dignity:

"The proceedings of to-day make me feel glad at my heart because we are friends. It has been a long time since the red men met in such a council. When our forefathers met in this way they kindled the sacred fire at their councils, to which all the red men of the various tribes flocked to have a smoke, and peacefully transact their business. In shaking hands they extend the whole arm to each other. The Cherokee is the oldest brother of the Indian tribes. To them is entrusted the white path and the key of peace. My young brothers, the head men of the

various tribes are now sitting before me. It is our duty to assist
each other in promoting peace and welfare. All nations should
go hand in hand, and always have a good talk."[12]

In the general palaver that followed, Mr. Tatum states,
each chief would "utter a sentence, or part of one, and then
wait for it to be interpreted into different languages." This
naturally slowed things down considerably, but it gave the
interpreters time to impart to their fellow tribesmen a
clearer knowledge of what had been said, and enabled the
recorders to take it all down word for word. Such a procedure contrasts markedly with the method of instantaneous
interpretation used today in such gatherings as the United
Nations—but Indians were rarely in a hurry and it served
the needs of the time.

What records the Indians themselves kept of such
palavers are to be found in their wampum belts. And, as
might be expected, these records were extremely condensed.
Even so, some of these wampum belts, still preserved, have
as many as 5,000 or 6,000 colored shell beads worked into
the body fabric of deer or other animal skin. The meaningful figures and curious designs each tell their own story.

With many of the Eastern tribes such wampum belts
were housed in wampum lodges, constructed for that specific purpose. With others they might be placed in hollow
logs, or even in caves to protect them against time and the
elements. Sometimes these aboriginal records were watched
over by appointed wampum keepers or guards.

As mentioned earlier, only on rare occasions did the
tribal spokesman speak more than once on any single issue
pending before a given council. His words summarized the
actions or policy of his people, reflecting their ultimate will

TYPICAL **INDIAN COUNCIL:** The painting by John Mix Stanley, shown on the
opposite page, depicts Red Jacket defending himself against a charge of
witchcraft.

or decision. But there were times when such restraints were thrown to the winds.

Such a situation arose at the memorable Indian council held in 1793 at Miami Rapids, in the Ohio country. For months a loosely knit but determined group of Indian tribes had been on the warpath in protest against the ceaseless encroachments of the whites. Government troops had been sent to the scene, with devastating effects. For three consecutive days Joseph Brant, the brilliant Mohawk chief and orator, had pleaded with his own countrymen as well as the United States government for paths of peace, but to no avail.

The troops had been ordered to quell the uprising at any costs. In desperation Joseph Brant, known to the Indians as Thayendanegea, sent the following message to "The Commissioner of the United States," as the voice of his kinsmen:

> "Brothers: You have talked to us about concessions. It appears strange that you expect any from us, who have only been defending our just rights against your invasions. We want peace. Restore to us our country, and we shall be enemies no longer . . .
>
> "Brothers: We desire you to consider that our only demand is the peaceable possession of a small part of our once great country. Look back and view the lands from whence we have been driven to this spot. We can retreat no farther, because the country behind hardly affords food for its present inhabitants; and we have therefore resolved to leave our bones in this small space, to which we now are consigned."[13]

What a philippic! Needless to say, war continued— and with a ferocity seldom previously experienced by either Indians or whites.

# With the
# Early Colonials

**T**HE
literature which covers the past 300 years of life in the New World falls into three general periods. First is the era of discovery and exploration. The second is that of colonization, during which time European powers extended their control over great sections of the western hemisphere. Lastly, and that with which we are presently concerned, is the period which saw the establishment of our own United States and of the Dominion of Canada. In all three of these epochs the American Indian has played an outstanding role.

First of the white invaders to range over the boundless American wilds were the Spanish and the French. Urged on by their thirst for gold and expanding empire, the Spanish dons quickly laid out territorial claims more vast than they dared to assume elsewhere. The first French explorations were along the north Atlantic seaboard and the area about the St. Lawrence River. They built fortified trading posts at Quebec and Montreal, and from these vantage points pressed westward in the hope of discovering the long-sought Northwest Passage to the coveted spice islands of India. In small boats they plied their way through the Great Lakes region toward the headwaters of the Mississippi River. Then, turning south, they planted the flag of their country in a domain they called Louisiana in honor of their king.

In turn, the English, stern and puritanic, explored and established their colonies along North America's Atlantic shores. In the main these were intended for their surplus populations: those who, ill at ease in the homeland, came to America with the one thought in mind of making this their home. This spelled the difference in the territorial aims of these European rivals.

This same era is memorable elsewhere in the world for its intellectual and religious activities. It has been termed the age of the Renaissance. During this period many of Europe's universities were founded, along with innumerable religious orders of many kinds.

Outstanding among the fraternities for the training of missionaries, authorized by the Papacy at Rome, were the Jesuit and the Franciscan orders, termed the Black Friars and the Grey Friars because of the color of their robes. Each of these fraternities sent systematic reports back to their superiors in Europe of their experiences in the New World, and it is from such reports, especially the so-called "Jesuit Relations," that much of the information in this study has been derived.

Following the trails blazed by hunters and trappers, and often blazing their own, these devout missionaries penetrated to the wildest of America's frontiers. Here they built their chapels, preached their faith, baptized their converts and impressed the authority of their doctrines and church dogmas upon the minds of the credulous aborigines. It is from the firsthand record of such a missionary, Father Sebastian Rasles, in 1723, that we pick up the picture of one of these primitive Catholic parishes, located on the wild banks of the Kennebec River, many miles south of Montreal in what is now the state of Maine.

Father Rasles' report, written with obvious but naive pride, reads as follows:

> "The [Indian] village in which I live is called Nanrantsouak [now known as Norridgewock], and is situated on the banks of a river [the Kennebec] which empties into the sea, at the distance of thirty leagues below. I have erected a Church there, which is neat and elegantly ornamented. I have indeed, thought it my duty to spare nothing either in the decoration of the building itself, or the beauty of those articles which are used in our holy ceremonies. Vestments, chasubles, copes and holy vessels, all are highly appropriate, and would be esteemed so even in our churches in Europe.
>
> "I have also formed a little choir of about forty young Indians, who assist at Divine Service in cassocks and surplices. They have each their own appropriate functions as much to serve in the Holy Sacrifice of the Mass, as to chant the Divine Offices for the consecration of the Holy Sacrament, and for the processions which they make with the crowds of Indians, who often come from a long distance to engage in these exercises; and you will be edified by the beautiful order they observe and the devotion they show."[14]

Incidentally, Father Rasles had this to say about the speech of the Indians:

> "It cannot be denied that the language of the Savages has real beauties; and there is an indescribable force in their style and manner of expression. I am going to quote you an example. If I should ask you why God created you, you would answer me that it was for the purpose of knowing him, loving him, and serving him, and by this means to merit eternal glory. If I should put the same question to a Savage, he would answer thus, in the style of his own language: 'The great Spirit has thought of us: *Let them know me, let them love me, let them honor me, and let them obey me; for then I will make them enter my glorious happiness.*' "[15]

It was toward a similar center, far up in the inhospitable Hudson's Bay region, that another faithful Jesuit father in his loaded birchbark canoe was making his way when suddenly stopped by a band of Indians who refused to let him go farther. The black-gowned father demanded that he be taken before their chief, so that he might explain his destination and the purpose of his mission. But even as he made the demand the Huron chief, whose name was

Sesibahowra, stood before him. With the chief were about a score of trim canoes, filled with armed warriors.

Undismayed, the missionary gave a salute of guns in honor of Chief Sesibahowra and called for a council. Familiar with Indian customs, he proceeded to kindle a council fire. Gifts of the usual sort, cheap knives, gaudy blankets, beads and other trinkets, were spread before the wondering eyes of the Indians.

Following the customary preliminaries, the missionary addressed the Indians in their own language, which he had learned in France:

> "It is not to purchase the passage of this river . . . that I am pleased to regale thee with two presents [to the Chief]. The Frenchmen, having delivered this whole country from the in-cursions of the Iroquois, your foes, well deserve to be accorded the right to go and come with entire freedom through this region . . .
>
> "As your friend, ally, and kinsman, I give you a mat to cover the graves of your dead who were slain by the Iroquois, your enemies; and to you who escaped their fires and their cruelty, it will say you shall live in the future.
>
> "Onnontio [a name used by the Indians for the governor of Canada] has wrested the war hatchet from their hands. Your country was dead; he has restored it to life . . . Hunt, fish, and trade in all directions, without fear of being discovered by your enemies, either from the noise of your guns, the odor of your tobacco or the smoke of your fires."[16]

Throughout this speech the Indians sat in respectful silence, attentive to every word, with eyes riveted on their chief's face. After a few moments of reflection Sesibahowra indicated that for the time being he had nothing to say. However, he let it be known that on the morrow a response would be forthcoming. Meanwhile, with typical Indian courtesy, a feast was made ready in honor of the visiting friar.

The following day the council reconvened and an Indian spokesman, chosen for the occasion, stepped forth to deliver the sentiments of his nation. Thanks to the *Jesuit Relations* we have some of this Huron speech as it was delivered so many years ago:

> "Today, my Father, the sun shines upon us; and, favoring us with thy benign presence, thou givest us the brightest day that this country has ever seen.

"Never have our fathers or our forefathers had such happiness. How fortunate are we to be born at this time, for the free enjoyment of the blessings that thou bestowest upon us! The Frenchman places us under great obligations; in giving us peace, he restores us all to life.

"But he makes the debt much heavier by consenting to instruct us and make us Christians. We shall regard him as the one through whom we can escape eternal punishment after death."[17]

How much more there may have been to this native speech we do not know. This is all that was found recorded in this work. Nor can we be certain if it was taken down *verbatim* at the time. But we do know that the Tironian method of note taking, comparable to present-day shorthand, was the common accomplishment of many of the trained missionaries of that day. And the Indian flavor of the words, even after translation from the French, speaks for itself in their native stateliness and beauty.

Having concluded his formal welcome, the tribal orator took his place among his people and lapsed into silence. He had spoken. When appetites were satisfied and the calumet of friendship had gone the rounds for the last time, embers of the council fire were covered, mutual farewells were said, and the missionary went on his way unrestrained.

Characteristic of the rigors experienced by men and women in this same Huron country, another record, relating the burning of a little Catholic chapel operated by a group of Ursuline Sisters, has been preserved for history.

The incident occurred just after Iroquois raiders, predatory rivals and enemies of the Hurons, had swept through the lands occupied by the latter and left a trail of devastation in their wake. The small chapel cherished by the virgin sisters of Ursula, together with their converts, lay in ashes. During the foray a hundred or more Huron warriors had been killed, their people driven from their homes, and their corn fields mercilessly laid waste.

When this human tempest had passed a little band of Huron refugees gathered where the chapel had been to express their grief for the losses sustained. With a delicacy surprising in a savage accustomed to bloodshed and acts of brutality often involving unbelievable physical suffering, Taiaeronk, their spokesman, tried to comfort the nuns. Three thousand miles from their native homeland they listened to words that might have found their counterpart in that other old lament of a desolate people in a strange land:

> "Holy Virgins, you see before you miserable carcasses, the remnant of a country that once was flourishing and that now is no more, the country of the Hurons.
>
> "We have been devoured and gnawed to the very bones by war and famine. These carcasses are able to stand only because you support them . . . Look upon us on all sides, and consider whether there is anything in us that does not compel us to weep for ourselves.
>
> "Alas! This sad incident that has happened to you increases our woes and renews our tears . . .
>
> "Let us weep, let us weep my beloved countrymen; yes, let us weep for our misfortunes which were solely ours before, but which we now share in common with these innocent maids . . .
>
> "We have come here for the purpose of consoling you; and, before coming here, we have entered into your hearts, to see what might afflict you still more since your fire, so as to apply some remedy for it.
>
> "Your hearts do not sorrow for the loss of earthly goods; we see that they are raised too high in the desire for heavenly blessings . . .
>
> "We fear but one thing which would be a misfortune to us; we fear that, when the news of this accident . . . reaches France, it will affect your relatives more than it does yourselves; we fear that they will recall you and that you will be moved by their tears . . .
>
> "Courage, Holy Virgins! Do not allow yourselves to be persuaded by the love of kindred; and show now that the charity that you have for us is stronger than the ties of nature."[18]

Whether this speech, like the one which just precedes it, is preserved accurately word for word is beside the point. At least it is an eloquent and convincing instance of the strong attachment of the Indians for those who came unselfishly to American shores to share the hardships and privations of primitive life in an attempt to bring light and knowledge to more backward peoples. When the report of this tragedy reached France funds were quickly raised for rebuilding the Ursuline Chapel in the wilds of Canada.

# Iroquois Spokesmen

**I**NTER-
national boundaries usually rest on imaginary lines, less than paper-thin. The birds of the air ignore them and wild animals defy their restraint, much as have many of the Indian tribes of the past.

Throughout much of the era of exploration and colonization by the whites the Iroquois, persistent rivals of the Hurons, roamed at will over the open country west of what today is New England, as far as the Hudson's Bay area and to the headwaters of the Mississippi. This they regarded as their hunting grounds, regardless of others who resided in those regions.

From very early times this people comprised what has been termed the Iroquois Confederacy, a loosely knit league of Indian tribes, more or less related, composed of the Seneca, Cayuga, Oneida, Mohawk and Onondaga. Though often called the Five Civilized Nations because of their advanced stage of collective action, they were in many respects as barbarous as the wildest tribes of the continent.

For many months towards the end of the 17th Century complaints had poured into the headquarters of M. de le Barra, French governor of Canada, about the unceasing interference of Iroquois braves with the French traders who supplied the Miami, the Shawnee and other of the French-Indian allies in this vast land to the west. Since the area was rich in furs and offered an open market for French commodities, such a situation was not to be tolerated. Consequently, in 1684 de le Barra equipped a sizable army of frontiersmen to crush this troublesome Confederacy.

However, a ruinous epidemic of sickness hit the French forces and decimated their ranks. To cover up his weakness de le Barra called for an open council to be held at Kaihohage, a fortified trading post in the west. In opening the council he made this bold threat: "If my words do not produce the desired effect . . . I shall be obliged to join with the Governor of New York, who is commanded by his master to assist me."

This was a mere bluff, of course, and the Onondaga knew it. They were fully aware of the depleted ranks of the French, as well as of the rivalry between the French and the English in all Indian relations.

Throughout de le Barra's insolent address Grangula, chief of the Onondaga, sat motionless, his eyes focused on the end of his calumet, not showing the slightest emotion. Though advanced in years, he had lost little of his earlier vitality. He also had at hand some 2,000 warriors, a match for any force that the French might produce.

When the governor had finished his harangue Grangula arose. He strode several times around the council-ring, apparently for effect. Then he drew himself up to his full height.

"Onondio!" said he. "I honor you, and the warriors that are with me all likewise honor you. Your interpreter has finished your speech; I now begin mine. My words make haste to reach your ears. Harken to them!

"Onondio! You must have believed when you left Quebec

that the sun had burnt up all the forest, which renders our country inaccessible to the French, or that the lakes had so far overflown their banks that they had surrounded our castles [homes] . . . Yes, surely you must have dreamed so, and the curiosity of seeing so great a wonder has brought you so far. Now you are undeceived. I, and the warriors here present, are come to assure you that the Senecas, Cayugas, Onondagas, Oneidas and Mohawks are yet alive . . .

"Hear, Onondio! I do not sleep. I have my eyes open. The sun which enlightened me, discovers to me a great captain at the head of a company of soldiers, who speaks as if he were dreaming. He says, that he only came to the lake to smoke on the great calumet with the Onondagas. But Garangula [Grangula] says that it was to the contrary; that it was to knock them on the head, if sickness had not weakened the arms of the French.

"Hear, Onondio! Take care for the future that so great a number of soldiers as appear there, do not choke the tree of peace planted in so small a fort. It will be a great loss, if, after it has so easily taken root, you should stop its growth."[19]

At this point Grangula made it clear that his people had no intention of bowing to French demands, nor would they consent to the building of a new fortified post at Kaihohage. Nevertheless, with that grace common to Indian social life, Grangula invited de le Barra and his attendants to join him in a feast prepared for all. De le Barra refused and left the council, much chagrined by his defeat.

For a full decade following the abortive council between Governor de le Barra and Grangula at Kaihohage the struggle between the French and the British for control of America's fur trade continued unabated.

In 1694 Dekanisora, another of the chosen spokesmen for the Onondaga Nation, visited Montreal at the head of a delegation of sachems and chiefs of the Iroquois Confederacy. Also assembled at this seat of French government in America were many of the leading ecclesiastics and officers of the province, met to consider ways and means of relieving the strife on the western frontiers. In keeping with traditional French hospitality many of these visitors, both red men and white, were entertained at the governor's table. Among them Dekanisora was an outstanding guest of honor.

The personal bearing of this noted Indian speaker was

quite impressive. Atop the grey locks which fell to his shoulders he wore a laced beaver hat. This, together with a gold-trimmed red coat, both given to him by the governor of New York, the colony on the Hudson, made him an outstanding figure in this elite company.

The real purpose of this memorable council was to discover which of the colonial contestants, French or British, the Iroquois Confederacy would support. In the meantime, however, the canny Dekanisora and some of his tribal sachems had already paid a visit to Colonel Fletcher's quarters at Albany.

As others at Montreal grew more and more heated in their demands that the Iroquois support the French interests, the Onondaga chieftain sat in meditative and inscrutable silence. When his turn to speak came he rose with calm dignity.

> "Father [addressed, of course, to Onondio]. If we do not conclude a peace now, it will be your fault. We have already taken the hatchet of the [Hudson] River Indians whom we incited to the war. But we must tell you that you are a bad man. You are inconsistent. You are not to be trusted. We have had war together a long time. Still, though you occasioned the war, we never hated the house of Oghuesse [the Montreal gentleman]. Let him undertake the toilsome journey to Onondaga. If he will come, he shall be welcome . . .
>
> "You have almost eaten us up. Our best men are killed in this bloody war. But we forget what is past. Before this we once threw the hatchet into the river of Kaihohage, but you fished it up, and treacherously surprised our people at Cadaraqui.
>
> "After that you sent to us to have our prisoners restored. Then the hatchet was thrown up to the sky, but you kept a string fastened to the helve, and pulled it down, and fell upon our people again. This we revenged to some purpose, by the destruction of your people in the island of Montreal . . .
>
> "Onondio! We will not permit any settlement at Cadaraqui. You have had your fires there thrice extinguished. We will not consent to your building that fort; but the passage through the river shall be free and clear.
>
> "We make the sun clean, and drive away all clouds and darkness, that we may see the light without interruption."[20]

Such parts of this Themistoclean speech as have been preserved will be found in B. B. Thatcher's little two-volume work, *Indian Biography*, published in 1837. Again, however, its original must be looked for in European archives, not in American.

The imagery used in Dekanisora's truly eloquent speech is typically Indian. His reference to the Indians' having thrown the tomahawk "to the sky" merely meant that they wanted peace. When he said, in conclusion, "We make the sun clean," he simply implied the necessity of clarity on the part of all in regard to the issues at hand. So far the road was still open to compromise.

But as to the building of a French fort at Cadaraqui, his people's decision was unequivocal. It could not be questioned. It was "NO", accompanied with strong gestures!

# The Golden Age
# of Indian Eloquence

**E**VERY

society that has long endured has enjoyed what historians like to call its "Golden Age." The Chinese look back to the time of Confucius as the era when their people reached the zenith of their culture. With the Greeks it was in the time of Pericles. The Romans experienced it during the reign of Augustus Caesar.

The Golden Age of classical Greece embraced less than a single generation; yet, in that brief time, this heroic people produced more poets, artists, statesmen, philosophers and orators of distinction than has any other race during twice this period.

To a lesser degree this was also true of the American Indians during the last half of the swashbuckling 18th Century. Here in the New World the native genius of the red men gave birth to an exceptional number of distinguished masters of the speech arts—men such as Joseph

**PONTIAC** (Ottawa): "If you are English, we declare war against you."

Brant, Pontiac, Tarhe, Red Jacket, Logan, Farmer's Brother, Cornplanter and Little Turtle. Hence this era might truly be called the Golden Age of Indian eloquence. But it must not be forgotten that at the same time Europe had her Elder and Younger Pitt and Edmund Burke, along with her so-called "enlightened despots," such as Peter the Great. And the trend of history on American shores was rapidly being moulded by the acts and words of such white men as Washington, Franklin, Hamilton, Patrick Henry, Jonathan Edwards and a score of others worthy of any age.

Seldom has a century experienced such a flowering of articulatory talent.

Today, in America, Pontiac is almost a household word. It is the name of numerous cities in the United States, as well as that of a popular motor vehicle. But originally it was the name of a great Indian chieftain whose reach for power was monumental.

Pontiac seems to have been an Ottawa chief. According to his own testimony he was born somewhere along the banks of the Maumee River in Ohio. Today this stream wanders sluggishly in a northeasterly direction, finding its outlet into Lake Erie at or near Toledo.

From early childhood Pontiac was the inveterate enemy of the English. And he remained so until his dying day. He first appears on the stage of military action at the memorable defeat of General Braddock at Fort Duquesne, in the year 1755. Pontiac is said to have taken a decisive part in this rout at the head of his Indian braves. From that time on, like Napoleon, his passion for conquest swelled.

Later, as the leader of one of the largest bands of Indian warriors ever to be assembled, Pontiac challenged England's tightening grip on the great Ohio Valley in response to his French loyalties. He also resented Britain's expansion into the Hudson's Bay region and the northwest where his own aspirations for power lay. By the early 1760s, as chief of a confederacy moulded somewhat after that of the Iroquois League, he was openly propagating his conspiracy against the white man's advance on this continent.

An adapt at organization as well as a master of the
fine art of oratorical appeal, Pontiac informed his Indian
followers that in a vision he had received a message direct
from the Great Spirit in which three things were demanded
from all red men. First, having gone so far down the white
man's road, they were to return to the ways of their forefathers and were to use only their native weapons, the bow
and arrow, in acquiring their food. Second, they were to
refuse to trade their furs for the white man's articles of
commerce, and thus force him into bankruptcy. And third,
they were to combine their forces and sweep this white
scourge into the eastern sea.

Pontiac's plans called for simultaneous attack on all
of the British forts and trading posts throughout the frontier
West. Each tribe was to attack its nearest post, kill the
armed defenders and then fall upon the unarmed settlements. No mercy was to be shown, regardless of age or
sex. Death was to be the common lot of all whites.

This long-smouldering storm first hit the garrison of
Presque Isle, Michigan. For two full days every trick and
device known to savage warfare was pitted against the fort
and its defenders, including firebrands thrown against the
timbers. In the end the Indians were victorious and the
fort was consumed by flames. One after another, trading
posts and forts previously thought impregnable were
attacked and destroyed by the Indians. The atrocities committed on both sides beggar description. Defenseless men,
women and children were scalped alive and thrown into
the flames to be consumed.

But Fort Detroit, the Gilbraltar of the West, was reserved for Pontiac's own hand. Naturally, he looked to his
followers for both assistance and advice—and these included
his Canadian allies, white as well as red. In a formal
council, uninformed of the Peace of Paris, 1763, by which
France ceded all of her territorial claims in Canada to the
British, Pontiac launched the following philippic against
the Canadians as traitors to his cause:

"My Brothers!" he declared. "I have no doubt but this war
is very troublesome to you, and that my warriors, who are
continually passing through your settlements, frequently kill
your cattle and injure your property.

**JOSEPH BRANT** (Mohawk): "We can retreat no farther . . . we have resolved to leave our bones in this small spot."

"I am sorry for it and I hope you do not think I am pleased
with this conduct of my young men. And as proof of my friendship, recollect the war you had seventeen years ago [1746] and
the part I took in it . . .

"Did I not join you, and go to his [your enemy's] camp
and say to him, if he wished to kill the French, he must pass
over my body and the bodies of my young men? Did I not
take hold of the tomahawk with you and aid you in fighting
your battles? . . .

"Why do you think I would turn my arms against you?
Am I not that same French Pontiac who assisted you seventeen
years ago? . . .

"My Brothers! I begin to grow tired of this bad meat
[the English] which is upon our lands. I begin to see that this
is not your case, for instead of assisting us in our war with the
English, you are actually assisting them . . .

"This year they must all perish. The Master of Life so
orders it. His will is known to us, and we must do as he says . . .
You will tell them all we do and say. You carry our counsels
and plans to them. Now take your choice. You must be entirely
French, like ourselves, or entirely English.

"If you are French, take this belt [a war belt drawn from
beneath Pontiac's body blanket] for yourselves and your young
men and join us. If you are English, we declare war against
you . . . Let us have your answer."21

When he had finished his embittered speech the leader
of the Canadians strode toward Pontiac and put into his
hand a copy of the treaty of 1763 which bore the great seal
of the king of France. While his interpreter read it aloud
Pontiac stood as rigid as a stone statue. His expression
changed from one of expectancy to one of anger; then to
despair.

Perhaps at this moment the Ottawa chief saw his
aspirations for power commencing to crumble beneath him.
Despite the odds, however, he laid a determined attack
against Fort Detroit's sturdy walls. They held.

A few more moons and Pontiac was found dead,
murdered by a Kaskaskian Indian, a martyr to his people's
struggle for freedom.

Thayendanegea, better known to most of us as Joseph
Brant, was a chief of the Mohawk tribe, and a member of
the wolf clan. Throughout the border wars which attended
the American Revolutionary period this brilliant half-breed,
Indian-reared, was ever active on behalf of his people. He

first gained prominence when but a youth of about thirteen years of age. Because of certain personal exploits he won for himself the Indian title "Pine Tree Chief," a cherished mark of rank which he carried to his grave.

In certain of these border wars young Brant served under Sir William Johnson, a British commander. Much taken with the dusky youth, Johnson at his own expense placed him in Dr. Wheetlock's charity school at Lebanon, Connecticut. Here he learned to read and write English and became unusually fluent in its use.

Twice in his mature years Joseph Brant crossed the Atlantic to England on missions affecting the welfare of his people. The first of these trips was in 1776, the year that the American colonists declared their independence from the British Crown. The second was in 1785, following the acknowledgement of the independence of the thirteen American colonies. These visits abroad extended Thayendanegea's understanding of the problems of his day and added to the value of his services to his people.

Of his second visit to Britain a letter dated December 12, 1785, and published in London in part reads thus: "Monday last, Colonel Joseph Brant, the celebrated King of the Mohawks, arrived in this city [Salisbury] from America, and after dining with Colonel De Peister at the headquarters here, proceeded immediately on his journey to London."

The chief purpose of this second visit by Joseph Brant, to the Court of St. James, was to request an extensive land grant for his people north of Lake Erie, an area still under the British Crown. Fortunately his plea, as presented to His Majesty's Secretary for Colonial Affairs, has been preserved for us.

Of all his numerous speeches, spread as they are over many pages of history, this petition seems to illustrate the oratorical talent of Thayendanegea better than any other.

"My Lord, I am happy at the honor of being before your Lordship . . .

"The cause of my coming to England being of the most serious consequence to the whole Indian Confederacy, I intreat your Lordship patiently to hear and listen to what I am going to say.

"We hope it is a truth well known in this country, what a faithful part we took in their behalf in the late dispute with the Americans: and though we have been told peace has long since been concluded between you and them, it is not finally settled with us, which causes great uneasiness through all of the Indian nations . . .

". . . We were struck with astonishment at hearing we were forgot in the treaty [Treaty of Paris of 1763]. Notwithstanding the manner we were told this, we could not believe it possible such firm friends and allies could be so neglected by a nation remarkable for its honor and glory . . . For this reason we applied to the King's Commander-in-chief, in Canada in a friendly and private way, wishing not to let those people in rebellion [the colonists] know the concern and trouble we were under. From the time of delivering that speech, near three years, we have had no answer, and remain in a state of great suspense and uneasiness of mind.

". . . It is, my Lord, the earnest desire of the Five United Nations, and the whole Indian Confederacy, that I may have an answer to that speech . . ."[22]

Much to the credit of His Majesty's Government, response was quickly forthcoming. Within two weeks thereafter Thayendanegea again was on his way back home with the promise of an immense Canadian land grant in his possession.

Presented in clear, forceful English, despite his Mohawk background, this speech merits the most intensive study for style and choice of words. It should be remembered that it was attuned primarily to British ears; hence it was almost devoid of that rhetoric and symbolism so effective with American Indian council techniques. For judgment as to its true oratorical worth the student should, of course, examine the complete copy of which the above is but a brief excerpt.

A third Indian oration, cherished by every school boy of a generation ago, stands in striking contrast to those already cited in this chapter. Its main charm is its human appeal—the message of Logan, the Mingo *(He Who Lived Out of Bounds)*.

Logan was a noted Cayuga chief, whose people dwelt in the upper northwestern part of New York State. He was a proud member of the minor confederacy composed of several Indian tribes, including the Shawnee, the Delaware and the Iowa, as well as his own tribe.

Except as a peacemaker, Logan took little or no part in the French-English wars before 1760. An extremely temperate Indian, he had no use for the white man's fire-water. He was both shrewd and resourceful, a fitting successor to his father, who also was a chief of the Cayuga tribe. All through that troubled era he was looked upon as the friend of the whites, until the occurrence of the following tragic episode.

In the spring of 1774 certain depredations were committed on the nearby white settlements. The raids were blamed on "irresponsible" Indians claimed to be connected with Logan's people. Whether this was true or not may never be known, but the white frontiersmen demanded "justice." "Revenge" would have been a more fitting term!

Under the leadership of Colonel Cressap a posse was formed to hunt down the offenders. They concealed themselves on the banks of a stream frequently used by the Cayuga. Soon an Indian canoe, loaded with Logan's immediate relatives, came towards them. A volley from the guns of the white men, fired without warning, wiped all out.

A short time thereafter Logan's brother and sister were murdered in cold blood. Logan's love for the whites froze in his veins. Blood feuds and revenge were as natural to the Indian as breathing. Thenceforth Logan became the whites' deadly enemy.

The first retaliation by this noted chief netted no less than thirteen scalps, six of which were jerked from the heads of defenseless children. Three times Logan repeated such attacks, defying every effort of the whites to entrap him. Finally he secreted himself among the transient Shawnee villages of the far West. Later, the following message, pinned to the head of his war club, was delivered to Governor Dunmore of Virginia:

> "I appeal to any white man to say, if he ever entered Logan's cabin hungry, and he gave him no meat; if ever he came cold and naked, and he clothed him not.
> "During the course of the last long and bloody war, Logan remained idle in his cabin, an advocate of peace. Such was my love for the whites, that my countrymen pointed at me as they passed and said, 'Logan is the friend of the white man.'

"I had even thought to have lived with you, but for the injuries of one man, Colonel Cressap, who last spring, in cold blood, and unprovoked, murdered all the relatives of Logan, not even sparing my women and children.

"There runs not a drop of my blood in the veins of any living creature. This called on me for revenge. I have sought it: I have killed many; I have glutted my vengeance; for my country I rejoice at the beams of peace.

"But do not harbor a thought that mine is the joy of fear. Logan never knew fear. He will not turn on his heel to save his life. Who is there to mourn for Logan? Not one!"[23]

It was Thomas Jefferson who, while preparing his celebrated *Notes On Virginia,* published in 1784, wrote in regard to this war-club message: "I may challenge the whole orations of Demosthenes and Cicero, or any more eminent orator . . . to produce a single passage, superior to the speech of Logan."

Though this gem of Indian self-vindication was by no means a formal oration, since it had no audience, its poignant eloquence may well be ranked with Demosthenes' "Oration on the Crown" and William Jennings Bryan's "The Cross of Gold."

# The Silver-Tongued Red Jacket

W**ITHOUT** doubt the most outstanding Indian orator of the 18th Century was Red Jacket. Being a Seneca, he was also a member of the Iroquois Confederacy, whose interests he served throughout his life. The fame of this distinguished chief rests on little else than on his supreme gift of speech, the impelling power of his words. In this regard he stood head and shoulders above the leading Indian spokesmen of his day.

A poet not too distant from Red Jacket's time characterized him in the following words:

". . . with a smile whose blessing would,
like the patriarch's, soothe a dying hour;
With voice as low, as gentle, and caressing,
As e'er won maiden's lips in moonlight bower;
With look, like patient Job's, eschewing evil;

**RED JACKET** (Seneca): "Now the tree of friendship is decaying; its limbs are fast falling off."

With motions, graceful as a bird's in air;
Thou art, in sober truth, the veriest devil
That e'er clenched fingers in a captive's hair."[24]

Of himself Red Jacket once exclaimed: "A warrior! I am an orator! I was born an orator!"

The tribal name of this distinguished Seneca was Sagoyewatha; meaning, in the native Indian tongue, "He who keeps his tribe awake." And keep his tribe awake he did, until his lips were stilled by death.

Placid and conservative in temperament, Red Jacket appears to have possessed a remarkable memory. This stood him in good stead when speaking, as he frequently did, about past tribal experiences. His quick wit and ready repartee were equally valuable attributes when it came to debate.

From early boyhood Sagoyewatha could see nothing good in the white man's civilization. This naturally brought him into violent conflict with the growing power of the European intruders who surrounded his people on every side. He became a recognized reactionary on most public policies, especially those related to the Indian's welfare.

Although an avowed pagan, in the broad sense of that word, Red Jacket was far from narrow-minded in his human sympathies. Nor was he a non-believer in the Great Spirit, which the Indian held to have created all things, both animate and inanimate. Early in life he discovered that if he were to adopt the white man's "improved" mode of life, with all of its benefits and handicaps, he would have to subscribe to the Christian way of living as advocated by the missionaries, with all of its "blessings" and its drawbacks. These two issues challenged his thought at every turn; and already we know his answer.

Various white governments, French, English and American, encouraged the infiltration of Christianity among the Indians for obvious reasons. Hence, when a recognized religious organization, Protestant or Catholic, expressed a desire to establish a missionary post among them, a government agent usually assisted in conducting the negotiations.

Red Jacket played the featured role in just such a situation
when a Moravian missionary named Cram applied for
such a post among the Seneca. The headquarters of the
Moravians at that time was in Massachusetts, with numerous outposts farther west.

On opening this particular council the government
agent spoke first:

> "Brothers of the Six Nations: I rejoice to meet you at this
> time, and thank the Great Spirit that he has preserved you in
> health, and given me another opportunity of taking you by the
> hand.
> "Brothers: The person who sits by me is a friend who has
> come a great distance to hold a talk with you. He will inform
> you what his business is, and it is my request that you would
> listen with attention to his words."

With the recognition of the tribe's leading chief, Cram
was given permission to speak. Within five minutes, however, he found his hopes of success blasted by the obdurate
Red Jacket. Poorly acquainted with Indian council technique, Cram began his presentation in this way:

> "My Friends: I am thankful for the opportunity afforded us
> of uniting together at this time. I had a great desire to see you,
> and inquire into your state and welfare. For this purpose I
> have traveled a great distance, being sent by your old friends,
> the Boston Missionary Society . . .
> "Brothers: I have not come to get your lands or your
> money, but to enlighten your minds, and to instruct you how
> to worship the Great Spirit agreeably to his mind and will . . .
> There is but one religion, and but one way to serve God, and
> if you do not embrace the right way you cannot be happy
> hereafter."

While Cram continued to expound his religious precepts Red Jacket sat in respectful silence, scarcely moving
a muscle. Pointing out that already he had visited many of
the smaller Seneca villages to good effect, the missionary
stated that now he had come to request the approval of
Sagoyewatha for a mission station here, since this great
chief stood so high in the esteem of his people.

"I hope," he concluded, "that you will give me your
answer before we part."

All looked to Red Jacket as he stood up. Some of his
sachems favored the proposal; others were sternly opposed.

So friendly was Sagoyewatha's manner and tone at the outset that one might have thought he, too, was ready to assent. But only for a moment.

Crouching over the astounded missionary, leering into his eyes like an aroused demon, Red Jacket poured forth a storm of withering invective, mingled with chilling disgust:

"Friend and Brother: It was the will of the Great Spirit that we should meet together this day. He orders all things, and has given us a fine day for our council. He has taken his garment [the clouds] from before the sun, and caused it to shine with brightness upon us. Our eyes are opened that we see clearly; our ears are unstopped, that we have been able to hear distinctly the words you have spoken. For all these favors we thank the Great Spirit; and him *only*.

"Brother: This council fire was kindled by you. It was at your request that we came together at this time. We have listened with attention to what you have said. You requested us to speak our minds freely . . .

"Brother: Listen to what we say. There was a time when our forefathers owned this great island [the North American continent]. Their seats extended from the rising to the setting sun. The Great Spirit had made it for the use of Indians. He had created the buffalo, the deer, and other animals for food . . . Their skins served us for clothing . . . If we had some disputes about our hunting ground, they were generally settled without the shedding of much blood. But an evil day came upon us. Your forefathers crossed the great water and landed on this island. Their numbers were small. They found friends and not enemies . . .

"The white people, Brother, had now found our country. Tidings were carried back, and more came amongst us . . . We took them to be friends. They called us brothers. We believed them, and gave them a larger seat . . . They wanted more land; they wanted our country . . .

"Brother: Continue to listen. You say that you are sent to instruct us how to worship the Great Spirit agreeably to his mind, and, if we do not take hold of the religion which you white people teach, we shall be unhappy hereafter . . . How do we know this to be true? We understand that your religion is written in a book. If it was intended for us as well as you, why has not the Great Spirit given to us, and not only to us, but why did he not give to our forefathers, the knowledge of that book, with the means of understanding it rightly? We only know what you tell us about it . . .

"Brother: . . . We also have a religion, which was given to our forefathers, and has been handed down to us their children. We worship in that way. It teaches us to be thankful for all the favors we receive; to love each other, and to be united. We never quarrel about religion . . .

". . . The Great Spirit does right. He knows what is best for his children; we are satisfied."[25]

This, of course, was a definite refusal, and, having finished his speech, Red Jacket extended his swarthy hand to the missionary in farewell. But Cram, stung to the quick by defeat, refused to take it. He left the council-ring without even so much as covering the embers of the fire which had been kindled at his request.

Today, however, those who search history and literature for an understanding of the essence of the red man's religious faith frequently consult the records of this council to ponder the Seneca chief's simple exposition of his people's beliefs.

Scarcely had Red Jacket disposed of the threatened missionary invasion before he became involved with a new challenge. The Ogden Land Company, headed by certain shrewd "promoters," wanted more Seneca land. This company, as a commercial lumber agency, had applied to the head council of the Iroquois League for an added slice of the Indians' rapidly diminishing domain. If granted, of course, this had to be with the consent of the federal government.

To discuss the demand a combined council of all members of the Iroquois Confederacy had been called. The great Seneca council-house, near Buffalo, New York (the home of Red Jacket), was chosen for the meeting place, and the gathering, assembled in the spring of 1819, is said to have been one of the largest conclaves ever to have been held by the Five Civilized Nations.

Among the Indian leaders present were the eminent Cornplanter, Farmer's Brother, Little Turtle and numerous others, recognized orators in their own right. For days the deliberations continued. Some of the sachems and chiefs were for the transaction; others stood squarely opposed to it. Red Jacket was chosen as the League's spokesman.

Keenly aware of his responsibilities to his people, he began to speak with unhesitating words and perfect assurance. He turned the attention of his fellow tribesmen to their own ancient glories. He reminded them of the broad expanse of land they once occupied. Their rapt interest was obvious. With perfect timing, Sagoyewatha began to enumerate the long list of tribal heroes, the mention of whose names caused his listeners' breasts to swell with pride. This technique is well known to every master of the speech arts.

Sure of their interest and sympathy now, Red Jacket's whole manner suddenly changed. With thundering voice and impressive gestures he drove his own deep-seated convictions home to the hearts of his red brothers. This was *his* will, born of long experience with the whites—not theirs. But his prevailed.

Then, facing the white petitioners, he almost snarled:

> "Look back to the first settlement by the whites, and then look at our present condition. Formerly, we continued to grow in numbers and in strength. What has become of the Indians who extended to the salt waters? They have been driven back and become few, while you [the whites] have been growing numerous and powerful. This land is ours from the God of heaven. It was given to us. We cannot make land. Driven back and reduced as we are, you wish to cramp us more and more . . ."

At this point Red Jacket drew from beneath his blood-red cloak a huge strip of wampum which he had secured from his tribal wampum-lodge for this purpose. Holding it up at arm's length, he shouted:

> "I have told you of the treaty we made with the United States. Here is the belt of wampum that confirmed that treaty. Here, too, is the parchment. You know its contents [pledging never again to disturb the Seneca in the possession of their lands]. I will not open it. Now the tree of friendship is decaying; its limbs are fast falling off. You [pointing to the government agent] are at fault."

The council's atmosphere became electrical. By a mere wave of the hand, as with Pontiac at Fortress Detroit, it could have been turned into a holocaust of death had Sagoyewatha been so minded. However, he allowed fevered emotions to cool as he turned his venomous attack on Mr. Ogden personally. The remainder of this speech, as recorded, reads thus:

> "Brother: You recollect when you first came to this ground that you told us you had bought the preemptive right—a right to purchase [our lands], given you by the government. Remem-

ber my reply . . . I then told you as long as I lived, you must not come forward to explain that right. You have come. See me before you. You have heard our reply to the commissioner sent by the president. I again repeat that, one and all, chiefs and warriors, we are of the same mind. We will not part with any of our reservations. Do not make your application anew, nor in any other shape. Let us hear no more of it. Let us part as we met—in friendship . . ."[26]

Regarding this memorable council, Mr. Ogden left this statement: "It is evident that the best translations of Indian oratory must fail to express the beauty and simplicity of the originals . . . especially such an original as Red Jacket." "It has been my good fortune," he continued, "to hear him a few times, but only of late years, and when his powers were enfeebled by age . . . But I shall never forget the impression made on me the first time I saw him in council. I can give no adequate idea of the strong impression it made on my mind, though conveyed through the medium of an illiterate interpreter. Even in this mangled form, it was a splendid oration."

Life's tides seemingly have a way of running in extremes. So it was with Red Jacket. While most of his early years were triumphant, the closing years were humiliating, indeed. As he advanced in age the eloquent old chief traveled extensively among the towns and cities of the Atlantic seaboard states. But his listeners were fewer. As with many another who has outlived his usefulness, he finally fell from tribal grace and suffered demotion from his chieftainship.

Twenty-six of the chiefs of his people, who earlier had sat spellbound by Sagoyewatha's words, signed the document which brought this disgrace. Ironically enough, he was charged with being a disturber in council, for opposing improvements for his nation, for having blocked Indian children from going to school, for having taken goods which belonged to others, for having left his wife because she had united with Christians. But worst of all, he was charged with having killed a deer and kept it in his own cabin, refusing to share it with those of his tribe who were starving —an unpardonable offense for a chief.

Bowed with many wintry snows, Red Jacket's defense

in council was a sad parody of his former eloquence. Stripped of his chief's bonnet and adorning feathers, his closing words were these: "When I am gone to the other world—when the Great Spirit calls me, who among my people can take my place? Many years I have guided the nation."

On January 21, 1830, this silver-tongued American's worn-out frame was laid to rest in his native village, near Buffalo. Said a reporter who was present at the time, "Well might his people weep. He who lay before them was indeed the 'Last of the Senecas.' "

# Voices from
# the South

## South

of the winding Ohio River lies one of the choicest regions of
North America. Threaded by hundreds of flowing streams
and jeweled by as many pine-clad mountains, it provided an
ideal home for the primitive American Indians because of
its mild climate, its fertile soil, and its abundance of wild
life. Half a millennium ago you could have traveled from
end to end of this vast area without meeting a single pale-
face. Today, however, you can go through much of this
same country and not meet a single red man.

Here are to be found the relics of the ancient Mound
Builders, a highly developed people about whom we know
but little today.

To the best of our knowledge the aborigines who
occupied this southern area immediately before the coming
of the whites were the Cherokee and the Creeks. Both spoke
what has been called the Muskhogean tongue, possibly an

offshoot of the Iroquois language. Each of these Indian groups had their sub-clans, like other tribes. They were tall, well-built people, graceful in movement, amiable in disposition and fond of music. Proud of their ancestry, they were valiant in war and much given to public speaking.

The Cherokee hunting grounds of that day covered an area greater than that of England itself. Their country included most of the Tennessee Valley to the headwaters of that river, as well as parts of what today are western Virginia and the Carolinas.

The hunting grounds claimed by the Creeks were similarly extensive. They stretched through what now comprises southern Georgia, Alabama and on into the Florida Everglades—a region of constant, conflicting claims between Great Britain and Spain.

The same rivalries between England and France for the control of the American fur trade in the north persisted actively in the south. Here, too, tribe was set against tribe, and red man against white man in the continuing struggle for colonial empires.[27]

In general the Creeks favored the American colonists and their English brethren, while the Cherokee leaned to French support. Consequently, the voices of these southern Indian chiefs were frequently raised in council over the question of war and peace, land treaties and alliances—and they were not less eloquent than their northern cousins.

Little Carpenter (Attakullaculla) was a Cherokee chief, born about the year 1700, who represented his people in council through the troubled years which preceded and followed the American revolution. Like Joseph Brant, at about the age of 30 he was taken to England in 1730 by Sir Alexander Cumming for social and colonial purposes. He it was who spoke the will of his people at the great council held at Hopeville where a treaty was made with the British by the Cherokee Nation in the year 1755.

Little Carpenter, like Red Jacket, was of medium height and size, but powerful when it came to the use of language. He, too, like Red Jacket in later life became addicted to the use of rum, and because of this was frequently unable to

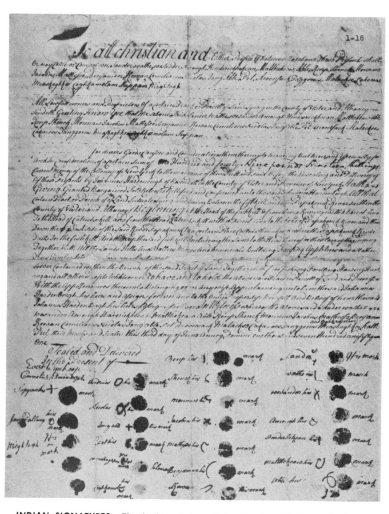

**INDIAN SIGNATURES:** The Indians "signed" treaties by affixing their finger-prints next to their names, as shown in this document dated 1751 and now in the Huntington Library.

perform as his tribe's spokesman when needed. Brave and daring in times of danger, however, Little Carpenter always placed the welfare of his tribe before his own.

One of Attakullaculla's outstanding speeches was the result of an occasion on which his tribe became involved in a charge of treaty violation. Apparently some sort of treaty or agreement had been entered into between the Cherokee peoples and the province of Old Virginia, guaranteeing the "safe conduct" of certain Cherokee emissaries *en route* to and from French trading centers in Canada, so long as white settlers' interests were safeguarded.

But something occurred. Either going to or coming from Canada, violence was committed by someone. The Virginians blamed the Indians; the Indians blamed the Virginians. A five-year war resulted. Finally the Virginian forces seized the initiative and ravaged the Indian country, destroying fifteen Cherokee villages. Over 1,400 acres of Indian corn lands were laid waste and some 5,000 Cherokee men, women and children were driven into the mountains in their effort to escape the white "vengeance."

The Indians appealed for peace. A council for this purpose was called to meet at Fort George, where terms drawn up by the whites called for unconditional Cherokee surrender. Colonel Grant, the officer in charge, after satisfying himself that the sachems and chiefs assembled actually had the authority to commit their people to action, demanded that the Cherokee Nation drop its relations with the French and swear allegiance to the king of England.

This was done, in the presence of Man-Killer, the Raven, and Old Cesar, together with other ranking chiefs. But before Indian fingers were pressed to the white man's plastic wax in confirmation of the terms of the treaty, Little Carpenter arose to deliver the following speech:

"You live at the water-side and are in the light. We are in darkness; but hope that all will yet be clear.

"I have been constantly going about doing good, and though I am tired, yet I am come to see what can be done for my people, who are in great distress.

"As to what has happened, I believe it has been ordered by our Father above. We are of different color from the white people. They are superior to us. But one God is father of us all, and we hope what is passed will be forgotten. God Almighty

made all people. There is not a day but some are coming into,
and others going out of the world.

"The Great King told me the path should never be crooked,
but open for every one to pass and repass. As we all live in one
land, I hope we shall all love as one people."[28]

At first glance this speech might be regarded as both
evasive and very weak. But it is typically Indian. It is to
be noted that Little Carpenter first acknowledged the racial
superiority of the whites. This in itself was tantamount to
surrender. Next he said he was "tired." Tired of what?
Naturally he and his fellow chiefs suffered in seeing their
villages destroyed, the cornfields laid waste, and their people
killed. Of these losses they were "tired." Only such could
bring the Cherokee Nation to submission.

Moreover, the Indians in general were great believers
in the overshadowing providence of the Great Spirit. What
He said, they did; hence, at His hands, they accepted their
fate. Attakullaculla and his fellow chiefs stood ready to
acknowledge the sovereignty of the "Great King," as they
understood sovereignty. To them, of course, all would continue to "live in one land" and all were to "love as one
people." These assumptions were taken for granted. Hence
they stood ready to affix their fingerprints to the white
man's paper as had their fathers before them.

Through much of the American colonial period
the Creeks, whose hunting grounds lay to the east of the
Cherokee, were more or less friendly toward the British
and American colonists. But they, too, insisted on keeping
their communication lines open to the French trading posts
to the north, come what might. To have done otherwise
would have deprived them of many commodities which
they felt were essential to their welfare.

Nevertheless, when war broke out between the United
States and Great Britain in 1812, for tribal reasons the
Creeks threw in their lot with the English.

At the start of that century the Creek Nation was composed of sixty or more villages, containing about 20,000
souls in all. Outstanding among their chiefs was William

Weatherford, also known as Red Eagle, a half-breed of uncertain parentage.

After repeated attempts to restore peace the veteran Indian fighter, General Andrew Jackson, decided to apply his "scorched earth" policy. Within five brief months 2,000 braves lay dead and numerous Indian villages had been given to the flames. The Creek spirit of resistance was broken and a wail of distress arose from Red Eagle's people.

The last crushing defeat of their cause came at Big Horseshoe Bend on the banks of the Tallapoosa River. It was there that Red Eagle made his last stand. So terrific were the Indian losses in that battle that all surviving Creek chiefs, except Red Eagle, sued for peace at any price.

Defeated, but not conquered, Red Eagle fled to the mountains with his few remaining followers. Then one day, starved and hopeless, he strode into General Jackson's camp and surrendered. His words of surrender were typically Indian and untinged by fear:

> "I am in your power; do with me as you please. I am a soldier. I have done the white people all the harm I could; I have fought them, and fought them bravely. If I had an army, I would yet fight and contend to the last; but I have none; my people are all gone. I can do no more than weep over the misfortunes of my nation. Once I could animate my warriors to battle; but I cannot animate the dead. My warriors can no longer hear my voice: their bones are at *Talladega*, *Tallushatches*, *Emuckfaw*, and *Tohopeka*. I have not surrendered myself thoughtlessly. While there were chances of success I never left my post, nor supplicated peace; but my people are now gone, and I ask it for my nation and for myself. On the miseries and misfortunes brought on my country, I look back with deepest sorrow, and I wish to avert still greater calamities. If I had been left to contend with the Georgia army alone, I would have raised my corn on one bank of the river and fought them on the other; but your people have destroyed my nation. You are a brave man; I rely on your generosity. You will exact no terms of a conquered people, but such as they should accede to: whatever they may be, it would be madness and folly to oppose. If they are opposed, you will find me among the sternest enforcers of obedience. Those who would still hold out, can only be influenced by a mean spirit of revenge; and to this they must not, and shall not sacrifice the last remnant of their country."[29]

Had Red Eagle been able to foresee the ultimate fate of his people he might have continued to fight in spite of his reasons for surrendering. The Creek and Cherokee nations were broken up and their populations moved under military guard beyond the Mississippi River. There, along with other tribes from the east, they were settled in what was called Indian Territory, now the State of Oklahoma. Here the major portion of their descendants dwell today.

No American who has been to school needs any introduction to the Marquis de Lafayette, friend of George Washington. His name is emblazoned forever on the pages of American history as one of those patriots who helped form the infant republic.

But few people of any country have ever heard of Pushmataha, another friend of America. Of humble Indian extraction, he was born about 1765 somewhere along the banks of Noxuba Creek, in what now is the state of Mississippi. Along with his numerous military exploits, Pushmataha became well known throughout the South for his gift of speech in and out of council. Andrew Jackson once referred to him as "the greatest and bravest Indian I have ever known."

During the War of 1812 this bold Choctaw chief led some 500 of his tribe's braves into the fray against the English.

At the ten-day Indian council held when the conflict broke out, Pushmataha declared:

> "The Creeks were once our friends. They have joined the English and we must follow different trails. When our fathers took the hand of Washington, they told him the Choctaw would always be friends of his nation, and Pushmataha cannot be false to their promises."

Despite their ancient ties with the Creeks and the British, the Choctaw followed their leader and cast in their lot with the Thirteen Fires.* They served ably at the Battle of New Orleans.

After the war was over and Lafayette visited Washington, D. C., as national guest of honor, Pushmataha was invited to be present. The two leaders met on the speakers' platform in the Capital City in 1825. When he was invited

---

*The thirteen original states of the Union, later referred to as the "Fifteen Fires."

**PUSHMATAHA** (Choctaw): "The earth will part us forever."

to speak, as Indian orator of the day, Pushmataha addressed himself to the distinguished Frenchman:

> "Nearly fifty snows have melted since you drew your sword as a champion of Washington. With him you fought the enemies of America. You mingled your blood with that of the enemy, and proved yourself a warrior. After you finished that war, you returned to your own country, and now you are come back to re-visit the land where you are honored by a numerous and powerful people.
>
> "You see everywhere the children of those by whose side you went to battle, crowding around you and shaking your hand as the hand of a father. We have heard these things told us in our villages, and our hearts longed to see you.
>
> "We have come; we have taken you by the hand and are satisfied. This is the first time we have seen you; it will probably be the last. We have no more to say. The earth will part us forever."[30]

For a moment all was silent as the white and bronzed hands of these representatives of different hemispheres met. Each glanced into the other's eyes, then turned and went his own way.

Today Pushmataha's remains lie at rest in the Congressional Cemetery in Washington, as one of the nation's honored dead. It was almost a century after his death, while searching for examples of eloquence for his *The World's Best Orations*, that William Jennings Bryan came upon the above words in the archives of the National Capital.

# Heroes of the
# Old Northwest

T HE
"Old Northwest" was that portion of North America that
lay to the north of the Ohio River and east of the great
Mississippi. This was the area of our nation's new "public
domain," first occupied after the winning of independence
from Great Britain.

Today this territory comprises Ohio, Indiana, Illinois,
Michigan and Wisconsin and contains about one-fourth of
the population of the United States. It is the greatest pro-
ductive corn belt of the entire world. Also from this section
the country draws its main supply of coal, iron and
hardwoods.

From the Indian point of view the white man's conquest
of this region logically falls into two periods. The first
covers the decade from about 1785 to 1795. Within this
brief span were held the two great Indian councils of
Greenville: one in 1790, the other in 1795. The second

period covered the era of Tecumseh's conspiracy, supported by his disaffected brother, The Prophet.

The Councils of Greenville offer an excellent opportunity for the study of Indian oratory as it existed at that time. Almost complete records were kept of the main speeches given, taken down in translation by trained government interpreters. These records were intended for the use of members of the United States Senate, which was empowered to act upon all treaties entered into by the federal government. These speeches now may be found in the *American State Papers* (Indian Relations) covering the years mentioned.

Gathered at the two great conclaves mentioned were some of the best examples of Indian intellect. The problems to be faced involved the interests of almost all the Indian tribes of the Old Northwest. Chiefs and warriors of every rank from every quarter east of the Mississippi were present.

To match the assemblage of primitive brains and brawn at the council of 1795, which lasted from June 16 to August 10, the government had its ranking Indian fighter and statesman, General Anthony Wayne, along with his armed legions. Twelve Indian tribes were represented: Wyandot, Delaware, Shawnee, Ottawa, Chippewa, Potawatami, Miami, Eel River, Wea, Kickapoo, Piankashaw and Kaskaskia. Both sides were ready for any eventuality.

The treaty which concluded this great two-month palaver was embodied in a parchment nearly two and a half feet in width and fully seven feet long. Like that pictured on Page 63, it bears the fingerprints of scores of the Indian leaders of that day. This priceless document is now lodged in the archives of the United States Department of State.

Adequate preparation on the part of the government preceded the opening of the council. A large crew of woodsmen, armed with axes, cleared an area approximately ten acres in size of all trees and brushwood. An enormous palaver house capable of accommodating at least 1,200 persons was erected; camping and sanitation facilities were provided. Many tons of food supplies, together with the usual gifts expected by leading chiefs, were on hand.

General Wayne himself opened the council by first passing the calumet of peace among all those present. Then he said:

> "I take you all by the hand as brothers, assembled for the good work of peace. I thank the Great Spirit for this glorious sun . . . and for permitting so many of us to assemble here this day . . . The Great Spirit has favored us with a clear sky and a refreshing breeze for the happy occasion."[31]

Pointing out how he had had the council ground cleared of all brush and rubbish and how he had opened roads from all directions so that all invited might readily find their way hither, he went on to cite the hearty wishes of President Washington that "peace and brotherly love" might prevail with all.

Naturally there were many uninvited persons on the fringes of this great gathering—illicit rum sellers and greedy land speculators. There were also transients like Jacob Carmichael, a legitimate Indian trader who could read and write. From his notebook we learn that a Potawatami chief, named The Sun, had come to the council a bit early. Somewhat restive, he went to General Wayne with this inquiry, taken down verbatim by Carmichael:

> "Brother! It is some time since we left our wives and families: we have come a long distance and have been several days here. We wish to know when the treaty will commence . . ."[32]

General Wayne's response was that the talks would start as soon as the Wyandot and Shawnee delegates arrived. This seemed to satisfy The Sun.

Chief Tarhe was a Wyandot, an experienced speaker on many public occasions which affected the vital interests of his race. He was well known to such men as Joseph Brant, Pontiac, Red Jacket, Cornplanter, Farmer's Brother, Little Turtle and other lesser lights who shed glory on the red man's reputation as an eloquent orator.

Actually, Tarhe appears to have been chosen by the Indians gathered at Greenville as the one best suited to

**JACOB CARMICHAEL'S JOURNAL:** This page contains a translation of the inquiry of The Sun, a Potawatomi chief, in regard to a pending treaty. The Journal is now in the Huntington Library.

express their collective desires at the great council, much like the keynote speaker at a national political party convention. Previous to June 16, as stated above, there had been numerous tribal gatherings of the Indians present, trying to work out their many problems and concerns. To synchronize their interests into a single brief statement was Tarhe's task.

This was the gist of his message, when he addressed the council on behalf of seventeen tribal groups:

"Elder Brother: Now listen to us! The Great Spirit above has appointed this day for us to meet together. I shall now deliver my sentiments to you, the Fifteen Fires. I view you lying in a gore of blood; it is me, an Indian, who has caused it. Our tomahawk yet remains in your head; the English gave it to me to place there.

"Elder Brother: I now take the tomahawk out of your head; but, with so much care, that you shall not feel pain or injury. I will now tear a big tree up by the roots, and throw the hatchet into the cavity which they occupied, where the waters will wash it away where it can never be found. . . .

"Brother[s]: Listen to us, all Indians, who now speak to you! The bones which lie scattered of your ancient warriors, who fell in defence of the present cause, we gather all together, and bury them now; and place this white board over them, that they may never again be seen by our posterity. [Here a white and blue wampum belt was presented by Chief Tarhe to General Wayne]. . . .

"Brother: Listen to us Indians; I told you just now, that we were upon business of the greatest moment; I now conclude the great good works we have been employed in, and with *this* I cover the whole earth, that it may appear white, and shine all over the world. I hope the Great Spirit will have pity on us, and make this work lasting."[33]

While it takes but a few moments to read the portion of Tarhe's speech here presented, it took the Indian orator approximately two hours to say what he had to say, each statement being laboriously interpreted into the languages of the tribes represented so that all could understand fully as the palaver proceeded.

After days of discussion, mixed with many dangers, the Treaty of Greenville was drawn up and signed. Then arose the question as to which tribal orator should voice the

**LITTLE TURTLE** (Miami): "Your younger brothers are of opinion, you take too much of their lands away."

gratitude of the Indians for the new assurances given by the United States Government. Naturally great rivalry appeared among the several tribal groups present for this honor.

This privilege finally fell to Little Turtle, chief of the Miami. It will be remembered that it was this tribe whose homes and hunting grounds so recently had been ravaged by war. What would Little Turtle say?

Born of a family of chieftains in the Sciota country, Little Turtle had risen to prominence at the time of the St. Clair defeats of the whites in the winter of 1790-1791. His leadership had cost the government no less than 38 officers and men killed in action, in addition to more than 250 wounded. In turn Little Turtle's band of warriors went almost unscathed.

Unpredictable in thought and action, Little Turtle had appeared at the council early. General Wayne knew him well as a tricky, sly, shrewd and ruthless savage, so he was carefully watched. What did he have in mind?

They soon found out when the Miami chief arose to address them:

"Elder Brother, *and all you present:* I am going to say a few words, in the name of the Pattawatamies, Weas, and Kickapoos. It is well known to you all, that people are appointed on these occasions to speak the sentiments of others; therefore am I appointed for these three nations.

"Elder Brother: You told your younger brothers, when we first assembled, that peace was your object; you swore your interpreters before us, to the faithful discharge of their duty, and told them the Great Spirit would punish them, did they not perform it. You told us, that it was not you, but the President of the Fifteen Fires of the United States, who spoke to us; that, whatever he should say, should be firm and lasting; that it was impossible he should say what was not true. Rest assured, that your younger brothers, the Miamies, Ottawas, Chippewas, Pattawatamies, Shawnese, Weas, Kickapoos, Piankeshaws, and Kaskaskias, are well pleased with your words, and are persuaded of their sincerity. . . . [Here a wampum belt was presented to General Wayne as a pledge of loyalty.]³⁴

From this point on, for an hour or more, Little Turtle played artfully on the fears and prejudices of his red kinsmen. First he appealed to their racial pride, then to the fears growing out of the many aggressions of the whites. At times his expressions were amiable and friendly; at others they were austere and threatening. Then he came to the point:

> "Elder Brother: You have told us to speak our minds freely, and we now do it. [He scanned the boundary laid down in the signed treaty.] This line takes in the greater and best part of your brothers' hunting ground, therefore, your younger brothers are of opinion, you take too much of their lands away. . . . the Miamies, the proprietors of those lands, and all your younger brothers present, wish to run the line as you mentioned, to fort Recovery, and to continue it along the road; from thence to fort Hamilton, on the great Miami river. This is what your brothers request you to do, and you may rest assured of the free navigation of that river, from thence to its mouth, forever."[34]

To say the least, Anthony Wayne was nonplused at these words. Had the treaty not already been signed? Applause on the part of the Indians burst forth from tribal groups here and there, evidently in support of Little Turtle's belated demand.

The atmosphere grew tense. The wrong word, an inadvertent gesture, and the council of peace might suddenly turn into a bloody conflict.

General Wayne stood up. Quite calmly, he said:

> "I have listened to you with attention; and have heard your observations upon the general boundary line proposed by me, as well as upon the proposed reservations. If my ears did not deceive me, I have heard all the other nations give their assent to the general boundary line. . . .
>
> "You say that the general boundary line, as proposed by me, will take away some of your best hunting grounds; and propose to alter it. . . .
>
> "This would be a very crooked, as well as a very difficult line to follow; because, there are several roads . . . . some of them several miles apart, which might certainly be productive of unpleasant mistakes and differences; that which I propose will be free from all difficulty and uncertainty . . . . . . . The United States of America grant liberty to all the Indian tribes to hunt within the territory ceded to the United States . . . . so long as they demean themselves peaceably. . . ."[35]

# The Twin
# Conspirators

Like
the Old World's Darius, Alexander the Great, Hannibal,
Caesar and Napoleon, the New World had its empire
dreamers. Even American Indians could covet power. Of
this ilk were Massassoit of New England, Powhatan of
old Virginia, Pontiac of the Maumee country, and even
Tecumseh and his one-eyed brother, The Prophet.

In the ten years which followed the signing of the
Treaty of Greenville discontent accumulated among the
Indians. But the mass movement of the whites to the west
and south would not be stayed.

So far as is known Tecumseh and his brother had no
part in the Council of 1795; hence they felt in no way
bound by its terms. Moreover, everything white was as
loathsome to these two ambitious leaders as it had been to
Red Jacket and others.

The mother of these two brothers apparently was of

Creek descent, while the father seems to have been a Shawnee. Two sons born to this fateful union, together with the father, evidently had been killed by the whites. This, together with numerous other grievances, told and retold at their mother's knee, called loudly upon these two bold spirits for blood revenge.

The decade following 1795 saw a new generation of young Indians rise to power, inexperienced in the ways of their forefathers. Also the tribes of the great plains beyond the Mississippi were in commotion because of the reports of white aggression which constantly sifted through from their eastern cousins. Here lay a potential new empire, more than half a million square miles in extent, ready for leadership. Toward it Tecumseh's eyes turned with fierce ambition.

Better known among his kinsmen as Tenskwatawa, The Prophet, like Mahomet, apparently was subject to mental disturbances. In one such seizure he is said to have fallen to the ground as though dead. Upon being carried to his native village, however, he revived and announced that he had been to the spirit world where he had seen the veil of the future lifted. He declared that he had returned with a message from the "Father of Life," to the effect that all red men should combine and clear their native lands of the growing white scourge. He accepted it as a divine mission.

The memorable eclipse of the sun on June 16, 1806, provided an excellent opportunity for The Prophet to demonstrate his supernatural powers. (In all probability he had runners trailing the scientists in the field and knew that for which they had come.)

As high noon of that dramatic day approached The Prophet, dressed in a dark gown and surrounded by his followers, stepped to the door of his cabin. Like Joshua of old, with hand pointed toward the zenith, he commanded the sun to cover its face.

A thin mist dimmed its rim. Gradually the entire disk went black. The Indians watched with awe and fear. Within the hour Tenskwatawa commanded that the sun

**THE PROPHET** (Creek): "Our hatchets are broken; our bows are snapped; our fires are extinguished."

again give light. As the eclipse passed he turned to his followers and said, "Did I not prophesy aright?"

After that his word was accepted as law by many of his countrymen.

Months later, and far to the eastward, we again catch a glimpse of Tenskwatawa's method of fomenting unrest among his red cousins. We also obtain a sampling of his oratorical ability.

For years a missionary had been at work among the Tuscarora, a dependent branch of the Iroquois Confederacy. But the cunning apostle from the west sent messengers before him to arouse expectancy and prepare the ground for his seed of subversion. In due time The Prophet announced his intended visit.

Naturally, the Tuscarora arranged a council fire. Their guest was to be welcomed, whatever his mission might be. It was planned to hold the council in the tribal palaver house, but so many Indians gathered to listen that this proved too small. So the meeting was held in the open, close beside a stream and overshadowed by trees. The first touch of autumn frost had set the nearby hillsides aglow with a riot of color, providing a picturesque setting. The Indians waited with the calm patience of their race. Present, too, was their own missionary.

Suddenly, as if by magic, Tenskwatawa stood in their midst. Over his left shoulder was thrown a shield of soft white deer skin. In his hand was his ever-present tomahawk. He eyed the gathering boldly.

"Men of the Woods!" he cried, in the voice of an inspired prophet. "Hear what the Great Spirit says to his children who have forsaken him!

"There was a time when our fathers owned this island. Their lands extended from the rising to the setting sun. The Great Spirit made it for their use. He made the buffalo and the deer for their food . . . He sent the rain upon the earth, and it produced corn. All this he did for his red children . . .

"Red Men of the Woods! Have you not heard at evening, and sometimes in the dead of night, those mournful sounds that steal through the deep valleys and along the mountain sides? These are the wailings of those spirits whose bones have been turned up by the plow of the white man, and left to the mercy of the rain and wind. They call upon you to avenge them, that they may enjoy their blissful paradise far beyond the blue hills.

"Hear me, O deluded people, for the last time! This wide region was once your inheritance; but now the cry of the revelry of war is no more heard on the shores of the majestic Hudson, or on the sweet banks of the silver Mohawk.

"The eastern tribes have long since disappeared—even the forests that sheltered them are laid low; and scarcely a trace of our nation remains, except here and there the Indian name of a stream, or a village. And such, sooner or later, will be the fate of other tribes; in a little while they will go the way that their brethren have gone.

"They will vanish like a vapor from the face of the earth; their very history will be lost in forgetfulness, and the places that now know them will know them no more. We are driven back until we can retreat no farther; our hatchets are broken; our bows are snapped; our fires are extinguished; a little longer and the white man will cease to persecute us, for we shall cease to exist."[36]

This basic appeal strongly stirred the emotions of those present. It called for action—but action of a nature which the Tuscarora were not ready to give. They were devoted to their missionary and when their vote was taken this was made clear to Tenskwatawa.

Leaping from the council-ring, with a storm of anathemas on his lips, The Prophet disappeared among the shadows of the forest as mysteriously as he had come.

Tecumseh's so-called "conspiracy" was a plan to organize all Indian tribes of the west into one giant confederacy, much like that envisaged by Pontiac. To achieve this end he and his one-eyed brother, The Prophet, traveled widely among their people, encouraging them to united action.

Usually dressed in a white buckskin blouse and beaded leggings, with a feather-tipped blue and red band about his brow, he was known wherever he appeared.

Volumes have been written about the activities of these two bold "conspirators." And any treatise on the Indian speech arts which failed to recognize their skill in this respect would be remiss, indeed. Thus, the fact that they apparently were not invited to be present at the Council of

**TECUMSEH** (Creek): "Our object is to let our affairs be transacted by warriors."

Greenville was no oversight on the part of the government.

Tecumseh's mission seemed to carry him everywhere. At one time we find him deep in the Creek country, the home of Chief Big Warrior, far to the south at the village of Tukabatchi. At that time, it should be remembered, the Cherokee and Creek nations were having their troubles with the British and Americans who soon were to fly at each other's throats in the War of 1812.

Tecumseh wanted Creek support for his ambitions in the north. To this end he made direct approach for the help of Big Warrior. As the debate strung out in council, however, Big Warrior's braves gave little evidence of warming up to Tecumseh's appeal. Exasperated, he pointed a menacing finger at Big Warrior.

> "Your blood is white," he roared. "You have taken my talk, and the sticks, and the wampum, and the hatchet, but you do not mean to fight. I know the reason. You do not believe the Great Spirit has sent me. You shall know. I leave Tuckhabatchee directly, and shall go straight to Detroit. When I arrive there, I will stamp on the ground with my foot and shake down every house in Tuckhabatchee."[37]

So saying, Tecumseh took his belligerent leave. Scarcely had time enough passed for him to have reached Detroit before a disastrous earthquake struck Big Warrior's region in apparent fulfillment of his prophecy.

Like his brother, The Prophet, twice Tecumseh was cited before Governor William Henry Harrison for his openly subversive behavior. On one of these occasions the chief insolently responded with seventy-five or more of his armed warriors by his side. On another he was entertained for ten days at the governor's headquarters, every courtesy being shown to him, in an effort to obtain his loyalty. For this hearing Governor Harrison had employed a special interpreter, and it is from this occasion that we have the following speech delivered in the Shawnee language by Tecumseh.

> "Brother! I wish you to listen to me well. As I think you do not clearly understand what I before said to you, I will explain it again.
>
> "Brother! Since the peace [of Greenville in 1795] was made, you have killed some of the Shawnees, Winnebagoes, Dela-

wares and Miamies; and you have taken our lands from us; and I do not see how we can remain at peace with you, if you continue to do so. . . . You take tribes aside, and advise them not to come into this measure [the confederacy]; and, until our design is accomplished, we do not wish to accept your invitation to go to see the president. . . .

"Brother! You ought to know what you are doing with the Indians. . . . It is a very bad thing; and we do not like it. . . . We have endeavored to level all distinctions—to destroy village chiefs by whom all mischief is done. It is they who sell our lands to the Americans. Our object is to let our affairs be transacted by warriors. . . .

"Brother! . . . If the land is not restored to us, you will see, when we return to our homes, how it will be settled. We shall have a great council, at which all the tribes will be present, when we shall show to those who sold, that they had no right to the claim they set up; and we will see what will be done with those chiefs . . ."[38]

This was a bold threat but Tecumseh meant it. Already negotiations had been under way with many of the dissatisfied tribes for just such a council, and even with the British across the Canadian line. When the storm broke it came with a fury characteristic of Indian warfare. Tippecanoe and the Indian battle of the Thames lay just ahead. Who actually dealt Tecumseh's death blow we do not know, but we do know that he was as fearless a warrior as he was an orator.

# Defenders of
# the Mississippi

**W**HEN
the Napoleonic Wars closed in 1815 America turned its
back on Europe and settled down to the task of developing
its own internal resources. The British had been driven out
of New Orleans by Andrew Jackson and William Henry
Harrison had leveled Tecumseh's ambitions to the dust. The
young nation stood face to face with its third era of westward expansion.

The generation which followed Tecumseh's fall marked
a hectic period in American life. Fearful that unless they
made haste all the worthwhile lands of the West would be
occupied by others, many inexperienced and ill-equipped
Easterners set forth on the overland trail. Many perished
from hunger, thirst, heat, cold—or Indian arrows.

Meanwhile, a succession of hard winters had hit the
northern states, particularly those of New England. Crops
were poor and sickness prevailed on every hand. Hence an

escape psychology seized upon the public mind and to "move out" came to be a mania. Not only families, but whole communities, caught the "fever" to go West. Many had little or nothing to lose and everything to gain. Among these emigrants were two Jones families, residents of Maine, and incidentally ancestors of the writer.

Writing back to Unity, Maine, home of the Joneses, Peter Moulton penned these words: "I was sixteen days on the way [to Columbus, Ohio] and it is not likely that Thomas [Jones] and family will arrive before next Monday evening." As to the land itself, Peter Moulton continued: "From Cleveland I came across the country to Columbus by stage and believe me I actually wept . . . on seeing this wonderful country and reflecting that I had spent the flower of my days in so inhospitable a region as Maine."[39]

Such letters, carried back East by stage, fanned the flames that lay back of the westward surge in the second quarter of the 19th Century. Roadways were cut through the forests and canals were dug to facilitate travel with a national enthusiasm. Not only was the generation on the move, it was egged on by a new spirit of swagger and bombastic self-confidence.

It has been remarked of this era that our new West confidently believed its rivers were the longest, the grandest, and the muddiest on the earth. The men who plied them were the bravest and boldest of mankind. Moreover, it was seriously proclaimed that these river pilots could spit farther and straighter, and swear louder and more profanely than any others. In fact, when their boilers exploded, as they frequently did, they blew their passengers higher into the air than did the river steamers in any other land. Superlatives had become commonplace.

It was this egotistical, overbearing, cocksure spirit that the Indian tribes bordering on the Mississippi now had to meet.

What were these Indians like? Big Elk is a good example.


The remains of Black Buffalo, a deceased Teton Sioux, were to be buried near the Portage Des Sioux. Because of his recognized eloquence the Omaha tribal orator, Big Elk, whose people dwelt on the west side of the Great River, had been asked to deliver a speech befitting the occasion.

In keeping with custom, a great number of peaceful Indians had gathered to pay their last respects to their beloved chief. Also on hand were numerous friendly frontier families, men, women and children, as well as certain public officials.

During much of his address to the mourners Big Elk appeared to be talking to himself. His words seemed more of a reflection:

"Do not grieve—misfortunes will happen to the wisest and best of men. Death will come, and always comes out of season; it is the command of the Great Spirit, and all nations and people must obey.

"What is passed, and cannot be prevented, should not be grieved for. Be not discouraged or displeased then, that in visiting your father here, you have lost your chief.

"A misfortune of this kind may never again befall you, but this would have attended you perhaps at your own village. Five times I have visited this land, and never returned with sorrow or pain. Misfortunes do not flourish particularly in our path—they grow everywhere.

"What a misfortune for me," he continued in a jocular vein, "that I could not have died this day, instead of the chief that lies before us. The trifling loss my nation would have sustained in my death, would have been doubly paid for by the honours of my burial—they would have wiped off everything like regret.

"Instead of being covered with a cloud of sorrow—my warriors would have felt the sunshine of joy in their hearts. To me it would have been a most glorious occurrence.

"Hereafter, when I die at home, instead of a noble grave and a grand procession, the rolling music and the thundering cannon [evidently addressed to the whites], with a flag waving at my head, I shall be wrapped in a robe, (an old robe, perhaps) and hoisted on a slender scaffold to the whistling winds, soon to be blown down to the earth—my flesh to be devoured by the wolves, and my bones rattled on the plain by the wild beasts.

"Chief of the soldiers [to officials standing by]—your labors have not been in vain:—your attention shall not be forgotten. My nation shall know the respect that is paid over the dead. When I return I will echo the sound of your guns."[40]

This is all that history has preserved of this splendid tribute to the memory of Black Buffalo. Whether there were responses by others the chronicle does not tell us. But the simple words uttered by this unsophisticated savage

express basic truths common to all men. Death does
"always come out of season," and that which "cannot be
prevented, should not be grieved for."

To the Indian mind death is merely an intermediary
experience, not something final. His concept of being em-
braces a pre-existence as well as an after-existence. Hence
he has no fear of death.

The intelligent Indian knows no hell or purgatory, and
no horror of eternal punishment for sin, except as these
concepts have been acquired from elsewhere. He killed to
protect himself or for revenge, and with no fear of punishment in another world.

It might be added here that most white men feared
no future punishment for killing an Indian for whatever
reason—if any.

Early one spring day of 1827, while snow was still on
the ground in this upper Illinois country, an incident
occurred which threw the countryside into a frenzy. A
group of whites had tapped the sugar trees on a neighboring
Indian reservation. Discovered by Red Bird (Wanig-Suchka)
and his Winnebago fellow tribesmen, there was immediate
trouble.

The Indians insisted that the white men leave their
lands and go home. This was refused. Words, little understood, grew hot. Shots rang out and some of the whites fell
dead. Within hours the whites had unleashed a typical
manhunt. Certain Winnebago were captured and promptly
"executed."

When this news reached the Winnebago headquarters
the entire tribe was incensed beyond bounds. A special
council was quickly called and demands for revenge ran
high. As leading chief, Red Bird carried out the council's
orders. With two of his trusted braves he made a raid on
Prairie du Chien. Two white men, together with a helpless
baby, were killed. A few days later the same party attacked
a boatload of whites on the Mississippi River. Four frontiersmen were killed and two others injured before they could
escape.

Troops were rushed into the Winnebago country. This

changed the picture completely. Rather than precipitate what he knew would be a hopeless struggle, Red Bird surrendered himself on behalf of his people.

In appearing before the authorities Red Bird wore all his native finery, ready for execution. One side of his face was painted a deep red, the other white and green. Around his neck was a collar of blue wampum, interwoven with white and trimmed with panther claws. From his shoulders fell a white elk skin, ornamented with strands of colored wampum, and his feet were encased in decorated moccasins. On his shoulders rested two tiny stuffed red birds, representative of the name he bore. Across his breast two eagle feathers, one white, one black, were meaningfully suspended in opposite directions. Pressed close to his heart was his cherished calumet, and in the other hand he held a white flag. Said he emotionlessly:

> "I am ready. I do not wish to be put in irons. Let me be free. I have given away my life. It is gone like that [with a wave of his hand]. I would not take it back. It is gone."[41]

"Where is the oration?" you ask.

"Does it always take a volume of words to comprise eloquence?" is the querying reply.

"Eloquence," once said Lord Cecil, "is vehement simplicity."


In pioneer days, it should be remembered, big get-together occasions were few and far between. But when such celebrations came the hornyhanded toilers of the time poured forth in herds to enjoy the rare diversion. Especially was this true when news went abroad that an individual of Black Hawk's fame was to speak.

Black Hawk was a member of the Sauk and Fox tribe, a contemporary of Red Bird and Big Elk. He was born in 1767 at the Sauk village at the mouth of the Rock River, Illinois. As an individual he came to be one of the most troublesome Indians of his time.

He first made history for himself by invading the Osage country at the head of a band of restless Indian youths. With his own hands he took the scalp of one of his own

**BLACK HAWK** (Sauk and Fox): "I am a man!"

redskin cousins. Two years later he again invaded that same country. This time he returned with no less than seven scalps to his credit. But on this ill-fated expedition he lost his father, together with some of his younger braves. Through deeds such as these he rose to chieftainship, with Keokuk, a fellow tribesman, as his main rival.

Toward the end of his life, however, like Red Jacket, Black Hawk was demoted from the rank of chief. He was charged with indiscretion in connection with the so-called Black Hawk War. It is said that when this impetuous leader was informed of the decision of his tribe he broke into a fit of rage and slapped his robe across the face of Chief Keokuk with a force that made his rival stagger.

"I am a man!" he cried heatedly. "An old man! I will not conform to the counsels of anyone. I will act for myself—no one shall govern me. . . ."

Many are the stories that have been written about Black Hawk. One records a speech he gave at a 4th of July celebration near old Fort Madison, where he died at the age of 71.

Naturally, numerous speeches preceded that given by the famous Indian, but when his turn came the chairman introduced him with fitting tribute to his accomplishments —every word of which went straight to his heart. Black Hawk commenced to speak in a voice full of resonance and power. But as he proceeded age began to tell and he all but lost his self control. Many old people had huddled close to the platform, anxious to look into the face of him who had been the terror of their earlier years.

The speech, as transcribed, was as follows:

"Brothers! It has pleased the Great Spirit that I am here today. I have eaten with my white friends. The earth is our mother; we are on it, with the Great Spirit above us. It is good. I hope we are all friends here.

"A few winters ago I was fighting against you. I did wrong, perhaps; but that is past; it is buried; let it be forgotten.

"Rock River was a beautiful country. I liked my towns, my cornfields, and the home of my people. I fought for it. It is now yours; keep it as we did; it will produce you good crops.

"I thank the Great Spirit that I am now friendly with my white brethren; we are here together; we have eaten together; we are friends; it is His wish and mine. I thank you for your friendship.

"I was once a great warrior. I am now poor. Keokuk has

been the cause of my present situation; but do not attach blame to him.

"I am now old. I have looked upon the Mississippi since I have been a child. I love the Great River. I have dwelt upon its banks from the time I was an infant. I look upon it now. I shake hands with you, and as it is my wish, I hope you are my friends."[42]

Black Hawk's clear eye scanned the eastern skyline, once his cherished home. A flood of joyous memories flooded his wild soul. Pinned to the banks of the great Mississippi close by were the flatboats of those who had come from its eastern shores. There once rode only the more graceful canoes of the red men. Black Hawk's voice broke.

"I hope you are my friends," he concluded, took his seat, and lapsed into dignified silence.

It is a truism that individuals of like talents seldom bear amiable attitudes toward each other. This certainly was true of Black Hawk and Keokuk.

Keokuk was thirteen years Black Hawk's junior, although both lived to a ripe old age. His name, which means "he who moves about alertly," faithfully typified his actions. Like Black Hawk, he was born on the banks of the Rock River on the east side of the Mississippi, a fact of which he was unendingly proud.

To some Keokuk appeared sly and given to duplicity. His social influence, like many another, rested largely on his speech powers, recognized from an early period. In middle life he traveled extensively in the East, visiting Washington, D.C., and elsewhere. In Boston he was once the special guest of the governor of Massachusetts at a great banquet at which he was invited to speak. At that time a live Indian was almost as much of a curiosity in the East as would be a wooden cigar store Indian today.

After the Black Hawk Purchase in 1832 the Indians of necessity had to go. When the time came for the remnant of the Sauk and Fox tribes to be moved Keokuk, their now aged orator chief, was chosen to voice their sad farewell to the land which had sustained their ancestors from time unknown.

**KEOKUK** (Sauk and Fox): "The time for us to go has come."

Crestfallen and dejected, he appeared like a broken reed. There was little left now to sustain his interest in life. His words were so low and disconsolate as to be barely audible to those who stood close by.

"Brother! [said he] My people and myself have come to shake hands with you. The time for us to go has come. We do not feel glad to leave this country which we have lived in so long.

"The many moons and sunny days we have lived here will long be remembered by us. The Great Spirit has smiled upon us and made us glad. But we have agreed to go.

"We go to a country we know but little of. Our new home will be beyond a great river on the way to the setting sun. We will build our wigwams there in another land where we hope the Great Spirit will smile upon us, as he has here.

"The men we leave here in possession of these lands cannot say Keokuk and his people have ever taken up the tomahawk . . . against them. We have always been for peace with you, and you have been kind to us. In peace we bid you goodbye. May the Great Spirit smile upon you in this land, and upon us in the new land to which we go. We will think of you and you must think of us. If you come to see us, we will divide our supply of venison with you and we will gladly welcome you."[43]

Keokuk's lips ceased to move. All turned to go. Old and young, along with their women and children, moved silently into the darkness. Today their numbers are scattered throughout the West, even to the shores of the Pacific.*

---

* While the members of the Sauk and Fox tribes today are widely scattered, about 500 of them still reside on their small reservation in Tama County, Iowa, about thirty miles east of Marshalltown. The Indian language is still spoken in many of the homes there, though most of the children attend school regularly where English is taught.

# Where Sky
# Meets Prairie

**W**HEN
Thomas Jefferson, third president of the United States,
purchased much of the area west of the Mississippi River
in 1803 he thought he had secured enough room in this new
territory to absorb the nation's surplus populations for centuries to come. However, scarcely three generations had
passed before this land, too, was occupied by the white
avalanche.

Thousands of primitive Indians, still living as their
forefathers had for centuries, made this region their home.
De Soto had entered this wonderland and had been charmed
by its magnitude. Coronado penetrated it as far to the
west as where Santa Fe now stands. But Coronado was
seeking the Seven Golden Cities, found only the stone-and-
adobe villages of the Pueblo Indians, and returned to
Mexico empty-handed and disappointed.

The expedition of Lewis and Clark pressed its way to

the base of the Rocky Mountains and beyond, keeping careful note of what they saw. By their discoveries these explorers opened the eyes of the world to the possibilities of the vast Pacific Northwest—but mostly from the point of view of agriculture and stock raising. The event which really set the world afire with lust was the discovery of gold at Sutter's Mill, in California, on January 24, 1848.

Previous to that memorable event California is said to have had less than 1,000 white persons within its boundaries. Two years later the bay area near San Francisco alone had no less than 100,000 whites who had come from all parts of the world. Today, a little more than a century after, California boasts a population in excess of 17,000,000.

Among the most peaceful Indian peoples of the Pacific Northwest was the Dwamish tribe, a small body of the Salish group, occupants of the Puget Sound region. There they had dwelt for generations in comparative isolation, satisfied with the provisions of Nature. But, as with their eastern cousins, trouble soon knocked at their door. Their enviable climate, together with the white man's greed for gold, proved to be their undoing.

By 1855, the year of the Port Elliott Treaty with the United States, the lands of the Dwamish peoples were at stake—demanded by the whites. And when Chief Seattle (Seathl) touched the pen which inked the terms of this treaty his people were doomed to reservation confinement, an act which gave birth to one of the best known Indian orations on record.

Seattle, for whom the Washington city later was named, was a dignified and stately Indian of Salishan stock. Born about 1790, he was nearly 65 years of age when he signed the treaty mentioned, and he had always been regarded as a friend of the whites, even by the fur traders who came from Vancouver long before the national boundary had been settled.

To Isaac Stephens, governor of the Oregon Territory and official representative of the federal government, Chief Seattle spoke the mind of his people:

"Yonder sky that has wept tears of compassion on our fathers for centuries untold, and which, to us, looks eternal, may change. Today is fair, tomorrow it may be overcast with clouds. My words are like the stars that never change. What Seattle says, the great chief Washington can rely upon, with as much certainty as our paleface brothers can rely upon the return of the seasons.

"The son of the White Chief says that his father sends us greetings of friendship and good will. This is kind, for we know he has little need of our friendship in return, because his people are many. They are like the grass that covers the vast prairies. My people are few, and resemble the scattering trees of a storm-swept plain. . . .

"There was a time when our people covered the whole land as the waves of the wind-ruffled sea cover its shell-paved floor. But that time has long since passed away with the greatness of tribes now almost forgotten. I will not mourn over our untimely decay, nor reproach my paleface brothers with hastening it. . . .

"Your religion was written on tablets of stone, by the iron finger of your God, lest you forget it. The red men could never remember it or comprehend it. Our religion is the traditions of our ancestors, the dreams of our old men, given them by the Great Spirit, and the visions of our sachems, and is written in the hearts of our people. . . .

"Every part of this country is sacred to my people. Every hillside, every valley, every plain and grove has been hallowed by some fond memory or some sad experience of my tribe. Even the rocks which seem to lie dumb as they swelter in the sun . . . thrill with memories of past events connected with the fate of my people. . . .

"The braves, fond mothers, glad-hearted maidens, and even little children, who lived here . . . still love these solitudes. Their deep fastnesses at eventide grow shadowy with the presence of dusty spirits. When the last red man shall have perished from the earth and his memory among the white men shall have become a myth, these shores shall swarm with the invisible dead of my tribe. . . .

"At night when the streets of your cities and villages shall be silent, and you think them deserted, they will throng with the returning hosts that once filled and still love this beautiful land.

"The white man will never be alone. Let him be just and deal kindly with my people, for the dead are not altogether powerless. Dead, did I say? There is no death, only a change of worlds."[44]

Delivered in a calm, even voice, this speech expressed no hatred toward the whites, despite the fact that many ills suffered by the Dwamish people were attributable directly to white intrusion. But there is an ironic bitterness in the words, and there are no nobler in any language. Seattle and his people were bowing to the inevitable, but their pride

**CHIEF SEATTLE** (Dwamish): "The white man will never be alone . . . for the dead are not altogether powerless."

of race and ancestry could not be concealed. *The old order changeth, yielding place to the new.* One phase of the Indian's role in the drama of life had ended. But the Indian had been and would ever be—if not in this world, most certainly in another.

Though greatly abbreviated here, this speech of Seattle's is well worthy of study. Here is dignified pathos and a calm acceptance of a tragic destiny. The poignant words seem to reflect a stoic sense of fatalism.

Indeed, after scanning the various orations considered in this study one is inclined to wonder if that primitive child of Nature, the American Indian, was not given a clearer insight into the workings of destiny than any other people on earth. The Indian *knew* when his sun had set for the last time!

With the discovery of gold in the West the demand for tools, equipment and supplies quickly outstripped the ability of wagons to convey them. Transportation of that vintage quickly became obsolete, and the demand for rail transportation had to be satisfied. But the lands to be crossed included the vast hunting grounds of the Plains Indians. It was here that the buffalo, the very basis of Indian existence, roamed at will. These great shaggy beasts supplied not only the red man's food, but his shelter, clothing and tools as well.

With the conclusion of the Civil War a rail line already had reached Fort Laramie, Wyoming, as early as 1866. But trouble had been brewing in that part of the West for a generation or more. In 1851 a great council had been held at Fort Laramie with the Indians of this western country with a view to opening up the Powder River area where gold and other precious metals had been found. The treaty entered into at this time gave only the right to pass through the Indian lands, not the right to exploit its animal or mineral resources. Moreover, this right had been granted only for a period of ten years.

By 1866 this pact was five years extinct, but the whites were still going through Indian territory. Hence, when the federal government asked for its renewal there was considerable anxiety on the Indian side of the fence.

Two of the leading Indian chiefs of this high country, Sitting Bull and Red Cloud, made it clear that they were unalterably opposed to the proposal. It meant more forts, not less, in the Indian country, along with more white depredations of many kinds.

Red Cloud was an Oglala Teton Sioux, a master of Indian strategy in warfare. Adept in natural lore, he knew little of the white man's ways, other than those learned in the hard school of actual experience. Born near the upper forks of the La Platte River in Nebraska, in 1822, he knew that region well. For two long years he had defeated every attempt of the whites to drive their proposed railway into the Powder River country. Supported by large numbers of red men, he had captured and held prisoner numerous of the government troops sent to protect the workers on this road. Even the forces housed at Fort Phil Kearney, many miles away, scarcely dared to leave their stockades to harvest hay for the horses, so deadly were Red Cloud's attacks.

At the second council at Fort Laramie Red Cloud thus addressed his people:

> "Hear ye, Dakotas! When the Great Father at Washington sent us his chief soldier [General Harney] to ask for a path through our hunting grounds, a way for his iron road to the mountains and the western sea, we were told that they wished merely to pass through our country, not to tarry among us, but to seek for gold in the far west. Our old chiefs thought to show their friendship and good will, when they allowed this dangerous snake in our midst. . . .
>
> "Yet before the ashes of the council fire are cold, the Great Father is building his forts among us. You have heard the sound of the white soldier's ax upon the Little Piney. His presence here is an insult and a threat. It is an insult to the spirits of our ancestors. Are we then to give up their sacred graves to be plowed for corn? Dakotas, I am for war!"[45]

And war it was. There could be only one reaction to such words. War spread over the plains like a devastating prairie fire—and before it was brought to a close millions of dollars of public money had been expended, together with the lives of thousands of men of both races.

For the Indians of the plains the years 1865-1867 were, indeed, decisive ones. Here was where history was being

**RED CLOUD** (Sioux): "Are we then to give up their sacred graves to be plowed for corn? Dakotas, I am for war!"

made. Hence many of the newspapers throughout the eastern cities sent competent reporters to cover the exciting
events in this great prairie country.

Another great Indian council was in the making, that
at Fort Kearney, on the banks of the North La Platte, about
300 miles west of what today is the city of Omaha. In
keeping with custom the government commissioners came
early in order to arrange the details of the occasion. The
council had been set for early September, but it just had
to wait while the Indians settled a dispute that had arisen
among themselves.

Turkey Foot, a Sioux under-chief, had captured six
white persons, all women and children. He wanted to trade
these captives at the pending council for his own nephew
and one favorite Cheyenne squaw, held in captivity by the
whites.

As the Indians began to gather for the conclave, one of
the reporters in attendance wrote that "It was a thrilling
sight to see the long straggling lines of advance Indians
hastening to the powwow the night of the 15th inst.
[September 1867]."

"Ahead of all rode the [Indian] peace makers, clad in
the picturesque costumes of the red nomad of the American
desert. Behind these came the women, prisoners captured
the latter part of July, 35 miles east of Fort Kearney. These
white women, sitting astride the Indian ponies, holding their
puny suffering infants in their arms, had ridden four days.
They looked weary, yet somewhat animated at the prospect
of being so soon among friends and kindred people. On the
other side rode their captors."

In this same long winding column there were numerous Indian chiefs of distinction, including Spotted Tail,
Standing Elk, Swift Bear, Black Bear, Turkey Foot, Pawnee
Killer and The-Man-That-Walks-Under-The-Water. There
was also the brave Big Mouth, a chief of the Brulé Sioux,
of Oglala descent, and a spokesman soon to address the
assembled council. All these were on their way to meet the
commissioners, who sat ready to receive them, flanked by
a motley crowd of plainsmen.

Like most such Indian councils, the sessions dragged on
for days. At first Big Mouth, who was drunk much of the
time, refused to even so much as enter the council grounds.

Finally, having sobered enough to speak, he strode one day into the council-ring. Without preamble, and almost off-hand, he gave expression to the following epic:

"My friends and my people, open wide your ears and listen.

"Toward the north there are many Ogallallas [Oglala Sioux], to the south there are Ogallallas, and I, with my people stand between. I wish to succeed to make peace between my people and the pale-faces.

"This day you, General Harney, tell me, did the Great Spirit send you here? Do you tell the truth? You are a great chief also. I hope that the Great Spirit sent you to us.

"All you who are sitting here in council, I want to advise you. Be quiet! Behave yourselves! Leave the whites alone! . . . The whites are as numerous as the grass. You are few and weak. What do you amount to? If the whites kill one of your number, you weep and feel very sad. But if you kill one of the whites, who is [there] that weeps for them? [Laughter]

"I speak this for the good of my people; and now, you whites, I speak to you.

"Stop that Powder River road; that is the cause of our troubles. That great evil grows daily. It is just like prairie grass; the evil is spreading among all the nations.

"Red Cloud and The-Man-Afraid-Of-His-Horse had a talk with General Sanborn last spring at Laramie. Did you [General Sanborn] tell the Great Father what I said?

"Here are the Sioux on the one side and the Cheyenne on the other side. I stand between two fires. And you, after talking and talking, and after making treaties, and after we have listened to you, go and make the evil larger.

"You set the prairie on fire. My Great Father [the President] told me through men like you that he would give twenty years annuities for these two roads, the Powder River Road and the Smoky Hill Road. Where are these annuities? I stand before the palefaces and the Indians."[46]

Not as eloquent as most Indian speeches, this one by Big Mouth nevertheless had its effect. In time the annuities were paid. President U. S. Grant felt it to be much cheaper to pay the Indians than longer to fight. So peace finally again settled over the great plains—at least for a while.

Satank (*Setangya*, "Sitting Bear") was ranking chief of the Kiowa Nation, the tribe which killed more of the "Forty-niners" *en route* to California than did any other of the redskins of those disturbing days. Satank's right hand was

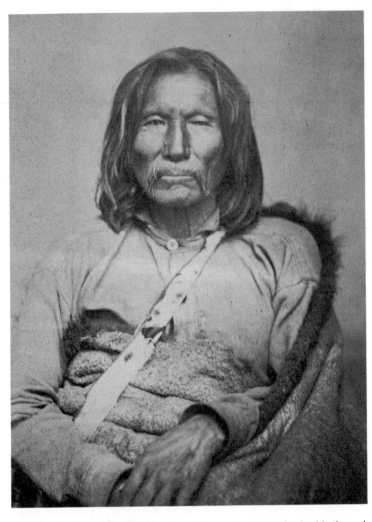

**SATANK** (Kiowa): "The green grass shall no more be stained with the red blood of the pale-faces."

a sub-chief named Satanta ("White Bear"). The latter, having been convicted of ruthlessly killing numerous Texans on their own native soil, was imprisoned and doomed to be executed. But he dodged the noose by committing suicide. He it was who said of the Texans: "If the Great Father at Washington wants my braves to cease attacks across the Texas border, he will have to remove Texas far enough away so my young men can't find it."

Satank was shrewd, unscrupulous, totally fearless, and a master of Indian warfare. He has often been compared to Pontiac, or even Geronimo, for his unpredictable behavior. He once, by sheer muscular power, tore from his wrists irons which had been welded there, then leaped with bared dagger at the guard who held him prisoner.

Of the many chiefs who signed the memorable Medicine Lodge Treaty of 1867, restoring an uncertain peace to the southern plains, Satank's fingerprints stood first. Later, suspected of criminal duplicity, an order was issued for his arrest. Alerted by his bodyguard, Satank· met the officers at the door of his tepee. They did not suspect, of course, that he had his swiftest pony hidden in the shrubbery nearby. Seizing the initiative, he addressed them calmly but boldly:

"It has made me very glad to meet you who are the commissioners sent by the Great Spirit to see us. You have had much talk by our chiefs, and you are no doubt tired of it. Many of them have put themselves forward and have filled you with their sayings. I have kept back and said nothing. . . .

"Before leaving, however, as I now intend to do, I come to say that the Kiowas and Comanches have made with you a peace, and they intend to keep it. If it brings plenty to us, we will of course like it all the better. If it brings prosperity or adversity, we will not abandon it. It is our contract and it shall stand. . . .

"You have not tried, as many others have done, to make a new bargain merely to get the advantage. You have not asked to make our annuities smaller, but, unasked, you have made them larger. You have not withdrawn a single gift, but you have . . . provided more guarantees for our education and comfort.

"When we saw these things, we said among ourselves, 'These are the men of the past.' We at once gave you our hearts. You now have them. You know what is best for us. Do for us what is best. Teach us the road to travel, and we will not depart from it forever. For your sakes the green grass shall

**SATANTA** (Kiowa): ''If the Great Father . . . wants my braves to cease attacks across the Texas border, he will have to remove Texas far enough away so my young men can't find it.''

no more be stained with the red blood of the pale-faces. Your
people shall again be our people, and peace shall be between
us forever."[47]

With this, before his listeners realized what he was up
to, Satank leaped to the back of his hidden pony and was
gone. The officers stared after him stupidly, having failed
to serve their subpoena, and in another moment their quarry
had vanished, swallowed up in the vastness of the prairie.
Only the echo of his closing words remained: *"Teach us
the road to travel, and we will not depart from it forever."*

The last illustration of Indian oratory born of this
troubled plains war period comes from the Idaho highlands.
Of all Indian tribes to resort to the warpath, the peace-
loving Nez Percé were the last. On first meeting them in
their high Walla Walla country, near the headwaters of the
Columbia River, Captain Bonneville declared that this people
were more like a group of saints than savages, so devoted
were they to justice and right.

But the time came when they, too, were caught in the
swirl of the white man's ceaseless advance into the West.
In 1863 the Nez Percé were called upon to yield their
hunting grounds by treaty right for settlement purposes by
the federal government. This they did and moved into
northern Idaho. Again, in 1877, at the Council of Lapwai,
they were confronted with the demand for another removal.
But this time their leaders, headed by the distinguished
Chief Joseph, could not be brought to accept the terms of
the proposed treaty. Thereafter, the Nez Percé were hunted
down like dogs.

When war broke out with the Nez Percé the balance
of power was clearly with the government forces. Armies
closed in on the Indians both from the west and the east,
each determined to fight it out to the finish.

Then occurred one of the most daring marathons known
to history. At the head of his little band of braves, burdened
by women and children, Chief Joseph, a master of Indian
strategy, strove to form a junction with his friend Sitting
Bull, then a refugee in Canada. He was fully 1,300 miles

**CHIEF JOSEPH** (Nez Percé): ''Looking Glass is dead.''

distant, separated by a tangle of mountain fastnesses and almost impenetrable forests. In front of him was Colonel Miles, behind him was General Howard, and on his flank was Colonel Sturgis. In spite of this fact Chief Joseph brought his people to within fifty miles of the Canadian border, their objective point.

There, with most of his warriors killed and starvation staring his thinned ranks in the face, like Red Eagle, the Seminole, Chief Joseph finally was brought to bay. Then, and then only, would he surrender. His words, written in scrawled English, were brought to General Howard, commander of the United States forces. One of the finest examples of Indian eloquence, the message read:

> "Tell General Howard I know his heart.
> "What he told me before I have in my heart. I am tired of fighting. Our chiefs are killed. Looking Glass is dead. . . . It is the young men who say yes or no. He who led the young men is dead. It is cold and we have no blankets. The little children are freezing to death. My people, some of them, have run away to the hills, and have no blankets, no food; no one knows where they are—perhaps freezing to death. I want to have time to look for my children and see how many of them I can find. Maybe I shall find them among the dead. Hear me, my chiefs. I am tired; my heart is sick and sad. From where the sun now stands I will fight no more forever."[48]

The gripping power of these words is matched only by those which fell from the lips of the Galilean on Golgotha's Hill. They carry the same note of self-denial and unconquered despair. Later, however, Chief Joseph came to be an intimate friend of two United States presidents, William McKinley and Theodore Roosevelt.

# Eloquent Indian Women

**I**T IS
popularly believed that the average Indian woman occupied
a menial position in native Indian society. She is considered by many to have been downtrodden, slavishly
treated and abused by men. This is probably because she
is usually pictured in the act of performing all the domestic
drudgery of Indian camp or village life. When her people
were on the move, as was common in their nomadic life,
she was required to carry heavy loads. And setting up or
taking down the tepee was usually her task, sometimes
assisted by her children. But has this not been true of
women in all primitive societies?

It must not be thought, however, that the performance
of such tasks gave these first American mothers an ignoble
status in their communities. Iroquois and Creek women
were sometimes chosen as leaders of their clans or tribes.
Among the Plains Indians women were loved and honored

by their "lords and masters," and their advice was frequently sought. Pueblo women not only shared an equal
status with the men, but usually owned the homes in which
they lived after marriage. And not infrequently Indian
women have spoken out eloquently on behalf of their tribes
in matters of government or policy.

Celsa Apapas was a Cupeño Indian woman, raised in
the San Luis Rey Valley, California, near the old mission
of the same name. Founded in 1798, San Luis Rey Mission
was one of the most prosperous of all the Franciscan institutions which stretched from San Diego to Sonoma, 800 miles
to the north. It gained worldwide fame through Helen Hunt
Jackson's tragic story of Ramona, which pictured the stigma
which went with being Indian in those days.

At one time the mission controlled no less than 30,000
acres of land, held in its possession by royal grant. Its
broad expanses supported 26,000 cattle, 25,000 sheep and
2,200 or more horses and mules. The mission also found
employment for no less than 2,800 persons, old and young.
In addition to its land and stock San Luis Rey was richly
furnished, had a large library of valuable books, and an
accumulation of vessels and jewels of gold and silver that
made it almost fabulously wealthy.

The discovery of raw gold in California changed all
this, however. In 1850 the people, now predominantly
white American, applied for admission into the Union.
Then followed the federalization of the lands of California
and the rush of land-grabbers and promoters which naturally
attended this move.

Civil courts were set up with power to determine land
ownership. The Indians of San Luis Rey Valley were soon
notified that the lands which they occupied had been purchased by a company from the East, and they must move.
They were instructed to select a new home, suitable to their
needs, which the government would allocate to them. But
where could that be?

A long council followed, at which Celsa Apapas, who
spoke not only her own tribal language but Spanish and
English as well, was chosen to interpret the words of

Cecilio Blacktooth, "captain" of the Cupeños living at Warner's Hot Springs at the turn of the century, to the government commissioners.

> "We thank you for coming here to talk to us in a way we can understand. It is the first time anyone has done so. You ask us to think what place we like next best to this place, where we always lived. You see that graveyard out there? There are our fathers and our grandfathers. You see that Eagle-nest mountain and that Rabbit-hole mountain? When God made them, He gave us this place. We have always been here. We do not care for any other place. . . . If you give us the best place in the world, it is not so good for us as this. . . . This is our home. . . . We cannot live anywhere else. We were born here and our fathers are buried here. . . . We want this place and not any other. . . .
>
> "There is no other place for us. We do not want you to buy any other place. If you will not buy this place, we will go into the mountains like quail, and die there, the old people and the women and children. Let the Government be glad and proud. It can kill us. We do not fight. We do what it says. If we cannot live here, we want to go into the mountains and die. We do not want any other home."[49]

Celsa Apapas' plea was, of course, futile. The rich San Luis Rey Valley was taken over by the whites. The Indians were moved to what now is the Pala Reservation, at the base of Mount Palomar, where today the white man stares into the heavens through the largest telescope in the world —his thoughts, perhaps, on other worlds which he can invade and from which he can evict their native occupants. Incidentally, it was the Sequoya League, noted for its philanthropic work, which purchased for the displaced Cupeños the small area in which they now live.

Pio Pico was the last of the Mexican governors of California. His estates were immense. The smallest of his ranches, called El Rancho Paso de Bartolo, about fifteen miles east of the growing pueblo of Los Angeles, comprised some 16,000 acres. Pio Pico's adobe house was flanked by *El Camino Real*, the famous footpath across mountain and desert followed by the Franciscan fathers as they trekked from mission to mission.

Although California came into the Union in 1850, it was many years before the Stars and Stripes were raised over this palatial old Mexican residence. But about 1930 a service club in the local community decided that this strange omission should be rectified. A celebration was arranged for the formal occasion and Warcaziwin, a full-blooded Sioux Indian woman, was invited to be the speaker. In the Sioux language the name of Warcaziwin means Sunflower.

When the American flag was unfurled to the evening breeze over the Pico house, this Indian lady stepped forth from the portico in calm dignity. Her garments were of white buckskin, cut to fit with the neatness of a Parisian gown. On her brow were slight strands of colored beads. Her feet were shod in elaborately decorated moccasins. In her hand she carried a small United States flag. She made a graceful and impressive figure as she addressed the audience in a soft, well-modulated voice that nonetheless carried its message to the farthest corner of the spacious patio:

"Mr. Chairman and friends! We like to put full reliance upon Americans. We like to think of our American historians as being true and exact in their words. But it is a sad commentary upon our American history to have to say that to date the native American does not occupy his just and sure place in America.

"In other words, American history has not been told in full, because our histories are inadequate in that they have paid little attention to the record of the native Indian who has been making history thousands of years before the advent of the white man to these shores. . . .

"He came representing what is known as the Age of Iron. I am told . . . that you cannot measure culture chronologically. You cannot say that because one people all belong to the Stone Age they have not made their contribution to human culture. As a matter of fact, when the whites reached these shores they had just arrived at the emergence of what historians have termed the Dark Ages.

"For centuries in Europe both children and women occupied a low social position. On the other hand, they, the white men, found the Indian woman and child occupying a very high social position.

"Those from England, coming to the west, found a people having a very high form of government. It is to the great Five Civilized Nations, the Iroquois Confederacy, that you owe, in a measure, many principles embodied in your Constitution. . . .

"Farther to the west there was a great series of Indian tribes which possessed a fine type of social organization. I now am speaking of the Plains peoples.

"We are wont in history to read of the warlike tribes of the plains, and particularly of the warlike Sioux. The Indians have

WARCAZIWIN (Sioux): "It is to the great Five Civilized Nations . . . that you owe . . . many of the principles embodied in your Constitution."

suffered from so many such misrepresentations that it seems at times that error would become stronger than truth. Again, we know that truth must be there betimes.

"The Sioux are not a warlike people. They never tried to make a science of war . . . as it is today. Today we see all of the ingenuity of man, all of the inventiveness and craftiness of man turned to ends of destruction.

"The Sioux's only efforts at warfare were to keep his boundaries intact. . . . Evils such as drinking, gambling, and poverty were almost unknown among them.

"Just remember—there was not a profane word in the Sioux language. Should a family awaken and find someone in their tepee, they would not let him go until he had his fill of food and sleep. They were a very hospitable people."[50]

As Sunflower turned to reenter the old Pio Pico home, now a California State Historical Monument, a thunderous applause broke forth from all present.

Lake Mohonk is one of the most charming small bodies of water in upper New York State. Its forest-studded environs are replete with history. Many years ago a prominent Quaker family, longtime friends of the American Indians, established themselves on its shores by founding what has since come to be known as Lake Mohonk Mountain House. From 1883 to the present time Mohonk Mountain House has served annually as a conference center on Indian concerns, with many ranking government officials attending.

In October, 1929, the theme of the conference was "How to Safeguard the Indian Home." The agenda for that year was packed to the limit. Consequently the chairman informed all invited guest speakers that there were but 800 minutes available for the six specialized sessions scheduled. This meant that all must be correspondingly brief in their addresses.

Toward the close of things someone raised the question of why the conference had not heard from one real Indian American—those supposedly the most interested. In fact, there were but two Indians present, neither of them scheduled speakers: a Mrs. Gertrude S. Bonnin, president of the Indian Defense Association, and another unnamed. Mrs. Bonnin was invited to speak.

Mrs. Bonnin, whose Indian name was Zitkala-Sa, had

left the Sioux Reservation in her early 'teens to seek admission at a little Quaker academy near Wabash, Indiana. Slight of form, but with an intelligent eye, she was readily admitted. From there she proceeded to Earlham College, another Quaker institution, located in Richmond, Indiana. Here, under its department of speech, she acquitted herself so well that in her junior year she was chosen to represent the college in the all-state intercollegiate oratorical contest at Indianapolis. Miss Simmons, as she was then known, won second place for her alma mater.

Press reports of the occasion said, "The slight, dark-skinned girl, dressed in black, who sat at the end of the row of speakers, had been gazed upon with curiosity. It was noticed that her face showed in delicate but firm lines the cut of her Indian extraction. . . . As she began to speak . . . her voice was clear and sweet; her language was that of a cultivated young woman."[51]

Thirty years later this same gifted woman rose at the great Mohonk Conference to plead the cause of the American Indian home. Without notes or script, she clearly and concisely revealed the true facts of Indian home life—a definite surprise to many of the whites present. This, in part, was her statement:

"The purpose of our organization is to help Indians help themselves. And we have been searching around how we shall preserve our homes, how we shall preserve our home ties, how we shall keep father and mother and the children together in their homes.

"This summer I had a wonderful experience in visiting North Carolina, seeing the activities of the mountain peoples. . . . I was inspired to see those mountain people, with limited resources, doing so much, salvaging lives which seemed so crushed; and I thought, why, this could apply to the Indian people on their various reservations. . . .

"There is a difference between the mountain folk and the Indian reservation. The Indian has his property; he still has land; he still has a little home, whether it be a square house or tepee.

"Right there we can teach them the doctrine of the preservation of the American home. Home is home, wherever it may be, and the children's love for their parents and the parents' love for the children brings a heart tie superior to anything the missionary can do for us. . . .

"This Government functions through laws. Who makes these laws? Men make these laws. Citizens of America make these laws. . . . It would be well, I think . . . if we would

become interested in looking over these laws written upon our
statute books affecting the Indian people and cancel the obsolete
and unnecessary laws, and in their place suggest and cause to
be enacted laws that shall meet the constructive plans that have
been heard discussed here today. . . .

"Someone asked me when I was addressing an audience,
after this fashion: 'Are you a civilized Indian?' [Laughter]
I told them I did not know because civilization is very hard to
define and to understand. I don't know what you mean by
civilization. We send our little Indian boys and girls to school
and when they come back talking English, they come
back swearing. There is no swear word in the Indian languages,
and I haven't yet learned to swear."[52]

With this Mrs. Bonnin took her seat amidst a deafening
applause. Mrs. Daniel Smiley, hostess of the conference,
ran to Mrs. Bonnin and kissed her on the cheek in impulsive
tribute.

# The Old Guard Yields

T HE LAST great Indian council held under the supervision of the federal government was in strange contrast to many which had gone before. It was held in the late fall of 1909 at the Little Big Horn council grounds in Montana.

Many of the older chiefs and sachems of bygone days had been invited to attend this "last roundup" for a final talkfest. This time there were no peace treaties to be drawn up, no agreements to be met, no demands to be made, no gratuities to be dispensed. It was simply a get-together of the "old guard" for purposes of reminiscence—all expenses paid.

A huge tent had been erected and numerous seats set up in the proverbial semicircle of the time-honored Indian council. All of the rules common to such conclaves were to be strictly observed.

The council was formally opened by the government

agent who had called it. With befitting dignity he first
lit the council fire. Next he touched a live coal to the bowl
of a filled calumet, took a few puffs, and blew the smoke
upward into the air. Then he passed the pipe to a nearby
ranking chief, who did likewise. After the calumet had
gone the rounds the council was considered in session.

Almost immediately a friendly rivalry arose among
the several tribes assembled as to whose chief was to give
the opening address. The lot fell to the Kiowa-Apache.
This meant that Apache John (Koon-kah-za-chy) would be
the first to speak.

Dressed in full Indian regalia, feathers and all, Apache
John rose to his feet. Though in his sixties, he was still
well preserved. His voice was not particularly strong, but
it sufficed for the occasion. Speaking in his native tongue,
which was translated as he proceeded, he began by telling
of his childhood days and how he learned the art of Indian
warfare from his father. He told of his first battle and how
he had been urged by his father never to run from danger.
Eventually he came to the core of his thought: how his life
had been changed after meeting the government's Indian
Commissioner in Washington. There he was informed of a
better way to live—the way of peace. He had tried this
way. Since then, said he, his people had prospered. Now
he was head of the Kiowa-Apache Nation. Thus saying, he
yielded the council-ring.

There were other speakers. And, of course, there had
to be a final speaker. To close this last great roundup the
choice fell upon the shoulders of Chief Plenty Coups
(Aleck-shea-ahoos), of the Crow tribe.

The Crows were Plains Indians, great hunters and
warriors, located largely in Montana. Proud of his heritage,
Chief Plenty Coups began his farewell address with obvious
emotion:

> "The ground on which we stand is sacred ground. It is the
> dust and blood of our ancestors. On these plains the Great White
> Father at Washington sent his soldiers armed with long knives
> and rifles to slay the Indian. Many of them sleep on yonder
> hill where Pahaska—White Chief of the Long Hair [General
> Custer]—so bravely fought and fell. A few more passing suns
> will see us here no more, and our dust and bones will mingle
> with these same prairies. I see as in a vision the dying spark

of our council fires, the ashes cold and white. I see no longer
the curling smoke rising from our lodge poles. I hear no longer
the songs of the women as they prepare the meal. The antelope
have gone; the buffalo wallows are empty. Only the wail of the
coyote is heard. The white man's medicine is stronger than
ours; his iron horse rushes over the buffalo trail. He talks to
us through his 'whispering spirit' [the telephone]. We are
like birds with a broken wing. My heart is cold within me. My
eyes are growing dim—I am old. . . ."[53]

In this same vein Chief Plenty Coups continued for an
hour or more, his thoughts ever pointed nostalgically toward
the past. His words were couched in the same fatalistic
style and robed in the same metaphors characteristic of
Indian council-fire oratory. But this was one of the chief
purposes for which this Little Big Horn Council had been
called.

Scarcely had it culminated, however, when one of those
freak storms, common to high mountain country at that
time of year, struck the camp ground. Its attack was furious.
Those not already beyond its reach were forced to take
shelter under the nearby cliffs. It seemed a dramatic and
wholly fitting orchestral finale by Nature as the curtain fell
on the red man's final council.

Albert Thayer Freeman, a young man of unusual
speaking ability, was a member of the Flathead Indian tribe.
Born in the high Rocky Mountain country, in his boyhood
he had ranged over the great Pacific West with his father
from the Gulf of Mexico to Alaska, living the life of his
primitive ancestors. When the United States entered the
first World War young Freeman enlisted and served his
nation overseas.

On his return to America he applied for admission to
De Pauw University at Greencastle, Indiana, and was
promptly accepted. Here his gift of speech was quickly
discovered. Like Gertrude Simmons (Mrs. Bonnin), he was
chosen to represent his university in the intercollegiate
oratorical contest, held at Indianapolis. There he won first
prize. Later he continued his studies at the University of
Southern California, where he qualified for the Master of
Arts degree in the field of religion.

**SEQUOYAH** (Cherokee): The great Cherokee leader is shown here with a scroll of the alphabet he invented so that the words of the white man might be written down and read by his people.

Freeman's De Pauw oration, a written document, reads thus in part:

> "I am an American Indian—one of three hundred thousand—pleading for justice.
>
> "Surely a nation turning a sympathetic face toward Belgium will heed, too, the appalling drama of my people. The tragedy is no less pitiable because without hateful intent. Neither government nor citizen have purposed it. It is simply the narrative of a nature-race thrust aside by a mighty civilization. . . .
>
> "No wonder we are not the strong . . . people who entered these reservations a half century ago! No wonder the 'music of our life has gone out!' No wonder we are heartbroken and disconsolate! No wonder that under the 'doom of perpetual childhood' we 'croon about our dead past.' . . .
>
> "About fifty per cent of my people are illiterate—the most untutored race in America. . . . What does the word Indian suggest? A skulking savage, with a tomahawk in one hand and a dripping scalp in the other. We are denounced as crafty and treacherous in our inmost nature. I can never forget the day that my blood chilled when the school children taunted me, 'You low-lived, savage Kickapoo. Kill the dirty Indian!' And this in Boston, sacred in the traditions of old Faneuil Hall. . . .
>
> "Will the people of America heed this prayer? Economically, a ruthless system has been brought upon him [the Indian]—dependence, spoliation, ruin; socially, the fate of a damning banishment . . . and the ignominy of a bloody name. . . .
>
> "Surely we will not withhold from him the opportunity to make his life as 'heroic as a statue cast in bronze!' "[54]

Years after this the present writer was in his own study—his nose, as usual, buried in a book. It was night, dark and quiet. Noiselessly, someone entered the room. I did not hear anything, but the strange feeling of another's presence crept over me. I raised my eyes. There, as motionless as his "statue in bronze," stood Albert Thayer Freeman. I must have appeared startled. He smiled.

"White man afraid?" he asked gently. "Indian never knows fear."

The name Sequoyah (Sikwayi) will be honored so long as men have interest in alphabets and the art of speech. Born about the year 1760, Sequoyah, who was also known as George Gist, seems to have been a "halfbreed." His mother is said to have been a Cherokee woman of mixed blood, but his father may have been a German trader named Guess, sometimes spelled Guest or Gist.

Reared in an Indian wigwam, it appears that Sequoyah never went to school. Hence, where he got the inspiration to invent his valued alphabet, by means of which the Cherokee language might be written and read, still remains a mystery. Be that as it may, the time came when his name was to be honored by the placement of his statue in the so-called American Hall of Fame.

Federal law provides that every state has the privilege of ascribing this honor to a limited number of its citizens. In 1917, ten years after its admission into the Union, the state of Oklahoma, once known as Indian Territory, decided to avail itself of this opportunity. By legislative enactment it chose Sequoyah as its son to be so honored.

Houston B. Teehee, also a Cherokee Indian, was selected to speak for the state at the dedication of the statue. Mr. Teehee was a unique character. What *he* did in his school days we do not know, but that he was adept in the art of oratory remains unquestioned.

Early in life he was elected mayor of his home town, Tahlequah (*Talikwa*, the capital of the Cherokee Nation in the northeastern Indian Territory, now incorporated with the state of Oklahoma). Later he stood for a seat in his state's legislature and won it. Then he studied law, and in due time was appointed to the supreme bench of Oklahoma. His pleadings at the bar, always based on Indian justice, almost without exception won favorable verdicts. When asked to dedicate the marble statue of Sequoyah in the rotunda of Statuary Hall, Washington, D.C., Mr. Teehee accepted the invitation with deep personal pride. On June 6, 1917, with the hall crowded to its outer walls, he addressed the assembly in these words:

"It is with a feeling of genuine pleasure, not unmixed with a pride common to the citizenship of Oklahoma . . . that I respond on this occasion. . . .

"When these proceedings shall have been disseminated through the medium of the press, and have been brought to the notice of the Indian of America, he, too, will be thrilled with a peculiar pride and will join us in according to . . . his race a rightful place in the history of his country. . . .

"It is significant that that State, intended to have been the great mobilization camp and home of the red man, should have chosen . . . one of her sons for this signal honor. . . .

**HOUSTON B. TEEHEE** (Cherokee): "At last my people are no longer strangers to their native soil."

". . . when the red man sees in this historic Hall of Fame
a figure of his race, standing erect as of yore, and touching elbow
with elbow with the most noted of the pale faces, with poet and
patriot, orator and philosopher, statesman and soldier, he will
forget these artistic decorations and, rising to his full stature in
exultant joy, exclaim to his pale-face brother, 'At last my people
are no longer strangers to their native soil—the land of the free,
the home of the brave'."[55]

For moments after Judge Teehee's voice ceased to be
heard hundreds stood in silence, as other hundreds had
stood mute at the conclusion of the majestic words uttered
at Gettysburg.

Except for our Sequoia National Park in California, the
name Sequoyah is now but a memory. But not so with the
recently elected headman of the Navajo peoples, Raymond
Nakai, a modern of the moderns.

Now in his middle forties, Nakai is an Indian of tremendous drive and energy. As a man of practical affairs
and a public speaker he has few rivals among red men of
today. Following his election on April 13, 1963, fully
10,000 of his fellow tribesmen and citizens gathered at
Window Rock, Arizona, to listen to his inaugural address.

The Navajo, far from being a "vanishing people," are
the largest Indian tribe in the United States. Because of
their stubborn resistance to the white advance through their
country a century ago, the entire tribe was forcibly removed
to the Pecos River Valley, New Mexico, under military
guard. At that time they numbered in all about 20,000.

By the Treaty of Fort Wingate of 1867, however, this
noble-hearted people was permitted to return to their mountain home of turquoise skies. Today their population nears
the 100,000 mark, a gain of more than 400 per cent. They
have long substituted sober industry for their ancient
adeptness at warfare.

An area comprising several acres had been cleared for
the occasion of Raymond Nakai's inauguration. At the crest
of this area, flanked by rising ground, a large platform had
been built. This accommodated the 74 members of Mr.
Nakai's Tribal Council, together with other distinguished
guests. On the platform was a speaker's stand, equipped

with numerous broadcast sets and loud-speakers. Well accustomed to this type of opportunity, the new leader arose and in clear, forceful English addressed his expectant audience:

> "My fellow citizens: . . . The goal toward which I propose to lead the Navajo people is the goal of all true Americans. . . .
>
> "To achieve this goal I propose first, that the Navajo nation adopt a written constitution, with a Bill of Rights protecting the individual's freedom of speech, association and religion. . . .
>
> "In my administration, agents will not be sent out . . . to tell the Navajos they cannot worship God in the way they desire. . . .
>
> "Only he who makes his people strong, is strong; and only he who rules free men is great. This shall be the motto of my administration. . . .
>
> "I will engage economists to give economic advice, engineers to give engineering advice, and lawyers to give legal advice. For political advice I will go to the Navajo people. . . .
>
> "I shall propose a greatly tightened administration of the fiscal affairs of the Tribe, with full controls. . . . I will root out wherever found any instances of kickbacks, graft. . . . or conflicts . . . among the Tribal staff, and . . . set up adequate criminal penalties for such misconduct. . . .
>
> "To the States [the Navajo reservation extends over parts of Utah, Colorado, New Mexico and Arizona] also I hold out the hand of friendship. Let us have no more jurisdictional quarrels. . . .
>
> "Now as new workmen, we enter upon the great unfinished edifice of the Navajo Tribe . . . It is a better world we have to build, the one where every Navajo shall stand erect beside his fellow Americans as an equal among equals.
>
> "Councilors and friends! The tools are ready and the task is tremendous. Let us now go to work together!"[56]

As to the value of this "Inaugural" in terms of eloquence, the head of the Office of Indian Administration at Gallup, New Mexico, had this to say: "In view of the fact that Mr. Nakai made his address in English only, it is doubtful that this speech can be taken as an example of traditional Navajo oratory."

To this, let us point out that words are thoughts cloaked in vocal sounds. Some sounds may seem more musical than others, some more sonorous and majestic. But many listeners hear with the mind as well as with the ears.

# The New Citizen

**I**N PRESENTING
this picture of American Indian eloquence we have quoted
from the words of thirty or more outstanding red men.
Some of these were famous warriors, others were messengers of peace. Some of the speeches were carefully planned
in advance (at least their purport and tenor); others were
more or less spontaneous. That of Gertrude Simmons
Bonnin at the Lake Mohonk council is a good example of the
latter type—an address conceived for the moment.

Each of these speeches had its own mission to perform.
Some, of course, were heard by many listeners in a mangled
form since they were translations from the original tribal
language and thus often lost the true force of the original
words. Others have been presented in English as they are
preserved to us today from the free and easy "field translations" of government recorders.

Some of these speeches were the products of untrained

minds. Others were made by the holders of college degrees. But whether formally educated or not, many of these speakers were great thinkers—even to the point of genius. Among these might be named Joseph Brant, Pontiac, Red Jacket, Tecumseh, Keokuk, Red Cloud, Joseph Nez Percé and Houston B. Teehee. All have left much more than their "thumbprints" on the ceaselessly unrolling and unerasable scroll of history.

In the long past we have fought with the Indian and have betrayed him. In spite of this, he has made many contribtuions to the welfare and beauty of the world—not all of them merely material. Today the Indian is a citizen of the United States, and eventually, no doubt, will be fully absorbed into the white man's type of culture and civilization. But every effort should be made not only to guarantee his future but to enshrine his past. The Indian is proud of his race and his traditions. He should never be permitted to forget them.

Nor should we, his fellow citizens in the America that was destined to come about from that early day back in the misty past when the first primitive red hunter made his way across the frozen ice of Bering Strait into the unknown Western Hemisphere.

# Notes and References

1. This document, from the W. C. Wyman Papers, is reproduced with the kind permission of the Huntington Library, San Marino, Calif.

2. Bancroft, Hubert H. *The Native Races.* A. L. Bancroft & Co. San Francisco. 1886. III, 552.

3. Adair, James. *The History of the American Indians.* Edwin & Charles Dilly. London. 1775. 27-28, 63.

4. De Forest, John W. *History of the Indians of Connecticut.* W. J. Hamersley. Hartford. 1851. 42.

5. Harvey, Henry. *History of the Shawnee Indians.* Cincinnati. 1855. 12.

6. Hale, Horatio E. (Ed.) *The Iroquois Book of Rites.* D. G. Brinton. Philadelphia. 1883. 102-103.

7. Kroeber, A. L. *Anthropology.* Harcourt, Brace & Co. New York. 1948. 213.

8. Stone, William L. *Life and Times of Sa-Go-Ye-Wat-Ha, or Red Jacket.* J. Munsell. Albany. 1866. 431-432.

9. Schoolcraft, Henry R. *The Red Man of America.* Lippencot, Grambo Co. Philadelphia. 1847. 54.

10. Caleb Atwater's statement, taken from the W. C. Wyman Papers, is reproduced with the kind permission of the Huntington Library, San Marino, Calif.

11. Heckenwelder, Rev. John. *History, Manners, and Customs of The Indian Nations.* Memoirs of the Historical Society of Pennsylvania. Philadelphia. 1876. XII, 132.

12. Tatum, Lawrie. *Our Red Brothers*. John C. Winston Co. Philadelphia. 1899. 109-110.

13. Stone, William L. *Life of Joseph Brant*. J. Munsell. Albany. 1864. II, 354-355.

14. Allen, William. *The History of Norridgewock*. Edward J. Peet. Norridgewock, Me. 1849. 227-228. (This is a curious old publication. The copy consulted was loaned to the writer by courtesy of Colby College, Waterville, Me.)

15. Kenton, Edna (Ed.) *The Indians of North America*. Harcourt, Brace & Co. New York. 1899. II, 368.

16. Thwaites, Reuben G. (Ed.) *The Jesuit Relations and Allied Documents*. Burrows Book Sellers. Cleveland. 1899. XXXVIII, 173-176.

17. Ibid. Vol. 67, 195.

18. Ibid. Vol. 36, 177.

19. Ibid. Vol. 36, 215-219.

20. Thatcher, B. B. *Indian Biography*. Harper & Brothers. New York. 1837. II, 42-45.

21. Ibid., 117-118. (See also: Parkman, Francis. *The Conspiracy of Pontiac*. Little, Brown & Co. Boston. 1897-1898.)

22. Stone, William L. *Life of Joseph Brant*. J. Munsell. Albany. 1864. II, 249, 253-255.

23. Jefferson, Thomas. *The Writings of Thomas Jefferson*. Taylor & Maury. Washington. 1854. VIII, 308-309.

24. This little personality sketch in rhyme is taken from B. B. Thatcher's *Indian Biography*, II, 301 (see reference above). Red Jacket was not a big man, as some have thought. He was of medium height and weight but unusually swift of foot. He served the British as a message carrier, for which he was awarded a bright red jacket similar to those worn by the king's soldiers.

25. Stone, William L. *Life and Times of Sa-Go-Ye-Wat-Ha, or Red Jacket*. J. Munsell. Albany. 1866. 272-276.

26. Ibid., 370-372.

27. The records of some of these undercover agreements entered into by European nations with certain American Indian tribes present a gruesome picture of what all too often took place on the colonial frontiers. From a Seneca village called Tioga went this message from a British envoy to his government in London: "I hereby send to your Excellency . . . eight packages of scalps, cured, dried, hooped, and painted with all the triumphal marks." Package 1 contained "forty-three scalps of Congress soldiers"; also "sixty-two

farmers, killed in their houses . . . at night." Package 2 carried
the scalps of 98 farmers "killed in their houses . . . fighting for
their lives and family." Parcel 7 contained 211 girls' scalps, "big
and little." This report is taken from B. B. Thatcher's *Indian
Biography*, Vol. II, 316-318.

28. Thatcher, B. B. *Indian Biography*. Harper & Brothers. New York.
    1837. II, 162.

29. Howe, Henry. *Historical Collections of the Great West*. Henry
    Howe, Publisher. Cincinnati. 1853. I, 265.

30. Bryan, William J. *The World's Famous Orations*. Funk & Wag-
    nalls Co. New York. 1906. VIII, 19-21.

31. American State Papers. (*Indian Affairs*, Vol. I). Gales & Seaton.
    Washington. 1832. IV, 564.

32. The Journal of Jacob Carmichael, dated 1795, is the property of
    the Huntington Library, San Marino, Calif., by whose kind per-
    mission the quotation appearing in this book is published.

33. American State Papers. (*Indian Affairs*, Vol. I). Gales & Seaton.
    Washington. 1832. IV, 571.

34. Ibid., 576.

35. Ibid., 578.

36. Frost, John. *Thrilling Adventures Among the Indians*. John C.
    Potter & Co. Philadelphia. 1851. 181-182.

37. Bureau of Ethnology. *14th Annual Report: 1892-93*. Government
    Printing Office. Washington. 1896. Pt. 2, 687.

38. Dillin, John B. *History of Indiana*. Bingham & Doughty. Indi-
    anapolis. 1859. 442-444.

39. Vickery III, James H. *A History of the Town of Unity*. Falmouth
    Publishing House. Manchester. 1954. 178.

40. Thwaites, Reuben G. (Ed.) *Early Western Travels: 1748-1846*.
    (Bradbury's Travels in the Interior of America: 1809-1811.)
    Arthur H. Clark Co. Cleveland. 1904. V, 222-223.

41. *Michigan Pioneer and Historical Records*. Robert Smith & Co.
    Lansing. X, 170.

42. Drake, Benjamin. *The Great Indian Chiefs of the West, or Life
    and Adventures of Black Hawk*. H. M. Halison. Cincinnati.
    1856. 243-244.

43. Fulton, A. R. *The Red Men of Iowa*. Mills & Co. Des Moines.
    1882. 238.

44. The speech of Chief Seathl (Seattle) from which these excerpts were taken was kindly sent to the author by Mr. Leonard Ware, chief correspondent for the U.S. Bureau of Indian Affairs.

45. Eastman, Charles A. *Indian Heroes and Great Chieftains.* Little, Brown & Co. Boston. 1918. 16.

46. This speech by Big Mouth is taken from one of the unnamed newspaper clippings found in the cabin mentioned in the preface to this work. It is dated September 18, 1867, and is ascribed to a "Special Correspondent."

47. This speech is also taken from the newspaper clippings mentioned above. It appeared in *The Cincinnati Commerical*, but the date is missing.

48. Howard, Helen A., & McGrath, Dan L. *War Chief Joseph.* Caxton Printers, Ltd. Caldwell. 1941. 282.

49. Engelhardt, Zephyrin. *San Luis Rey Mission.* James H. Barry Co. San Francisco. 1921. 192. See also: Robinson, W. W. *Land in California.* University of California Press. Berkeley & Los Angeles. 1948. 20-21. *Warner's Ranch Report.* (Typed). Congressional Commission. Los Angeles. 1902. 30-32.

50. This address was taken down stenographically while being delivered. The excerpts used here are published with Warcaziwin's permission.

51. These words are from *The Earlhamite*, March 16, 1896, official bulletin of Earlham College, Richmond, Ind., and are quoted here by the kind permission of that institution.

52. The *Report of the 35th Lake Mohonk Conference on the Indians*, Oct. 16-18, 1929, is the source from which these excerpts are taken. Mrs. Bonnin's words are quoted here with the kind permission of Mr. A. Keith Smiley, manager of Lake Mohonk Mountain House.

53. Dixon, Joseph K. *The Vanishing Race.* Doubleday, Page & Co. Garden City. 1913. 189.

54. This part of Albert Thayer Freeman's speech, "The American Indian's Appeal," was supplied to the author by De Pauw University for use in this book. All efforts to locate Mr. Freeman himself failed.

55. *House Document No. 240.* 68th Congress, 1st Session. *Statue of Sequoyah.* Government Printing Office. Washington. 1924. 40-47.

56. The printed copy of Raymond Nakai's inaugural address, from which these excerpts are taken, was acquired from Navajo Tribal Headquarters, Window Rock, Ariz. The excerpts are published with Mr. Nakai's personal consent.

# SEOUL MAN

## A MEMOIR OF CARS, CULTURE, CRISIS, AND UNEXPECTED HILARITY INSIDE A KOREAN CORPORATE TITAN

# FRANK AHRENS

**HARPER BUSINESS**

*An Imprint of* HarperCollins*Publishers*

HarperCollins books may be purchased for educational, business, or sales promotional use. For information, please e-mail the Special Markets Department at SPsales@harpercollins.com.

FIRST EDITION

*Designed by William Ruoto*
*Sunburst image courtesy of Kritchanut/Shutterstock*

Library of Congress Cataloging-in-Publication Data
Names: Ahrens, Frank, author.
 Title: Seoul man: a memoir of cars, culture, crisis, and unexpected hilarity inside a Korean corporate titan / Frank Ahrens.
 Description: New York : HarperBusiness, 2016. | Description based on print version record and CIP data provided by publisher; resource not viewed.
 Identifiers: LCCN 2016016111 (print) | LCCN 2015042560 (ebook) | ISBN 9780062405265 (ebook) | ISBN 9780062405241 (hardback) | ISBN 9780062405258 (paperback).
 Subjects: LCSH: Hyŏndae Chonghap Sangsa (Korea) | Automobile industry and Trade—Korea (South) | Corporate culture—Korea (South) | International business enterprises—Korea (South) | BISAC: BIOGRAPHY & AUTOBIOGRAPHY / Business. | BUSINESS & ECONOMICS / International / General. | BUSINESS & ECONOMICS / Industries / Automobile Industry.
 Classification: LCC HD9710.K62 (print) | LCC HD9710.K62 A37 2016 (ebook) |
 DDC 338.7/629222095195—dc23
 LC record available at https://lccn.loc.gov/2016016111

16 17 18 19 20   OV/RRD   10 9 8 7 6 5 4 3 2 1

TO MY WIFE, REBEKAH,
AND MY DAUGHTERS,
ANNABELLE AND PENELOPE

# CONTENTS

# 1
## ALMOST, NOT QUITE

Punishingly peppy K-pop music pounded in my ears. Secondhand cigarette smoke filled my lungs; my crisp blue dress shirt was now soaked with my own sweat and splattered with beef drippings and mysterious sauces that had been served with dinner earlier in the evening. Flashing colored lights cut through the dark, windowless room I'd been packed into with a dozen yelling, clapping, laughing, hugging Koreans. A karaoke screen on a wall projected animations of saucer-eyed children and song lyrics in English and Korean. My wife must be somewhere in the room, but she seemed to have slipped just beyond my reach as I was jostled by the exuberant crowd that shout-sang along with the two Koreans sharing a microphone as some Korean pop tune played. When they weren't shouting or singing, they were downing shots of whatever it was the older Korean ladies kept bringing in little green bottles. Drank, that is, whatever wasn't spilled on the floor or on each other.

And here I was: sopping wet, laughing, singing incoherently and hugging people I'd met only five days earlier. Welcome to Korea.

I had expected South Korea to be more sterile. I'd had this feeling that South Korea existed thirty or so years in the future, where things are cleaner and more orderly, the way Japan used to seem. With its booming growth, strong democracy, ultrafast Internet, supersmart students, and all the sleek, impeccably groomed Koreans I saw using next-generation Samsung and LG electronics in the TV ads I watched online, South Korea turned out to be that, but it also turned out to be something else: a gritty, bare-knuckled uppercut to the jaw. The noise, the crowds, the traffic, the powerful smells, the nonstop visual stimulation—the all-night partying, the street protests, the fistfights in Parliament—all combined to stagger me on my feet moments after I'd stepped into the ring.

It's a lot to process, so you have to start somewhere. If you're going to talk about the way South Korea hits you, you must begin with *kimchi*. It insists.

You catch your first whiff before you're outside Incheon International Airport, almost immediately after you deplane. To a Korean, *kimchi* smells like home. It's the rocket fuel of their great leap forward, 150 years of industrialization pressure-packed into fifty years. To a foreigner, *kimchi* is at first only a smelly food, a pungent combination of fermented vegetables—cabbage, radishes, or cucumbers—and spices, chief of which is garlic. Traditionally made, it steeps in a jar buried in the ground for months, where its awesome olfactory power builds. Unleashed on every Korean meal, including breakfast, it stings the nostrils of the uninitiated, causing recoil. It comes in many types and doesn't smell like just one thing. Some *kimchi* smells like cabbage, if the power of that cabbage were intensified a hundredfold. Some *kimchi* smells like vinegar and chilies. Some *kimchi* has almost no smell. Some *kimchi* smells like feet. *Kimchi* exhaust—twenty people who just ate *kimchi* for lunch packed into an elevator, exhaling—has a metallic smell, a top note of iron filings that hits like an anvil and can induce a wooziness over the span of just a few floors. Today's Koreans have separate *kimchi* refrigerators in their homes to isolate the aroma. Sure, it's cliché to talk about the smell of *kimchi*, but to not do so would be to fail at describing an integral part of nearly every Korean's daily life and an essential staple of their cultural identity. *Kimchi* is to Koreans what hamburgers are to Americans, only more so. Americans (most, anyway) don't eat hamburgers with every meal. *Kimchi* is a reliable place locator. If someone blindfolds you and flies you to a mystery location and you get off the plane and smell a hamburger, you could be almost anyplace in the world. You get off the plane and smell *kimchi*, there's a really good chance you've landed in Korea. If there were a global prize for a bona fide national dish and staple of cultural identity, *kimchi* would win it. Its smell is terrifically, aggressively, proudly Korean and probably the first bridge that foreigners must at least attempt to cross if they want to know something about this place.

My wife, Rebekah, and I arrived in Seoul in October 2010 after a thirteen-hour nonstop flight from Washington, D.C. (middle seats, middle aisle). Rebekah was about to begin a two-year posting in the U.S. Foreign Service at the American embassy in Seoul. I was to take over as director of global PR for Hyundai Motor Company. We had both left the *Washington Post* in Washington, D.C.

We had been married for only three months and were still getting to know each other and wedded life when Rebekah and I uprooted ourselves and moved to a foreign country, taking new jobs in new careers. I had left a steady twenty-one-year career as a journalist—the last eighteen years at the *Washington Post*—to make one leap into public relations and another leap to living outside America for the first time in my life. Rebekah, the youngest child of a New Zealander Presbyterian minister emigrated to the U.S., had never spent eighteen years in any one place. A preacher's itinerant vocation moved the family around in Rebekah's youth and either instilled or complemented a restlessness that was already in her. Unlike most American kids, she was spoiling to see the world, and had already lived in China, Japan, Lebanon, and France before we met. For me, going to Korea was going to the moon. For her, it was just the next spot on an ambitious itinerary.

What did we know about South Korea coming in? Little more than most Americans do: it's the most wired nation on earth, the kids are ultrahigh academic achievers, and they eat *kimchi*. Surrounded by our LG flat-screen TVs, Samsung smartphones, and Hyundai and Kia cars, most Americans know Korea for its powerhouse consumer brands—and perhaps for the murderous Kim dynasty in the North whose periodic outbursts alternate between lethal threats and farce. Had I been asked to name famous Koreans or Korean-Americans before I arrived in Seoul, it would have made for a short list: U.N. secretary-general Ban Ki-moon, a few baseball players and actors. My late father was a Korean War vet, so I'd learned a little bit about the war from him. Depending on the time of year, Seoul is thirteen or fourteen hours ahead of Washington; Korea literally is in the future. Soon after our arrival, we stopped saying "South Korea." We simply called it "Korea," because that's what South Koreans call it. They distinguish the country to the north as Book Han. Book means "north" and Han is short for Han-Gook, which is what South Koreans call their country. South Koreans see North Korea as simply the northern part of South Korea, waiting to be reunified. This drives North Korea nuts, so it calls South Korea Nam Chosun, which means, as you might imagine, "Southern North Korea."

In our first few days in Korea, we managed a cursory look around Seoul, a ten-million-person Asian megacity split by the Han River into Gangbuk, the older part of Seoul north of the river, and Gangnam, the newer, southern part of Seoul. Gangnam—think Fifth Avenue meets Beverly Hills—was made famous by K-pop star Psy's YouTube pop hit of 2012, which has enjoyed more than two billion views on YouTube. Many of Korea's richest citizens live here; all of them shop here. Democratic, exuberant, luxurious Gangnam, south of the river, exists because of decades of labor by Koreans north of the river, who rebuilt the country from ashes, in privation, directed by the strongman who ran the country. At once, Gangnam feels like the place where Korea is heading, and gives a hint of the centuries of tradition it is leaving behind.

Seoul is surrounded by mountains; indeed, most of Korea is mountainous, and the hills reminded me of my home state of West Virginia. Washington, D.C., is at essentially the same latitude as Seoul, so the climates are similar: sultry summers paired with bitingly cold, short winter days that ensure diligent Korean salarymen go to work in the dark and come home in the dark for nearly half of each year. When we arrived in Korea in October, the hills were bursting into familiar shades of orange, yellow, and red.

Seoul lacks the signature skyscraper common in other Asian megacities—the twin Petronas Towers in Kuala Lumpur, for instance. Instead, Seoul's defining architectural feature is its clusters of beige twenty-story apartment buildings—most with a big identifying number on the side—built like hills, one behind the other, marching into the distance. These are the homes of the millions of Koreans who have moved from the countryside to seek prosperity in the megacity. Nestled between mountains, with flat land scarce, Seoul became a vertical city.

Half of the entire country's population of 50 million people make Greater Seoul their home. The next biggest city in Korea has only 3.5 million people. In many ways, Korea is a city-state, like Singapore, but with more land. Seoul is the white-hot center of Korea in almost every way that matters, from politics to taste-making trends. And, in many ways, it is the culture engine for much of East Asia, which ravenously consumes K-Pop and Korean TV dramas. DVDs and flash drives of the soap operas even find their way into North Korea, through its bribe-friendly border with China, giving a few of the 25 million North Koreans, shut off from the world, a tantalizing and agonizing vision of what life is like in the well-fed, beautiful, unfathomably rich South. Seoul is also home to Korea's beauty belt—scores of plastic surgery clinics that make Koreans, per capita, the world's most cosmetically altered people. It is home to the nation's best universities and the massive conglomerates that drive its economy. Understanding Seoul is crucial to understanding Korea; it is the shimmering reservoir of the country's endlessly striving aspirations—the best Korea has to offer.

The U.S. embassy is located in the center of Seoul's older downtown district, just down the street from the country's largest and most important historic palace, the seat of a glorious dynasty that ruled Korea for five hundred years. The traditionally Korean curved roof of Gyeongbok Palace—gracefully upturned at the ends like a hat—is an unmistakably ancient and Asian design, stately and handsome. The palace is, as movie directors would say, Seoul's establishing shot. Rebekah's first week as a Foreign Service officer at the embassy consisted of getting to know her American and Korean local-hire coworkers and learning the daily work of a consular officer. Basically, her job was to sit in a chair behind a customer service window for eight hours per day, conducting up to 250 interviews (in Korean) with Koreans who had applied for visas to visit the U.S.—to go to school, for instance. Her job was to determine if their reasons were legitimate.

My job was at the twin towers of Hyundai Motor Group, about forty-five minutes south of the embassy in a part of Seoul called Yangjae, alongside the country's major north-south highway, which Hyundai's founder built in 1970. Unlike Rebekah's neighborhood, there were few traditional structures to be found near my workplace, which grew over the past thirty years as Seoulites sprawled southward out of the city. Next to my office was a supermarket, perhaps Korea's largest. Across the street, the headquarters of the country's trade promotion agency. Down the street was a Costco, a Saturday morning destination for thousands of Koreans and dozens of ex-pats, whose cars snaked around the building, waiting for a parking space.

Hyundai Motor Group is Korea's second-largest company, behind Samsung. It is made up of Hyundai Motor, Kia Motors, and more than thirty affiliate companies, including auto parts makers, a steel company, and a defense company. I worked for Hyundai Motor only, part of a family-owned conglomerate, or *chaebol*, which are similar to the Japanese *zaibatsu*. The *chaebol* powered the rapid growth of Korea and made it what it is today, the world's thirteenth-largest economy. The *chaebol* are composed of dozens of affiliate businesses—some related to the group's main business, others not. Through a complicated governance structure that enables family control with small amounts of share ownership, the *chaebol* are handed down from generation to generation. (Though there are other companies in Korea called Hyundai—more on that later—for brevity's sake, I'll refer to my employer, Hyundai Motor, as simply Hyundai.)

Each of the big *chaebol* faces a pivotal transition, as all stand on the cusp of being handed down to the third or fourth generations of their founders. One popular joke goes that in

North Korea they hand down governments from father to son. In the South, they hand down companies. Most inside Korea expect—and many outside Korea hope—the coming corporate successions will mark a change in the management style and personality of the *chaebol* toward a more international, less insular feel. Most of the heirs are fluent in English, a first for the *chaebol*. Because of their outsize influence on the Korean economy, the *chaebol* will continue to drive Korea's remarkable growth story. But Korea is at a crossroads and its future prosperity is not assured. Much of Korea's future rests on the shoulders of a handful of men in their thirties and forties, the heirs to the great *chaebol*. One of them hired me.

Not only is Korea nearly homogenous—at 97 percent ethnic Korean—but it is also probably the third-most homogenous country on the planet, after Japan and North Korea. Indeed, according to the government, the family names Kim, Lee, and Park are attached to half of the people there. Even Koreans joke that the perfect Korean name is Kim Lee Park. Such was my confusion that first week at work as I met numerous new Korean colleagues, almost all introducing themselves with some variation of this nomenclature. The highlight of my first few days as Hyundai's director of global PR consisted of being shuttled around from office to office at headquarters, meeting an endless stream of Mr. Kims, Mr. Lees, and Mr. Parks, making some small talk, trying to comprehend the frequent broken English, bowing and smiling a lot, accepting business cards with both hands, as is the custom, and then coming back to my office with a stack of cards and absolutely no idea who was who. My global PR team was feverishly preparing to host several top-flight European automotive journalists and had no time to brief their new *waygookin*, or foreigner, who—as I would come to find out—was not quite their boss.

On the Friday night at the end of my first week of work, my

team invited me to a welcome dinner. In truth, it was my boss Mr. Lee who invited me and my team to dinner. I had not met or even heard of Mr. Lee until my first day; I had to write "my boss" on his business card so I could remember who he was. Compounding my confusion, to my untrained eyes, Mr. Lee looked no different than any other Hyundai executive at headquarters: male, middle-aged, medium height, medium build, black hair, no facial hair. He dressed like other executives, too: dark suit, white shirt, red or blue tie. Mr. Lee was more fine-boned than many men his age and, though not an outgoing man, walked with a bit of a swagger at times. While not outwardly emotive, Mr. Lee would in fact show much kindness to his out-of-place American PR director. On the times when he drove the two of us to lunch, without my asking, he would flip his car radio from a K-pop station to one of the two Seoul radio stations that broadcast in English. I would come to find that Mr. Lee enjoyed good-natured teasing when drinking with colleagues.

Mr. Lee had planned a customary Korean work night out for the team, the sort of forced socialization, I would come to realize, that was common in Asian business. Your availability to the company begins before eight a.m. Monday and ends on Friday night pretty much when your boss decides it's time to call it quits for the week.

And now Rebekah and I were about to get our first taste of real Korea. More like a force-feeding, really.

The twist was that I had brought Rebekah to dinner. This was wholly unexpected by my team, as wives do not attend work social functions. As it was explained to me, if my wife and I hosted, say, the one-hundred-day party for our newborn—a Korean custom—the wife of my team leader might attend. But every other work-social function, like this dinner, she would not attend. It just wasn't done, and it was understood implicitly by the Koreans, as most things are.

Not yet aware of this custom, Rebekah and I met the team at a Korean barbecue restaurant, where the meat is brought to the table raw and cooked over a tub of hot coals or a grill in the middle of the table. Every square inch of the table is covered with small bowls of side dishes: greens and noodles and pickled things and tubers and pickled tubers and the ever-present *kimchi*. But no barbecue sauce.

"Korean barbecue" was the first example of a phenomenon our State Department sponsors told us about the day we arrived in Seoul: "Welcome to Korea, the land of Almost, Not Quite." What they meant was that Korea, or at least Seoul, looks familiar to Westerners accustomed to large cities. But as you dive in, you find things are just a little . . . off. Barbecue with no barbecue sauce. Backing into parking spaces is the rule rather than the exception. No trash cans in any public space: office, sidewalk, theater, anywhere. The utter absence of voice mail. Cleaning women showing up in the men's bathroom while it's occupied. Dark tint on *every* car's windows. Business attire worn in the office with bedroom slippers and shower sandals. Green flashing lights on ambulances. Car navigation screens showing live TV that drivers watch *while they're driving*. No individual dishes at meals; instead, everyone helps themselves from communal plates. Another State Department friend summed it up this way: "If you live in a foreign country and you have to take a rickshaw to work every day, you're, like, 'Okay, this is my life. I take a rickshaw to work.' And you ratchet down your expectations accordingly. But here in Korea, everything looks like it should meet your expectations and when it doesn't, it's all the more frustrating." The frustration goes both ways. For Koreans, all these things are normal, and my colleagues quickly grew tired of hearing me discover and comment on these mundane (to them) realizations.

We gathered around a table in a private room, as is the custom for business dinners. Mr. Lee sat in the middle of one long side of the table, which is the seat always occupied by the highest-status person in the room. I sat across from him.

The evening started off pleasantly enough, but once the *soju* came out, things got Korean. *Soju* is the national drink of Korea. It is clear alcohol, typically made from rice or barley, but can also be made from sweet potatoes and other foods. Alcohol content varies by brand but hovers around 28 proof (or "degree," as the Koreans say). It comes in small green bottles about the size of an old-style Coke bottle, and the Korean government keeps the price artificially low at about $1 per bottle, so all Koreans can afford their birthright: constant access to a momentary escape from their hard lives. And their lives are plenty hard. When they were a country as poor as the poorest in Africa sixty years ago, their lives were hard in a daily survival kind of way. Now that Korea is a rich country, Koreans' lives are a different kind of hard, with all the physical and psychological problems caused by a lifetime of constant competition. So they get drunk on *soju*.

*Soju*—like vodka in Russia—is more than just a drink. It is the means to team building at work and relationship bonding outside of work. Ideally the two become one. At one Hyundai dinner I attended, an executive rose to make his toast, as each male guest is typically expected to do, and shouted to the group. He raised his glass and asked, rhetorically: "Is this *soju*?"

"No!" they shouted back.

"Is this our spirit?"

"Yes!" they replied.

I had been warned and had read about the Korean drinking culture. Indeed, during my first interview with Hyundai, I was asked, "Do you drink alcohol? Your team will want to show respect to you by giving you drinks." I told my Korean interviewer that I enjoy a good beer and, I glibly added, I was sure there were other ways my team could demonstrate their respect.

I was wrong.

By most reports, Koreans drink more alcohol than anyone on earth. By a lot. According to a 2014 European survey, Koreans downed an average of eleven shots of alcohol per week. This made them number one in the world by more than double their closest rival, Russia, where the average citizen downs only five shots per week.

Problem number one: I myself am not really a drinker. Neither is my wife. That is to say, we don't get drunk, for reasons of faith and health. One of my favorite things to do is go out with a couple of buddies and, over the course of a three- or four-hour evening, enjoy two, maybe three excellent beers—say, a pale ale or an IPA or a copper ale. A Korean executive once asked me exasperatedly, "Don't you drink?" "I drink beer," I replied. "Ha!" he spat. I soon came to understand Koreans don't really consider beer alcohol, so skewed, by American grown-up standards, has perception become within the Korean drinking culture.

Each guest at our welcome dinner table had a shot glass for *soju* and a larger glass—about the size of a bathroom sink glass—for beer. Both were kept full. And then emptied. And then filled, and so on. In Korea, it is polite to pour the drinks for your tablemates and considered rude if their glasses go empty. You pour either with two hands on the bottle or the right hand on the bottle and the left hand respectfully touching your right elbow. The person receiving the drink holds their glass respectfully with two hands. Then they return the pour. My new teammates would either toast "*Geonbae*," which means "To your health," or "*Wehayo*," which simply means "To your . . ." (fill in the blank: to your health, to your business success, whatever).

Pretty soon, everyone was shouting "One shot!" and downing the *soju* shots. As the welcome dinner progressed and everyone got drunker and more red-faced, variations on the one shot appeared: the "love shot," where two drinkers loop arms, their faces close together, and down the shot; the shot where you prove you've downed your shot by turning the glass upside down over your head; and the Korean "bomb shot," called a boilermaker in the States, where you drop your shot of *soju* into your beer, down it all in one drink, and rattle the glasses to prove they're empty while the rest of your drinking mates cheer.

The ringleader was Ben, my team leader. Self-confident and tall, Ben was, like most Hyundai men his age, a Hyundai lifer and a patriot. "First job, last job," they would all say. Once, when asked why he liked working for Hyundai, Ben said, "It makes me proud to help make Korea strong." Ben was the entertainer in chief for our global PR team; in terms of drinking, he was our enabler in chief. Like many Koreans in business, Ben had taken an English first name because Koreans fear their Korean names are too difficult for Westerners to pronounce. Ben and I were about the same age and, despite our radically different backgrounds, shared a couple of touchstones, including eighties rock. His favorite band was Queen.

As a team leader, it was Ben's job to execute Hyundai executives' orders, wherever they may come. Imagine team leaders like army sergeants, carrying out an officer's orders. If the Hyundai executive—in this case, my boss—orders and hosts the dinner, it is the team leader's job to carry out his commanding officer's orders. But that's the Western way of looking at it. I would come to understand that Ben thought of himself like a father or a big brother to his subordinate team members. Ben's attitude was just one of the many profound ways the concept of Confucianism—Korea's de facto national religion—weaves its way into every strand of Korean life.

Ben was also emblematic of Korean working stiffs in another way: He was a *gireogi appa*, or "goose daddy." In the way that male geese fly far from their nests for long periods of time to gather food for their families, as the folklore goes, Korean *gireogi appa* sacrifice time with their families in order to provide for them by furthering their careers with Hyundai. This means living on opposite sides of the world, sometimes for years, missing births, anniversaries, and huge chunks of childhoods, save for a couple short visits per year, to take the job Hyundai has assigned. In Ben's case, his family had followed him to a Hyundai posting years earlier in the U.S. and stayed behind when he was recalled to Korea. His computer screensaver at work showed the current time in his family's U.S. time zone. He saw his wife and kids once, maybe twice a year.

For this evening's activities, Ben's job was to incite heavy drinking and high-volume merriment, and he ran quite a show. There was yelling, and lots of it. Laughing, and cross-talking, and team members mocking each other, and *"Wehayo!"* shouted three times in a hearty toast, and people running around the table to pour *soju* for each other—and especially for my boss, Mr. Lee—who sat quieter but still amused and fully invested—to show their respect for him. For some reason, one of my team members showed her affection for us by joyfully pinching us with two fingers, like a crab's claw.

At one point I asked Rebekah, "Have you ever seen anything like this before?" The last time I had seen anyone drinking this way was during quarter-beer nights at West Virginia University in the 1980s. But at least Rebekah knew what was coming.

"Sure," she said. "Remember, I lived in Asia for four years."

Rebekah was one of those rare American kids who, when they graduate from college, can't wait to get out of the country. Not because she hated America but because she felt claustrophobic. From her earliest adulthood, Rebekah sought overseas adventure. Right out of college, she found a job with a Lebanese trading company in Hong Kong. After two years cavorting with other young, glamorous ex-pats, she was not ready to come home yet. So she went to Sendai, Japan, for two years, where she taught English to Japanese high school girls, bridging the cultural gap in inventive ways, such as leading them in a production of *Pippi Longstocking.*

Rebekah understood that, throughout East Asia, drinking is not only a social pastime; it is a tool for conducting business and for developing tight bonds among employees and business partners. And so here was my almost, not quite introduction to Korean salaryman culture. Before I worked in Korea, I held many of the classic white American stereotypes about Asians: hardworking, good students, quiet, and reserved. More likely to be found in the lab or the orchestra than in politics or sports. Indeed, during my first week at Hyundai, it was remarkable how quiet office life was. Most workers stayed at their desks working or huddled in quiet meetings. There were few desk-side conversations that did not relate to work, little laughing, and none of the loud cross-newsroom bonhomie I enjoyed at the *Post.*

And yet here, outside of work on a Friday night, I was surrounded by a dozen cavorting Korean party animals. Unlike in the U.S., with its more relaxed offices, work culture and after-work behavior weren't all that different. In Korea, I came to learn, you behave one way at work and another outside of work, and often the two behaviors are jarringly extreme.

Just when I thought the commotion in our private room had reached its pitch, someone pushed a button on the table summoning the waitress and *more meat* was ordered. A guy with tongs humped in another bucket of red-hot coals and set it into the recess in the middle of the table as the waitress fixed a grill over the coals and plopped down more pieces of red uncooked sirloin, slicing them up with a pair of scissors while we watched. While smoke rose from the sizzling beef, and sparking hot coals were hauled perilously close to bare skin, and there was laughing and jostling and amid all this commotion, I hadn't noticed that one of my team members had wheeled in a cart lined with two rows of glasses: a row of full beer glasses holding up a row of full *soju* shot glasses on top, each shot glass balanced on the lips of two glasses.

I was told it was my honor to take the customary metal Korean chopsticks and lightly tap the first shot glass in the row, thereby triggering a chain reaction that would drop each shot glass into a glass of beer, which would then be handed out to all the guests, who would down the bomb shot. I was told it was very tricky and only real Koreans can do it. That was a lie, if a well-intentioned one, as it's almost impossible *not* to make the chain reaction happen. But after I did it, I was welcomed, in a way, to Korea. Just to make sure we were both properly blooded, Rebekah was required to do her own chain reaction, too. My team members quickly adapted to her presence and welcomed her at the dinner, probably understanding I didn't know the custom.

After two hours of this saturnalia, we were shocked to discover that we had completed only round one of the evening. Round two is *noraebang*, which means "song room," which means karaoke. Bright lights, more drinking, and lots of enthusiastic singing.

Problem number two: I don't really *do* karaoke. And that's an issue because karaoke is no joke in Asia. Every year, there are reports from the Philippines or Thailand or China or Japan about stabbings because someone was intolerably butchering a version of Frank Sinatra's "My Way," which is an anthem of Asian salarymen—because, I think, Asian salarymen don't get to do anything their way. In Korea, I came to learn, karaoke is a standard part of an evening's entertainment, regardless of age, gender, professional, or social status. And everyone has their go-to karaoke song.

We all piled out of the restaurant into the street and walked to a nearby *noraebang*, laughing and talking loudly in Korean and English. We crammed into a windowless room with banquettes. Thick plastic-covered songbooks in English and Korean were handed around. The music started and one of my team members began singing while everyone else started clapping and signing along. Ben ordered *soju* and the action escalated over the next few songs as the strobe lights kicked in and the dancing started.

Naturally, my boss sang "My Way." I sang a couple of English songs, a little bit of Billy Joel because no Clash was available. After an hour or so, exhausted, bloated from ingesting pounds of grilled meat, head spinning, clothes infused with cigarette smoke and sweat (much of it mine), my wife and I begged out and asked to be driven home. The team was disappointed, but we insisted. Apparently, there could have been a round three in the offing.

Escorted into the mercifully crisp and smoke-free autumn air by the most junior member of the team, Eduardo, we waited for the black Hyundai sedan to take us home. Eduardo was a young Korean, new to Hyundai, who had spent several years growing up outside of Korea. His father, a doctor, practiced overseas and Eduardo had attended American school in Peru and had lived in California. He spoke English like an American without a regional accent. Because of this and his junior status on the team, Eduardo had been assigned by Ben to be my man Friday, as it were. Not only was he to help me with whatever work tasks I needed, but he would also help me schedule maintenance for my car with Korean-speaking mechanics, take emergency phone calls from the gas station when my company credit card no longer worked, and inform me, on the QT and after the fact, why I shouldn't make self-deprecating jokes in front of my team.

Eduardo became my invaluable Tenzing Norgay. Without

Norgay, Sir Edmund Hillary would never have scaled Everest. Without Eduardo, I never would have come to understand the admittedly small bit of this incredibly complex and ancient culture. And I probably would have been sacked from Hyundai within six months.

While we were waiting for our driver outside the *noreabang*, Eduardo, who always had one foot in Korean culture and the other outside, was apologetic about the whole evening. "Sir," Eduardo said—he always called me "sir," and still does—"I'm sorry about all this Korean bullshit."

"No worries," I slurred, my temples pounding. I felt like I'd been blown through a jet engine and then used to mop the floor of a frat house the morning after an epic party. Rebekah and I piled into the backseat of the car and slumped together, holding hands. Our silent Korean driver weaved through the endless red brake lights of Seoul traffic, as seemingly heavy at eleven p.m. as it had been in morning rush hour. Through the tinted windows of our sedan we saw sidewalks packed with well-dressed Koreans window-shopping and taking selfies. Dancing videos promoting products and Korean soap operas stretched several stories high on the sides of buildings, turning darkness into a pulsing, multicolored daylight. We caught the iron-filing whiff of *kimchi* exhaust on our driver's breath. I would try, but I wasn't sure I was ever going to get used to its smell. Rebekah and I looked at each other with the same question on our faces. Where were we headed? *Home?*

# 2

## THREE MIDLIFE CRISES

On my first morning of work at Hyundai, at a little after seven a.m. on a Monday in early October 2010, I walked into the brightly lit, marble-floored multistory atrium of the headquarters lobby. With gleaming new Hyundai and Kia models on raised stands all around me, I stood there mystified, entranced, over-whelmed, the lone Caucasian standing stock-still as hundreds of Koreans streamed around me, like an endless school of fish flowing past a rock stuck in a stream. A young Korean colleague noticed my profound sense of lostness and came over to help. He knew what I was thinking, laughed, and said, in lightly accented English, "Too many Koreans!"

If you're new to almost anywhere in Asia, nothing prepares you for the crushing multitude of bodies seemingly packed into every available space. Seoul is the third-densest big city in the world, trailing only Delhi and Mumbai.

Koreans seemed to thrive on this closeness. One of the first things I noticed in my new country is how physically intimate Koreans are with their friends of the same sex. Walking through the lobby on my first day of work, I saw several pairs of (and here I was guessing) heterosexual women walking arm-in-arm. It is common to see a young salaryman walking with an arm slung around the shoulder of his male friend, in a way that looks antique, like *Huck Finn*, to Americans. We Americans, on the other hand, like our personal space, even with our closest of friends. Koreans seemed at home in crowds and comfortable being up close. This was going to take some getting used to.

Part of the power of Seoul's density comes from its monolithic population. Everyone in Korea of course does not look alike, and you learn to see that the longer you live there, but they look alike enough to a newcomer that it creates an overwhelming feeling of being the only Other in a sea of sameness. I wasn't just the only American in the Hyundai lobby on my first morning. I was the only American at Hyundai headquarters, full stop. Of the few thousand employees who worked there, fewer than a dozen were non-Koreans. So I already stood out. At six foot two, white, and XL size, even more so.

But, as much as it felt that way at the moment, I was not alone. When I arrived in Korea and at Hyundai, all three of us—the country, the company, and I—were heading into uncharted territory: our midlife crises.

These were not the hedonistic, leave-your-wife-and-get-a-Corvette midlife crises. These were the kind where you realize you've spent your entire adult life pushing, climbing, and striving toward something and then, in your forties, pulling up like a distance runner taking a break, putting your hands on your hips, and taking a look around. Evaluating where you are and comparing it to where you thought you'd be. Who you are and comparing it to who you thought you'd be. In the worst cases, wondering, "Is this all there is?" In the best cases, trying to figure out your second act.

In 2010, Hyundai Motor was forty-three years old, having been established in 1967. I was forty-six, having been established in 1963. And although South Korea became its own nation in 1948, the late forties and fifties were a terrible, directionless time for the fledgling country, which took the worse end of a brutal three-year war waged by North Korea and afterward staggered through two inept administrations, corruption, internecine squabbling, and abject poverty. Modern South Korea, the beginning of what we see today, did not start until military strongman Park Chung-hee's coup in 1961 put the nation on its path to prosperity and modernity. In this respect, in 2010, South Korea was only forty-nine years old.

We were all trying to engineer the next stage of our lives. The stakes were high.

Hyundai could keep chugging along, cranking out very good if unremarkable cheap cars. Or it could try something radical and untested and aspire to become something much more than what it was and what people expected it to be. If Hyundai faltered, its moment might not come again. Soon it could be bypassed by waves of Chinese economy cars and might never rise above the level of being the Brand That's Almost As Good As Toyota.

Korea could rest on its laurels, congratulating itself for how far it had come so quickly—maybe the fastest industrialized development in history—and enjoy the fact that Samsung, Hyundai, and LG Electronics had become global brands. But the country knew that if it started coasting, it faced the prospect of becoming another Japan: zero population growth coupled with a swelling over–sixty-five population weighing down a stagnant economy overly dependent on national champion conglomerates that may be past their prime. Korea's leaders understood that just doing more of what got Korea to where it was in 2010 was not enough if the country was going to write the next chapter of its remarkable growth story. Korea had to become something else besides what it was.

If I washed out as a PR executive in a foreign company, we'd still have Rebekah's Foreign Service job, free housing for two years, and a grand adventure. But I didn't want to wash out. I had only fifteen to twenty prime earning years left and was heading a family for the first time. If I could succeed at this job, I could set us on solid financial footing for years to come in a way I never could on a journalist's salary. More important, I was starting a family late in life. Most middle-aged family men had already made their radical change from bachelorhood to husband and father in their twenties and thirties. I was a forty-six-year-old first-time newlywed. Like an old stag deer, I had long settled into my life patterns, wearing footpaths around Washington, between friends, and within the *Post*. Now, for the first time in my adult life, I had to pay attention to someone else's opinion of me. And start a new career. And do it in a foreign country. That was my midlife crisis.

The big question was: How would Hyundai, Korea, or I know if we had made it through our midlife crises? How would we know if we had succeeded in writing a second act? With businesses and governments, you can establish quantifiable measurements, or KPIs—key performance indicators, as they're called. Former South Korean president Lee Myung-bak campaigned on a catchy "747" platform: he wanted to achieve 7 percent GDP growth, reach a $40,000 per capita income, and make Korea the world's seventh-largest economy. Hyundai worked to achieve a top-three quality ranking among its global competitors. But would Korea have to look beyond GDP growth and employment? Would Hyundai's midlife transition require new metrics? What about me? How would I know—*when* would I know—if I'd done it? What were my KPIs?

It was my great good fortune to have arrived at Hyundai at the moment it was launching its grand experiment and just as Korea began trying to reimagine itself. My global PR team would be instrumental in Hyundai's next big step, and I had a press box seat for the beginning of Korea's attempted transformation. The number of foreign executives who had worked at the big Korean *chaebol*—ever—could be counted on two hands. This was history being made, and I had insider access that almost no other *waygookin* could or would have.

## HYUNDAI'S MAKEOVER

When I joined Hyundai, the company was a couple of years into a strong run of growing sales and increasing reputation around the globe, especially in the U.S. The world's biggest automakers—Chevrolet, Volkswagen, Toyota, Nissan, Honda—saw Hyundai as you might see a car coming up fast in your rearview mirror.

Starting in 2008, Hyundai began an aggressive overseas capacity expansion. It raised new automotive manufacturing plants in the Czech Republic, India, and China and had blueprints for new plants that would open in the next few years in Russia and Brazil. In 2008, Hyundai sold 2.8 million cars globally. By the end of 2013, it was 4.7 million. Combined with its sister company, Kia, Hyundai had become the world's fifth-largest automaker, trailing only GM, Toyota, Volkswagen, and—barely—Ford. Even without Kia, Hyundai's global market share was 5 percent, the same as Fiat Chrysler's and bigger than Honda's. In the U.S., Hyundai sold nearly 540,000 cars in 2010—more than Dodge.

To me, as with most Americans who hadn't paid close attention to the Korean auto industry during the 2000s, Hyundai still had the air of a joke about it. It entered the U.S. market in 1985 with the low-priced Excel and followed with other inexpensive models and chirpy advertising. They were seen as a cheaper, pluckier alternative to Japanese cars, already well established in the States.

But as the eighties turned into the nineties, the first Hyundai cars aged poorly. Subsequent generations of offerings to the U.S. market were badly turned out, with low quality and rust problems. The nadir came in 1998 when Hyundai sold only a little more than 90,000 cars in the U.S. Hyundai became to the nineties what Yugo had been to the eighties: a punch line.

So it's no surprise that most Americans missed Hyundai's radical management philosophy shift in 1999. Switching from a manufacture-and-export model, Hyundai established an aggressive and sprawling quality management regime, appointed a vice chairman of quality, ramped up R & D efforts, benchmarked the best Japanese competitors, and set seemingly unrealistic goals. As former Hyundai Motor America CEO John Krafcik used to say: "We keep setting targets we don't know how we can meet." Even better, Hyundai's head of R & D once told reporters: "We make 7 million cars a year and we have to have the same quality as BMW, which makes only 2 million." Mass production is the killer of quality: the more cars you make, the greater the chance of quality problems. Yet Hyundai demanded elite, European levels of quality in its cars and expected its designers, engineers, and manufacturers to deliver. By 2009 this strategy was beginning to pay off. Hyundai's quality was becoming the equal, if not superior in some metrics, to that of its Japanese rivals.

The quality improvements came incrementally over a decade. But in 2009, in one grand and unexpected flourish, Hyundai shocked the auto industry when it debuted a groundbreaking new design on its big-selling Sonata sedan. Called "Fluidic Sculpture," the look was all curves and swoops. In one move, Hyundai had leaped from bland fast follower to industry design leader, forcing competitors such as Nissan and Toyota to overhaul or at least examine their own cars' designs.

Critics favorably compared the new Sonata's design to the Mercedes C-class. A bold character line swept along the side of the Sonata—Hyundai designers called it the "orchid stroke"—and it arced like a javelin in flight, giving the car a look of tension and velocity. Some Hyundai lifers considered the Fluidic Sculpture Sonata the first car of Hyundai's modern era.

In subsequent years, new models, such as Hyundai's Veloster, adopted the stylish and sporty new design. Existing models, such as Elantra and Accent, were redesigned to the Fluidic Sculpture form. For the first time, Hyundai had a distinct family look, one that was directly contributing to sales and, more important in the auto industry, to "conquests"—winning new buyers from other auto brands. A big chunk of Hyundai's staggering 20 percent 2011 sales increase in the U.S. was attributable to Fluidic Sculpture. It was an astounding concept: people were buying Hyundai cars for their *looks*.

The new design helped Hyundai's sales, but so did risky management thinking. When other automakers radically cut back on new product development during the Great Recession of 2008–2009—and while two of America's Big Three were in bankruptcy—cash-rich Hyundai stepped on the gas and raced ahead with new product development. That meant that when the financial gloom began to lift in late 2009 and 2010, Hyundai had one of the industry's youngest lineups of cars—striking new models that made the competition look old and stodgy. And it didn't hurt that a relatively weak Korean currency made car prices in the U.S. and other overseas markets competitive.

Shortly after I arrived in Korea in 2010, *Car and Driver* put the Hyundai Sonata on its annual list of Ten Best Cars—the first time any Hyundai had cracked the *Car and Driver* list. And yet, in late 2010, just as the company appeared to outsiders to be settling in for a long and profitable run as a high-quality volume carmaker, finally the equal to its Japanese rivals, continuing to build new factories and someday challenging to be the world's biggest automaker—maybe even become the new Toyota—internally, Hyundai was planning something altogether different and much, much riskier.

Hyundai had looked around the auto industry and noticed a few things. If you go to a motor show in Shanghai or Beijing or Guangzhou, you'll see the Chinese brands: SAIC, BYD, Great Wall, Geely, and so on. The reason you don't see them on the streets of North America or Europe is they're not good enough. Not high enough quality, not safe enough, not enough features. Yet. But soon they will be. And, thanks to tight cooperation with the Chinese government, they will be sold at prices that automakers such as Hyundai cannot beat without taking a loss. Hyundai knew that lower-priced rivals would come in soon at the bottom of its lineup and that the company could not compete on price.

Second, Hyundai looked at its Japanese rivals' attempts to create luxury brands: Toyota's Lexus, Nissan's Infiniti, and Honda's Acura. They offer seriously mixed results. Only Lexus is a true success, and it took years for it to become profitable—setting up an entirely new "sales channel," or dealerships and infrastructure, to support a new luxury brand is extraordinarily expensive. Furthermore, not one of those luxury brands added one ounce of prestige—or, in auto industry argot, "halo"—to its parent brand. No buyer thinks better of their Toyota because the same company also makes Lexus. In fact, the opposite may be true. Nissan, for instance, worried that its Infiniti premium brand was being harmed by the fact that customers know it is made by Nissan.

So Hyundai decided upon a radical and untested idea: it would not split its most expensive cars off into a separate Lexus-like brand, condemning its cheaper cars to a permanent ghetto under the Hyundai "H" logo. Instead, it would keep all of its cars, from its low-cost subcompact to its luxury sedans, under one Hyundai badge and it would attempt to haul the entire brand *upmarket*. This would give it some breathing room at the bottom of its lineup, allow it to extend the upper range of its lineup and gradually raise all prices over time. No other automaker had tried this.

As audacious and perhaps even foolhardy as this may have seemed at first glance—"You're talking about *Hyundai* going up-market? Really?"—in some ways, Hyundai may have been the only major automaker positioned to carry this off. Because Hyundai is so young, it is largely unburdened by history. Unlike Ford or Dodge or Mercedes or even Toyota, Hyundai doesn't have to overcome one hundred years of brand perception. Hyundai has been in the consciousness of the U.S. and Europe for only a little more than twenty-five years. For the first fifteen or so, the brand was a joke. Then, for the past ten years, it was good. Going forward, there was no reason it couldn't be anything it wanted. In markets where Hyundai has been for only ten or fifteen years, such as China, it is *already* considered a premium brand.

Hyundai's other takeaway from its analysis of the global auto industry's future was the marketing miracle that was Audi. Until the 1990s, Audi was the poor-selling stodgy uncle of German cars—basically overpriced Volkswagens. Then Audi underwent a radical makeover, putting design at the forefront and giving itself a corporate identity: maker of gorgeous luxury cars. The designer behind the vanguard car of the sleek new look, the Audi TT sports coupe, was a hip, bespectacled German named Peter Schreyer who dressed only in all black.

So, in 2006, Hyundai went and got Schreyer.

Schreyer's first job was head of design for Kia; in 2013 he was put in charge of Hyundai, too. Audi is now the world's number two–selling luxury car badge. The thing is, until recently, Audis had not been particularly great cars, as judged by initial quality, reliability, and cost-to-maintain measurements, but they are beautiful and benefit from cachet-driven advertising and a premium image. This lesson was not lost on Hyundai. Good design doesn't just sell cars; it establishes a brand presence and value and it is the way customers interact with your product. All you have to do is look at Apple to know how important design is.

Aiming upmarket was a big risk. It was one thing for Hyundai and Korea to match blows with Toyota and Japan. The auto industry could easily do the math and understand that if Hyundai kept building factories, it could sell as many cars as Toyota before long. But to aim for Audi, BMW, Mercedes-Benz? And to try to compete on something as tough to quantify as brand? That was a kind of chutzpah that maybe the rest of the world didn't yet understand about Hyundai.

Hyundai set on course its grand ambition only three months after I started. Over the three years I was there, the company's progress—and missteps—toward becoming a premium brand would be marked at every auto show, when Hyundai unveiled a new car that instantly exceeded or fell below the expectations it was setting for itself. It would be marked by every Car of the Year Award a Hyundai won—or didn't win. It would be marked by every slide up or down the industry-wide quality ratings, every recall, every good or bad car review. This would be a long, uphill trudge, marked by signposts along the way. They would tell us if the idea was working—if customers were buying the idea that Hyundai could be more than what it was. It they didn't, or if market conditions and other factors changed in the coming years and it made sense for Hyundai to change tack and spin off a luxury sub-brand, the company was sensible and nimble enough to do it. But for now, this was the plan. Hyundai was all in. It's hard to think of a major global company that had set itself higher stakes. This would have been like Walmart suddenly trying to convince its customers it was Neiman Marcus. Would anyone buy that?

This task is even tougher, and more costly, than it sounds. Going upscale would require more than marketing savvy and slick advertising. To succeed, to elevate its brand—and its prices—Hyundai needed to make significantly better cars. Better-looking, higher-performance, world-class quality. From its cheapest to its most expensive cars. What I didn't know when I arrived at Hyundai was that they were already on the drawing board, being tested in wind tunnels and getting polished for their big motor show rollouts.

This would be the launch of Hyundai's second act, and it was beginning just as I arrived. I suppose in one sense, Hyundai *was* getting a shiny new car for its midlife crisis.

## KOREA'S BURDEN OF SUCCESS

At the same time that Hyundai was devising its next move, Korea began a serious midlife soul-searching about its future, questioning the very methods that had made it an economic success. In an amazingly short time—by will of a strongman leader and a military-like social structure that mobilized a pliant citizenry of "industrial warriors"— Korea had grown from one of the world's poorest nations into one of the richest and smartest.

This rapid industrialization—maybe the fastest in world history—came at a high cost. It created a society where nearly everything is a competition. From fifteen-hour study days for children to fifteen-hour workdays for their fathers, Korea had turned itself into a Jacob's ladder—a climb for something never achievable, on a ladder that just keeps repeating itself.

It's why Korean parents pay tens of thousands of dollars for after-school private academies, or *hagwons*, that go until ten p.m. so their children can ace the annual college entrance exam and get into a top Korean university. It's why Koreans flock to plastic surgery—to make a better you. And it's why Korea has one of the world's highest rates of suicide. There is a spate of youth suicides after the annual college entrance exam, and more and more elderly Koreans are killing themselves either because they have been abandoned by their money- and status-obsessed children or they don't want to be a burden on them.

Then there is the feeling among Koreans that for all of the country's achievements, for all of their personal sacrifices, they are always in danger of slipping behind. Just when Korea seems on the brink of becoming what it sees as a first-rate nation, something like the *Sewol* ferry disaster of April 2014 happens and they feel they're back to square one. Nearly three hundred people—most students—died when the ferry capsized. The *Sewol* was found to be carrying three times its allowable weight of freight and was top-heavy when it executed a hard turn to starboard. For Koreans— their own harshest critics—the deaths were the result of Korea's *pali-pali*, or "quick-quick" culture: Do things fast instead of well, cut corners, maximize profits. It's how Korea grew so quickly. It's how ferry disasters happen. It's how Hyundai grew so rapidly in the 1980s and it's why the cars' quality went downhill so fast in the 1990s. Hyundai had its come-to-Jesus moment in 1999 when it committed to quality improvement. Now it is Korea's moment.

By 2010 this was beginning to happen. Loudly in the media, and in public protests, and in government, and even within the *chaebol* themselves, there was growing realization that the country could not take the next step in its hoped-for growth by keeping up business as usual. The country could no longer rely solely on the *chaebol*. Koreans were beginning to realize that their economy must diversify from its manufacture-and-export model and develop the country's practically nonexistent service sector and start-up incubators—to build a robust knowledge economy.

Korea's other midlife crisis was more ghastly: when it looked in the mirror, it could see itself starting to resemble Japan. For a Korean of today, whose grandparents can tell stories of the brutal Japanese occupation of the Korean Peninsula in the first half of the last century, there is no worse fate.

Japan's rise to postwar prosperity came on the backs of its family-owned conglomerates: the *zaibatsu*. Mitsubishi, Kawasaki, Nissan, and Panasonic became world leaders and household names. In the 1980s, media stories alarmed Americans that a rising Japan was buying up the scuffling U.S. economy in chunks of land and handfuls of skyscrapers. But by the beginning of the 1990s, the insulated business philosophy of Japan, corporate paralysis owing to an overimportance placed on consensus, the bursting of an asset bubble brought on by easy money, and the creeping ossification of the great companies helped bring on two decades of economic stagnation. Korea had a front-row seat for this and took copious notes.

Thanks to its increased standard of living after World War II, Japanese people also began living longer. By the 1990s, Japan's societal graying was becoming a major problem. Korea, which began its economic growth about fifteen years after Japan, started seeing the same problem in the twenty-first century. Paying for their children's *hagwons* and universities; footing wedding bills that can easily top $200,000 (for middle-class families); buying keeping-up-with-the-Kims luxury goods; and forking over Manhattan-level housing expenses has left Korean parents with little or no retirement savings and a total dependency on their children. Korean elderly, who should have been at the top of the Confucian hierarchy, were being abandoned by their children, who had grown up only in prosperity.

Hence, by 2013, half of Korea's elderly were poor, the highest rate in the industrialized world. This may seem shocking and even unbelievable to foreigners who've never visited Korea and think of it as only an iridescent futurescape where everyone wears a Samsung wrist phone and has a wall-sized LG flat screen. It is that. But it is also the other thing. A heartbreakingly common sight is the hunched-over *halmoni*, or "grandmother," pulling a cart of flattened cardboard boxes through the streets of Seoul, trading them for the pennies they bring.

There is a utility to ethnic and cultural unity when building your nation, especially under dictatorial rule: most people believe the same thing and they pull in the same direction. But mature democracies and economies are diverse: they draw insight and energy from immigrants, and they allow them to assimilate. Businesses are not vassals of the government and don't always align themselves with the national interest.

But how would Korea get from here to there? It may have begun in 2012 when Park Geun-hye, daughter of the man who built modern Korea, ran for president. She talked about building a "creative economy" that would be diversified, encouraging entrepreneurialism, venture capital, and a real service sector. This was a radical departure from her father's relentless message of "Build, build, build; produce, produce, produce . . . ," but Korea was in a different place now and needed a different path to its future. Koreans believed and elected her. At the same time, the people of Seoul voted in as mayor a nonpolitician, a lifelong social activist who had been imprisoned for four months for protesting the iron rule of, ironically, Park Geun-hye's strongman father. Instead of

preaching longer hours, harder work, higher targets, more diligence, Mayor Park Won-soon had radical ideas about creating a
"sharing economy" and talked about quality of life, work-life balance, and institutionalizing siestas for his government workers.

At the same moment Korea was wrestling with this midlife
crisis, jarring—and deadly—upheaval was coming on all sides
of the peninsula's geography, in Japan, China, and North Korea.
This reinforced Korea's self-image as a small country sandwiched
between large, powerful, and aggressive ones, ones that often controlled Korea's fate.

As if to illustrate this point, one month after we arrived
in Seoul in 2010, North Korea attacked. The South Korean
navy was holding live-fire exercises near a small South Korean
island called Yeonpyeong, which sits just inside the South's
side of the two countries' western maritime border. The North
considered the exercises a military provocation and opened
fire, shelling Yeonpyeong. The South retaliated, and although
the exchange lasted only two hours, four South Koreans—two
marines and two civilians—were killed. Yeonpyeong is only
about seventy miles from Seoul; it was the closest Rebekah
or I had ever been to military action. The day of the shelling, before we knew what was happening, I could see South
Korean fighter jets scrambling over Hyundai headquarters.
The sound is distinctive—closer to the ground and faster than
a commercial jet—and it was a chilling reminder that Seoul is
only thirty miles south of the border with North Korea, well
within the range of that nation's weaponry. The North's attack
was over before we heard about it in Seoul, but it became a
bracing reminder that the country to the north was a hostile
and unpredictable Stalinist police state with 1 million soldiers
and a nuclear capability that was still technically at war with
the country that was now our home.

## ME: THE PLANETS ALIGN

When I started at the *Washington Post* in 1992, the paper had more than 800,000 daily readers. I watched that number fall below 800,000, then 700,000, then 600,000. At the same time, the *Post* and other big newspapers were building terrific online sites, but their ad revenue remained, at best, a fraction of newspaper ad revenue. In the early 2000s, the *Post* newsroom had its first-ever "voluntary early retirement," or buyout. Then another. And another. A newsroom that had nearly 1,000 journalists at its peak in the early 1990s was closing in on half that by 2008.

I was a business reporter and part of my beat was covering the media industry and the Washington Post Company. I read the *Post*'s earnings reports. I watched ad revenue shrink and shrink some more. The cratering was general across the U.S. newspaper industry. This was bad news for my life plan. I had stumbled through a mechanical engineering degree at West Virginia University and, faced with the prospect of spending a career as a mediocre, unhappy engineer, looked for a way out. I found it when I wandered over to the student newspaper with an offer to take pictures, as I'd done for my high school yearbook. I realized instantly I loved the newsroom atmosphere, even if it was only a student newsroom in a ramshackle old white house in danger of coming down on itself at any moment. I stopped taking pictures and started writing. I loved the feeling of being in the know, and the agonizing thrill of writing. After that, all I ever wanted out of life was to be a journalist, and a journalist at the *Washington Post*, home of the industry's best writers. But, after several years in my dream job, I had to admit that it looked like my beloved industry wasn't coming back. I started looking for a Plan B and, squarely in middle age, it had better be sooner rather than later. I knew too many journalists in their fifties who were finding it difficult to make a professional life after the *Post*.

What I definitely was not looking for was a wife. I was neutral, at best, on marriage. I was already forty-four and never married. If a wife dropped out of the sky into my lap, I'd consider it. But I wasn't looking.

Rebekah Davis fell out of the sky in early 2008 but missed my lap.

She had been hired as the *Post*'s foreign desk administrator, meaning she ran the paper's foreign bureaus, handling the needs of the foreign correspondents, overseeing the department's budget and generally making tough things happen. For instance, having the savvy and know-how to get cash to the paper's fixer in Pakistan so the *Post*'s reporter could do his job.

I spotted Rebekah right away in the newsroom—who wouldn't?—and made it a point to meet her. Over the next few weeks we went out several times. At work we sat at our desks in different parts of the *Post* newsroom tapping out funny and flirtatious messages back and forth, getting to know each other.

Then, one night at a restaurant, she dropped it on me: the Friend Talk.

I'd both given and received the Friend Talk before. At forty-four, there was something especially humiliating about getting it. Come to think of it, there was something especially humiliating about "dating" at forty-four. Maybe that was the larger issue.

At any rate, I wasn't having it. One benefit of being middle-aged was that you no longer have time for wasting time. I knew what I wanted, and it was not to be Rebekah's friend.

"Well, I'm disappointed," I said, "but I'm not going to be your friend."

Silence.

"I don't mean I'm going to be your enemy, or that I hate you," I explained. "What I mean is that I'm not going to continue to hang out with you and message you at work. You're beautiful,

I think you're terrific, and I want to date you. And if you don't want that, that's fine. But I can't pretend I'll be happy just being your friend. It'll make me miserable a thousand ways."

As a younger man, I had moped for months after women who were not romantically interested in me but liked me well enough to spend time with me. I hoped if I hung around long enough and was charming enough, eventually I'd win them over. Usually these efforts ended when they got boyfriends and wanted us all to hang out.

"Oh," she said.

I tend to explain relationships in terms of the solar system. Call it a quirk.

If a person is the sun, I told Rebekah, when you're young, you have "friends" all the way out to Pluto. Roommate friends, first-job friends, bar friends. You're certain they'll be in your life forever, orbiting as sure and steady as the planets. In truth, they're held to you by weak gravity. As you get older, they break free and spin off. You don't have the time or effort to try to keep them. The friends you keep are in the tight orbits, close to the sun; think of them like Mercury and Venus, where the gravity is strong. You may have a couple in Earth orbit. Once you hit Mars, you're outside the orbit of grown-up friends.

Rebekah pretended to understand my strained metaphor, but mostly she respected it. I was deeply disappointed. But I knew it was better to absorb the short, sharp shock of pain now than drag it out for months.

The next day at the *Post*, we didn't message each other.

A couple of days after that, we chanced upon each other in the hallway. We chatted amiably about nothing for a few minutes and then started to walk in opposite directions.

She called back over her shoulder, "I miss my messages."

"Well," I responded, walking off, "that's life on Mars."

A few days later I got a text on my phone. It was from Rebekah. It read: "What if I'm tired of life on Mars?"

I wish I could claim that the entire solar-system-to-life-on-Mars-line was a grand, elegant, and elaborate gambit to win Rebekah. In my telling of the story, it usually is. But it was not. It was an immediate and brutally honest bit of emotional self-preservation in response to getting dumped.

And yet, it had led to this point where Rebekah wanted to come back.

There was the proof, in digital type on the screen of the phone in my hand. An open invitation to the thing I wanted most.

Naturally, I waited several hours before I replied.

But reply I did. I remember being outrageously happy when tapping out that text.

And so we began dating. The first thing you notice about Rebekah is that she's beautiful. Soon after, you discover she has a great wit and sound comedic timing. Must have come from her theater work in college. She gives off a Jennifer Aniston–esque vibe. Even more remarkable is her resilience in not only adapting to but excelling in tough circumstances. A preacher's family is not a rich one and you seek bargains everywhere. For a time Rebekah's family car was a cheaply acquired 1970s station wagon whose previous job was serving as a hearse. It sounds Gothic to you and me, but she happily recalls sleeping with her two siblings in the vehicle's casket-length rear on long road trips—sans any sort of restraining devices, of course. As a young woman, Rebekah worked her way through college, three jobs at a time. She worked retail and at a law firm during the day and did her homework while running a country club front desk at nights, fending off the boozy male club members slouching on her counter, trying to impress her. She had the drive to win a scholarship to study in Beirut and the chops to get into a graduate program in Paris.

Of the many things I admire about Rebekah is her directness in knowing what she wants. I tend to be a muller, fully examining a situation, turning it over and over, trying to get my head completely around it before I take action. Rebekah says during this time I'm in my "shell." Ultimately, I pop out and we move forward. Maybe not as fast as she'd like, but eventually.

Rebekah gets a quicker read on situations than I do and knows what she wants. Sometimes this produces friction in our union: Rebekah wonders why I won't move forward. I worry that we're not as expert on a situation as we think we are.

After a couple months of dating, over dinner, Rebekah told me she wanted to be married and have a family. As we moved forward, she said, if I felt that was not the future I wanted, I needed to let her know so she could move on.

Rebekah clearly did not want to be married to anybody just to be married; she'd had that chance before and skipped it. She didn't know if I was the right guy, but she let me know—rightfully—that I owed her the decency of telling her if I didn't want the same thing she did.

I felt like a relationship cop had just read my Miranda rights.

It was the best thing that could have happened to me. If Rebekah hadn't put her foot down, I would most likely have done as I'd done before: hit a cruising altitude in the relationship where I was fine dating exclusively and long-term without any particular goal in mind. Rebekah would've rightly got sick of the inaction and we'd have just . . . drifted apart, what I'd allowed to happen so many times before.

I saw the wisdom of Rebekah's argument and realized nothing truly worth having in life comes easily or without some kind of leap. Aside from being attracted to each other, enjoying spending time together, and being in love, we shared the most fundamental of connections: our faith. We are both Christians and knew this meant we would be in accord—or at least start from the same point—on the most crucial of topics that either make or break marriages, from worldview to money to raising children. Every Christian has a testimony and mine is this: I received Christ my freshman year of college, read the Bible assiduously, attended church, and tried to live right. But within a couple years my innate selfishness, lack of discipline, and human desire overtook my faith and I fell away from it for more than two decades. I dated a number of women. I cared deeply for many but treated others poorly, and for that I will always be sorry. I was mired in narcissism, pursuing my own empty compulsions and separated from God. It was Rebekah who brought me back to church and to God. It is the most important of the many ways she has saved me. I am still narcissistic and selfish. The difference now is that I care that I am, I seek forgiveness for these and my manifold other sins, and I pray for the strength to change. Faith in a fallen world is a constant struggle, sustained only by the grace of God.

So even though Rebekah and I felt bonded on the big issues that would hold us together, a more prosaic one threatened to stuff the union before it could take off: Where would we live?

Rebekah took the job at the *Post* so she could be in Washington while applying to the U.S. Foreign Service. The Foreign Service was actually the safety school of Rebekah's career options. Her career of choice was spy. She had applied to—and actually been offered a directorate of operations job with—the CIA. Then the Agency began the security clearance process. She took multiple polygraphs in unmarked and otherwise nondescript Northern Virginia buildings. The Agency interviewed Rebekah's family and friends all over the country. She learned of these interviews only when she got puzzled calls from friends saying, "Hey, this is going to sound crazy, but this CIA guy came to my house . . ." And she waited. And waited. To survive, she took various jobs, such as the one at the *Post*. Cannily, on a parallel track, she started the application process to the Foreign Service, a job that would still mean a career overseas but one with less intrigue. Finally, after nearly three years waiting on the Agency, she lost patience and decided to pursue the Foreign Service. It is a decision for which I am ever thankful. Dinner conversations would have gone like this:

"How was your day, honey?"

Silence.

By the time Rebekah and I met, she had already passed two of the Foreign Service's three rigorous entrance exams. If she passed the brutal oral exam and got a security clearance, she told me clearly she would accept a job, which most likely would lead to a posting abroad. That was what she wanted.

I, on the other hand, had never lived overseas and frankly had no desire to do so. Where I was in life, I was as comfortable as a worn recliner. I liked my America and my conveniences. I liked being able to easily drive to a football game at my alma mater and get a satisfyingly large diet soda beverage—with ice—nearly every mile along the way, happily ensconced in my satellite radio-equipped, fairly taxed, cheap-gas-drinking car. And I knew that if I moved to many places overseas, I'd miss the little things about America. You know: the freedom of expression, assembly, and religion; the rule of law, free and fair elections, and the comforting knowledge that we'd already had our civil war. Those sorts of things. But I could see where my newspaper industry was going. And, having neither siblings nor living parents, nothing tethered me to any one place. I wanted to see where this woman, and this life, would take me.

In mid–2009, Rebekah was accepted into the U.S. Foreign Service, which I had come to realize was an impressive accomplishment. New officers get what's called a bid list that shows which jobs will be available when their posting is set to begin. Each officer must rank every job in order of preference and can ask to be sent to a particular one. But in the end it's called a service for a reason, and you go where your country sends you.

Rebekah got the bid list for her first posting in November, right around my birthday. We joked, sort of, that it was the worst birthday present I'd ever received. There were about one hundred jobs on the list in about seventy-five cities all over the world. I'd never heard of half the cities. Most of those I had heard of were usually in the news for the wrong reasons. Where was the Paris and Rome of the glamorous Foreign Service? Instead we saw Port Moresby and Malabo. This was the first of several ways we became disabused of the Foreign Service's grandeur.

Rebekah and I agreed that the best posting would be Seoul. We knew it was first-world modern and had heard that it was clean and amazingly safe, the simmering threat from the North notwithstanding. Rebekah had lived and worked in East Asia and was intimate with Confucian culture. We liked the potential for regional travel. And because of its size and status, home to global companies, Seoul offered the possibility that I could continue something approximating my career—communications of some sort at a high level. Rebekah would bid on Seoul, but going there was not up to us. It was the State Department's decision.

A month after getting the bid list, in December 2009, Rebekah and I joined her classmates for "flag day," a Foreign Service tradition where each member of the entire incoming class gets their first posting, in front of everyone, friends and family included. It is a dramatic and anxious event, with each posting called out along with the name of the officer being sent there. The officer comes to the front of the room and receives a small flag of their assigned country. There are tears of joy, relief, and unhappiness. You see newly minted officers exulting in their posting, imagining it as the first step toward an eventual ambassadorship. You see others wanly taking the flag of their assigned country, suddenly sure that joining the Foreign Service was the worst decision of their lives. We were prepared for anything: Rebekah was bidding for one of only two jobs available in Seoul.

State Department officials started reading down the list and, just a few names in, the first Seoul job went to one of Rebekah's classmates. Rebekah and I were not allowed to sit together, so we exchanged nervous looks across the big room. More names and more cities were read off. I kept crossing names off the list of jobs I held. One Seoul posting remained, but so were jobs in Port Moresby, Papua New Guinea; Sana'a, Yemen; and Accra, Ghana. "Well," I thought, "in for a dime, in for a dollar." I'd never lived in a place where I'd be assigned an armed escort every time I left my house and was not allowed to travel at night, but, hey, life's an adventure, right? *Right?*

The list was now down to the last twenty or so postings. That left one Seoul and nineteen not-Seouls.

Then, suddenly, magically, prayerfully, we heard: "Seoul, Republic of Korea: Rebekah Davis."

Up until right before that moment, I'm not certain I had fully realized that, for the first time, I was putting my life and immediate destiny in the hands of someone besides me. I liked choosing where I would live and, to an extent, where I would work. What I experienced was the feeling of utter relief in being sent to Seoul combined with a terrible dread of what could have happened. This may be how people who walk away from plane crashes feel.

Now we could move ahead with our next task: all I had to do now was find a job for me in Korea.

It's a natural transition for journalists to move into what used to be called PR but what we now like to call communications. Same skills—reporting, building source networks, writing, use of multimedia, storytelling—but now you're an advocate. Some journalists aren't comfortable with that, so they never make the leap or fail when they do.

I loved journalism, but as I grew older I came to see it more as a craft than as a calling or as a religion the way many of my former colleagues and friends do. My religion is my religion. I was already looking into communications jobs in Washington, D.C., before I met Rebekah. I would never have thought about doing a communications job overseas until Rebekah's posting to Seoul forced me to think about jobs in Korea at the same time I was covering the financial crisis for the *Post* in 2009 and assiduously following economic indicators.

Auto sales are a good bellwether for consumer confidence, especially in the U.S., so I watched them closely to try to understand if the country was starting to claw its way out of the Great Recession. But, thanks to Hyundai, just watching auto sales gave no clear answer. A pattern started to emerge. At the first of every month, when automakers report their sales, I'd see pretty much the same thing: Chevrolet down 10 percent, Ford down 8 percent, Toyota down 7 percent, Hyundai . . . *up* 5 percent.

This put Hyundai on my radar. A series of phone calls to sources in the auto industry confirmed that Hyundai was indeed swimming against the tide of decline in the auto industry and the general economy and was making its competitors nervous.

I got in touch with the company and, before I knew it, was interviewing for the job of director of global PR, a position that had—coincidentally?—just been vacated.

I was following a familiar route for ex-pats: getting a job outside the U.S. that I never could have gotten at home. I never could have entered GM or Ford at a director level of corporate communications in my first job out of journalism knowing—technically speaking—absolutely nothing about corporate communications.

But in Korea I had certain advantages desirable to a Korean company. I was a native English speaker and would be dealing with auto reporters from all over the world, the majority of whom speak English. Also, hiring me would show foreign journalists that Hyundai was a global company. My job was part show pony, and I knew that going in. But I was determined to make it more than that. I just didn't know how.

I signed a two-year contract with Hyundai. Rebekah's State Department posting was for two years. That was all we planned to stay in Seoul.

Before Rebekah and I left for Korea, we had one more thing to do.

We were married in July 2010, outdoors, at a historic mansion in a Washington suburb. Rebekah's father, Ivan, a Presbyterian minister, walked Rebekah down the aisle, then turned around and hitched us. Rebekah shimmered in the low-angle, late-afternoon sunlight. Instead of throwing rice, our guests blew soap bubbles. The photos looked terrific.

# 3

## AT WORK: ALIEN PLANET

Hyundai's headquarters is two rectangular towers, each topping twenty stories. At first glance, the buildings look identical save for the blue Hyundai name and logo atop one and the red Kia name and logo atop the other, but a lengthier inspection will confirm that the Kia building is slightly shorter and slightly thinner. It's this way on purpose. Hyundai bought Kia out of bankruptcy in 1998 and purchased the smaller tower from another company, then the two companies moved in together in 2000. But the newly merged companies were too big for one building, so Hyundai built a second, larger, but matching tower right next door. Hyundai, which has always sold more vehicles than Kia, moved into the new, bigger tower and Kia got the smaller one. This is the physical embodiment of the little brother feeling many Kia folk have.

The headquarters also presents itself as a useful corporate metaphor: the twin towers are joined by the three-story glass atrium lobby I had encountered on my first morning at the company. As a fellow Hyundai executive explained to me, this is a good way to think about how the two companies relate to each other. As with all other automakers with multiple brands, such as GM and Volkswagen, Hyundai and Kia cars share R & D, car platforms, engines, and transmissions. That was the atrium part of our corporate metaphor: a shared space. But after that the companies—and cars—are purposely quite separate. Hyundai and Kia each have their own separate sales, marketing, advertising, product development, design, and PR teams, in addition to different target markets, brand images, and strategies. As head of global PR for Hyundai, I spoke only for Hyundai. I did not speak for Kia. Those are the separate towers.

As an illustration, the platform of a Hyundai Sonata and Kia Optima are the same. But the exterior and interior designs, the features, even the tunings of engine and suspension, are different, built for different kinds of drivers in different markets around the world, all of whom have different driving desires. That's why auto magazines will test a Sonata versus an Optima and record measurable differences, such as zero-to-60 acceleration times, and subjective ones, such as steering feel.

My office was on the eighteenth floor of the Hyundai tower. I was trying to get to know my team members and my job. There were plenty of obstacles.

Starting with what to call each other.

Korean workplaces are formal and hierarchical, thanks to Confucianism. A boss could refer to a subordinate by their first name. But the subordinate would always—even outside of work—refer to their boss by title and last name.

I didn't know this at first, and didn't know how to address my boss by his Korean title, so I just used "Mr. Lee," which was fine. My junior colleagues were having a much tougher time with me.

Shortly after I arrived, two junior members of another team screwed up their courage and blurted out, "We don't know what to call you!" They didn't know if I wanted to be called "Ahrens Ee Sa" (Ahrens Director) or "Mr. Ahrens" or what. Further complicating issues was name order. In Korean as in many Asian cultures, last names come first. Because I was Frank Ahrens, I was "Mr. Frank" to many Koreans.

Then there was the alphabet issue.

Unlike the Chinese and Japanese languages, Korean is based on an alphabet, not thousands of ideograms that require memorization. The Korean alphabet, Hangul, has twenty-four letters; it is simple and efficient and can be learned by a foreigner in an afternoon.

But my name is spelled using a Latin alphabet. So, as all cultures do, Koreans phonetically convert non-Korean names into Korean. Problem is, Latin languages have some sounds that Korean does not, and vice versa. There is no *F* sound in Korean. So they substitute *P*. There's no hard *K* sound, so they substitute a sound that is somewhere between *G* and *K*. Korean doesn't strictly differentiate between *R* and *L* sounds; instead, there's one sound somewhere in between. Basically, my name was a landmine for Korean speakers. As a result, "Frank Ahrens" ended up looking like "프랭크에이렌스" on my business card and, if you tried to say it by looking at the Korean letters, sounding like "Puh-lan-guh Ah-lee-laen-sz."

Some of my Korean colleagues, such as Ben, my team leader, took English first names, which I remembered more easily than their Korean first names. But some of my Korean colleagues did not know their Korean coworkers' English first names. So there was a lot of me saying:

"William told me . . ."

And my Korean colleagues asking:

"Who?"

"William."

"Who's that?"

"You know, William who works on the overseas marketing team. Tall, funny."

"Oh, you mean Dae Hyun."

"I guess."

It got no easier in writing. The common Korean surname "림" sounds like "Lim," "Rim," or "Rhim." So sometimes I would get an e-mail explaining I needed to talk to "Mr. Lim" and later would get an e-mail from someone else saying I needed to speak to "Mr. Rhim." It took me a while to realize it was the same guy with multiple English phonetic spellings of his name.

Finally, I complicated matters even more with three little words: "Call me Frank."

I told this to pretty much everybody from the first day I got to Hyundai. This gesture was meant to create an egalitarian feeling on my team, flatten rank, and try to reduce some of the executive status I was trying on for the first time. In other words, I was attempting to establish a Western workplace in an Eastern culture.

This was among my first of more than a few mistakes.

"Call me Frank" made some of my team members uncomfortable and drained me of some of my rank and status. They didn't *want* to call me Frank, not only because it didn't feel right, but because it made them feel like they were working for someone of lesser status than all the other directors. This was a workplace where bowing to one another was a routine part of the workday, from quick dipping of heads in the elevator to a higher-ranking colleague to deep bows in front of visiting VIPs. Status was coin of the realm. "Call me Frank" was chump change.

In my team—Hyundai's global PR team—Ben, my team leader, was the highest-ranking member just below me, and Eduardo was the most junior member. In between, and of different ranks, were about seven members, depending on who was rotating on and off the team. It was an unusual team and probably the most international at Hyundai: every member had traveled outside of Korea and several had lived overseas, including in the U.S., either as Hyundai employees or as students. It had a fairly even male-female split, another oddity at male-dominated Hyundai. All the men on the team had completed their compulsory twenty-one to twenty-four months of military service, required of all able-bodied Korean men. One had been an officer in charge of fifty men and tank maintenance. Both Ben and a junior member of my team, Ike, had been KATUSA, which stands for Korean Augmentation to the U.S. Army. An elite number of Korean conscripts with excellent English skills are chosen for this branch and do their time embedded in a U.S. Army unit, not a Korean one. As a result, outgoing, whip-smart Ike was, along with Eduardo, the most American of the lot.

Every member of the team spoke and wrote English ranging in quality from superb to pretty good. Some spoke a third language. Many had attended one of the top three universities in Korea and had been chosen for the global PR team because of their English skills, not for their PR skills or even interest. Instead of hiring specialists for certain positions, the big Korean *chaebol*, like many big Western firms, hired college graduates with gilt-edged CVs and assigned them to teams. Hyundai HR worked to match preference with work but couldn't always. So that's why, at times during my three years at Hyundai, I had PR team members with degrees in mechanical engineering, French, and Scandinavian language studies. Hyundai likes generalists, one of my team members explained to me, and rotates promising young hires among different teams as they're promoted; the idea is to create a well-rounded automotive executive.

Despite Korea's workplace formality, what Hyundai and I were going to call each other had to take a backseat to the business at hand: bringing hundreds of foreign journalists to Korea.

When I arrived in October 2010, Hyundai was getting a lot of interest from journalists outside of Korea. Hyundai recognized correctly that its cars were becoming well known around the world, but journalists and car buyers were less familiar with Hyundai.

People didn't even know how to pronounce our name. In Korean, you say the *Y* sound, so it's pronounced "HYUN-day." But Hyundai Motor America, our subsidiary in the U.S., had spent decades teaching customers the name is "Hyundai, like Sunday." No *Y*. If you go to England, it sounds like "HI-yun-die." Why, I can't tell you. In Thailand, it was repeated back to me sounding something like, "Hee-yun-dee." This is not a problem that Ford has.

My global PR team was trying to introduce the company to the world's motoring media—if not getting them to pronounce our name right—by conducting nothing short of a massive, ongoing journalist airlift. We brought scores of journalists each year to Korea, scooping them up from all around the world and having them delivered to us.

The Hyundai subsidiaries around the world would identify several top motoring journalists in their country and we'd fly them to Korea for a three- or four-day program to learn about Hyundai—actually see its facilities up-close and appreciate its scale, understand that it was a top global automaker—and to learn about Korean culture. In addition to selecting the most widely read and influential journalists, we'd pick jurors for that country's Car of the Year awards, which every automaker covets.

This kind of program is standard procedure in the auto industry, and motoring journalists routinely accept these trips, which almost always include business-class flights and top-end hotels. The former *Washington Post* journalist in me instantly recoiled against this idea. But that lasted only about five minutes. As a PR man, I came to understand that these get-to-know-you trips are a powerful tool for getting your message out. And, to be fair, motoring journalists are literally traveling to auto company events all around the world every week and could not do so if their magazines were forced to pay the bills.

Throughout the remainder of 2010, all of 2011, and well into 2012, we had journalist visits almost every week, save for the summer and year-end holiday times. Our throughput was impressive and looked that way in the results we reported to management. One week it'd be a group of journalists from Spain. The next week, Germany. The week after, Thailand; then Malaysia, the U.K., the Czech Republic, Turkey, and so on. Eventually, we'd cycle back through a country to hit a second round of journalists. There was nothing secret about these trips; the journalists wrote about them in great detail and in many languages.

These three- and four-day visits typically started at the journalists' hotel in Seoul at seven thirty or eight a.m., when we'd load them onto a big Hyundai tour bus and haul them to headquarters for presentations and on-the-record interviews with the key executives in charge of their country's sales, marketing, and product development. This impressed the journalists, who were able to ask questions about upcoming models, sales targets, and marketing plans directly to the executives in charge of them—unlike many other automakers, which gave the journalists access only to PR flacks like me.

On other days during their visit, we'd load the journalists back onto the bus for a full-day trip to Hyundai's nearest factory, its steel plant, or its R & D facility.

Hyundai's R & D complex is about ninety minutes south of

Seoul, in a rural district called Namyang. Everyone calls it the Namyang R&D center, or just "Namyang." Its very existence is remarkable and a testament to the will of the company. Former R & D vice chairman H. S. Lee was assigned the task of building the R & D center in Namyang and related the improbable story of its creation to some visiting German journalists over dinner one night in Seoul. The pharaoh Cheops himself would have been proud of the feat.

Hyundai owned a big chunk of land in Namyang, and then-chairman Chung Ju-yung, Hyundai's founder, ordered Lee to erect the R & D center there. Like all major automakers' R & D centers, Hyundai's would need several test tracks with multiple road surfaces, a high-speed oval track, large indoor facilities for crash tests, a design center, a pilot plant—basically, a miniature assembly line factory where prototypes are built—and, of course, security to make sure the competitors don't snoop.

But when Lee drilled down into the ground at Namyang, he hit water. It wasn't a marsh, but it wasn't far off. "But this," Lee said, "is where the chairman said 'Build it.'" So Lee did. Over the next several months, thousands of dump trucks carrying dirt drove into the site. They dumped their loads, and bulldozers spread it out and built it up. Eventually, Lee erected a ten-foot-high, multi-acre, flat-topped pyramid. Then he let it settle. After Lee had his building site, he needed security. He knew that Hyundai was clearing trees at another site for a different project. Instead of allowing those trees to go to pulp, Lee ordered some 10,000 of them dug up and replanted around Namyang in what was basically a reforestation project. This is the Hyundai way of doing things.

With its own steel plant, parts suppliers, factories, and distribution system, Hyundai is largely a vertically integrated company, as it is called in business. This is not a new notion. More than one hundred years ago, Henry Ford had this idea. He owned mines in Michigan and Minnesota that sent iron ore to his River Rouge plant in Dearborn, Michigan. There, a mill turned the iron ore into steel that became the chassis, fenders, and parts of the Ford vehicles that rolled off the Rouge assembly line and were shipped to Ford-owned dealers around the country. Ford controlled the entire automaking process, from the ore in the ground to the car lots themselves. Because business trends change as routinely and often nonsensically as fashion, vertical integration became obsolete in late-twentieth-century manufacturing philosophy. It was replaced by outsourcing, with manufacturers buying steel from steelmakers, parts from suppliers, and so on and divesting themselves of any business no longer considered core.

Even though Hyundai does buy some parts from non-Hyundai suppliers, it either has not gone through, or will never go through, the transition to full outsourcing. Neither vertical integration nor outsourcing is the empirically superior method. What's superior is which method works for you. For Hyundai, working in a homogenous society with a top-down command-and-control system, vertical integration is efficient, accountable, and the best way, Hyundai believes, to ensure automobile quality from molten iron to finished product in the showroom. And, as the company chairman, you can get your company and its vertically integrated affiliates to turn on a dime if need be, a luxury not enjoyed by manufacturers dependent upon a sprawling network of outsourced firms, each with their own interest at heart. And, in point of fact, some of the world's biggest companies, such as Apple, place such pressure on their suppliers through sheer market share and tough negotiation that, in essence, they can act like vertically integrated companies. When Steve Jobs decided, only weeks before the release of the first iPhone, to redesign its touch screen, the Chinese manufacturer woke up thousands of workers in the middle of the night, fed them, and put them on assembly lines the moment the first new screens arrived from the U.S.

Indeed, though Korean companies are famous for their 'round-the-clock work hours and employer demands, they do not differ that much from Apple and some other Silicon Valley tech companies. Both Apple and Hyundai have been led by charismatic figures who get the final say. Both companies ask high performance and long hours from their employees. Both create an inward culture where employees stay for a long time and don't routinely mix with peers at rival companies. And both Apple and Hyundai are successful.

From a PR perspective, these journalist visits allowed us to tell a compelling company narrative of carmaking. In a single day, we could start reporters at Hyundai's steel plant, where they would watch huge slabs of glowing orange molten steel being stretched, cooled, and wound into twenty-two-ton coils, each one almost twice as tall as a man and more than a kilometer long when stretched out. Then we'd drive them to a nearby Hyundai assembly line factory, where they'd watch those same steel coils unspooled and fed into great stamping machines of unfathomable pneumatic power. At the other end of the factory, brand-new Sonatas would roll off the line, built with those coils of Hyundai steel and Hyundai parts. No other automaker could put on a show like this. We took plenty of pictures of the visiting journalists to give to them as mementos and to include in the reports to our bosses. In Korea, instead of "cheese," you instruct photo subjects to "say 'kimchi!' "

As exciting as it was to see all this, for the first few months these tours were the toughest part of my job. I was confined with a busload of journalists who asked a lot of questions about Hyundai. And I was expected to have answers and sound confident. I was barely keeping my head above water.

Hyundai Motor Group was a vast conglomerate with 80,000 employees all over the world, two car brands, multiple affiliate companies, a rich and complicated history often foreign to outsiders, multiple factories and models, a brand philosophy that needed explaining and, because it was so young and new to self-promotion, Hyundai was probably the most unknown of all global auto brands. I didn't speak for Kia, but I had to provide a sensible explanation of the difference between Hyundai and Kia. I didn't work for the shipbuilders Hyundai Heavy Industries, but I had to be able to explain the difference between that company and Hyundai Motor. I wasn't born in Korea, but I had to be able to provide a CliffsNotes version of the country's history and Confucianism. These were things baked into the DNA of Hyundai employees and Koreans. But I had to learn them, and fast, cramming my head full of facts whenever I was back at my desk or home on my computer.

It was only my journalism experience that prevented me from looking (too) foolish and embarrassing my new company. Journalists pride themselves on becoming "instant experts" on almost any topic. It's sort of a joke, because we know we're not, but it's also not a joke. Mostly, we are quick studies who can gain a passable knowledge of a new topic pretty quickly and write about it with authority, because that's what we're trained to do. I don't know how many mornings I walked into work at the *Post*, got assigned a story on a topic I'd never even heard of, and, by the end of the day, had produced a *Post*-worthy story.

This is how a lot of journalism gets done.

After having somehow formed an answer to a question from a journalist on one of the bus trips early in my time at Hyundai, he asked, "How long have you worked here?"

Sheepishly, I answered, "Um, two weeks."

"Two weeks!" he repeated. "It sounds like two years!"

And this is how a lot of PR gets done.

These long days with journalists from all over the world allowed me to hone my PR skills in another way: deftly moving on when one of them would say something shockingly racist. It happens more often than you might think. One eye-opening thing about living overseas was the casual, conversation-level bigotry and racism I so frequently encountered. I'd be talking to a journalist from, say, a country in the Middle East, Africa, Eastern Europe, Southeast Asia, or practically anywhere. This may have been an educated man, possibly schooled in England or the U.S. I'd been enjoying the conversation, learning about his country, sharing a few laughs, and then, out of nowhere, he'd drop a caustic anti-Semitic remark. Or a hateful characterization of another tribe that lived in his country. And, for some reason, he just assumed that I agreed. It would have been, strictly speaking, bad PR to have called him a racist jerk or punched him in the nose. So I learned how to move on. I felt bad letting it slide, but realized it was part of my job. Indeed, my exposure to global journalists educated me on numerous cross-border and inter-ethnic hatreds I'd had no idea existed. When I'd mention this to my Korean colleagues later, some would invariably respond: Americans are so hypocritical. You think the same things, but you just don't say them. My response to that was: That may be true, but there is a value in not saying a toxic thing, even if you may believe it. Saying it gives others license to say it, too, perpetuating the evil.

At the end of a day's tour with the journalists, we'd usually go directly to a dinner, always hosted by a senior Hyundai executive. The dinners were often held in the Gangnam district. The sidewalks were full of arm-in-arm salarymen staggering from round two to round three and packs of music fans hoping to catch a glimpse of their K-pop heroes at restaurants and clubs.

Some nights we'd take the foreign journalists to a Western

restaurant to boast of how international Seoul was. Other nights we'd take them to an upscale Korean restaurant, with seemingly limitless courses of food; sometimes we'd sit on chairs, other times on the floor. For VIP journalists, we'd often offer after-dinner entertainment. Typically, this was a trio of Korean musicians dressed in *hanbok*, or the traditional attire. For women, a *hanbok* looks something like a brightly colored silk, empire-waist dress. For men, it is a tunic with billowy sleeves, loose pants or tights, and a broad-brimmed hat. The musicians plucked at ancient Korean string instruments and kept time on a small drum. In a wonderfully intentioned attempt to make foreign visitors feel at home in Korea, these musicians would often break into instrumental versions of Beatles and ABBA songs. Unfortunately, the incongruous mix of culture, instrument, and tune often caused the journalists to laugh and comment on how bizarre Korea was. After a while I recommended that the traditional Korean musicians play traditional tunes, which we explained in programs given to the journalists. The journalists wanted to feel like they were in someplace foreign and authentic, and this worked out better.

Despite its electric feel, Gangnam at night meant, for me, the end of a day that began six a.m. and would not end until I pulled into my driveway nine thirty or ten p.m. This was not terribly helpful to a young marriage. Rebekah, keeping U.S. government hours at the embassy, would be home by five thirty p.m. and would have read, cooked, and bonded with Apple TV, watching *Friday Night Lights* and *Bones*. Several nights a week she lived a life more appropriate to a single professional woman, which is not what she signed up for when she got married. Often she was asleep when I dragged myself in, bleary-eyed, tie askew, smelling of Korean barbecue. Her forbearance was remarkable.

I felt pulled between my home life and my work obligations. There were dinners each night during the week for each group of visiting journalists, which meant I could stay out until ten p.m. three nights a week if I wanted. I had to figure out which dinners were absolutely critical I attend—typically the ones my bosses attended—and which ones my team leader could handle. On the one hand, if I went to all the dinners, it created tension at home. If I begged out on too many dinners, it created tension with my team.

Being out of the office for fifteen-hour days two or three days a week was exhausting. But being in the office for normal eleven- or twelve-hour working days could be exhausting, too, as I tried to learn a new culture and the folkways of Korean business; tried to form alliances with other executives; tried to figure out exactly how to relate to my boss, Mr. Lee, who was kind to me but not very talkative; and—for the first time in my life—tried to really understand how to succeed in a business environment.

It turns out, spending two decades in a newspaper newsroom not only does not prepare you for corporate life—it is probably the worst training for it, this side of a Marxist summer camp.

Newsrooms are horizontal structures full of, essentially, inde-pendent contractors—reporters who usually do their best work alone and not always on the company's schedule. This is even more so in the era of digital journalism, where journalists pack up and take their audiences with them from one publication to the next. Journalists are either born or bred to be at least skeptical of, and frequently openly hostile toward, authority structures of all types: governments, corporations, religions, the armed forces. Historically insulated from the world of commerce by their em-ployer newspapers—which, until recently, enjoyed local monopo-lies on advertising markets—journalists, even business journalists, are traditionally indifferent to or even dismissive of what has been called the "business side" of their newspapers. By their code, they are chasing the truth, revenue be damned. It was considered a badge of honor if you wrote a story so critical of a business that it led to the business withdrawing its advertising from the newspaper. Such a thing would be—should be—grounds for dismissal in a normal business. The atmosphere of the newsroom is informal. My Korean colleagues at Hyundai were incredulous when I told them there were only four levels between me and my boss, the *Post*'s executive editor. And that I called him by his first name. At the *Post*, we e-messaged bits of breaking "Did you see?" information and trivia back and forth among each other all day. In journalism, information is not necessarily judged for its usefulness; just being in the loop with the latest Internet meme or political gossip is currency in itself. At Hyundai, pretty soon after I arrived, I was upbraided by one of my senior team members for interrupting her work with trivial information I'd seen on the Internet—even though it was about the auto industry—that I was distributing to the team. If it didn't pertain directly to the doing of one's job, such information was a distraction.

Corporations—and Korean corporations are similar in structure to most in America and much of the developed world—are vertical structures. They are hierarchical and frequently operate in silos. Everyone works toward goals that are in the best interest of the company. (If I'd said I'd tailored my reporting at the *Post* to be in the best interest of the Washington Post Company—my employer—I would have, and should have, been fired. This is the upside-down world of journalism.) Korea's Confucianism adds a workplace formality to its corporations and can create a powerful motivational force that is absent in America.

If it's not already obvious how unprepared I was to work in a corporation, here is the only detail you need to learn: I didn't know how to use Microsoft Office, a necessary evil for virtually everyone else on the planet. Yet I had never sent or received an e-mail in Outlook, had never made an Excel spreadsheet, had never drafted a PowerPoint presentation. The *Washington Post* newsroom, like most, used a customized content-management system designed to bring text, pictures, and advertising together into a publishable format and used IBM e-mail software. Microsoft Office is used by more than 1 billion people worldwide. It is the beating heart of business. And I had never touched it.

"Okay," I thought. "While I'm scuffling to communicate with other teams using PowerPoint and spreadsheets, at least I know how to use e-mail."

Wrong again!

In the West, we use e-mail for everything, from official documents to relationship break-up notes. In a Confucian society, form matters as much as function, style as much as substance; often more. Thus, e-mail is not thought of as just one more value-neutral delivery system, as it is in the West. Instead, it has been assigned a higher rank: for official communication. Younger Hyundai employees, who have grown up with a more Western view of e-mail's neutrality, are sometimes scolded for using e-mail to send around informal notes to fellow team members.

Not only should an e-mail in Korea contain a greeting and eschew casual language, it is important to e-mail the right person. And that doesn't necessarily mean the person who has the information you need.

If I e-mailed a coworker of lesser rank on another team, there's a good chance they would not e-mail me back, but not out of rudeness. First of all, it was highly uncommon for an executive to e-mail anyone below him but his Team Leader; further, e-mailing from higher rank to lower rank or from team to team can almost be seen as subversive.

Let's say that I, as a director, wanted some information that I knew an assistant manager on another team had. Instead of my e-mailing them directly, it was proper form for me to tell one of the assistant managers on my team—or, better, tell my team leader to tell one of my assistant managers—to contact the assistant manager on the other team to get the information and relay it to me.

A few times, I e-mailed juniors on other teams and they answered, but typically to tell me that my e-mail made them uncomfortable because they were afraid their team leader would ask why they were exchanging e-mails with an executive on another team and would I please stop?

I was eventually able to master Korean e-mail style. I never mastered lunch.

Lunch at Hyundai headquarters is exactly—exactly—from noon to one p.m. Several thousand Hyundai, Kia, and affiliate workers in the two towers rush to the massive cafeteria to form long lines to get trays and pick one of a few choices of Korean food for lunch.

Toward the end of my time at Hyundai, the lunch choice got a little more diversified and a Western counter was added to the cafeteria, where, if you were among the first couple hundred employees in that line, you could get a hamburger and a soda with no ice in a small cup from a fountain. This choice proved so popular that employees packed the hallway outside the cafeteria door nearest the Western stand and shoved, chest to back, like they were trying to board a Tokyo subway to get in at 12:01 when the doors opened and claim their burgers. I once asked a colleague why Hyundai didn't stagger lunch hour to ease the crush: for example, odd-numbered floors could eat from 11:30 to 12:30, even-numbered floors from noon to 1:00. He believed the idea that lunch is at noon is so ingrained in the Korean business brain there was no changing it. To paraphrase Peter Drucker, culture eats strategy for lunch.

Staff-level employees ate in the big cafeteria. The handful of non-Koreans at headquarters—about seven of us—could eat in the "foreigner's café," a small room with a few tables and a limited daily menu of what the Koreans thought Westerners would like to eat. This was a good effort by Human Resources, but imagine an American short-order cook trying to prepare quality Korean food.

I ate with my team the first couple days in the big cafeteria, making a go of trying Korean food. Then they told me I could—probably should—eat in the executive cafeteria. There, we sat at tables with white tablecloths and were served by waitresses. Typically, a senior executive and his top junior executives would all walk to the executive cafeteria right at noon and sit at the same table each day. Per Confucian custom, the waitress would serve the table's senior executive first, then everyone else after. Everyone would be done eating by 12:30 easily, but would wait if the senior executive was not finished. When he finished, he rose, everyone else at the table rose, and they all left.

I ate several times with my boss and his other junior executives, and they certainly tried to be hospitable, but the problem was language. If I was at the table, they felt compelled to speak English, and their English did not lend itself to the long, wandering conversations I was used to at the *Post*. There was a lot of this:

Boss: "I'm going to Brazil."

Me, hopeful that an English conversation was about to commence: "Oh, really? Why?"

Boss (pausing): "To check the situation."

Me (realizing that was the end of the conversation): "I see."

Eventually, everyone at the table would lapse back into Korean and I'd be left out. I didn't blame them. I was the obstacle to conversation at the table and I felt bad about it. To the quite natural question "Why don't you learn Korean?" I would plead the following: I was trying to learn a new job, a new career, a new culture, and a new corporate culture all at once. It was, frankly, overwhelming, and I wasn't doing so well at it. I didn't have the bandwidth to take up a new language as well.

It was just awkward all around, and so I started coming to lunch in the executive dining room by myself at around twelve thirty, after everyone else had eaten and left. I'd catch a quick nap in my office chair—it's completely common and even encouraged to see people sleeping at their desks at lunchtime in Korea, either with their heads down on their desks or leaning back in their chairs—and then head down to the dining room as everyone was walking out. I know this created the impression that I didn't want to eat with Koreans, but I just couldn't bear the awkwardness of those stilted and uncomfortable and frequently silent lunches.

But eating alone did not solve the problem of actual lunch. I'd sit down at the table by myself and try to guess what they would bring me.

Usually it was a tray packed with food, twice the normal amount, that was a surprising mix of Korean and Western food from every meal. So I'd have, say, a bowl of Korean soup with a huge unshelled prawn floating in it, waffles, *kimchi*, noodles, Korean sirloin, French fries, and sometimes—and this was my favorite—a hot dog (no bun) with one end split into four slivers so it blossomed like a lily. The lengths to which the serving staff went to accommodate and please me was stunning and unheard-of in the West.

The problem here was that many of the side-dish staples of the Korean lunch—the pickled foods, the fish jerky, the bean sprouts, the shredded squid with chili pepper, the lotus roots, the cold noodles, the *kimchi*—were not to my liking nor filling. A small cooked fish was also typically offered, served whole, which meant I had to use chopsticks, which I was just learning, to pick out the fish's dozens of sliver-like bones. I ended up with about a fingernail's worth of fish and a fistful of frustration. This meant that the only things I could really eat were the beef and the noodles. So every day my lunch was meat and starch.

My eventual solution was to bring my lunch from home or get in my car and drive ten minutes to the closest Subway or Outback Steakhouse or Tony Roma's, where I could get a turkey sub or a chicken Caesar salad.

The other choice for lunch hour was a workout in Hyundai's well-appointed gym.

I decided to take advantage of the gym on one of my first days at Hyundai. When I walked into the locker room with my gym bag, I got some curious looks: first, because I forgot to take off my shoes and put them in a small locker at the front of the locker room; second, because I was carrying a gym bag. I quickly realized that everyone working out in the gym was wearing the same gray shirt-and-shorts set. Workout clothes, including socks, were provided in the locker room by the company.

But even before I tried on the shorts, I knew it was folly. I was able to pull up the Korean XL shorts to my mid-thighs, where they stopped. The shirt was a second skin. I looked like a bursting bratwurst and could barely move. I peeled out of the company togs before too many people saw me, pulled on my own gym clothes, and worked out. I never really fit Korea. Too big.

After the workout, I walked into the shower room with my towel and found rows of showerheads along two walls with only symbolic dividers between them. There was no privacy. There was a large soaking pool and smaller, floor-level sinks where you could sit and wash. Naked Korean men were everywhere, chatting amiably in the pools, joking while waiting in line for the showers. Not an optimal time to start recognizing coworkers.

For me, anyway. For everyone else, it was as routine as working together in the cubicles upstairs. Same-sex public nudity in Korea and other East Asian countries is simply part of the culture, from the required military service for men to the gyms at work to the mass public spas, called *jjimjilbang*. At one high-end Korean resort Rebekah and I visited in the southern beach city of Busan, Rebekah got into animated conversations in Korean with a succession of hotel employees who marched into the sauna where she was seated, alone, wearing a bikini, shouting: "Suit off!" It didn't matter that there was nobody else in the sauna: the hotel's rule said that everyone using the sauna must be nude, regardless of how they feel about public nudity. She was eventually allowed to keep her suit on because she was a foreigner, but there was initially no recognition by the hotel staff that not everyone feels comfortable with public nudity. For the Korean managers, it was simply a rule, like the rule that said you had to wear a swimming cap in the pool, and because it was a rule it superseded any moral or modesty reasons anyone might have for not wanting to strip down in public.

I would come to learn that showing skin in public was just one more way East and West were opposite. Where Westerners may feel uncomfortable in the all-nude same-sex Korean bathhouses, they would think nothing of wearing a revealing bikini or Speedo on a public beach. Koreans, on the other hand, are so much more modest about revealing themselves to the opposite gender that you'll often see them swimming at the beach in shorts and shirts instead of revealing swimwear.

Many Westerners, like me, find public nudity uncomfortable. It's one thing to briefly drop your towel while stepping in and out of an enclosed shower at a gym where no one knows you, as you may at a gym in the West. Here at Hyundai, I was naked around men I would be working with thirty minutes later as if nothing extraordinary had just happened. As uncomfortable as this made me feel, I came to realize it was all part of the teamwork that Hyundai—and Korea—engendered. Without this sense of bonding, this soldiers-in-a-common-cause environment, Hyundai could not have come so far so quickly, and could not take its next great leap forward.

# 4

## AT HOME: ALTERNATE UNIVERSE

If my work life was 100 percent Korean, the home life that Rebekah and I shared in Korea was, quite bizarrely, about as American as it could be.

That's because we lived on a U.S. military base. Smack in the middle of Seoul.

The U.S. Army Garrison Yongsan is a 620-acre, 17,000-service-member American military base situated on what must be some of the most valuable real estate in all of East Asia. It is located in the southern tip of Gangbuk, north of the Han River. If you look at a Google map of Seoul, you'll see a large, unlabeled, empty gray patch. That's the base. It was built by the Japanese, who occupied the Korean Peninsula from 1910 to 1945, and was taken over by the Yanks after World War II. It is the base of the Combined Forces Command, the joint military forces of the U.S. and the Republic of Korea, the principal deterrent against the sixty-year threat of North Korean invasion.

Unlike almost every other State Department posting overseas, Foreign Service officers assigned to the U.S. embassy in Seoul live on the military base, chiefly because that's where the housing is. In other countries, Foreign Service officers live "on the economy," as they call it, in everything ranging from high-rise luxury apartments in the safest countries to well-fortified compounds in more dangerous places where they lock the high gates at night and post armed guards.

This military base was where Rebekah and I would begin our marriage.

Embassy housing on the Yongsan base consisted of identical one-story homes that came in pairs; two long houses side by side, joined by a common wall to create the effect of one very long house. They have spacious yards—a thing rarely seen in Seoul—and are neatly arranged along the kind of quiet, pleasant, tree-lined streets that once populated the suburban American imagination. They are not fancy but they are big. We had a three-bedroom, two-bath house with a large living room, kitchen, dining room, and den. The house's size elicited gasps from our Korean guests as they entered. It looked every bit like the post–World War II suburbia that visionary developer William Levitt intended when he broke ground for his first suburban tracts on Long Island.

Our general store on-base was the PX. When non-military people hear the term "PX," images from old war movies or *Beetle Bailey* cartoons probably come to mind: long wooden shelves stocked with tins of food, boots, and supplies, all colored Army olive drab, overseen by a gruff quartermaster.

Today's PX, the kind found on Yongsan, is indistinguishable from a small Walmart or Target. Embassy and military personnel are issued ration cards with a fixed dollar amount per month to prevent mass purchases intended for resale on the black market off-base. No one gets inside without a ration card. There, we bought everything from our toiletries to Christmas presents to household supplies to a plasma flat-screen TV to a bowling shirt I still wear today.

On Saturdays, I exercised at the base gym along with American and Korean military personnel. The contrast could not have been more jarring. Over here were the American soldiers, sailors, and marines—black, white, Latino, male, and female—wearing all manner of workout gear, most of it designed to flatter. Thick and ropey muscles were covered in tattoos that depicted mayhem in images and promised worse in blunt language. The great weights they lifted clanged like church bells when they hit the ground. These were the guys I saw carrying bucket-sized packages of nutritional supplements out of the PX. On the other side of the gym were the Korean soldiers: slender, all male, all Korean, all with similar jet-black haircuts. They wore matching workout outfits, gray T-shirts that read ARMY neatly tucked into black shorts. They exercised quietly.

The base also has a commissary, which is military-speak for "giant supermarket." Everything but the most exotic cooking goods is for sale. To further create the home-away-from-home feel for military personnel, the base has a food court with Subway, Burger King, Starbucks, Taco Bell, and so on. TVs hang from the walls of the food court, showing the American Forces Network, which carries major U.S. sports programming. On base there is also a driving range; a movie theater; a dog park; a large hotel called the Dragon Hill Lodge ("Yongsan" means "Dragon Hill"); a football field; a swimming pool; an elementary, middle, and high school; a chapel; and of course housing for officers and soldiers. The military housing ranges from small single-family homes to duplexes to garden apartments. The base feels like a leafy, quiet small town with a couple of stoplight crossroads and traffic moving along at 25 mph. A small town that is surrounded by a twelve-foot concrete wall topped with razor wire. If your head isn't yet fully wrapped around the oddity that is Yongsan, try this: Think of New York's Central Park as a Korean military base full of Koreans.

Leaving the base and entering Korea each morning, then exiting Korea and reentering America each night, felt like moving between alternate mirror-image universes. As I grew into my work life, I became more Korean at the office; as the sole American, it was impossible not to experience some degree of assimilation. My home life, on the other hand, became even more American than it had been back in America. From Fox News and *American Idol* on the TVs at the food court to Katy Perry and Miley Cyrus on American Forces Network radio in my car, I was reintroduced to mainstream, Top 40 culture after decades spent loitering on the alty fringe of entertainment. More to the point, living among U.S. military personnel and the constant reminders of duty, sacrifice, and military threat can't help but boost your patriotism. The Fourth of July on a U.S. military base bears greater significance than it does on the Mall in Washington, D.C. My daily switch from home life in America to work in the heart of Korea reminded me of the *Star Trek* episode where the crew passes into an alternate universe with an identical starship *Enterprise*, an identical Captain Kirk, and so on. Identical, that is, until you realize—wait a minute—Spock has a goatee. At first both worlds look pretty much the same, but the longer you live in each, the more jarring their differences.

To ease each day's shock to my system, I established a comfortable morning routine, as I'm wont to do. I awoke in the dark at 6:00 a.m., kissed my sleeping wife good-bye, and left the house with my bagel, banana, and granola bar. I hit the Burger King drive-through on base when it opened at 6:30 a.m. to get my morning large Diet Coke. Then I drove off base and south toward Hyundai, crossing the Han River on the Jamsu Bridge, the lower level of a two-tier span, which scenically sits about ten feet above the fast-flowing water. Halfway across the bridge, I'd pull over and stop to eat my breakfast, watching the sun rise to my left and the hikers and bikers pass by on my right, and listen to the previous day's podcast of ESPN's *Mike & Mike* show. One thing I quickly found out about myself, and it surely surprised me, is that I can handle massive upheaval in my life—new wife, new job, new country, new whatever—if I can just maintain a couple of small, familiar tethers to my old life.

Being able to start the day with an American-sized beverage—not findable off base in Seoul, a city of 10 million—and some radio sports banter did the trick. At 7:00 a.m., Seoul's English-language radio news came on my car radio. This was my cue to finish breakfast, start the car, and drive the rest of the way to work. I would arrive at my desk, usually by 7:20 a.m. or so, aware that more than half of my colleagues were already at work. My bosses certainly were. The chairman legendarily arrived at 6:30 each morning, which meant his top executives had to be there no later than 6:20 a.m. A senior executive once showed me the morning alarm he had set on his iPhone. It awoke him at 4:20 a.m. each workday to ensure he got to the office before the chairman. So, in this way, I was a slacker.

This routine is not unusual in the business world, East or West, but it was a bucket of cold water in the face of a former journalist. For my entire newspaper career, my day—and the days of practically every journalist who worked at a morning newspaper—started when I'd amble into work at around 10:00 a.m. I'd done a college internship at an evening paper, which meant I had to be at work by 6:00 a.m. I vowed never to endure that again. I even turned down a job at an evening newspaper simply because of the hours. Now, at Hyundai, I was working evening newspaper hours again long after most U.S. evening newspapers had disappeared.

Given that our home life was sealed off from Korea because we lived on a U.S. military base, Rebekah and I wanted to acculturate ourselves as much as possible to our new country. We both loved dogs, so we figured we could learn a little about Korea by getting a Korean dog.

We had done some research and discovered a native Korean dog called a Jindo, which is largely unheard-of outside of Korea. It's almost impossible to export them because they are a protected national treasure. They are raised on Jindo Island, off the southwest coast of the Korean Peninsula. The Jindo—or, in Korean, *jindo gae* (*gae* means "dog")—is a medium-size dog, about thirty pounds, usually white or tan. It has medium-length fur, a curled, furry tail, and a face like a Husky's. It is universally described by Koreans as loyal, like the Japanese Akita, although its personality is closer to that of the grumpy Shiba Inu. Originally bred to be a hunting dog, it is highly athletic and intelligent.

Online, we found a no-kill shelter in a city called Asan, south of Seoul. It was run by Koreans and ex-pat volunteers. On the website was a striking white Jindo called Lily.

Rebekah and I made the ninety-minute drive to Asan in three hours, thanks to typical Korean traffic. The shelter was a ramshackle but well-intentioned collection of cages and fenced-off areas with more than a hundred dogs yapping excitedly.

We found Lily, leashed her, and took her out for a test drive. She interacted nicely with us and seemed so happy to have a walk, pulling—we thought—enthusiastically at her leash. She was bright-eyed and springy, with a pink tongue wagging happily as she trotted about. She had a little scratch on a hindquarter, but it seemed minor. Her backstory was more troubling.

Lily, who was probably less than two years old, had been

found wandering in the countryside and brought to the shelter. We had been told she had escaped from a dog farm, where she was being bred to be sold to a dog restaurant, which are a lot less common in Korea than they used to be but can still be found off the main strips in Seoul. The type of dog typically raised for meat in Korea is a midsize yellowish Spitz-like dog called a *nureongi*. The dog has no formal name: *neurongi* means only "yellow one." But other dogs, including the Jindo, are bred for meat, too. Some believe that Jindo meat has a superior taste. Eating dog meat has been a sore point in the country since the outside world got its first good look into Korea during the 1988 Olympics, the same year Korea became a democracy. Aware that the practice would draw international criticism, the Korean government banned dog restaurants, although the move was widely flouted. Dog meat is typically served in stew and is most popular during the summer, when it is thought to give an extra boost in the wilt of August. It is a practice that survives largely because of a subset of older Koreans who guard it as a cultural practice and resent being told what to do by outsiders. But young Koreans have little interest in dog stew and are forming more family-member relationships to their pet dogs as in the West.

After spending about an hour with Lily at the shelter, we told them we'd take her and paid the $50 adoption fee. "What a great deal," we told ourselves.

On the way back to the base, Lily, in a strange environment, slept curled up in the dark in Rebekah's lap in the backseat of the black Hyundai Grandeur company car I drove. She peed once. Lily, not Rebekah.

When we got home, Lily bolted around the house, sniffing out her new surroundings, adapting pretty quickly. We tucked her into a dog bed in the kitchen, closed the doors, and made a note to check the scratch on her hindquarter when we woke up.

By the next morning, the scratch, thanks to Lily's overnight worrying, had gotten bigger: a bright red wound that looked infected. We took her to the vet on base.

While we were waiting for the vet to arrive, another person showed up with a German shepherd. We had never seen Lily interact with another dog, so we cautiously let her approach the shepherd while both dogs were leashed. I left some slack in Lily's leash.

Lily sensed the slack and struck. She was a white fur lightning bolt that shot straight at the neck of the shepherd, which was a good thirty pounds heavier. The spookiest thing was Lily didn't growl, didn't bark. She just silently attacked.

We were all startled, and a vet tech on the scene reacted quickest, grabbing two handfuls of the back of Lily's neck, pulling her off the shepherd, and subduing her. The other dog was unhurt, and Rebekah and I chalked it up to Lily's unfamiliarity with a new situation and discomfort caused by her wound.

Lily was not violent with us, but she was a chewer. My wife's first Kindle, a pair of prescription sunglasses, and several pairs of shoes, in addition to furniture hems, a wooden door frame, chair legs, and practically anything nonliving fell victim to Lily. Her diligence when it came to destruction was without equal. Were she loosed on the North Koreans today, the peninsula would be united under Seoul's rule tomorrow. I began to think of Lily as a weaponized house pet. But I also soon could not think of our household without her.

Lily rode around with us on base in our Hyundai, sitting or lying happily in the backseat. She became well known to the young Korean women who worked at the drive-through window at the Burger King. To the young ladies who worked there, Lily was beautiful and exotic—a Korean *jindo gae* owned by Americans. And maybe a signal that the *waygookin* were trying to fit into their new country.

So it quickly came to pass that, two months after arriving in Seoul, Rebekah and I spent our first Christmas as a married couple on a U.S. military base in East Asia, 10,000 miles from our friends and family. We found a very good English-speaking, Bible-teaching church near the base that turned out to be the most multicultural place we frequented in Seoul: Americans were joined in worship with Koreans, Indians, Africans of many nations, and representatives of several other nationalities. If you survey Koreans, you'll find about one-quarter identify as Christian, another one-quarter as Buddhist, and the rest as "none." An ancient shamanistic tradition that focuses on luck still runs through the culture, as it does elsewhere in Asia. Many minimize its role in modern Korea, but not a few expectant mothers still consult fortune-tellers to determine "lucky" birth dates for their unborn children and schedule cesareans accordingly. I knew one young Korean man who, following two accidents as a small child, was taken by his father to a fortune-teller who gave the boy a new, "luckier" name.

Rebekah and I sent a photo Christmas card of us and Lily posing in front of the fireplace in our home. You don't have to look very closely to see that my smile has the hint of a struggle to it. It took all my effort to restrain Lily in one position for the one-sixtieth of a second required to take the photo.

We hosted our first Christmas party at our house. We were able to buy a seven-foot live Christmas tree from the Boy Scout troop organized on the base, another nice reminder of home. In typical American style, we invited friends from different spheres of our lives. I invited my Korean team and a fellow Korean executive from Hyundai who had befriended me. Rebekah invited American and Korean embassy staff she worked with. We invited people from our church.

We set out a serve-yourself buffet. Koreans call this a "standing party" to differentiate it from a dinner party. The first sign I knew something was a bit off was when the senior Korean women on my team—professional, accomplished women—prepared a plate of food for the Korean executive in attendance. My team leader got him his drink. I was a little offended by it, especially the American feminist in me. I wanted to say, "You don't have to serve him. This is a party. We're not at work; everyone's the same." But I didn't. Confucianism doesn't take days off. Even if you're not at work, your boss is still deserving of your service and respect.

The second tip-off was that none of my team members brought spouses or dates. As far as they were concerned, this was a work party at an executive's house.

If it weren't obvious by their actions, I came to understand that the Koreans were not comfortable at this kind of a party. Almost no one on my team mixed with any of the other guests.

I turned to a more senior member of my team who, like Eduardo, patiently fielded my relentless and frustrated questions about his culture, and asked him what was going on. "Sir," he said, "we don't go to parties where we don't know everyone."

I told him that an American party is considered a success if strangers meet and strike up friendships or other relationships. He explained that most Koreans make their friends for life in school; Korean colleagues I knew even attended grade-school reunions. Sometimes Koreans made friends early on in their workplace, he said, but not always.

"But how do you make friends as an adult?" I asked him.

"We don't, sir," he said.

This was also Lily's first party. We let her mix with the guests for a little while, but it made some people uncomfortable. So we parked Lily in a bedroom. Which was fine until we heard a scratching sound. We went to the bedroom and found Lily chewing at the door, trying to get out where the people were.

Ike, my KATUSA team member, loved dogs and volunteered to stay in the bedroom with Lily and occupy her while everyone else enjoyed the party.

He stayed with her for more than an hour until Ben, my team leader, determined the team had put in a dutifully long enough appearance, and they all left. I came to understand: the Korean sitting alone in the bedroom with the wild dog had more fun than any other Korean at the party.

# 5

## DETROIT: SHOWTIME

It was a bitingly cold early morning in Detroit in January 2011. The wind drove wispy snow devils across the empty suburban parking lot outside my hotel as the gray sky brightened. I watched the icy show for a bit, silently repeating parts of a speech in my head, and then got back to dressing for the day. On the television in my room, a reporter was speaking from the floor of the Cobo Center, the vast convention hall in downtown Detroit. Already, a flurry of activity had commenced behind and around the reporter as workers finished setting up for the biggest, most important motor show in America.

This was the stage Hyundai chose to launch its transformation from auto industry joke only ten years earlier to premium brand. It would happen today, in a speech by Hyundai's vice chairman, son of the chairman and grandson of Hyundai's founder. In many ways Detroit was the first big step on Hyundai's uphill climb. Success or failure here would be the first signpost in the company's quest to change the way people thought about it. The environment could not have been more unforgiving and the stakes could not have been higher. The dream was that Hyundai's less expensive cars would rival those of Volkswagen and that its most expensive cars would compete against BMW, Audi, and Mercedes-Benz. This was a daredevil stunt and would be hard to pull off—like, say, a caveman discovering fire on a Monday and inventing the wheel on the following Thursday.

But it was no more audacious an achievement than what Hyundai, and Korea, had already pulled off.

After an armistice was signed in 1953, ending the fighting in the Korean War, South Korea was one of the poorest nations on earth. Indeed, until 1974, Stalinist North Korea, propped up by the communist regimes of China and the Soviet Union, was a richer country, impossible as that seems now. Just as bad, South Korea was a political mess as the people starved and the nation languished.

In 1961, Major General Park Chung-hee, director general of army operations, had seen enough and took power in a military coup. He ruled as dictator until he was assassinated by his own head of intelligence in 1979. (It's easy to forget that democracy didn't come to South Korea until 1987.) Chung was the builder of modern Korea and opinion is still deeply divided about him. On the one hand, Korea's prosperity today is largely owing to the policies he put in place. On the other hand, Park was a dictator who rewrote the constitution to declare himself president for life and tortured political opponents. Pretty much all you need to know about the character of Park Chung-hee can be learned from this amazing story: in 1974 he was giving a speech in Seoul when a Japanese-born North Korean sympathizer burst into the hall firing a gun, trying to kill the president. He missed Park but shot Park's wife. After the gunman was subdued and Park's injured wife was carried from the stage, Park resumed his speech. When he finished, he picked up his wife's shoes and purse and left. His wife died the next morning.

It is impossible to overstate the dire condition of South Korea when Park Chung-hee took over the government in 1961. A year earlier the South Korean annual mean income per person was $155, slightly higher than Sierra Leone's and substantially less than Zambia's. More than 11 percent of the entire population of what would become South Korea was killed during the Korean War. Half of all South Korean housing and 80 percent of public buildings and infrastructure had been destroyed, according to U.S. military estimates. The uncontrolled Han River flooded periodically, killing and displacing war survivors; other refugees who returned to Seoul after the armistice to find their houses destroyed joined others to build shantytowns, called "moon villages," on Seoul's mountains. Unclean sanitary conditions led to widespread disease and further deaths. Photos from that time show Seoulites, wearing impossibly large Asian conical hats—the diameter of an umbrella—trying to scratch sustenance from the earth and the Han.

Park Chung-hee realized South Korea had few natural resources; most are in the North. What it had was manpower and an adherence to Confucian ideology. When combined, they provided labor and the required motivational and organizational might. Park had 25 million Koreans dedicated to marching relentlessly and around the clock toward one destination: making South Korea a strong country. Park called them his industrial soldiers. They could make things.

Park decreed that South Korea would grow by manufacture and export. First, by manufacturing things the unskilled labor could master, like textiles. Then bigger and more value-rich items. Shortly after he took over, Park exported coal miners and nurses to labor-starved Germany for work; possibly in return, Park got a regime-sustaining loan from Germany.

South Korean economic and governmental prosperity would go hand in hand. The banks did the government's bidding. As it was explained by a Korean friend, "In the old days, if you wanted to start a fertilizer company, you did not go to the bank to get a loan. You went to the president to make your case. If he decided yes, he would call a bank and order them to loan you money."

This was a climate of enormous opportunity for industrious young men like Chung Ju-yung, who started an auto repair shop in Seoul in 1940, under Japanese colonial occupation. The story goes that Chung would con the Japanese occupiers by telling them they needed new parts for their cars. He'd then take off the old, fully functioning parts, shine them up, put them back on, and charge the Japanese for new parts.

Chung took his earnings from the repair shop and, after liberation from the Japanese, set up the Hyundai Group in 1946, which started life as a construction company, winning government contracts to rebuild Korea in the wake of the war. During the Korean War, Chung was forced to leave Seoul for the southern city of Busan and picked up what work he could from the United Nations forces fighting the North Korean invasion. The war left Seoul and much of the South an impoverished smoking ruin. But that, and generous foreign aid and loans apportioned by South Korea's new government, provided Chung with his opportunity of a lifetime. He rebooted Hyundai (which means "modern" in Korean) and built dams, the country's first major highway, and the world's largest shipyard. He won a contract to build his first ship before he had ever built a ship or indeed a shipyard. He built them both simultaneously and delivered the ship two years early. It was a project of enormous chutzpah and Pharaonic use of human capital and it became the template for the Hyundai that would follow.

Chung and other nation builders—Lee Byung-chull, who started Samsung, and Koo In-hwoi, who launched LG Electronics, originally Lucky-Goldstar—were the Carnegies, Rockefellers, and Vanderbilts of modern Korea. These companies continue to control sectors of Korea's economy in similar proportion to what America's Gilded Age oligarchs did in their day.

The Korean plutocrats built their businesses in the same way: assembling massive "groups" of frequently unrelated companies, always with a goal of getting bigger. This was partly to one-up their nearest rival, but it was also because the government would concentrate its economic incentives and direct low-interest loans at the country's biggest companies in a policy of creating national champions. Focusing on total revenue rather than profit, the *chaebol* piled up debt with easy loans to buy or create company after company. The empire would be passed down from father to son in Confucian fashion.

Chung Ju-yung built the Hyundai Group on ten core values. Number ten is: "Serve our nation and society."

By 1967 the greater Hyundai Group was made up of affiliate companies that built ships, dams and bridges, nuclear plants, and elevators and provided numerous other sundry products and services. That year it added an automaker to the *chaebol*, founding Hyundai Motor Company. For the first seven years of its life, Hyundai Motor built cars for other automakers; for instance, Hyundai Motor assembled the Ford Cortina, which was sold inside and outside Korea.

In 1974, with help from British manufacturing experts, an Italian designer, and a Japanese engine, Hyundai launched Korea's first car of its own, the little Pony hatchback. Over the next thirty years, Hyundai became the dominant carmaker in Korea, owning almost the entire market, thanks to government protectionism. Up until that point, Hyundai showed little interest in building its cars anywhere but Korea.

Flash-forward to the 1997 Asian monetary crisis, which began in Thailand and spread across Asia. It hit Korea hard. The debt-laden *chaebol*—their clustered affiliates dependent on one another for cash flow and saddled with high-interest, short-term foreign loans—fell like dominoes. Twenty percent of the *chaebol* collapsed. One of the Korean businesses felled by the crisis was Kia, at the time an independent automaker. This gave an opportunistic Hyundai the chance to buy Kia out of bankruptcy and instantly capture a near monopoly of the Korean auto market.

During the 1997 crisis, ordinary Koreans tried to help their government out of trouble in ways that seem inconceivable in industrialized nations in the late twentieth century. Thousands gave the government their gold jewelry. To greater effect came a bailout from the International Monetary Fund. The IMF and a liberal Korean government agreed that the *chaebol* were too big, had too much debt, and must be broken up.

By 1999 the Hyundai Group had split into three smaller conglomerates: Hyundai Motor Group, along with its auto-affiliated businesses; Hyundai Heavy, the ship builder; and a smaller Hyundai Group, which got the construction company and other catch-all businesses. Split in one sense, but not all: each of the three smaller *chaebol*, and other family businesses, would go to one of the six surviving sons of Hyundai founder Chung Ju-yung.

Even though they were split, the major *chaebol* came roaring back in their new forms. The impact of the *chaebol* on Korean life and the Korean economy is almost impossible to comprehend for anyone in the West. Korea is a physically small country, with about 50 million people, so the *chaebol* have outsized impact. In 2012, Samsung and Hyundai—Korea's two largest *chaebol*—accounted for 50 percent of all the profits of companies listed on the Korean stock exchange. That was nearly double from only three years earlier. But these companies weren't just big in Korea.

By the turn of the millennium, Samsung's annual profits had topped those of any of the giant Japanese companies, a fact that shocked and galled Japan.

Even though the *chaebol* family owners individually hold comparatively small amounts of stock in their businesses, they are able to retain control of their empires thanks to complex cross-shareholding arrangements linking one company to the others. This structure is unfamiliar and murky to Westerners and is the cause of what is known as the "Korean discount," meaning that the stock of big Korean companies such as Samsung and Hyundai trades for less than its real value because of the opacity. Then there is the Korean side to the story. In the wake of the 1997 IMF crisis, the formerly big conglomerates found their individual companies weak and vulnerable to being picked off, one by one, by foreign takeover firms. Interlocking the *chaebol* created an entity too big and seemingly too complex to be swallowed at once. Think of dozens of small fish swimming closely together to create the impression of a much bigger fish to potential predators.

The *chaebol* have also drawn criticism for a business practice called "tunneling," meaning the awarding of contracts to related conglomerate businesses without a public tender. But many of the *chaebol*, like Hyundai, are vertically integrated enterprises. In a corporate ecosystem like that, tunneling is efficient. And, in fact, in response to public criticism and new laws, tunneling is less prevalent than it used to be.

Hyundai's business will become more and more global in the years to come. When I was still at Hyundai, the company switched to international accounting standards. Much more globalism is anticipated when the third generation takes over the company. And, for the first time, large shareholder groups are no longer marching in lockstep to what the conglomerate chairmen decree. But don't expect the great Asian conglomerates to completely mimic their Western counterparts in terms of corporate governance anytime soon, if ever. The Eastern conglomerates have prospered by following Asian corporate values, adjusting to their historical mean after being force-fed Western business practice after the IMF crisis. Traditionally, Asian corporate giants have not had access to capital markets or been subject to Western-style market regulation, so they have relied on political and family networks in authoritarian political systems—the personal relationship that is at the heart of every Asian business deal. On the one hand, the *Economist* wrote in 2015, this leads to cronyism. On the other, the *Economist* allowed, it enables long-term decision making. Companies are not forced to scramble for quarter-on-quarter earnings as Western public firms must. Regardless of which system is better, East and West have very different concepts of how corporations should be structured. There is more ill will to be gained and less progress to be made when condescendingly trying to force Western values upon Asia, either at the corporate or individual level.

Hyundai founder Chung Ju-yung's plan to pass on his empire to his sons was perfect, except for one problem: Hyundai Motor. It was being run by one of Chung's brothers, and the great man wanted his brother out. At the urging of his father, Chung Mong-koo—the oldest living son, who was heading the car company's main parts supplier—forced his uncle out of a job and took over Hyundai Motor.

Chung Ju-yung died in 2001 after a colorful life that saw an unsuccessful presidential bid, the creation of a joint economic zone just across the border in North Korea, company picnics where he wrestled his employees, and a lasting legacy as one of the men who literally built modern Korea in concrete and steel.

Now, Chung Mong-koo was in charge of the biggest of his father's companies. It was his turn.

Let us return to the corporate metaphor of the twin Hyundai headquarters towers. If you were to complete the metaphor accurately, you would build a bridge at the top, linking the Hyundai and Kia towers, and put a seat at the apex. On that seat would sit one man and one man only: the chairman.

Hyundai Motor Group chairman Chung Mong-koo was born in 1938. He speaks very little English. In the entire time I worked at Hyundai, I spoke to him only once. It took place when a number of executives were lined up in the lobby of Hyundai headquarters waiting to meet some arriving VIP journalists. The chairman, deciding to greet them as well, emerged from an elevator I didn't even know existed, spotted me, walked straight toward me with his hand out, smiled, and said, "Staff!" Yes, sir, Mr. Chairman. That's right. I'm on your staff. I should have said, *"Annyeong hashimnikka,"* the formal greeting, but I choked and blew it.

Short and stocky, the chairman is old-school Korea, direct and authoritarian but with a ready smile that conveys charisma. Chung Mong-koo was not the most polished of Chung Ju-yung's boys—indeed, in younger days he was known as "the farmer" for his rough mannerisms. Like many Korean business leaders, he's been called a "bulldozer" and a "tank."

But Chung Mong-koo was smart enough to realize Hyundai's desire for international growth was being doomed by its poor quality. He is the man who is responsible for Hyundai's high-quality reputation today. Chung is responsible for building most of Hyundai's factories outside of Korea so the company would not be brought to its knees each year by the country's annually striking militant labor unions. Chung is responsible for investing in new product development during the 2008 global financial crisis, giving Hyundai a jump-start on its competitors when the crisis began to lift. In short, Chung Mong-koo is responsible for taking the car company that his father established as just one more company in the family conglomerate and turning it into a world-class automaker.

Chairman Chung commands authority. He once visited a motor show I was working, sending everyone into high-panic preparations. After his inspection of our booth, the chairman decided to stroll the convention center floor to check out the competition. Unlike other car company CEOs who do this and take a couple top aides with them, our chairman was followed by his top executives, which meant—per Confucian custom—that they had to be accompanied by *their* top executives, and so on and so on, down the hierarchy. I climbed to the second floor of our booth to watch this play out: there was the chairman making his way through a parting motor show crowd, at least twenty dark-suited men following, some taking notes. The effect was that of a long, black eel snaking its way through a crowd of startled media and competitors. PR-wise this was bad optics: it looked imperial. But there was nothing I could do about it.

One day—no one but the Chung family knows, and they aren't telling—Chung Mong-koo will pass down Hyundai Motor Group to his only son, Vice Chairman Chung Eui-sun, who will become head of the world's fifth-largest automaker and an $85 billion company. Chung Eui-sun already is a billionaire, as is his father. But that's where most of the obvious similarities between the two ends.

Chung Eui-sun, born in 1970, has the task of taking Hyundai to a higher goal, something even harder than improving its vehicle quality: improving its brand to an extent that consumers will start to think of Hyundai like Audi. Chung did his undergraduate work at the prestigious Korea University in Seoul but then got his master's in business management administration at the University of San Francisco. He then worked for five years in New

York and San Francisco before returning home. I'm sure there was never any question that he would take up the family business. As the only male heir to the Hyundai automotive empire, Chung Eui-sun had no choice, from the time he was a boy, to be chairman. He has two daughters and, luckily, like his father, only one son, so there will be no question who continues the Hyundai Motor Group dynasty.

Unlike his father, Chung Eui-sun speaks nearly fluent English with a light Korean accent. He has an easygoing, ingenuous manner, not at all imperious in the fashion of other Korean corporate heads. He is confident and comfortable enough in his own skin that, when asked a question he doesn't know, will turn to a nearby colleague for help. In addition to social gatherings with his top executives, he puts on good-natured nights out for the rank-and-file Hyundai employees, renting a theater for a movie showing, dinner, and *noraebang*, inviting not only his top executives in a particular division but also representative employees who are only in their early years at the company. He is more physically fit than his father, has a good sense of humor, enjoys watching Britain's *Top Gear* motoring show, and has a much more restrained style at the Korean drinking dinner. He has, naturally, his own go-to *noraebang* songs. There was one detail about the vice chairman I found especially telling and promising. Like most other high-level Hyundai executives, he rode in a top-of-the-line Hyundai Equus luxury sedan. But unlike the others, which are black, the vice chairman's was dark blue. In a society such as Korea's, this is a radical, even revolutionary color choice. It suggests to me that Chung Eui-sun, even within a highly ordered culture and corporate structure, is and will be his own man. And may even have a little streak of rebelliousness in him.

As a businessman, Chung Eui-sun rose through the company

ranks working in several jobs at Kia as well as Hyundai, learning the business from the ground up. So far his signature on the two marques has been in their design and branding. Understanding that the great auto brands also are among the most beautiful and distinctively designed, with a family look—think BMW, Audi, Porsche—it was Chung Eui-sun who lured Audi's Peter Schreyer to Kia. Schreyer redesigned the Kia line, giving it a distinctive grille, known as the "tiger nose." Chung took the extraordinary step of promoting the non-Korean Schreyer to a president's position in 2013, overseeing both Kia and Hyundai design. Now vice chairman of Hyundai Motor, Chung Eui-sun is in charge of the automaker's daily operations.

When he interviewed me for the job in July 2010 in his office in Seoul, Vice Chairman Chung referenced the Twitter feed for financial news I ran at the *Washington Post* and asked me how I'd built my audience. He then went on to note other major corporations that had not handled their digital communications optimally during various crises and asked my opinion about that. It was clear to me from the interview that the vice chairman was aware of which way the media was heading and the need for Hyundai's global PR team to digitally engage with journalists.

At this point you have just read a longer profile of Chung Eui-sun than has appeared anywhere, at any time ever, in English, at least on my watch. As a Hyundai PR man, this was one of my greatest frustrations. Here I had a perfectly media-genic top executive, the heir to the company, who would be approachable and engaging with the world motoring and business press—and I could not use him. In Korean corporate culture, the spotlight should fall on the product principally, and if it falls on any one person, it should be the chairman. It's okay for lower-ranking executives to give media interviews about their business operations—say, the head of international sales or a power-train engineer. But only one person speaks for the company, and that's the chairman. And my chairman did not speak English. And, per custom and culture, his son, who did speak English, could not do interviews. There is a famous (in Korea) photo of Hyundai founder Chung Ju-yung walking to work one morning in the 1970s trailed by all of his sons. In a Confucian culture, children, juniors, and lessers literally walk in the footsteps of their parents, seniors, and superiors.

My inability to market my vice chairman to the media was correctly diagnosed by an auto reporter at a global business paper, who told me: "Every other automaker has one top guy who can tell the brand's story—Alan Mulally at Ford, Carlos Ghosn at Nissan, Sergio Marchionne at Fiat. Hyundai is the only one that doesn't." When I conveyed this observation to a colleague, he was dismissive. "They are salaryman CEOs," he said. "Chairman is owner." And that was that.

I liked Vice Chairman Chung and his inquisitive, unassuming manner. Unlike every Korean who worked for him, I was at ease around the vice chairman—probably because I didn't have the cultural burden of being deferential. I was looking forward to working closely with him and found that opportunity when it was decided by top management that Vice Chairman Chung would step briefly into the spotlight and deliver the corporate speech to the 2011 Detroit Auto Show, announcing Hyundai's bold plan to elevate its brand to stand alongside the world's greatest cars.

It was a heavily symbolic moment utterly lost on all the Americans in the audience but freighted with meaning for the Koreans. Here was the Hyundai heir who would one day lead the company. At the Detroit Auto Show, he was going to take that first step by announcing the company's new brand direction.

I got a rough draft of the vice chairman's speech about a week before the show, written by the marketing division, whose job it was to launch the new branding campaign. It was my job to hone its message and craft it into clear English that would be easily understandable to native speakers and at the same time be easily pronounceable by a nonnative speaker working off a TelePrompTer. In addition, it should be interesting, compelling and, hopefully, quote-worthy to the media members in attendance.

Most speeches given by executives at motor shows tend to focus on whatever new car is being introduced. Sometimes sales figures or company performance will be mentioned: solid facts and figures, along with some superlatives thrown in. With this speech we had to do something much harder: we had to roll out an idea. We had to debut a new slogan and the "brand concept" behind it.

After working on the speech for a couple days, instead of passing all my edits back up the chain of command, I e-mailed the vice chairman directly, unknowingly violating cultural policy and knocking a bunch of noses out of joint. During my interview in July, the vice chairman told me I could contact him directly, so I took him at his word. He responded immediately and we worked on the speech.

Once I was finished, I took what seemed to me the very natural step of telling him I'd like him to read it out loud and identify any words or phrases that he was uncomfortable with. I also told him I'd like to hear him give the speech to me. He agreed. As his head of global public relations, it was my job to protect my vice chairman and make him look as good as possible.

During our rehearsal in his office at Hyundai headquarters, the vice chairman sat behind his desk and read the speech aloud a couple of times. Then he asked me to read it so I could show him where pauses and stresses should fall. He said he felt comfortable with it.

When I told my colleagues that I'd asked the vice chairman to rehearse, they could not believe it. It was like I'd asked Confucius himself to drop and give me twenty push-ups.

When my counterparts at Hyundai Motor America found out that I had gotten the vice chairman to agree to a rehearsal, they praised me for a great breakthrough, an achievement that would make all the PR departments look good. Unfortunately, it turned out to be the last time I worked with the vice chairman one-on-one with a speech. Although the vice chairman appreciated my willingness to contact him directly, my naïve action was not appreciated by a number of people because I had broken the chain of command.

I came to understand, as I came to understand corporate life in general, that it wasn't so much a turf issue as it was a looping-in issue. Put simply, the vice chairman and I had approved changes to the speech that the marketing department and my boss didn't know about. Afterward, I followed the chain of command when writing speeches for the vice chairman. This is the nature of all big companies. I know it makes things run smoother and everyone gets in the loop and everyone's turf is protected, but I can't help but feel like something straightforward and even intimate is lost.

## LIGHTS UP

The media days of a big motor show are held immediately before the show opens to the public. Every automaker invites automotive journalists to the booth where the company's cars are debuted, although calling it a "booth" is a big understatement. Today's auto show booths are multimedia performance stages with sound and light shows, live entertainment, two-story digital screens, concert-loud speaker systems, giveaway swag, and—oh, yeah—cars.

Each automaker has a set press conference time, usually fifteen to twenty minutes, and they are stacked back-to-back, usually at adjacent booths, so the media can travel from booth to booth and see every press conference. Usually, each automaker's press conference consists of a couple of short speeches, some video, an entertainment element, and the new product reveal.

The day before an automaker's press conference is rehearsal, often a twenty-hour day inside the gaping convention halls that host auto shows. Automakers are practicing at show volume all at the same time. Videos on massive screens and walls play while up-tempo music blares from all sides and mashes together into a cacophony. Every automaker likes to add an element of show-manship to their debut, so last-minute details—bands, singers, dancers, dancing sheets, choreographed car ballets, you name it—are rehearsed and fine-tuned. Some elements are scrapped al-together and new things are cobbled together at the last minute. All of this is occurring as every other automaker at every other booth, dozens within eyesight and earshot, are doing the same— some secreted behind huge curtains—and as workers are assem-bling booths and the hall itself at the last minute, with rolling cranes and forklifts and duct tape everywhere. It is a maelstrom of light, noise, and action, the smell of rubber and leather, and a real adrenaline rush. It's showbiz.

The auto industry's yearly calendar is driven by the world's major motor shows. Each year kicks off with Detroit in Janu-ary, followed by Geneva in March, alternating between Beijing and Shanghai in April, New York in May, alternating again be-tween Paris and Frankfurt in September, and then closing with Los Angeles in late November. Each of the shows takes on and proudly displays its national identity. Almost each one is, and is designed to be, a powerful home-court advantage for the native automakers. Detroit is about the Big Three. Frankfurt: VW and the German luxe brands. Paris: Renault and Peugeot. This is one reason why many auto journalists and industry folks like the Geneva show best of all. Like its home nation, the Geneva show is neutral. Switzerland has no national automakers, so no one gets a home-court advantage. Every automaker more or less has the same square footage and the same chance to attract attention. And because Geneva is on the border with France, the entrecôte is delicious. The motor shows in Beijing and Shanghai, like China, are brassier than any others in the world. A writer once remarked about China: It often mistakes gigantism for greatness. As standard practice, every automaker at every motor show surrounds its new cars with attractive female models. (The São Paulo show is the winner in this category.) At the Beijing show one year, one Chinese automaker surrounded one of its new cars with *ten* scantily clad dancing female models. And a mime. Because that wasn't enough, they were all painted gold from head to toe. At another Chinese show, we had to cut short a media interview with one of our executives, because even when shouting he couldn't make himself heard over the pounding music at the Chinese automaker's booth next to ours, cranked up to distortion levels.

Detroit is probably the world's second-largest motor show, in the ways these things are measured, after Frankfurt. At the Hyundai booth the day before the Detroit show in January 2011, John Krafcik, who helmed Hyundai's U.S. subsidiary from 2008 through 2013 and doubled Hyundai's U.S. market share, rehearsed repeatedly. Krafcik, a former MIT and Ford star, has a boyish look and enthusiasm despite his white hair. He is an expert communicator and became a favorite of the U.S. motoring media, elevating Hyundai's brand status to new heights and, most important, giving a face to an often faceless company, at least outside of Korea. Krafcik is an expert communicator because he works at it. At the rehearsal for the Detroit show, where he would speak after Vice Chairman Chung, Krafcik went through his speech several times. The vice chairman did not. He was too busy, I was told. He felt he would be ready. I said okay and crossed my fingers.

The next day arrived and it was Hyundai's turn for its press conference. In my head I had been repeating the key takeaways of the vice chairman's speech since I got up that morning and opened my hotel room curtains to the wintry suburban tableau outside my window. Was there any fine-tuning I could do? Were there any words the vice chairman would stumble over? If his speech was a flop, Hyundai's new vision for its brand would suffer a false start and be lost in the din of our competitors' press conferences, most of which would be given by their executives: big, enthusiastic, native-English-speaking CEOs. Maybe our soft-spoken Korean wouldn't stand a chance.

To add some dazzle to the vice chairman's presentation, Hyundai was debuting a fun new sports coupe called Veloster, a funky thing with one door on the driver's side and two on the passenger's side. This was a wholly unexpected kind of car from Hyundai, which was known as the sensible-shoes carmaker. Veloster would be one of the product vanguards of Hyundai's brand elevation.

Moments before the Hyundai press conference started, as more than three hundred media people packed the booth, the vice chairman walked in, his wireless mike already in place, and sat down in the first chair in the front row. I stood in the back, watched, and silently rooted for him.

The show opened with lights and sound, a get-amped feel. When the vice chairman was introduced, he walked to his mark on the stage and began with some welcoming pleasantries. Then he hit the red meat of the speech.

"Today, customers do not believe that expensive cars with unnecessary technology are premium," he said. "Instead, they want their core needs fulfilled at an accessible price and with a car that exceeds their expectations; a car that reflects their values and the times in which they live."

If journalists asked me later to elaborate on this idea, I found an easy visual answer: I held up an iPhone. The iPhone, I said, works out of the box, is beautiful, is intuitive, and doesn't confuse a user with too many gadgets and gimmicks. Bonus: it makes you feel cool to use it. That's what we wanted Hyundai cars to be. In the past, automakers just kept larding shiny trim and sometimes goofy features on cars in the hopes of making them "premium." Consumers have seen through this. They want what they want, they want it to work, and that's it. Simplicity, elegance, functionality. That's what the vice chairman was talking about in his speech.

"They want a new kind of premium," Vice Chairman Chung continued. "We call it 'Modern Premium.'" There. He had introduced the brand philosophy that would guide the company forward.

Then he threw the media a curve: "Our goal is not to become the biggest car company," he said. This was surprising, even shocking, especially given what Korea had just spent the past fifty years doing. Everyone just assumed that Hyundai's goal was to be the next Toyota—to keep pumping out solid, high-quality affordable cars until it hit number one in global sales.

Instead the vice chairman said, "Our goal is to become the most-loved car company and a trusted lifetime partner of our owners."

This was the key thought and the engine that Hyundai needed to propel its brand higher in value. In a larger sense, it was indicative of the upshift Korea as a whole was beginning to recognize it must make in order to begin the next chapter of its growth: to change the focus from quantity to quality.

A company emphasizing "brand" may sound like PR flim-flam, but I can assure you it is not. It is as valuable to a company as any tangible asset. Entire sprawling consultancies are built on forensically analyzing companies' financials, products, physical assets, management, distribution, marketing, and a dozen other factors and assigning an overall dollar value to the brand. When you read that Toyota's brand is worth $30 billion, that's not just a figure some guy pulled out of the sky. A team of MBAs from a company like Millward Brown spent weeks poring over Toyota's quarterlies and annual reports, examining the company's debt, assessing its position in the marketplace, watching workflow, interviewing executives, and so on.

That's because brand makes sales. People don't buy Apple products just because they look cool. They buy them because they love the brand. It's the same reason a rich guy doesn't say, "Look at my new watch." Instead, it's "Check out my new Rolex." Customers develop an affinity for a brand, and it keeps them buying within the brand. If you don't believe this, see if you don't notice a few Apple logos stuck to car windows like sports team emblems the next time you take a drive. When was the last time you saw a Team Microsoft window sticker?

Most consumers probably thought of Hyundai cars like washing machines: a necessary purchase based on price, not brand name. If Hyundai was going to take its brand upmarket, it had to change that. The Hyundai brand must begin to mean more to consumers than just reliable, cheap cars. Hyundai must have a character trait. Ours would be trying to get people to form an emotional attachment to the Hyundai brand—literally, to fall in love with us.

General Motors, in its heyday in the 1960s, when it had a

staggering half of the U.S. auto market, did a brilliant job of this, driven by Alfred P. Sloan's famous phrase "A car for every purse and purpose." GM customers would be cultivated as young men by Chevrolet, the cheapest and sportiest of GM cars. As the men aged and grew in wealth and status, they stayed within the GM family of cars, trading up for more and more prestigious brands. The Chevy owner traded up for a Pontiac, then a Buick, then an Oldsmobile, and finally, when he had "made it," a Cadillac. For other kinds of buyers, GM's marketing was genius at creating brand loyalty. My father, for instance, topped out as an Oldsmobile man. From the 1960s until GM killed the brand in 2004, my dad would buy only white four-door Oldsmobile Delta 88s, the brand's large family sedan. During his prime years as a traveling salesman, he traded them in every two years. There was no telling him that his Delta 88 was the same under the skin as the same-size Buick and Pontiac. He was an Olds man and nothing would change that.

Here's how I came to explain the concept of buying a brand to journalists who visited Hyundai: Let's say you're in the market for a midsize family car. Normally you'd compare car to car, putting a Toyota Camry alongside a Hyundai Sonata alongside a Ford Fusion and choose based on whatever your criteria are. I told the journalists, if we do our job right, you'll say: "I need a new car. Let me first look at Hyundai and see what cars they have that might fit my need." You go to the Hyundai brand first and see if we have a suitable midsize family car. If we do, great. If we don't, okay, fine. You exit the brand and look elsewhere. But we got you to shop the Hyundai *brand* first before looking at our competitors. *That's* what it means to improve a brand value.

The vice chairman finished his speech without a hiccup. He got big applause and the lineup of colorful Velosters on stage behind him graced the next day's *Wall Street Journal*. Maybe he really was a one-take guy. I was so proud of him. I'd never attempt a speech in Korean. I walked up to him, smiled, clapped him on the back, and said, "Great job!" The corner of my eye caught one of my senior team members wincing as I did this. Do. Not. Touch. Vice. Chairman! But I didn't care.

The company had put its vision out there: it was clear how high we were aiming. The motoring media took our message—delivered on the Big Three's home court—mulled it over, and opined. Some thought we could pull it off. Others were skeptical that we could do it, but even they respected our brass for trying. And no one laughed at the idea that Hyundai could be something more than it was. As the first step in Hyundai's attempt to raise its image, Detroit had to be considered a success.

On the plane ride back to Korea, I bumped into Vice Chairman Chung waiting for the bathroom and he told me that he was very comfortable saying the speech as I'd edited it. I went back to my seat happy to have weathered my first big test. And happy to be heading, as odd as it still sounded in my head, home to Korea.

# 6

## THE KOREAN CODES

A few months before I left Hyundai and Korea, I was dining with my team. One of my junior female team members, whose English was quite good and who had lived for a short while in the States, was sitting to my left, next to the napkins. I asked her to pass me one.

She did and then asked me, "Did you ask me to hand you the napkins because in your culture it's considered rude to reach in front of someone while they're eating?"

"Yes," I said, "that's right."

"In our culture, it's considered rude to interrupt someone while they're eating to ask them to hand you something," she replied. *That* was why Koreans had been jabbing their hands in front of me at meals for the previous three years, I realized.

But there it was, finally explained to me so clearly that even I could understand: each culture—Korean and American, Eastern and Western—had been behaving in a way it believed to be polite, only to actually be behaving in the rudest way possible to the other culture. It was a small example of what I came to realize was the larger truth: Korean and American, East and West, have entirely different ways of looking at and understanding the meaning of the same thing. And although each side probably believes its intent is clear to the other side, oftentimes it could not be more opaque.

I came to explain it this way: if you set a glass on a table in between an American and a Korean, they will both see a glass. But it will mean very different things to each of them. To the American, the glass will mean "thing that will soon provide me with a refreshing beverage." To the Korean, the glass will mean "thing that I must fill and serve to my seniors to show my respect for them."

This concept, thought of in another way, is not unfamiliar to us in our highly politicized America. Republicans and Democrats will look at, say, the same social problem yet have two totally different interpretations of how it came to be and how to solve it.

If the Napkin Episode, as I came to call it, had happened a few months after I'd arrived in Korea, my three-plus years there might have gone more smoothly for me and for everyone around me.

It's not just that Americans and Koreans speak different languages. The language is only the mechanical representation of the divide and is in fact the easiest chasm to bridge. I had always considered myself a superior communicator. I had made my living at a high level doing just that for two decades, making complicated stories clear and easy to understand for a general readership.

But in the East, my record was mixed. To the English-speaking foreign journalists who visited Korea, I was still a good communicator. They often found me a welcome relief from my colleagues, whose Korean-accented English the foreign journalists—who were not native English speakers, either—sometimes found diffi-cult to understand.

But to my Korean colleagues I was a poor communicator, at least for a large part of my stay there. Part of the problem was my quirks. I sometimes use double negatives. I'm sorry, but I can't not do it. For a native English speaker, this was not a problem. For others, it was a source of pure confusion. The bigger problem was that I didn't think through how to respond when I didn't understand something I was being told. "So, wait," I'd respond in exasperation. "Are you telling me it can't be done?"

"No, sir."

"No, it can't be done, or no, it can be done?"

"Yes, sir."

I was putting my poor colleagues through an Abbott and Costello routine, and no one was laughing.

I still remember how puzzled I was the first time one of my team members referred to my "American accent." "What accent?" I said. "We don't have accents. Brits have accents. Australians have accents. Even Canadians. We don't." To me, the British accent is a deviation from the norm—accent-free American English. But to a Korean, and to most of the world's population, American English is just another kind of English accent.

This realization shocked me more than it would have had my ignorance been only linguistic. But embedded in my response, although I didn't realize it at the time, was my belief that America is the industry standard for the world. Not just for English but in everything: politics, power, sports, entertainment, finance, you name it. It's America's world and everyone else is just playing in it. It didn't take long living on the far side of the world to disabuse me of this notion. Yes, America was still by far the world's rich-est and most militarily powerful country, and American movies got big audiences in Seoul. But over here, Beijing and Tokyo had much more impact on Koreans' daily lives than Washington. No one followed the NFL. Whole epochs of American and Western history were unknown. In the wake of the Great Recession, there was a general feeling that the West was in decline and that the twenty-first century would belong to Asia, not America.

I was feeling more than befuddlement over the way I sounded. This was a symptom of a much deeper dislocation I was feeling and confusion over the way I thought about America's place in the world.

It turned out that the biggest reason for my poor communication wasn't my American accent or lack of Korean fluency. It was my inability to understand the basic codes of Korea: Confucianism and Koreanness.

If you're going to live in Korea, it is important and simply good manners to at least try to learn these codes, or understand that they exist, even if you don't learn to speak Korean. If you're going to do business in Korea or with Koreans, it is vital.

Confucianism, named for sixth century B.C. Chinese philosopher Confucius, is a quasi-religion but mostly it is a way of ordering society via a hierarchy based on age, wealth, social status, birth, gender, and other factors. An example of this is filial piety, the devotion to parents and elders, usually meaning obedience well into a child's young adult years. Today's Confucianism is known as neo-Confucianism, a form that has purged the mystical elements of Taoism and Buddhism that crept into the original doctrine during the Chinese Han dynasty in the first two centuries of the first millennium A.D.

I knew a Korean woman who went to graduate school in the U.S. who was required by her parents back in Seoul to have a video conversation with them every night at the same time—and she obeyed. Even modern Korean women will rarely go against their parents' wishes, especially their fathers' wishes, when it comes to spouse selection.

Confucianism does not limit filial piety to strictly family relations. Expanded to a concept of "respect for the elder/senior," it suffuses Korean society everywhere: from the workplace, where junior employees often see their bosses as fathers and vice versa, to business contracts, which are rarely equal. This is the *gap-eul* relationship of Confucianism, or "higher to lower." In every relationship, one person is superior and the other is inferior, either in age, rank, income, status, whatever. In geopolitical terms, this goes back to ancient times when China was the *gap*, or the superior, to which Korea, the *eul*, or the inferior, paid tribute to the Chinese royal court. It carries forth even to modern Korean contracts, where companies are *gap* and employees are *eul*. So you always know where you stand. It is one reason why a Korean might ask your age shortly after meeting you. They are not being rude, although they may seem to be by Western standards. Instead, they are trying to determine your age relative to theirs and thus your hierarchical relationship to them—partly, at least, to know how to address you. The Korean language, like Japanese, has multiple levels of speech, which range from highly honorific to intimate, depending on whom you are addressing. These manifest in verb endings. One verb ending is used in conversations between male coworkers, another between female coworkers, another when older people speak to younger people, another when a shopkeeper is speaking to customers, and so on. That's why it's said the Korean alphabet is easy to learn but the language is difficult.

Anyone who has ever flown on one of the great Asian airlines or stayed at a big hotel in Seoul or Tokyo has been the beneficiary of the Confucian *gap-eul* relationship. The consumer, especially the business- or first-class one, is the *gap* and the service providers are the *eul*. This explains the constant bowing and smiling, the graceful and measured gesturing reminiscent of a spokesmodel and the ever-attendant service so complete that Westerners unfamiliar with it can mistake it for obsequiousness.

Relationships are so important in Korea that they can overshadow personal identity. For instance, it's much more common to hear women refer affectionately to each other as *eonni*, Korean for older and younger sister, rather than use each other's names. A younger brother would usually call his older brother *hyung* in public rather than use his name, which would be considered a challenge to his authority. Girls who want to flirt with a boy will call him *oppa*, or "older brother to a girl." One adult Korean-American woman swore she didn't even know the names of her aunts and uncles because she only called them by their family titles. In the West, our names are our identities. In the East, identities are inextricably tied to our relationships to others.

Koreanness is the result, at least partly, of the application of Confucianism to the Korean people and how they have conformed to it. It is also the result of a highly competitive and homogeneous culture, where the pressure to fit into the crowd—a crowd that is always striving to be smarter, better-looking, more prestigious, and richer—is enormous.

A present and constant confluence of Confucianism and Koreanness, and one that was causing me the most friction at work in the months after I arrived in Korea, was the custom of *hoesik* (pronounced "hway-shik"), or "staff dinner." It turned out that the welcome saturnalia my team threw for us at the end of my first week at the company was not just for special occasions. It was simply the way business dinners went in Korea.

Westerners get just as drunk as Asians. But I soon learned there was a purpose to the Asian drunkenness—or, as they like to call it, the "drinking culture." It was supposed to lead to closer teamwork back at the office, better productivity, and the creation of real affection between colleagues. The biggest struggle Westerners tend to find with this practice is not just the excessive drinking but the shattering of the boundary between professional and personal lives. In Korea, at *hoesik*, you bond with one another over delicious beef sizzling on a hot-coal grill at your table, emptying one green bottle of *soju* after the next, repeatedly toasting each other, ribbing and laughing with each other, and then following it up with karaoke, of course. The next morning at work, everyone commiserates in the smoking room at work with the same hangover. As it was explained to me by a fellow Hyundai executive: "Everybody same level of drunk, everybody same." If you didn't get drunk, or refused to drink, you made everyone else uncomfortable, disrupted the harmony, and puffed yourself up in their eyes. *Hoesik* is driven by the relentless Korean competitiveness. One drinker may ask another, "How many bottles of *soju* do you drink?" The other may reply, "Four!" And the first will shoot back, "Per hour?"

At *hoesik*, the woes of the salaryman's life spill forth from Hyundai executives: starting early, staying late, tough boss, working all your life for one company, being reassigned to foreign countries at a moment's notice, feeling like a number, being yelled at, striving to make money to pay for after-school tutoring and the best universities for your children. Maybe it sounded miserable, but it was a shared misery, and everyone at these dinners had the same points of reference, the same shared culture and experience, the same dreams and disappointments, and within those grew a love for each other. On a larger scale, the drinking culture has created a strong nationalistic bond among Koreans of multiple generations and is partly to credit for the pull-together spirit that lifted the country out of poverty.

I came to see the value of the *hoesik* and the drinking culture within Hyundai and Korea despite the clear health risks to self and society. And, to be fair, today's *hoesik* is trending milder and less frequent compared to those of years past. A little.

But even though I eventually understood why the Koreans drink like they do, I needed to find a way around it in order to save my liver, my marriage, and my faith.

When our global PR team entertained journalists from Muslim countries, my team members and Hyundai executives, who have done business in Muslim countries since almost the beginning of Hyundai, knew better than to serve alcohol at dinners. We didn't want to put the journalists in the awkward position of having to refuse our liquor, which would have meant refusing our hospitality, which is as grave an error in Muslim and Arab cultures as it is in Korea. So unless a Muslim journalist was from a more Westernized Arab nation—say, the United Arab Emirates—and asked for *soju*, alcohol was off-limits. It was easy for the Koreans to understand that alcohol was against the Muslim religion. That was the rule, and you followed it.

It was more difficult for them to grasp the idea that drunkenness is discouraged in Christianity, even though drinking alcohol is not. In the Korean drinking culture, drinking equals getting drunk. Why else would one drink? My stance was especially confusing because so many Koreans, and many of my colleagues at Hyundai, went to Christian churches.

Basically, the early conversations with my Hyundai colleagues went like this:

Me: "I don't want to get drunk."

Korean colleague: "For health?"

I could have said yes, or made up a reason, but that would have been a lie and it would have denied my faith. I could have told them about genetic predispositions and my alcoholic father, who drank two six-packs a night for decades, turning him into a mean drunk. Or not. I actually had a more relevant answer, although it proved less understandable.

Me: "Well, health, sure, but mostly because the Bible teaches me not to."

This answer provoked a variety of responses, from sympathy to puzzlement to accusation. For those who were offended, not only was I disrupting the group harmony by not getting drunk, but I was also acting holier-than-thou and, worse, telling them, if they also went to church, that they were poor Christians.

If my Hyundai coworkers were curious about the biblical instruction on drunkenness, I was happy to share it: Romans 13:13; Ephesians 5:18. Otherwise, I just tried to defuse the situation. There would have been no problem if I objected to eating dog or to one of the other peripheral Korean activities. But to object to the excesses of the Korean drinking culture was, basically, to spit in my host country's face. I was keenly aware of this and wanted desperately to avoid it.

I consulted experts for their opinions. An American who spent years in Korea told me that, when no one was looking, she'd dump her shot glass full of *soju* into her soup, refill the glass with water, and toast away, skipping over the soup course. A Korean executive told me he once filled his shot glass with "cider," or the Korean soft drink similar to Sprite, but his colleagues saw the carbonation bubbles. Busted, he was forced to drink even more *soju*.

I eventually found a solution for *hoesik*. As waitresses streamed in and out with food and hot coals, amid the laughing and teasing and arms thrown around colleagues' shoulders, I poured *soju* for my boss, and poured for those around me, and let others pour for me, and partook in the endless toasts each salaryman was required to make. For each toast, each time everyone else did a bottoms-up shot of *soju*, I took one sip from my shot glass. By the end of the night, my colleagues may have had ten or twelve shots of *soju*; I had a total of one or two.

My strategy became known and understood, mostly because my boss said it was okay. I was there, I was participating, I was honoring the process. Indeed, I was not invited or required to attend every *hoesik* because of my stance. But I, as always, had been afforded a foreigner get-out-of-jail-free card that none of my Korean colleagues had.

At one dinner, one of my Korean colleagues slipped into the seat next to mine, leaned over, and whispered: "I do not like to drink, either. But if I do not, it will hurt my career."

Fitting in at work was not limited to drinking. It also included mandatory extra-work activities, such as an annual Saturday morning team-building hike, to which I had no religious objections, only selfish ones.

During my first spring at Hyundai, I found out that our entire international sales division was required to meet at a mountain near headquarters at 7:30 a.m. the following Saturday for a team-building hike. "You're kidding" was my response. Nobody was kidding. I asked several pointless and prickly questions: "If this is mandatory, why aren't they holding it during work hours?" And so on. Pointless. The hike was happening and attendance was required. These outside-of-work team-building activities are common at Korean companies—and at American ones, too. It was my background as a journalist that made me ignorant of the practice. If you tried to get American journos on an early Saturday morning team-building hike, well, I can only imagine the snarkiness and derision that would spew forth on Twitter in the days before the hike, forcing embarrassed executives to call it off.

I showed up at the appointed mountain on the following Saturday, which was sunny and cool but not cold. I wore typical American hiking wear: cargo shorts and a college sweatshirt. First off, I was the only hiker there wearing shorts (aside from a Kiwi Hyundai executive who happened to be in town and decided to lark along). Second, all the Koreans were dressed like they were about to assault K2; top-end, brand-name Lycra gear, the best hiking boots, even walking poles. This was to hike a

2,000-foot-high hill. With paths. We lined up in our work teams and started with group calisthenics, which are unavoidable in Asia. They were affably led by a Hyundai colleague who did his required military service in the Korean marines, and he broadcast instructions through a handheld PA. As an American, who had grown up with grainy video images of mass communist calisthenics and strongmen with bullhorns, it was hard not to laugh at what I thought was a caricature of this one-people behavior. Yet it is not caricature. It just is. Then we attacked the summit the same way we attacked work: hard and fast. I could not keep up, and became a sorry, wheezing drag on the procession. Of more than three hundred Hyundai hikers, the only American was the last one to the top of the hill. My team leader kindly stuck with me, making him the second-to-the-last up, when he easily could have left me. With each step, I got more and more resentful that I was forced to endure this extra-work activity, when, in reality I was angry with myself for being unable to compete.

Blunt as it was, here I was in the middle of a live-action metaphor for what Hyundai was trying to do with its brand and what Koreans saw as their lot in life: a never-ending uphill climb. It was how they got to where they are; it was how they would get to where they were going: the top. Like me, everyone else climbing the hill—Hyundai's automaker competitors, Korea's regional rivals—would have to stop a few times to catch their breath. I looked around at my Korean colleagues. They did not stop.

After we came back down the hill, we were treated to a delicious open-air lunch of grilled duck. Even though it was barely noon, the *soju* was flowing and guys were standing on benches, leading team cheers and toasting each other with love shots.

I could enjoy neither the duck nor the camaraderie. Sweaty, sore, and sullen, all I wanted to do was leave. I told this to one of my team members. "We can't leave before our boss leaves," she said, meaning the division's top executive, whose exuberant toasts indicated he had no intention of leaving anytime soon.

"But I'm dying here," I lamely protested.

"We're all dying," she replied sternly.

I am not proud of this behavior and attitude when it comes over me and I allow it to show. It is ungenerous and un-Christian and it is among the things I'd like most to change about myself. Rebekah has a phrase she uses when I act like this: "You've got peppercorns in your soul."

Around this time, I caught wind of a rumor going around that I was giving up and going back to America. I never heard where the rumor came from, nor did I care. The fact that it was out there was challenge enough. Hyundai, and Korea, were going to be stuck with this *waygookin* for at least two years.

Something had to change in me before next year's hill climb.

# 7

## READING THE AIR

Going along with others for the betterment of the whole is a concept that was embedded in Korean culture from the earliest ages. To reference *Star Trek* again: "The needs of the many outweigh the needs of the few."

A female Korean friend once told me, "In Korea, we teach our children do not be outstanding." This was surprising to me, given the society's emphasis on educational excellence. But then I thought for a moment.

I said, "I think you mean to say, 'We teach our children not to stand out from the crowd,' right?"

"Yes, that's right," she laughed.

I told her, "In the U.S., we teach our children to do everything they can *to* stand out from the crowd."

Westerners would call the Korean practice "mindless conformity." Easterners would call it "harmony." My Western definition of conformity was nonoperative in Korea. American workers crave positive and public feedback from their bosses just for doing their jobs. When I applied my "attaboy" management style to Korea and singled out my individual team members for praise, they were mortified. To a person, they would reply, "It was a team effort." Boldly expressing individuality for the sake of it—or basking in selfish public glory—was not a sign of independence and accomplishment, as it was in the U.S. It was rude and inconsiderate to all those around you.

I felt this when I told my boss and my team that Rebekah and I planned our two-week 2011 vacation for May. First of all, no one in Korea who has a job takes a two-week vacation, and certainly not two consecutive weeks together. It would be inconsiderate to ask your team members to carry your work for that long. Furthermore, Hyundai employees are expected to take their vacations in July or August. Finally, the higher up the corporate ladder you climb, the less vacation you are expected to take. That's not different from the U.S. You don't see a lot of American CEOs checking out of work for two-week stretches. However, it was almost impossible for Rebekah to take two weeks off from her consular work at the embassy in the summertime: that is the peak season of visa processing for Korean travel to the U.S. So we chose May. My boss never said anything about our vacation plans other than okay, but when I returned after our two weeks in Cambodia and Thailand, my team taught me the meaning of the Korean word and skill *noonchi*.

*Noonchi* translates to "eye measure," but a better definition is "reading the air." The closest translation to English is reading body language. But *noonchi* is more subtle and complex than that. If you tell your supervisor you want to take one of your allotted days off and he says yes, you'd better use your *noonchi* to interpret his face, his tone of voice, his current job status, his ambitions, his estimate of the abilities and mind-set of your fellow team members, your work and social rank relative to him, *his* work and social rank relative to *his* boss, the circumstances of his personal life, and on and on in order to determine if he really means no. Smart corporate climbers must have finely tuned *noonchi*.

The trip to Thailand and Cambodia was a terrific, eye-opening, exotic time. There was much I wanted to share.

The Monday after we returned, I walked from my office to my team's cubicle area and effused, "Good morning, everyone!"

I got a few muted "Good mornings" and a couple of briefly upturned faces with awkward smiles, and that was it.

I hung there in the silence waiting for someone—anyone—to simply ask, "How was your vacation?"

Nothing. Even a novice *noonchi* reader like myself knew what that meant.

Back I went to my office, lesson received, muttering to myself, "It was great! Thanks for asking!"

But it was I who had failed, not only as an outsider, but also as a manager, to see things from my team's point of view. When the big, refreshed, tanned American came bumptiously bounding into the office to share photos and tales from his amazing two-week vacation, they were thinking: "What about us? We had to work while you were on your TWO-WEEK VACATION."

It was becoming clear to me that I had a lot of learning and changing to do, or else I would remain frustrated and angry all the time. If I was going to stick it out for two years here, I was going to have to adapt to a totally different definition of what it meant to be crowded, what it meant to be rude, what it meant to be considerate, what it meant to be a team player—and learn a thousand other lessons, quickly. Rebekah, veteran of East Asia, warned me that I should probably try to tone down my act a little to fit in. I tend to speak loudly. Even as a child, my mother advised me, "Your voice carries." I enjoy laughing and having animated conversations with people, including those I've just met. People might describe me as "garrulous." On top of that, given my history as a journalist and occasional humorist at the *Washington Post*, I liked to riff on topics, make jokes, and spread opinions with the focus and subtlety of a runaway fire hose.

In short, I was, as Rebekah termed it, an "America bomb" dropped smack into the middle of an Eastern, harmonious, formal workplace culture.

### HAN AND JEONG

I found most of my Hyundai executive colleagues eager for our visiting foreign journalists to truly understand Korean culture. On the long bus rides with journalists, at *hoesik*, during tours of historic Korean sites, the journalists and I learned about two critical concepts that form the base of Koreanness: *han* and *jeong*.

*Han* is a concept that was probably birthed by the first foreign invasion of the Korean peninsula millennia ago and was pounded deeper into the Korean psyche in the ensuing years with each of the hundreds of successive invasions, pillages, indignities, injustices, and setbacks at the hands of a superior opponent in a constant battle against insurmountable odds. One writer called it "collective melancholy." That helps get at the concept, because it introduces the concept of bondedness. *Han* is felt individually but it is experienced collectively. It's a feeling that we're all in this together, we've all been wronged, and we all wait for justice. It's simplistic to strictly call it pessimism, because Korea's entire stunning modern growth story is built on implied optimism, even if the results were achieved with head-down, sometimes joyless doggedness. Indeed, plenty of people who've studied the Korean success story attribute much of it to *han*. After surviving hundreds of invasions over history, beating Toyota and Apple at their own games is, to use the Korean expression, "like eating rice cakes while lying down."

In her smart and funny 2014 book, *The Birth of Korean Cool: How One Nation Is Conquering the World Through Pop Culture*, in a chapter hilariously titled, "The Wrath of Han," Euny Hong describes it like this:

> *Han* doesn't just mean that you hate people who have wronged you for generations. It also means that random people in your life can spark the flame of *han*. Someone who cuts you off in traffic or disappoints you with his or her friendship can unleash the anger of generations. I have never seen so many roadside fist fights, or so many people permanently shunning their friends, as in Korea.

*Han* lingers in the Korean soul, and then it boils up with great wailing grief, when a tragedy strikes the nation, such as the 2014 ferry disaster. In such a homogeneous society, the 250 high school students who died on that ferry are everyone's children. *Han* manifests itself in the unashamed displays of public mourning seen in the wake of the catastrophe. You can hear the subtext in the tears: "Not again. Why us? *Why us?*" *Han* manifests itself in the physical scuffles that break out in Parliament: "Oh, no. This will be on the international news tomorrow."

The happier companion to *han*, the *yin* to its *yang*, is *jeong*.

At one of our dinners with foreign journalists, one of my very friendly Hyundai executive colleagues, who had worked in several foreign countries for the company, rose at the table and told the journalists that in order to understand Korea, they must understand *jeong*.

Trying to explain *jeong* in English to non-Koreans may be close to impossible. There is no English equivalent to the feeling.

But it is essential that foreigners understand that it exists and that it matters deeply to Koreans. Indeed, a Korean friend mentioned to me, it is considered a drawback in Korean culture if someone is too analytical or too rational. If they are not emotional or passionate—if they don't show the *jeong*—they are considered lacking a vital ethnic trait.

In succinct English, the Hyundai executive told the journalists, "*Jeong* is, even if you hate someone's guts, you understand their situation." It is much more than just love. Once I learned about *jeong*, I started to understand a little better the way many South Koreans feel toward North Korea. On paper, it makes no sense to engage North Korea, to trust North Korea, to do anything but resist and work toward North Korea's downfall. But *jeong* softens the South Korean feeling toward the North. Logically, it makes no sense. Emotionally, it makes perfect sense.

After years of treating Korean-American patients, California psychiatrists Christopher K. Chung and Samson Cho published a paper titled: "Significance of '*Jeong*' in Korean Culture and Psychotherapy." They write:

> An even clearer understanding in this regard may come from *jeong*'s characteristics as a "centrifugal" tendency. The more common expression in Korean is "*jeong deulda*" rather than "I feel *jeong*." A literal translation would be "*jeong* has permeated." An even bolder translation would be "I am possessed by *jeong*." It is important to understand this in comparison to the English expressions of love, depression, hate, or anxiety; "I love you," "I feel nervous," or "I feel depressed." If love has a centripetal effect, then *jeong* has the opposite, i.e., centrifugal effect. . . . [*J*]*eong* affects the individual's ego boundary; an individual's "cell mem-

brane" becomes more permeable, so to speak, thinning the ego boundary.

This last sentence is crucial, as it dovetails perfectly with the Confucian concept of harmony—the diminution of the "I" for the "we." This extends outward to the loyalty and commitment Koreans feel toward friends and family members—to company and country—often without reason or assurance that it will be reciprocated. In the West, we institutionalize commitment with contracts. In Korea, *jeong* suggests commitment is understood.

It is important to note that *jeong* does not permeate to everyone. I was struck early and often in Korea by a lack of what we Westerners call common courtesy. No apologies are offered if someone bumps into you on the street. Merging into traffic requires aggression. Forget about elevator chitchat with a stranger. It would be considered rude to impose your conversation on a stranger. Another U.S. Foreign Service officer told the story of going to a busy Korean supermarket with his wife and infant son in a stroller. He walked ahead to open the door for his wife, but before she could push the stroller through, Koreans pushed past her and through the door her husband held open. I came to understand the binary relationship Koreans seemed to have with others: If you're a friend or family member, there's nothing a Korean won't do for you. If you're a stranger, you're invisible. Not because you hate him, but because you have no formal context for knowing him.

Anyone who spends more than a vacation in Korea will find that it is what sociologists would call an implicit, high-context culture. Like many things in Korea, this is the exact opposite of the U.S., which is an explicit, low-context culture, as many Western cultures are.

From a practical point of view, this means important cultural lessons in Korea are learned by osmosis as much as they are directly taught. It is much easier for this to occur in a homogeneous culture. To use Drs. Chung and Cho's language, the cell membranes of individuals in a homogeneous culture are much more permeable, and information flows more freely and rapidly among people than it does in a multicultural society, such as the U.S., where our cell membranes are not only of differing permeability, but they are also set up to repulse, rather than take in.

In a high-context culture, how a thing is communicated—the honorifics, the *noonchi*, the relationship of one person to another in terms of age, gender, social status, and so on—is just as vital as the information being communicated. In the West, this is not so. We could call this "style over substance." This is why American business e-mails are a few words long—"How's this look?"—and Korean e-mails are not: "Dear First Vice President Kim: Thank you for your earlier e-mail. I hope you are doing well today. We would very much like to receive your sincere opinion regarding the procedure for . . ."

I was often frustrated in Korea and at Hyundai by what I wasn't told. This had the effect of making me feel even more like an outsider and less informed than my most junior team member. The surprises ranged from important to trivial. One day during my first May at Hyundai, I walked in and every nonexecutive male employee was wearing a short-sleeve button-up shirt, in white or light blue, with no tie and no jacket. The massive and abrupt sartorial switch was jarring and a little disorienting. What was happening? Was I at the right company? I came to understand that, because Korea summers are so hot and because the Korean government forces big companies to keep their thermostats above 80 degrees to prevent summer brownouts (and sends around inspectors with thermometers to check), Korean offices are warm.

So the big companies take it easy on their male employees, allowing them to work in their shirtsleeves in the summer. (Women's dress, less restrictive but still professional, varies little throughout the year.) What startled me was the way the change came, as most changes do in Korea: big and all at once, like a scenery change in a play. One day a few thousand Korean men walked into Hyundai in pretty much the same dark suit, white shirt, and colored tie. The next day those same few thousand Korean men walked in all wearing pretty much the same dark pants and same light, short-sleeve, button-up shirt. It was like a performance-art prank was being played on the *waygookin*.

I came to understand, late in my time in Korea, that if you learn things implicitly by osmosis, you just assume everyone else does, too, so there's no need for explication. It's the same way I wouldn't think to tell a friend that the sky is blue. It's just obvious.

# 8
## CONSTANT COMPETITION

Implicitly, Koreans learn early that life is a constant competition. And for a long time everyone was aiming at the same prize: a prestigious, well-paying job at one of the big *chaebol*, a top government job, or a profession, such as medicine or the law. Korea has attacked education with a fury seen almost nowhere else in the world. Children start attending *hagwons* in elementary school and can stay in them through high school. The government outlawed *hagwon* teaching after ten p.m., but the *hagwons* merely began setting up out-of-classroom classrooms and teaching until midnight, because the parents insisted on it and paid for it, worried that their child could be losing a competitive edge to another. To combat this, the government pays snitches to rat out illegal *hagwons*.

*Hagwons* are expensive, and parents spend their salaries and run up big debt to pay for the best education for their children. All of this is geared toward the annual national college entrance exam in the fall. It's not an exaggeration to say Korean children work for years for one make-or-break day. SAT pressure in the U.S. is tough, but nothing like this. Official Korea honors each year's test takers by stopping construction around test sites for the day and even limiting air travel over Seoul so the students can concentrate. The test, as do most in the Korean education system, rewards disgorgement of facts and is starting to be questioned by many Koreans, who say it is an exercise in memorization rather than critical thinking.

The demands of managing their children's round-the-clock education schedules falls on Korean mothers, as fathers are committed to long working hours and drinking dinners during the week and often golf with the bosses on Saturdays. This—and the historically male-dominant culture—is why so few female executives exist in the *chaebol*. Like so many American working women, Korean women can sometimes juggle a full-time career with one kid in school, but if they have a second child, it's impossible, and they drop out of the workforce.

A good score on the national college entrance test allows entrance into one of the three Korean Ivies, or the "SKY" universities: Seoul National University, Korea University, and Yonsei University. A degree—any degree—from these schools almost guarantees a job at Samsung, Hyundai, or LG Electronics—or else a prestigious public service career. So much so that this process—from *hagwon* to college entrance test to SKYs to *chaebol*—even has a name. It is called "the right spec." Korean students assault their higher education strategically, such is the lifelong value of a diploma from one of the SKY universities and the connections you make there. For instance, if it is harder for a high school graduate to gain admission into Seoul National's engineering program than, say, one of the school's foreign language programs, a student will study the foreign language and even take their degree in it even though they may have loved engineering and have no interest at all in the foreign language. The value of a Seoul National degree is quantifiable: a study by the Korean Educational Development Institute found that graduates from Seoul National made on average 12 percent more than their colleagues from other Korean universities.

When younger Koreans asked me how the American higher education system differed from Korea's, I phrased it like this: in Korea, it seemed to me, a student aimed to get a degree from the best university possible so they could get a job at the best *chaebol* possible. Once there, they did the job assigned by the company, even if they hated it, to enjoy the lifestyle and prestige that job provided. The point was being at the big-name company. The U.S. Ivies still had undeniable clout, I said. But for everyone else, a student is more likely to think, "I would like to have a career in marine biology. Which universities will best prepare me for that?" And the student would apply to those universities, whether or not they are Ivies. The graduate would then try to get a job in marine biology. The point was pursuing the career you loved. Doesn't always work out, I said, but that's the ideal.

The annual college entrance test isn't kind to many Korean kids. Some take it year after sad year, even into their late twenties, in hopes of improvement. Surveys of Korean millennials, conducted by pollsters both inside and outside of Korea, find them to be pessimistic about their future and the direction of the country. A 2015 study showed Korean teens are the most stressed of those in thirty developed countries. Modern Korea was built on constant, diligent, hard work. Yet, the millennials say, hard work alone is not enough to succeed in today's Korea. That's partly because the country's overriding importance on education has created too many four-year college graduates. A stunning 65 percent of Koreans aged twenty-five to thirty-four hold four-year degrees.

About 40 percent of Americans of the same age hold a four- *or* two-year degree.

Competitive pressure is not limited to improvement of one's mind. Everything is a competition and every part of you can give you an advantage—or create a stumbling block.

One day at work, Eduardo came into my office to deliver the newspapers. But he was acting a little sheepish, like he wanted to tell me something. After a little prying, he blurted out, "Sir, I got a hair transplant!"

Eduardo was in his mid-twenties, with a full head of hair worn long enough to touch his collar and cover his ears and his forehead. If you looked at Eduardo's head, there was no place you could think of to put more hair.

"Wha . . . ?" I said. "How? Where?"

Eduardo told me that he'd gone to a doctor, who had chunked out a divot of hair from the back of his head and planted it just in front of his hairline, like sod. He pulled back his bangs to show me the transplant—and the stitches. It cost almost $3,000. It was paid for by his parents, who believed they were helping their son.

"Eduardo," I said. "You're not bald. You're nowhere close to bald. What were you thinking?"

Ah, Eduardo explained, he was worried that *eventually* he would become bald. He'd noticed hair coming out in the shower; I explained this was a natural part of showering. But his sister had teased him about going bald. And when he looked closely, he could see a receding hairline. He wanted to take, in the managerial-speak of Koreans, "countermeasures." He'd already consulted his fellow team members at work to get their advice; to a person, he said, they believed he was acting smartly and correctly. Eduardo kept trying to persuade me that it was a good idea and no one could understand why I didn't get it.

This was my first up-close brush with what is often called

"lookism," the Korean obsession with appearance. If you think Americans are at the extreme when worrying about, and spending for, their appearance, well, you're wrong. We look like a nation of derelicts and slobs compared to the Koreans. A Korean friend at a big *chaebol*—who happened to shave his head—told me that before he was offered his job, the company's HR person awkwardly asked if he would consider wearing a wig because his bald head might make coworkers uncomfortable. He declined, to his credit.

Korean women consider, perhaps rightly so, their skin the most flawless in the world. They work to make it so. An executive at L'Oréal told me that South Korean women use on average three times as many daily skin care products as Western women. It's no surprise that the richest man in Korea is the head of Samsung. But the second-richest? Not the head of Hyundai Motor or LG Electronics. It's the chairman of a company called Amore-Pacific. They produce skin care products, including the famous BB blemish-hiding cream that makes up as much as 15 percent of the Korean cosmetics market and is used by men and women.

This emphasis on looks has fueled Korea's plastic surgery industry, one of the world's biggest, best, and most pervasive in society. It is not only a way of life in Korea, it is an economic engine. There is a medical tourism booth in Incheon International Airport. Medical tourists come from all over Asia to Korea. Korea has the highest number of plastic surgeons per capita and the world's highest rate of cosmetic surgery. Buses and subway ads all over Seoul show highly graphic, often gruesome before-and-after photos.

Again, plastic surgery is not unique to Korea, as any resident of Hollywood can tell you. But the kind of surgery popular in each country tells you about the culture's priorities. In the U.S., liposuction and breast augmentation are the most popular procedures. In Korea, as throughout much of Northeast Asia, the face is the focus, which I suppose is the literal manifestation of the Asian concept of "face." The snow-smooth, poreless, perfected Korean woman's face is almost a point of national pride, like perfectly aligned, gleaming white American teeth and round Brazilian female bottoms.

Lately, the pervasiveness of plastic surgery among Korea's women has caused a lot of social reflection and self-criticism. The most popular procedure is blepharoplasty, or "double-eyelid" surgery. It is designed to create an upper eyelid and widen the eyes with the aim at making the recipient look more Caucasian. Gaining in popularity while I was in Korea were procedures on the jaw that I had never heard of, involving the shaving-down of bone to create a tapered chin, which was considered more attractive. Critics say such surgeries amount to cultural self-abnegation, the denial of Asian beauty in a quest for Western standards of beauty. Feminist writers decry Korean beauty pageants full of women so unified in their cosmetic enhancements that the contestants look like sisters.

Yet, there is a practical reason behind all this cutting: Korea's relentless competition. In Korea, as throughout much of Asia, a job applicant's résumé includes their headshot. Just writing that sentence probably breaks a few anti-discrimination laws in the U.S. Job applicants know that in Korea, as everywhere in the world, the better-looking of two equally qualified job seekers will likely get the position. So instead of being hypocritical, as Koreans would say Americans are by pretending looks don't matter, Koreans understand the system and try to succeed within it with attractive headshots on their job applications. To not choose plastic surgery, if it will improve your employment and life prospects, would be considered just as ill-advised as not paying for *hagwon* classes.

Fear of falling behind—this is what drives Hyundai. This is what drives Korea. Fear of falling behind your richer family member. Fear of falling behind your smarter classmate. Fear of falling behind your rival company. Fear of falling behind Japan.

Like China, Korea is still in its "new money" phase, and the characteristic trait of new money is showing off that you have it. It's understandable. Korea has been a rich country for only two generations. China, for only one generation. That's why 40 percent—that's *40 percent*—of all luxury goods purchased in France are by Chinese tourists. In Korea, it's why couples rent strangers to be wedding guests—it's an actual business—so their real guests will be impressed by the size of their weddings. It's why one of my young female colleagues kept a label on a sleeve of her camel hair coat stating that the coat had been "hand-sewn." "Oh, you forgot to take the label off your new coat," I said to her, thinking I was doing her a favor. She looked at me as you might at a clueless grandparent. "Oh, no," she said. "I want everyone to know it is hand-sewn."

The result of all this Koreanness and Confucianism is a nation of extraordinarily well-groomed, attractive, stylish, well-dressed, youthful-looking people. It is often startling to first-time foreign visitors. One of our saltier Australian journalist guests spent a couple days looking around Seoul and asked me in exasperation, "Where are all the scruffy Koreans?"

For the longest time, I couldn't reconcile the seeming paradox of Korea's intense competition and its intense conformity: everyone seems to need the latest and best phone, the right-brand winter jacket, the latest Prada bag. Finally it was explained to me by a Korean friend: "In the U.S., you compete to stand out from the crowd. In Korea, we compete to fit into the crowd."

## A SHRIMP BETWEEN TWO WHALES AND THE MADMEN NEXT DOOR

The hunger that drives Hyundai's uphill assault to become a premium brand—the same thing that pushes a bleary-eyed

Hyundai engineer to try one more way to solve a nettlesome problem at the end of a fifteen-hour day—originated centuries ago and has been reinforced by events ever since. It is a perpetual inferiority complex fueled by slights both real and imagined, and, despite this, by a surprising sense of confidence sometimes bordering on arrogance. It is hard for Americans to wrap our heads around the idea of a people sculpted by a millennium of experience when we think of a two-hundred-year-old building as historic. While Americans think of cycles of economic boom and bust that occur every few generations, the cycles in Asia run for hundreds of years, with glorious dynasties reigning for centuries, and violence and anarchy ruling for centuries more. And, as with many things in Korea, there is a paradox to this thought. In today's Korea, where the love is for anything new and next, from fashion trend to smartphone, you'd wonder why history has such purchase. Yet Korea cannot, and should not, shake its past.

Archaeologists estimate the first humans appeared on the Korean Peninsula more than 100,000 years ago. Humans that we would recognize today showed up by at least 6000 B.C., a few hundred years before Sumerians scratched out the world's first writing. The first Korean kingdom was founded, according to legend, in 2333 B.C. by Dangun, called a "grandson of heaven." But we don't have to delve into ancient mythology. We can stick to more recent historic facts. To begin to understand the way that Korea sees itself today, and the way it sees its two biggest neighbors, we need only step back to the Chosun, Korea's greatest dynasty.

Stretching from 1392 to the dawn of the twentieth century, the Chosun dynasty saw the unification of the Korean Peninsula, the invention of the Korean language used today, the rule of Korea's greatest king, the flowering of the sciences, the establishment of an efficient administrative bureaucracy, the entrenchment of Confucianism as the cultural norm and de facto national religion, and the isolationist policies that caused Korea to come to be known as the "hermit kingdom."

Western colonial powers probed at Korea, as they did much of Asia, during the twilight of the Chosun dynasty, in the mid-nineteenth century, as corruption and internecine power struggles ate away at the court. The French and Americans sent missionaries to Korea; Russian and German ships arrived, demanding trade. In 1866, America sent a suspiciously heavily armed side-wheel steamer named the *General Sherman*, laden with tin, glass, and cotton, demanding an opening of trade with Korea. It plowed uninvited up the Taedong River, bound for Pyongyang, now the capital of North Korea, despite warnings from the Koreans to halt. A battle ensued, and the *General Sherman* was sunk with loss of Korean and American lives. Five years later, the U.S. launched a military expedition to investigate the incident. Mutual suspicions and misinterpretation led to a U.S. assault on Korean fortifications at Gangwha Island on Korea's west coast, the gateway to the Chosun capital of Hanyang, now Seoul. The American sailors and marines killed nearly 250 Koreans and destroyed several forts before withdrawing. Korean isolationism didn't seem like such an odd policy, given this history.

But for hundreds of years before the Americans or Germans had ever heard of Korea, it was a coveted peninsula for both China and Japan. A buffer between the two, Korea was a tiny country that paid allegiance to one of its giant neighbors and feared the other. This is why Korea has always thought of itself as "a shrimp between two whales."

North Korea, on the other hand, is a much newer concept in Korean history. For most of Korea's past, the peninsula has largely been unified as one people. For hundreds and hundreds of years. It has been separated only since 1948. That's a drop in the Korean historical bucket, an anomaly. South Koreans believe reunification is inevitable, given enough time. Not for any particular reason, like an impending North Korean collapse, foreign intervention, or an internal coup. Just because it's inevitable, because both North and South Korean people are Koreans, sharing the same DNA, the same Confucian customs, and mostly the same language. Koreans believe strongly in the concept of race, and North and South Koreans are the same race. Despite their *pali-pali* nature, Koreans play the long game of history.

In the years following its birth right after World War II, South Korea competed against the North. But that race is long over. South Korea has eclipsed the North in every meaningful category. Even though it holds an existential threat over the South in a way that China and Japan do not, North Korea does not drive South Korea. Today, as it has been for thousands of years, it is China and Japan that loom like giants on either side of the Korean Peninsula. Despite a feeling among some that Korea is already bypassing Japan in many ways—in electronics, heavy manufacturing, pop culture, and even national reputation—Korea will never stop competing against Japan. As for China, Korea does not seek to best the authoritarian giant. Korea's goal is to diplomatically persuade Beijing to regard Seoul as an equal partner in the region and to join with the South in its efforts to reunify the peninsula. These are two mighty and simultaneous missions that Korea has set itself. But it is this rivalry with Japan and China that will push Korea over its midlife hump.

# 9
## ADMIRAL YI: KOREA'S GREATEST JAPAN FIGHTER

Yi Sun-sin was a promising young officer candidate in the Korean military. He had passed his exams in stellar fashion, impressing his senior officers, and only a cavalry test stood between him and what appeared to be a bright military future. But Yi broke a leg during the exam, ending his career before it started. Or so the examiners thought. Instead, Yi fashioned a field splint out of willow branches and completed the riding exam, announcing the character of the man that was to mark his career. Yi Sun-sin entered Korean military service in 1592, the same year Japan launched a massive invasion of the peninsula designed to take over Korea and eventually China.

Five years after its invasion of Korea, Japan held much of the peninsula, but the war against the Koreans and the Chinese, who had come to Korea's aid, had exacted such a high price on all sides that a truce was called while formal negotiations for a peace began. Any peace was doomed from the start, however, by a tragic comedy of miscommunication and bad translation. The Chinese Ming emperor was told by his court that Japan was a defeated minor nation ready to become a tributary of China: capable of some autonomy but essentially a vassal state. Meanwhile, the imperial regent of Japan, the warlord behind the invasions, was told that China was ready to surrender, so he issued the demands of a conqueror, which were untenable to China.

This misunderstanding led to Japan's second attempt to take the Korean Peninsula in 1597, the same year as the first performance of William Shakespeare's *Merry Wives of Windsor* and ten years before the first permanent British colony in the New World at Jamestown.

By this time, battle-hardened Yi Sun-sin had become Admiral Yi. He was Korea's greatest naval strategist and the sailor-warrior pride of the Chosun dynasty. In the prime of his career, this should have been Admiral Yi's greatest moment. But Japanese-instigated intrigue in the Chosun court and Yi's own headstrong behavior led to his firing and near execution. Yi was replaced by the shockingly incompetent Won Gyun. Without planning or preparation, Won sailed the entire Korean fleet toward the invading Japanese force, anchored off Busan, at the southeastern tip of Korea, in August 1597. Won was routed by the Japanese, who destroyed the Korean fleet save for a handful of ships under the control of a subordinate officer who prudently refused to follow Won. For his part, Won was killed by the Japanese after struggling ashore following the disastrous battle.

The Korean king hastily reinstated Admiral Yi as head of what was left of the navy. He assessed his situation: he had the thirteen ships and about two hundred badly demoralized sailors. Yet, only two months later, on October 26, 1597, Yi found himself forced into a last stand against the mighty Japanese fleet as it sailed around the Korea Peninsula to the west coast and China. He had one chance: to lure the Japanese into the narrow Myeong-nyang Strait, off the southwest corner of Korea, and stop them there. If he failed, the Japanese would have unfettered access to the west coast of Korea—the only part of the peninsula still held by Koreans—and a clear route of attack across the Yellow Sea to China.

The Japanese armada sailed 133 warships and some 200 supply ships. Yi had 13 ships, total. But he had an intimate knowledge of his country and a keen strategic mind.

Yi knew that the Myeongnyang Strait was too narrow for the Japanese force to outflank Yi's thirteen ships, which forced a head-on conflict and immediately reduced the Japanese advantage. The tactic of using a narrow passageway to withstand a vastly superior force dated to at least Thermopylae.

Yi knew something else about the strait: it had rough currents, which inhibited maneuvers and compelled the mighty Japanese force to break off and attack in smaller groups of boats, further leveling the odds. But Yi's secret weapon was the tidal flow in the strait. Its currents changed direction every three hours. The Japanese did not know this.

Twelve of Yi's boats anchored reluctantly at the north end of the strait, still shell-shocked from the rout two months earlier and spooked by the size of the looming armada. They watched the Japanese fleet crowd its way in, riding the current north. Yi probed the enemy, sailing only his flagship forward and loosing cannon and arrow fire on the lead ships. Inspired by this show of aggressiveness, Yi's twelve other ships followed, engaging the Japanese. The battle commenced.

By this time, the currents had begun to shift and flow swiftly southward, surprising the Japanese. Their ships drifted backward and collided with each other. Confusion engulfed the Japanese. Yi ordered a full-out attack, and his thirteen ships rode the force of the current directly into the foundering Japanese ships. Densely packed, it was a target-rich environment for Yi's cannons and archers. The Japanese ships that weren't destroyed or sunk on their own retreated. By battle's end, the Japanese had lost thirty-one warships and Yi had lost none. Japanese sailors who had leapt from their sinking ships were consumed by the tide, which flowed so swiftly that it produced a roaring sound. For this reason—and possibly for the immense loss of Japanese life—Myeongnyang became known as the "Screaming Strait."

Admiral Yi's victorious last stand shocked the Japanese and helped turn the course of the war, essentially blocking off the Yellow Sea. More important, it gave the Chinese enough security at home to allow its navy to move its ships away from defending its harbors to join Admiral Yi's fighting fleet. This created a balanced force to oppose the Japanese at sea and cut off naval supply lines to invading Japanese ground forces in Korea.

One year later, Admiral Yi struck the final blow of the war, joining with a Chinese commander to lead an armada of 150 Korean and Chinese ships against 500 Japanese ships that were attempting to break out of an allied blockade at the southern tip of Korea and re-form with the rest of their navy. Again Yi effectively used his home court advantage, deploying intelligence gleaned from local fisherman spies and his ability to maneuver the Japanese into a narrow strait. He used his technologically superior cannons to keep the Japanese at arm's length, foiling their chief naval tactic, which was boarding and hand-to-hand combat. By the end of this battle, the Japanese had lost more than half of their ships. The war was effectively over.

But Yi would not live to see it. Struck down by a bullet during the battle, Yi issued a final command to his eldest son and nephew, who saw Yi fall: "We are about to win the war—keep beating my war drums. Do not announce my death." Yi's nephew donned his uncle's armor and led the fleet's flagship in victory in disguise.

In *The Influence of the Sea on the Political History of Japan* (1921), British Royal Navy admiral and historian G. A. Ballard wrote of Yi: "It is always difficult for Englishmen to admit that Nelson ever had an equal in his profession, but if any man is entitled to be so regarded, it should surely be this great naval commander of the Asiatic race who never knew defeat and died in the presence of the enemy; of whose movements a track-chart might be compiled from the wrecks of hundreds of Japanese ships lying with their valiant crews at the bottom of the sea, off the Korean peninsula."

Today, Admiral Yi can be seen in defiant statuary on the main street of Seoul, within sight of the president's residence. He is Korea's greatest military hero and the embodiment of the spirit still felt by many Koreans: "We may be small, but we are smart, we are courageous, and we are relentless."

And lest you think Admiral Yi is lost to dusty Korean history and remembered only glancingly when today's Seoulites walk past his statue, if at all, you are wrong. In 2014, a Korean studio released a big-budget epic recounting Admiral Yi's 1597 stand against the Japanese, called *The Admiral: Roaring Currents*. Not only did it break every box office record in Korea, it became the highest-grossing Korean-language film in North American history.

Admiral Yi-ism works its way into many parts of daily Korean life. Rebekah and I had a young American friend who was working as a copy editor at the English-language version of one of the big Korean daily newspapers. His job, he joked, "is putting a headline on yet another story about how Korea is better than Japan."

There's a larger point to the Admiral Yi story: the constant, frequently irritating, sometimes violent presence of Japan on Korea's life. It is unavoidable. And it's something many Koreans just can't forget or let go, and for good reason. Enough Koreans remain alive who remember the most recent time Japan set its sights on Korea: the period from 1910 until 1945, when Japan ran Korea as a subjugated colony.

In the nineteenth century, Korea was still a protectorate of China and paid yearly tribute to the Ming dynasty. Which is why the Chosun court recoiled in diplomatic horror and indignation in 1868 when the Japanese sent Korea a message saying a new government had been established in Japan. As harmless and indeed neighborly of a gesture as that sounds, the Koreans took it as a grave insult. Why? Because the missive contained the Chinese characters for "royal decree." None but the Chinese emperor was allowed to use these symbols, the Koreans believed, and their use by the Japanese was arrogant and intolerable self-aggrandizement, equating themselves to the Chinese. The Koreans refused to receive the letter or recognize the new Japanese government. Diplomacy failed to resolve the stand-off between Japan and Korea, and in 1875, with relations between the two countries still poor, a small Japanese warship patrolled too near the Korean island of Gangwha, a hot spot since the battle with the Americans only a decade earlier, and sent a small boat ashore in search of drinkable water, the Japanese later said. A nearby Korean fortress interpreted the presence of the warship and the landing party as an act of hostility and opened fire.

Unlike the Korean hermit kingdom, Japan had been opening to the West and importing the latest technology—chiefly, modern weaponry. The Japanese warship returned the volley with superior firepower, destroying the Korean guns, and sent marines ashore to clean up before retreating. As a result, the following year Korea was forced to sign a treaty opening up the country to trade with Japan. Once they had a foothold in Korea, the far stronger Japanese expanded their influence, forcing the politically unstable Korea to sign a number of unequal treaties. In 1910, Japan took the final step: it annexed the Korean Peninsula to an empire the Japanese were planning to significantly expand by military means.

The colonization, like many, was a combination of modernization and brutality. The Japanese brought in technology and built infrastructure. At the same time, Koreans were forced to take Japanese surnames, learn Japanese, accommodate as many as 1 million Japanese immigrants, and watch their land-ownership system get overturned. Once World War II started, millions of Koreans were conscripted to work at Japanese war-effort factories at home, in Japan, and elsewhere in the Japanese battle theater. At the same time, hundreds of thousands of Korean males volunteered to serve in the Japanese military, and while some rose to the highest ranks and ended up fighting the Americans and Allied Forces in the Pacific, most were distrusted by the Japanese and relegated to noncombat laboring roles until the very end of the war. Some Koreans serving in the Japanese imperial forces were killed not by enemies but by suspicious Japanese.

For Korean females, the war was equally brutal. Once a foreign territory had come under Japanese control, it was customary for the military to establish "comfort stations" for the Japanese soldiers. There, women coerced or kidnapped from other Japanese-occupied territories—Korea and China, mostly—were forced to have sex with Japanese soldiers. They were called "comfort women," or sex slaves, as former Secretary of State Hillary Clinton termed them.

The issue became a significant roadblock to better relations between Korea and Japan for years, with heated accusations flying back and forth. But the two sides began talking in earnest in early 2015 with a mind toward resolving the issue, and, days before the year ended, they announced an agreement to break the stalemate. Japan, which believed it had apologized sufficiently for its past and denied its government had any part in running the comfort women system, apologized anew and acknowledged its military was involved. Japan agreed to pay about $8 million to the forty-some surviving Korean comfort women, and both sides agreed to stop criticizing each other.

Despite the deal on the comfort women, relations between Korea and Japan have remained tense since the 2012 election of Shinzo Abe as Japanese prime minister. Koreans reacted viscerally to Abe's elevation, fearing the earliest reawakenings of Japanese imperialism. During a prior one-year tenure as PM in 2006 to 2007, Abe had shown his nationalist stripes. Before becoming prime minister, he followed other PMs and visited Japan's Yasukuni Shrine, the third rail of Japanese-Korean-Chinese politics. The shrine houses the remains of Japanese war dead from many eras—including more than 1,000 war criminals from World War II. In Japan, a politician's visit to the shrine is a patriotic duty; in Korea and China, it is a Japanese slap in the face.

Since its defeat in World War II, Japan's military policy has been pacifist. The country could defend itself against invasion but not extend its military beyond Japan's shores. Shortly after Abe was elected, he began flexing Japanese military muscle in small but symbolic ways. The Japanese military sent its first military aid overseas since World War II. A year later it sold military planes to India, the first sale of Japanese military hardware to another nation since World War II. At the same time, Japan would coordinate disaster relief in the Philippines, something no Korean could object to.

Before I left Korea, I was discussing Abe with a Korean friend. Almost every Korean I talked to had a highly negative opinion about Abe, and many saw him as the beginning of something bad for Korea. Their fear only increased as Abe faced a slumping economy at home and attendant rising nationalism. Some, like one of my Korean friends—a rational, highly educated, well-traveled executive—worried that Abe might revive Japan's expansionist past and gaze hungrily west across the sea to Korea.

I was incredulous.

"Come on," I said to my friend, "this is the twenty-first century. After all that Japan suffered in World War II, after seventy years of being a model world citizen, you actually think Japan might militarize again?"

My friend, who had a much fuller and personal grasp of Korea's history than I did, and whose grandparents grew up during the Japanese occupation of Korea, simply said, "Could be first step."

Because relations between the two countries have been so sour, and because of Korea's high tariffs on imported cars—designed to protect its domestic automakers, such as Hyundai—it was almost impossible to buy a Japanese car in Korea until very recently. The first Japanese brand to open dealerships in Korea was Lexus, in 2000, to tap into affluent Koreans' increasing taste for luxury goods. In 2013, Korean auto journalists shocked the nation, and certainly Hyundai, when they selected the Toyota Camry as Korea's Car of the Year. Koreans, especially younger ones, are buying Japanese cars.

The converse so far has not been true.

Hyundai tried selling cars in Japan but to little effect, thanks to that country's even tighter protectionist laws. Hyundai's efforts in Japan were not for wont of trying, however. The company established a technical research center in Japan, which not only benefits Hyundai but is a show of good faith that automakers typically make in foreign countries where they plan to make a long-term commitment. But the import climate proved too hostile for Hyundai and it stopped selling, or trying to sell, cars in Japan in 2009. Hyundai's failure to crack the Japanese car market is not unique: 90 percent of all car sales in Japan are by Japanese automakers. By comparison, cars made by the Big Three amount to about 45 percent of the U.S. market.

Nevertheless, when Hyundai decided in 1999 to improve the quality of its cars, it looked to Japan. Toyota, Honda, and Nissan were the industry benchmark for high-quality volume carmakers. They had built deservedly great reputations for making automobiles with outstanding fit and finish, groundbreaking production methods, and terrific engineering. Hyundai had to at least rise to their level to be considered a global contender.

By 2010, Hyundai was getting there. Its gains in quality—and sales, especially in the U.S.—were being noticed with nervousness in the Japanese car industry, which was having its own problems. Toyota was just digging out of an image crisis of epic proportions in the U.S., with quality flaws leading to massive recalls, accidents, lawsuits, and relentless, pile-on media coverage—including from yours truly, when he was at the *Washington Post*—regarding something that came to be called "unintended acceleration." Suddenly, mighty Toyota seemed vulnerable. Some journalists and thinkers began talking about Hyundai as the New Toyota and Korea as the New Japan.

A year later, with Toyota still reeling, a cascade of tragedies enveloped Japan.

The Tohoku earthquake of March 11, 2011, five months after Rebekah and I arrived in Korea, was the biggest to hit Japan since modern records were kept more than one hundred years ago. It triggered a tsunami that struck shore hours later and flooded the Fukushima nuclear reactor near Sendai, in the north of Japan, unleashing radioactivity into the water and air.

Nearly 16,000 people died and another 2,600 went missing, according to the final records. The impact of these triple disasters had significant impact not only on Japan but on the region, crippling Japan's economy for most of the year, especially its mighty auto industry.

And they impacted our family life.

Rebekah and I were driving around the military base in Seoul two days after the quake struck, and she got a phone call from one of her bosses at the embassy. She asked if Rebekah could possibly be ready to fly to Japan the next day to help with a region-wide State Department effort being mobilized for the stricken country. Of course, Rebekah said.

Then her boss embarrassedly asked: "And how much do you weigh?" There was a chance Rebekah and her colleagues would be airlifted from the U.S. embassy in Tokyo to Sendai to help find and evacuate Americans. For that to happen, the U.S. government needed to know the total weight of all the personnel in Japan so it would know how many helicopters to send.

The next day Rebekah was in a war room at the U.S. embassy in Tokyo. She and her State Department colleagues had one major goal: to find Americans. Communications between several areas of Japan and the outside world were cut off, and the U.S. embassy was besieged with frantic calls and e-mails from people in the States unable to get in touch with their friends and relatives in Japan. U.S. citizens in foreign countries are encouraged to register with the U.S. embassy in their host country precisely for this reason: so your government can find you in emergencies and put you back in touch with your family.

We of course were nervous for Rebekah to be sent into a disaster zone with an unknown radiation hazard. But she retained conversational Japanese from her time there as a teacher. She would be a valuable asset.

Also, and this is in no way to glamorize the assignment, one of the reasons that people join the Foreign Service is to try to make a difference in times of crisis. For part of her posting in Seoul, Rebekah directly helped her countrymen in distress. Lots of Americans travel the world on spiritual or self-discovery quests. A surprising number of them end up in Seoul, out of money, perhaps struggling with a mental illness, and sleeping in the train station while losing touch with family members back home, who are worried sick. At the end of their rope, the families call the U.S. embassy in desperation. Rebekah and her embassy colleagues helped these Americans, putting fathers back in touch with lost sons and solving seemingly insurmountable paperwork problems with the Korean government that prevented destitute Americans from being repatriated.

But much of her posting was in the visa window at the embassy. Intellectually, she knew that granting visas to Koreans who wanted to work and study in the U.S. was an important job and made many dreams come true. But it was a dull grind and there was no way to see the end result of her efforts.

Here in Japan, she loved the Tokyo embassy esprit de corps with her fellow officers from Seoul and around the region. Putting an American student on the phone with her crying mother back in the States—this was satisfying. For the first time as a U.S. Foreign Service officer, she felt like her job mattered. If there were any doubt she was in a danger zone, the aftershocks that shook the hotel at night reminded her.

In the days that passed following the receding of the tsunami waters, Rebekah and her Foreign Service colleagues were able to locate many Americans as they wandered out of their refuges and found a telephone. But just as many Americans in Japan had not registered with the U.S. embassy, and Rebekah and her colleagues leaned on the Japanese officials for help, they had their own priority: find missing Japanese citizens, of which there were tens of thousands.

Rebekah and her colleagues exchanged increasingly frantic calls and e-mails with one family of a twenty-four-year-old American woman who was in Japan to teach English. The family was able to get in touch with their daughter's friends and others who knew her, but their daughter had not been found. Feeling helpless on the far side of the world, the American family readied to board a plane to Japan to look for their daughter. But just before they did, Rebekah and her colleagues delivered the terrible news that Japanese authorities had finally found the body of the young English teacher.

Rebekah came home after two weeks, after being wanded by Korean officials at Seoul's Incheon Airport and found to be radiation-free, which was no small relief to both of us. It was an intensely emotional time for Rebekah, full of both great joy and sorrow for the families of the Americans in Japan and the Japanese themselves.

But Rebekah's emotional stake ran deeper. At one point in her life, she was a twenty-five-year-old English teacher in Japan. She lived and worked in Sendai, a city that had been obliterated by the tsunami. It was not lost on her that it could have been her family that had received that awful phone call from the U.S. embassy.

Rebekah had come to love Japan from her time teaching there. Returning as a Foreign Service officer to see the destruction and terrible human toll was heartbreaking for her.

"Japanese people were calling us at the embassy, terrified about the radiation," Rebekah recalled later. "They were saying, 'Our government is not telling us the truth about the radiation. Please help us.'"

It was this feeling of helplessness and fear of the unknown that stayed with Rebekah.

"We had planes waiting for us at the airport to take us out if the radiation became a problem," she said. "But they didn't."

The Japanese tragedies also threw into sharp relief the differences between Japan and Korea.

For instance, in the aftermath of the disasters, world newspapers were filled with unbelievable photos of hundreds of Japanese patiently standing in long, single lines, waiting for fresh drinking water. Unbelievable to anyone, that is, outside of Japan.

One of my Korean team members, seeing one of these photos, joked, "If those were Koreans, no one would be in line. They'd all be shoving up to the front."

It's not for nothing the Japanese have often been called the British of Asia, so impeccable are their manners and civilized behavior. But you may never know what a Japanese person really thinks of you. And because Japan is a culture of "yes," because saying "no" is seen as an insult, you may get something promised to you that can never be delivered.

The Koreans, on the other hand, are often called the Irish of Asia, and it's not just for the drinking, which the Japanese (and Chinese) can easily match. In the right setting, you'll hear what Koreans have on their mind. If you have a blemish on your face, colleagues will helpfully point it out all day, because they want what is best for you. Conversely, if you're looking especially good, you may be told you're having "a good face day."

But I came to admire this bluntness and directness. If you're a tourist in a country, then you'd want to be in a place like Japan, possibly the most mannered nation in the world, because you're only ever going to get surface-deep with the locals and it doesn't matter what they really think of you.

But if you're going to work and live every day with colleagues, then you'd better be certain they mean what they say. And generally I found Koreans did, tough as it could make daily life for both Korean and foreigner. Frequently my non-Korean Hyundai colleagues from around the world would e-mail or phone me in Seoul to complain or lament that their Korean bosses had told them they had "failed" at some task rather than informing them in a more gentle, more Western fashion that their performance could be improved. Koreans actually pride themselves on this sort of socially enforced toughness. It has been one of the keys to their rapid ascent.

Comparing corporate behavior at the rival countries' national champion automakers tells you a lot about national personality.

Both Hyundai and Toyota use the Japanese-created "just in time" manufacturing system, which reduces the overhead of excess inventory. Both are Confucian in corporate hierarchy. Both are run by scions of their founders.

But after that, national character takes over. If Toyota CEO Akio Toyoda is scheduled to speak at the 2020 Detroit Auto Show, unless he is dead, you can bet your life he will be there. If Hyundai vice chairman Chung is scheduled to speak at next year's Detroit Auto Show, you may not know he'll be there until he mounts the stage. Most likely the vice chairman's visit has been scheduled and canceled a half dozen times in the month beforehand, sending executives and staff scurrying this way and that to initiate and then halt preparations. This is quite sensibly to ensure that the vice chairman is exactly where he needs to be, tending to the most important thing in the company at that moment.

Things are well planned at Hyundai, but they actually *happen* at the last minute, in an all-hands-on-deck crisis mode.

Turns out, this has its benefits for the consumer.

A former Hyundai executive who worked for years at one of Hyundai's keenest rivals, put it this way: Everyone in the auto industry takes about four years to build a car, from first idea until it rolls off the assembly line. At most automakers, the final design is locked in place eighteen months before that car rolls off the line. This leaves adequate time for marketing, advertising, dealership training, and so on. "At Hyundai," he said, "we're literally making changes on the car until a month before it comes off the assembly line."

Of course, this causes chaos. But it means that when a customer buys a "new" car from one of Hyundai's rivals, that car is really eighteen months old and no longer on the cutting edge of the industry. When you buy a Hyundai car, it's so up-to-date, the paint is barely dry, and there are a few thousand sleepless, exhausted Koreans to thank for it.

# 10

## SEJONG THE GREAT: GIVE-AND-TAKE WITH CHINA

China has a much different and far more patriarchal relationship with Korea than does Japan. Unlike Korea and Japan, which are separated by the East Sea of Korea (which the Japanese call the Sea of Japan), the Korean Peninsula is connected to China, and the border between the two peoples has moved back and forth since at least the fourth century B.C., capturing members of Chinese and Korean ethnicity under alternating flags as the Chinese waged various invasions and Korean dynasties rose and fell. Successive Chinese dynasties understood that the Korean Peninsula was not only a trade market but also an important defense against invaders.

Most of the inhabitants of the Korean Peninsula—by then unified under the first great Korean dynasty, the Silla—became tributaries of China's Tang dynasty in the seventh century. The Chinese saw themselves as emperors of the entire world, with

China at the center. The Koreans had little choice but to agree, sending yearly tribute to the Chinese emperor in return for nominal protection. This recognized Korea as the smaller and lesser state to China's dominant position. Trade and culture flowed from China to Korea.

The ties between China and Korea became set in stone during Korea's Chosun dynasty, thanks to its founder, Yi Song-gye (no relation to the later Admiral Yi), who ruled from 1392 to 1398. He cultivated close relations with China's Ming dynasty and imported technology and ideas. But of all the ideas Korea absorbed from China, none was more powerful or durable than the institutionalization of Confucianism in Korean culture. Confucianism had come to Korea from China in the sixth century A.D. Eight hundred years later, King Yi made it the official Chosun state religion.

Despite the weaving of Confucianism into Korean DNA, it could be argued Yi's greatest contribution to Korea was his bloodline. His great-grandson became Korea's most remarkable man: Sejong the Great.

Born in 1397, Sejong was the youngest of three sons of the third king of the Chosun dynasty. Bookish and inquisitive, Sejong was not destined for the throne. That right belonged to his oldest brother, who proved to be an excellent man of leisure but not a worthy successor. Sejong's father removed his oldest son from the line of succession and the middle brother became a monk, clearing the way for Sejong to take the Chosun crown in 1418, at age twenty-one.

Korea, like many other cultures, was a caste society, based on birth or, as it was called in ancient Korea, "bone rank." It was impossible to rise above your birth rank. Sejong broke open this idea. He astounded his royal advisers on his second day on the throne, seeking input from all ranks. He appointed the lower classes to civil service jobs. He felt it was critical that the people have the ear of the king and asked to hear directly from them.

In order to facilitate this, Sejong did nothing less than invent the modern written Korean language, Hangul. Before Sejong, only the ruling classes knew how to read and write. There was a spoken Korean language, but the written language of the Korean court was Chinese, and the few literate Koreans used a pared-down version of Chinese known as *hanja*, borrowing Chinese characters to transcribe spoken Korean. A literate underclass was considered potentially restive and politically dangerous, and some of Sejong's advisers opposed the spread of written language to the peasants. So the king worked on his language in secret, possibly with some help from trusted members of his Hall of Worthies researchers. In 1443 or 1444, records indicate, Sejong debuted his twenty-eight-letter phonic alphabet. (Four letters have become obsolete.) Hangul is simple and was designed that way so uneducated peasants—and even American executives—could learn it. Korea was still five hundred years away from becoming a democracy, but its earliest seeds were sown here. Sejong promoted the idea that one could advance on merit, not just privilege.

Under Sejong, the arts and sciences prospered, with the advancement of astronomy, agriculture, weaponry, metallurgy, and printing. (Contrary to popular notion, Gutenberg did not invent movable type. He advanced it and mass-produced the first printed book, the Bible, but movable type was in use in China in the eleventh century and metal movable type appeared in Korea a century after the Chinese invention.) One of Korea's greatest inventors under Sejong was a natural-born engineer named Jang Yeong-sil who had come from the lowest classes. Had Jang been born under any previous Korean king, he would have, at best, been a village tinkerer. But Sejong recognized Jang's genius and gave him a place at the Chosun court. Yang went on to invent water clocks and sundials to mark the passing of time and celestial globes to track the path of the heavens a generation before da Vinci created his wonders in Italy.

Sejong was a voluminous reader of Mencius, an ancient Chinese philosopher who, legend has it, was taught Confucianism by Confucius's nephew. Mencius applied Confucianism to government, writing that the good of the commoner was the highest goal of a rightly venerated king, who should act as a steward. In his inauguration speech, Sejong promised to rule benevolently, which he believed would create a harmonious state. For all of Sejong's radical ideas about caste, his Confucianism did not destroy the hierarchy; instead, it clarified and rationalized it. At the same time he and his father introduced a crucial concept to Korea's Confucianism that holds to this day: it will reward a person with a good idea if he plays by the rules. This is most clearly seen in Korea's great *chaebol*, which hire the best output of Korea's top universities and place them into a command-and-control, top-down structure. On its surface, such a structure may appear to be the enemy of creativity. And, indeed, such a system can prove an effective killing ground for new ideas if only for the number of hurdles the fledgling idea must span. But the system also applies discipline and rigor to creativity, which—left without it—can flail about aimlessly, produce nothing, and end up being rewarded simply for its existence, as has been seen in too many failed American dot-coms. Korean corporate Confucianism takes new ideas, wrestles with them, roughs them up, and—if they're still standing—propels them to success with resources unavailable outside the *chaebol*.

At Hyundai, an example of this process was the sporty Veloster coupe, which debuted on the stage behind Vice Chairman Chung at the 2011 Detroit Auto Show. Because of its weird nature—one door on the driver's side and two on the passenger's side—and its sleek but unusual hatchback design, the Veloster was never meant for the production line. Instead, it was rolled out at the 2007 Seoul motor show as a just-for-fun concept car. The press reaction, particularly from the Korean media, was highly favorable, however, catching Hyundai by surprise. So the company researched the car's possible market segment, considered features and pricing, studied potential competitors, and found only one— the well-liked but decidedly retro Mini—and decided there was room for a sexy, modern-looking rival. The view from the top of Hyundai was not pro-Veloster, but the concept and the research won the day. Hyundai introduced the production-model Veloster in 2012 and wowed critics with its creative design, which proved to have a lasting impact. In the auto business, a "halo" car is typically the brand's most expensive model, and although its sales are respectable if modest, the car is meant to throw a halo over the other models, which in theory benefit from the halo's fairy dust. The classic halo car is the Chevrolet Corvette, a world-class supercar that shares nothing with the bread and butter of the Chevy lineup—its pickup trucks and sensible sedans and SUVs—except the brand name. For many critics, Veloster was a "reverse halo": a $22,000 high-mileage car whose design and sexiness were so profound as to make people think differently about the entire Hyundai lineup.

In many ways, the Veloster epitomized the version of Confucianism shared by China and Korea: Confucianism as an efficient means to order civil society and the bureaucratic process and to get things done. When Japan imported Confucianism via Korea in the sixth century A.D., scholars hewed to the Confucian principles of harmony and humaneness. Yet Japan never adopted Confucianism's elaborate exam culture meant to ensure competent civilian administration, which is still embedded in China and Korea. This was the way of the scholar-bureaucrat. Instead, over time, Japan's brand of Confucianism became a way to validate the country's Japan-ness. It elevated the samurai, who stood atop the Confucian hierarchy, creating the warrior-bureaucrat. Chinese-Korean Confucianism values duty to parents and loyalty to a ruler. If a conflict exists between the two, generally duty to parents outweighs duty to ruler. In Japan's version of Confucianism, however, there is no conflict. Duty to parents means absolute loyalty to a ruler. This, combined with Japan's intense chauvinism, effectively nationalized and militarized Confucianism in Japan.

I understood the similarities between Korea's and China's Confucian social organization and understood that both Korea and China had suffered under Japanese invasion and occupation, uniting them in an enemy-of-my-enemy way.

Now, whether this history has any bearing on why Hyundai sells more cars in China than anywhere else in the world is open to debate.

As Hyundai's biggest market (the U.S. is number two, Korea is number three), China accounts for nearly 25 percent of the company's total global sales. Hyundai built its first factory in China, near Beijing, in 2002, added two more in the following years, and in 2014 said it would build a fourth and fifth plant, bringing Hyundai's combined manufacturing capacity in China to 1.4 million cars per year.

Chinese car buyers have embraced Hyundai, as they have most imported cars. China has its own massive auto industry, with more than 170 automakers. This is radically different in scale but no different in practice from the early U.S. automotive industry, when dozens of automakers sprang up, competed, and died off. The concept of a Big Three is relatively recent and dates only to American Motors' subsumption into Chrysler in the 1980s.

Western auto analysts expect a rapid consolidation of the Chinese auto market in the coming years, with eventually five to eight of the biggest brands, such as BYD, SAIC, Geely, and Chery, buying up the smaller ones and surviving. China has great plans for its domestic auto market. In the medium term—say, ten to twenty years— Beijing wants five of the world's top-ten-selling brands to be Chinese.

But they have a long way to go. First, they have to convince Chinese buyers. Many are newly affluent and, as is the custom with new-money cultures around the world, that which is foreign is seen as more luxurious and preferential.

The top-selling foreign automakers in China are GM and Volkswagen. The combination of German brands—VW, Mercedes, BMW, and Audi—account for nearly one-quarter of all sales. Sales of Chinese brands—from those 170-some automakers—account for about 40 percent of the market. Hyundai and Kia combine for about 9 percent of the market.

Hyundai, like all automakers, quickly learned the Chinese auto buyers' preference, and it is for bling. Even if Chinese buyers are purchasing a bargain-priced family car, they want it to look prestigious. To cater to the Chinese buyers, Hyundai in 2013 launched a Chinese version of the Elantra, its biggest-selling car around the world. The Chinese Elantra, called Langdong, is slightly longer but more important replaces the subtle Hyundai hexagonal grille with a shining chrome grille. The Langdong is one of Hyundai's biggest-selling models in China.

The Chinese auto market, like most of its markets, is a tricky bargain for foreign companies. The hundreds of millions of potential customers, many of whom are growing richer and more global by the second, is irresistible. But in order to reach them, foreign companies must wade through the often impenetrable Chinese bureaucracy, deal with corruption and outright intellectual property theft, and—at least in the case of the auto industry—partner with Chinese automakers, many of which are owned by the state.

Beijing requires all foreign automakers to form a 50–50 joint-venture (JV) partnership with domestic automakers if they want to do business in China. It's not always a one-to-one partnership: more than one foreign automaker will partner with a Chinese automaker or a holding company. Each of these JVs requires government approval. The reality of this creates strange alliances. One foreign automaker may end up in a partnership with a Chinese automaker that is also partnered with one of the foreign automaker's competitors. For instance, Chinese automaker Dongfeng has JVs with Nissan, Honda, and Kia—all direct competitors with each other. Many of the state-owned automakers, such as Chery, survive on state subsidies and profits from their JV partner. This is a market inefficiency, one of the many found in the planned, centralized Chinese economy that places social stability above economic goals. And this is simply the price of doing business in China.

As a resident of Seoul for more than three years, I was immersed in Korean culture, but my geopolitical center of gravity was China. There was no way it could be otherwise. I spent more time reading and thinking about China in those years in Korea than I had in my entire life. China is the great sun in Asia, illuminating the hemisphere, keeping objects in orbit around it, and at times giving off the vague threat of going supernova at any moment.

My first trip to China came in spring 2011, when Rebekah and I decided to take a long weekend trip. We joked about the oddness of our new lives—"popping off to Shanghai for a weekend"—and although we didn't feel like international jet-setters, it probably looked that way on Facebook.

As China's financial center, Shanghai feels like New York, especially in the get-rich 1980s: rich, fast, smart, and almost independent of the nation's capital. It throbs with materialistic avarice.

Rebekah and I had lunch at an outdoor café in the trendy and expensive Xintiandi shopping district. Our waiter was a young, really, *really* wired Chinese guy with very good English and an affable if in-your-face style.

He found out that we were Americans and delighted in telling us how much he loved "he-men" Americans, such as George W. Bush and John Cena, the WWE wrestler. He whipped out his camera phone and showed us a selfie he'd taken with the world's richest man, Carlos Slim, who of course had visited his café a month earlier. And he was struck with Rebekah.

He told me he'd seen a lot of American women but that I had "picked the best."

"You must be successful," he added, obviously missing my movie-star looks. "You CEO?"

That night Rebekah and I had one of the better dinners we've had, ever, at a restaurant on the western bank of the Huangpu River, overlooking the multicolored lights playfully dancing up and down the skyscrapers of Pudong across the river. On the balcony of the restaurant, large Chinese flags flapped in the breeze, a characteristically Chinese juxtaposition with the skillfully prepared Western meal we were enjoying. After dinner, we held hands and walked along the Bund, or west bank of the river, with the European architecture of the French Concession to our left and the Jetsons-like futurescape of Pudong glimmering to our right. It was February, but the temperatures were in the sixties. It was impossible not to feel like you were walking in the past and looking into the future. This is the moment when China seduces a tourist.

But as cosmopolitan and romantic as Shanghai felt, we remembered we were in China when we returned to our hotel. Rebekah noticed her Kindle had been tampered with. Someone had entered our room, taken the e-book reader from its leather case, fiddled with the back, and awkwardly returned it to its case. We were reminded of a story told to us by Foreign Service friends in Seoul who had been posted to Moscow during the latter years of the Soviet Union. They'd return to their apartment and find a cigarette butt floating in the toilet, left there on purpose to let them know they were being monitored by the state. This episode, and several articles I read by foreign businesspeople traveling to China who'd had their electronics tampered with and hacked, led me, on subsequent business trips to China, to never let my electronics out of my sight. I'm sure I looked a little pretentious carrying my iPad all around motor shows, but it gave me peace of mind.

Going to China was not easy for me. I was a Cold War kid, and was raised to fear and oppose communism, whether Sov or ChiComm. But my suspicion of China was not only legacy-based; I kept up with the news. I recognized that the Chinese version of communism was different from the Soviet version, had lifted hundreds of millions of Chinese out of poverty for the first time, had provided a massive export market and jobs to the U.S. and was open to the outside world in a way the USSR never was. Nevertheless, China is totalitarian, brooks no political dissent, and shackles free speech and worship. I was ambivalent about spending my money on a holiday trip—a nonnecessary visit— that would, in its almost incalculably small way, I acknowledged, go toward propping up a regime that I believed oppresses its citizens.

But curiosity got the better of me, so we decided to make the most of our chance. We hired a young female Chinese tour guide, Julie, to show us Zhujiajiao, a 1,700-year-old town about an hour outside of Shanghai built around a number of streams, canals, and small rivers. It has become a tourist site and is promoted as "the Venice of Shanghai." We visited homes and bridges built during the time of the Italian Renaissance and took a canal boat ride. We pushed our way through narrow streets lined with vendors selling trinkets and Chinese food as the old lady shopkeepers came out from behind their goods and grabbed us by the arms, physically dragging us toward their stalls in a rural replay of Shanghai's relentless quest for lucre. Fried silkworms sizzled on hot grills; their pungent smell of burned hair filled the air. At the "Setting-fish-free Bridge," locals sold small carp in bags filled with water. You were supposed to let them go in the river, which would bring good luck and carry away your bad luck with the fish. It's unclear if your bad luck got passed on to the next customer, because we could see people downstream scooping up the carp with nets for resale.

During our half-day tour, I got a chance to quiz Julie—Rebekah would say "interrogate"—about issues of the day, including political freedom, Internet openness, and Chinese hacking. As a tour guide for Westerners, I knew she'd be ready with answers; I just wanted to hear what those answers were.

I asked her about the Chinese government blocking Facebook. "We do not need it," she said. "We have our own Facebook," referring to Renren, which began life in 2005 as Xiaonei.com, or "On Campus," a Facebook clone that assiduously copied Facebook's layout and shades of blue.

When the conversation turned to politics, Julie opined that there eventually will be more than one party in China, but that change "will only come from the top." Like most Chinese, she had never heard of the Tiananmen Square massacre of 1989; it is censored from textbooks. Asked about democracy, Julie said that poorer, less-educated rural Chinese "are not ready for it," which is the party line. She said the best form of political system is "freedom with controls," but the thing she said that still sticks in my mind years later, because it's a piece of social engineering genius by Beijing, is this quote: "We have enough freedom." If a government can get enough of its people to believe that, it's won.

I tried, vainly, to explain that to a Westerner, certainly an American, there is no such thing as "enough" freedom. Political freedom is a binary thing for us: either you're free or you're not. Naturally, certain revelations about the activities of the National Security Agency and other U.S. government agencies have tempered this binary view a bit. Nevertheless, when Americans step into a voting booth, they have a real, legally protected choice, and that's not naïveté.

The Chinese government has walked the delicate line of supplying its people with economic freedom while withholding political freedom. This was Deng Xiaoping's masterpiece. He believed that an open economy leads to efficient markets, but an open political system leads only to chaos. Deng's—and now Beijing's—wager is that its people will trade stability and economic prosperity for political freedom. Given China's long history of eras of great advancement followed by epochs of savagery and destitution, one after the other, the utmost goal of the ruling People's Party in Beijing is stability. That governs every decision it makes, and those who interact with China must understand that.

China is not unique in trying to run a country this way. One of the most eye-opening things this West Virginia bumpkin realized in his travels outside of the U.S. is just how many people are willing to shave off a little, or more than a little, personal freedom in exchange for prosperity and stability. If your country was recently poor and unstable, that makes more sense than it might to an American. You'll see that bargain in Singapore, which is a modern, prosperous, quality-of-life paradise—as long as you don't break a law. Then you'll be subject to the country's laws, which Westerners see as disproportionate and draconian but which Singaporeans see as a just price for living in what they believe is a civilized fashion. You'll even see that bargain in Korea, where voters are not allowed to Tweet pictures of themselves in front of campaign posters of political candidates, because the government feels it could unduly influence the outcome of an election. Korean voters are not even allowed to give the ubiquitous-in-Asia peace sign in photographs posted to social media on election days, because Korean candidates are identified by numbers, and the two-finger peace sign could be seen as an endorsement of candidate number two.

I certainly saw the allure of China and the attractiveness for Hyundai and all automakers. I had felt the seemingly limitless optimism, openness, and enthusiasm of its next generation, who are certain they're riding the wave of the next big thing. I had treated a group of auto journalists to a spectacular meal at a restaurant off Tiananmen Square with a striking view of Mao's mausoleum, the Monument to the People's Heroes, and the Forbidden City in the distance, all spectacularly illuminated at night. Six hundred years of history lay before us, both glorious and tragic, right at the heart of China, the great, throbbing story of the twenty-first century. I had also experienced the pollution; Chinese automakers' blatant and unapologetic rip-offs of Western car designs on display at Chinese auto shows; the state's control over its citizens' information and opinions; and even the unvarnished hunger for money and advantage that leads someone to violate a foreign tourist's personal electronics.

I kept coming back to what was, for me, the most telling—and seductive—paradox that is China: although the communist party is officially atheist, nowhere in the world is Christianity—evangelical, Bible-based Christianity—growing faster. There is a surging hunger for it. The state authorizes an antiseptic form of Christian worship, but once Chinese Christians compare that to what they're reading in the new Bibles passed out by missionaries, they find the state's offering wanting. So they are organizing underground churches by the hundreds. The state crackdown on these unauthorized churches ranges from annoyance level—shutting off the electricity to the building hosting the church—to imprisonment. And yet the churches are still growing. As one Chinese pastor put it, "We sing sitting down to keep our voices low, so the neighbors won't complain to the authorities." In other words, as long as the churches do not threaten China's stability, they can continue, albeit sitting down. Perhaps one day they will be able to stand up.

# 11

## THE DANGEROUS COUSINS KIM

A few months after we had settled in Korea, Rebekah and I got a chance to visit the demilitarized zone, or DMZ, which separates North and South Korea. It is the most heavily defended border in the world. In theory it's still a live battlefield; only a cease-fire preserves the peace between the two Koreas. At the same time it's a tourist attraction. The USO runs one-day bus tours that leave from Seoul every day, only adding to the bizarreness of the whole thing. I couldn't help but think of the Civil War tourists who rode out from Washington with picnic lunches to watch the battles in Northern Virginia.

Rebekah and I took a Saturday tour to Panmunjom, the aban-doned village on the border where the armistice was signed in 1953. The DMZ itself is not the border. The DMZ is a strip of land run-ning the width of the country roughly along the 38th parallel and is four kilometers wide, two kilometers on each side of the border. It largely is a no-man's-land, but it is not barren. It is a remarkable and verdant wildlife preserve, home to several rare species. And it's not entirely absent of people. A South Korean propaganda effort has placed about 250 farmers inside the DMZ. In return for tilling the first land that would fall to invading North Korean forces, the government pays each farmer nearly $90,000 per year.

A row of humble one-story huts straddles the actual border at Panmunjom. Each hut has two doors, one opening into North Korea, the other into South Korea. Looming over the huts on each side of the border are large, modern government structures. Inside the big building on the South side, our tour is told by U.S. military officials that, once outdoors, we will take several steps to get to the huts. We are warned to keep our arms at our sides and not to point or gesture at anything. We are being photographed by the North and are told that pictures of pointing tourists can easily be turned into North Korean propaganda.

The scene is a mixture of tension and absurdity. We walk inside one hut and see a conference table astride the border that bisects the building. A line is painted on the floor. Once we walk past the table, we are in North Korea. Our guide tells us not to wander too closely to the door opening into North Korea, as it has been flung open by soldiers who have snatched tourists. We are told stories about past negotiations where North Korean agents have surreptitiously sawed down the chair legs on the South's side of the conference table the night before talks so the South's representatives would have a literally lower position in negotiations with the North.

Outside, on the ground, a short concrete curb defines the border between the two warring nations. Snow had fallen in the days before our tour. It was shoveled from the ground on the South side of the curb and on the North side, but the snow remained piled on top of the curb itself. I suppose if one party were to shovel the curb, it could be construed as an incursion.

It's easy to think of North Korea as a joke, because it has done so many childish things. Over the years the South has discovered several tunnels dug under the DMZ by the North for spy infiltration. Caught red-handed digging one tunnel, the North told the South, no, the tunnel was not for spying on the South. They were just mining for coal, the North said. And, in perhaps history's lamest attempt to hide evidence, the North painted the tunnel walls black and hoped the South would buy it. In a more recent example, instead of simply ignoring the 2014 Hollywood farce *The Interview*—whose admittedly tasteless plot involved assassinating the North Korean leader—North Korea petulantly hacked Sony Pictures, the film's studio, causing embarrassing internal e-mails to be leaked and costing millions in security and brand damage, not to mention the studio head's job.

North Korea is no joke to the South. In 1968, North Korean commandos ordered to kill President Park Chung-hee got within 100 meters of the presidential residence, called the Blue House for its roof color, before being stopped by security forces. Six years later came the second attempt on Park's life, by the North Korean sympathizer who killed Park's wife. In 1983, North Koreans tried to kill South Korean president Chun Doo-hwan during a state visit to Rangoon by planting a bomb in a ceiling of a building he was scheduled to visit. He was delayed in traffic but the bomb went off anyway, killing several senior advisers already there. In 1987, ostensibly upset that it had been denied the honor of hosting any of the 1988 Olympic games that went to Seoul, North Korean agents exploded a bomb on a Korean Air flight, killing 115. In 2006, North Korea detonated a nuclear bomb, repeating the exercise in 2009, 2013, and 2016. The spring before we arrived in Korea, in 2010, a North Korean torpedo sank the South Korean corvette *Cheonan*, killing forty-six sailors.

When we visited the DMZ, Kim Jong-il had been supreme leader for seventeen years, having inherited the dictatorship from his father, Kim Il-sung, who was installed by the Soviets after they took the northern part of the Korean Peninsula from the Japanese in 1945. Kim Il-sung advocated the political and economic policy of *juche*, or self-reliance, cutting off his people from the outside world and virtually severing trade. He also built the gulags that continue to this day and engineered a cult of personality around him. Kim Jong-il took over the country at his father's death in 1994. On his watch, as many as 600,000 North Koreans starved during a famine caused by incompetence. Health experts visiting the country determined that chronic malnourishment caused North Koreans to be, on average, three inches shorter than their genetic cousins in the South. The country adopted a military-first policy. Kim Jong-il repeatedly outfoxed and embarrassed Seoul with bogus olive branches.

So, the longer one lives in Korea, the less funny North Korea gets.

As bellicose as North Korea can be, threatening to turn South Korea into a "lake of fire" every few months, a full-scale attack from the North was a theoretical if remote possibility. More worrisome to me was a rogue North Korean commander or an accident loosing a missile at one or both of the prime targets in the South: downtown Seoul, where my wife worked at the U.S. embassy, and the U.S. military base where we lived. The rest of the world thinks North Korea is crazy and unpredictable. South Korea does not. It believes the North is calculating. The South's thinking seems to come down to this: the South will respond gravely to the North's verbal threats and even endure the occasional fatal military action, such as the Yeonpyeong shelling, because the South believes the North is not reckless enough to launch a full-scale attack on the South, since the North would be obliterated in a counterattack by combined U.S.–South Korean forces. So South Koreans learn to live with the North and continue to absorb its occasional deadly attacks. It's like living next door to a bully.

Less physically threatening to those of us who lived in Seoul but more horrifying were the North's gulags. As recounted by numerous North Korean defectors, these camps are for political enemies of the North Korean regime, although most of the prisoners don't even know that. Kim Il-Sung believed that political prisoners must be punished to their third generation. They are the longest continuously operating gulags on the planet. People are born, live, and die in these squalid camps, where mothers turn on their own children for scraps of food and never know why they are there or what exists outside the camps. So lowly are they regarded, they are not even given the privilege of learning about their Dear Leader. As far as they know, life is simply a brutal cage with no escape and no explanation.

Ever since the cessation of the Korean War, South Korean presidents have tried to figure out how to handle North Korea, often in league with the U.S. Some, such as conservative president Lee Myung-bak have hewed to the U.S. hard line that insists no quarter be given to the North until it abandons its nuclear desires. Under these administrations, there is no talk of rapprochement with the North. Other South Korean presidents, such as liberal Kim Dae-jung, have tried to pacify the North. Kim launched what he called the "Sunshine Policy" of engagement that led to the building of a vacation resort of sorts in the North open to tourists from the South and an industrial complex just over the border in the North where businesses from the South set up shop using cheap North Korean labor. The glimmering apex of the Sunshine Policy was the 2000 summit between President Kim Dae-jung and North Korean dictator Kim Jong-il, something few would have believed possible. For all this, Kim Dae-jung was awarded the Nobel Peace Prize in 2000 and South Korea swelled with pride.

But the Nobel committee acted before all the facts were in. As criminals do, the North simply took advantage of the South's good intentions. The North reneged on agreements, treating the industrial complex like a political tool and randomly barring South Korean businesses from it from time to time; and a South Korean tourist was even shot to death at the North Korean resort, closing it. Three years after the summit, an investigation showed that Kim Dae-jung only got Kim Jong-il to the negotiating table with a secret payment of $150 million. The Nobel Prize became a farce. By 2010, the South Korean government declared the Sunshine Policy a failure.

Many in the West don't understand the South Korean government's occasional impulse to placate the North when clear evidence appears to uniformly repudiate the idea. Western ex-pats living in South Korea don't understand what appears to be the general indifference to the North Korean gulags and the lack of any desire to challenge the North on its human rights abuses.

Yet, for many in the South, these policies make perfect sense. Despite the Stalinist government, North Korean citizens are still Koreans, and elderly South Koreans still have living relatives in the North whom they haven't seen since 1953. And, as was explained once to me by a middle-aged Korean friend who'd lived through conservative and liberal presidents, when the South has a liberal government that attempts to reach out to the North, general tensions in the South are lower. Furthermore, he said, it's good for the economy: if it looks to the outside world like North and South are on the brink of war, or not even on speaking terms, foreign investors will find much friendlier places to put their money.

Here's how I came to think about it: the North Korean regime deserves not one more day in power. The nuclear threat to the entire region is real and escalating. It has been a state sponsor of terror. The regime is guilty of the longest-running human rights atrocities in modern history. The South has received criticism for appearing to pander to and appease the North, only to be gulled—or attacked outright—each time. And some wonder why the loudest critics of the North's gulags come from outside of the South. But after living on the peninsula for more than three years and seeing the many ways people learn to live with this constant threat—a threat faced by no one in the U.S.—I came to believe that I don't have the right to judge how anyone in the South thinks about or behaves toward the North. Koreans just have to get on with their lives in the same way that a few generations of Russians and Americans did with the threat of global nuclear annihilation hanging over their heads.

### THE DICTATOR DIES

I was heading to lunch on Monday, December 19, 2011, around noon when BBC news, which I always had on the TV in my office, announced that North Korean dictator Kim Jong-il had died. South Korea immediately went on military alert. At Hyundai, it looked like business as usual. If this had happened in America, people would be up from their desks, forming little knots of conversation all around the office. Not here. Everyone was still at their desks. Maybe they were furiously messaging back and forth, but maybe not. Hyundai had no dealerships in North Korea. I briefly chatted with Ben, my team leader, about Kim's death, and he thought it was worrisome, as Kim had been—despite his savagery—a known quantity.

That night, when I pulled up to the security checkpoint at the main entrance to the base where we lived to show them my ID,

Henry the guard greeted me with his usual beaming smile and inquiry about my family's health. Henry—"My name is Henry! You can call me Henry!" he said the first time I met him—was a lovely older Korean man who took his job swiping ID cards and verifying identity quite seriously. "I have a very important job!" he once told me. He was always trying to improve his English by asking Rebekah and me about new words he'd learned. That night I said, "Wow, that was big news about Kim Jong-il, wasn't it?"

"What news?" Henry asked.

"That he died," I said. "It was announced today at noon."

"Really?" he asked, astonished. "I had not heard! Good. I am glad he is dead!"

I was the one who was astonished. How was it possible that eight hours had passed since it was announced on national news that South Korea's greatest enemy had died and Henry had not heard? Had he missed the news? Had no one thought to tell him? Was it simply not a big deal for South Koreans? I had no answers and drove home, puzzled as ever about the place where I lived, about its priorities, about how information travels (or doesn't); about this great, shadowy other culture that existed outside the walls of the military base and beyond my realm of comprehension. It was moments like these that made me realize I could live here for forty years, learn the language inside out, and still not understand Korea.

Kim Jong-il was succeeded by one of his sons, Kim Jong-un, who was such a mystery that news agencies could only report at the time that he was in his late twenties or early thirties. The new dictator attended a Swiss boarding school as a youth, where he apparently was obsessed with Michael Jordan, but any hopes that he would be a new-generation, Western-friendly reformer were quickly quashed. Kim wasted no time in consolidating his power by executing enemies and the perceived disloyal within his inner circles. These eventually took a darkly absurd turn: he executed one senior official by blowing him apart with an antiaircraft gun. Stories even leaked out that Kim executed enemies by feeding them to packs of wild dogs. Fantastical and impossible to verify, such tales nevertheless stoked Kim's cult of personality within the country and his air of unpredictability to the rest of the world, both of which he doubtless aimed to cultivate.

Kim does all of this to keep control of North Korea's 1 million-man army. As long as he is successful at this, any sort of people-led internal coup is impossible. People often asked me, "What are the Kims trying to achieve in North Korea? Do they want to attack the South? Use the nuclear threat to extort outside aid?"

Kim Il-sung, the founder of North Korea and the first of the Kim dynasty, was a revolutionary and may in fact have wanted to create a true Marxist state. He belonged to the Chinese Communist Party and served in the Soviet Red Army. But his son and now his grandson have only one goal in mind: the survival of the regime. When you see all of North Korea's moves as designed to hold on to power, they start to make grim but logical sense.

One day, though, the Kim regime is destined to fall, one way or the other. When that happens, there will be many beneficiaries, chief of whom are the prisoners of the gulags and the rest of the 25 million imprisoned North Koreans who will finally taste freedom—and a steady diet of healthy food. Hyundai will also benefit. Aside from profligate military spending and disproportionate allocation to make North Korea's capital Pyongyang into a Potemkin village for propaganda purposes, much of the infrastructure in the rest of North Korea is crumbling or nonexistent. When reunification happens, billions of dollars in South Korean government, private-sector, and foreign construction aid will flow into the North. Korea's leading maker of big trucks needed for this kind of construction is Hyundai's little-thought-of commercial vehicle division, whose day will have finally come. Hyundai also happens to have an entire engineering and construction affiliate—practiced at building nuclear reactors, ports, high-rises, highways, and dams all over the world—that could probably rebuild North Korea on its own.

# 12

## "THIS DOESN'T RATTLE"

It was at the 2011 Detroit Auto Show in America, the auto industry's taste-making market, that Hyundai had boldly stated that it
aspired to become a premium automaker. It set stakes improbably
high. Now, nine months later, it was time for Hyundai to make
its assault on Europe, where the true targets lay. Hyundai already
made cars easily the equal in quality and value of anything the
Big Three produced. If we were going to become a true premium
brand, it wasn't adequate to be as good as Ford or Chevy. We had
to be as good as Volkswagen, Mercedes, and BMW. We weren't
laughed off the stage in Detroit, but the Germans were a tougher
crowd. They guarded the superiority of their cars like Americans
guard their freedom: as a birthright and a fundamental compo-
nent of their national identity.

International motor shows around the world—even the
biggest—are usually contained to a connecting series of massive
convention center buildings. Frankfurt took it to another level.

The 2011 Frankfurt motor show occupied several connected halls; in addition, outside the halls, each German automaker built its own huge stand-alone pavilion. Audi's was so big, it had its own two-level track inside, where new Audis zipped around for media members to see. I remember walking around the Frankfurt show that year as Europe's economy and auto sales were falling to pieces—with 50 percent youth unemployment in Spain, Greece defaulting every other day, and even stalwart, sober Germany struggling—and thinking, "What recession?"

This show was terribly important to Hyundai. We were unveiling an all-new version of our best-selling car in Europe, the i30. The i30 was an economical and agreeable if unspectacular five-door hatchback that Hyundai had sold in Europe for years. The new i30 was something altogether different. It was designed to head-on challenge Europe's gold standard of affordable cars: the Volkswagen Golf.

Plenty of automotive writers will tell you that the Golf is the world's best car, pound for pound. Not only do they love its practical aspects, such as its roominess and features, but they also love to drive it. The Golf has an auto enthusiast's tight suspension, a peppy engine, and just the right touch in steering; in automotive parlance, the car gives great "feedback" from the road surface. Drivers agree. The Golf is perennially Europe's best-selling car. Nominally, the Hyundai i30 was a competitor to the Golf, occupying the same segment, or size, but that's where the comparisons stopped. No one hated the i30, but no one considered it a serious rival to the Golf. Globally, Volkswagen itself is a monolith, a fact that would surprise most Americans. VW has by far the largest share of the European car market, accounting for more than one-quarter of all sales, and has pulled even with Toyota as the world's biggest automaker. What's holding the German titan back from making Toyota the permanent number two automaker is the U.S. VW has never given Americans a compelling reason to buy its cars. With only 2 percent of the U.S. market, VW has a far greater chunk of the American mindshare, thanks to its clever ads and agreeable imaging, than actual sales.

But in Europe, VW is a monarch. And if Hyundai was going to carry off this "Modern Premium" brand elevation that the vice chairman had launched earlier in the year in Detroit, Hyundai had to make a dent in the European automotive psyche. In the way that Hyundai had benchmarked the Japanese automakers a decade earlier for quality, we were now benchmarking the Europeans for brand—that alchemic combination of quality, performance, legacy, prestige, and coolness. The i30 would be a key measure of how Hyundai's upmarket aspirations would play in Europe, another marker along our uphill path to premium. How much work had Hyundai put into the i30 to make sure all the details were dead-solid perfect? This much: a female member of Hyundai's i30 product team had spent literally months of her life folded into the back of an i30 as it was blasted with water hoses, frozen in subzero temperatures, and roasted in desert-level temperatures. Why? Because the new i30 had a clever gizmo on its rear hatch: when you put the car into reverse, the Hyundai *H* logo pivoted up and a small backup camera extended, like a machine gun from behind the headlight of James Bond's Aston Martin. This wow-factor feature was actually a complicated electrical-mechanical device that opened and closed to the outside elements, meaning it could not break down, it could not freeze shut, it could not leak, and it could not stick. To make sure none of those things happened—not just the first time a driver put the car into reverse, but ever, during the whole life of the car—a human being had to monitor hundreds of hours of all-weather testing from inside the hatchback, as this young Hyundai woman had.

Hyundai's press conference at the Frankfurt show would

launch the i30. Although it was September, it was unseasonably hot. Hyundai's booth was at the end of a long hallway lined by the Italians. You had to walk past the supercars of Ferrari, Maserati, and Lamborghini—and their leather-clad female models, looking like they'd wandered out of a high-end BDSM party—to get to the Hyundai booth. Some three hundred journalists packed into Hyundai's space to see the i30, raising the temperature to sweltering. Stagehands opened outside doors on either side of the stage in a vain attempt to coax a cross breeze.

Vice Chairman Chung was on hand to give the press conference's main speech, signaling the new i30's significance. The show started, the vice chairman walked onstage, hit his mark, opened his mouth, and started talking. And nothing came out. His wireless headset would not work. After an awkward few seconds that seemed to last forever, the head of Hyundai's European operations, a man with a backup plan, gave the vice chairman a handheld microphone. Mercifully, it worked. My one-take vice chairman was utterly unflustered: he restarted his speech and we were off.

After the presser, journalists streamed around the i30. It was completely redesigned from its predecessor and followed Hyundai's Fluidic Sculpture styling. Even though it was a five-door hatchback, the i30 was graceful and aggressive at the same time, with a muscular rear haunch propelling the car forward at a dynamic, rakish angle. I still think of it as the most beautiful Hyundai of the first Fluidic Sculpture era.

The i30 started with a platform shared with other Hyundai cars of the same size, but that was it. Everything else was new. The interior and exterior were designed at Hyundai's European design center in Frankfurt. It was assembled by Europeans at Hyundai's plant in the Czech Republic. And now it was being sold to Europeans as a plausible alternative to the mighty Golf.

Hyundai wanted Europeans to know the car was made for them, by them, on the Continent. The i30 embodied Hyundai's philosophy of designing and building, as completely as possible, its cars within the markets they are destined for. Some other carmakers had what is called a "world car" philosophy: Make a car vanilla enough that it will theoretically sell everywhere in the world. Hyundai, per its character, went the opposite way. Before a region-specific car was launched, Hyundai designers, engineers, and product teams spent months in the target market, learning not only the customer preferences there but absorbing the culture and ethos of the place. In the years before Hyundai launched its Eon subcompact in India, for instance, Hyundai designers spent weeks traversing the country, touring ancient architecture, making sketches of temples, examining the curve of lotus flowers, talking to Indians, looking for universally understood design elements in the culture that might be referenced and signified in the Eon as well as features that Indians wanted in their cars. Eon, for instance, had a higher ceiling than its segment rivals. Why? Sikh turbans. Hyundai did the same for new cars built specifically for and in the Russian, Chinese, and Brazilian markets.

Hyundai even made modifications for the U.S. market. My car in Korea, for instance, the large Hyundai Grandeur sedan, had a glossy black surface on its center console, a finish known in the industry as "piano black." The same car sold in the U.S. as the Azera has a matte finish. The first Azeras shipped to the U.S. also had the piano black finish, but too many customers complained that they showed smudgy fingerprints. So the Azera product team switched to the matte finish for the U.S. cars, which doesn't show fingerprints as obviously. Your first question may be "Don't Koreans care about fingerprint smudges?" The answer, I think, is that Korean drivers simply don't have smudgy fingers. Koreans rarely eat in their cars, and Americans have made a culture of the practice. A Hyundai colleague told the story of her time as an exchange student in the U.S. She and her host family went through a McDonald's drive-through to pick up dinner, which was familiar enough to her. But when they started eating in the car, she said, "I was horrified."

It's easy to see, then, that building a successful car for a particular market is like writing a dissertation on its culture and sociology.

The initial reaction from the automotive press milling about the i30 in Frankfurt was positive. They said it was a sign of the company's maturation and upmarket ambitions, satisfyingly conveying our messaging. But no amount of praise from auto journalists could compare to what shockingly came next. As a PR guy, I wish I could claim credit for it, because it would have been a career maker. But I cannot.

It is common for rival automaker CEOs to stroll the floor of motor shows checking out the competition, usually with a few top executives in tow. These visits are designed to *not* make news. The CEOs meander somewhat detachedly around their competition, not showing too much enthusiasm, not asking too many questions. That's what usually happens.

Usually.

Shortly after our i30 press conference concluded, VW CEO Martin Winterkorn appeared at our booth. Six feet tall and fit like a slab of Black Forest oak, with silver hair and all-business mien, Winterkorn was a striding example of Teutonic gravity. He is a colossus in the auto industry. Or, rather, he was, before a hard-to-believe scandal would come to rock VW and end Winterkorn's career. In 2015 it was discovered—partly by some engineers at my alma mater, West Virginia University, no less—that VW had been cheating diesel emissions tests all over the world. Their engineers had gotten too clever and invented an algorithm for their diesel cars that told the car when it was being tested for emissions. When it detected that the car was hooked up to a tester, the algorithm switched on the car's emissions controls, making the exhaust cleaner. When the test was over, the algorithm switched off the emissions controls—improving gas mileage and performance but also increasing the car's pollution by as much as 40 percent. It was a calamitous bet. When the cheat was discovered, it shocked the auto industry and destroyed the confidence of thousands of people who had bought the diesel VWs specifically because they were told VW diesels pollute less than gasoline-powered cars. For them, this was more than a carmaker trying to hide a defective part or putting off a recall: VW had desecrated their religion. As of this writing, it's unclear how dire VW's fate will be. Toyota's sales rebounded from its crisis. But this one is worse. VW's stock was punished; the company may face billions of dollars in fines from multiple governments (the cheating algorithm was installed in at least 11 million cars around the world): the brand was crippled; a pall was cast on diesel cars everywhere; and some VW officials may even end up in jail.

It would turn out that, back in 2011, when Winterkorn stepped into our booth in Frankfurt, the diesel deception had already been in place for more than two years. Engineers at other automakers were wondering how VW was making such clean-diesel cars and just assumed VW had better engineers. Such was VW's reputation for world-beating technology and engineering.

Winterkorn was the personification of this supremacy, and his every move was watched. When he came to our booth, he was accompanied by Klaus Bischoff, his head of design. Winterkorn circled the blue i30, peering down over his aristocratic, hawk-like nose, surveying it as a lion might a downed antelope. He pulled a pen from his pocket and probed at the car's open hatchback.

Then he walked around the front of the car, opened the driver-side door, and got in.

Inside, Winterkorn appeared to forget where and who he was. It seems hard to imagine, because dozens of auto journalists were watching him, amazed by what was happening in front of them. This was a mountain-comes-to-Muhammad moment. All I could think was that, in his mind, he was no longer the CEO of the world's number two automaker. Instead, he seemed to be a young engineer again, unguarded, incapable of stopping himself from curiously probing a fellow student's very interesting-looking experiment.

Winterkorn grabbed the i30's steering wheel, reached underneath, and flipped the lever that allows a driver to adjust the wheel up and down. He flipped it again. He called out to his chief designer and began barking questions in German:

"Bischoff!"

Bischoff walked over.

Winterkorn: "This doesn't rattle."

Bischoff tried the lever. It didn't rattle.

Winterkorn, somewhat sternly: "BMW can't do it, we can't do it," meaning neither BMW nor VW could prevent their steering wheel adjustment levers from rattling.

"We had a solution," Bischoff responded, surely regretting the words as they were coming out of his mouth, "but it was too expensive." Brilliant. I could not have summed up Hyundai's value proposition better or more succinctly.

Winterkorn snapped, *"Warum kann's der?"* Or: "Why can they do it?" Then he gave the i30's driver's-side vanity mirror cover a little ticked-off flip back and forth and exited the vehicle.

This scene would have been remarkable enough had it played out only in front of the assembled automotive journalists and stunned Hyundai employees. But it was not. Turned out, it was all being filmed. Seconds after Winterkorn settled into the i30's driver's seat, a video shooter popped into the backseat and filmed over Winterkorn's right shoulder. The video posted to YouTube almost immediately. Winterkorn never realized what was happening. Or, amazingly, never cared. What unfolded was beyond anything anyone at Hyundai could have ever hoped for or thought up—no guerrilla marketing team would have chanced it—and it probably sent beautifully engineered office chairs flying from windows of VW's Wolfsburg headquarters the next day as the YouTube numbers kept piling up.

It is hard to explain to someone outside the auto industry the impact this had. The video has nearly 2 million views. Articles were written about it. It became lore on the motor show circuit, with auto journalists still mentioning it to me two years after it happened. Looking back, I believe the "Winterkorn Incident," as I came to think of it, did as much for Hyundai's aspirations to move upmarket as anything else I saw during my three years at the company.

A few giddy hours after we had ruined Martin Winterkorn's motor show, we held our media reception. Some two hundred reporters showed up for free food and drink, and a number of our Korean and European executives mingled. The vice chairman shocked everyone and showed up, too. He worked the room like a pro, answering journalists' questions and offering frank appraisals of his company's strengths and weaknesses. Reporters asked about the Winterkorn Incident, and he was gracious and demure in response, complimenting the VW brand. I was thrilled to see him winning over the reporters, but a little dispirited as well, thinking, "If I could get you to do this all the time, we'd be the most popular auto brand in the world," all the while knowing it was impossible.

Toward the end of the evening, my boss, Mr. Lee, pulled me

aside and, out of nowhere, offered me the chance to spend a few months working back in the U.S. in 2013. This had never been broached; it had never occurred to me. Mostly because my contract ran only until October 2012, when Rebekah's posting in Seoul was set to end and she'd be sent to another assignment, most likely back to the U.S. for several months to learn another foreign language before being sent overseas again. I had mentioned this to my boss—in passing, I believed. Apparently, Hyundai had taken it to heart and had a longer-term plan for me.

"I know that your wife will return to the U.S. after her two years at the embassy in Seoul," he said. "I will work it out so that you can work from there for a few months while she's there."

I could barely believe what I was hearing. This was shockingly generous and, I believed, a real sign of how Westernized and progressive the company was striving to become. I thanked him profusely and called Rebekah as soon as I could to tell her the good news. She was equally floored. We could not believe the blessing. We started to sketch out what an additional two years would look like with me in Korea and Rebekah . . . somewhere else. Could it work out? Would the State Department accommodate her? Would it be possible for Rebekah to extend her posting in Korea? Those were questions for a later time. Right now Rebekah and I talked and laughed together on the phone—me in Germany, her in Korea—like two kids who just got told the next year will have an extra Christmas.

# 13

## THE CHAIRMAN ARRIVES

One Sunday evening several months after we'd got Lily, our Korean Jindo dog, Rebekah and I pulled up to our house after returning from a weekend trip. We had hired a neighborhood boy to walk Lily a couple times a day and feed her. While in the house, Lily would be kept in the combination kitchen and breakfast nook, a large area with a tile floor and lockable doors at each end. We had done this before with Lily to good effect.

Rebekah was first in the door and I followed with suitcases. She walked out of my sight toward the back of the house and the kitchen to see Lily. The next thing I heard was Rebekah shriek.

I dropped the suitcases and hurriedly rushed to Rebekah to see her stopped in her tracks and looking at something neither of us could initially process: a hole in the bottom right of the still-locked wooden kitchen door, about nine inches high and twelve inches wide. The edges of the hole were sharp wooden shards; sawdust was piled on the floor on either side of the door.

Our first thought was that someone had broken in and harmed Lily. Panicked, I called, "Lily! *Where are you?*"

Lily, it turned out, was in the kitchen. She poked her head through the hole in the door. Then she hopped through the hole and ran up to us, affectionately. It became instantly clear to both of us what had happened. In the twenty-four hours since she had last been walked and fed by the neighbor boy, Lily had systematically and relentlessly chewed a hole in the wooden kitchen door because she wanted out.

This was remarkable. We had seen her gnaw around doorframes and on various items, but never through a piece of wood with the raw, ceaseless determination of John Henry battling the steam drill.

This was not a solid hardwood door, but it was not a hollow-core door, either. It had heft to it. It stood between her and what she wanted, which was the other side. I photographed the door and produced the picture upon request, because no one ever believes me when I tell the story.

It was at this moment that, finally, Lily's true character came into sharp focus. She was the Terminator. And she was in our house.

There's a line from the first *Terminator* movie that described the Arnold Schwarzenegger killing machine:

Listen, and understand. That Terminator is out there. It can't be bargained with. It can't be reasoned with. It doesn't feel pity, or remorse, or fear. And it absolutely will not stop, ever, until you are dead.

That was our Lily. It was chilling to watch how dispassionately she pursued her savagery and depredation: never a bark, never a threatening move. Only the swift, silent velocity of cold-blooded purpose.

It's worth noting that the South Korean military's alert status, like the U.S. DEFCON system, is called Jindogae, or "Jindo dog." Jindogae 1 is the highest level of alert, meaning an attack is imminent.

Lily was always at Jindogae 1.

On the day after Thanksgiving 2011, Rebekah and I had returned from shopping on base. Lily was in the backyard. We had several bags to carry in, so I propped open the front door. Rebekah, unaware that the front door was open, let Lily in the back door and, in a second, she was out the front door and loose, off her leash. I didn't realize this until, standing at the trunk of our car, I looked down and saw her looking up at me, tongue wagging.

A cold chill hit me. All sorts of terrible scenarios ran through my head. I put down the bag of groceries slowly, so as not to startle her. I felt like I was looking at a two-year-old who had somehow gotten hold of a loaded gun. "Easy, Lily," I said, as I slowly went for her collar . . .

. . . and she was off!

Lily ran toward the back of the neighbor's house, sure that this was a game. I spent the next five minutes futilely trying to catch her as she darted back and forth just out of my reach, toying with me. Then she sprinted to the front of a neighbor's house and out of view, toward the sidewalk, as I ran behind. My eye tracked upward and saw three small neighbor girls walking on the sidewalk with their tiny white Maltese in front of them.

"Oh, God, no," I thought. We were at Jindogae 1.

I didn't see it start, but I heard the screams. Three little girls shrieking in terror, pretty much the worst sound in the world. As I rounded the corner of the house, I saw Lily with the Maltese clamped in her mouth, trying to shake it to death.

I don't know how I did it, because all I remember is a violently twisting, furry storm of teeth and white fur, but I managed to pull the little Maltese, "Pokey," from Lily's jaws and set it down as I held Lily's collar. Lily was still silent. No barking, no growling. The girls were hysterical. Pokey, somehow not dead, sat on the sidewalk shaking. Rebekah by now had heard the commotion and came running.

Short of blowing up a neighbor's house, this is the worst kind of neighbor you can be: your dog attacks the neighbor's dog in front of his three little girls, probably traumatizing them for life. Forget about the vet bill: Send me the therapy bills. The girls' father, a Korean-American U.S. Army colonel, was, as you might expect from his training, levelheaded, calm in a crisis, and reasonable. Pokey was taken to the vet and worked on; Lily had somehow sheared layers of skin apart with her puncture wounds and shaking. Over the next several days, we paid plenty of visits to the colonel's household to check on Pokey—*"Please, Pokey, don't die!"*—and repeatedly told the girls how sorry we were.

Pokey would come to make a full recovery and the family bore us no ill will. But of course the attack had to be reported, and the judgment of the U.S. embassy was swift: Lily could no longer live on base. We were heartbroken in the way that parents of criminals and drug addicts are. But we could no longer avoid the fact: Lily was a killer.

Lily's last night with us, I left the house on some errand and turned to look at our front window. There was Lily, standing on her hind legs, front paws on the back of the sofa, looking out at me as she always did when I came or left. A few steps behind her stood Rebekah, sobbing.

A year after we got her for only $50—and she ended up conservatively costing us about $5,000 in ruined products, wasted training, home repairs, and vet costs—we drove Lily back to the shelter, finally admitting to ourselves what everyone else could see all along: that Lily was too wild to be a pet. If she were lucky, her best-case outcome would be adoption by a Korean farmer and chained to a stake, serving as a guard dog. Later we came to joke that we'd let a wolf live in our house for a year. And we told ourselves that we gave Lily maybe the best year of her life: shelter, food, warmth, and a target-rich environment.

I was not ready to bond with another dog after Lily. But Rebekah needed a dog. This provided a critical lesson to understanding my wife. If she has something to love, and you take it away from her, you'd better get her something else to love right away. The absence of Lily caused her to change, and I feared she might be dipping into depression.

The house did feel too quiet and stagnant. I relented. We'd get another dog. But where? Through a Korean-American diplomat friend at the U.S. embassy, Rebekah learned that Samsung, the Korean electronics giant, as one of their corporate social responsibility or charity programs, trained service dogs for the blind and other needy Koreans. Bred at a beautiful, state-of-the-art complex outside of Seoul, the Samsung guide dogs, mostly Labrador retrievers, spend the first two years of their lives in training and then are given to the blind. The training to be a service dog is so rigorous: only 30 percent graduate. The rest are put up for adoption. We had the chance to adopt one, but only because the mother of Rebekah's Korean-American friend was friends with the Samsung chairman's wife's niece or something.

Rebekah and her friend went to the dog training site a few days before Christmas 2011. She met four Labs that had been selected for her. Among them was a one-and-a-half-year-old male golden Labrador named Chae Um, a common Korean boy's name that means "fill up." We came to understand how well it suited him. He ran directly to Rebekah, kept shoving his head into her knee, and then sat on her foot. Then licked her.

The bond was instant and complete. Chae Um was wonderfully trained and docile and already had all the classic lovable Lab traits; he was just too playful to be a service dog. He was not only the anti-Lily—he got along with everyone—he was balm for the wound of losing Lily.

Rebekah and Chae Um came home and my wife was happy again. We decided we'd keep his commands in Korean, because that's how he learned them: "Sit" is *Anja*." But we wanted to give him a Western name. We knew it had to sound like Chae Um so he wouldn't get confused. We considered "Charlie," "Chips," and so on.

A couple days after we got Chae Um, I was driving home from Hyundai one night after having what I came to call a particularly "Korean" day at work, meaning it was a combination of my inability to communicate with my team members, their frustration with me and my frustration with them, and the whole Confucian corporate hierarchy that I found so difficult to comprehend and manage. I was feeling particularly foreign and a little peevish. Maybe I had a few peppercorns in my soul.

I walked into the house and told Rebekah, "Honey, I know what we're going to call this dog. We're going to call him 'Chairman.'" It was a perfect combination of homage to my Korean employer and gentle subversion. It sounded a lot like "Chae Um" and the dog responded instantly to his new name. Plus, it's just hilarious to call a dog "Chairman."

Most of my Korean team members had met Lily, knew how her sad story ended with us, and also knew we'd gotten a new dog to replace her. I confess I took some puckish glee in telling them our new dog's name. Their reaction was a combination of delight and horror. So deeply freighted was my dog's name that, whenever friends at work would message me to ask about Chairman, they would type, "How is Ch*****n?" I don't know if they were worried their messages were being monitored or if they were behaving like ultra-Orthodox Jews, who spell God's name "G-d" to show the ultimate respect.

Chairman filled the Lily-shaped hole in our lives. We drove him around the base and he sat up in the backseat, just like Lily.

A few weeks after we got Chairman, my wife, the dog, and I visited the Burger King drive-through. In the window was the employee who I saw most often, a charmingly friendly young woman called Yu Chin, who was maybe nineteen. Yu Chin gave us our drinks with her customary cheer: "Hello, sir!" she always chirped.

Just as we were about to drive off, Yu Chin's happy face suddenly morphed into what I could only think of as an exaggerated cartoon sad face.

"Sir," she said, "what happened to Rlirly?"

It took us a moment to translate in our heads, but then we realized she wanted to know what had happened to Lily. It seemed Yu Chin had waited weeks to screw up her courage to address an older social superior—and a foreigner—and ask a highly personal question. It was courageous.

I gave an answer I had pretty much waited my whole life to give. "Lily went to live on a farm," which was close enough to the truth. Her sad face turned happy again and Rebekah and I drove off, laughing at the improbability of it, but also astounded and moved by what had just happened.

# 14
## SEOUL SURPRISES

By age twenty-seven, Park Geun-hye, daughter of the man who built modern Korea, had lost both of her parents to assassins. When her mother was killed in 1974, she was twenty-two and became the nation's de facto first lady to her strongman father. When she was told of her father's murder five years later, her first question was "Is North Korea attacking?" This sort of iron nationalistic sentiment and pragmatism in the face of tragedy mirrored her father's and won her admiration around the country, along with sympathy. She became a star in Korean politics by the 2000s, even expressing measured regret for the treatment of political dissidents under her father's rule. She resuscitated a failing conservative party as its head, earning the title "Queen of Elections." She made her first bid for the presidency in 2007 but narrowly lost to Lee Myung-bak, a Hyundai man. By the end of Lee's term five years later, he had become so unpopular—even within his own conservative party—that Park, then the head of the same party, cannily gave the party a different name to distance herself from the toxic president. Personally, Park remains something of an enigma. Despite a lifetime in the public eye, Park has maintained tight privacy, and many Koreans feel they don't really know her even though she has been a constant presence in their lives. An anomaly among major world political figures, Park has remained single, saying repeatedly she is married to Korea.

In 2012, Park made a second run at the presidency. Initially, Koreans wondered if it would be more of the same conservative party dogma: Play tough with North Korea, befriend the *chaebol*, set ambitious economic growth targets, stay cozy with the U.S. Opponents darkly hinted that if Park were elected, she would mimic her father's autocratic ways, and democracy and transparent government would suffer.

Instead, Park spoke of different things.

One of Park's campaign planks called for the establishment of a "creative economy" in Korea. She recognized that the country could no longer keep doing business solely as it had done. It had to diversify, evolving from a stable, manufacture-and-export economy where innovation and employment came from the mighty *chaebol* in a top-down fashion, into an entrepreneurial, risk-taking economy where ideas came from the ground up and found the economic funding to grow. Korea needed a more robust start-up scene. It needed big-money venture capital. It needed, most of all, its well-educated youth to opt out of the "right spec" and follow their own dreams apart from lifelong employment at Samsung, Hyundai, and LG.

Park promised government-backed venture capital funds to help entrepreneurs launch their businesses. She lured Western tech titans such as Bill Gates and Mark Zuckerberg to personal meetings to pick their brains on how to find and nurture their analogs in Korea. She visited the U.S. to talk to venture capitalists and learn the secret of the U.S. success. She openly questioned the future of the very corporate titans that her father helped build, and that built modern Korea: "The past economic model designed to catch up with advanced economies drove Korea's rapid growth, but it has lost steam," she said. Koreans believed, and elected her.

At the same time President Park was trying to coax Korea through its midlife crisis and into its second act, the same thing was happening in the Seoul city government—basically, the proving ground for the Korean presidency—where another remarkable political transformation was playing out and under dramatic circumstances.

The mayor of Seoul, Oh Se-hoon, was seen as a rising star in the national conservative party and popular enough to have won a second four-year term in 2010. He was a polished, well-educated man who looked great in a suit and fit the time-honored mold of what a grown-up Korean leader should look like. The previous mayor of Seoul had become president, as had some of his predecessors, and Oh had similar ambitions—until he staked his office on a foolish stunt. The liberal party, which controlled the Seoul City Council, wanted the city to provide free lunches for all schoolkids. Mayor Oh wanted a more limited program. The issue was put to a referendum. As a way of trying to defeat the referendum, I guess, an overconfident Mayor Oh said he would resign if it passed. The referendum failed to draw enough voters to make it valid, meaning the liberal free-lunch-for-all plan went through. Mayor Oh was bound to follow through on his vow, and he resigned.

This proved to be a turning point for Seoul. A special election was held two months later and, literally out of nowhere, an older lifelong liberal social activist named Park Won-soon won the election. He had been imprisoned during youthful democratic protests against the Park Chung-hee dictatorship. He had since built a gilt-edged left-wing résumé, heading a watchdog group that fought government corruption; establishing a foundation to promote volunteerism and community service; and heading a commission to examine human-rights abuses in Korea, whether they came at the hand of foreign occupiers, such as the Japanese, or domestic dictatorships.

Park, now Mayor Park, was swept into office on a wave of dissatisfaction with the status quo in Korea. He was backed by a strong block of angry young voters who had spent their lives doing as they were told: studying until midnight and competing at school, following the well-trod path that made Korea great. Now they found themselves among the tens of thousands of similarly high-qualified applicants for a limited number of jobs at Samsung and Hyundai. They wanted change.

Like President Park, Mayor Park understood the need to diversify Korea's economy. He traveled to Silicon Valley and lured venture-capital money to Seoul. Grasping the coming sharing economy, Mayor Park initiated a range of sharing businesses and services in Seoul, including the creation of a city-funded sharing-economy business incubator. He said he would convert a disused downtown Seoul highway overpass built in the 1970s into an elevated walking park, Seoul's equivalent of New York City's High Line. This was the kind of mayor that Seoul had never seen before. Citizens of big European and Scandinavian cities were used to this kind of municipal administrator, but not Koreans, who have been taught that life is an uphill climb to make Korea great.

One of Park's first acts as mayor was to renovate the mayor's office, replacing solid walls with glass ones, making the office literally transparent. He live-streamed his inauguration on the Internet, showing his new-media savvy. Outside the mayor's office, he commissioned an eight-foot-high red and white sculpture, loosely based on a human ear, that includes a microphone and recorder. Seoulites can walk up to the ear and record their complaints into the microphone.

At the time, I could not believe Seoul elected this guy. He was so un-Korean. I figured he'd run up a big deficit with lots of free-ride government programs and get tossed out in the next Seoul mayoral election, replaced by another upright, conservative mayor who had worn ties since childhood. I figured the people of Seoul would come to realize their infatuation with Mayor Park was little more than a midlife-crisis fling.

# 15

## ALMOST, NOT QUITE ENGLISH

Early one morning I was sitting in my office at Hyundai, enjoying the quaint daily habit of reading the physical copies of the *Korea Herald*, the Asian edition of the *Wall Street Journal*, and the *Financial Times*. Of course, I already knew the night before if any of these papers had news about Hyundai. But as a former newspaperman I still enjoyed the serendipity of cruising through a newspaper and seeing stories I would never run across on the news pushes I had set up to send alerts about Hyundai and the auto industry.

I certainly never would have seen what I saw that cold winter morning.

Leafing through the Asian *Wall Street Journal*, which is tabloid-size, I came across a full-page ad for Hyundai. Unless a company's ad is addressing an issue or expecting to make some news, PR departments rarely see their own company's ads before they appear in print or on TV. Big, global image campaigns, sure, because PR will probably write a press release about them. But anything below that bar, probably not. That's standard in business. PR often feels like it's late to the table—that important public-perception decisions have been made by other departments and are faits accompli by the time they reach PR, which is tasked to release the information and defend it to the media.

I was delighted to see a nice ad for Hyundai in the *Journal*. It was an ad touting the Hyundai Tucson SUV's high residual value, often a key buying consideration. Delighted, that is, until I read the headline, which stretched across the page:

Years doesn't diminish the value of a Hyundai.

"Oh, no," I said.

My eyes darted to the right of the *Journal*, where the *Financial Times* lay, suddenly menacingly, on my conference table. It's a broadsheet paper, meaning it's twice as big as the *Journal*. I trepidatiously opened it, and leafed through the pages, and . . . oh, no.

There was the same full-page Hyundai ad, only twice as big. The headline also was twice as big:

# Years doesn't diminish the value of a Hyundai.

All the work the company had been doing, trying to persuade car buyers that Hyundai was striving toward a new, better image—that we were raising our quality in everything we did—had just taken a hit in print. Over the previous year, the company had made some big strides along the uphill path toward becoming a premium brand: the Detroit Auto Show, the Winterkorn Incident. This bungled newspaper ad was a stumble over an exposed root. Fixing this problem may not have been part of Hyundai's plan to become a premium brand, but it was part of mine.

Overreaction? Maybe. I plead guilty as a former newspaper reporter and editor who spent twenty years of his life trying to make English clear and correct. Fixing incorrect written English is nothing short of a cause with me. It affects me physically. For instance, because they make me laugh, I always catch misplaced modifiers.

This headline wasn't making me laugh; it was making me sick. Not just because of my personal peccadilloes but because, as a major global automaker, this sort of thing should not happen.

The way English is produced at Korean companies—and this is probably true of most non-English-speaking companies around the world—typically follows a system: the content is written in the native tongue, in this case Korean. Then it is sent out to a local translation agency. These agencies, at least in Seoul, have widely varying competence. Although many of them employ native English speakers, some are native English speakers from the U.S., some native-English speakers from Australia, some native English speakers from Canada, and so on. You can see the problem. Or these translation agencies employ Koreans who are, in theory, bilingual, fluent in Korean and English. But there are two problems here: first, which English are they fluent in, American or British? Second, Korean grammar is different from English grammar. For instance, in Korean, the verb comes toward the end of the sentence, unlike in English. That's why Korean translated into English invariably is in the passive, not active, voice, which creates deadly run-on prose. The passive voice always takes too long to get to the point. This is one of the elements of "Konglish," or Korean English.

After the translation agencies return the content to the company translated into a kind of English, the originating teams at Hyundai would publish it in the form of a product brochure, or ad, or text on a film, or a corporate website. The alternative is that the copy is written in-house, in English, by a bilingual Korean. But unless that person reads and writes native-level English, again, you often get Konglish. In addition, there was no one filter through which all English generated by Hyundai headquarters must pass, so that meant there was no one standard of English. Aside from the fact that we were publishing incorrect English, we were publishing English written in many voices.

Because Koreans are schooled in English from childhood, many Koreans think they have a good command of English. Instead, what they have is "test English," which is taught generally by Koreans, not native English speakers, and is geared for achievement on the national college entrance exam, not for daily use with native speakers. As Eduardo once told me, "Sir, it may be hard for us to speak and write Western English, but we can diagram the hell out of a sentence." Thus, Konglish may be unclear or baroque to English speakers, and the Koreans are at a loss to understand why.

A couple examples that I ran across during my time editing copy at Hyundai:

I am confident to say that the greatest dedication you have made would be a stepping-stone for the exceptional total brand experience before and after sales as well as during the ownership of Hyundai car.

And:

Recognizing such desperate efforts for quality improvement, many customers are turning to Hyundai.

I am not including these examples to get easy laughs or take cheap shots. It is only to illustrate how hard it is for nonnative speakers to understand exactly what native-standard English looks like. The translation labyrinth aside, the larger issue was that Koreans were trying to write publication-level text in a language that was not their own. It's difficult for anyone to work in a foreign language. You try writing marketing copy in Korean. Because I had never learned a foreign language, I had no gauge of how difficult this was. A Korean trying to learn English is not like an English speaker trying to learn Spanish. At least English and Spanish share the same alphabet and sounds. It's more like an English speaker trying to learn Chinese and execute it at business-level proficiency. Good luck with that.

Add to this the issue of tone between cultures: references that one culture will instantly get will be unfamiliar to the other. Touchstone emotions vary widely. Representations of deeply held love and sentiment in the East, for instance, may seem childlike and saccharine to Western consumers. Worse, even though East and West may more or less understand the definition of a word, all the rest of that word's freight—connotation, context, racial signifiers, and so on—can easily get lost in translation. For example, in the summer of 2012, Korean Air opened a new route to Kenya. In ads for the service, Korean Air wrote: "Fly to Nairobi with Korean Air and enjoy the grand Africa savanna, the safari tour, and the indigenous people full of primitive energy." Turned into a subject of Twitter mockery, Korean Air quickly apologized. Some good-natured Kenyans took it in stride, one Tweeting, "Thinking of lion hunting today and maybe some elephant baiting to deal with my #PrimitiveEnergy."

The offense goes both ways. I was lecturing to an MBA class at Seoul's Yonsei University once and wanted to outline Hyundai's family ownership. I grabbed the first colored marker I saw and began writing the names of prominent family members on the whiteboard. I turned around to make a point to the class and saw one Korean student had his hand up.

"Yes?" I said.

"Why did you write their names in red?" he asked.

"Oh, no," I thought. The minute he asked the question, I realized: in Korea, and in some other Asian countries, using red ink to write a name indicates death. I apologized profusely, explaining my faux pas to the Western students in the class, then erased all the red names, rewrote them in black, and moved on.

I became acutely aware of how hard it is to operate—especially in a business environment—in another language when I fully realized my burden on my Korean team members, who were forced to communicate with me in English. At one point I asked one of my junior team members, who spoke okay English, wrote it better, and was always trying to improve, "When you have to write to me in English, is it 50 percent or 500 percent harder than Korean for you?" He didn't even pause before answering: "Five hundred percent, sir."

Part of my job was to edit the official English correspondence of my higher-ups, write speeches for them, and generally deal with English generated by my bosses—and I was pleased to do that. But as it dawned on me that there were dozens of teams at headquarters generating English for external consumption, I realized neither I nor my team could edit it all, nor should we. We needed a dedicated English editor.

I alerted my team leader about the incorrect headlines on the Hyundai ads in the Asian *Wall Street Journal* and *Financial Times* ads, and he told me he would inform the team responsible for the ad. I asked: "And then what?" "It's not our team's responsibility," I was told.

This was true, but it irked me. If I see a person about to get run over by a bus, I'm not going to say, "Well, that's another team's responsibility." I'm going to try to get them out of the way of the bus. There is a saying throughout the big Korean *chaebol* that actually translates across most corporate cultures: "No one ever got fired for not doing something." Risk taking is rarely rewarded at big companies, and an employee is best thought of and rewarded by working diligently for their team and helping to meet their team's goals. The hiring of an English editor introduced all sorts of variables and risk into the system that could result in negative outcomes for those responsible. Furthermore, as the English editor would interact with a number of teams from both inside and outside my team's division, it raised numerous reporting problems.

In hindsight, I have come to understand the reluctance to hiring a silo breaker. For all the outside criticism of silos within companies, some siloing must exist, otherwise every team would experience mission creep, goals could not be defined, no one would take responsibility, and nothing would get done.

But I was too new to corporate life and too aggrieved to let anything like the bureaucratic process get in the way of doing what I knew was right.

To me, it made perfect sense that we hire an English editor and that that person should be a member of my team, because we produced most of the English at Hyundai; because our team was often asked informally to correct English from other departments and could not handle all the requests; and because I was the only native English-speaking executive at the entire headquarters, and it made sense that I should supervise the English editor.

My team leader and senior team leadership were opposed. They had several reasons, all of them valid. But none won the argument that an English editor was not needed.

If I could have done it over, knowing what I know now, I

would still have pushed stridently for the English editor, but I would have done it differently. I would have created a short but persuasive report, with examples of incorrect English produced by various teams at headquarters; then I would have cited examples of our competitors getting their English right; then I would have cited an expert estimating the loss in brand value Hyundai was suffering due to its flawed corporate English skills. I would have presented it to my boss and we would have discussed which team the English editor should be assigned to. Then, if it was decided the English editor should indeed be on my team, I would have worked with my team leader (he would no longer oppose the position, because our boss had agreed to it) on exactly the way the English editor would be integrated into our team and what their duties would and would not be, and the rest of the team would have been briefed accordingly.

This would have taken a couple months to accomplish. Instead, it took several months of arguing with my team leader before I finally went around him and showed some examples of bad English to my boss. He agreed it was a problem that needed to be fixed, and sent me off to HR to get them to create a position.

With some time and distance, I can see that my team members who were opposed to the idea were not just opposed to the idea itself; they were opposed to *the way I was presenting the idea*. By this time I realized I was living in a high-context culture—that how I said and did something was just as important as what I said and did. I guess I just thought I was too far down the road toward getting what we needed and there was no point in turning back.

I plowed ahead, got the slot approved by HR, and began the interview process. I settled on one finalist and had her brought in for an interview.

Her Western name was Aurelia, and I had seen her résumé: she was the daughter of a Korean diplomat and had attended high school and college in the U.S. She had had internships at major U.S. broadcasters. She was a young woman; I could tell from the headshot on her résumé.

When I met Aurelia in the Hyundai interview room, she was dressed appropriately for a Korean interview: featureless charcoal-gray suit, white shirt buttoned up, no noticeable jewelry. She was nearly shaking with nerves.

The interview room was set up in the corporate style: two tables facing each other, with a gap of maybe eight feet in between. My place was set up at one of the tables. A folded tent of cardboard was printed with my name and title; there was water and juice. Aurelia was to sit at the other table, facing me, a Grand Canyon of unease between us.

"This poor young person does not need any more intimidation," I thought, so I came to her side, pulled out the chair next to her and sat down. The HR manager was alarmed. "That is your chair over there, sir," he told me. "I'm good here, thanks," I said, and sent him away, breaking all sorts of corporate and cultural formalities in the process.

Aurelia calmed down and gave a fine interview. She would later tell me my move to her side of the table put her at ease. I later gave her a writing test in which I'd hidden a couple Easter eggs: hard-to-find errors that must be found by a good editor. She nailed them.

Integrating Aurelia into the team proved difficult. There was plenty of blame to go around, and I take my share of it. But some of the team members didn't make it easy on her, either. I had failed in defining exactly what her role would be in relation to our team. The team asked me: "Will she edit only English generated by our team?"

"No, she would edit English generated by any team that wants to use her," I replied.

"How can we make the other teams use her?"

"We can't. We can tell the other teams about her and strongly encourage them to use her."

"But there is no process for that."

"We'll find a way."

"Well, because she is a contractor, we will not show her sensitive company information."

"You must, because she has to edit it and she is a part of our team."

"No she isn't."

"Yes she is."

"Her English may be good, but her Korean is not."

"She was not hired to be a Korean editor."

And then: "She is young and this is her first real job. Why doesn't she have to do the same kind of menial jobs every entry-level employee at Hyundai has to do, like bringing the newspapers up from the mailroom in the morning?"

"Because she was hired for a specific skill."

"But we don't do that here."

"Well, we just did."

You can see how it went: basically, bullheaded foreign executive versus lifelong Hyundai employees who knew and followed the Hyundai way of doing things, and this was most definitely not that. I was certain the team would not help integrate Aurelia— would not spread the word about her—and she would be deemed a failure. Worse, Aurelia would be emotionally damaged by the fiasco.

It was, to be honest, a bumpy start. There were conflicting directions, cold shoulders, and hurt feelings. Aurelia's dedication, good humor, and undeniable value to the company won the day.

And I took a lesson in humility. I admitted to my team leader that I had handled her integration clumsily. He began to see her value and helped spread the word about her to other teams. As young Aurelia proved both her competence—her English was equal to mine—and her flexibility, dozens of other teams sought out her skills. They became grateful for her ability. One team of Hyundai engineers had proposed an article to a technical publication that was rejected because of its poor English. They turned to Aurelia, she helped them whip it into shape, and the piece was accepted. I had hoped by the end of her first year that she would have worked with a handful of other teams. Instead, thanks to her resourcefulness, her fighting spirit, and a maturity beyond her years, she more than doubled my expectations.

At one point I told Aurelia, "You have saved this company millions of dollars in brand value simply by correcting English." The bungled language in the Hyundai newspaper ads was only a one-day embarrassment. The positive change that resulted from it—the hiring of an English editor—would be lasting.

But that wasn't my ultimate satisfaction with Aurelia's hiring. That came on a day not too long before I left Korea. I took several of the junior members of my team out for lunch. As we were walking to a nearby restaurant, I looked behind me to see one of the other young women on my team walking close by Aurelia, her arm slung around Aurelia's neck, the two of them laughing. She had been accepted.

## "BUT . . . REPORTERS WILL JUST CALL US."

I had a hard time finding a lot of information about Hyundai when I was researching the company before I was hired. As a journalist, the first thing you do when looking at a company is go to the media website, where you'll find press releases, photos, videos, financial information, company history, biographies of the top executives, statements about corporate governance, and the e-mail addresses and phone numbers of the company PR people. It was easy to find the media site of Hyundai Motor America. But I couldn't find the media site for Hyundai's headquarters. It was puzzling.

About five minutes after I started my job at Hyundai in October 2010, I found out why I couldn't find the headquarters' media site. There wasn't one. Hyundai was, in fact, the only major global automaker that did not have an English-language media site. They had one in Korean, for the Korean media, but nothing for the English-speaking world. All we had in English was a list of press releases. A media site is like a front door to a company for journalists. Ours was effectively closed.

To me, this seemed like Job One. My team needed to build an English-language media site, stat. If we were truly going to be a premium automaker, this was basic blocking and tackling. This was an easily achieved marker along the way to Hyundai's drive to become a premium brand, or so I thought. Some senior members of my team objected to the idea of creating an English media site, questioned its necessity, or wondered who the target audience would be. I found it difficult to understand how to answer their objections and questions: Would you question why human beings need oxygen? One of my team members even said, "But if we put our contact information on the Internet, reporters will just call us." I was speechless. We *were* in PR, right?

The problem was, my incredulity and outrage were putting the cart before the horse. I didn't yet understand how, why, and at what speed things move in a corporation. My view was: Problem? Fix it. But despite what I initially thought, some of my team members were not actually trying to stop my idea. (Well, a couple were. The English-language media site would mean more work for my team and, more important, greater potential for making a mistake they could be blamed for.) Instead, most of the people on my team were asking smart questions about how best to build the site, what it should look like, and whom it should serve, and raised legitimate questions about the risk versus the benefits of the additional public exposure such a site would bring. As a corporate outsider, I did not yet understand this. And, in many ways, I was still thinking like a journalist: Make information available to journalists. Soon I would come to think like a company employee: Is this in the best interest of the company? One way of thinking is right for one job; the other way is right for the other job.

After several months of frustration, I eventually learned how to get it done. I made a brief and effective PowerPoint presentation to my boss showing him screenshots of what we had—our meager list of press releases—and the sophisticated, full-service, world-class media sites that our competitors, specifically our Japanese competitors, had. "Theirs look like a news site," my boss said, correctly. He was a smart man and got it right away. He authorized the building of Hyundai's first English-language media site. We contracted with a Web designer and started the meetings. Of course, the designers spoke only Korean, so my two best junior English-speaking team members, Ike and Eduardo, were assigned to the project to make sure the designers understood my ideas and directions and to ride herd on the designers, making sure they nailed down the details. They did more than that: they gave me valuable ideas about how to improve the site and even took the lead in eventually upgrading it a year after it was launched.

Several months after the website process got off to a rocky start, it was launched, just before a key motor show. At the same time I put Hyundai headquarters on Twitter, slowly and cautiously. This was risky territory for all concerned, but pretty quickly my team and others saw the value of having an English-language media site—although no one on my team wanted their contact information on the site. I learned to pick my battles. I don't think I ever won over anyone to the value of Twitter, even though Hyundai Motor America used it to great success. But that's okay. I came to see the cautious side of it: with a Twitter feed, Hyundai opened itself up to negative and attack Tweets it couldn't delete. This, too, is a part of brand management and protection.

### WHO BROUGHT THE BGM?

The hiring of our English editor and the building of our website— and my daily, often tortured, often hilarious clashes with almost, not quite English—caused a philosophical question to bubble up in my mind. The Konglish and incorrect English produced in Korea, however jarring to native English speakers like me, was just fine in the alternate universe in which hundreds of millions of people reside and where Korea, Inc., does a lot of business: the huge swath of the world's people who are not native English speakers but nevertheless speak some version of English, the language of global business.

The philosophical question was: Whose English is it now, anyway?

There are still plenty of people in native-English-speaking nations such as the U.K. and the U.S. who are appalled at what is happening to "correct" English in their countries, thanks to generations of immigration and the assimilation of their languages into ours.

To them I would say: You should see what's happening *outside* your countries.

When I was back in the U.S. and my mother was still alive, she bemoaned the "corruption" of English by foreign languages. Even though my mother was well read, she had never lived outside of West Virginia and had not encountered a lot of people not like her. Also, as with many older folks, as she aged, she became more fearful of a lot of things.

I used to joke that she was afraid she was going to wake up one morning and everyone was going to be speaking Spanish except her. I assured her that's not how languages change. I noted that she ordered fettuccine in restaurants, using it like it was an English word. I told her the wonderful thing about English is how malleable it is and within that is its strength. Much like the U.S. itself, English defeats revolutions by absorbing them.

Once I moved to Korea, my take on English got a lot less liberal, at least at first.

Suddenly, here I was, a lone protector of my language, besieged on all sides by a fusillade of incoherent, casually applied, and brazenly reckless English sentences.

But if I was going to be intellectually consistent, I came to realize, I had to endorse and even celebrate what nonnative English speakers are doing to my language. If it was okay for English to change within the boundaries of my own country—let's be honest, if it's okay for fast-food restaurants to invent Spanish-sounding words like *quesarito* and American travel magazines to invent "glamping"—it must be okay for it to change outside the U.S. I just felt like I had so much less . . . control. Out here in the rest of the world, it's everybody's English, and there's nothing particularly special about it, as there is to me. For me, English is as much a part of my being as my spine. For the rest of the world, it's only a tool. I wasn't as initially okay with this as I thought I might be.

Koreans, possibly because of the *pali-pali* ethos, modify and abbreviate every language they come in contact with. Because Korea is a homogeneous society with the bulk of its people plugged into the same mass media delivery systems, abbreviations spring up and are spread instantly throughout the Korean body, and are therefore understood by everyone. So it goes with English in Korea.

Koreans use easy-to-understand shortenings such as "aircon" and "biz." Others are harder to decrypt. "Backdancer" is a musical group's backup dancer, and "combi" is a sportcoat-and-slacks combination. Every digital camera is a "dika," from the first sounds of "digital" and "camera." You use a "dika" to take a "selca" (self-camera) photo, not a selfie. And every beer restaurant is a "Hof." (This one's a bit of a maze. The Hofbräuhaus is a famous and historic Munich brewery. But "Hof" doesn't mean "beer"; it means "court." "Bräu" means "beer." It must have been an original mistranslation that just stuck.)

To learn the culture, I had to learn Korean English. If you were to say that many people at Hyundai speak English, you would be correct. But that would be the fact of the situation, not the truth. Just because a Korean "spoke English," I could not assume they knew all the English words I did, or the idioms or the jokes. In order to "speak English" with Koreans who "speak English," I had to learn the English that Koreans know. I had to learn the Korean English vocabulary.

As in England, a Korean "diary" is your calendar or schedule, not your personal journal. "Fancy" is fine stationery. "Glamor" means a buxom woman. "Sharp" is any mechanical pencil. Every overcoat, regardless of brand, is a "Burberry"; every clear carbonated beverage is a "cider," even if it's not cider. A "mind control" book is not meant to turn you into a brainwasher; it is a self-improvement book to help you learn to control your own mind. Window-shopping is "eye-shopping." Men's dress shirts are "Y-shirts," because they are invariably white, which sounded to the occupying Japanese like the letter Y, and it stuck. Women with attractive curves are said to have the desired "S-shape." Once at dinner, one of my colleagues, a little tipsy and well meaning, complimented Rebekah (she was not there) by saying "she has the perfect S-shape!" My favorite Konglish word? "Stamina." For the first year I was in Korea, I kept hearing that certain foods, like a kind of chicken soup, were good for "stamina," and this was followed by chuckling from the men at the table. "Sure, you guys work such long hours, you need your stamina," I thought, and ate up. Then I came to realize that when Koreans say "stamina," they mean sexual stamina.

And if you thought the U.S. military and federal bureaucracy love acronyms, well, you've never been to Korea. My wife Rebekah's Korean staff at the U.S. embassy was amazed that she had never heard of "BGM," as in "Who's going to bring the BGM to the party?" That's "background music," of course. I bounced this off my Korean team members and, of course, they knew what BGM was. They asked: "Don't you?" I said that, yes, Americans know of the concept of background music but we had never felt a need to come up with an abbreviation for it. Just doesn't seem to come up in conversation that much.

Now, thanks to the ubiquity of smartphones, Asians are leading the way in all but eliminating written language. Texting apps got bigger faster in Asia than in the U.S. and are the preferred method of communication. As a journalist, I covered a lot of new technology, and I never saw "uptake," or widespread acceptance of new technology, like I saw in Korea.

KakaoTalk launched as a free messaging app in Korea in March 2010. Within three years it was installed on 93 percent of the smartphones in Korea. American kids drive grown-ups crazy with text language—"SMH" and "LOL" and so on—but Asian kids and adults are way beyond that. They're speaking in pictures only—emojis and the like. Americans use emojis to punctuate text conversations with clever little emotional icons. Asians are having entire text-free conversations in emojis only. The Japanese messaging app Line allows users to type in text and Line translates it to a smiling face or frowning face: you type "Happy birthday" and it picks an image. I note that the logical extension of this trend means we'll eventually be communicating feelings only, not ideas. My wife points out we're returning to hieroglyphics.

In the end, when it came to "my" language, I still stood watch over official Hyundai documents, such as press releases. But in every other case I just went with the flow. I had spent my life using language to make a living, and chose that path because language fascinates me. It was interesting and usually fun to learn what foreigners were doing to English. It was mind-blowing to me that a Korean and, say, a Turk who each learned English as a second language might understand each other better than I would understand either of them when they spoke English. There's a sort of global English out there, and native speakers must learn it to do business when they are away from home.

# 16

## CAR OF THE YEAR

On the lunar calendar, which is observed throughout East Asia, 2012 was the Year of the Black Dragon. A rotation of twelve animals populates the lunar calendar, so the Year of the Dragon comes once every twelve years. In Chinese astrology, the dragon is the luckiest symbol. Once every sixty years, the Black Dragon appears, its rareness intensifying its power, or so goes the marketing spin. So, if you were a believer in the Chinese zodiac, 2012 should have been a very good year.

As it happened, 2012 was shaping up pretty well for me and for Hyundai. A little more than a year after my hiring, I was finally figuring out the folkways of Hyundai. I'd hired a Korean tutor to make an attempt at learning the language. Hyundai sales were up and the brand was humming along. I was learning how to manage my team, working with the more enthusiastic members and working around those I was simply unable to win over. During my first year and a half of marriage, I had spent more waking time with my team leader, Ben, than I had with my wife. And like a couple that took a while to understand how to make their marriage work, Ben and I were starting to wear off each other's rough edges and sync up better. I had made a couple good friends at work. Eunju was one of the only female executives at the Hyundai Motor Group. Both outsiders, she and I bonded pretty quickly. She was Korean but, as the daughter of a diplomat, had grown up and lived mostly overseas. She spoke Korean, but it wasn't her best language. She had the cultural advantage at work that I did not have, but I had a gender advantage she did not have. She was direct and hilarious, and we had plenty of good meals together. The other was Jinho, probably the best friend I made at the company. A middle-aged manager, Jinho was soft-spoken and savvy. He had worked overseas for Hyundai and had a fine mastery of English. He helped me through many rough patches, from showing me how to make a winning PowerPoint presentation that would persuade my boss to approve an idea to dispensing sage career advice.

For the first time at Hyundai, I felt like an executive—that is to say, someone who leads and produces results.

The Black Dragon's mojo started working for Hyundai almost from the very beginning of 2012. At the Detroit Auto Show in January—in the very hall where Hyundai had announced its upstart and improbable vision of becoming a premium automaker one year earlier—the Hyundai Elantra shocked everyone by winning the coveted North American Car of the Year award, one of the world's most important auto prizes. I crowded into the basement of Cobo Center in downtown Detroit with about five hundred other auto industry types for the 7:30 a.m. awards ceremony, a yearly ritual in the U.S. auto industry. Everyone expected that the winner would be the Ford Focus parked in front of us, sitting beside the Elantra and the other finalist, a Volkswagen Passat.

The Focus had been the media darling of the season and received strong praise for its performance and handling.

I was so convinced we wouldn't win that when the envelope was opened and the emcee said, "Hyundai Elantra!" I experienced a nanosecond of aphasia and was certain he'd said "Ford Focus!"

All two dozen or so Koreans in the room cheered. The rest of the room gasped. It was completely unexpected: everyone thought the Elantra was a B-plus car across the board, while the Focus had A-level road chops. But the jurors were impressed with Elantra's overall package and premium features not found in similarly priced rivals, such as heated rear seats.

Elantra goes a long way toward explaining how different today's Hyundai is from yesterday's Hyundai and why the company has the ability to execute its upmarket strategy if it maintains its will. The Car of the Year Elantra was a pivot point between Hyundai, a car sales company, and Hyundai, a brand company. This award represented several big strides on Hyundai's climb up the premium brand hill. The company's wins were starting to accumulate into a noticeable pile. I started getting queries from automotive journalists suddenly keen to write about us. They all had the same questions: "How are you doing it? What is Hyundai's special sauce?"

Elantra's tale began in 2007, when Hyundai's designers were battling with Hyundai's formidable finance teams. Hyundai's finance department almost always got the last word in any interdepartmental argument. That's how Hyundai became one of the world's most profitable automakers, according to *Forbes* and other business publications. To understand how impressive it was that the North American Car of the Year Elantra even existed, you need to realize that every car you see on the road from every automaker is a compromise between designers, engineers, and product development teams. And then finance has its say. It is like this at every automaker.

To illustrate what I mean, I'll exaggerate a bit for effect, but it's not much of an exaggeration.

If automotive designers—at Hyundai, Ford, Fiat, wherever—had the last word, every car would look like the Batmobile. It would have $900 pavement-chewing, gas-guzzling twenty-two-inch tires. (Most car tires are about seventeen inches and you know what they cost.) The wheels would be pushed out to the edges of the chassis to create a wide, aggressive look, making it impossible to park. Every car would have a belt line—or the bottom of the side windows—raised so high that the windows would be mere slivers of glass, impossible to see out of but unquestionably sleek. It might have a matte finish instead of a glossy one. Great look, but you have to wash it by hand. Every production car would look like a futuristic concept car: gorgeous, but way too expensive and impractical.

If engineers had their way, every engine would be turbo-charged and every suspension would handle like it belonged on a Formula 1 racer, partly because it used forward-looking radar to sense the road surface ahead and make driving-feel adjustments automatically. The car would be built with exotic, super-strong materials, making it safe and light. Inside, eye-tracking and gesture-recognition sensors would allow the driver to change songs, turn up the volume, and raise cabin temperature by looking at holographic logos on the windshield and waving their hand in front of the dashboard. At the Detroit Auto Show in 2013, Hyundai showed a concept car that had all these gesture- and eye-tracking gizmos. Someday your car will, too. But right now they're too expensive.

It is the job of the product developers to bring the designers and engineers back down to earth to create a car that contains as many of the features and cutting-edge pieces of technology as possible but remains cost-competitive with its rivals in its particular segment. The product developers will tell engineers, for instance, "We know you want a sealed underside to the car to decrease drag and gain incremental gas mileage, but doing so will push its price too high above its competitors. So, no."

And it is the job of the finance teams to crush everyone's dreams to keep the company's overall profits high. Even at Hyundai, where the chairman is treated like a demigod, even he usually defers to Finance, because they're the minders of profit and loss. It's the rare case when the call comes from the top floor that overrides Finance.

In the case of the new Elantra, in 2007 the finance guys were telling the designers to simply give the car a less expensive facelift and be done with it. The designers, meanwhile, were pushing for a complete redesign, like the Sonata was getting, based on the company's new image-making Fluidic Sculpture design principles. Standard throughout the auto industry, cars get a complete makeover about once every five years, a time period known as a car's "cycle." About halfway through that cycle, cars get a "facelift," which usually means only a new grille, some new wheels and taillights, and maybe some new features inside. (America is the world's only market that perpetuates the fiction of new models every year. Nowhere else in the world is a 2016 Honda Accord or 2017 Chevy Malibu marketed.)

A merely face-lifted Elantra would make cost sense. A complete redesign would be expensive and cut into the already thin profit margins that every automaker endures on their lowest-priced cars.

At every point in Hyundai's history up to this moment, this decision would have been a slam-dunk for the finance guys: facelift only. But not this time. Hyundai's designers insisted. If Fluidic Sculpture is truly going to be a brand design going forward, and if Hyundai really wanted to create a consistent family look—like Audi, BMW, Mercedes, and even Chevy—and if Hyundai really wanted to become a "modern premium" brand, Hyundai's designers said, a simple face-lift on the Elantra would not do.

The problem was Elantra's platform: the car frame, suspension, axles, and basic infrastructure. Hyundai's designers said Elantra's platform was too short to accept the bold, curving strokes and character lines that marked Hyundai's new Fluidic Sculpture. Trying to apply Fluidic Sculpture to a face-lifted Elantra on the current platform would be a design disaster. Generally, customers do not buy ugly cars.

What was required was a new platform. Hyundai shares platforms with Kia to keep down costs, but a new platform—even if it's shared with a sister car—is extraordinarily expensive. Many parts do not translate from one platform to the next. New platforms require new steel molds, new welding instructions for the robotic welders on an assembly line, new training for workers.

But Hyundai's designers won the day. Top management decided to invest for the long run, making a real commitment to Fluidic Sculpture, "modern premium," and—in the largest sense—brand elevation. Elantra's styling was even bolder than Sonata's. The deeply creased character lines flowed up the side length of the car and ran seamlessly into taillights that curved organically around the car's rear corners. You were sure it was a coupe, from the aggressive angle of it, but saw four doors. And, through some alchemy of physics, the designers had given the Elantra—solidly slotted in the compact car segment—so much interior room that it was classified by the U.S. EPA as a midsize car, like Sonata.

It was Oh Suk-geun, Hyundai's former chief designer at the time, who proudly told me the Elantra story along with a reporter. A trim, smiling, slightly elfin figure with black-rimmed glasses who grew up loving Aston Martins, Oh was the father of the Fluidic Sculpture design. Up until then, he said, Hyundai had been a fast-follower company. This is how many Asian companies rose to prominence: copying an innovative product developed by another company and making it quickly and cheaply. But with the new Elantra, Oh said, Hyundai was proving it, too, could innovate. Korea was experiencing a pivot point, too. A generation earlier, Japan had evolved from fast follower to innovator. Now Korea, with its curved-screen Samsung TVs and design-leading cars, was taking the next step.

By 2012, when the Elantra's product developers and designers were starting to figure out what the next version—which wouldn't come out until at least 2015—would look like, they went through the customary process of benchmarking competitors to see what they needed to improve on the Elantra to bring it up to its rivals' level. For the past forty years, Hyundai had gone through this process with every car, taking small steps toward the industry's best cars but remaining far behind.

One of Elantra's product executives told me about this process and said, "Now, when we're benchmarking this Elantra, we can't find any competitors." It was said with a sort of amazement, not arrogance. This was how far Hyundai had come.

The decision to go all in on Elantra paid off in spades. Awards are nice, but they don't sell cars. The product must sell itself. The new Fluidic Sculpture Elantra, which debuted in 2011, quickly became Hyundai's best-selling car worldwide. It increased the previous Elantra's selling power so much that, by the end of 2011, *Forbes* magazine reckoned the Elantra was the second best-selling car in the entire world, behind only the ubiquitous Toyota Corolla.

Not long after the Elantra's big win in Detroit, spring came to

Seoul, and with it the annual Saturday-morning team-building hill climb that had crushed me the previous year. I again showed up in my shorts and college sweatshirt. But that was the only similarity. If there was any sign that my 2012 was different than my 2011 and that my life in Korea was starting to change, forget about learning the culture, building a website, or winning awards: it was all about the hill climb. This time I was carrying twenty fewer pounds and a better attitude. I gladly participated in the bullhorn-led warm-up calisthenics, which now seemed not at all odd. I made the summit in the middle of the pack, ahead of even a couple of my younger team members, including Eduardo, whom I teased mercilessly as he huffed to the top. When we arrived at the grilled duck lunch, at the same open-air restaurant as the year before, my boss invited me to sit with the other executives at the head table. I was handed a microphone and encouraged to make a toast. I drew cheers and laughter with a little butchered Korean. On the drive home afterward, I thought, "That was fun."

# 17

## BYE, BYE, BABY

With the summer of 2012 coming, Rebekah and I found ourselves in a hotel room in London with her parents next door. They were celebrating their fortieth anniversary with their first trip to the motherland. Rebekah is the only member of her family not born in New Zealand; the rest are Kiwis. Rebekah's father, mother, and older brother and sister came to the U.S. in 1976 so her father could attend a seminary in Mississippi. They had, quite literally, never seen a black person in real life before coming to the U.S., and they set down right in the geographic focal point of the U.S. civil rights struggle only a generation after the worst of the mayhem. Although Rebekah's parents became U.S. citizens and moved to North Carolina long ago, they—especially her mother—maintain ties to their heritage in the British Isles. Rebekah and I joined them and we all packed into a Hyundai station wagon and spent a very fun, very British week driving around England's Lake District, the Cotswolds, and London.

One night in our hotel room in London, while I was reading, Rebekah told me she was late.

"Late for what?" I asked, not looking up from my computer. "We're already in for the night."

"No," she said, with pantomime exaggeration, "*late*."

"Oh," I said. A beat. "Oh! Oh! *Late* late!"

"Yes, my dense husband," she didn't say but doubtless thought.

Without telling her parents, Rebekah and I slipped out of the hotel and walked to a nearby drugstore. We scanned the aisle for an early pregnancy test, which this pharmacy kept not only near the birth control but also some very adult toys. One-stop shopping, I thought.

We returned to our hotel room and Rebekah took the test. She came out of the bathroom smiling a smile I'd not seen before. It seemed to have a mind of its own: unrestrained, dancing, laughing nervously, animated by the joy of what the little white stick had just told her. The test was positive. I was instantly overwhelmed. I thought I didn't show it, but Rebekah told me later I did a poor job hiding it. Rebekah was setting the mental clock ahead about nine months; our baby would be born, God willing, in January 2013. I was setting the mental clock ahead eighteen years: I'd be sixty-eight when our baby entered college. "Welcome," the chirpy university representative would say to me as we dropped off our son or daughter in 2031. "And you're the grandfather?"

The hard part was keeping the secret from the grandparents-to-be for the next few days of the vacation. Because of the high risk of first-trimester miscarriages, we decided not to tell anyone for several weeks. We needed a code name to refer to our unborn baby. We found one of those websites that compares your baby's size to produce at certain weeks during the pregnancy. The first time we checked in, at four weeks, the site told us that our child was as big as a poppy seed. Not only did this blow our minds and illustrate the magnificence of God's work, it gave us a name: we'd call our unborn baby "Poppy."

Back in Seoul, Rebekah took a blood test at the U.S. embassy medical unit that confirmed her pregnancy and estimated the due date at January 24, 2013. We had to find a Korean ob-gyn, because the embassy didn't have one. Our doctor recommended a female Korean ob-gyn named Dr. Choi, who was located just off base and spoke English.

Our first visit to Dr. Choi revealed that she was an ob-gyn *and* plastic surgeon. Korean pragmatism. It simply makes sense to have the doctor who delivers your baby do your tummy tuck afterward. Of course, this odd-to-us combination put us off, in the way that you never want to eat at a sushi-and-ribs restaurant. It usually means they don't do either well.

But we didn't have a lot of choice. Dr. Choi's English was capable and well-meaning, but she did not have what Westerners expect in a bedside manner. In the U.S. we shop for doctors, rate them online, and treat them like service providers. We want information and engagement and to be treated like intelligent equals. We want to know what our doctors are doing before they do it. In Korea, patients rarely ask questions of doctors, as they are near the top of the Confucian hierarchy. You simply do what they say. My wife's Korean coworkers at the U.S. embassy would come back from their doctors with bags full of pills. "What are those?" my wife would ask. "I don't know," the Koreans would say. "The doctor just said to take them." This creates a culture clash when U.S. embassy personnel are referred to Korean specialists. They've reported Korean doctors walking out of the room when the Americans start asking questions.

As such, Korean doctors don't always explain to the patient what's coming next. In one of our early follow-up visits to Dr. Choi, we were sitting at her desk, looking at the photocopied handouts she gave us regarding prenatal care. Then Dr. Choi said, "Come in here," and led us to a room next to her office without telling us where we were going or what was going to happen there. In the room was an exam table tilted up at an angle and fitted with foot stirrups. "Get on, please, and take off underwear," Dr. Choi told Rebekah, smiling. "Okay," we realized, "it's some kind of exam."

As Rebekah complied, she started to ask, "What are you . . ." Dr. Choi then began doing two things simultaneously: giving instructions on what Rebekah should do during our baby's delivery that sounded very important while probing Rebekah with a cold and uncomfortable scope.

In the next moment a color television hanging on the wall flickered on, showing a wet, pinkish scene. It took us a second, but we realized with shock that we were looking at Rebekah's innermost thoughts, live. I gasped. Rebekah grabbed my hand. Meanwhile, Dr. Choi was chatting amiably about contractions and pushing, all the while guiding her *camera* scope on its appointed rounds. It was one of the most surreal—if medically fascinating—experiences either of us had had.

By the end of summer, Rebekah's two-year posting to Seoul was nearing its end. Several months earlier, the bid list for Rebekah's next tour had come out. It became clear to us that if Rebekah was going to remain in the Foreign Service, this was going to be our routine every two years: seeing the list of all the places we might be sent next, angling to find the best city and job for Rebekah, trying to find something for me, and praying for a positive outcome.

We initially thought I would spend only two years at Hyundai in Seoul, to coincide with Rebekah's two-year embassy posting, but now my job was looking more promising. And with his offer of letting me work from the U.S. when Rebekah was there, Mr.

Lee told us that Hyundai wanted to keep me for another couple of years. I had gotten to that point in my job where I had started to understand how to do it, had seen the things that needed to be done, and realized it would take more than two years to do them. Rebekah and I thought and prayed long and hard on it, and we decided that I'd sign on for another two years. The key was figuring out where Rebekah would work next. It turned out that the Foreign Service doesn't allow first-tour officers to do consecutive postings in the same country, so the ideal solution—another Seoul tour—was out. We contemplated other options: Rebekah would bid on a one-year posting in Iraq, Afghanistan, or Pakistan that would be "linked," or followed by, another two-year posting back in Seoul. This would keep us together for two of the following three years. The downside? Well, the intense amount of daily danger in any of those three countries—while pregnant—and the isolation of effectively being a prisoner in a heavily fortified U.S. compound subject to enemy shelling. She bid on the combination posting but lost out on the Iraq job she was shooting for. In hindsight, thank God.

There was nothing suitable or available in nearby China or Japan, so our next best open job that Rebekah was qualified to apply for was in Jakarta, capital of Indonesia, a six-and-a-half-hour plane ride from Seoul. Years ago Rebekah had been to Jakarta on a short business trip. My only impression of the country came from the film *The Year of Living Dangerously*, which was not exactly upbeat. Rebekah put in a bid for an economics officer's job in Jakarta.

After several months of anxious waiting, the news came: the State Department granted our wish and gave Rebekah Jakarta. It was a terrific job: Rebekah would be an economics officer with a portfolio in science. No more drudgery in the embassy's visa window. In her second Foreign Service tour, Rebekah would be working on vital issues in a bilateral relationship with a key strategic ally.

Rebekah would be sent back to Washington for several months to learn Indonesia's main language, Bahasa, and study up on her new country and job. She would also be pregnant and without her husband. But she had friends in Washington and her parents lived in North Carolina. We told ourselves we'd manage with Skype. And I would be joining her in Washington from Christmas 2012 until May of 2013, thanks to the telecommuting deal my boss had graciously arranged. It worked out perfectly: I would be with Rebekah for the birth and first four months of our baby's life, before I had to return to Korea. After that, we'd "commute" as frequently as possible between Seoul and Jakarta.

This all looked good on paper; we thought we'd planned out every eventuality. We figured being separated would be tough but manageable. We knew plenty of ex-pat married couples who pulled it off, even for years. We told ourselves we were doing it for our family's future. Probably the greatest benefit of the ex-pat life is that it frequently comes with no housing expenses: either the U.S. government or your foreign employer pays for housing. That's why it's so seductive for some Americans and why, like us, they're willing to trade what seems like just a little time away from family and friends, even from each other, for financial rewards.

With Rebekah leaving Korea at the end of August—and taking Chairman with her!—I was getting kicked off the comfortable U.S. military base where we had lived for the past two years. I had to find housing in Seoul "on the economy," as the U.S. government phrase goes. I knew I'd be able to find a fine, modern apartment in Itaewon, the most international of Seoul neighborhoods, which abuts the U.S. base. What broke my heart was losing access to the base and shopping rights at the PX and commissary. The base was my American refuge, my comfort food. Now that would be gone.

I could get our friends who still lived on base to sign me on as a guest, but there was no way I could keep PX and commissary rights: the U.S. military took away my ration card when Rebekah left. So that meant I had to stock up on U.S. goods on my last days on base. It wasn't that I didn't like Korean products; I used some. But if I wanted any U.S. products, the prices on the Korean economy were exorbitant. A $2 box of Quaker Oats at the little store in Itaewon that sold some U.S. goods cost $12. I could order U.S. goods online and have them shipped to the embassy, but that would have required one of Rebekah's coworkers to lug a big box back to the base and sign me on as a guest so I could pick it up. It was much easier and less of an imposition on others if I just bought what I needed for the next two years at the PX and commissary while I still could and took it to my new apartment.

If I was planning on being at Hyundai until October 2014, I had to figure out how much stuff I'd need. I checked how long it took me to go through a roll of toilet tissue, for instance. It turned out to be one week per roll, my research showed, so I multiplied that by 104 and added 20 percent to allow for unanticipated gastric events, and bought that many rolls of toilet paper. I did the same for toothpaste, shaving cream, deodorant, and all my toiletries. I assembled a decent-sized pharmacy of almost any over-the-counter medication I thought I'd need. I also bought a fifty-inch flat-screen TV and a bunch of electrical transformers to run all my media, appliances, and lamps, because Korea operates on 220 volts, not 110 volts like the U.S. Basically, I had assembled a Little PX in my apartment overlooking the bustling Korean neighborhood of Itaewon, and could have run a fine black market.

Thus established, I got on a plane with Rebekah at the end of August 2012 and we flew together back to the States. Hyundai allowed me to work from Washington for a couple weeks while I helped Rebekah get set up and to see how this telecommuting arrangement would work come January. The two weeks back in D.C. were wonderful. We ate at our favorite restaurants, saw family and friends, and introduced Chairman to America. We had to explain his Korean commands several times at dog parks. My team and I spent the two weeks sending documents back and forth as we prepared for the big Paris motor show and the unveiling of our revolutionary hydrogen fuel cell car and the surprise announcement that Hyundai was returning to racing, also set for the Paris show.

At the end of the two weeks, Rebekah and Chairman dropped me off at Dulles International Airport. Amid tears, we told each other I'd be back for Christmas and the birth of our child, and that three and a half months apart wasn't so long. We could do this, we said. I gave Rebekah one last hug, and the bump in her belly pressed into my stomach. I gave Poppy a little squeeze and turned to walk into the terminal. Rebekah got back in our car and drove off as Chairman watched me through the window. "Doesn't feel right," I remember thinking. Now, like my team leader Ben, I was a goose daddy, or *gireogi appa*.

# 18

## NOT HERE, NOT NOW

Despite our painful separation—Rebekah and I had never been apart for longer than a week since we'd been married—neither of us initially had time to dwell on it.

Rebekah started right in on Bahasa language classes at the State Department's Foreign Service Institute in suburban Virginia. Bahasa would prove to be much easier to learn than Korean, and Rebekah has a facility for languages, but the long classroom hours were no fun in a second trimester. Meanwhile, she had to set up a household for her and Chairman, which meant lugging things up and down the three flights to her apartment on her own. How she got the Christmas tree up there when she was eight months pregnant is still a mystery but a testament to her determination.

Back in Seoul, I was preparing for the longest business trip I'd ever taken. By now I was used to travel. In 2012, I would log 150,000 air miles. Soon, I would have to add pages to my passport. But the trips I took were usually there-and-back jaunts that involved flying a long way to spend a short amount of time somewhere, like my seventeen-hours-in-Delhi trip. This trip, in September 2012, would be a monster.

I'd fly from Seoul to the Paris motor show and spend several days there. Then to the Middle East launch of Hyundai's new Santa Fe in Muscat, Oman. After that, I'd head to Hyundai's Middle East headquarters in Dubai for meetings; then to Istanbul to see Hyundai's nearby Turkey factory; then to Prague to see Hyundai's Czech Republic factory; and finally back to Seoul.

Our performance at the Paris motor show was the best I saw at any show during my time at Hyundai. My boss, Mr. Lee, nailed his speech. The first motor show speech I saw him give nearly two years earlier was stiff and hard to understand, with awkward pronunciations and off-syllable emphases. In Paris he was relaxed and conversational. Several months into my own poor attempts to learn his language, I could fully appreciate his growing mastery of mine. An appreciative Parisian media applauded that we rolled the three i30s out in the national colors of blue, white, and red. The tone of the media coverage was highly favorable. There was a feeling that Hyundai had some serious momentum and was raising more than just its market share.

After the Hyundai press conference, I was trying to find a quiet corner of the motor show. I had a call to make.

At the same moment back in Washington, Rebekah was heading into an appointment at her ob-gyn. She was at five months, and her doctor said she should be able to determine our baby's gender. Washington was five hours behind Paris, so we worked out the time when we could be on the phone together while she was in the doctor's office. Unable to find anywhere near the Hyundai booth or inside the hall where I could hear well, I skulked out the back of the huge convention hall and found a cafeteria. Waitresses stacked trays noisily, and conversations in French sailed around me, but it would have to do. I tucked myself into a corner and pressed the phone to my ear.

Rebekah was on the line.

"Okay, I'm on the table," she said. "They're putting the goo on my stomach."

I closed my eyes, picturing the ultrasound transducer sliding over my wife's bulging lubricated belly.

"We're getting a picture . . ." Rebekah said.

Then, in the background, I heard the nurse say, "Are you ready?"

"Yes," Rebekah said. A silence.

"You're having a girl!"

"We're having a baby girl!" Rebekah said.

I pressed the phone against my ear, aching for my wife. "We're having a baby girl!" I repeated, grinning. "A little girl."

When you're not a parent, and you ask expectant parents if they want a boy or a girl, and they say, "We don't care, as long as it's healthy," you think: "Bunk." Because how could you *not* have a preference? But once you're expecting a child yourself, and the cosmic complexity of the process fully impacts you, and you learn all the terrible things that could go wrong not only with your baby but also with your wife, "Gender of Child" is about number 103 on the list of things you think about.

We were having a girl and that was wonderful. And it was a relief. Naming a boy would have been impossible. If my suggested boy names and Rebekah's suggested boy names were placed into a Venn diagram, not only would there be no overlap, the two circles wouldn't even touch. First of all, and completely unfairly, I might add, Rebekah ruled out all the names from the *Star Trek* canon, including the real ones, such as "Tiberius." On girl names, there was at least some possibility of compromise.

The good news carried me through the remainder of my

business trip. Along the way, I picked up some souvenirs I would eventually give our daughter and tell her, "Daddy got you these presents during a business trip when he found out you were going to be a girl." In Paris, naturally, I picked up a little Eiffel Tower; in Dubai, a stuffed camel. Prague supplied a small Bohemian crystal globe; Istanbul, a handmade glass bowl.

The separation from Rebekah marked the beginning of an unanticipated divergence in the two major streams of my life. I was doing the best work of my time at Hyundai, but at the same time my personal life was taking a turn for the worse.

On my own in Seoul, the days settled into a pattern: Face-Time with Rebekah in the morning, who was thirteen hours behind me in Washington and just going to bed; work for eleven hours; home to Itaewon; pick up take-out dinner; and then Skype with Rebekah, who had just woken up. Then watch an hour of something on Apple TV and go to bed. Repeat. On Saturdays I'd beg one of our friends to sign me onto the military base as a guest, where I'd drop off dry cleaning, work out at the gym, have lunch at the food court, use the Wi-Fi, get a haircut, and see a movie at the theater. On Sundays I'd go to church in the morning and, in the evening, go to a Bible study group on base. Sometimes, our friends on base would invite me over for a cookout or meal, but the longer I lived in Korea, the fewer friends I had on base. Their tours were ending, as Rebekah's had, and they were reposting elsewhere. Slowly but surely, the tethers to my American life in Korea were slipping from my hands, one after the next. The alternative would be to take the opportunity to throw myself fully into Korean life. But I couldn't handle any more raucous, late-night *hoesiks* than the ones I had to attend for work. A trip to the sprawling COEX Mall in downtown Seoul was too crowded and too loud for me. And Rebekah and I'd learned the folly of trying to take a leisurely weekend drive in the countryside. My isolated, repetitive daily routine was entirely my choice, but it beat the alternative. But we told ourselves we had to make it for only four months, until I could fly to Washington in December.

In October I had to fly to Brazil for the São Paulo motor show. The vice chairman would attend. The trip to Brazil is the longest anybody in Hyundai's overseas division ever has to make. It's the farthest you can travel and still stay on the planet: a twelve-hour flight from Seoul either to Los Angeles or Paris, followed immediately by a twelve-hour flight to São Paulo. It was one of those business trips where you're away for five days but spend only two or three nights in a hotel. It was punishing and stressful.

But it was more than the trip. It had been about six weeks since Rebekah and I had separated. I tried to bury myself in work, but Rebekah and our baby kept intruding into my thoughts during the day. Nights were worse. The bed in my Itaewon apartment—the one we shared at our house on base—was so achingly barren, I slept toward one edge so I would feel the empty bed on only one side. I felt like I had an emotional phantom limb.

I had considered myself lucky in bachelorhood and marriage. When I was single, maybe because I am an only child, maybe because I never longed for marriage, I was not lonely. I'm good at occupying myself and never felt the lack of a partner. I never felt half-full. Then I got married and realized what it was like to be happily coupled with someone. But that feeling had a flip side. I was now separated from my mate. I knew that she was weathering a pregnancy without me, and that made me feel like a bad husband, in addition to a lonely one.

All this was brewing in my mind, along with some volatile brain chemistry, evidently, when I came home the night before the Brazil trip. I had been at the office late, finishing up some work for the trip, and was feeling pressed to pack and try to get some sleep before the flight the next morning. I had a brief Skype call with Rebekah. She asked if I was okay. I said sure, just distracted.

I pulled out my green suitcase and followed my familiar routine of packing for a long trip. I turned out the lights, climbed into bed, pulled up the covers, and closed my eyes. The door to my bedroom wasn't quite closed enough. I got up, closed it, and got back into bed. Still not right. I got back up, moved it again. I smoothed the covers. It was quiet. I realized I was clicking my teeth. I felt like I'd had too much caffeine. I'd had a large diet soda with dinner, chalked it up to that, and rolled over, trying to will myself to sleep.

And then I felt it in my feet.

"Oh, no," I thought. "Not now. Not here."

I knew what it was as soon as it started and knew I was helpless to stop it. It was a panic attack. It always starts in my feet and rises through my body. The sensation is hard to describe. Imagine the times you've had a restless leg, that feeling of involuntary twitchiness. Instead of affecting your whole leg at once, it starts in your foot, then climbs to your knee, then your thigh. If you're lying down, you must sit up, but as soon as you do, you desperately want to lie down again. You must get outdoors, but the moment you do, it's unbearable, so you must retreat back inside. It feels safe and comfortable nowhere.

Then the feeling rises up into your torso, waking a kind of jumpiness in your gut and expanding toward your chest. The feeling around your heart is fullness and tightness. Involuntarily, you start breathing from the diaphragm, hoping that will stop its advance at the neck. This is crucial. You're certain that if this spreading, all-consuming feeling of unease reaches your head, you'll die, although you rationally know you won't. This all happens over the course of a few minutes. It's accompanied by a feeling of growing terror. No one knows until the moments before death what the end feels like, but during a panic attack you're sure this is it. It's the feeling of sliding away from life. Not a dramatic, instant end, like a brain hemorrhage. Instead, a gradual dimming and, with it, the odd need for grim resolution. Let the end come, if only to stop this unbearable feeling.

I suffered my first panic attack in early 1997. I was living in Washington and working at the *Post*. My mother and father were both back in my hometown of Charleston, West Virginia. My mom, then seventy-three, had scheduled cataract surgery a couple months earlier—her first visit to a doctor in probably twenty-five years. She took tests to determine her ability to undergo surgery. They found Mom's cholesterol was a how-are-you-not-dead 355 and she had system-wide clogged arteries. Her doctors advised immediate bypass surgery. She and I spent the next two months in torturous discussions and fights on the phone and back in Charleston, with me urging her to get the surgery and her putting it off. She raised larger questions, such as "At my age, what's the point?" and "How much longer do I have, anyway?" It's not a lot of fun for even an adult child to hear a parent say these things.

As this was going on, my dad experienced chest pain and had gone to the hospital, where they determined the main artery into his heart was 90 percent blocked. He would have bypass surgery the morning after his diagnosis. Unlike Mom, Dad, then sixty-four, grabbed the bypass procedure with both hands and jumped on. Ten days after a quadruple bypass, Dad was home climbing stairs, feeling better than he had in years, and evangelizing for bypass surgery. His example helped Mom, who—despite her fears—agreed to have her own bypass. I prepared to drive from Washington to Charleston for her surgery, and the night before was packing my bags.

That's when my first panic attack hit. After thirty minutes of suffering symptoms I was dead certain were telling me I was having a heart attack, I drove myself (not the best idea) to a hospital in suburban Maryland. After a thorough checkup, including an EEG, the doctors determined I was having a panic attack—which, up until about a couple of hours before, I didn't believe in. They gave me a Valium tablet, told me to go home and sleep, and see my doctor the next day for antianxiety medication.

My doctor concurred and put me on antianxiety meds. Over the years I've tried several, with varying degrees of success, and have had only one other full-blown attack. Eventually I settled on a drug called Sertraline.

I'm not going to detour into an exegesis on anxiety. There are plenty of excellent ones out there. No one's attacks are the same, but they do share some traits. Mine are not as bad or frequent as those suffered by many other folks. I've adopted a pretty simple mind-set: Treat the worst and learn to live with the rest. It's always there, lurking, waiting to climb up from the soles of my feet. Sometimes I can feel it gathering and can will it back down. But it will never go away, I reckon. Even writing these words, I can feel it wanting to stir.

The problem with antianxiety medication is that its effectiveness is unknowable. If you're on medication and you don't have panic attacks, you don't know if the medication is stopping them or simply that you haven't had one for whatever reason. So, in early 2012, I hadn't had an attack in more than a decade and I felt like getting a daily medication out of my life. Under the embassy doctor's care, I dosed off the Sertraline over the course of a month. For months I was fine.

And then, all of a sudden on that October night, I wasn't.

The biggest fear I had of moving off base was a medical emergency. It was not a fear of Korean health care. It is among the world's best, with excellent facilities and top-grade personnel. If I managed to get to a Korean hospital, I was certain I'd be well cared for. My fear was isolation. Let's say I fell and hit my head in my apartment. Who would find me? How long would it take? Let's say I thought I was having a panic attack but then sharp pains started shooting down my left arm. I could call 119, Seoul's version of 911, but was it certain I would get an operator who could speak English? If I did, could I give them directions to my apartment or tell them to take me to the hospital that I knew had some English speakers on staff? Or would I try to stumble out into the street and hail a cab to the hospital? Once I moved off base and began living alone again, I felt like I had no floor beneath me. Rebekah and I never really spoke about it, but we both understood it: for two years, we were hoping and praying that neither of us would get gravely ill or injured.

As the awful hours passed that night, and the fear coursed through my body and kept surging up in waves of anxiety—it felt like a blackout was impending—I tried to think straight. I didn't call Rebekah even though it was daytime in Washington, partly because I didn't want to worry her—there was nothing she could do—but also because I couldn't stand to speak to her, or to anyone. That's the wicked nature of the attacks. They fully consume their victims, making it unbearable to do anything besides endure them.

With shaky hands, I called up the website of a local hospital on my phone and programmed the route from my apartment in case I had to show it to a taxi driver or confused neighbor I would have to wake up. All I could do was lie down, pray, keep telling myself it was "only" a panic attack, and wait for the first gray streaks of morning, which I knew, along with the passing hours, would bring relief.

After an interminable wait, day broke and the worst had passed. But now I had another problem.

My flight to Brazil was meant to take off in just a few hours.

I knew bloody well that any corporate culture would have a hard time understanding "Sorry, can't go: panic attack" as an excuse. I also knew that my attacks could come in multiples, like earthquake aftershocks, and was not about to get into a claustrophobic environment like an airplane for the next twenty-four hours without some help. I knew I could handle the noon flight if I could just get my hands on some Ativan, a powerful, fast-acting drug that stops panic attacks in their tracks and leaves you feeling drained but functional.

My only hope was the U.S. embassy doctor. Our previous embassy doctor had just left Seoul for another posting. He was replaced by a doctor whom Rebekah and I had met only once. And technically, because my wife was no longer posted to the embassy in Seoul, he probably was not supposed to treat me. I called Ben, my team leader, and spilled it all. I told him I was trying to get the drugs that would allow me to make the trip. But I might not get them. If I couldn't get them, I couldn't get on the plane. To his credit, he told me to take care of my health and that he'd explain to our bosses if I couldn't go. I was grateful.

I called the embassy as soon as the doctor's office opened. I told the doctor what had happened and, thank God, he understood right away, telling me to come in immediately. He gave me several of the tiny, dot-sized Ativan tablets. The attack had subsided, but I could feel another one lurking. I took two pills, thanked him profusely, went home, and finished packing. Thanks to him, two hours later I slumped into my seat—feeling like a wrung-out dishrag—and took off on a twenty-four-hour trip to Brazil. The Ativan would not leave my side during the entire trip to Brazil; I carried the orange plastic bottle in my pants pocket. I was still on such a knife edge that even the realization that I had accidentally left the pills in my hotel room and was unable to get to them in a matter of minutes could trigger another attack. Once back in

Seoul, I went back on my old meds and will be on them until I die.

Ex-pats have their own *jeong*, even if it may not feel as emotional as Korean *jeong*. There is a sense of bonding among ex-pats of any sort, which explains why immigrant communities form by geography: to build a support system. You find yourself going out of your way to help ex-pats you may not know particularly well. When you're an ex-pat, away from people who love and care for you and away from safety systems you know how to navigate, the small kindnesses done for you by sympathetic ex-pats feel like winning lottery tickets. I will remember the U.S. embassy doctor's kindness forever.

Back in the States, Rebekah moved into her eighth month. Her pregnancy was healthy and largely free of problems. There was one thing: our little girl was sitting upright, facing outward. We joked that she was riding around in Mommy's tummy and trying to look out at the world. More seriously, if she did not turn, she would have to come out by cesarean. We were agnostic on delivery method, other than wanting the most help, the latest technology, and the best drugs. But natural versus cesarean made no philosophical difference to us. The thing is, a cesarean delivery is major surgery: essentially, the mother is cut in half and complications can happen.

To take our minds off that, we focused on settling on a name for our little girl. Like all expectant parents, we sent each other a stream of "What do you think about . . . ?" e-mails. One day in Seoul, as I was driving around at lunchtime, I flipped to one of the two English-language radio stations. One of the hosts was named Annabelle.

Huh, I thought. Annabelle Ahrens. Sounds nice together. The more I said it to myself, the more I liked it. It was traditional but not musty, and it would give our daughter some flexibility as she grew and her personality formed. She could be called Annabelle, or Anna, or Belle or even Bella. I bounced it off Rebekah and she liked it right away. Now all we needed was a middle name.

We wanted our little girl to have a middle name that expressed our faith and what we prayed would be hers, too. We considered the so-called virtue names found in the New Testament—Faith, Hope, Charity, and so on—but thought them too common and old-fashioned.

I was in my Seoul apartment one December evening after work, talking to my wife on the phone. I was looking out of my fifth-floor picture windows across my neighborhood of Itaewon. Because of its proximity to the U.S. military base, Itaewon was once known only as Seoul's red-light district. Some of that remains along a steep side street called Hooker Hill and its attendant seedy bars. In recent years, however, Itaewon had begun gentrifying, adding Nike, Adidas, and other Western retail outlets, along with high-end Korean skin care stores, restaurants, bars, and coffee shops, all of which crowd the *ajumma*s and *ajusshi*s (older Korean women and men) who haul their hand-pulled, wheeled souvenir trollies to their sidewalk spots each day, creating a vibrant street bazaar. The result of all this commerce was a dense packing of brightly colored signs like you see in photographs of most big Asian cities, some in Korean, some in English, lighting up the Itaewon night. From my apartment window, signs flashed for "Rio" and "DVD" and "Mr. Kebab" and "Richard Copycat" and "Cozy Massage."

Speaking to Rebekah, I idly scanned the signs until my eyes lit on one: "Café Jubilee." It was not a massage parlor, thankfully. It was a chocolatier.

I started laughing.

"What is it?" Rebekah asked.

"What do you think about 'Annabelle Jubilee'?"

Rebekah howled with laughter. "I like it! I really like it!"

In the Judeo-Christian tradition, the Jubilee is a regular, special year of universal pardon and forgiveness of debts. In ancient Israel, as recorded in Leviticus, Jubilee occurs every fiftieth year, and slaves and prisoners were to be set free. In the American South, January 1, 1863, became known as Jubilee Day as the Emancipation Proclamation became law. Many evangelical churches adopted "Jubilee" into their names to expand the word from earthly to heavenly meaning. Rather than a forgiveness of earthly debt, the true Jubilee is God's forgiveness of our sins through the redemption of Christ. The name was Christian, and it was Southern, as are Rebekah and I. It was genteel and it was pleasantly quaint. Even if you didn't know the word's history, as a name for a baby girl, it made people laugh with delight. It was a happy name. She would be Annabelle Jubilee Ahrens.

# 19

## *SANG MOO WAYGOOKIN*

My two-year contract with Hyundai was coming to an end and there were some things I needed if I was going to sign another deal. Hyundai had made it pretty clear they wanted me to stay another two years, so I felt like I had a position of strength going into negotiations. Neither of my predecessors, a Canadian and a Brit, had risen above the rank of director despite several years in the job. To show that a non-Korean could rise at Hyundai headquarters, I wanted a promotion to vice president. I felt I had earned it and it would send a good message to the media.

There was another thing I needed. Shortly after I came to Hyundai, I learned I was not quite the boss of my global PR team. Below me was Ben, my team leader. Above him, though, was not me, but Mr. Lee, my boss. I was to the side between the two of them, a horizontal line in an otherwise vertical organizational chart. Like my predecessors in the job, I did not have evaluation authority over my team—the stick to the carrot. This meant that, in order to get done the things that I wanted, I either had to persuade and cajole my team or I needed an order from my boss. My team was polite and helpful to me, and a number of them went way above and beyond to help me through rough patches in my three years at Hyundai, but even the most helpful ones knew the score. Not that it mattered to me, but no one bowed to me in the morning when they came into the office, as other team members did to their Korean bosses. I didn't realize where I stood in the organization before my hire because I simply didn't think to ask. I didn't know how companies were structured or how Asian companies dealt with foreigners. I wasn't the only one surprised by my station. My boss didn't realize it, and neither did some other executives. But not long after I discovered my position, I told myself: "If I re-up for another two years with Hyundai, if I am going to be a real executive, this is something that's going to change. I need job performance evaluation authority with my team." Without this, my authority had fewer teeth.

To make my case, I crafted an impressive PowerPoint presentation: my PowerPoint skills were finely honed by now. I made my case in sequential, logical order. I rehearsed at home what I would say to the head of HR in our meeting. Then the big day came. I marched in with my PowerPoint and assertively but respectfully made my case. The head of HR listened politely and nodded through the overlong presentation. Once I was finished—master negotiator!—the head of HR said, "The vice chairman has already approved your promotion to vice president." And my other requests, including evaluation authority, were granted. I had not heard of another non-Korean at Hyundai who had evaluation authority over Koreans.

It was humbling, in a number of ways. I correctly felt my puffery deflated. But I also was grateful for the vice chairman's act.

This told me that the man who had hired me felt I was doing a good job. Two years after my cold-shower transition from journalism to PR, from newspaper to corporate culture, from America to Korea, I was succeeding. I felt loyal to the vice chairman and to the company.

Was this it? Was this the sign that I'd navigated the shoals of middle-age transition and made the leap to my next life?

My promotion, coincidentally, helped solve, for some, a two-year-old problem: what to call me. Quite charmingly, after I was promoted to vice president, or *sang moo* in Korean, some of my team members simply took the first sound of my first name (remember, Koreans substitute the *P* sound for *F*), added it to my title, and started calling me "Poo Sang Moo," which sounds like a pet name I might call my wife.

However, the I'm-on-a-roll-at-work feeling didn't last for long.

A month after I signed my new deal, Hyundai's PR people were earning their paychecks. Hyundai and Kia announced that about 900,000 cars had been sold in the U.S. and Canada with false mileage estimates on their window stickers. Every U.S. car consumer is familiar with the numbers—Environmental Protection Agency estimates for gas mileage in city, highway, and combined driving. In Hyundai's case, the numbers for several models were too high by 1 to 2 miles per gallon. Even though every rational car buyer understands the estimates are just that—estimates—and could be achieved only under ideal driving conditions, this would be seen as a breach of trust between Hyundai and its consumers. Furthermore, Hyundai Motor America had aggressively marketed a "4 x 40" campaign: four of its models were rated at 40 miles per gallon on the highway, the highest in the industry. It was embarrassing and potentially disastrous for our brand. A brand's tenuous hold on its customers is trust.

Immediately, we had a reputation problem. We knew there

would be a further EPA investigation and probably a substantial fine, and of course the class-action lawsuit mills would heave into motion to get their cut. This could seriously damage the two years of progress Hyundai had made in pushing its upmarket ambitions into the public eye. This was more than a stumble over a tree root on a long uphill hike, as the ungrammatical Hyundai newspaper ad had been. This was the sickening feeling of a cliff-side path giving way under your feet.

What most consumers don't know is that the U.S. is just about the only country where the government doesn't test the mileage of new cars. In other countries, either the government or a government-appointed agent actually drives the new cars, runs tests, and comes up with mileage estimates.

In the United States the EPA issues guidelines for testing and tells the automakers to use the guidelines to determine the mileage estimates on their own. Then the EPA "certifies" those estimates and occasionally randomly tests vehicles to see if the estimates match up.

In the months prior to our announcement, the EPA had been getting complaints from some Hyundai owners that some of our cars were not hitting the window sticker mileage estimates. The EPA did its own tests and found a discrepancy between its results and ours.

Our engineers met with the EPA engineers and the methods were reviewed. On November 2, Hyundai and Kia said that a procedural error had caused the discrepancy and both companies printed new window stickers with the lower mileage estimates. A technical explanation would take pages, but essentially it came down to this: because the EPA doesn't spell out exactly how all these tests are to be conducted, the agency tells automakers to use "good engineering judgment." Hyundai engineers did so in one test designed to estimate the impact of tire-rolling resistance, wind drag, and friction on gas mileage. They made their tests, then made their good-faith judgments and came up with their data. The variables they had to contend with, and judgments they had to make, were legion. In my three-plus years at Hyundai, I saw everyone—engineers, designers, salespeople—pushed hard for results. But I never witnessed anyone cheating or being ordered to cheat or doing it on their own.

But at this moment none of this mattered. All that mattered was that it looked like we fudged the numbers.

The company's first response would be the most critical. It had to take ownership of the problem and provide a solution.

In what would become a best-practices case study in the industry, Hyundai Motor America simultaneously announced the bad news of the mileage reduction *and* the good news of a consumer compensation plan. Hyundai would issue debit cards to the owners of the affected vehicles that would be good for as long as they owned their cars. These cards would reimburse owners for the extra gas the owners would have to buy because their cars didn't get quite the mileage promised, plus an additional 15 percent to compensate for the inconvenience. It came down to about $88 per owner per year. "We're going to make it right," Hyundai's U.S. CEO John Krafcik said.

Hyundai eventually delivered several hundred thousand debit cards to its customers, paid a $100 million fine, lost $200 million in greenhouse-gas emission credits, and spent $50 million on testing improvements. Judges ruled the class-action suits settled for $400 million, or about $325 per owner.

Hyundai was not the only automaker to get tripped up by the EPA's guidelines. A year later Ford had to shave 6 miles per gallon off its C-Max hybrid and 7 miles per gallon off its Lincoln MKZ hybrid. BMW had to lower the mileage of its Mini Cooper. And even luxury leader Mercedes-Benz was forced to lower the mileage on two of its vehicles.

Automakers want customers to have accurate mileage estimates. But the EPA must do its part and reform. It's time for the agency to get in step with the rest of the world and start testing cars itself. If not that, then it should clarify its testing procedures to make certain that companies aren't penalized hundreds of millions of dollars in fines, lawsuits, and reputational value simply because the EPA's byzantine testing guidelines force engineers to exercise "good engineering judgment," only to find out later it isn't good enough for the EPA.

### SECOND GENESIS

There is a saying in the auto industry that goes something like this: "Good product fixes everything." Automakers refer to their lineup of cars as "product." Not "the product," just "product." And the saying reflects the fundamental, visceral core of the industry: new cars are shiny, pretty things that distract us and move us emotionally. A car company can weather a number of public problems—recalls, mediocre quality ratings, gas-guzzler labeling—if it just keeps rolling out great product and it keeps hinting at even better product in the pipeline. The red meat of the latter is the "spy shot."

Auto magazines pay photographers well to get the first pictures of an automaker's next models before they hit the street. Photographers with long telephoto lenses stake out R & D centers, desert test tracks, and well-known cold-weather testing sites used by automakers in Sweden and Finland. The automakers respond by cloaking their cars in high-tech camouflage. This includes not only bulky black padding that makes the cars look like Special Forces vehicles but also shape-distorting black-and-white spidery decals that look like album covers for 1960s psychedelic bands and even fake body parts draped over the car meant to hide its shape—like throwing a tent over a supermodel. These are often painted matte black, which absorbs a camera's focus-finding infrared light, sometimes rendering a fuzzy picture.

Automakers have a love-hate relationship with spy shots. On the one hand they spoil an automaker's reveal. On the other, especially in the Internet era, they can build enormous buzz for an upcoming model, more than any PR operation could crank out.

In late November, three weeks after our EPA crisis broke, we got a little gift of good product. The first spy shots of Hyundai's next Genesis started appearing online.

The first Genesis, launched in 2008, was Hyundai's maiden attempt to create a luxury sports sedan. Since 1999, Hyundai had sold its flagship sedan, Equus, in Korea. But it was seen largely as a plush limousine for executives to be driven about in. Genesis was built as a direct challenge to the Lexus sedans trickling into Korea and dominating the market in the U.S. The car announced Hyundai's ambitions and was regarded as a terrific value—priced well below comparable BMWs and Audis. It even won the U.S. car of the year award against a weak field. Nevertheless, it was seen as a paint-by-numbers near-luxury car. A fine try, but nothing terribly innovative.

The industry was watching to see what Hyundai would do to Genesis when it came time for a makeover. Would Hyundai play it safe—dress up the exterior and add some features? Or would the company try to create a truly distinctive luxury car, one that would make the Germans nervous? Inside the company, the second Genesis was the Hail Mary, the car upon which so many hopes had been pinned. Hyundai had been working for four years to create product that would effectively showcase the aspirations it had for its brand. If it was seen as only a slightly nicer version of the first Genesis, much of the brand momentum gained since the vice chairman's Detroit Auto Show speech would be lost. It would be said that Hyundai was all talk and no walk. The next Genesis would be the most important car Hyundai had made in years.

In November 2012, three weeks after the EPA crisis hit, the first spy shots and video of the next Genesis prototype started popping up on the Internet. They spread quickly, to favorable reaction. Commenters compared the styling, even under all the camo, to top-end German luxury sedans. A couple months later, gearhead drool started pooling on the Internet when more spy shots appeared of the Genesis prototype racing hard through the demanding curves of the legendary Nürburgring racetrack in western Germany. This track, which twists for fifteen hair-raising miles through the forest, is known as the "Green Hell." If you're an automaker with real sports car ambitions, you must test on the 'ring. It is a station of the cross.

I started getting e-mails from auto journalists asking about the new Genesis instead of the EPA issue. The next Genesis looked like great product.

## READY FOR TAKEOFF

I landed at Dulles International Airport outside of Washington a few days before Christmas 2012. Remarkably, the media coverage of the EPA issue started turning favorable. Not only for the gas reimbursement idea but also because Krafcik opened the Hyundai press conference at the Los Angeles Auto Show, the first after the EPA news broke, by addressing it head-on. Before talking about the company's new cars on display, Krafcik reported how many customers the company had contacted regarding the EPA issue and how many had asked for the debit card and other marks of progress the company was making toward hopefully winning back its customers' trust. If this crisis had to happen to Hyundai anywhere in the world outside of Korea, we were lucky it happened in the U.S. Krafcik always liked the media and had built up tremendous goodwill and capital with reporters by being accessible and forthright during his time at the top of the company. He even Tweeted with them.

I felt good about the past year. We had hired our English editor, launched the company's first English-language media site, put our PR team on social media, and were making solid steps in coordinating our global PR activities around the world. And I felt great about the year ahead. I was heading into 2013 with a promotion and reinforced upper-management backing. A new Genesis was coming and that was going to be fun to promote. And, most important to me, I was going home to see my wife and the birth of our daughter. This next year would be a good one.

A freezing wind whipped around Dulles as I stood outside waiting for Rebekah to drive up. I thought to film it so I could remember the moment. I saw our little red Hyundai Veloster approaching and held up my iPhone. Rebekah pulled to the curb; I could see Chairman riding shotgun. Rebekah put down the passenger's-side window and Chairman—all ungainly seventy-some pounds of him—*heaved* himself airborne through the window like a B-25 struggling to get off a carrier deck. He hit the ground and ran to me, squeezing between my legs. Rebekah got out and came around the car. Wow, was she pregnant! I hugged her and looked down. "Honey, something's come between us."

There's only one good thing about being separated from someone you love for an extended time: there is never a sweeter reunion. When we got back to the apartment, I flopped down on the bed, exhausted, with a feeling of earned rest. Chairman joined me and did something he'd never done before. He snuggled in next to me and pressed the top of his furry golden head into my cheek and kept it there. Poo Sang Moo drifted off like that, with the homey sound of Rebekah arranging Christmas decorations elsewhere in the apartment, feeling happy, content, loved.

# 20
## THE 2013 MODEL

On Monday night, January 14, 2013, at about seven p.m., I was sitting in a bedroom that Rebekah and I had made into a nursery in our rental apartment in Arlington, Virginia. I was talking to members of my team back in Seoul via conference call at nine a.m. the next morning, their time. We were coordinating upcoming events, talking about the Detroit Auto Show that I was going to skip to stay home with my very pregnant wife. Rebekah and I were just back from dinner. Our little girl was due in nine days and we were packing in as many dinners out and movies as we could before she arrived.

Before dinner, Rebekah noticed some wetness in her pants. It was not enough to indicate that her water had broken, but she decided to call the doctor anyway. She talked to her doctor while I spoke to my team. After a few minutes Rebekah came into the bedroom and silently handed me a piece of scrap paper on which was written: "Doc says we need to go to the hospital."

"OhmyGodI'vegottagotothehospital!" I spluttered to my team, and hung up, panicked. Rebekah tried to counsel calm. "It's probably nothing," she said. "They'll check me out and send me home." She was so confident of this that she refused to change out of her flip-flops and sweats.

The go-bag had been packed and in the car for a week. We put Chairman in his travel crate in the apartment—the one that had carried him from Seoul to the U.S.—and headed out into the cold night to the hospital.

We got to the hospital, and waited. And waited. And were tested. And waited some more. By two a.m., we were exhausted, hoping to get sent home. Instead, the doctor came in and said, "Your fluid levels are getting low, so we should just go ahead and deliver your baby. We'll schedule the cesarean for six a.m."

Wait. Wha . . . ?

This was it. In a few hours we were going to be parents. Annabelle wasn't due until January 24. We weren't ready! To cover our nerves, we joked: What about all the movies we were going to see during the next nine days? Pretty quickly, I came to this conclusion: As a forty-nine-year-old first-time father, I was grateful that I would get nine extra days with my daughter. And right now my main concern was Rebekah. I had done enough reading to be justifiably worried about what my wife was about to undergo. Rebekah and I prayed for a smooth delivery, a healthy baby girl, and a safe Rebekah.

A few hours later, doctors took Rebekah into the delivery room. A few moments after that, in my hospital scrubs, I followed. The room was full of happily chatting medical professionals and a battery of technology, with lights flashing and sounds beeping and buzzing reassuringly. I almost asked them to wheel in some more technology, even if it was unnecessary, just to make me feel better. I would take any comfort at that point.

I was led around behind Rebekah, who was lying on her back, a blue cloth curtain raised over her neck so neither she nor I could see the surgery. She was already numb from the waist down with the anesthetic, but saw me and groggily said, "Oh, good. It's you." I sat on a stool that was provided to me and held her hand and stroked her hair. Rebekah would later say she never felt pain per se but felt a great deal of pressure and discomfort, aware that her midsection was being manipulated in extreme ways as they pulled a baby out of her gut.

I was worried about Rebekah, although none of those attending to her seemed worried about anything. That actually was more soothing than all the technology. I was curious about the surgery. I had watched a fluoroscope—like an X-ray video—of my mother getting stents placed in her femoral arteries years earlier. It was fascinating. The doctor's description of what she was doing to Rebekah beyond that blue curtain only made me want to see.

"Should Dad look?" I asked, beginning to rise off my stool.

"No!" shouted all eight or nine people in unison. I sat back down. In retrospect, I didn't need to have the image of my wife being cut in two in my head. I still hadn't been able to shake the interior shots of my wife I'd seen in Dr. Choi's office back in Seoul.

In a matter of only a few minutes, it seemed, it was over. The doctor removed our baby girl from my wife's midsection and handed her to a nurse. I heard her first—she screamed out a good cry—and then I peeked around the curtain in front of my wife's face to see her placed on the scale, naked, wriggly, covered in gray slime. Our baby girl. She had the exact same turned-up nose that had so charmed us when it showed up in the ultrasound pictures.

"Ten fingers and ten toes!" the nurse gleefully announced.

I can't and won't attempt to write anything elegiac about the first few moments a parent spends with their baby. It's been written before and better by countless others. I'll only make two observations: for me, it was like a switch had flipped in my head and, I guess, in my heart. Here was this tiny human whom I'd just met, whom I understood was made by God in the image of God, yet with whom I had no relationship in any way that we think of it. But I instinctively knew that I would do anything to protect her. I would take a bullet for her. In the coming days, I realized I could not allow even the *thought* of harm coming to her to slither into my mind. If even the first few motes of such a thought began forming, I found myself involuntarily shaking my head, trying to rattle them out, like sand in my ears.

Second, my heart burst with love and admiration for Rebekah. I had never seen anybody do anything more amazing, scary, dangerous, and heroic than Rebekah had just done. In many ways it cast any and all accomplishments I'd gathered in my life into pale relief. What had I possibly done to equal that? Write a front-page story? By the time I left journalism, robots were writing newspaper stories. I had never—would never—take on such a months-long, risky, constantly burdensome, and selfless task as Rebekah had when she became pregnant. I was in Korea for months five through eight of Rebekah's pregnancy, and she always wanted to put on a good face for me on Skype, so I thought her pregnancy was going swimmingly, completely unaware of all the things pregnant women—even in healthy pregnancies—deal with: the perpetual exhaustion; the suppressed immune system leading to more colds and sinus infections; the shifting baby pressing on Rebekah's round ligament (her what?), causing the occasional stabbing abdominal pain; and the utterly random, mysterious pains pregnant women wake up with in the mornings and that stick around for days before disappearing. Adding to Rebekah's heroism was this fact: she gets awful migraines. Debilitating, three-day, can't-move, can't-stand-light, vomiting migraines. Has for years. She's tried every possible prophylaxis to little effect. The one thing that works is a drug called Relpax. If Rebekah feels a migraine coming on and gets to her Relpax fast enough, it frequently—but not always—stops the pain before it can spread from the point behind her eye or up her neck to envelop her head in a blinding agony. But here's the rub: pregnant women can't take Relpax. So, during her pregnancy, much of it spent by herself, when Rebekah felt a migraine coming on, she couldn't reach for the one thing that might stop it. Imagine knowing that relief was within your grasp—seeing it on your medicine cabinet shelf—and being unable to take it because it may harm the child you're carrying. Instead, you simply have to accept the fact you've got three days of misery ahead of you, with only largely ineffective Tylenol in the offing. That's called selflessness. This, to me, was awesome, as in: I was full of awe. I felt utterly, eternally bound to her. Single people are always told by parents that having children puts life into perspective. Part of what they mean is the way it binds the parents together in ways unknowable before the pregnancy and even unknown to their children.

In the hours right after Annabelle was born, Rebekah was taken to her room and began the arduous healing process from the cesarean. Nurses brought the baby to our room and we took our first family pictures and called Rebekah's mom and dad and . . . *Chairman!*

We had totally forgot about Chairman, who had been in his crate for about fourteen hours by this point. I raced home and heard him barking, hoarsely, from outside. Once I got inside, I saw that poor Chairman had soiled himself. I let him out of his crate without thinking and his poo-soaked Labrador tail spattered the apartment's walls like Jackson Pollock attacking a canvas. Jackson Poo-lock, we called him. It was hard not to laugh. A fine preparation for what was ahead of us, I thought.

Soon enough, Rebekah's mom and dad arrived to see their first grandchild. Then Rebekah and Annabelle came home, Chairman met and sniffed his new baby sister, and we set up our little family.

I worked hard to be a new father and found myself surprised by some of what I would later realize were the no-duh moments of parenting. ("Wait a minute. You mean we have to give her a bath *every* night?") I also worked hard to be Hyundai's head of global PR. I stayed in touch with my team and other colleagues back in Korea through a daily dump of e-mails that arrived in my in-box overnight, sent by my colleagues in Korea. One morning, I opened a devastating e-mail from Eduardo: He was leaving Hyundai. My man Friday, my trusted navigator of Korean culture and corporate life, my good friend. Leaving. In any workplace, you can typically count your true allies on one hand. As the only American at Hyundai, they were even more precious. And now I was losing one.

Eduardo was getting married and thinking about joining his wife's family business. Or he was considering buying wholesale hotel supplies and retailing them to hotels. Or anything besides Hyundai and the *chaebol* life. Eduardo had been with Hyundai for a little more than two years and had become a trusted part of our team. He was smart and savvy and could negotiate a sharp deal with outside vendors, such as website designers. Thanks to his international childhood and excellent language skills (Korean, English, and Spanish), he had a bright future at Hyundai. I could easily see him as a manager at one of our overseas affiliates in a few years. By the time Eduardo was in his fifties, it was not impossible to see him as a president of Hyundai Motor Spain or the like.

But that was just the point. One day Eduardo came into my office and summed up his frustration with the *chaebol* life. "Sir," he said, "I know what my salary's going to be twenty years from now." For generations of Koreans who grew up in the privation of the 1950s, the 1960s, and even 1970s, this knowledge was comfort. They knew that once they managed to get hired by Hyundai or Samsung or one of the other *chaebol*, they were set for life, assuming they didn't commit a massive screwup. Whole lives were planned around this fact, and offspring were encouraged to follow the same arc of security and prestige. Hyundai's slogan for a time was "Hyundai for life." It was more than a tagline meant to sell cars. It was an accurate description of the lives of generations of Koreans.

But it was not for Eduardo. Eduardo was a natural entrepreneur, not a company man. In university, he'd run a couple of pop-up bars, haggling with beer distributors as a twenty-year-old. He wasn't sure exactly what was next for him after Hyundai, but it would be something more on his own terms.

I was in Washington when Eduardo left Hyundai. In his good-bye e-mail, he wrote: "Sir, when you first came, I was going through a rough time . . . and I was in hell. However talking to you and hanging out with you was sort of a vacation for me. Felt like going to States for a few minutes. I was your right hand, but in a way, you have given me a lot of support too."

He concluded: "I sincerely hope that Rebekah and Annabelle will always be healthy and right next to you . . . I also wish you become a president somewhere, so you could give me a job when I go bankrupt."

Without realizing it, Eduardo, by quitting Hyundai and striking out for the territory ahead, was a symbol of what Korea must become in order to launch the next chapter of its remarkable growth story. Eduardo might become the very guy whom President Park and Mayor Park both described when they talked about the need for Korean entrepreneurs to start their own businesses.

Eduardo was aiming to become, probably without thinking of it, the vanguard of the next chapter of Korea's great growth story—and possibly an answer to its midlife crisis.

Only a few years earlier, I had scoffed at the idea of having a midlife crisis of my own. As a young-feeling bachelor with a great job, my own house, and a 6-speed, 270-horsepower car, to me, my forties and fifties were going to be nothing more than the next decades, hopefully with a little more money. Unmarried, childless, the stakes were low. I had little to lose and therefore little to fear. I knew I wouldn't live forever, but such ghoulish thoughts rarely crossed my mind. I was focused on the next home improvement I'd make, the next story I'd write, the next date I'd go on. I was moving forward, I suppose, but denying an end. Now, as a new father, I had everything to lose. But it was more than that. The birth of my child not only marked the beginning of her life but, in a real and meaningful way, the beginning of the end of mine.

The late Christopher Hitchens wrote that, upon seeing his baby son, he realized, "I knew at once that my own funeral director had suddenly, but quite unmistakably, stepped onto the stage." My reaction to Annabelle's birth wasn't quite as morbid as that, but I was hit with an unexpected and instant gut punch of mortality—mine. It lingers to this day and I suspect it will forever. Part of this comes from being an older dad, but a larger part, I think, comes from finally, after all these years, really having something to live for. I've come to realize that parents wish for immortality just as they did when they were single, but for different reasons. Now it's so they can spend forever with their children. My faith teaches of eternal life with God through the salvation of Christ, and the Bible speaks of maintaining our identities in heaven; Moses and Elijah, long dead, appeared to some of the apostles during Jesus's transfiguration on the mountain. I want more than anything to spend eternity with my wife and child, and there is biblical hope to believe I will, but for now I am stuck in this failing corporeal body in this fallen world, and I am occasionally lashed with the horror that one day I'll lose everything that matters to me. Losing a house? A car? A job? Now utterly meaningless by comparison. This is the other part of the perspective you always hear parents talking about. If anyone asked, I'd encourage prospective parents to have children earlier than I did, not necessarily because you'll have more energy—you will—but so you can spend more time with them. Barely a week goes by that I don't catch myself silently watching Annabelle playing, or eating, or doing nothing and think, "I wish I just had ten more years with you."

When I let these silent thoughts slip into words, Rebekah, in her typically straightforward way, tells me: "You have trouble with the whole 'circle of life' thing."

But, oh, how baby Annabelle chased those dreaded moments away. Before we had our baby, one of our friends gave us some lasting advice, which I pass along to every expectant parent. "Everyone tells you how hard it is to have a baby, and it is," she said. "But no one ever tells you how much fun it is." Rebekah and I had always laughed a lot; it is one of the best parts of our marriage. But we never laughed so much until we had Annabelle. She's a ham and a crack-up by nature, which was probably inevitable, given her parentage. She got the most giggles as an infant, it seemed, by presenting me with a fully loaded, pestilent diaper when it was my turn to change her. She'd lie there on her changing table, laughing and gurgling away as I hazmatted the evil thing to the diaper bin. "Yuck it up now, laughing girl," I'd tell her. "In about thirty years, you'll see how much fun it is changing Daddy's diapers."

And even the difficulties she had learning to sleep made for unforgettable moments. Annabelle wouldn't sleep in her crib. Just wouldn't. She wanted to be near us. By way of a solution, we took the mattress from her Pack 'n Play and put it on one of the beds in the apartment, shoved up against the headboard and wall. We piled pillows at the bottom, safeguarding her on three sides. Then we lay down next to her on the bed, which soothed her. I usually wrapped my arm around her—she curled up right inside my forearm and biceps—and pulled our faces close together. We'd both go to sleep with her quiet, warm breath brushing my face.

After four sweet but sleep-deprived months in Washington with my wife and new baby girl, it came time for me to return to Seoul. Rebekah still had three months of leave from the State Department remaining before she had to fly to her new posting in Jakarta in August, separating us again, so there was no point in extending the separation at the front end. So before I flew back to Korea, we took Chairman to live with Rebekah's mom and dad in North Carolina; we called it his summer camp. Then Rebekah, Annabelle, and I boarded a plane to Seoul. It was Annabelle's first transpacific flight, at four months.

I didn't know how I would be greeted at headquarters after my "vacation in America," as I had been told some back in Korea were calling it. About a month into my four-month telecommute in the U.S., I started to sense a distance growing between me and my team. It was understandable, given the fourteen-hour time difference and the fact that our working hours overlapped only early in my morning or late in my night. The weekly teleconferences with team leadership tapered off as I began to feel I was inconveniencing them by forcing them to sit around a speakerphone and keep me up to speed.

I hadn't realized at the time—or, more likely, hadn't wanted to realize—what damage my four-month telecommute could do to the crucial force of bonding that holds together every Korean team. Sacrifice, willing or otherwise, is always called on—more from the culture than the company—from every team member for the greater good of the team as a whole. I'd seen the resentment during my two-week vacations. But this, I hoped, was different. I'd still be working, just on the other side of the world. Truth was, however, no matter how much work I was doing, I was not physically part of the daily life of my team or of headquarters. The news that I was going to work in America for four months was at first greeted with shock—no one had ever heard of Hyundai doing this before—and then, understandably growing resentment. Some of my colleagues used the opportunity to carp about my special treatment.

Before returning to Korea, I turned to Jinho, my trusted adviser at work. In Korean fashion, Jinho was direct. He told me that if he had been offered the same deal, he would have refused, even though it would have meant missing the birth of his child and leaving his wife on her own. Such is the expected commitment to company. At the time I thought it unnecessarily harsh and particularly Korean. But now, with a few more years of business life under my belt, it's hard for me to imagine how many other companies, anywhere in the world, would allow one of their executives to do what I did.

The idea of teleworking boomed with the explosion of high-speed Internet. We were told we would all have a perfect work-life balance, that flexibility was the future and rigidity and routine were the past. We were told that the need for workers to gather in one place every day was an idea as archaic as the Industrial Revolution. Turns out not quite and not for everybody. At about the same time I was not-quite-launching Hyundai's telework experiment, Marissa Mayer was taking over at Yahoo and ending telework at the company. She talked about the need for face-to-face contact and in-person collaboration. And, let's be honest, a dozen or thousands of miles from our offices, we probably work a little less and a little less hard. If there's slack, we will take it.

Despite its ongoing and sincere efforts to move from a car-selling company to a brand company, the heart of Hyundai was the assembly line. There would be no brand if there weren't cars, and there would be no cars if an assembly line worker tried to telework. "Soft" work, in marketing, PR, or accounting was less assembly line oriented, but the ethos ran through the company. And as I was finding out, something is missed when somebody—especially the boss—is not in the office. I was on the other side of the planet and so was my authority.

But it was a hit I was willing to take. Not only did my wife and new daughter need me, I couldn't imagine being parted from them. If Hyundai had said, "You need to come back now or lose your job," it would have been an easy choice. So I decided to endure the backbiting, focus on doing as much good work as I could, enjoy Rebekah and Annabelle, and try to rebuild bridges when I returned to Korea at the beginning of May. A Korean friend at Hyundai gave me a long exegesis on zero-sum Korean envy, even teaching me a cultural saying: "When your cousin buys land, your stomach starts to turn." But I think anyone at any company would have looked askance at my special treatment.

Jinho told me flatly that people didn't like that I'd spent four months working in Washington, away from headquarters. "Who?" I asked. "Everyone who knows," he responded.

Part of me wanted to hold people to account for talking behind my back and undercutting my authority while I was gone. There is no doubt that some of it happened because I was a foreigner. While I was gone, I was told that one of my team members—no longer with the company, thankfully—said to the others, with unintentional irony, "We don't need more foreigners on the global PR team." But I tried to think of most of it as "soldier talk," the same kind of blowing off of steam that enlisted personnel must be allowed regarding their commanding officers when they're not around. Everyone—regardless of culture, country, or century—gripes about their boss. Instead of seeking retribution, I remembered being told at Hyundai that it is the duty of the boss to make good relations with his team, not just the other way around. This is the reciprocal nature of the Confucian hierarchy that is often unknown to outsiders. Something a former president of Hyundai said stuck in my mind: "Yesterday's leader says, 'I will lead you there.' Today's leader says, 'We will get there together.'" I talked to Rebekah, prayed a lot about it, and went back to work at headquarters.

I called a meeting with my senior team members. They brought their notebooks, as you do when called to the boss's office, and sat down across from me. I could feel the tension. I drew a deep breath and told them I wanted to sincerely apologize for my bullying Western style of management, for not appreciating the Korean and Hyundai way of doing things. They, who I guess were expecting to be yelled at, were shocked. One spoke for all when she said, "We are surprised by this." Ben, my team leader, was gracious and said he understood that in my position it must feel like "I am on an island." "That's all I wanted to say," I told them, "that and I'm looking forward to the rest of 2013."

A few moments later one of my junior team members e-mailed me to say she overheard one of the senior team members wondering suspiciously "what I was up to." That was okay, I thought. I felt like I had done the right thing and tried to clear the air. It was time to move forward.

Rebekah had no job to go to in Korea. She was stuck inside a small apartment in a cramped urban neighborhood of Seoul with a five-month-old baby, no car, and almost no friends. The crowded sidewalks and narrow, hilly streets of my Itaewon neighborhood were not stroller-friendly. Nap times were worse. We were employing the "cry it out" method. It works if you've got the stomach for it. After a while I can turn Annabelle's crying into white noise. But not Rebekah. It tears her heart out. So when she was letting Annabelle cry it out in her crib at the back of our apartment, Rebekah had to sit outside on the tiny balcony at the front of the apartment, out of earshot, fiddling on her laptop. If it was raining, she had to drape a towel over her head. I got lots of sad-Rebekah selfies when I was at work.

One night I returned to the apartment to find Rebekah collapsed on the sofa. "I'm tired, I'm bored, and I'm lonely," she said.

We rented Rebekah a car to get her some mobility and got in touch with the Filipino cleaning lady who'd worked with us when we lived on base. She babysat Annabelle to let Rebekah get out of the house occasionally. But what saved Rebekah's sanity was yet another small kindness extended by a fellow ex-pat. One of the families at our church in Seoul was German, sent by the father's company to manage the Korean branch of the business. Part of his compensation package included membership in the Seoul Club, an old-style city club with a restaurant, bar, gym, and, most important, pool. Rebekah and her German girlfriend would go to the pool at least once a week while sitters watched the children. I'm convinced that one seemingly prosaic thing allowed Rebekah to get through the two months in Seoul.

As our time together as a family in Seoul came to an end, we braced to be separated again. Rebekah and Annabelle would fly back to Washington, where Rebekah would do another month of training for her new job in Indonesia. At the beginning of August, she and Annabelle—and Chairman, back from summer camp— would fly to Jakarta. As we had planned it, I would stay in Seoul and Rebekah and Annabelle would be in Jakarta for more than a year, until the end of my contract, in October 2014. We would be a Skype family, and I would try to fly to Jakarta for a few days each month. It seemed like a plan. I wasn't sure if Annabelle had bonded with me yet and I didn't know how she would respond to me on Skype. I wanted to give her something like a memory key to remember me when she saw me on the computer screen, in addition to hopefully recognizing my face. I tried a bunch of songs and eventually discovered her name works nicely as the lyrics to the "Ode to Joy" choral movement in Beethoven's Ninth Symphony. That would be our little song.

If all went according to plan, by the end of our first four years of marriage, Rebekah and I would have been apart for nearly half of it. We rationalized the separation because both of our careers were going so well, because we were saving money, because we were each having intriguing overseas experiences, because . . . well, because we thought we could handle it. Because we thought none of us, now including Annabelle, would be the worse for wear for it. There were times when we thought we'd never make two years in Korea; yet we did. Surely we could manage another fifteen months or so of this lifestyle, then finally figure out a way we could be together by the time Annabelle was starting to be conscious of the separation.

I put a Hyundai calendar on the wall of my Itaewon apartment. It was July 2013. By the time this calendar ended, I'd have only a little more than nine months until we were reunited as a family. In the meantime, I'd make the six-and-a-half-hour flight from Seoul to Jakarta—"commuting," we called it—for a long weekend once a month.

In the in-between times, when I was alone in Seoul, my life shrank down to a point. Work, home, dinner, Skype, TV, bed. Repeat. My colleagues joked that I must be enjoying my bachelor life, but I was not. It turned out I was no good on my own anymore. But it was more than loneliness. I lacked accountability. When I was with Rebekah and Annabelle, I wanted to be a better man and tried to act accordingly. Left adrift on my own, it was too easy to slip back into my old slothful, selfish ways. This would probably surprise friends who had known me for years, because I had never evinced a desire for family life, or accountability, for that matter. But now I had no energy for any sort of sustaining human interaction other than with my family, and no personal ideal for which to strive. It all felt hollow and farcical to me; I couldn't pretend I was having a good time while separated from my family and knowing my wife was in need. I was in endurance mode only. On Sunday nights, after Rebekah and I had hung up on Skype, I'd draw through another week on the calendar with an orange marker—aware that I had simultaneously brought our reunion one week closer and sliced one more week off my life— turn out the lights, and go to bed.

# 21

## GENESIS AND SONATA

I was nearly vibrating with anticipation. It was a midsummer morning during 2013. After months of talking about it, after planning PR campaigns for it, after seeing spy shots of it on the Internet, I was finally going to get my first in-person look at the second-generation Genesis, the car upon which Hyundai's premium-brand aspirations had been pinned. I had been aching to see the car in person. In the auto industry—heck, in life—there is really nothing to compare with the first in-person look at an all-new car. Unlike a face-lift—a refresh of an existing model—an all-new car is a whole-cloth new creation. Renderings and spy photos of new cars are titillating, but they do not provide the all-senses thrill of seeing the car in person, cleaner and shinier than it ever will be again. The smell of fresh rubber tires mixes with that of new leather when the door is flung open, forming a heady, intoxicating perfume of promise and plenty. Pop the hood and the light industrial aroma of fluids and lubricants reminds us that the object of our affection is a machine, one with which—even in the digital age—we have a unique relationship. These gorgeous machines transport us away from bad things and toward good ones, wrapping us in a private cocoon of our preferences: our seat settings, our ideal climate, the soundtrack of our life's milestones. We fall in and out of love in these machines, we make the first and last trips of our lives in them, we ride for miles and miles of contented silence in them, happy merely to be sharing the intimate space with the person next to us.

Strictly speaking, I didn't have to see or even drive the new Genesis to promote it to the media. All the time in PR you promote people or things you've never met or seen. All I needed were the car's specs to show how superior it was to the previous Genesis and to show how it stacked up to its German rivals. But I felt that in order to convincingly persuade journalists of how good—not just how important—this car was, I needed to see it, to touch it, to sit in it. Mostly I just wanted to. I drove to Hyundai's Namyang R & D facility, south of Seoul, and walked into the big design presentation hall. The building is a dramatic, domed, skylit structure. It was sunny that day, and the louvered windows shot the room full of light.

The doors to the big room opened, and I saw the car by itself, sitting in profile. My first thought was that the designers had pulled a trick on me and driven in an Audi A7, one of the most beautiful cars on the road. Nope. This was the next Genesis. The first thing that came out of my mouth was "Whoa." I walked around it a couple times. It was good from every angle. Genesis had a brushed-chrome hexagonal grille. Car companies spend a lot of money and time—years, even—thinking about and perfecting their grilles. They are the first part of a car you see on the road and are the face of the brand. The best ones are memorable. Think of the "twin kidney" BMW grilles, the three-pointed star in the Mercedes grille, and the diagonal bar across the Volvo grille. Hyundai wanted an equally recognizable and memorable grille, so it was decided that the Hyundai face would be a six-sided grille— sometimes with different proportions and materials, but always a hexagon. The Genesis hood was long, a characteristic of high-performance rear-wheel-drive European sedans like Jaguars, with hoods lengthy enough for landing strips. It had gorgeous volumes of sheet metal along the sides, contoured to reflect the light just right. And it had an aggressive fastback trunk, giving it an elegant and sporty look. The new Genesis would be the first Hyundai to feature what we were calling the Fluidic Sculpture 2.0 look, a muscular, upmarket refinement of the Fluidic Sculpture design that astounded the auto industry four years earlier.

I opened the driver's-side door and felt a satisfying heft but an easy pivot. I climbed inside and shut the door with a muffled *whoomp*, solid as a safe. The leather seat was bolstered just right to hold you steady when accelerating out of a turn. The interior was roomy, understated, and elegant, with high-end, unflashy materials and a makes-sense cockpit layout. My fingers wrapped around the steering wheel in a way that felt more comfortable than in other cars. I was told that was because this Genesis had an ergonomically designed steering wheel. Hyundai engineers realized that human hands, when wrapped around a steering wheel, do not naturally form a circle, the typical cross-sectional shape of a steering wheel. Instead they form something like an angled oval, and that's how Hyundai engineers had designed the new Genesis steering wheel. Genesis was loaded with invisible, functional details like this.

The car was the design manifestation of Vice Chairman Chung's pronouncement in Detroit more than two years earlier when he launched Hyundai's grand aspirations: "Today, customers do not believe that expensive cars with unnecessary technology are premium." The Elantra Car of the Year win in Detroit one year after the vice chairman's speech was thrilling. The Winterkorn Incident in Frankfurt was satisfying. The favorable press was nice. But the Genesis was *product*. The designers, engineers, and product teams had done it. If there was one Hyundai that could take the brand to the next level—to make people really think differently about Hyundai—this was it. Of course, this was only one PR man's opinion. The test that mattered would come months later, when we put Genesis into the hands of automotive writers for the first time. An hour or so later I left the hall, upbeat about the car and the direction of the brand.

A few weeks later I walked into the same hall with the same sense of anticipation. This day I would see the new Sonata. Genesis was going to be a halo car for the brand, establishing the design direction and premium-brand aspirations. But Sonata was our meat and potatoes after Elantra, our biggest seller. In the U.S., Hyundai would sell ten times as many Sonatas in a year than Genesis sedans. The previous Sonata had caused a splash, so expectations for the new Sonata were sky-high. Critics wondered: Could Hyundai keep up its design leadership, or was it a one-hit wonder?

The doors opened again, the sunlight streamed, and there was the new Sonata. I didn't say it out loud, but the first thought that popped into my mind was:

"Oh."

The new Sonata was sitting next to a new Genesis. It was undeniable, for the first time in Hyundai's history, that these two cars belonged to the same family in the way it is undeniable that all Audis and Benzes belong to the same family. That was good. The new Sonata was handsome. It had strong, sharp lines around its nose and daytime running lights under the headlights that gave it the feel of a European touring car. Its interior resembled the more expensive cabin of the new Genesis. It had new features.

It was superior in every measurable way to its predecessor, in performance, safety, fuel economy, and even price.

And yet . . .

Hyundai's designers had taken the powerfully arcing "orchid stroke" character line on the previous Sonata's side—the one that drew comparisons to the Mercedes C-class cars—and flattened it out, Honda-style. The just-over-the-top shiny chrome grille was redesigned into a signature hexagonal shape and changed to brushed chrome to give it a statelier look and so it would fit into the family. Everyone acknowledged the previous Sonata's styling was polarizing, but it stood out among its bland competitors, such as the Toyota Camry, the Honda Accord, and the Chevrolet Malibu. The buzz around the company was that the previous Sonata, which had wowed the pants off of American motoring journalists and made it a success among American customers, was too wild for Korean customers, who were turning to the more conservative Kia Optima. This is a calculus every global automaker must make, as buyers' tastes are so varied across the world. Will a new design gain sales in one market but hurt sales in another? I had an uneasy feeling in my stomach about this Sonata. I was afraid that auto writers and customers would see the new Sonata and think that Hyundai had settled back into the pack of its competitors rather than leaping out in front of it. Yes, the new Genesis would be on American roads, but it would be outnumbered by ten times as many of the lower-priced new Sonatas. I was afraid it was the new Sonata, rather than the new Genesis, that customers would think of when they thought of Hyundai. If it didn't quite feel like slipping back down the hill that Hyundai was trying to climb, it did feel like a rest on a trailside bench. And that didn't feel like Hyundai; it was certainly not the experience I'd had during the Hyundai team-building mountain climbs.

# 22

## JAKARTA IS NO SEOUL

On our first day together in Jakarta, Rebekah and I passed through two fortified security gates at the entrance of our apartment compound, greeted the smiling soldier holding a machine gun, and stepped out into the riotous Indonesian morning. It was September just south of the equator, and the sun pushed the temperature past 90 degrees. The humidity clung like a damp wool blanket. We could barely hear each other over the lanes of traffic rushing by—a seemingly endless stream of cars, scooters, and covered three-wheeled buggies known as *bajaj*, powered by howling motorcycle engines. Vehicles zoomed past in a sort of self-regulated, organic flow of moving bumper-to-bumper traffic, obeying a seemingly telepathic, driver-to-driver control system. How does every starling in a murmuration of hundreds know to turn left at the same moment? I don't know. Same way Indonesian drivers know how to get around Jakarta without constantly bashing into each other. The smell of gasoline exhaust and the odor of burning wood, likely from smoldering rice husks in fields outside of the city, hung in the air. As we began walking along the broken sidewalk, a green lizard about six inches long scurried out of a hole, scuttled under our feet, and disappeared into another gaping crack.

Rebekah and I looked at each other and laughed, breaking something of a subsurface tension between us. Each of us knew separately that this was going to be our greatest challenge yet as a married couple and, now, as parents to an infant. We had exhaustively talked through all the logistics, planned my first few long weekend visits from Seoul to Jakarta, and gotten everything set up as best we knew how. We had approached this rationally as an obstacle to be hurdled and as a discomfort to be mitigated, much in the way I had stocked up my pantry back in Seoul when forced to leave the plenty of the U.S. military base. We were consciously separating our family by thousands of miles and creating, we acknowledged, a physical distance between us. We knew that. What we had not banked on was the emotional distance.

You don't see a lot of lizards on the sidewalks of Gangnam. None, actually. Our new friend underfoot was not only a reminder of the vast difference between Seoul and Jakarta; he was one of many points that drove home a big takeaway from living in the Eastern hemisphere: the word "Asia" is almost meaningless. The countries of East Asia can on the surface seem pretty similar to an outsider. After a while you learn of the cultural rifts and historic grievances, along with intense nationalism, that divide Korea, Japan, and China. But once you start comparing East Asia to Southeast or South Asia, "Asia" becomes little more than a gross bucket into which dozens of cultures and more than 2 billion people are wrongly dumped, no more descriptive or insightful about what they are like than "Caucasian" helps you understand the people of North America and Europe.

Seoul has four seasons; Jakarta has two, dry and flooding. Seoul has Confucianism; Jakarta is the capital of the world's largest Muslim country. Korea is a geographically small land filled with a homogeneous people who speak one language; Indonesia is an archipelago of more than two hundred islands stretching for two thousand miles, filled with three hundred ethnicities and seven hundred languages. At first contact, Koreans can feel overly mannered and a bit distant; Indonesians are instantly artless and familiar. In Seoul, state-of-the-art video displays in store windows enchant sidewalk shoppers. In Jakarta, beggars hold on strings monkeys that dance for coins. Korea is First World; Indonesia is developing Third World. In Seoul, I was a *waygookin*. In Jakarta, I was a *bule*, or white foreigner.

Rebekah embraced most things about Indonesia in a way she did not in Korea. She loved the hot temperature, even if the humidity played havoc with her hair. She loved the smiling warmth of the people. She loved that she wouldn't be stuck in a visa window for a year, as she'd been at the U.S. embassy in Korea. In Jakarta, Rebekah would be a science and technology officer, with a portfolio that included maritime issues, such as illegal fishing, shark fin poaching, and coral restoration. She would meet with her counterparts in the Indonesian government to advance her government's position. She was, at last, a real diplomat.

She was also instantly in charge of a household staff.

Ex-pats will often say their favorite part about living in developing countries is the ability to afford household help. But this is an entirely new concept to most Americans, whose only exposure to housing staff is *Downton Abbey*. Through references from U.S. embassy diplomats already in Jakarta and those who were leaving post, even before Rebekah arrived in Jakarta, she'd already hired a live-in nanny for Annabelle, a housekeeper who would come from nine to five each weekday, and a driver. All for about $700 per month, the going Jakarta market rate. It was our first taste of pricing disparity between the First and Third Worlds.

Tri was our nanny. She was a sweet, smiling single mother in her late twenties who came from a village outside of Jakarta. She had been left by her husband and was the sole earner for her and her son. She would live with us during the week while her mother watched the boy and return home on the weekend. She had the ability to instantly make Annabelle smile. She would be the first person to see our daughter walk, and the first to hear her talk.

Sati was in her early forties and would run the household. She'd shop with money Rebekah gave her, walk Chairman, cook dinner—including dishes for the weekend—do laundry, and clean. Sati had worked for several Western diplomat families and had even gone on vacation with them to watch the children. She, too, lived outside of Jakarta, and had a son and a daughter and a husband who could not find work, making her the family's breadwinner. She would sometimes ride to and from work in a puttering *bajaj*.

Our driver was Pak Wandi, "Pak" being the polite and familiar Bahasa word for "Mr." Pak Wandi didn't have a lot of English, but his knowledge of the streets of Jakarta would best Garmin and Google Maps. Like many Third World megacities, Jakarta, with a population of 11 million, grew organically and without plans. GPS was useless. You navigated by landmark, moving from one neighborhood to the other, counting how many highway overpasses you'd driven beneath and then, when you were pretty sure you were close to your destination, you'd slow the car, pull over, roll down the window, and ask a local. Pak Wandi was a middle-aged Indonesian with a trimmed mustache and a seemingly stern bearing whose face animated into a handsome smile at the sight of Annabelle.

Considering we'd hired them sight unseen, we felt really lucky with Tri, Sati, and Wandi. Our one concern was Tri's English, or lack of it. Sati's English was good, but it was Tri who spent the most time with Annabelle during the day. Living as an ex-pat, you learn pretty quickly how to communicate in simple words, gestures, and sketches. Tri fully comprehended what we told her; that wasn't the problem. We worried that Annabelle's language skills might develop slowly. In retrospect, this was typical first-time-parent overreaction. Between Rebekah and Rebekah's embassy friends, Sati and nightly Skype calls with Dad, Annabelle heard plenty of complex English. And besides, she was only nine months old. This wasn't going to keep her out of Harvard. Her dad's hillbilly genes would take care of that.

Rebekah's new home was in a high-security U.S. government housing compound surrounded by a tall brick wall strung with concertina wire, like the U.S. military base back in Seoul. Each time we drove in and out of the compound, the car had to pass through a twelve-foot-high security box made of steel bars with sliding gates front and back as guards used mirrors to look under the car for bombs, then popped the trunk and hood. There is a violent Islamist movement in Indonesia: a 2002 bombing on the resort island of Bali killed more than two hundred. For this reason, and due to the fact that Americans should not drink Indonesian tap water for fear of parasites, Jakarta is designated by the State Department as a "hardship" post, which bumped Rebekah's salary up a bit.

Inside the compound were about six four-story garden apartments around a driveway and small courtyard planted with towering palm trees that dropped surprisingly heavy six-foot fronds and stunning flowering shrubs that would probably win prizes at garden shows in the U.S. but were run-of-the-mill flora in ridiculously verdant Indonesia. Embassy personnel shared the compound with U.S. Marines who guarded the embassy, and every morning at six a.m. jarheads would be out in the courtyard, doing pull-ups and push-ups. In both Seoul and Jakarta, Marines kept my family safe. If those guys wanted to *"Hoo-wah!"* at six in the morning and politely flirt with Rebekah at the embassy, it was fine with me.

Unlike the U.S. base in Seoul, which covered more than six hundred acres and felt like a small town you could walk and drive around in, the compound in Jakarta was the size of two football fields and felt tighter. The broken sidewalks and car fumes outside the complex did not make for pleasant baby strolling or dog walking. So Annabelle and Chairman did lap after lap around the complex driveway led by us, Tri, and Sati.

Rebekah's apartment had three bedrooms, tile floors, and dark wood cabinets throughout. Built probably during the 1950s, Jakarta's wet weather had taken its customary toll: the building was streaked with soot and mold on the outside and mildew was an occasional smell. Around the back of the compound, grim, dirty servants' quarters had been built to accompany the apartments. No one lived in them anymore, but Pak Wandi and the other drivers liked to hang out back there and talk and nap during the day, and Sati, a Muslim, would often use one of the small rooms to pray. The high humidity and frequent, violent cloudbursts combined to create a feeling of general dampness in Jakarta, even when the sun was out.

From time to time, even inside the safety of the walled compound, there were unexpected reminders that my family was living in an authentically tropical climate. During one of my visits from Seoul, I was walking Chairman on a patio at the back of the compound and noticed him quickly lifting his feet, one after the other, like he was walking on hot coals. Before I could figure out why, I felt a sting on an ankle, then another and another. I looked down and saw dozens of red ants swarming up my sneakers and socks. They were on Chairman's paws, too, biting through the fur. If this had been a horror movie, this would have been the part when the camera does a fast zoom out, pulling back to show Chairman and me standing in a surging sea of thousands of biting fire ants. I yanked Chairman out of there and spent the next several minutes washing the red marauders out of his paws.

Given that Jakarta traffic could turn a three-mile trip into a three-hour nightmare, Rebekah was lucky that her new home was only a fifteen-minute walk from the U.S. embassy.

Her whole life, Rebekah had only ever wanted to do one thing: work overseas or in the international sector. The Foreign Service allowed her to do that. Now, in Jakarta, she had one tour under her belt and understood the State Department's peculiar, often vexing folkways. She had mastered its endless paperwork. She was making good contacts elsewhere in the service and maintained a professional "hallway reputation," eschewing gossip and bad work habits. In Jakarta she was meeting with high-level Indonesian government officials who worked on science and technology and they regarded her highly, as an emissary from the U.S. government who deserved attention and respect. She would take to her new job with vigor.

Only weeks after she arrived, Rebekah put on a successful public seminar on shark fin fishing, a key element of the embassy's public diplomacy initiative. Several species of sharks around Indonesia are in danger of becoming extinct because shark fins, usually served as soup, are considered a delicacy throughout much of Asia. Shark fin soup is served at prestigious events, such as weddings. Despite the lack of any scientific proof, shark fin soup is believed to increase sexual potency, lower cholesterol, improve skin tone, and impart other benefits, especially in China. Shark finners typically strip the fins from a shark and leave it to die, a cruel and indefensible process. This has led to a growing number of bans on shark fin soup. When I was running my team at Hyundai, I would not allow it to be served at business dinners.

For other parts of her job, Rebekah traveled to faraway parts of the Indonesian archipelago, planting mangroves and doing market-entry evaluations for potential U.S. investment. Her section inside the embassy was an important one, meaning her work was noticed and well regarded. As I enjoyed telling her about the new Hyundai cars I was seeing, she loved telling me about the colorful characters she was meeting and dealing with. Her work intersected with officials in the Indonesian government, with people at U.S. NGOs, and with private-sector U.S. corporations. As a U.S. diplomat and as a natural and skilled communicator, Rebekah could build bridges among parties that others could not. The job was not always comfortable, but it was gratifying and vital and hands-on experiential in the way Foreign Service jobs are supposed to be. By turns, the service took her to pink coral reefs so gorgeous they could hardly be believed and to an island so remote it required two plane rides and a two-hour drive over mountainous jungle roads so perilous and twisty, she lost her lunch on the roadside. She made good friends at the embassy, where she found an esprit de corps similar to what she experienced during her post-tsunami time in Tokyo. On her off hours, she went to parties at the embassy deputy chief of mission's home, a sprawling Dutch compound dating from that country's early-nineteenth-century colonization of Indonesia, filled with exotic artifacts—and fascinating stories—from a career in the Foreign Service. Here, finally, was what Rebekah had thirsted for most of her adult life. She was, in many ways, living her ideal overseas life.

But the professional satisfaction Rebekah derived from her work and the richness of her tropical ex-pat life conspired to highlight the one thing missing from her life: her husband. It was a weekend getaway Rebekah planned that brought it home to us.

She had rented a three-story guesthouse surrounded by rice paddies a few hours outside of Jakarta in the Indonesian countryside, more than enough room for Rebekah, me, Sati, and Annabelle. By day, Annabelle toddled around the breezy, open-air villa, weaving around wicker furniture and padding across cool tile floors, holding Sati's hands. At ten months, Annabelle was crawling up stairs and walking almost on her own. They splashed in the villa's pool and took in the staggeringly lush scenery. Indonesia may be the world's most biodiverse country, and this place demonstrated that fact with an almost vulgar glee. At their edges, the carefully laid-out rice paddies surrounding the villa were overtaken by a high-canopy rain forest that displayed all shades of green. The jungle blared with the peculiar and often startling calls of winged and legged animals. Some were recognizable. Others might prove a stern challenge to taxonomy. Nighttime noises only deepened the mystery. The effect was to place a guest out of time, in a previous century, and beyond civilization. I know all of this because Rebekah recorded it on iPhone video and e-mailed it to me. I couldn't make it down from Seoul for their trip. My experience of the sumptuous weekend was sterile, detached, edited. When they returned to Jakarta, Rebekah recounted the trip and she and I laughed over Annabelle's antics, but we both realized this was the beginning of a problem. I was watching my daughter grow up on Skype and thirty-second iPhone videos. One parent was living her child's life; the other was just watching it. Skype and Apple FaceTime and the other modern tools for maintaining contact are technological miracles that seemed like science fiction only twenty years ago. And there is no doubt it is better to see your loved ones than not. Yet, at the same time, the video link only emphasizes the distance between you and others, acting as an unavoidable real-time reminder that you are indisputably apart. Video swells the ache.

On the other end of my video link was this tiny, stunning on-camera presence that I could not touch. Annabelle was born with almost no hair and had very little for the first year of her life. This focused all attention on the brown, luminous, doe-like eyes that dominated her face and quizzically probed her mother's computer screen. Transfixed more by the moving colors than by any recognition of her father, I was only a human face to Annabelle. On Skype we had no connection: my oh-so-clever "Ode to Joy" trick wasn't working.

Rebekah and I had at least anticipated this problem with Annabelle and tried to steel ourselves for it. But there was another problem we had not foreseen. With a live-in nanny, a housekeeper, and her mother focused on her, Annabelle was exceptionally well taken care of. But no one was taking care of Rebekah. As her husband, that was my job, and I was failing.

When I was in Seoul and Rebekah was on her own in the U.S., even pregnant, she was lonely but felt safe and had her parents in a nearby state. Her only professional responsibility was language class. In Jakarta, the entire weight of making sure our child stayed alive fell on her while she was trying to execute diplomacy on behalf of her government and look after the needs of a household staff. For five nights a week Tri shared the apartment with Rebekah but, per custom, retreated to her room after Annabelle went to sleep. She would not have felt comfortable hanging out with the boss after work hours. Despite Rebekah's work friends, she had no ally, no one who was always, unequivocally, on her side 24–7. She had no intimate support. She had no one to wake up to or snuggle with while watching TV. Rebekah had no husband.

Any parent will tell you the time you most need your spouse

is when your child is sick. No one wants to be the sole safety net, the lone decision maker for a child in pain and misery. You need someone to consult with. Someone whose face you can search for answers. Someone who will defuse the situation or say, yes, we need to call the doctor now. There is no greater feeling of isolation and helplessness than what a lone parent feels with a sick or injured child.

Going in, veteran Jakarta parents had told us to expect Annabelle to contract a "funky rash" from time to time. Given the heat and humidity and who-knows-what in the air and bathwater, that was not a surprise, nor terribly worrisome. But what would happen if Annabelle got really sick or was badly injured? The U.S. embassy had a doctor, nurses, and a well-equipped office open during business hours. In Korea, if our medical situation exceeded the capacity of the embassy doctor, we had a U.S. military hospital on base and access to some of the world's best health care moments away in Seoul. In Jakarta, that was not the case. There were big hospitals, but the level of care so poor and the English-speaking ability so spotty that the U.S. embassy urged its employees to avoid them. Instead, the embassy recommended use of a handful of small clinics called "SOS" scattered around the city. But they had no ability to handle serious or longer-term conditions or do surgery. This meant that the best option for Annabelle—if she needed serious medical help—was a six-hour medevac helicopter ride to Singapore. On my own in Seoul, I had felt cut off from medical care. But that was only by language. In Jakarta, Annabelle—and Rebekah—could truly be in danger if things turned badly and they had to build in a six-hour gap until top-level medical care was available. And things could turn bad for any number of reasons: a car or pedestrian accident on the city's crowded streets; a mosquito bite that leads to dengue, a disease that can cause hemorrhagic fever; the faint but still real threat of domestic terrorism; getting caught in a violent public protest . . . Even a minor language problem with a member of our household staff or the compound guards when every second counted could lead to disastrous consequences for our daughter. This was the reality of Jakarta.

Our fears were realized in a terrifying manner one weekend night in Jakarta when Rebekah was alone with Annabelle. Tri and Sati had gone home for the weekend. I was in Seoul. Annabelle was sick with a cold, and Rebekah was trying to administer liquid Tylenol through an eyedropper, a familiar drill for parents. She had done it several times before but now, possibly because Annabelle was crying and gulping air, as Rebekah squeezed the sticky pink liquid into the back of Annabelle's mouth, something went wrong. Annabelle tried to gasp but couldn't get air in. Her eyes got big and her mouth gaped as she writhed in Rebekah's arms. Mere seconds were passing but it seemed like hours to Rebekah since Annabelle had breathed. There was no food stuck in her mouth, so there was nothing Rebekah could reach in and pull out. More seconds ticked by as Annabelle silently gaped and heaved. Her little pink lips began to turn purple. Not knowing what to do and having no one to call to for help, Rebekah remembered her infant choking training and flipped Annabelle over on one hand while striking her upper back with an open palm, hoping it might somehow open an airway. After another few seconds Annabelle drew a big gulp of air and resumed breathing normally. Before long, with full, pink lips, Annabelle was cooing and cuddling Mommy, who could barely hold her in badly shaking arms. "I thought she was going to die," Rebekah told me the next morning by Skype.

I sat alone in my apartment in Seoul, staring into my laptop screen, listening to the story in rapt, impotent horror. Rebekah spoke while Annabelle snuggled in close on a sofa in their apartment in Jakarta, 3,300 miles away from where I was. Annabelle was seemingly no worse for wear. But this brought no sense of relief. Instead, it convicted and shamed me. I didn't feel like part of a cool twenty-first-century, ex-pat, jet-setter family. I felt like an absent father who hadn't been there for his wife during the scariest moment of her young motherhood. My dereliction of duty as a husband and as a father had not really hit me until that moment. I'm certain that I would not have reacted better or more swiftly than Rebekah did had I been there when Annabelle choked. But that wasn't the point. I would have been there. Dads are supposed to *be there*. What was I doing? What were *we* doing?

What Rebekah and I were doing, we were finally forced to realize, was trading time together as a family for nothing more than money. And that was a devil's bargain.

# 23

## ESCAPE PLAN

Rebekah and I could speak of little else other than how to get the family back together. I had seen my wife's personality start to change once before, when we were forced to get rid of Lily. Now I was seeing it change again. Rebekah was lonely. Despite all of our planning, despite our rational attempts to create workarounds for our family separation, a growing realization began to overtake us. It didn't look like we were going to make it living apart for another year. When I was able to visit in Jakarta for three or four days at a time, Annabelle wasn't comfortable with me, at least not initially. She wouldn't sit next to me until the last day of my visit. During playtime, she crawled away from me on the floor. When I'd pick Annabelle up to cuddle her, she'd cry and reach for Rebekah, or Sati, or Tri. It was heartbreaking.

On a Sunday night during one of my commutes to Jakarta, Rebekah and I sat on a sofa in her living room and ran through our options as we saw them. She could quit her job with the Foreign Service and bring Annabelle to Seoul, where we'd ride out the rest of my contract. The problem there was threefold. First, we'd lose Rebekah's U.S. government health insurance, which covered me as well. Second, Rebekah really didn't want to come back to my little apartment in Seoul again with a one-year-old, no job, and no friends. Finally, what would happen after my contract ended? When I signed my second contract, I had told Hyundai that four years in Korea would be enough and that I'd like them to find me a job in the U.S. or Europe. But any such job was likely to be a step down from my current one and there was no guarantee there would even be one available.

I broached the idea of just quitting Hyundai and moving to Jakarta without a job. With government-supplied housing, we could live on Rebekah's salary through her two-year posting. But what about after that? We could see where her next posting would take her. But we doubted it would be as easy for me to find as good of a job as I had at Hyundai, so I'd either be out of work again or lucky to score a job in the embassy mail room. Or she could quit the Foreign Service and we'd head back to the States with a baby and both of us looking for work. Good luck with that.

We concluded there was no solution that enabled both of us to keep our jobs, or for me to keep my higher-salary job without Rebekah being miserably cooped up in Korea. My faith instructs me to turn to prayer first, acknowledging God's sovereignty in all things. Instead, as a prideful human, believing I had control over the situation, I turned to prayer only when I was out of options.

Rebekah and I began to pray together but we were interrupted by a knock on the front door. It was Pak Wandi, ready to drive me to the airport. Time to leave my family again. I would catch the 10:05 p.m. Korean Air flight from Jakarta, touching down in Seoul at 7:05 Monday morning. I'd rush home, take a shower, and get to work a little more than an hour late. Another of my too-short visits was over, leaving me hungry for more and unsettled about the future.

Annabelle was long asleep, so I patted Chairman, hugged Rebekah, and slid into the backseat of the silver minivan. As Pak Wandi drove, I silently stared out of a window at the scooters zipping noisily by. Festive flashing lights and billboards cut through the hazy, damp Indonesian darkness. "There has to be an answer," I thought. "Something we're missing."

I had some time before my flight once I got to Soekarno-Hatta International Airport, named for another strongman who'd built his country during the 1960s, like Korea's Park Chung-hee. I typed out an e-mail to an old *Washington Post* colleague named Jeff Birnbaum. Jeff was a top-tier Washington journalist for the *Wall Street Journal* and *Fortune* for many years before coming to the *Post*'s business section. It was only an accident of fate that briefly made me his editor, a task I was in no way prepared for. Jeff and I had one big thing in common: like me, he had left journalism for PR a few years earlier. Now he was heading the practice at BGR Group, a well-regarded lobbying and PR firm back home in Washington, D.C. I hadn't spoken to Jeff for months and knew little about his firm and even less about doing PR in an agency setup, servicing multiple clients. I gave him a brief update on our situation, saying that Rebekah and I were both doing well professionally but that the separation was tougher than we expected. I had no expectations but suppose in hindsight I was fishing a little bit. I sent the e-mail, packed away my iPad, and got on the flight. When I landed in Seoul and opened my e-mail, I saw Jeff's reply:

> Thanks for the note. I'm glad to hear all is well except for that terrible separation. How long are you locked into your current gig? I'm looking to hire a senior colleague.

I couldn't believe it. Could this be the answer to prayer, late as it was offered up?

I forwarded the e-mail right away to Rebekah in Jakarta. I wrote, "Ready to go back to D.C.?"

I got back in touch with Jeff and told him my particulars and that I'd discuss things with Rebekah. But to me it already felt like a foregone conclusion, if Jeff's firm would have me. This was the only way I could see of getting the family back together without taking an economic hit—if we could work it out so Rebekah could transfer from the embassy in Jakarta to State Department headquarters, or "Main State," back in D.C. My big concern was Hyundai. I had signed a contract that ran until October 2014. Would the company let me out of the contract early? Would there be legal or monetary penalties? I had no idea what my employee rights were in Korea.

I needed to hire a lawyer. But this time I prayed first.

# 24

## THE JUDGMENT OF GENESIS

My arrival in Korea coincided almost perfectly with Hyundai's grand and risky gambit to remake itself as a premium brand, a quest launched at the Detroit Auto Show in January 2011. I didn't know it at the time—it was three years off—but the first ground-up, one-hundred-percent-new car that that was meant to carry these premium aspirations would be the second-generation Hyundai Genesis. The arc that started at the beginning of 2011 would conclude at the end of 2013 with the launch of the new Genesis and, as it was increasingly seeming, with my time at Hyundai.

After years of research, engineering, design sketches, clay models, prototypes, tests, executive decisions, and finally assembly, it was time to turn the new Genesis over to the public. Its first test would be the harshest: my team would host a group of top-tier U.S. motoring journalists in Korea. They would be the first foreigners in the world to test-drive Genesis.

Genesis was the bar that Hyundai had set for itself. Although it was unfair to judge an entire company on the basis of one car, in reality, if Genesis failed to excite—if Hyundai failed to make the pivot from value-for-money automaker to premium car builder—then Hyundai's metaphorical midlife crisis would turn into an actual one. If Genesis was ho-hum, if it were judged a less-than-premium vehicle, Hyundai would have to wait three more years—until its next Equus luxury sedan was released—to try again. This would be a disastrous setback for the company's strategy and, not to mention, sales. If Genesis did not satisfy, it would not sell.

The big engineering advances between the old and new Genesis had less to do with features or gimmicks. The car did have an automatic braking function that would stop the Genesis on its own if a person ran in front. It even had an industry-first carbon dioxide sensor. If the carbon dioxide level inside the car got too high, the new Genesis would automatically open the vents to prevent the driver from getting drowsy.

But the heart of the next-gen Genesis was improved drivability. Hyundai wanted to build a car that could run the road with the German luxe sedans. To do this, Hyundai engineers had to reduce what is known in the industry as NVH, or noise, vibration, and harshness. To achieve this, engineers started anew. The new Genesis shared no common parts with the previous one, making it more expensive to produce. British racing legend Lotus was brought in to improve the steering feel of the new Genesis, to increase road feedback, and to maximize response and driving pleasure of the driver. A new eight-speed transmission was introduced to match the eight-speed gearboxes found in Audis, BMWs, Bentleys, and Jaguars. A new all-wheel-drive system was built for Genesis to give it better handling and improve sales in snowy North America. The amount of high-strength steel—

made by Hyundai Steel—in the new Genesis was significantly increased to improve its safety, rigidity, and feel of tightness on the road. In the previous Genesis, the suspension on the left and right sides of the car were linked. In the new Genesis, left- and right-side suspension were independent, allowing it to better adjust to road conditions and improve handling. Every joint and gap was insulated and caulked to eliminate road noise.

We brought the U.S. auto journalists to Korea. For the next week I would have to place my escape plan and thoughts of family reunion on hold. This required my full attention. Hyundai, Genesis, and my vice chairman deserved that. We put the journalists up at a luxury hotel in Gangnam, hoping to impress them with the best that Korea had to offer. We took them to top-end restaurants. We had designers and engineers give them briefings on what they'd done with the new car. Then it was money time. We took the journalists to the test track at the Namyang R&D center and put them behind the wheel of the new Genesis. But, to prove our point, we needed to do more than that. If we wanted the new Genesis to compete with the best of Europe, that had to start right here. At our test track, we lined up the new Genesis next to an old Genesis, the obvious comparison. But next to these we parked a Mercedes E-class and a BMW 5-series, our new chief rivals. We wanted the journalists to see how much better than its predecessor the new Genesis was, and then we wanted them to step right out of the new Genesis and into the Benz and BMW. This would be like an up-and-coming chef opening a new restaurant and placing his signature dish before an influential food critic—then inviting the town's most established chefs to come over to do the same. What we were doing was nuts.

The journalists appreciated our chutzpah and, admittedly, the chance to zip around in the high-end German cars as well. No test drive ever lasts long enough for an auto journalist; this is true if you let them have the car for a month. But we gave them more time with our new Genesis than we typically gave visiting media, and we let them take it on a couple of different test tracks, with curves and straightaways. This was my first chance to drive the new Genesis, too. Even non-gearheads can tell when they're riding in a luxury car. The body feels tighter, quieter. The high-tech, well-damped suspension barely transmitted road bumps that would rattle your teeth in a cheaper car. After a couple of turns in the new Genesis, I thought, "I can feel the money."

You don't get a lot of meaningful instant feedback from auto journalists right after a test drive. So I held my breath for the next couple of weeks until the reviews started to appear, trading anxious e-mails with my colleagues back in the States.

Finally they came out. *Autoweek* wrote, "The coming Genesis is worthy of spearheading Hyundai's new aim of including more premium luxury in its lineup." Of his time on the test track, the *Automobile* magazine writer said, "The Genesis is a willing partner as we try to keep a smooth line and generate as much speed as possible on the brief straightaways. The AWD system adds stability, and the new steering system is an upgrade. The car goes where it is directed." Even *Car and Driver*, the tone setter for U.S. auto criticism and always tough to please, wrote: "Hyundai might not have the know-how to threaten the BMW 5-series just yet, but this new Genesis is precisely the kind of experience that moves the Koreans one step closer to their goal."

Phew. We made it through the initial gauntlet. Had we received a raft of Hyundai-should-stick-to-making-Elantras reviews, it would have been calamitous. Instead, the critics liked the new Genesis. Some even thought it showed we were pulling off the great brand-elevation experiment. Truth is, it was only a first step. With this kind of aspiration, every next model that Hyundai churns out must be a significant improvement over its predecessor. Yet that is exactly the kind of challenge Hyundai is always setting for itself. No one had written that we'd made a car that would blow the doors off the Germans. But we hadn't expected that. Our best hope was that the new Genesis would be taken seriously as a premium car and would be a worthy challenge to the world's best cars. That, the initial reviews had confirmed. I had to admit, wryly, there was a tone of "almost, not quite" to some of the reviews. "Three years here in Korea and I'm still getting that," I mused. But I quickly brushed that aside. Given the huge chasm we were hoping to ford in just one generational jump of a vehicle, for the first time in a couple weeks I felt like I could breathe. I hoped the engineers and product teams who had put years of their lives into the new Genesis felt the same way.

Now, I could turn my attention back to my family and our plan.

## 25
### FINDING HOME

For the past four years of our lives, as soon as Rebekah was accepted into the Foreign Service, it felt like we had spent more time planning and coordinating the logistics of our lives than actually living them. Each State Department posting was a months-long process of bid lists, uncertainty, false starts, lobbying, and maddening silences as we waited for a government bureaucracy to decide our fates. When we were separated, we spent hours scouring airline schedules and fees, trying to time ticket purchases to get the best price for the not-cheap transoceanic flights. Now here we went again, trying to execute our highest-degree-of-difficulty maneuver yet: a simultaneous escape from jobs in Seoul and Jakarta and a unified splashdown into two new jobs back in Washington. The job offer waiting for me in Washington would mean nothing if we couldn't extract ourselves from our current roles in Asia.

Rebekah was optimistic she could get something called a

"compassionate curtailment" from the State Department. In the Foreign Service, a curtailment means you're leaving your assigned posting before you're supposed to. The compassionate curtailment allows officers to leave a post for any number of personal reasons: for example, a death or illness in the family, or a spousal separation, like we had. We had seen a couple of compassionate curtailments approved while we were in Korea, and they enabled families to get back together. If Rebekah got one, she would be free to apply for jobs—of which there usually were many—at State Department headquarters in Washington. Rebekah felt good about where things were headed.

Meanwhile, I found my Korean lawyer. I had only had good dealings with my bosses at Hyundai, and Human Resources had bent over backward for three years accommodating my unusual situation. But a contract is a contract, and you never know how counterparties will react. A Korean labor lawyer looked at my contract and told me he thought the chance was minimal but not nonexistent that Hyundai would try to hold me to the contract. I was not as confident as Rebekah about my transition out of my job.

At the same time, after my initial euphoria wore off, I had to wrestle with the nature of exactly what kind of job I'd be doing back in Washington. There are essentially two kinds of PR jobs: in-house and agency. In-house PR was what I had done at Hyundai. At Hyundai, I had been able to treat my job as I'd treated a news beat back at the *Post*: I dug in deep, got to know everything about it, tried to develop a mastery. That fit my personality. At an agency, two things are true: First, you have to bring in clients, which I'd never done before. Second, you have to work for multiple clients. One day it could be a white-hat client. The next day, maybe not. That troubled me.

Going into Hyundai, I knew I liked cars, and my mechanical

engineering degree helped me know how they worked. I knew that practically every new car these days is a pretty good, very safe car, leagues better in quality and safety than my dad's Oldsmobile Delta 88s. The longer I worked at Hyundai, the better I got to know the quality and commitment of the people who worked there, the easier it got to do PR for the company.

At Hyundai, I'd been approached by plenty of PR agencies hoping to win business from us. I knew the tone of the pitches I received, ranging from earnest to unctuous to even desperate. We'd rebuffed most of them. Now I'd be the guy making the pitches. I had to determine if I had the stomach for that.

Helping matters was the fact that I'd be going to work for a former colleague and friend. BGR had a number of international clients, which appealed to me. Many were long-term clients, which told me the firm valued relationships. I thought I had a reasonable chance to bring in some Korean business eventually. And, bottom line, all the meetings and e-mails and hallway chatter and lunchtime conversations would be in *English*. That as much as anything else swung the balance.

In truth, the overwhelming desire to get the family back together made most of these concerns secondary, or at least a can I could kick down the road. Rebekah could not hold on much longer without support from her husband, and I could not hold on much longer being a stranger to Annabelle. When you have a family, you don't always get to choose your dream job. You hope that you're lucky enough to do a job that (a) provides for your family, (b) is legal, and (c) allows you to sleep at night.

Maybe this was the sign that I'd made it through my midlife crisis and become something else, maybe something better; that I was manning up and walking away from a job that I was good at to take a flyer on an unknown gig for the greater good of getting the family back together. Maybe this was it.

BGR made its offer. Now it was time to tell Hyundai. I gulped hard and went to see Hyundai's HR head, who had helped recruit me three years earlier.

I started by telling him how well Hyundai had treated and supported me and how grateful I was to have the opportunity—maybe a once-in-a-lifetime opportunity—to have had my job. But, I continued, "you know the situation I have with my family, with me here and my wife and daughter in Indonesia."

He did, he said.

"Well, I'm being recruited by a PR firm back in Washington, D.C.," I said. "They want me to start January 1. And I need to take the offer."

The first words that came out of his mouth: "I understand. Family must come first."

I was floored. I didn't know what to expect, but this was not it. It was generous, understanding, and gracious. Who knows, maybe they expected I'd bolt when Rebekah left Seoul. Maybe they'd got one more year out of me than they thought they would. The head of HR said they'd start the separation paperwork and ask me for some recommendations for my replacement, then told me the company would miss me.

I immediately got in the elevator and went back to my office. I walked to the area where my team sat and asked them to join me in my office right away. They looked at each other in a puzzled fashion—a couple sighed with annoyance—and they trundled in.

I shut the door and told them. Stunned silence until Ben, my team leader, broke the ice with a laugh and called me an "asshole" for leaving. He immediately followed up by saying he completely understood my situation—as he would, with his wife and children still living in the States—and most of the rest of the team congratulated me and said they understood. Those who didn't probably thought this was just another incident of the American always getting what he wanted—a promotion, four months in the U.S. with his wife, an early exit from his contract—at the expense of the team and the company. If I put myself in their shoes, I could see that point of view. I had tried my best to smooth that over but could not.

I said good-bye to my team and my friends at Hyundai on December 6, 2013, three years and two months after I walked into the headquarters lobby, the lone American, hopelessly adrift in a sea of Koreans. As I walked out, I saw things differently. Now everyone looked like individuals. I saw a couple young women walking arm in arm through the lobby and realized I would miss that kind custom. I might even miss the smell of *kimchi*, if not the taste. I had accomplished a lot at Hyundai, but could have done more if I'd been smarter about it earlier in my time there. But this was not a time for reflection. I was an arrow pointed south toward Jakarta. The next day I was on a plane, headed to my family.

I'd like to write that the reunion was instantly sweet, but it was not. I had work to do in building a relationship with my eleven-month-old daughter, to whom I was largely a stranger. She was learning to walk and talk, could recognize individuals, and was communicating basic desires. She was becoming, in a word, interactive. Aside from the fact that I was unfamiliar to her, she was not accustomed to men. She was being raised by three women: Rebekah, Tri, and Sati. She had almost no meaningful interaction with men, so I had to get her used to my size, my smell, the deeper sound of my voice, the hair on my chest—everything. The good news was I didn't have to start my new job back in Washington until just after the New Year, so I had a month in Jakarta with no job, which meant I could spend all day with Annabelle.

Tri and Sati were terrific. Although Tri was the primary caregiver, whenever Sati had a free moment she wouldn't take it for herself: she'd get down on the floor to play with Annabelle and Tri and me. As for Tri, one day I was looking for something in the apartment and glanced into her bedroom. On the nightstand, next to her bed, was a well-worn and dog-eared paperback English dictionary. She was trying to improve her English. Neither Rebekah nor I had ever said anything to her about our concerns regarding Annabelle's language development, but maybe she'd overheard us talking. Or maybe she had just taken it upon herself. In either case, I was deeply moved.

At home during the day in Jakarta, I was able to play with Annabelle, get to know Sati and Tri better, take Annabelle to a pool for a swim, and walk over to the embassy and have lunch with my wife. Rebekah and I both realized our ex-pat lifestyle, and all the perks that went with it, was coming to an end. Rebekah was simply happy to have her husband back in her house. For both of us—and for most families, I'm sure—being separated felt deeply unnatural: each of us was single without being single; each was married without a spouse.

Now it was Rebekah's turn to engineer her exit. Her request received support from the embassy in Jakarta and a cable announcing her curtailment was sent to Foggy Bottom.

And then it all went south.

One day after her request was sent to State, Rebekah got an e-mail from the State Department saying her curtailment was being strongly opposed. This was the beginning of a wrenching, two-month churn through the confusing—and what eventually felt spiteful—bureaucratic machinery of State. Rebekah appealed to various entities and would get encouraging strategy from one that would be rejected by another. By now it was January 2014, I had gone to Washington to start my new job, and Rebekah was trying to manage this on her own while still being a U.S. diplomat in Jakarta and trying to find good new positions for her three household staff members. And it wasn't lost on us that, once again, our family was separated.

Throughout January in Jakarta, Rebekah would routinely awake in the morning to a negative or even hostile e-mail that had arrived overnight from the State Department in Washington as communications volleyed from one side of the globe to the other. She and her career adviser cobbled together one plan that was given the preliminary okay by the higher-ups—raising our spirits—only to have them change their minds two days later and rescind it, dashing them once again. At one point the State Department warned Rebekah that if she somehow managed to get a curtailment from Jakarta, she would be reassigned elsewhere overseas instead of being allowed to return to Washington. This was the part that felt spiteful.

Finally we pulled the rip cord. With the help of the embassy in Jakarta, Rebekah got a short-term leave of absence. It would protect her job for the time being and give us a few months to mull over the options. She and Annabelle would come to Washington, where she would continue her appeal in person with the full intention of remaining in the Foreign Service. She didn't want to walk away from the only career she'd ever wanted and had worked years to achieve—and had turned out to be very good at.

We asked Sati to come with us to the States. The fact that she was older and had traveled outside Indonesia with previous Western employers made her the better choice over Tri. Both Tri and Pak Wandi were very worried when we told them Rebekah was leaving—she was their only income—but we found each of them equally paying jobs with Western diplomats. When Tri had to say good-bye to Annabelle, she squeezed her hard and sobbed.

For Sati, it was the windfall of a lifetime. In the U.S. we'd pay her four times what she was making in Jakarta. We wanted her to stay at least until we had a prayed-for second child. The money she would earn from us would be a life changer for Sati, her husband, and their two children. It would literally lift them into the middle class and set them up for future generations. We were delighted to have Sati help us in the States, but also happy we could help her.

Rebekah, Annabelle, and Sati arrived at Dulles International Airport in early February 2014. I caught the moment with a photograph of a tiny, colorfully dressed, and slightly dazed Annabelle, only thirteen months old, standing by herself in the middle of the airport's vast, gray arrival area. At last we were all together and would be for the foreseeable future. We all squeezed into a small rental apartment and spent our Saturdays house hunting. It was especially fun to take Sati with us simply to experience her awe at walking into empty suburban Washington homes that, for us, were of average size and amenities but, for Sati, may as well have been palaces.

I settled into my new job at BGR. Documents were in English. I could attend meetings on my own and understand what was being said. We all addressed each other by our first names, even our bosses. I could walk outside my office and there were a dozen good lunch options within five minutes.

But events did not turn out as happily for Rebekah. It became clear that there were no options that would allow Rebekah to get a job at State Department headquarters in Washington. As far as they were concerned, her job—and the only job she could have in the Foreign Service—was back in Jakarta. She could either return to that one or resign.

It was finally the end. Rebekah was not going back to Jakarta. State would never tell Rebekah why her compassionate curtailment application had been rejected and why so many others were approved. It didn't matter. She tendered her resignation from the only career she'd ever really wanted. This was a crushing blow for

Rebekah. When she was younger, she'd taken jobs overseas just so she could live overseas. None had been a career. The Foreign Service posting in Jakarta was the first time Rebekah had a career in a foreign country—her dream life. I had once walked away from the only career I had ever wanted—a job at the *Washington Post*—but my professional arc from the declining *Post* only pointed upward: better salary, more adventure, new experience. For Rebekah there was no professional promise in her future. She was, at least for the time being, going to be a stay-at-home mom. We valued that and were glad Annabelle would have one parent with her at home, but Rebekah and I knew it was not going to be professionally satisfying. My wife was taking a major hit for our family.

You might think the State Department was finished with us. You'd be wrong. Another overnight e-mail, this one from Jakarta to Washington. Rebekah awoke before me one morning in February, then came back into the bedroom to wake me up.

"Sati has to go home," she said, her face fallen.

The U.S. embassy in Jakarta said that Sati's visa status, which allowed her to live and work in the U.S., was dependent on Rebekah's continued employment with the State Department. Now that she'd resigned, Sati's visa was no longer valid. She had to return to Jakarta immediately.

I spent a day talking to an immigration lawyer and learned nothing promising. We would miss Sati terribly, but for us, losing her was an inconvenience. For Sati and her family, losing us meant a return to near poverty in Indonesia. Her family's future of economic assurance, a college education for her daughter, a house they could own—all evaporated in a five-minute conversation in our apartment.

"This was always my dream," she told us heartbreakingly. "Now it is gone."

The next day I drove Sati back to Dulles Airport and put her on a flight to Jakarta. Driving home alone, I realized that our ex-pat adventure was truly over. All the ties to our frustrating, dangerous, gorgeous, glamorous, absurd, exciting three-plus years had now been cut. It was all just pictures on an iPhone and Facebook updates. It was jarring to have been a corporate executive in Seoul and to have been a diplomat in Jakarta and then, within a few weeks, suddenly become an agency PR man and stay-at-home mom living on a cul de sac in suburban Washington. The truth was, I quickly realized, it didn't matter whether we lived in Seoul, Jakarta, or Arlington. Even though so much of our previous three years had been defined by exotic geography, we were not a place. What we were, in fact, was a family. Wherever we were.

A couple months after Rebekah and Annabelle arrived back in Washington, the three of us were puttering around our little rented apartment. I was sitting on a low inflatable sofa—my furniture had not arrived from Korea yet—and Annabelle walked up to me and stood between my legs, putting her hands on my knees. She didn't have anything particular she wanted to say or that she wanted from me. She just wanted to stand there, touch her daddy, and make some tongue-clicking noises she had been experimenting with. A total throwaway moment in most parents' lives, barely noticeable, but for me it was a revelation. Only a few months earlier, back in Jakarta, Annabelle cried each time I tried to hold her, and wobbled off to her mother or Sati or Tri. Now here she stood before me, sure-footed, comfortable with her father, gently patting his knees, and clicking away. Seated, I was the same height that she was, and instead of looking down at her, as I usually did, I got a different view. This was one of those moments when her face hit a certain angle, or when she threw me a certain look, and it felt like she'd suddenly crossed an age threshold. She was only fourteen months old, but her pinched baby features were growing and migrating apart on her face, like tiny continents slowly traveling to their eventual destinations on a globe. I felt like I was getting a glimpse of what she was going to look like as an adult—a glimpse of her future. Years telescoped out ahead of me as I sat there probing her face, extrapolating. I could see her as a little girl, as a teenager, as a young woman, as a mother. "You're it," I thought. "You're the proof that I made the turn—that I made it through my midlife crisis." Annabelle was the proof that I'd written—that God had written—a second act for my life that was something wonderful, and unimaginably better than the first one.

# EPILOGUE

Change happens *pali-pali*, or quick-quick, in Korea, faster than in the U.S. When Rebekah and I arrived in Seoul at the end of 2010, we could count on one hand the number of high-quality Western-fare restaurants we found that weren't located in luxury hotels. By the time I left three years later, because of new laws, new entrepreneurs, and new fads among Koreans, I could get an excellent craft beer on tap and top-drawer bar food at any of a number of microbreweries that had sprung up around the city.

The birth of the microbreweries—sweet relief to long-suffering Korean beer drinkers—was emblematic of how much had changed while I was in Korea and how much is still changing. I came to understand—and appreciate—that I had lived in Korea during one of the young nation's true pivot points.

On the first day we were in Korea, our Foreign Service sponsors told us that Korea is the land of "almost, not quite." I took that to mean it's almost, not quite like the U.S. and that American standards of comfort, quality, and convenience were not to be found. I laughed about it, admittedly a little smugly. This was the natural if unfortunate reaction of a West Virginia provincial tossed into the deep end of internationalism, thrashing about for anything to keep his head above water.

But the longer I stayed in Korea—and after I left—I came to realize that "almost, not quite" really meant that Korea and Hyundai were almost but not quite the next things they were about to become. For all the daily frustration to be felt as the only American in a foreign corporation, for all the hardships we endured as a family, it turned out to be a privilege to watch this country and this company transform into their next incarnations—to work through their midlife crises before my eyes.

As I write this, in late 2015, change continues in the lives of Hyundai, Korea, and myself. We are all different entities today than when we first intersected in 2010. Each of us has tallied the early results of our urgent and labored efforts to evolve. Each of us stands at the brink of something new, perhaps something great.

## HYUNDAI: A BUMPY ROAD BUT POINTED UP

After Hyundai opened its Brazil and China factories in 2012, the company said it would take a break from its rapid expansion of the previous few years and renew efforts to maintain and improve its high quality. This was Chairman Chung's decision, and although there was some whispered internal dissent, what the chairman said went, as usual. Hyundai never directly expressed it, but we—and many in the industry—believed that Toyota's terrible quality problems that led to the unintended acceleration, massive recalls, terrible PR, and billion-dollar fine were at least partly caused by the company building too many factories too quickly. It is hard to keep a lid on quality across a global network when you're putting up factories fast in a bid to remain the world's top-selling brand. That's part of the reason why we always said that Hyundai's goal was never to be the world's biggest-selling brand; instead, we wanted to be the most-loved car brand, even though that might sound cheesy to some hard-bitten Western journalists.

The chairman's reticence about continuing rapid expansion was certainly understandable, given how jealously Hyundai guarded its hard-won quality gains. But Hyundai's competitors did not stop expanding, so Hyundai lost market share in some regions, including in the U.S. This spawned a spate of what's-wrong-with-Hyundai stories that dulled some of the media shimmer we had enjoyed in previous years.

The bigger problem was SUVs. When Hyundai introduced its Fluidic Sculpture Sonata in 2011, the midsize family sedan was the hottest segment in the industry. The Sonata was a beautiful design, to be sure, but it hit at the right time and rode the wave up. By 2014, with gas prices plummeting on falling global oil production costs, consumer tastes were swinging away from midsize sedans and toward SUVs of all sizes. Hyundai had built a sedan-heavy lineup and was caught flat-footed by the consumer sentiment shift. When Hyundai introduced its new Santa Fe in 2012, it came in two versions: one with two rows of seats and one with three rows. This allowed Hyundai to scrap its poor-selling big SUV, the Veracruz. But this left Hyundai with only two SUVs in its entire U.S. lineup, the Santa Fe and an aging Tucson, introduced in 2010. By comparison, Nissan had six SUVs and Chevrolet had five. Even Mercedes had five.

Then there was the new Sonata with the more conservative design. It has sold well enough, but not as well as the previous, sexier version. Part of the problem was the segment decline: even the Toyota Camry, America's best-selling car, saw a sales drop from 2014 to 2015 as consumers moved away from sedans and toward SUVs. But the new Sonata's slump was worse. It's always hard to pin down one sure reason why a car succeeds or fails, but the reviews of the new Sonata were pretty consistent: this is a terrific car to drive and own, it's packed full of features, it's better than the previous one—but it will absolutely not stand out from the pack. There was a feeling that some of the previous Sonata's design magic—that alchemic combination of lines and surfaces—had been lost.

These were Hyundai's vehicle problems. But the company suffered a big corporate black eye in 2014 as well. Hyundai announced it was spending *$10 billion* to buy a piece of land in Seoul's trendy Gangnam district to build a new hundred-story corporate headquarters. Not only was the sale price high, it was three times the land's appraised value, so badly did Hyundai want the plot. What's more, it was revealed, Hyundai had asked its board of directors to approve the purchase without telling them the purchase price. They complied, confirming the worst impressions of the powerful, chairmen-ruled *chaebol* and their puppet boards.

By the end of 2015, though, it looked like Hyundai was getting back on track. The chairman finally relented and Kia announced it would build a factory in Mexico, which likely will also produce Hyundai vehicles. I would not be surprised to see Hyundai build a second plant in the U.S., probably near its Alabama factory. Hyundai introduced a new Tucson that got good reviews and scored top safety marks. Hyundai promised a fun little SUV to compete with Nissan's funky Juke, and hinted at a Genesis luxury SUV to compete directly with Audi and Mercedes SUVs. But these will likely be at least a couple years out.

The new Genesis sedan—the flagship vehicle of Hyundai's grand ambition to raise its brand to German-level premium status—turned out to be a home run. Through 2015 it continued to outsell its predecessor. By this time every publication had a chance to test drive the new Genesis, compare it to its rivals, and conduct long-term testing. These reviews were even more favorable than the ones we'd gotten from the first journalists we'd brought to Korea to drive Genesis back in 2013.

AutoGuide.com pitted the new Genesis against the Jaguar XF—and judged Genesis the superior vehicle. The Car Connection called it a "legitimate alternative to the heavyweights," meaning the German rivals for which it gunned.

*MotorWeek* wrote that Genesis "has the potential of being a brand-changing vehicle, if they can follow up with additional models in the same vein."

In November 2015, Hyundai announced plans to do just that, but under a new, separate Genesis luxury brand. This surprised the auto industry—and me. Hyundai was creating its own Lexus.

I spent more than three years telling reporters the one thing Hyundai did *not* want to do was create its own Lexus-like luxury brand. Instead, we wanted to raise the entire brand to premium status, something that had never been tried before. Now, had all that been rendered meaningless? And what would this mean for Hyundai? Would Hyundai forever be consigned to the "value for money" category, with no hope to climb to premium?

But after talking to some people at Hyundai, I was reminded of what we told reporters who asked if we planned to create a luxury brand: "We don't, but the customers will ultimately decide for us."

They did. The Genesis always wore a Hyundai H logo on the trunk and a special winged Genesis logo on the hood. In the years following its introduction in the U.S., many Genesis owners would ask their Hyundai dealer to remove the Hyundai H from the trunk and replace it with a winged logo.

By the time the second-generation Genesis came out, the H had all but disappeared from the car. The critical reception and strong sales for the new Genesis convinced Hyundai that the Genesis name could carry its own lineup of six luxury vehicles. The new Genesis would be renamed G80. The next Equus would be renamed G90. The Genesis brand would include a luxury SUV, a small sedan aimed directly at the BMW 3 Series and other vehicles, all carrying the "G" alphanumeric naming and all on the road by 2020.

Markets and consumer preferences change. Only foolish, hidebound companies do not change with them. An improved economy and cheap gas drives the desire for luxury cars in the U.S. Hyundai believed elevating the entire brand was the right strategy for 2011. Splitting off a Genesis luxury brand is the right strategy for 2015 and beyond. Characteristically, Hyundai will go its own way even with its new luxury brand. Unlike its Japanese rivals, Hyundai will save money—and increase profit margin—by not setting up new dealerships for its Genesis models, at least not at first. Instead, it will continue to sell the Genesis models out of Hyundai dealerships and offer its luxury customers special treatment designed to save their time, believing that's what wealthy luxury car buyers really value, rather than fancy dealerships with marble floors.

I don't believe Hyundai will give up attempting to elevate the Hyundai brand, either. In late 2015, Hyundai showed its new Elantra, the successor to the top-selling version that won the Car of the Year award in Detroit in 2012. Not only does the new Elantra have a completely remade exterior design that critics termed upscale, and that mimics some of the Genesis's best styling moves, but Hyundai also packed the new Elantra with features found on the Genesis and other luxury cars.

To compete with high-performance luxe cars, Hyundai established an "N" sub-brand for souped-up versions of its cars, like the Mercedes AMG performance brand. Hyundai announced its intentions powerfully by building a testing facility at Germany's fabled Nürburgring racetrack. It is a gleaming structure with a mirrored surface that reflects sunlight like a beacon, an impossible-to-miss metaphor for Hyundai's ambitions.

With the new headquarters, Hyundai learned a tough corporate lesson. After the outcry from foreign shareholders who felt they had been kept in the dark about what the company was doing with their money, Hyundai established its first—and Korea's first—board-level committee designed to protect the interests of non-family shareholders. This seems like an obvious, long-overdue step to appeal to Western investors, but for Korea it marked a huge cultural shift. In the past, in Korea's Confucian hierarchy, a *chaebol* chairman answered to no one, and it was almost considered a privilege to invest in his company. That is changing, one more sign of how Korea will continue to adapt to global norms while retaining its character: the company is, after all, still going to build its headquarters. Hyundai insiders might have been surprised by the caustic outside reaction, even from Koreans, to the expensive land purchase. Inside Hyundai, it probably made perfect sense: Hyundai, playing the long game as usual, sees its new building as a hundred-year headquarters, a way to get all of its affiliates under one roof, a showcase for its new premium vehicles, and a landmark anchor for the next phase of Seoul's growth. If this had been communicated well to major shareholders in advance, if they had been told that the Korean government was promising to punish the *chaebol* unless they spent some of their massive cash reserves—if it had been accompanied by a shareholder dividend and if the biggest shareholders had been enfranchised in the decision—it all might have gone a lot more smoothly for Hyundai. The black eye was not a failure of strategy or vision; it was a failure of communication, with share-holders and with the media.

This is one of the things I hope and believe will change when Vice Chairman Chung Eui-sun—son of the current chairman, grandson of Hyundai's founder, and the man who hired me—takes over the company. This may happen before this book is published; it may happen five years or more from now. Vice Chairman Chung is decisive—that is demonstrated by Hyundai's design direction—but I believe he is more collaborative, egalitarian, communicative, and perhaps even revolutionary than his father. The last trait is critical. In order to execute Hyundai's audacious plan to build premium cars, it needs to recapture some of the bold risk-taking spirit of Hyundai founder Chung Ju-yung, who sold his first ship before he had even built a shipyard. When you have suffered the privation that Korea only recently experienced, it is understandable to avoid risk, play it cautious, and hold on to what you've got. But that is a path toward stagnation, not innovation and leadership. I'm excited to see risky new product like the Genesis luxury brand. I'd like to see Hyundai distribute that feeling of adventure across the company: hiring more people from outside Hyundai, promoting more women to executive roles, getting more foreigners at headquarters, helping Hyundai's non-Korean employees outside of Korea—especially the managers—feel more enfranchised in the company and given more authority. In a 2014 interview with Bloomberg Business, Choi Myoung-wha—Hyundai's first female vice president—hinted at the changes that need to come in Korea's Confucian corporate culture when she told younger female colleagues, "Your manager is your boss, not your father." It takes more than good design to make a brand premium. It takes corporate culture change as well.

Can Hyundai become a maker of premium automobiles, someday the peer of the world's best cars? In the long game, I believe it can, but it will be under the chairmanship of Chung Eui-sun.

## KOREA: CHANGE EVERYTHING

When Eduardo, my right-hand man at Hyundai, left the company, he wasn't sure what he wanted to do. Within a few months he figured it out: Instead of devoting his life to a *chaebol*, Eduardo wanted to be a hotelier. With some backing, Eduardo opened a modern, twelve-unit boutique hotel on the vacation island of Jeju, off the southern coast of the Korean Peninsula. The hotel is already a success and he has plans for another. With this decision, Eduardo transformed himself into the very thing that Korea needs to achieve the next chapter in its historic growth story: a risk-taking entrepreneur in the service sector. The best part, at least as Eduardo sees it, is that now he's the boss. And as the boss in a Confucian workplace, he gets to assign English names to his Korean workers, just as his team leader had given him an English name back at Hyundai. Eduardo named one of his employees "Frank" and had a great time yelling at him when he screwed up. "Every time I see him," Eduardo wrote to me, "I miss you a lot."

Before the *chaebol* were players in the world marketplace, they were little more than faint ideas in the minds of risk-taking entrepreneurs. Chung Ju-yung, running his A-do Service Garage. Samsung's Lee Kun-hee telling his employees, "Change everything except your wife and kids." Move Chung and Lee into the twenty-first century, place them in a software design studio or a sharing-economy start-up in Seoul—or a boutique hotel on Jeju Island—and they will be the leaders of Korea's next economy.

Koreans understand this. In a February 2014 speech, President Park said, "Our past . . . way of growth that made us one of the world's 10 largest economies has now reached its limit." The export and manufacturing sector, led by all-powerful *chaebol*, has completely overshadowed the domestic consumer market and services industry, Park said. The president vowed to ease regulations on service-sector industries, such as finance and software, and sink government money into funding start-ups that would be appealing to outside investment. It has started to pay off. In 2015, Japan's SoftBank invested $1 billion in a Korean e-commerce firm called Coupang, valued at $5 billion. None of this means the end of *chaebol* like Hyundai. It means the birth of something else: a diversified economy. The Korean economy still has its issues: growth will continue to be pegged to the performance of the *chaebol* until diversification achieves critical mass. Korean household debt is high. Currency fluctuation has an outsize impact on the export-heavy economy. But the macro arrows are pointing the right way. In its 2015 Innovation Index, based on metrics such as R & D spending, education, number of high-tech companies, and patents, Bloomberg ranked Korea as the world's most innovative country. For a country that only two generations ago was making Mitsubishi knockoffs, this is astounding.

Politically, change is coming, too.

Constitutionally, the Korean president can serve only one five-year term, meaning Park Geun-hye is out after the 2017 election. Her successor may be U.N. secretary-general Ban Ki-moon, who tops polls of possible candidates. Or it may be Seoul mayor Park Won-soon, who has lured venture capitalists to his city and preaches the work-life balance. I was wrong about Mayor Park: Seoul voters did not toss out the crazy liberal after only one term, possibly because—even with all his crazy liberal ideas—he managed to cut the city's budget deficit. Instead, they affirmed his direction by reelecting him in 2014. Either way, the options for the country's next president look more progressive than previous ones.

At the cultural and even personal levels, change is coming fast, too.

Korea's relentless pursuit of education has caught up to it. The universities produce more four-year-degree graduates than the great *chaebol* can absorb, even though each year they make tens of thousands of new hires. This has had a few effects, one of which is a rise in multiculturalism. Although many college grads can't find work, there is also an unwillingness among some to do offered work they find beneath them. The upside to this is an influx of foreign labor, changing Korea's complexion. The highly educated class of young Korean females has created a shortage of brides for less-educated, often rural men. This has also contributed to immigration, as more Korean men are marrying Vietnamese, Chinese, Filipino, and Cambodian women. As many as 10 percent of all new marriages in Korea are now multicultural. This naturally foments tension in the largely homogeneous culture, and problems of assimilation occur. But long-term it will be a good thing.

Another by-product of the glut of college grads is that it pushes Koreans to seek international careers with foreign firms, making them more global. And it encourages others to abandon the "right spec"—in other words, to get any degree you can from the best university you can so you can get hired by a *chaebol*. Instead, Korean kids are starting to major in topics that interest them and that lead to careers they want to pursue. These young Koreans will contribute to the post-*chaebol* economy. "Gone are the days when a degree from the SKY universities guarantees entrance to a *chaebol*," a Korean friend told me.

When Rebekah and I threw our first Christmas party in Korea shortly after we arrived in 2010, we were struck by how little the Koreans mixed with the Americans. A Korean friend told me that Koreans tended not to make new friendships as adults. Now, thanks to the Internet, more Koreans are meeting others online who share their interests, forming up in clubs to bicycle, or work out, or go to baseball games. And to make new friends in adulthood.

Not even the revered Korean *hoesik*, or drinking dinner, is immune to change. Both the *chaebol* and the government are now warning against excessive *hoesiks*—what we would call binge drinking—in public service ads. Not only does binge drinking lead to early deaths, the ads say, it costs the Korean economy $20 billion annually in lost productivity. The ads indicate that the *hoesik* is not always a form of bonding; for nondrinkers it can be harassment. Don't think the *hoesik* is going away anytime soon; it's not. It's still a fundamental part of the Korean salaryman's life, and that's a fundamental part of the Korean culture. But now the costs of the practice are being acknowledged, and that's the first step.

All of this change—often radical, on-a-dime change—taught me that the greatest Korean trait turns out to be adaptability, the key to species and cultural survival. Add adaptability to other key Korean traits, such as diligence, loyalty, velocity, and *jeong*, and that's why I argue it makes sense to put your chips on Korea among the three major powers of East Asia. Korea has radically changed once in recent history—growing from foreign aid recipient to aid distributor—and can do it again. It has several factors in its favor. Unlike China, Korea is a democracy. This makes it more stable, more dynamic, and more innovative than authoritarian China. Korea's industrialized infrastructure is only fifty years old and is not yet facing a breakdown. Unlike the great *zaibatsu* in Japan, Korea's *chaebol* are still on the rise and have not yet hit cruising speed. Unlike Japan, Korea has great relations with the region's largest power, China. Unlike China, Korea has not built islands in the South China Sea that inflame its neighbors. Unlike Japan, Korea doesn't have a meaningful ultranationalist wing to destabilize regional politics. And Korea is the most U.S.-friendly power in the region.

The final factor in South Korea's long-term success is North Korea. Instead of being only a perpetual threat, North Korea is South Korea's eventual ace in the hole when the peninsula is reunited. It can give South Korea something that no other economy in the region has at the ready: an overnight doubling of landmass, access to natural resources, and an infusion of 25 million new citizens who are younger and have more children than their South Korean cousins, helping to defuse the South's demographic bomb. This will be more complicated than reuniting East and West Germany. Who knows how many North Koreans will become South Koreans and how many will melt away into China. And there will be other problems to resolve with China, which would share a border with America's best friend in the region. There would be an economic shock and a decade-long sag to the South Korean economy with the absorption of the North Koreans. The less-educated, unworldly North Koreans would be an underclass for a couple of generations. But in the long run, citizens of the two Koreas speak (mostly) the same language and they have the same DNA, heritage, culture, and customs. They are, in the end, Koreans. The North will collapse one day; the only questions are how dramatically and when. When that happens, South Korea—by then truly "Korea"—will be the beneficiary.

## ME: A NEW IDENTITY

When I am asked what it was like living overseas, I have a few brief go-to stories. Some are designed to explain, others just to get a laugh at my expense. It's what people want. But often the question prompts me to think of Tri, our nanny in Jakarta. I usually don't tell this story.

About a week after we were forced to put Sati on a plane and send her back to Indonesia, Rebekah's iPhone chimed, signaling a text message. It was from Sati. Without warning or context, in curt and cruel broken English, she texted: "Dear Mrs I hope you and Mr are fine. Tri already die this Friday." Shocked but unbelieving, thinking Sati must have made an errant keystroke or meant something else, we called and learned that Tri—only twenty-seven, the single mother of a young boy—had gotten sick with something that gave her a fever. Unable to pay for treatment at a clinic, her condition got worse until, a few days after she became ill, she died. That was all the information Sati had and all we were likely to get secondhand out of a rural Indonesian village on the other side of the planet. It seemed so senseless, almost absurd. For the want of—what? Maybe $100 of care and medication? Yet, for Tri and millions of Indonesians like her, spending that towering sum of money on herself was probably unimaginable. It is a tragic fact that in Indonesia, and all around the world, poor people die of things that should not kill them—that is, if they had access to good health care, the money or insurance to pay for it, and the knowledge and expectation that many illnesses can be cured. Early mortality is a grim and familiar presence in every one of these families. Dying of old age is a First World luxury. Tri held Annabelle through many crying nights and was a part of our family for a time. Annabelle was too young to remember Tri, but we do, and we will show Annabelle pictures of Tri one day and tell her about the woman who heard her first words and watched her take her first steps.

This was one of the many sobering experiences of living overseas, and a catalyst of the change I saw happening in myself. Now, as a husband and father and no longer an aging #YOLO bachelor; now, as an accountable member of a church family and no longer an outlier of the faith; now, as the leader of a business team and no longer a journalistic observer, I came to understand that my identity—the person I was becoming in my second act—was completely enmeshed with and dependent on others. I had become, odd as it sounds to say, a bit Korean.

In Korea's hierarchical Confucian culture, who you are at any given moment largely depends on your relationship to who's around. You are something like a cultural chameleon, adapting to environment, showing deference and respect in one direction, authority and leadership in another.

In the West we are taught that we are individuals above all. Our identities are either inherent in our being—expressed by gender, color, height, weight, intelligence—or they are handcrafted by accumulating things, money, connections, ideology, experience, fame. Either way, we stand at the center of our world and announce ourselves loudly.

This is how I lived most of my life. Now I have come to understand that my identity is in fact based on my relationship to God, my family, and others. My identity is not dependent on my profession, my salary, my nationality, my home state, my college sports teams, or anything else I used to think defined me.

I have become a husband and a father, and I'm good with that.

I read an awful lot about parents bemoaning the loss of their identities when becoming parents. They talk about no longer being able to enjoy their hobbies or have the kind of intense political conversations they had in grad school. I can sympathize. I used to ride a motorcycle. I really liked it. It was fun. But now that I'm a parent, I'm probably not going to ride a motorcycle again. I have too many people depending on me and it's one unnecessary risk, and an extra expense, I can cut out of my life while significantly lowering my wife's anxiety. But am I less of who I am because I no longer ride a bike? Of course not. Once I became a parent, I stopped doing a lot of the things I used to do when I was single—not just dating—and that's as it should be. I now answer to people other than myself. And it turns out that my selfishness as a single man was overrated. As a parent, I get to do so many more satisfying things with my family than I ever got to do when I was single. That's something I never saw when I was unattached; I surely did not believe it when my happily married friends explained it to me. Marriage and family, like the most important things in life, are leaps of faith.

But each day there's a payoff. More than a year since Annabelle and Rebekah returned from Jakarta and we were reunited as a family, I'm still grateful and thrilled when Annabelle climbs all over me in a restaurant booth or clings to my leg while I'm trying to walk around the house. When I was a stranger to Annabelle and she wouldn't let me hold her, I wasn't sure if she ever would. "Ode to Joy," with Annabelle's name as the lyrics, is finally part of our relationship: it's the song she requests when she's swinging. Do I sing it on a public playground? Yes, I do. At age two and a half, Annabelle's personality is forming each day, with surprising new bits like leaves shooting from a growing tree. On the downside, this means she has learned willful disobedience, and at times she tests and tasks us. On the upside, it means that she is learning the important things in life, such as how to tell a joke and how to totally melt her father.

"You know what, Daddy?"

"What, Annabelle?"

"I love spending time with you!"

In October 2015, our little family expanded, adding Penelope Honor. Annabelle has fully embraced her role as big sister, including giving her little sister a nickname a two-and-a-half-year-old can pronounce: "Nelpy."

It astounds me, when I think of it, that all of these early childhood memories I'm making with my daughters—ones that I will carry to my grave—they will probably never remember. I watch the girls and the scenes are etched into my brain like acid into rock. How is it possible they will forget all this? This is the point where Rebekah would probably refer to my circle-of-life issues again.

As for Rebekah, she still smarts from the forced separation from her career, like a bandage ripped off too soon. Blood still pools at the wound. She is a stay-at-home mother, which has enabled her to spend crucial developmental time with Annabelle and to build a solid support network of similarly situated mothers from our church. Like many places, the church is full of highly qualified, accomplished professional women who've made the tough choice—or been forced to make the choice—of sidelining, downsizing, or abandoning their careers for their families. Rebekah once pointed out that her circle of church friends includes a former diplomat, a senior-level government manager, a medevac helicopter nurse, a scientist who worked on Ebola, and a professional ballet dancer. This is the work-child choice that we fathers are almost never forced to make. Nevertheless, along with her like-situated friends, she is working to come to terms with it. In an e-mail to a friend, Rebekah wrote: "I've learned that my identity was rooted in my work, and that I was overly confident and prideful in my abilities, which didn't look awful on the outside, but I can see God has taught me through letting go that He is in charge, not me. I've learned that God gave me intelligence and the ability to have a career, but my energy and intellect is His to direct, and that by feeling empty without a work project is a sign of my priorities out of place. I still struggle with 'boredom,' especially on the intellectual side, but I have really come to learn that God is using this in a powerful way in my life." You can call it justification; Rebekah calls it learning to follow God's will instead of her own desires, as all Christians struggle to do.

I learned that I made the right decision to leave journalism.

I am still immersed in it by vocation and avocation and I respect many journalists. At the same time, I do not miss journalism. Toward the end of my time in journalism I became tired of writing about other people doing things and I wanted to do something of my own. Journalists are watchers, not participants. That's as it should be, and I think it suited the only child in me. I grew up observing rather than mixing it up with siblings. I was not a joiner. I put off marriage for so long because I feared things that could not be undone, such as having a child with someone. Marriage and parenthood were the first things I truly dove into completely. It took me a long time at Hyundai to abandon my observer status—which I know many of my colleagues felt and rightfully resented—and try to become a part of the team.

Once I did, I came to enjoy the business atmosphere more than the newsroom atmosphere—which was quite a surprise, because the newsroom atmosphere was the main reason I went into journalism. Businesses can screw up, deceive, and be, at their worst, forces for evil. But at their best, as I saw from the inside, businesses are optimistic and forward-looking and the best ones are filled with optimistic people. Newsrooms, on the other hand, can be pretty negative places, peppered with snarkiness, sarcasm, and a pelts-on-the-belt, "afflict the comfortable" mind-set. An old editor of mine liked to crack, "We don't write stories about the planes that land safely." That gets big laughs in a newsroom, but I am now less interested in dark humor and am much more open to positive, feel-good narratives and stories of uplifting experiences.

I am over negativity. I have lived long enough to see that negativity and pessimism cause repeating loops of misery. And while believing in and practicing optimism in no way assures good things will happen to you, your chances of recovery markedly improve when inevitable misfortune strikes. If you tell me that optimism is not a realistic way to live, trust me, you don't have to tell a Christian that we live in a fallen world. I probably think it's worse than you do. After all, God sent the world a savior and the world crucified Him. Logically, Christians should be the most realistic, Hobbesian people you know. Yet, to simply yield to a nihilism that asks "What's the point?" not only dishonors the life God gave us, it makes us miserable for the period we're privileged to walk the earth and it does nothing to bring anyone else to God.

On a more worldly level, I found I developed a taste for hopping on a plane in Seoul, disembarking in Muscat or some other exotic-sounding point on the globe, and speaking to an audience of journalists for those few moments when I was the voice of a major global automaker. That can be intoxicating, and the danger of pride must continually be checked. I learned I liked the car industry, especially working with designers and engineers, and still miss it. There was much Rebekah and I liked about living outside the U.S.—no one would be more surprised than me to learn that about myself—and I wonder if Annabelle will ask us why we lived in these cool places when she was too young to remember it. We'd love to do another turn overseas for the sake of the girls when they get older. I know we'd have a blast.

I returned to the States more impressed than ever by our flawed but potent principles of multiculturalism, tolerance, rule of law, inclusiveness, human rights, gender equality, and the embracing of risk. Here's something I came to love about America: when you fly into Dulles airport in Washington from overseas and head to Immigration, you see two lines, one for American citizens and one for noncitizens. If you took away the signs, I would dare you to identify which line was which.

Even though I found the Korean culture tough to live in as a foreigner and tough to penetrate, I made good Korean friends, and many showed great empathy for my fish-out-of-water troubles. Where I initially recoiled at the drinking dinner as merely a drunken bacchanal, I have come to understand it is a glue to Korean society and culture: the salaryman's life can be miserable, but it is a shared misery, and the *hoesik* makes it tolerable. And sometimes, just sometimes, I get a little nostalgic for sitting shoulder-to-shoulder around a sizzling grill full of beef in the middle of a table, sparks flying, *soju* flowing, while smoke and laughter fill the room. Just in that moment there is an undeniable warmth to the experience, the *jeong* permeates, and a *waygookin* can feel like just a little less of an outsider. I even ended up with my own go-to *noraebang* song, which is "Dancing Queen," because it's just funny to see a big American guy singing ABBA.

I have battle scars from my time in Korea, but each one tells a story and each one makes me stronger and a little more interesting, I think. On one of my last days at Hyundai, Ben, my team leader, said he believed my three-plus years at Hyundai were "like medicine." We often resist it, it doesn't always taste good, but it makes us better. There may be no better way I could phrase it.

# ACKNOWLEDGMENTS

The first person to believe in my writing was my late mother, Betty Lee Ahrens. The second was my twelfth-grade English teacher, Bonnie Maddox, who wrote on the final class paper I gave her, "Reconsider engineering. It will stifle you." That was charitable. More accurately, she should have written, "Reconsider engineering. It is too hard for you." The third person, and the one who had the most impact on the writer I became, is Gene Weingarten, who, before he became the first person to win two Pulitzer Prizes for feature writing, was known as the man who discovered Dave Barry.

In 1992, I was a nobody freelancer who pitched the *Washington Post* a story about a criminal Hare Krishna leader and his strange compound in West Virginia. "Perfect Weingarten story," someone must have said. Gene bought the story, edited it, and put it in the *Post*, still one of the highlights of my life. Gene was an activist editor, a man of great endurance, who each week somehow managed to manhandle a 4,000-word narrative feature into the *Post*'s Sunday Style section. Not every writer could stand up to Gene's muscular editing, but if you could, you'd be a better writer for it. Gene said every story should be about the meaning of life. That's not particularly helpful to the majority of journalists, who cover things like county zoning procedures in suburban bureaus, but I got his point. Within those prosaic beats, you could find stories that are in fact about the meaning of life. These are the toughest and most frustrating to write, but also the most rewarding. Gene gave me the tools to tell them.

Gene was part of the great *Miami Herald* migration of writers to the *Post* in the 1990s, and I feel privileged to have spent a time in their orbit and count them as friends. All of them—Joel Achenbach, Marc Fisher, Lynn Medford, Steve Reiss (sorry for all the semicolons, Dr. No!), and others—improved my writing either by instruction, example, or tough editing. Another, David Von Drehle, shared his tips for writing a book in one's spare time, and it was invaluable. Dave Barry contributed nothing to this book but I did break his glasses in a backyard football game once, so that's something.

Thanks go to former Washington Post Company CEO Don Graham for building a paper that held institutions accountable—and allowed tough reporting on itself—and for creating the kind of oxygen-rich newsroom atmosphere that allowed writers like those above, and even me, to flourish. I hope Jeff Bezos is doing the same. I must thank my two executive editors at the *Post*, Len Downie and Marcus Brauchli, for their support.

While I'm thanking journalists, I need to thank PR pros. The best are not liars, obfuscators, or shallow mouthpieces. They are deeply knowledgeable representatives of their companies and organizations and they respect a journalist trying to do his or her job. In my career at the *Post*, I encountered a few whom I'm indebted to—more than one prevented me from committing major mistakes in print and harming myself and my paper—and they provided outstanding role models for my current profession. I think of the late, great Barbara Brogliatti and her colleague, Scott Rowe, at Warner Bros.; John Spelich, formerly of Ali Baba and Disney; Scott Grogin, formerly of Fox Networks; and Amy Weiss of Weiss Public Affairs.

At Hyundai, I must first thank Vice Chairman Chung Eui-sun for hiring me, promoting me, and backing me. I hope very soon the world motoring media will get to know him, because they will be impressed. Also at Hyundai, I want to thank my global PR team, especially Ben, Antonio, and Ike. I also want to thank my good Korean friend who read the manuscript and worked hard to keep me from embarrassing myself too much. I am forever in your debt.

Here, a word about character identification: all characters in this book are real. Each character identified by first and last name is that person and can be found in an online search. For others, I have created pseudonyms to protect them from workplace and cultural backlash and because they are not public figures. There is one composite character, Jinho, who is a combination of two individuals who share traits and befriended me in similar ways. I created the composite for literary expediency.

BGR Group was the prime worldly actor in getting my family back together, and the founders—Haley Barbour, Lanny Griffith, and Ed Rogers—and my boss, Jeff Birnbaum, have my gratitude.

The first person to envision and believe in this book was my agent, Howard Yoon, of Ross Yoon in Washington, D.C. He took a rambling pile of pages and turned it into a sellable pitch. This book would not exist without my editor, Hollis Heimbouch, of HarperCollins, who turned the manuscript into a book. I knew as soon as I met her that I would like Hollis, because she shares her first name with a character in William Gibson books that I love.

I want to acknowledge the authors who came before me who added depth to my experience. No one who writes about Korea can do so without consulting two foundational texts: Don Oberdorfer and Robert Carlin's *The Two Koreas* and Michael Breen's *The Koreans*. If you're moving to Korea, read Mike's book the first week you're there. You'll thank me. Other books proved invaluable to making me smarter on both Koreas: Barbara Demick's *Nothing to Envy*, Suki Kim's *Without You, There Is No Us*, Bruce Cumings's *Korea's Place in the Sun*, Richard M. Steers's *Made in Korea*, Euny Hong's *The Birth of Korean Cool*, Daniel Tudor's *Korea: The Impossible Country*, Larry Diamond and Byung-Kook Kim's *Consolidating Democracy in South Korea*, Nicholas Eberstadt's *The End of North Korea*, Chol-hwan Kang and Pierre Rigoulot's *The Aquariums of Pyongyang*, and Blaine Harden's *Escape from Camp 14*. Tim Clissold's *Mr. China* and *Chinese Rules* helped me understand China, and early-twentieth-century British naval officer and historian George Alexander Ballard provided an unexpected nugget on Admiral Yi in *The Influence of the Sea on the Political History of Japan*.

No one was more important to the creation of this book than my wife, Rebekah, who was the first reader and whose opinion I trust more than anyone's. Not only did she help shape the book and clean up mistakes on U.S. diplomacy and East Asian politics and policy, but she also supported its writing by handling a toddler when I vanished into my study, and by going to sleep alone while I typed into the night. Finally, I must thank God for His provision and His great love and mercy. I hope I have honored it.

## ABOUT THE AUTHOR

FRANK AHRENS was a reporter at the *Washington Post* for eighteen years before joining Hyundai Motor Company for more than three years, eventually becoming a vice president. He lives in Washington, D.C.